# WHERE THE WIND LIVES

## By

## JACK WALKER

Library of Congress Cataloging-in-Publication Data
Walker, Jack, 1915
Where The Wind Lives : a novel / by Jack Walker.

ISBN 1-881825-07-8

Library of Congress Catalog Card Number: 94-72943

Copyright ©1995 by Jo Walker

*Historical Publications*
*15705 Hilcroft Cove*
*Austin, Texas 78717*

# DEDICATED

**To my son Bill . . .**

# About the Author

Jack Walker lived in the Texas Panhandle, growing up with cattle and oil fields as part of his life. After retiring from teaching Speech and Drama at West Texas State University, he and his wife Jo, along with their son, raised and raced registered quarter horses. Jack unexpectedly passed away shortly after the completion of this manuscript, his fourth novel.

# PART 1

## WEST OF FORT WORTH

# CHAPTER 1

Fauntleroy Finch had no more idea why he possessed unique speed and accuracy with firearms than why he was more than six feet tall and had icy blue eyes, strong white teeth, and straw colored hair that tended to curl a bit when it was damp.

Finch was a bit sensitive about his given name although he would never have admitted it. After all, it had been his mother's maiden name and her brother, T.T. Fauntleroy, was a Colonel in the First U.S. Dragoons. It was a proud name and one to be reckoned with come fighting time.

In fact, for more than half of his nineteen years Finch himself had been fighting in one way or another, for on the Texas frontier in the 1860's, the ability to use guns was as necessary as riding a horse.

His father had presented him with a new Sharps rifle and a 45 pistol on his twelfth birthday with the admonition: "Son, it's not enough to know how to use a gun—it's just as important to know when to use it."

Fauntleroy had lived scrupulously by his father's advice. Actually, the guns were no novelty to him even at twelve years of age, for he had been using his father's guns before that time, and had often amazed his father with his ability.

"I've never seen the like," he had overheard his father tell his mother. "The boy is plumb unnatural. He can pull a gun faster and shoot straighter than any man I ever saw."

"Oh, I hope they don't get him in trouble," his mother worried.

"More likely they'll get him out of trouble," his father said complacently. "He's level-headed, and I've never seen him excited."

Seven years later Finch rode into Austin on his best horse followed by a small pack mule carrying all of his earthly belongings.

As he rode down the streets of Austin that summer day in 1862 he looked about curiously. A few men lounged on the sidewalk, but movement was desultory, for the day was hot and the town was dusty. Suddenly there was a commotion at a hitching rail ahead, and a wildly plunging horse broke from the bunch tied to the rail. A rider was on the horse; he was clutching the saddle horn with all his might, and both reins were flapping. The man went over the horse's head, but he did not clear the saddle, for one foot was hooked firmly in a stirrup. The horse increased his speed and his bucking as the man fell from his back and his head hit the dirt street. It was a simple reflex action as Finch shot the horse in the head. There was a pile-up in the street as the horse fell, and the man that he had been dragging struggled to get to his feet.

A group of men quickly gathered about the fallen horse and man.

"You hurt bad?" one man asked anxiously.

"Not much," the man said, breathing deeply. "But I'd sure have been killed if somebody hadn't shot that horse."

"Who did shoot him?"

"I did." Finch was still sitting on his horse.

"That was good shootin', mister," the fallen horseman said. "And I appreciate it."

"Hated to kill that horse," Finch said. "But it looked like you was in for it if I didn't."

"I was in for it, all right," the man said grimly. "My foot was plumb through that stirrup. First time that ever happened."

"You shot that horse, huh?" A rather small man was looking at the horse's head, and then he looked up at Finch.

"That's right," Finch said tightly. There was something about the small man that made him wary.

"Then I reckon I'd better talk with you, young feller," the man said. "Come into the office with me." He nodded toward a small building and walked toward it, turning his back to Finch and the crowd.

Finch pulled his hat off and ran fingers through thinning yellow hair. He looked at the man's back and shrugged.

"Better foller him on in there, son," a bystander volunteered. "That's Captain Cates of the Texas Rangers."

Finch hesitated a second, then dismounted and tied his horse to the hitch rack. He followed the small man toward the shoddy office. His pace seemed leisurely, but his almost leonine stride made little noise on the boardwalk, and he was only a step behind the smaller man when he entered the office. Two other young men were sitting in the office when they entered. They glanced up with interest.

The Ranger captain stopped suddenly and whirled as his hand flashed toward his pistol; Finch very adroitly smashed him beside the head with his own pistol. The two men partially rose, and their hands were on their guns when Finch turned to them, his blue eyes gleaming.

"That'll do!" he said sternly. Both men gasped and quickly removed their hands from their pistols.

"What 'n hell you mean, bashin' the Cap'n, mister?"

"He was pulling a pistol," Finch said tightly. "Both of you saw it."

"We seen it all right, but I don't believe it. Captain Cates is the fastest man I ever seen with a pistol. You had your gun already out when he turned!"

"I didn't have my gun out," Finch said grimly. "And he isn't the fastest man you ever saw with a pistol, either! Now do you boys want to be friendly and help me bring the Captain around, or do you want me to put my pistol up and you try me? You two are too far away for me to bash with my pistol, so I'll have to shoot. But it's your choice."

"Hell, if you can shoot like you can draw, I shore do want to be your friend!"

"Me, too," the other chimed in.

Finch grinned fleetingly. "All right, then let's get the Captain up and get his head washed off. There's a sight of blood on it."

With that Finch turned his back to the two men and holstered his gun as he bent over the fallen captain.

It was fifteen minutes later when the captain began to stir and opened his eyes.

"What hit me?" were his first words.

"The young feller that's washing your hair out. He hit you with his pistol."

"That's crazy," the captain said as his voice gained strength. "He had his pistol in the holster. I saw to that."

"That's right, Cap'n," the older of the two men agreed. "But he shore got it out in one hell of a hurry."

The captain shook his head as if he were still dizzy. "Tom, you reckon that coffee is still hot back there on the stove?"

"I reckon. I'll fetch some if you and Matt don't want me to stay out here to protect you!" he said jokingly.

The captain glared at him. Matt and Finch grinned a bit as Tom left the room. He returned almost instantly with a pot and four enamel cups.

"We can use the desk for a table."

"Pull up a chair, young feller," the captain invited. "It ain't every day I get whopped over the head with a pistol. I'd like to have a drink with the man who done it."

"I'm right willing to do that, but I'd like to know—"

The captain held up his hand. "Now you just wait a minute, son. I still got a pretty bad headache, and I'd hate to do a lot of explaining. What's your name?"

"They call me Finch."

"What's your last name?"

"Finch is my last name."

"Then what'n hell is your first name?" The captain was brusque. His head throbbed.

"My first name is Fauntleroy. My last name is Finch. Fauntleroy Finch is my whole name. Given to me by my mother." Finch looked challengingly at the three men.

One of the young Rangers spoke up. "You any kin to old Too Tall Fauntleroy of the first Dragoons?"

Finch didn't answer.

The captain cleared his throat and nodded. "A nice name. Ahem—well, Finch. As I said, I ain't exactly used to getting banged over the head with a pistol. I was gonna stick my gun in your belly when I turned, just to show you what the Texas Rangers could do, but I reckon—Finch, just how the hell did you do that? I could have swore that your pistol was in the holster when we came in here."

"It was."

"Then how did you do it?" the Ranger asked.

"I don't know."

"You don't know?" The captain was incredulous.

"Nope. I reckon I've always been handy with any kind of firearm."

The captain looked at him in disbelief. Finally he spoke to the two men. "Tom, I reckon you and Matt have already met Finch. Finch, these two here is Matt and Tom. A couple of Rangers in my company. Not worth much of a damn, but all I could find. Now, Matt, you and Tom get plenty of ammunition, and we are all going out to the range for a while."

Thirty minutes later they were at the practice range just out of town. An hour later, the three Rangers were shaking their heads in disbelief.

"I wouldn't a believed it if I hadn't seen it," Matt said.

"Me neither," Tom agreed. "And that pistol just suddenly appears in his hand. You can't even see his hand move, and you have to look real careful to see the pistol when he's carryin' it in the holster. And that's a fact!"

"That's because it's a part of him. That old wooden stock is about the same color as his chaps."

"He's a freak!"

"I don't know about that. But I'll say one thing—that son-of-a-bitch is a magician with a pistol." Then Matt looked about quickly to see if he had been overheard and breathed a sigh of relief when he saw the captain and Finch standing under a tree a few yards away talking earnestly.

"Who taught you how to use them guns, young feller?" the captain asked Finch in wonder.

"Nobody much. My Pa, he gave me my first guns when I was pretty little."

"He good with 'em?"

"Average, I guess," Finch replied after a moment's hesitation.

"Where you from?"

"We had a ranch down southwest of Santone."

"Had one?"

"Still do, I reckon. Pa sent me into Santone to get supplies, and when I got back the ranch had been raided, and the folks were killed along with a couple of men who worked for us. They ran our cattle off and some of the horses."

"You find the men that done it?"

"Nope. They had a couple days head start and was pushin' em hard. I tracked 'em to the Rio Grande. They had crossed into Mexico."

"What you been doin' since?"

"Tried to round up enough strays and scattered cattle to restock the ranch. Couldn't get help after the war started; so I turned all the stock loose but my best horse and a pack mule. And here I am."

"You going back?"

"Don't know yet. Figgered I'd enlist in the army, maybe."

"You got a mad on agin the North?"

"Not about slaves, I reckon. We never owned any. Mom didn't hold with it. Neither did Pa, I reckon. But I don't like being pushed around, and it seems to me like the North is tryin' to do that to us."

"The North ain't pushin' Texans around nothin' like the Indians and outlaws, thieves, and them damn Comancheros. Since the war started and most of the Texas men gone off, every kind of varmint you can imagine is makin' the Texas frontier a pure hell."

"I know," Finch said. "They've raided us a couple of times since the folks were killed."

"They get off with anything?"

"Nope. I was close by."

The captain nodded understandingly. "They lost some men, huh?"

"Some," admitted Finch.

"You ever thought about bein' a Texas Ranger?"

"Nope."

"You could do a lot more for Texas with the Rangers than with the army."

Finch was silent a few moments, and the captain looked at him inquisitively. "How old are you, Finch?"

"Nineteen. You reckon I could qualify for a Ranger job? I do reckon I've got a mad at the kind of men that killed the folks and ruined our ranch."

"I think you can qualify, all right," Captain Cates said a bit sarcastically. "Come on."

He and Finch walked to where Matt and Tom were standing.

"Boys," the captain said jovially, "meet Fauntleroy Finch, our newest recruit in the Texas Rangers." Then with a ghost of a smile, the captain added, "I expect you boys will have to teach him to shoot a bit."

Finch was welcomed warmly by the other members of the Ranger company, all of whom were of varied backgrounds, but who shared several characteristics in common. They were almost all young, reckless, good with guns and horses; they possessed a penchant for fun and a zest for life, and they were absolutely fearless.

Captain Cates' company was authorized thirty men, but the number fluctuated, for the Texas frontier during the Civil War was almost lawless except for the Rangers. Bandits, thieves, Indians, and murderers rode the country constantly and raided, pillaged, killed, and looted with little fear—except of the Texas Rangers.

Almost every mission assigned the company was fraught with danger, but it seemed that the more perilous and impossible the mission, the more anxious the Rangers were to volunteer for it.

The Texas Rangers were the most solidly regimented group of law-men the world had ever seen, and any one of them would have invited a man to a gun fight if he had heard himself so described, for each Ranger was an individual, his own man, and he took no guff from any man, though they would have charged a grizzly bear with a club if Captain Cates had asked them to. Their fierce loyalty was rewarded by the sum of $40 per month, and all of the beans, bacon, coffee, and hard tack they could eat, when they were not too busy to eat. They wore no uniform but provided their own clothing, which usually consisted of a felt hat, heavy woolen shirt, corduroy or buckskin pants, and boots. They also furnished their own guns and horses, although the State did provide ammunition and would replace a Ranger's horse if it were killed or lost in the line of duty. They each had a little pack mule that would follow his master's horse like a faithful dog.

The Rangers were divided into messes of ten men each, and they took turns cooking. The simple fare was good enough to sustain hard, young bodies, and when on a scout, many of the men would simply pack hard tack, coffee, and jerky in their saddle bags and go for days at a time without warm food. They slept on the ground.

Though they were almost constantly chasing marauding Indians, bandits, Comancheros, or other killers, they occasionally had time for relaxation when the whole company was in camp. They whiled away the time playing cards, racing horses, shooting contests, fishing or hunting. They were a happy lot.

Finch was assigned to a mess that included Chico Baca, one of the most admired and respected members of the company. Chico was a smiling, happy-go-lucky Mexican who never seemed to have a worry in the world, and he always had money, which many of the Rangers wondered about, but never asked. Only Captain Cates knew that Chico came from one of the wealthiest and most respected families in Mexico. He spoke excellent English, but delighted in flavoring his speech with Spanish. And until Finch arrived, he was considered the fastest and most accurate man in the company with firearms. He and Finch quickly became friends.

The first time the entire company was in camp, Tom and Matt, both of whom had seen Finch's prowess with guns, urged a shooting match. Finch reluctantly participated, and it quickly became apparent that no one, not even Chico, could compete with him. In later contests, Finch would occasionally deliberately fumble his gun or miss his target and enjoyed the good natured kidding of the others when he did. Chico became his greatest friend, ally, and fan.

"Oh, I can outshoot Finch with my left hand," Chico Baca laughed. "But he ess mi amigo. I let heem win so he feel good!"

Finch's expertise with a gun spread quickly among the Rangers and was quite often proven in battle, yet not a single one of the young Rangers would have hesitated to challenge him had he felt reason to do so. Thus Fauntleroy Finch was becoming a legend among all the Ranger companies, and in truth, over the entire state of Texas, for he was quite often sent on missions that required skill, good judgment, and steel nerves.

Occasionally, he was accompanied by another Ranger, his preference always being Chico Baca, for the happy Mexican always made the trip a grand occasion. They scouted over the entire western and northern part of Texas and as far as Taos in the New Mexico territory. Once they even crossed into old Mexico where Chico was quite at home. Their crossing the river was strictly against international law, but they were after a notorious killer, and of course no one would recognize them as Texas Rangers.

Their first stop was at an adobe cantina where Chico was at home with his native tongue.

They sat in the dim interior of the cantina and drank sparingly of the liquid fire served there. The girls of the cantina were pretty and flirted outrageously with them. One was particularly intrigued with Finch's blond hair and blue eyes, while another plied her wiles on the cheerful, laughing Chico, who spent his money lavishly and bought drinks for the house at the least excuse.

Men came and went throughout the afternoon, but none resembled the man they were looking for. Later, when the cantina began to fill with thirsty Mexicans, Chico went to the bar and chatted a few minutes with the barman. He returned to Finch and said, "Come, mi amigo. We will sleep in a bed tonight."

Finch looked at him questioningly but said nothing. He simply rose and followed Chico up a stairway to a long hall with doors on each side. Chico looked at the numbers painted crudely on each. He stopped at one of the doors.

"Thees ess your sala, amigo. Mine ess next door. You yell if you need help."

"Why on earth do we need two rooms, Chico?"

"Ah, mi amigo! You will see. Chico read the eyes of the senoritas like you read the book. You see?"

Finch shook his head and entered the room. It was clean enough and had a wash basin and a pitcher with tepid water on a stand. The bed did look inviting, and he undressed, took a sponge bath, and lay down. He was almost immediately asleep, and he had no idea what time it was when he was awakened by a light knock on his door. He quickly covered himself and held his pistol under the covers.

"Come in, Chico," he invited.

The door opened. Much to his surprise, it was the pretty Mexican girl that had flirted so openly with him that afternoon. Her hair was still damp, and she had obviously just had a bath. Finch blinked and stared at her. She began to speak rapidly. Finch spoke little Spanish, but the sparkling dark eyes and the prevocational stance of the pretty senorita could be understood in any language. Finch moved over.

Finch and Chico dawdled in the village for several days. Each morning they rode about the countryside; in the afternoons and early evenings they whiled away the time in the cantina. Chico was greeted as "amigo" by almost all the men who came in. Each night a senorita came to their rooms.

Finch was becoming impatient. They had been gone too long, and they should be looking for their man.

"I figured he would show up here sometime," Finch observed glumly to Chico. "And we've got a good enough description of him."

"Si, amigo," Chico grinned. "But for now we enjoy life the Mexican way, no?"

"It's sure a nice way to spend some time," admitted Finch. "But we gotta get back sometime, or Captain Cates will send somebody to look for us."

"Nada," Chico chuckled. "El Capit n, he know Finch and Chico take care of themselves!"

"I hope so!" Finch said earnestly. "I'd sure hate for him to know we crossed that river."

"You worry too much, amigo," Chico said. "Let Chico worry for us!"

Finch went up to bed one night and left Chico down stairs in the cantina. He was awakened by a shot. He sat up quickly and looked at the peacefully sleeping girl by his side. The traces of a pleased smile still lingered on her face. Apparently she had not heard the shot. Finch quietly eased out of bed and slipped on his clothes. He had just shut the door behind him as Chico came up the stairs.

"What happened?" he asked with relief as he saw his friend.

"Not much, amigo. A gringo downstairs was drinking tequila and bragging that his partner would be back tomorrow, and they were going on another raid across the river. He wanted recruits. Said they had spent most of the money from the Birdwing herd."

"Birdwing!" Finch almost yelled as he grabbed Chico's arm. "Did you say Birdwing? That was our brand on the cattle that were rustled from our ranch."

"Si. I remember, amigo. You told me."

Finch dropped his hand from Chico's arm and started for the stair way.

"Espero, amigo," Chico said urgently. Finch halted but did not turn. "The gringo, he is gone. And a lot of hombres are downstairs. I teenk we wait."

"Why?" Finch demanded as he turned to Chico. "That must be one of the men who killed my folks."

"I know, amigo," Chico said almost sorrowfully. "And I hated to cheat you, but the alcalde ess mi amigo, and in Mexico they do not like one gringo to shoot anyone, even another gringo."

"What are you driving at, Chico?" demanded Finch.

"Well," Chico said. "When I hear him say Birdwing, I know it is him, so I accidentally spill his drink, and he call me a name—at least I teenk maybe he want to call me a name. And he start for his gun. So I shoot!"

"You killed him?"

"I said I was sorry to cheat you, amigo. But tomorrow his partner will be here. I teenk he ess the man we look for."

Finch just shook his head and said nothing.

"Now, you go back to your room. The alcalde will come, and I will explain. You will see. Nothing more will be done about it. Ess only one gringo killed by a Mexican. Nothing serious, you see?"

Finch shook his head again in bewilderment. Chico took his arm and led him back to his room.

"Go back to your senorita, mi amigo. She ess lonesome." Chico pushed Finch inside the room and closed the door.

Finch stood for several minutes; then he removed his clothing and got into bed. The girl reached for him sleepily, and he made savage love to her. She was startled, for always before he had been gentle. But she met his savagery with wild abandon and enthusiasm. It was dawn before they slept.

When Finch awakened again, he donned his clothes hurriedly and went to Chico's room. He did not knock but pushed the door open and stepped into the room. He stopped abruptly, for Chico was sound asleep, and another pretty Mexican girl had her head on his shoulder. He started to back quickly out of the room when Chico opened one eye and grinned.

"Buenos Dias, amigo. A short night, no? I meet you down stairs, and we eat the huevos and tocino, and then we find our hombre and cross the river, no?" Chico replaced the pistol he had been holding under the covers.

Finch nodded and backed out the door. Downstairs, the cook was already busy, and the barkeeper was making half-hearted gestures at cleaning up the place.

"What happened here last night?" Finch asked.

"No hablo ingles." The man shook his head slowly.

"He's a damn liar," the cook yelled from the kitchen. "He can, but he won't. I'm a gringo, mister. What you want to know?"

"I heard a shot down here last night." Finch walked to the door of the kitchen to see a bald headed and red-complexioned man, who was obviously not Mexican, moving energetically about. "I was wondering what happened."

"Wasn't here, myself," the cook said. "But I heard plenty about it. A Mexican shot a gringo, they said. Give him ever chance in the world, too. The Mex let him grab his gun and then shot him afore he cleared leather. Must a been mighty fast."

"What happened to the man who shot him?"

"Not a damn thing. Oh, they held a trial of sorts. The alcalde, he come down; but they was a dozen men who swore the Mex shot in self-defense, and I guess he did. Anyway, the shooter and the alcalde left, and the Mex was back in about an hour lookin' mighty pleased."

"They won't do anything to him, then?"

"Naw," the cook said complacently. "Might give him a medal. I hear tell the gringo he shot was a no good bastard anyway."

"Well," Finch started to say something further but stopped. "Cook us up a couple of big batches of bacon and eggs, will you?"

"You gonna eat both of 'em?"

"I've got a friend upstairs. He'll be down in a few minutes."

Finch sat at the table, and the cook brought plenty of coffee and two servings of bacon and eggs.

"You on the run?" he asked Finch amiably as he set the platters down.

"Just visiting," Finch answered.

"Wisht I was," the cook said wistfully. "Had a little woman trouble north of the river a couple of years ago and had to cross over. Ain't too bad, though. These Mexes know how to live."

The bacon and eggs were getting cold, and Chico still did not show; so Finch ate both batches. Finally Chico appeared, his smile as bright and sunny as the out of doors. He sat with Finch.

"You want more bacon and?" the cook yelled.

Chico waved negatively and poured himself a cup of coffee.

"Hear me, amigo, por favor," Chico said earnestly, which was very unusual for him. "I know how you must feel. And the partner of the man I killed last night is almost sure to be the one that was with them when they raided your ranch. But I had a long talk with the alcalde, you see. He knows my family. And today he will have his men on all the trails coming into town. They will catch our man and take him to the middle of the river. We will meet them there and take him to Captain Cates. You see?"

"But how—?"

"Do not worry, amigo. Let Chico do the worrying," he grinned. "Now let us say adios to our senoritas and ride across the river. We will meet the alcalde's men when they are at the middle of the river."

\* \* \* \* \* \*

Finch and Chico were lolling in the shade of a tree on the north side of the river when Chico suddenly exclaimed, "Caramba!"

Finch looked; the Mexicans were crossing the river, and one of them was leading a horse which carried a man who was bearded, bareheaded, and had his hands tied behind his back.

Chico and Finch hurriedly tightened their cinches and rode out to meet them. Ten days later they delivered the killer to Captain Cates.

It was early spring in 1866 when Captain Cates told Finch to bring in a couple of horse thieves that, at last report, had been seen in Fort Worth.

"I go with heem, mi Capitán?" Chico asked eagerly.

"You stay here," the captain said brusquely. "We may need you."

"But Finch, he might need me too."

"What for?" the captain said. "There ain't but two of 'em."

Finch left Austin early the next morning. He rode his best horse and was followed by his faithful little pack mule. He rode into Fort Worth at sundown a few days later. The town was situated in Tarrant County on the Trinity River. The stone court house was only partially completed, for all the workmen had left to enlist when the war between the states began. There were several vacant buildings around the square in which the courthouse was located, but the town was beginning to show signs of life again since the war was over. In 1865 there were only 250 people in Fort Worth, and most of the houses were vacant. As Finch rode, however, he noted that there was now a flour mill, a shoe cobbler shop, and a blacksmith shop, but not one saloon or rooming house.

As night was quickly falling, Finch decided to ride a few hundred yards to the edge of Clear Fork and make camp under some huge pecan trees. He picketed his saddle horse. The little mule, relieved of his pack, grazed contentedly nearby. Finch ate a good supper. He never minded being alone; in fact he occasionally preferred it. He spent a couple of peaceful hours beside his campfire and then rolled up in his blankets.

It was just after sunup when Finch finished his breakfast and was packing his mule that he heard the clear, ringing sound of iron on iron coming from the blacksmith shop. He grinned and quickly saddled his horse and rode toward the sound. The shop was open in front; a protruding roof, supported by tall cedar posts, reached the street edge. There was a bright fire glowing in the furnace, and the forge, when turned caused sparks to fly from it. As he had surmised the evening before, the blacksmith shop was the hub of activity in town, for already several men were lounging about the place, perhaps seeking warmth from the fire, but more likely seeking the companionship of other men. They were a nondescript lot, mostly buffalo hunters and men returning from the war, who had few roots anywhere.

Among them, however, was Buff Larrigan. A huge old mountain man wearing stained buckskins and a magnificent beard and long, snowy white hair, Buff had trapped in the mountains for many years and had both friends and enemies among the Indians. Every few years it was his want to skip the trappers' yearly rendezvous and return to civilization for a few days. "Keeps a man from turnin' into a varmint" was his explanation.

He spied Finch riding toward the shop and peered keenly at him. His blue eyes seemed puzzled as Finch dismounted. Then a smile creased his craggy features. "Never seen the lad afore, but I reckon I know who he is," Buff thought with satisfaction. The mountain telegraph traveled fast.

"Mornin'!" Finch spoke cheerfully as he rode up. The blacksmith looked up incuriously as he pounded a piece of red hot iron. Two or three of the other men grunted what they deemed to be a greeting.

The old mountain man said, "Light and set, lad. Give your saddle a rest."

"Lookin' for a couple of fellers," Finch said jovially. "One is ridin' a bay horse with three stockings, and the other is riding a grulla with a blaze face. Both wearing a 69 brand on the left hip. Any of you fellers seen 'em?"

Finch was greeted by a stony silence for several minutes, interrupted only by the banging of the smithy's sledge as he worked. Finally Buff Larrigan said, "And who be lookin' for 'em, me lad?"

"I am," Finch said shortly.

"And who might ye be, young feller?" Buff asked.

"Name's Finch."

"Uh huh!" Buff grunted in satisfaction as he squirted a stream of tobacco juice and rubbed his chin with a forefinger. "I ain't sure you want to find them two fellers. They got some bark on 'em. Friends of yourn, be they?" The Irish brogue was rich and thick.

"Nope," Finch grinned at the old man. "You seen 'em?"

The old fellow shrugged and said, "They came through a couple of days ago."

"Know where they are now?"

"Last time I heard 'em say anything about travellin', they was talkin about Dallas. That's a little settlement about twenty-five or thirty miles down river. But it don't amount to much and never will. So I expect they've moved on."

"They didn't go to Dallas." The blacksmith spoke for the first time. "I shod the grulla horse, and the feller said that it'd damn well better last to get him to Taos, and then he left without payin' me."

"They were headin' for Taos?" Finch arched an eyebrow at the smithy.

"That's what they said," the smith replied grumpily. "Wish that shoe'd come off the grulla before they get there—but it won't."

"Thanks!" Finch grinned at them as he turned his sorrel gelding and rode away.

"Now what you reckon that feller wants with them two hard cases?" asked one man of no one in particular.

"Don't know for shore," Buff said, "But if he's who I think he is, I'm just as glad I ain't ridin' a grulla hoss, begorra!"

# CHAPTER 2

Humphey Beatenbow was returning from the Civil War just before his twenty-fifth birthday. He was accompanied by Largo, his former slave, and for the past four years his friend and companion.

Humphrey was sturdily built and had coarse, wiry hair that had bronze tints in it when the sun struck it. His eyes were brown flecked and hawkish. His face was almost stern, and he rarely smiled. He was able to hold his left shoulder even with his right only with a conscious effort, for he still carried a musket ball from the battle of Chattanooga that pained him constantly.

Largo was a huge black man with bulging muscles, ebony skin, and a ready smile that showed glistening white teeth and twinkling eyes. Before the war he had been the Beatenbow blacksmith, and unofficially, the prime stud of the plantation. He adored his young master, and although he loved the plantation and enjoyed the young wenches tremendously, he quite willingly, even joyously, accompanied Humphrey when he went off to join the Confederate Army. During the four years of fighting, he had served as valet, confidant, and protector of sorts to Humphrey. He had, on more than one occasion, saved his master's life, and Humphrey had reciprocated. Their association grew from master-slave to friends, although neither of them would have suggested such a thing.

As they neared the Beatenbow plantation where both Humphrey and Largo had been born, Humphrey was impervious to the beauty of the budding Louisiana countryside with its majestic wild oaks and cypress trees, and to the damp, heavy air so laden with the aroma of jasmine, wild azalia, dogwood, and redbud.

His mind was on what he feared lay ahead. He had learned that both his parents were dead of consumption while he was recuperating from his wound in the crude army hospital. Only the slaves remained on the plantation, and of them, only Kate, the huge Negro woman who had been the Beatenbow cook since he could remember, had any sense of responsibility or proprietary interest in the place. His nebulous hope was that she had been able to cajole Sam, her elf-like mate, and some of the others to keep the place in decent condition.

This forlorn hope, however, was dashed as they drew nearer. The broad cotton fields that should have been planted lay fallow, and the weeds growing profusely indicated that the land had not been plowed for more than a year.

"God-a-mighty!" Humphrey whispered under his breath; but the phrase was not profanity; rather it was used to express incredulity, anger, surprise, joy, vexation, humor, or desperation, depending on the tone in which it was used. His father, a devout man, had used the phrase in the same ways. Humphrey had acquired it and could express almost any emotion with it.

Humphrey shook his head sadly as he and Largo rode toward the big house. He was somewhat surprised to see a garden plot and a few acres nearby that had been recently planted.

Kate greeted them profusely, and tears flowed down her fat face as she ran to them.

"I done told Sam you'd be back, Mars Hump!" she cried. "I just knowed you would!"

"Hello, Kate." Humphrey's greeting was cryptic. "The place is a mess."

"I know dat, Mars Hump," she wailed. "I done my best to get them no-good niggers to work, but dey jus' lolls around and don' do nothin'. But me and Sam, we got us a few acres planted to raise us some vittles. Sam, he take good care o' de livestock, and they in good shape. Don' know how de res' of de niggers been eatin' and don' care. They too lazy to live."

"Largo," Humphrey said, "you go and look over the cabins. I'm goin' to be out there directly. But first, I want to look about the house here."

"Yassuh, Mars Hump," Largo said quickly. "I do that right now."

As Humphrey inspected the big house, his depression deepened. Little had changed in the interior, and the many rooms both downstairs and up had apparently been well kept by Kate, but the house no longer seemed alive. Even his old bedroom evoked no nostalgia in him.

When he returned to the kitchen, Kate was energetically stirring something on the wood-burning stove.

"We got any whiskey, Kate?"

"Yas suh, Mars Hump. We has. I been keepin' it hid in de root cellar, and some vittles, too."

"Pour me a glass full. I'm goin' out to inspect the nigger quarters, and I'll drink it when I get back. Doubt I'll want anything to eat, though."

"Yassuh, Mars Hump, yassuh. But I fix yo somp'n good to eat, anyway."

Humphrey's face was grim as he inspected the slave quarters. Apparently, they had been neglected for four years. Some of the roofs were caving in, and there was generally an air of desertion and desolation. He was mildly surprised and deeply disturbed. The Beatenbow plantation had been able to boast of the finest Negro stock in the country when he was at home and his folks were alive. But now he realized that even the Beatenbow slaves were shiftless without supervision and direction.

The grown men and women ducked back into cabins as he approached. Several naked young blacks played in the dusty road that ran in front of the cabins. That would never have been allowed when the plantation was operating, for they were required to wear shifts and diapers as soon as they were able to go outside to play.

He met Largo at the far end of the cabin row.

"How many are left, Largo?" he asked.

"No idee, Mars Hump. They been comin' and goin' ever since they got freed up. A lot of 'em still here—most o' the wenches, but the bucks, they been leavin' and comin' back."

Humphrey could almost sympathize with them, for he, too, was at a loss to know what to do; the slaves had been anxious to try their new freedom, but found that freedom was much more than a piece of paper signed by the government.

Though many had left the plantation, most of them had come drifting back in the past few weeks.

The only bright spot was the stables and corrals. Sam had evidently spent most of his time keeping them in decent repair, and all the mules and thoroughbred mares were in good condition. Their breeding jack was in his stout pen, and Humphrey approached the stall of his prize stallion with some trepidation, but the big, black horse neighed his recognition; then tried to bite him when he reached through the bars to pet him. Humphrey laughed for the first time since he had been home.

"I'll take some of that vinegar out of you tomorrow, you black bastard," he promised fondly.

He started walking back toward the once fine mansion that had been the home of the Beatenbows for four generations. He stopped and sighed as he looked at the neglected lawns and gardens. For the first time in his life, he consciously wished that he had brothers or sisters. Maybe things would have been different.

"There's yo drink, Mars Hump," Kate said almost proudly as he entered the kitchen. "And I have yo somp'n good to eat right soon."

Humphrey accepted the glass without thanks. "Don't want anything to eat, Kate. I'm goin' up to my room. Don't want to be disturbed by anybody."

"Yassuh, Mars Hump. I don't let nobody bother yo," she said with a worried frown.

Humphrey sat on the bed in his room and sipped the whiskey. He wondered what he should do. What he could do. When he finished the whiskey, he lay back on the bed and stared at the ceiling. The future looked bleak, for with little money and the oppression of the North that was already being acutely felt throughout Louisiana, the future of the Beatenbow plantation did indeed look bleak.

He thought of the bustling, thriving plantation that was so vital and alive when he left. The comparison made him almost ill. He remembered a special friend of his in the army, a Texan, who had no particular feeling toward Negroes, but was simply fightin' because it seemed the thing to do. He was constantly extolling the virtues of his home state.

"Land for the taking," he bragged, "and cattle by the thousands just runnin' loose. Not a brand on 'em. I was one of the last men to leave for the war, and most of the ranchers had already signed up and turned their herds loose. Moved their women folks back east, most of 'em. Them cattle have had five years to multiply, and they'll be thicker than jackrabbits when I get back. I'm gonna round up a million and get me some land that stretches from here to yonder to run 'em on."

But he didn't. The same day Humphrey was wounded, his friend was killed. Humphrey actually knew little about him other than that he was from Texas. He didn't know whether he was married, had folks at home, or even what part of Texas he was from. Humphrey only knew that the Texan was an optimistic person who did not object to Largo's being with them. In fact, he had shown more friendliness toward Largo than Humphrey did.

Humphrey slept sporadically that night, and when he awakened, he was still tired. But sometime during the night he had reached a decision. When he was eating breakfast, he told Kate to have Largo saddle his black stud.

"Yassuh, Mars Hump. I tells 'im. But Sam he say that black stud gettin' awful mean. Ain't been rid since yo pa—"

"I'll ride 'im," Humphrey said. "Just tell Largo to saddle 'im."

When Humphrey finished his breakfast and walked down to the stables, he found Largo sweating profusely and the black stud tied securely to a stout post. The horse was breathing heavily and walling his eyes.

"That stud sho has gone mean, Mars Hump," Largo gasped. "Thought I never would get a saddle on 'im. He kicked and bit at me somp'n fierce."

Humphrey laughed. "Old Heck knows better than to rile me," he said confidently. "We've been through all that before, and horses have a good memory."

He walked up to the black and put his hand out, whereupon the stud pulled back mightily on his short tether. Humphrey promptly kicked him in the belly three times just as hard as he could. The horse seemed to settle down a bit, and Humphrey loosed the tether and quickly mounted. The horse turned his head and snapped viciously at Humphrey's leg. Although Humphrey sat a saddle sloppily, he was an excellent horseman, and he had ridden Old Heck before. He calmly hit the horse across his powerful jaws with the handle of a lead loaded quirt. The horse squealed his fury and reared high in the air. Humphrey applied the heavy end of the quirt again with a powerful blow between the horse's ears. Old Heck come back to earth with his forelegs spread wide apart and blood running from his mouth and nose.

"Got enough, old feller?" Humphrey said in a soothing voice.

Evidently Old Heck had had enough, for he started walking sedately away as Humphrey applied his spurs to the shiney sides.

"Tell Kate I'll be back for supper," he ordered Largo over his shoulder.

Largo watched in admiration as the man and horse disappeared into the trees.

Humphrey returned just before sundown and turned Old Heck over to Largo to unsaddle. Old Heck was actually docile, but Humphrey's face was grim, and he looked almost ill. His shoulder was sagging badly.

"Give 'im a good feed, Largo, and then come up to my room in about an hour."

"Yo means in the Big House, Mars Hump?" Largo asked in surprise. The only room he had ever seen in the Big House was the kitchen.

"That's what I mean," Humphrey said bluntly.

When he had eaten supper, he said to Kate, "Largo will be up in a few minutes. Send him to my room."

"To yo room, Mars Hump?" Kate was stunned.

"You heard me, Kate," Humphrey said grouchily.

When Largo came to Humphrey's room, he knocked timidly.

"Come in, Largo," Humphrey said. And then he explained the decision he had made and the steps he had taken.

"Have all the niggers out in front of the house early in the mornin'."

\* \* \* \* \* \*

Largo had the Negroes assembled on the shoddy lawn in front of the big house early the next morning. Humphrey walked out on the porch and looked at them. Many of the little ones had been born since he had been gone, but he noted with satisfaction that none were naked.

Humphrey's voice, always a little gruff, was almost harsh as he addressed those assembled.

"All right," he said. "The Beatenbow plantation is gone—and all of you are free. I'm headin' west—to Texas. If some of you want to go with me, I'd be right pleased. But it's up to you. You sure don't have to if you don't want to. I sold out yesterday to Mr. Farnham, who owns the place just south. I reckon he'll be glad to have as many of you as want, to stay here and help him out. I have no idea what to expect out west, but I hope we won't have any Yankees out there. If any of you come with me, you'll be free men and women. I'll pay you what I can, which won't be much—but more'n you've ever had before. Now those of you that want to stay, go back to your quarters. Those that think you want to go with me, follow Largo down to the blacksmith shop. I'll be down there directly."

With that, Humphrey turned his back to them and walked into the house. He had been standing straight when he talked to them, but when the door closed behind him, his right shoulder sagged. He leaned against a stairway for a moment and then made his way to the kitchen where old Kate stood with her hands on her hips and glared at him as he came into the kitchen. Sam, her wizened little mate sat timidly, his eyes almost hidden in his wrinkled face.

"I heard that Mars Hump," Kate said accusingly, and her huge body trembled with emotion. "And if'n yo thinks yo is gonna go off and leave me and Sam, even if we is wuthless niggers, then yo got another think a-comin'. I changed yo didies when yo was a little bubbin, and I watched yo grow up and go off to war—which near broke my heart. So we is gonna go with yo now, where ever it is, even if I has to spank yo bottom agin'!"

Humphrey grinned self-consciously. "I reckon I never even thought of leavin' you and Sam here," he admitted. "Now pour me a good stiff shot of whiskey, and I'm gonna go down to the shop and find out how many want to take a chance out west—with the Indians and all."

"Some will, and some won't," old Kate said philosophically as she poured Humphrey half a glass of brown liquid. "Them that does come, it'll be cause they wants to. Them that don't—yo'll be better off without."

"I reckon you're right, Kate. I don't want anyone with me that doesn't want to be!"

"Yo gonna see that little Terrell girl afore yo leave?"

"Why did you ask that, Kate?"

"Cause I knows she's had big eyes fo' yo since afore yo went off to war, and she was only twelve years old then."

Humphrey wanted to tell Old Kate to mind her own business, but at the same time he wanted to talk about Colette Terrell. They had grown up on adjoining plantations, and he had been enthralled since the first time he had seen the dark-eyed, straight-haired little tomboy. He had made many excuses to visit her plantation, but had not gone there since his return. She would be a grown woman by now, and being a practical man, he just couldn't see what a very beautiful sixteen year old girl would see in a twenty-four year old man with nothing but uncertainty and danger in his future. Besides that, her father, old Nate Terrell, had made no secret of his dislike for Humphrey Beatenbow, but Colette's mother had always welcomed him warmly. She was a gentle person with dark eyes and straight hair like her daughter, and Humphrey suspected, correctly, that she had a great deal of Indian and French blood.

"Well, God-a-mighty, Kate!" Humphrey said. "That girl wouldn't look twice at me. She's a lot too young for me, and besides, old man Terrell would run me off the place with a bull whip if he thought I—!"

"Hah!" old Kate snorted disdainfully. "I reckon they ain't nobody gonna run yo no place that yo don' wanta go. Yo is as bull headed as that jackass stud yo keeps here to pleasure them good mares and raise them big mules—and I reckon yo is jus' about as mean when yo riled up! Besides, she's a growed up young woman now. She been over her ever month since yo been gone wantin' to know did we hear from yo. She was mighty good to yore folks, too, afore they died. I reckon yo is gonna think she's some pretty lady when yo see her. I guess yo gonna like her even if she do sometimes talk like a field nigger and ride over the country like a wild Indian on that spotted mare of hers."

Humphrey laughed and drained his glass of whiskey. "Well, I guess I had better go down to the shop and see if anybody beside you and Sam and Largo is going west with me."

"Yo do that, Mars Hump. And yo stop by that Terrell place afore we leave. I thinks maybe we'll have another passenger if'n yo'll jus' behave yoself. Besides, yo gonna need a woman out there where they ain't gonna be nothin' but Indians and maybe a few black wenches that'll come with us."

"Now Kate, you know that I ain't gonna have anything to do with an Indian or a black woman!"

"Don' know no such thing, Mars Hump. I know a man—and animals too, is gonna breed. I reckon that's one o the reasons we're on this ol' earth, and I knows yo been breedin' since yo was twelve years old."

"Now, Kate!" Humphrey was aghast.

"I seen yo pester them high yella gals a lot of times, Mars Hump. But I never said nothin' cause yo Ma 'n Pa would a tanned yo good. And yo ought not to do that no more—yo needs a white woman to take care of yo!"

"That's crazy, Kate." Humphrey was flustered. "But maybe so I will go by the Terrell place before we leave."

\* \* \* \* \* \*

Largo had gathered a good crowd of blacks in front of the blacksmith shop. "They's ready, Mars Hump."

"You know why you're here," Humphrey said. "I'm goin' west—to Texas. Those that want to go, can. Those that don't, can live here as long as the man that now owns the place will let you. Those that go with me will be taking big chances. I knew some Texans in the war, and they say there ain't much there now but buffalo and Indians and land—at least not where I'm going. Those of you that want to go, let Largo know. He'll be your boss now, and you do what he tells you. First thing is to get some wagons covered and loaded with grub and tools and utensils. Then we need to pick the best of the mules and horses to take—and some brood mares and that jackass. We'll pull out as soon as Largo says we're ready."

Humphrey turned on his heel and walked back toward the house. He was afraid to watch lest all the blacks walk away. When he entered the kitchen door, old Kate and Sam were there. Kate was stirring something on the stove, and Sam was sitting in a cane bottomed chair grinning his toothless grin.

"Hello, Sam," Humphrey greeted him. "Where you been?"

"Ain't been nowhere, Mars Hump," Sam grinned, and his small black eyes twinkled. "Jes sittin' here watchin' Kate. But I reckon I's gonna go sommers—leastwise that's what Kate says."

"That's right. Were heading out west to Texas. Nothing out there but Indians and buffalo—and maybe trouble!"

"Then why we goin' Mars Hump?"

"I'm gonna build me a cattle ranch out there. There's plenty of free land, and I'll find the cattle."

"But we ain't never raised cattle, Mars Hump. We always raised cotton and niggers."

"Right, Sam. But it's time we changed that. You are free people now. That means you got a right to pick and choose who you want to bed down with."

"Do it really?" Sam grinned in delight.

Kate glared ferociously at him. "Yo go traipsin' after one of them young gals and yo'll find out who's got a right to pick and choose, yo no good nigger—sides, yo got more'n yo can take care of already."

"That's a fact," Sam admitted gloomily. "I was jes talkin', Kate."

Humphrey had been taking in the conversation with delight, and he laughed aloud. "Well, Sam, I reckon Kate has got us both figured pretty close. I guess we'd better just toe the mark—specially when Kate is around!"

"Now don't yo go funnin' me, Mars Hump. I's a free woman now, and yo can't sell me lak yo could afore. I jes know what men needs, that's all. Ain't like I was tryin' to boss nobody around!" Tears rolled down her fat black cheeks as she turned to the stove. Humphrey walked up behind her and put his hand on her shoulder.

"I know you weren't being bossy, Kate. You've always been good to me, and I'd never sell you anyway—not for a million dollars."

"Well," sniffed Kate. "You and Sam ort to get down to the corrals and see about loadin' things out. When we leavin'?"

"As soon as Largo says we're ready. Come on, Sam."

Sam and Humphrey left the kitchen, and Kate watched them as they made their way toward the corrals; then she sat at the table and put her head down on it as great sobs racked her huge, fat frame.

\* \* \* \* \* \*

Three days later Humphrey was satisfied that Largo was doing a good job of getting the wagons covered and loading tools and equipment of various kinds that would be necessary in building, farming, or ranching, and that old Kate and Sam were stocking enough provisions to furnish an army for a year. But Kate insisted that, even with buffalo meat plentiful, they would need a lot of provisions for the black men, women, and kids. There were several Negro men and women and a few youngsters gathered about and Humphrey assumed that they were the ones that had volunteered to go west with them.

Two of the youngsters, both boys, belonged to the oldest woman; and the youngest, a girl, belonged to the youngest black woman. Since slaves were not married, there was no sure way of telling who the father of each was. Humphrey suspected that the two older boys probably had been sired by Largo before the war, for their mother was one of the most comely of the wenches. The sire of the youngest girl, of course, could have been any one of the bucks that had been left behind, for Humphrey's father had been too frail to supervise the breeding program very carefully. Humphrey hoped, and indeed his hope was true, that the buck who claimed the wench was also the sire of her daughter. There was another young buck and an extremely dark young wench about fourteen years of age that wanted to make the trip, and Humphrey agreed. That left only Largo, who declared that he wanted no wench tagging along after him, but Humphrey could envision a lot of trouble if Largo took no woman.

"Now, Largo," he said sternly. "You are all free people, now. And that means that you've gotta act like whites as much as you can. You can't go beddin' down wenches that belong to other men! You've got to get your own. Fact is, I'm gonna stop at the first place that I come to that's got a preacher and have him marry every couple that's with us."

"Yo means, Mars Hump, that I can bed only one wench for the rest of my whole life?"

Humphrey smothered a smile. "That's right," he said sternly. "Now you go down to the quarters and pick you out a wench. If she don't want to come with us, let me know, and I'll talk to her."

"Well, all right, Mars Hump. I don't reckon I'll have no trouble gettin' one to go with me, but it shore will be a chore to keep from pesterin' them other wenches that are comin' along."

"They're gonna be married to their men, and you're gonna be married to your wench!" Humphrey said coldly. "And don't you ever let me catch you with any wench other than your own!"

"Yassuh, Mars Hump. I shore won't let yo catch me!" Largo said earnestly, and Humphrey looked at him keenly as the double meaning of Largo's answer dawned on him.

The next morning Largo brought an extremely comely wench with him to the blacksmith shop. She was very dark, but her nose was thin and almost aristocratic, her lips were full but not Negroid, and her figure was astonishingly full and lissome.

"This here is Maisie, Mars Hump," Largo introduced her. "She gwine to go with us. Told her about us havin' to get married and not bed nobody but each other. Don't know why, but she like dat!"

Humphrey looked at Maisie; she smiled shyly, showing very even, white teeth.

"Maisie, you understand that this trip may be dangerous and that you must marry Largo and not bed any other man than him?"

"Yassuh. I shore understands that, Mars Hump." Maisie's smile widened. "Largo done tole me, and he take care of me, too. And I don need to bed no other buck. Largo plenty fo' me. We done tried it out all right last night."

Humphrey could think of no answer to that; he shook his head and looked at Largo who grinned a bit sheepishly.

"Well, Largo when do you reckon we'll be able to start?"

"Three days, Mars Hump. I got it all figgered. This here is Thursday. We finish riggin' and loadin' ever'thing by late Saturday. We can rest up Sunday and start early Monday mornin'."

"How many wagons are we taking?"

"Eight, Mars Hump," Largo answered. "I figgered you for the lead wagon, and I already put a good bed in it. We'll put blacksmith an farmin' tools in the second wagon and let a buck drive the others They'll be loaded with vittles and some furniture. Maisie and me will bring up the rear with a wagon load of odds and ends that'll come in handy. And we'll tie that big jackass behind our wagon."

"Sounds like you have everything under control. But we'll want to take six or eight of our best mares with us, and I'll ride Old Heck myself. And throw in a few sacks of corn for him. We can't turn him loose to graze."

"Yassuh. I figgered you'd want to ride that big black stud, and that mean we need a couple more bucks, maybe three. One to drive yo wagon and somebody to herd them mares along behind the wagons—lessen yo wants to hitch some mares to the wagons."

"Ain't gonna have no mares of mine pullin' wagons, " Humphrey said sternly. "That's a job for mules. You'll just have to round up some more bucks."

"I can do that, Mars Hump. Fact is, I's already had several more pesterin' me to go. Trouble is, if we does lak yo say, them bucks ain't gonna have no wenches. What we gonna do about that?"

"They'll just have to do without," Humphrey said emphatically. "Maybe they won't like that, but it sure as hell won't kill 'em."

"Yassuh. I'll 'splain it to 'em. Don't know as they'll go though if'n they has to do without a wench."

"You convince 'em, Largo!"

"I reckon I can do that, Mars Hump," Largo grinned.

"There's one other thing, Largo. We're gonna need a lot of guns and ammunition, and I don't reckon there's another nigger in the bunch that ever shot a gun except you."

"That's a fact!" Largo admitted ruefully.

"Well, I'll bring down some rifles and ammunition, and we'll just have to lay over an extra day. You take the bucks down by the river and show 'em how to shoot a bit. At least, let 'em know which end of the rifle the bullet comes out of."

"Yassuh, Mars Hump. Anything else?"

"Be sure there's a good water barrel fixed to each wagon. I understand that we'll cross some country where there isn't much water."

"Yassuh, I'll do that. Hadn't thought of it."

"All right, " Humphrey said with finality. "Have everything all set, and we'll pull out next Tuesday morning early. And I'll be gone the rest of today—and maybe tomorrow. I'm gonna ride over to the Terrell place."

\* \* \* \* \* \*

Humphrey rode to the Terrell place with deep misgivings. Old Nate Terrell had never liked Humphrey, and he suspected correctly that it was because Colette and Mrs. Terrell thought that Humphrey Beaten bow was something special. If Nate Terrell had ever given the matter thought, he would not have considered himself a jealous man. He did, however, resent the fact that he was not able to raise the fine slaves, the Beatenbows always had. There was one thing, though, that he was inordinately proud of. There was no one to whom he had to take second place when it came to womenfolk. His wife had been, and indeed still was, the most beautiful and luxuriously endowed woman in the entire country. Her beauty was both inside and out, for she was a woman to whom others came for comfort and cheer. And now his daughter Colette was becoming, if possible, even more beautiful than her mother. She made friends easily and always seemed to be at ease in any situation. Many of the slaves came to her for solace, and she listened to them for hours. Often she would intercede in behalf of one. Nate half suspected that Humphrey Beatenbow had coveted his wife, and he knew that his wife had returned a great deal of the feeling that Humphrey could not hide when around her. But it was with Colette that Nate distrusted Humphrey most. He was certain that his wife would never be untrue to him. But he also knew that Humphrey was a randy youngster who screwed every high yeller and a lot of white girls before the war. And Nate boiled when Humphrey came near Colette, for even at ten or eleven years, she was a budding beauty. And now Colette was a young woman, sixteen years of age, fully developed, and a beauty if there ever was one. Humphrey Beatenbow probably hadn't changed any for the better since he went to the war four years before. Nate Terrell fumed when Humphrey was even near the place.

Although the Terrells had three other children, one daughter and two sons, Colette was the oldest and had always been her father's favorite, though he tried very hard, but in vain, to show no partiality. Colette was a constant delight to him, though he deplored her candid speech which she said was "just what other people thought but were afraid to say". Perhaps, Nate thought guiltily, that was a part of her charm, for her mother in their intimate moments often shocked him with her language and honest verbal expression of emotion and passion.

"I guess that's just the French part of them," he thought. "Maybe that is why I love them so much. But I do wish Colette wouldn't talk like that in front of others. The wife doesn't."

Luckily Nate was away that day when Humphrey rode up. The Terrell house was grand and well-kept, as the Beatenbow place had been before the war. Humphrey sighed as he looked about and then dismounted, tying the black stud to a sturdy shrub. He felt uneasy but determined as he walked up the gravel path to the door. Colette opened the door and ran to meet him.

"Humphrey! I'm glad you came. I was afraid you would leave and not say goodby."

Humphrey removed his hat. "I couldn't do that, Colette. I'm well—"

"Come on in the house, Humphrey. Mother has been worried about you too. We heard about you going off to that Texas place. She'll want to hear about it."

Humphrey followed Colette inside. The house was cool, well-ar ranged, and tastefully furnished. Mrs. Terrell was sitting on a screened in porch overlooking the river, and to Humphrey's surprise, another woman was with her. She was as fair as Mrs. Terrell was dark; yet she had the same dark eyes. There was a strong and strange resemblance, though the other woman looked much younger.

"How good to see you, Humphrey," Mrs. Terrell said with genuine pleasure as she rose and extended a well shaped and carefully tended hand. When Humphrey took her hand, she put her other arm around him and hugged him. Humphrey was terribly flustered.

"Humphrey, I want you to meet my sister, Maureen," Mrs. Terrell said. "I know she looks like my daughter," she laughed, "and she is almost young enough to be. She is only four years older than Colette."

"It sure is good to see you, Mrs. Terrell," Humphrey gulped, "and I'm right glad to meet you, too, Mrs.—"

"Maureen." The blond sister rose and extended her hand. "And I'm glad to meet you, too, Humphrey Beatenbow. Colette has told me about you."

"Well, I'm—I just wanted to come by to see you all," Humphrey said lamely.

Mrs. Terrell's laugh was delightful, and she hugged Humphrey again. "I know who you came to see." She pushed him away and looked up at him. "You've grown since you went away, Humphrey."

"Yes ma'am. I reckon I have. Beatenbows don't get full grown until after we are twenty—the men, that is."

"Well, the Terrell women get grown a lot faster than that," she said teasingly.

Humphrey grinned but could think of nothing to say. The three women were all standing, and Humphrey thought them the most beautiful he had ever seen. Colette, with her boundless energy and natural young beauty; Mrs. Terrell, with her mature poise and composure; and Maureen, who was so different, yet so much like the others. All three of them had the same dark eyes that could sparkle with merriment, flame with emotion, or envelop another human being with love and tenderness.

"Now, Humphrey, you sit and tell us all about this wonderful Texas place that you plan to go to."

Humphrey sat awkwardly and told them what he had heard of Texas and why he had decided to go there. "Our place just isn't home anymore. It's gone to ruin while I've been gone."

"I know," Mrs. Terrell said sadly. "Colette has been telling me about it. She has been going over there every few days, and she is always sad when she comes back home."

"Kate told me that Colette had been over a few times," Humphrey admitted. "I just wish—I mean—"

"Now," Mrs. Terrell interrupted with some finality. "Maureen and I have a lot of visiting to catch up on; so why don't you take Humphrey for a walk down by the creek, Colette. Your father won't be home until late; so there will be no need for you to hurry."

Humphrey looked at her gratefully. She smiled in return and left them.

"Come on, Humphrey. You want to put your horse in a stall while we're gone?"

"Maybe I ought to. He sometimes breaks his tether, and then there is hell—heck to pay."

"That stud is big and mean enough looking to raise a lot of hell," Colette laughed. "But I'll bet some of our mares would be glad if he did get loose."

Humphrey had been around slaves and animals all his life, and any sort of allusion to their mating did not in the least bother him, but at Colette's statement he felt his face grow hot.

Humphrey untied the stud and took the lead rope in one hand. Colette took his other, and they made their way toward the barn. Several former slaves looked at them curiously. Colette paid not the least bit of attention to them. When they reached the creek, Colette leaned against a tree. Both she and Humphrey were silent as they watched the muddy stream flow by.

"I didn't know you had an aunt," Humphrey finally broke the silence.

"I have three of them," Colette said absently. "They all live in New Orleans. But Maureen is my favorite. She's not much older than I am. Her husband was killed in the war."

"A lot of good men were killed in the war. Those of us that got back were just lucky, I guess."

"You intend to stay in Texas for good?" Colette asked suddenly.

"I reckon," Humphrey admitted. "I got no reason to come back here—unless it's to see some friends, if I have any left here."

"You gonna ride that black stud all the way to Texas?"

"Aim to. I never liked riding in a wagon."

"You're going to ride that black stud all day—what are you going to ride at night — a black wench?"

"God-a-mighty, Colette!" Humphrey was aghast. "That's a hell of a thing for a young lady to say."

"I'm not a young lady, Humphrey Beatenbow." Her black eyes flashed as she looked angrily at him. "I am a woman! A grown woman! I've been a woman since before you left for the war; only you were too stupid—or blinded by mother's good looks to notice me." She thrust out her chest, and the rounded breasts protruded invitingly through the thin material of her dress. "Well look now! If you took me with you, you wouldn't have anything to come back for."

Humphrey stood dumbfounded for a moment, and then he stepped forward and gathered her in his arms. "It may be a dangerous trip," he said huskily. He kissed her hungrily, and she returned his kisses with equal fervor.

"No more dangerous than what we're doing right now—in sight of the house. But I don't care if we do get caught. In fact, that's the reason Mama sent us down here. She knew this would happen!"

"She couldn't!" Humphrey gasped.

"She did!" Colette giggled. "And I'll bet she and Maureen are peeping out a window right now. When are we leaving for Texas? I think it's time you changed the color of the mount you ride at night."

Colette took his hand and led him toward the stables. There was a row of stalls inside, and one which had housed a horse with a particularly mean disposition was completely enclosed. Colette opened the door; the stall was empty, but there was clean straw on the floor. She turned to Humphrey and reached behind his back and locked the door from the inside.

Colette stood for a moment and looked into Humphrey's eyes. He felt that he was floating in the depths of her luminous, black eyes. Slowly, without moving her eyes from his, she began unbuttoning her dress.

"God-a-mighty!" Humphrey breathed hoarsely as he took her in his arms and gently lowered her to the straw covered stable floor.

An hour later when they were walking toward the house, hand in hand, Humphrey tried to be flippant, although he did, in fact, feel very humble and a little scared.

"You know, Colette," he said as he grinned sheepishly, "it never has been that way with me before. I mean, you're so—" He was suddenly at a loss for words, but he continued doggedly. "What I mean is—you're so good! And I even feel good about what we did. I never felt good about it before."

"I'm sure that must be a great compliment, Mr. Beatenbow," Colette said flippantly. "For I know you must have had a lot of women."

"Aww—Colette, I didn't mean—" Humphrey protested.

"Oh, yes you have. I know about you—slaves talk, you know," she said impishly. "But you will never know about me!"

"Even after we're married?"

"Even then! And what makes you think we are going to get married?"

"Why—God-a-mighty, Colette!" Humphrey sputtered. "We have to—I mean—well dammit, I've loved you ever since I can remember. And I love you now more than ever!"

Colette stopped walking and turned to him. "Humphrey Beatenbow, I've wanted to hear you say that since I was ten years old!"

"Well, I've said it," Humphrey said firmly. "Now let's get on with it."

They embraced in the gravel path that led to the house but were not aware of Colette's mother standing at the door until she slammed it after her. They parted quickly, Humphrey guiltily and Colette gleefully.

"Come into the house, you two," Mrs. Terrell said chidingly but with a smile in her voice. "The blacks are all peeping at you!"

They were still holding hands when they entered the house. Colette was radiant, and her fine dark eyes sparkled as she looked at her mother. Humphrey flushed guiltily and looked uncomfortable. Mrs. Terrell's eyes twinkled, and Maureen looked at them with dark eyes that shone with tenderness and a tinge of envy. Humphrey somehow felt that both of them knew what had happened. In their intuitive womanly wisdom, they did indeed know.

Humphrey blurted almost belligerently, "We're gonna get married."

Mrs. Terrell laughed merrily. "I've known that for years, and it may be sooner than you think if Colette's father sees that straw in her hair!"

\* \* \* \* \* \*

The departure was delayed a week in order to prepare for the wedding, but finally the deed was done. The bride was radiant, and the groom happy and determined. Colette's father proved not to be as obnoxious as Humphrey feared, and at last they were ready to depart.

Humphrey agreed to ride the first wagon with Colette, at least until they were well on their way. But Colette insisted on bringing her own saddle mare, which was tied to one of the wagons. As the wagons pulled around a bend west of the house, Colette and Humphrey turned to wave from the high front seat of the lead wagon. Then they both looked westward, and Humphrey reached for Colette's hand.

"God-a-mighty!" Humphrey said prayerfully. "What a week!"

Colette's laughter pealed in the clear morning air, and the occupants of the following wagons smiled.

# Chapter 3

Finch was at peace with the world as he rode his handsome, fox-eared sorrel gelding toward the Canadian River on his way to Taos that warm, spring day in 1866.

He had covered a lot of country and crossed a lot of streams, including the Washita River, the Pease, and the Salt Fork of Red River since he had left Fort Worth.

But he was in no hurry. The men he was after would still be in Taos, which suited him just fine, for his great friend Kit Carson lived there. Finch had served with Kit in several skirmishes with outlaws and Indians on the Texas frontier during his tenure as a Texas Ranger. Kit was fast becoming a legend in the west by virtue of his having guided Fremont, and his prowess as an Indian fighter and soldier in the Union Army. Actually, it was more than passing strange that the two men were friends. Kit was more than thirty years older than Finch and had fought for the North, while Finch was a Southerner. But on the frontier where Indians, renegades, and Comancheros were playing havoc with settlers and travelers, the two men had fought together and had recognized in each other a kindred spirit that knew no politics; and victory and survival were the primary objectives of those who sought to tame a lawless land.

In addition to the very pleasant prospect of visiting his old friend, Finch was looking forward with almost childish eagerness to seeing his beautiful valley again. Of course, the valley wasn't really his, but since he had first seen it some five years before, he had harbored the seemingly hopeless dream of having a home in it one day, and he visited it whenever possible. The valley lay on the north side of a river and was deeper than the land around it. It was an idyllic winter haven for all sorts of animals. He had seen wild mustangs, deer, antelope, coyote, foxes, and almost every other kind of wild creature grazing contentedly in the lush grass and wild flowers that were so abundant. There were, of course, many buffalo, and he had even seen an old mossy horned bull once, which was not surprising since most of the ranches in Texas had been abandoned by their owners when the war started in 1861, and the longhorns had scattered and multiplied all over Texas. The one that Finch had seen was even wearing a brand, which he did not recognize.

The valley sloped gently from north to south, and the tall grass reached to the cottonwoods at the bank of the river. The closer he came to the valley, the more he tended to urge his horse faster. Finally, he could stand it no longer; he pushed his horse into a lope, and the pack mule lumbered along behind. They reached the brow of a sloping hill where they stopped, and Finch looked eagerly as he feasted his eyes on the most beautiful place he had ever seen.

The sandy river bed was wide, but only a small stream of water ran down it. Giant cottonwoods grew on the banks, but on the great expanse between the banks, only a few bushes and small trees were visible. Those were bent downstream, and trash had collected on them, giving mute testimony to the raging power of the frequent head rises that churned down the river, sweeping everything eastward.

Finch sat for a few moments, letting his gaze travel up and down the river. He had never seen it without the blue haze that seemed to enshroud it, lending it an air of mystery. Finally, he urged his horse forward and rode to the river's edge. He very carefully eased his horse into the sandy river bed, for he knew from experience and from stories told around campfires how treacherous the quicksands were. The faithful pack mule followed obediently. As Finch crossed, a big area of sand would suddenly seem to bend under the weight of his horse, and he would spur forward rapidly until he reached solid sand again.

The crossing finally accomplished, he stopped on the north bank and looked westward. He could see the grove of giant cottonwood trees and headed for it.

Pulling up under the biggest tree, he unpacked and tied his mule to a sturdy tree. Then he rode north into his valley. It was everything he remembered it to be. Wild flowers were beginning to bloom, buffalo were plentiful, and he saw a big mule deer and the tracks of various other wild creatures. He stopped and sat for a moment, taking a deep breath as he looked about.

"I'm gonna run me some cattle here some day." Finch had the habit of many western men, when alone, of talking to his horse. "And maybe it won't be too long now." He patted the horse's neck. "And then you can grow old and fat here where the grass tickles your belly."

With a sigh he turned back to his camp. On the way he killed a young turkey and set about roasting it when he arrived.

The camp was a natural place with good cover, and Finch had camped there before. He knew that Indians were still plentiful. He also knew that his horse would warn him if any were near.

An hour later he had finished the turkey, and with a most agreeable feeling of contentment, he unrolled his blankets and slid in. He couldn't see the sky clearly through the thick, barren limbs of the cottonwood; so he moved his bed away from the tree and into the starshine. He gazed upward for a long time and sighed.

"Much obliged, Lord," he said softly and turned on his side and instantly slept.

Finch was wary as he rode into the village of Taos. His years on the frontier had made him superbly sensitive to danger, and for some reason that he could not fathom, he felt the hackles on his neck rise just a bit as he rode down the dusty street.

The center of activity was not hard to spot. Several horses stood tied to the rail in front of the Emporium saloon. Finch held up a moment as he scanned the street both ways. Then he rode to the saloon. He looked the horses over carefully and noted with satisfaction, but no surprise, that two of them wore the brands he was looking for. He dismounted. His tall frame was lithe and limber as he stepped to the board walk and entered the saloon. A cowboy lounging in a chair leaning against the saloon wall was whittling and chewing tobacco. He nodded and grunted at Finch as he passed. The cowboy pushed his hat back, yawned, and stretched, then jumped upright as he heard what seemed to him to be a shot and an echo from within the saloon. A moment later Finch emerged from the saloon; his face was very white, and he looked sick. He quickly mounted his horse and rode away. The cowboy rushed into the saloon.

"What the hell happened in here?" he demanded. Then he saw two men lying on the floor near the bar. The room was deathly quiet. Then the bartender seemed to come to himself.

"Them two gents there," he pointed to the men lying on the floor, "they tried to outdraw a Texas Ranger!"

The rest of the men seemed to come to life, and there was a babble of sound throughout the room.

"That feller looked like a kid, except he was tall."

"Told 'em he was a Texas Ranger and that they was under arrest."

"I thought he was gonna let 'em shoot 'im. They both had their guns half way out before he even moved, and then they was both fallin'. I looked at 'im just in time to see 'im slip that pistol back in the holster."

"Fastest thing I ever saw—can't say that, though, because I didn't even see it!"

One of the customers rose from a table and went to the two men. He rolled them over. "Got both of 'em plumb center. Doubt if Kit could a done any better."

"Even Kit couldn't match that feller. I've seen Kit draw and shoot. That Ranger ain't got no equal with a pistol."

Finch rode up to Kit Carson's house and hollered. A Mexican woman came to the door with three small ones clinging to her skirt. She looked at Finch and turned to say something to someone inside. Kit came to the door; a huge smile split his face as he hobbled down the graveled walk to Finch and extended his hand.

"Finch! It's good to see you, boy!"

"Good to see you, too, Kit," Finch said quietly.

"What brings you this way?" Kit shook Finch's hand vigorously and slapped him on the back.

"After a couple of horse thieves."

"Still Rangerin', huh?"

"Yep!"

"Found 'em yet?"

"I found 'em."

"Got 'em in the Taos jail?"

"Nope. They didn't want to go to jail."

"Oh." Kit paused only slightly. He understood. "Just as well, I reckon. They probably would have hung, anyway."

"I reckon," Finch agreed glumly.

"Come on in this house!"

Finch followed Kit into the cool interior of the house. Kit spoke to the woman in Spanish; she poured coffee into mugs and set them before the men as they sat at the table. Finch had removed his hat and exposed a very white forehead and his rapidly thinning blond hair, which he combed his fingers through several times.

"The wife knew it was you," Kit said proudly, "soon as she saw that hay colored hair and that long frame of yours. I been telling her about you."

Finch grinned self-consciously. "Looks like you been busy as usual, Kit." Finch nodded toward the woman and youngsters.

"You know me, Finch," Kit said proudly. "I've got a couple little 'uns that ain't here, and I got one all growed up, too. Older than you are. But that ain't all I been doin'. I been chasing bad Indians and visiting with some good ones, too."

"Heard about that," Finch said. "Heard you was appointed Indian agent for southeastern New Mexico Territory."

"That's a fact," Kit agreed. "Pierce appointed me, and then Buchanan, he reappointed me."

"Didn't know that," Finch said. "Reckon that gives you some say over the Indians out here—especially the Kiowa."

"I'm supposed to have say over all of 'em—but you know Indians! Black Bull is chief of the Kiowa and a friend of mine. Fact is, most of the Indian chiefs have visited me here, and I've been to their camps quite a bit too. Grey Eagle—he's a good friend of mine. He's Arapaho. And White Horse is chief of the Comanches, and he's a good Indian. I reckon me being able to speak their languages helps some too. Then I spent a whole winter with the Crows."

Finch and Kit talked long into the night, and although more than thirty years different in age, they bore striking resemblance which defied definition. Kit was short and dark, while Finch was tall and blond. Yet there was an aura about each man that emanated raw power and even danger.

They reminisced about the times they had hunted Comancheros, horse thieves, and Indians on the Texas border. Kit got up occasionally to refill their coffee cups, and as he walked, he limped badly, and his face sometimes contorted in pain.

"Still gimpy from that horse fallin' on you, huh, Kit?"

"Reckon I always will be," Kit replied glumly. "Wasn't his fault, though. A Indian bullet broke his leg when he was in a dead run. When you headin' back to Austin?"

"Tomorrow, I reckon. I got no more business here. And I need to take those two horses back."

"Too bad you had to kill them two fellers."

"It doesn't make me feel good," Finch replied glumly. "Never does. But sometimes I reckon it can't be helped."

"Committed suicide is what they done," Kit said. "I could a told 'em that. How long I known you, Finch? Five years—maybe six. Anyway you wasn't even growed up good when I first saw you down on Red River, and even then I never saw a man that could pull a pistol so fast and shoot as straight as you can."

"I know," Finch said tiredly. "Sometimes I almost wish I wasn't so handy with a pistol."

"Killin' don't get no easier with me either, Finch," Kit commiserated. "But men like us don't have much choice that is agreeable to us. I don't have any idea how many men I've done in—countin' Indians—and they're human, too. Reckon I'm getting old. I'd rather talk than fight—given the chance."

"Well." Finch rose to his feet and stretched his full height. "Reckon I'll be goin'; it's gettin' late. Give my regards to your wife."

"Bunk here on the floor," Kit invited. "Can't offer you a bed cause I got kids in all of 'em."

"Better not," Finch laughed. "I've got all my gear down at the Pavillion, and I need to stable those two horses that were stolen."

"Maybe it's just as well," Kit grinned. "I've told Maria so much about you that she thinks you're about the most stud she's likely to see. She'd probably be in your pallet before morning!"

"Not a chance, Kit! And you know it."

Finch moved with catlike grace as he picked up his saddle bags and strapped on his pistol which he had removed upon entering the house. "Anyway, I reckon I'll leave out early."

"Which way you goin' back?"

"I'll cut southeast until I hit the Canadian and follow it a good long ways, then cut across salt Fork of Red River, and then the Pease to Fort Worth, and stop there a few days."

"You watch your top knot goin' down the Canadian, Finch. I had a whole regiment of soldiers goin' down that river a couple of years ago. Just afore we got to that place where Bent fixed up an adobe pen to do some tradin', the Indians hit us. Never saw so many. They was comin' out of every bush; so we just tucked our tails and ran. Fact is, Bent's adobe walls saved us a lot of horses, and men, too!"

Finch laughed. "I'd like to have seen that, Kit. There must have been a passel of 'em."

"They was. But I ain't proud of that little fracas, though we did hurt 'em pretty bad. Anyway, they made me a Brevet Brigadier on account of that."

"I'll be darned, Kit. I didn't know I had been hobnobbin' with a general most of the night. Reckon I ought to have saluted—or somethin'!"

"Sure!" jeered Kit. "I can just see you salutin' anybody! Anyhow, I got nearly five thousand troops I can call out at any time. The Indians know that and pay it a bit of mind."

"They ought!" Finch exclaimed.

"Tell you what—" Kit's face brightened. "You say you are goin' to follow the Canadian a ways?"

"Figure to. I got my eye on a piece of land on the north side of that river, and I'm gonna run some cattle on it some day."

"Cattle? Hell, Finch, that country's covered with buffalo."

"I know it is now, but—"

"Come back in this house, Finch." Kit's voice was urgent.

Finch followed Kit back inside the house. Kit's limp was more pronounced as he poured coffee.

"Set down, man. Set down." Kit was excited. Finch was puzzled. "Know what!" Kit's excitement was growing. "You just said 'hello' to the next century, Finch."

"What do you mean, Kit?" Finch was bewildered.

"I mean cattle, Finch! That's what this western country was made for. The buffalo won't last—they're killin' 'em now by the millions, just for their hides—and if they didn't kill 'em, they'd eventually breed themselves out of existence—be so many of 'em they'd ruin the grass and starve to death. Cattle is the answer."

"I know that, Kit. We ran cattle in south Texas until we got wiped out by thieves. You can handle cattle, and there is money in them. But how long do you reckon it's gonna be before the Indians and buffalo will make room for cattle on the Canadian river?"

"What's the land like, Finch, that you got your eye on?"

Finch removed his hat again and ran his fingers through his hair. A serene, almost euphoric look came over his youthful face and blue eyes as he said in his soft, almost musical voice: "It is the most beautiful country the good Lord ever made, Kit. A big, green valley on the north side of the river where the big cottonwoods grow, and there are live streams all through it. I've seen mustangs in there, and, of course, a lot of buffalo. There are deer, antelope, wild turkey, coyotes—all kinds of varmints. Even saw an elk once."

"Sounds like some places I've seen!" Kit said enthusiastically. "Tell you what, Finch. It's just possible that you might run cattle there sooner than you think."

"How's that?" Finch leaned forward eagerly. Their coffee had grown cold.

"Well, now," Kit said. "Old Chief White Horse is the bull Indian around that part, and he is a friend of mine. He knows, too, that I can muster a lot of troops and that I won't put up with no foolishness from any of the Indians—and that means Arapaho, Comanche, Kiowa, or any others—"

"What are you drivin' at, Kit?"

"We-e-ll, now," Kit hesitated. "If I was to tell Chief White Horse that you was a friend of mine and that I'd take it kindly if he, and all the other tribes, didn't bother you none—well, he just might be agreeable to lettin' you run cattle there. Course, you'd need a big crew and would be takin' a awful chance—other tribes might raid you, and there'd be renegade Indians, and the buffalo would have to be hazed away all the time, but—"

"Hey, wait a minute, Kit!" Finch interrupted. "You don't mean now?"

"Damn right, Finch. Now! Soon as you can get a crew and a herd of cattle on it," Kit said firmly. "Tell you what! I'll ride out with you early tomorrow, today—and we'll see how it sounds to the Indians."

"Aw, hell, Kit, you aren't in any shape to ride all the way to the Canadian with that game leg."

"Won't have to," Kit said. "I'll just ride with you until we see an Indian, and I'll send 'im to Chief White Horse. He'll come to us."

"You mean—"

"Damn right —I mean!" Kit responded. "It ain't much too early for breakfast right now. I'll get the wife up to fix us some while you go down to the pavillion and get your gear and fix us up with a couple of horses and pack animals."

\* \* \* \* \* \*

Finch and Kit camped the first night under a pine tree near a small stream. Finch staked the horses to graze, including the two stolen ones which he had tied behind the pack animals. Kit's bad leg was hurting, and he did not protest when Finch took over the cooking chores. The night was clear, the stars were bright, and a crescent moon hung high in the clear sky. When they were in their bedrolls, Finch cupped his hands behind his head and looked at the star-filled sky.

"I tell you, Kit," Finch said softly, "on that place of mine on the Canadian, you can just about reach up and dust off those stars at night."

"Already own that place, do you, Finch?" Kit was testy.

"Guess I am a little ahead of myself," Finch agreed sheepishly. "How you reckon all those stars up there were made?"

"Well," Kit stirred, "I don't know how He done it, but the Man Upstairs shore did do a fine job of it."

"That's a fact," Finch agreed. "Makes a man feel cut down to size all right!"

"It does!" Kit agreed. "Now let's get some sleep."

There was a short silence, and Finch asked, "Kit, when do you reckon we'll meet up with an Indian?"

A soft snore answered him, and he grinned and rolled over on his side.

\* \* \* \* \* \*

It was almost noon the next day when they met a small band of Indians. They were Comanches, and Kit knew them. He spoke to them in their language for several minutes and then turned to Finch.

"They say they will take word to White Horse. We'll wait yonder under that big pine."

"How long do you think it will take to get word to him?"

"Not long. We're lucky. They're having some kind of big pow wow over on Mulberry Creek. That ain't but about ten miles from here. A lot of different tribes are there—and that's good."

"What do you reckon he'll say?" Finch asked nervously.

"Oh, he'll agree to lettin' you run cattle in your valley, all right," Kit said nonchalantly. "Only trouble is—whether his braves and the other tribes will pester you."

"That's what I'm afraid of, Kit."

"Afraid!" Kit raised his eyebrows. "I doubt if Fauntleroy Finch would be afraid of the devil himself."

Finch laughed. "Just hope I don't run into him. Let's go over to that pine tree and unpack."

After they were settled in camp, Finch made coffee and fried some bacon which they ate with hardtack as they waited. Kit napped, and Finch paced. Kit opened one eye and looked at Finch.

"Know what you remind me of, Finch?"

"What's that?" Finch stopped pacing and looked at Kit.

"One of them big, spotted cats they got from Africa and locked up in a cage in Kansas City."

"Well, I—" Finch stopped and pointed. "Here he comes."

Kit rose, and he and Finch were standing side by side as White Horse and six braves rode up. Kit raised his hand, palm out, and spoke in the Comanche language. White Horse grunted and slid from his horse. Kit motioned for him to sit, which he did, as Finch poured coffee for them. The braves were still mounted; Finch looked a question at Kit who shook his head almost imperceptibly. Finch then filled his own cup and joined Kit and White Horse, sitting cross-legged on the ground. The six braves remained on their horses and looked expressionlessly at the trio. Kit began the conversation with White Horse. Finch, who could understand a bit of the language, could garner some of the meaning as White Horse spoke in a mixture of Comanche and Spanish. The Comanche word for 'cow'

Tuh' Mon' Oh' came up frequently, and his own name was spoken several times. Chief White Horse grunted and pointed at Finch, and Kit laughed.

"Finch," Kit interpreted, "White Horse says your name is too hard to say; so he will call you 'Ice Eye'—in Comanche, of course. In their language that is Hut' se Pah Suh' Kahwe—Seems to me that's worse than Fauntleroy Finch, but I reckon it's easier in Comanche."

"Don't blame him for changing my name," Finch laughed. "I'd a done it long ago, except Ma was set on 'Fauntleroy'. (It was her maiden name.) She was a school teacher, you know, back in Missouri."

"I'll be durned," Kit said surprised. "Wondered how you come to talk so good. She learned you how, huh?"

"I reckon," Finch admitted. "What does White Horse say?"

"Nothing yet. You can't rush him, but once he gives his word, we can abide by it. He's gonna talk to some of his braves and the other chiefs about it."

White Horse rose and walked to his horse, then turned to speak briefly to Kit. Then he mounted, and he and his men rode away.

"What did he say?" Finch asked impatiently. "He said to wait here and he'll be back."

"How long do we have to wait?"

"Till Chief White Horse comes back," Kit said testily. "You oughta know you can't rush a Indian, Finch. Maybe so he'll be back in an hour, maybe tomorrow, maybe next week. We'll wait."

"Well, what's he doing?" Finch demanded.

"Talkin' to some of his medicine men and some other chiefs, I reckon. Finch, you just settle down—you're as nervous as a whore at a camp meetin'."

"I know it, Kit. But I want that land! I figured it'd be at least five years, and maybe even more, before I could even think about it, but now you—"

"I know, Finch," Kit said placatingly. "The closer a feller gets to what he wants, the faster he moves. But you know Indians—they're either fightin', waitin', eatin', or screwin', and they don't git in no hurry about anything but eatin'!"

"You're right, Kit. I'm like a little boy with his britches full of red ants. Waiting isn't easy."

"Well," Kit said philosophically. "Let's make the best of it. We got plenty of grub and water and a good bed. I reckon we're better off than some."

\* \* \* \* \* \*

To make the waiting endurable, Finch coaxed Kit to talk about his winter with the Crows; trapping with Jim Bridger; his visit with President Polk; guiding Fremont, his first wife, the Cheyenne woman, Rai Du; about the duel he fought on horseback with the Frenchman from Canada; about his oldest daughter by Rai-Du, who was two years older then Finch; and about the many campaigns he had participated in.

At first, it was apparent that Kit obliged by talking simply to alleviate Finch's restlessness, but as time passed, he seemed actually to like having an audience to reminisce.

"You remember me talking about Will Drannon, the kid I picked up in Kansas City and brought west—well, he turned out to be one of the best guides in the west and finally got to be the Indian killin'est son-of-a-bitch you ever saw."

"I saw him one time. What's he doing now?"

"Killin' Indians if he can find 'em. He'll take a lot of chances just to kill an Indian. Don't know why that is, either. Most Indians are good enough in their way. They just don't think like a white man—that is, all except the Tonkawas. They're cannibals, Finch. You know that? I got no use for 'em, and I put one down when I get the chance."

"I didn't know that!" Finch was horrified.

"It's a fact. They especially like babies, and they will toss one in the cook pot if it's handy. Actually, I knew one white man that was a cannibal. He'd take a fat squaw into the mountains for a winter of trappin', and when he come out he was mighty fat and perky, but there warn't no squaw. Human bones was found in his diggin's lots of times. He was called Mountain Phil."

"I can't believe that!" Finch was incredulous.

"Fact!" Kit said shortly. "He trapped for me one winter."

"Well," Finch said feelingly. "I sure wouldn't have gone into the mountains with him."

"I took him aside afore we left and told the son-of-a-bitch that the first time we got the least bit short of grub, I was gonna shoot him right between the eyes. I meant it, and he knew it. We didn't have no trouble. He died a couple of years ago up in Montana. A squaw probably poisoned him. Hope so!"

\* \* \* \* \* \*

After two days of interminable waiting, just as Kit and Finch were finishing breakfast, they saw Indians riding toward them. White Horse was in the lead. They rode up to the fire.

Kit greeted them in Comanche and then in a language that Finch could not identify. Kit turned to Finch and spoke in English.

"Finch, you know White Horse—he's chief of the Comanches; next to him is Grey Eagle, the Arapaho Chief; then there is Black Bull, chief of the Kiowas. Don't know the others, but I've seen the one on the roan horse; he's Cheyenne and some relation to my first wife, Rai-Du."

"How!" Finch held up his hand, palm out.

The Indians merely looked at him stonily. Finally White Horse started talking to Kit in Comanche. Black Bull added something in Kiowa, and Grey Eagle in Arapaho. Kit listened carefully as each spoke and nodded his head occasionally in understanding.

"What are they saying?" Finch asked.

"You can run cattle in your valley, Finch," Kit said over his shoulder. "But there is a few restrictions on it."

"Like what?"

Suddenly one of the Indian braves behind the chiefs spoke excitedly and pointed at Finch. The Indians turned to him, and Kit listened intently.

"What is he saying, Kit?"

"That's Big Elk. He says that you are Hut se Pah Suh Kawa (IceEye) and that you are a very good man in a fight. He's seen you before and fought against you in Texas. Says you shoot very straight."

Finch quickly stepped away from Kit and looked at the Indians expectantly.

"Not now, Finch!" Kit spoke urgently. "He's not mad. It was more of a compliment, and he don't want to fight now."

"Good!" Finch was relieved and stepped back beside Kit. The chiefs smiled broadly, as did Kit.

"What limits are they putting on me, Kit?"

"None that you can't abide. Just so they can hunt in your valley and camp there if they want to. They won't bother you, your cattle, or your people as long as you don't bother them. I reckon you will have a crew with you—that's what I told 'em."

"I'll have to have help, all right," Finch replied. "Quite a few men, especially at first. And I'll not bother them if they want to camp or hunt in my valley."

"Good!" Kit said enthusiastically. "It's settled then." He turned to the Indians and spoke rapidly. The chiefs dismounted and walked to Finch, and shook hands the white man's way.

"What do I do now, Kit?" Finch wanted to know.

"Just smile and act like a damn fool. I'll fix us some coffee, and then we'll pack up."

"Where are we going?"

"I'm goin' back to Taos," Kit said almost jovially. "But old Ice Eye is goin' back with these chiefs so they can show you around the camp and let it be known that you're off limits to their braves and to the other tribes."

Finch waved to Kit as he left leading a packhorse. Then he looked inquiringly at White Horse who spoke to him in Comanche and gestured for him to ride beside him. Black Bull and Grey Eagle moved their horses abreast of them. Finch wondered where they were taking him, but he shrugged philosophically; Kit would not have sent him to his death, and the Indians jabbered affably. Finch could understand only an occasional word or phrase, but nothing seemed to be antagonistic or threatening; so he relaxed and began to enjoy the country.

Six hours later they topped a ridge and saw a great Indian camp near a creek below. Chief White Horse smiled at Finch and said, "This Indian pow wow." He gestured at the scene below.

Finch was startled that the chief had spoken in broken English. He started to reply to White Horse but stopped as the chief seemed to be absorbed in the sight below. The scene was one of apparent bedlam; Indians were running everywhere, some were fighting, and others were reeling and obviously very drunk.

"We wait," White Horse said and motioned the other Indians to dismount. "Soon they eat," White Horse spoke to Finch, and Finch wondered just how much English the chief did understand.

As they waited for the pow wow to settle down, the Indians engaged in desultory conversation. Finch could occasionally hear the words Hut' Se Pah Suh' Kahwe (Ice Eye) and Tuh' Mor Oh' (cow). He wondered how Kit had ever learned all the Indian dialects and if he ever could! The jabbering irritated Finch, but he held his annoyance inside. He wondered how much of the Indian's life was spent in just waiting. Finally, however, the frenetic activity in the huge Indian camp began to slow, and lines began to form about the cooking fires. Eventually most of the Indians were seated cross-legged on the ground, although many of the drunkest lay sprawled where they had fallen.

"Soon we go," White Horse said to Finch as he motioned the others to mount. When all were mounted, White Horse indicated that Finch was to ride beside him as they rode toward camp. As they approached, the camp grew quiet, and all eyes were on the oncoming riders. At the edge of the camp, White Horse raised his hand, commanding the riders to stop. Finch glanced around and saw that the other chiefs had also raised their hands. When the camp was completely silent, White Horse motioned Finch closer to his side, and they began to ride among the seated and sprawled Indians. As they rode, White Horse spoke almost continuously and occasionally reached over to put his hand on Finch's shoulder. Finch could understand a few words such as Hites (friend), Carson, Ice Eye, and cow. Finch saw no enmity evinced by the Indian braves or women. Only a curious interest as if he were an unusual animal.

Finally, White Horse stopped near the middle of the camp and spoke forcefully for a moment, then again placed his hand on Finch's shoulder.

"Hites. Hut' se Pah Suh' Kahwe Comanche Hites!" he said in a loud, stern voice, and then he turned toward the biggest teepee in camp. Finch saw that the other chiefs were riding away in different directions. He supposed they were going to their own teepees.

As White Horse and Finch neared the big teepee, they stopped a few paces away, and White Horse uttered a guttural sound. Instantly, an attractive older Indian woman came to the teepee entrance and looked at White Horse and Finch. She showed no surprise or other emotion. White Horse grunted and gestured toward her. She stepped outside the teepee and called to the interior. Immediately three other Indian women emerged. They were all young and comely. White Horse spoke in Comanche to the older woman. Finch gathered that at least the older woman and one or two, or possibly all three, of the others were his wives.

White Horse dismounted and motioned Finch to follow him inside the teepee. It was dark until Finch's eyes adjusted to the gloom, and then he could see that the women had followed them.

White Horse sat on a buffalo rug on the ground and motioned Finch to do the same. Finch obeyed and looked about the teepee curiously. Bedding, mostly buffalo robes, was placed around the edges of the teepee. In the middle was a fire, and over it was a kettle in which some savory dish was cooking. He looked at the women. The older one averted her eyes. The others looked at him curiously and met his gaze boldly. They smiled at him with twinkling dark eyes and very white teeth. Finch returned the smile, but quickly wiped it off his face as White Horse grunted and motioned toward the cook pot. The older woman dipped a bowl in the pot and handed it to White Horse. One of the younger ones did the same for Finch. Finch wished he knew how to say 'thank you' in Comanche.

White Horse picked pieces of meat from his bowl and chewed noisily, then gulped the soup when the meat was gone. "Kit was sure right about them eating in a hurry," Finch thought as he did his best to match White Horse. He looked again at the women. One of them was smiling at him teasingly and flirtatiously. Finch quickly looked away and drained his bowl of soup.

\* \* \* \* \* \*

Black Bull and Grey Eagle came to the teepee of White Horse after it was dark. They sat around the fire and talked for hours after the women had retired to their pallets around the teepee walls. Finch could piece together only scraps of the conversation, but he surmised, correctly, that they were talking about him, for the Comanche terms for Ice Eye, cow, friend, and valley were often heard. Since he could not enter into the conversation, he let his eyes wander about the teepee. He was startled to see a pair of very black eyes peeking from the cover of one of the buffalo robe pallets. They smiled at him but quickly disappeared when Finch looked.

It was late when the other chiefs left. Finch declined the invitation of White Horse, made by signs, to sleep in the teepee. He made it known, also by signs, that he would sleep down by the creek. He walked cautiously through the camp, occasionally stumbling over the prostrate form of a drunken Indian. Finally, however, he found his gear, removed his bedroll, and made his way toward the creek. There was still a whisker of a moon, and Finch could barely make out a fairly large pool under the overhanging tree. Quietly, he unrolled his bed, then divested himself of his clothing and slipped noiselessly into the water. He swam about for a few minutes and then got out to dry himself in the cool gentle wind. As he stood, he could make out some movement in the water and surmised that he had disturbed a beaver at his nocturnal tasks.

As soon as he felt dry, he crawled into his bedroll. He was in that blissful state of relaxation that precedes sleep when he felt a movement at his side. He sat up quickly, his pistol in his hand, when suddenly against his naked chest he felt a small, soft hand that was warm but still damp from a creek bath.

Quickly Finch looked about, but it was almost completely dark under the tree. There was no doubt that there was a woman beside him, but what on earth could he do! Yelling was out of the question; besides, another small hand had softly covered his mouth and was gently pushing him back to a supine position.

Finch sighed and replaced his pistol. He had no doubt now that this was the smiling Indian girl that had been in White Horse's teepee. His wife? His daughter? No way to tell, and as the soft, warm hand slid down his naked chest, Finch decided it didn't make much difference. He relaxed and opened the covers for her to enter. Her body was small and firm, but soft, with small, taut breasts and delightfully rounded hips. Finch groaned in ecstasy as she slid under him and arched her body to meet his. Moments later she uttered a small cry of pain or pleasure, but Finch didn't care which, for he was experiencing a degree of sheer animal pleasure that he had never felt before. A moment later she relaxed under him as if she had suddenly died, and Finch sprawled atop her in total exhaustion. They lay inertly for a few moments; then the small body began to squirm under him, and almost immediately he became a stud again.

\* \* \* \* \* \*

It was near sunup when Finch awakened, sighed deeply, and turned to look at his now empty bedroll. He was not surprised as he felt about and found the bedroll cool except where he had lain. He cupped his hands behind his head and gazed into the tree above. He wondered idly which of White Horse's women had come to him in the night. He could not find it in his heart to regret it, for on the frontier women were scarce. If the woman were one of White Horse's wives, which he doubted, then White Horse was one lucky Indian. If it were his daughter, then she was extremely experienced or had more native talent than any woman had a right to have. In any case, White Horse might have a blue-eyed child or grandchild in about nine months! And that probably meant guns and shooting, and possibly the loss of his valley, or even his life! No. He wouldn't lose that valley! He'd—!

Finch sighed again and began to dress. Two hours later he rode away from the teepee of White Horse, and as he did, White Horse raised his hand, palm out, and four pairs of feminine eyes followed him as he rode away. One pair of eyes held a gleaming smile of satisfaction. But Finch did not look back. He was headed toward his valley!

# CHAPTER 4

Finch rode into Fort Worth about mid-afternoon. He was riding his sorrel gelding and leading the two stolen horses. The pack mule trailed behind.

All the horses were tired, for it had rained most of the night before, and the ground was soft. The sorrel had a loose shoe, and Finch rode directly to the blacksmith shop. The smithy had his forge going and was pounding red hot metal. Several men were lounging in the shade of the overhang. Finch recognized some of them that he had seen on his way to Taos. The old buffalo hunter and mountain man in the soiled buckskins raised his whittling knife in salute, and others grunted a greeting as Finch rode up.

"Howdy!" Finch said cheerfully as he dismounted. "Any chance of getting a loose shoe fixed?"

"Shore can," the smithy said. "I'm about through here now. It ain't that grulla, is it?"

"Nope," Finch smiled. "It's my saddle horse."

Finch tied the sorrel to the post of the shed and led the stolen horses to a nearby wagon and tied them to the wheel. Then he sauntered back to the shed.

"Bring that sorrel on in here," the smith invited, "and I'll take care of his loose shoe. Shoe's still tight on that grulla, huh?"

"Tight as a jug!" Finch grinned.

"Reckon you wouldn't want to pay me for puttin' them shoes on 'im, would you?" the smithy said in jest, for he didn't expect to be paid.

"I sure will pay," Finch said. "That good shoeing job probably saved me a lot of trouble."

"I'll be damned!" the smithy said in disbelief.

"Where is them two hard cases that was ridin' them two horses when they came through here a couple of weeks ago, me lad?" the old Irish buffalo hunter asked.

Finch hesitated a moment before replying. "They didn't want to come back."

"Oh, I see!" the old fellow said understandingly.

"Hey! Look!" Another man pointed to some wagons that were making a hard time of it as they pulled through the deep mire of the street. All of the men were looking at the caravan, and Finch grinned broadly as the big jack tied to the last wagon brayed his defiance to the world and reared back on his lead rope, only to slip and fall on his side in the mud. He righted himself after being dragged a few yards, continuing to bray with every forced step. The men in the shed laughed loudly.

"That feller that's ramroddin' that outfit has got his hands full," another man observed. "What you reckon he's doin' out this way?"

The blacksmith clinched a final nail on Finch's sorrel and dropped the horse's foot to the ground, then straightened, holding his back and grunting as he did so.

"No tellin'," the smithy said. "Quite a few people comin' back since the war is over. Looks like they're from back east, though; got a lot of blacks in them wagons. He's got a loose rim on one wheel. Mebbe so I'll have me a job to do."

"Them wagons is heavy loaded, and he's got some good thoroughbred mares tied to each one. It's a wonder they got through from the east with all them carpetbaggers and black soldiers so damn uppity and stoppin' everybody."

"Well, they ain't goin' much further today. Them wagon wheels is sinkin' a foot deep in that black mud, and them mules is about tuckered."

As the caravan neared the blacksmith shop, Finch noticed a stockily built young man with a beard who carried one shoulder lower than the other. He was riding a beautiful black stallion beside the lead wagon. A few yards away, he held up is hand, and the wagons stopped. He spoke to the small, wizened black man driving the wagon. Finch took a quick breath and forgot to breathe for a moment, for beside the little black man sat the most startlingly beautiful woman he had ever seen. She had long, straight hair as black as a crow and classic features with dark eyes that twinkled merrily and mischievously. Even though she was seated, Finch could see that her figure was slender, but ripe and full. He gaped and was brought back to earth only by the voice of the man on the black stallion.

"Hold 'em up a minute," he told the driver. Then he rode to the blacksmith shop and dismounted. He looked at the non-descript group of men under the shed. His wise, tired eyes belied his youth. No one spoke until Finch broke the silence.

"Howdy, friend!" Finch said, "I reckon some of us would help if need be."

"I'm obliged," the young man said and extended his hand. "My name is Humphrey Beatenbow."

All eyes were on Finch and Beatenbow, and although Finch was a good four inches taller, not a man was aware of it, but all of them knew instinctively that they were looking at two strong men.

"They call me Finch." Finch shook the proffered hand. The clasp of each man was strong. "Looks like you're havin' a tough go of it."

"I am," admitted Humphrey. "Right now I'm lookin' for a smithy to fix my wagon wheel. Got an anvil and forge in one of the wagons, and one of my niggers is a good smithy, but I hate to unload in this mud."

"Don't blame you for that!" Finch said feelingly. "And I reckon you've come to the right place. Smithy here has just finished with my horse. Goin' far?"

"Don't know how far we're goin'," Humphrey said tiredly. "But we've been a hell of a long ways."

"Uh-oh!" exclaimed the blacksmith as he pointed with his tongs. "Here comes trouble!"

All the men looked in the direction the blacksmith pointed. Three men were riding purposefully toward them. Two were white, and one was black. Humphrey looked at them closely and shook his head in resignation.

"Figured we wasn't through with that bunch," he said grimly. "They stopped us a few miles east of here and was gonna search our wagons. Don't know what for. Said they was state police. The big one on the right is the stud. The little weasel-eyed one in the middle is the shooter, and the black is just along cause he thinks bein' a free man gives him a right to anything he wants."

The three men were only a few paces away when Humphrey stopped talking. They halted their horses and looked at Humphrey. The big man smiled maliciously. Finch flashed a glance at the lead wagon and saw that the beautiful woman now held a shotgun, and her eyes were sparkling angrily.

"Thought you had skeered us off, huh?" the big man sneered. "Havin' a bunch of niggers pokin' rifles at us out there in the woods. Well, you didn't—and you ain't gonna! We're back in civilization now, and we got witnesses. We're gonna search them wagons."

"You're not gonna search my wagons!" Humphrey said firmly.

"Just who are you, Mister?" Finch's soft voice carried to all the men.

The three riders looked at Finch in surprise. "We're state police," the big man said importantly. "And just who might you be, Junior?"

"I'm a Texas Ranger," Finch said softly.

"Well, now!—Ain't you somethin'!" the big man laughed harshly. "Maybe you was a Texas Ranger—though I didn't know they made little kids Rangers—but you ain't a Texas Ranger no more, at least you won't be for long. The government is disbanding 'em, and now we're takin' over."

"Not my wagons, you're not!" Humphrey said sharply.

"Let me take 'em Cade!" urged weasel-eye. "Won't be no trouble at all. One is a kid, and the other is a cripple. I can—"

"That'll do!" Finch's voice cut like a whip as he stepped a couple of paces away from Humphrey.

Every man under the shed looked at Finch. There suddenly was an aura, like an icy fog, of feral danger incarnate about him. His blue eyes seemed to be shooting sparks. The old mountain man felt a chill run up his back, and his neck hairs bristled. The three men on the horses were taken aback. But only briefly.

"Now just who pulled your chain, Junior?" the big one sneered.

"I said, that'll do!" Finch's voice had lowered, but it still carried like a cold wind. "Now git!"

"Like hell!" Weasel-eye grabbed for his gun, and there were two shots that sounded almost as one. After a sliver of quiet, there was another shot.

The two white men were knocked from their horses, and the black was swaying in the saddle holding a bleeding right shoulder. His gun lay in the mud at his horse's feet. Finch had backed away a couple of steps and was thumbing the empty shell cases out of his pistol. His face was pale, but his hands were rock steady. There was absolute quiet under the shed. Humphrey Beatenbow was the first to move. The woman on the wagon seat looked first at Finch, her dark eyes unfathomable. Humphrey knelt by the men a moment and then rose and looked at Finch in awe.

"God-a-mighty, man! Do you know what you just did? These men are dead."

"I know," Finch said grimly. "But the black only has a busted shoulder."

"Well, what'd you do it for?" Humphrey demanded.

"Because the two whites were faster than most, especially the little one. But the black was slow, and I had time to cripple him."

"I mean," Humphrey said angrily, "what did you kill 'em for?"

"Because," Finch said quietly, "if I hadn't, you and I would both be dead by now."

After a moment of silence, Humphrey took a deep breath. "I reckon you're right," he said as he shook his head sadly. "But I was hopin' I'd seen all the killin' I'd ever see when the war was over."

"I don't like it either, Beatenbow!" Finch said angrily. "But some times that is the only way. I am sorry the woman had to see it."

Finch looked at the woman on the wagon. She was looking at him, and her eyes were soft and sympathetic.

"What about these two?" Humphrey nodded to the fallen men and the wounded black.

"Begorra! You two fellers go on down to the crick where it's dry under the trees and cool off," the old Irishman said matter of factly. "We'll plant the two of 'em, and we'll patch the black up—or string him up— hatever suits you."

"Patch him up!" Humphrey said firmly. "And thanks," he added.

The smithy spoke up. "I'll fix the wagon. Won't take more'n a hour or so."

Humphrey nodded absently, mounted the black stallion, and rode toward the creek. Finch tightened the cinch on the sorrel and followed. Humphrey stopped and called back.

"You that was ridin' in the broke wagon, get in another wagon, and all of you follow us. We'll camp for the night down by the river, and somebody can come back after the wagon when it's ready."

With that, Humphrey and Finch rode abreast toward the trees by the creek. The wagons followed.

When they were out of hearing range, there was an audible sigh from the men under the shed.

"Faith and the lad is quicker than a mountain trout with that pistol of his!" The thick Irish brogue identified the buffalo hunter. "Begorra! I don't think another man alive could beat him—leastwise, I never seen one that could, and I been around a bit, too!"

"I've never seen the likes of that kind of shootin', and I've lived in Texas most of my life," another observed, disbelief in his voice.

"You ain't likely to see it again, neither," said the buffalo hunter as he squirted a stream of tobacco juice. "That's Fauntleroy Finch!"

"The Texas Ranger!"

"I reckon he's a lot of other things, too. His folks was killed by renegades when he was fourteen, and he's been fightin' Indians and rustlers since then. He got in the Rangers when he was nineteen, about four years ago. Since then, he's been huntin' horse thieves, Comancheros, renegade Indians, and other riffraff. He's a friend of Kit Carson's, too! And I don't know what else he is."

"I didn't even notice he was wearin' a pistol."

"Me neither. But I was watchin' when he reloaded. He shore wasn't none nervous."

"Nobody knows how many men he's killed—and they say he's real good natured and likes to have a lot of fun. Don't never kill nobody 'less he has to."

"Well, I've heard a lot about a kid Ranger named Fauntleroy Finch. I guess with a name like that he was bound to be a fighter."

"You notice he got the squint-eyed one first, then the stud? Why didn't he kill that damn nigger?"

"That nigger was so slow with his pistol, most anybody could of took him. Fauntleroy Finch don't like to kill, and he had time to bust his shoulder."

"Well," the old buffalo man said. "I've heard a lot of men say he's got no equal with a pistol. I reckon I'll believe that now. Let's get them men buried."

\* \* \* \* \* \*

The blacks started making camp and getting fires going.

"Come on into the wagon, Finch," Humphrey invited. "I want you to meet my wife and maybe so we can talk a bit."

Finch was unaccountably reluctant to follow Humphrey into the wagon, but he did. The wagon was fitted with all the comforts possible in the restricted place. There was a small table, some very low chairs, and a thick, comfortable looking bed. On one of the chairs sat the woman that Finch had seen on the wagon seat holding the shotgun. She stood as they entered. The canvas top made it necessary for Finch to stoop, but Humphrey could stand almost upright. The woman did not reach the top of the canvas.

"Finch, this is my wife, Colette."

Standing, Colette revealed her statuesque beauty. Finch looked at her, his breath coming in short gasps. She was much younger than she had seemed when holding the shotgun.

"I'm real glad to meet you, Mrs. Beatenbow," Finch said clumsily. "And I can't tell you how sorry I am about what happened up at the blacksmith shop!"

"Please call me, Colette, Finch" she said as she extended her hand. It was soft and firm, and Finch felt the electricity flow all the way up his arm. He gulped. "And," Colette continued, "if what happened hadn't happened, I'd either be a widow or a killer."

"Yes, ma'am," Finch said. "I reckon you would. All the same I wish I hadn't had to do it. But it's a rough life out here and—"

"Please!" Colette interrupted softly and looked at Finch with large, gentle, black eyes. "All of us have to live the life we were born to live. I'm just grateful that you were there, Finch. I'll be your friend forever because of today." She squeezed his hand gently.

"Yes, ma'am," Finch said with obvious relief and gratefulness. "I reckon I'm mighty glad of that!"

"Make yourself at home, Finch," Humphrey invited. "We've got an extra chair, and I've got a bottle of snake medicine around here some place, I think."

Humphrey stuck his head out the back of the wagon and called. "Kate, bring us some glasses, and as soon as the coffee is done, bring us a pot."

Finch removed his hat and ran his fingers through his hair, which was difficult in a stooped position. Then he unbelted his gun and put it on the floor of the wagon. Colette looked at him inquiringly but said nothing. Then she reached under the wagon seat and removed a bottle with brown liquid in it. Finch could see that it had not been opened.

"Here, Finch, have a seat." Humphrey pushed a chair toward him, and Finch sat just as a huge Negro woman appeared at the back of the wagon.

"Here is yo glasses, Mars Hump," she said. "I'll have coffee too, in no time at all."

"Thanks, Kate," Humphrey said absently as he sat and handed Finch a glass, then with only slight hesitation, handed one to Colette. Colette poured. She filled the men's glasses almost half full and poured a dab in hers. Then, she too sat. There was a short silence; Humphrey and Finch took a gulp of their drinks, and Colette took a dainty sip. Humphrey cleared his throat noisily.

"Finch," he began hesitantly. "I'm sorry I lost my temper up there a while ago. Didn't aim to and don't usually do that. It's just that I don't like to see men killed, though I've done my share of it, and may have to do more. And I will if I have to—but I don't like it."

"Me neither!" Finch said feelingly. "And I don't blame you for losing your temper. It always makes me a little sick."

"You two forget this afternoon!" Colette said quietly, her voice gentle and sympathetic. "Men do what they have to do!"

"I know," Humphrey said glumly. "And I know what would have happened if Finch hadn't done what he did. I don't think I could have beat either one of the two whites."

"Well, now," Finch said with a grin. "I don't know about that. With that shotgun that Mrs. Beaten—Colette was holdin', I expect those men would have had a handful."

Humphrey looked at Colette inquiringly.

"You gave me that shotgun for protection, Humphrey," Colette said archly. "And I thought the time had come for me to do some protecting."

"God-a-mighty!" Humphrey was aghast. "You might have been killed, Colette!"

Finch smiled, and Humphrey emptied his glass.

"Well, I wasn't," Colette said lightly. "And neither were you—thanks to Finch. Finch! That's a nice name, but you must have another one, too."

"Yes, ma'am, I do," Finch gulped. "My whole name is Fauntleroy Finch. Ma named me." Finch emptied his glass. Colette giggled delightedly.

"Fauntleroy! I like that. I'll bet your mother read a lot."

"Yes ma'am, she did. She was a school teacher once."

"Would you mind if I called you Fauntleroy?"

"I reckon you can call me anything you want, Mrs.—Colette. But I'd just as soon the men folks called me Finch."

"Finch it is," Humphrey said in a business-like way. "Now, Finch you saw my outfit today. We've come all the way from the Beatenbow plantation in Louisiana. It was a great place in its time, but it was a plumb mess when I got back from the war. My folks had died, and there wasn't anybody to run it. So I sold out and headed for Texas. Some of my army buddies thought it was a great place. Can't say I'm much impressed up to now. But anyway, we're here—but I don't know where we're goin'. You know this country?"

"Most of it," Finch said. "I've ridden it since I was big enough. We had a ranch down close to San Antone, but rustlers cleaned us out and killed my folks. I was gone at the time. Since joining the Rangers, I've chased over most of the plains country west of here and parts of New Mexico territory."

"What I'm lookin' for is land," Humphrey said earnestly. "I've heard there is a lot of free land in Texas."

"There's land," Finch conceded. "And it is free for the taking. The big problem is keeping it."

"How's that?"

"The Indians are still runnin' wild," Finch said. "And there's renegade whites, horse thieves, Comancheros! You name it. There's riff raff all west of Forth Worth. They'll kill you or steal you blind, run off your stock—anything. I've been chasin' them for four years."

"What's a Comanchero?" Colette wanted to know.

"Most any human that is mean!" Finch said almost savagely. "They come up from Mexico and headquarter in the Palo Duro canyon. A lot of Mexicans, renegade whites, and Indians, and other vermin. They trade with the Indians, but they also rob and steal, and kidnap. No tellin' how many whites they've killed or how many women and children they've stolen and taken to Mexico!"

"How horrible!" Colette gasped.

"It is," Finch agreed. That's why I don't recommend goin' very far west of here."

"Well now, Finch," Humphrey said. "I've got a pretty good crew myself. All niggers, I'll admit. They were once Beatenbow slaves. But they are free people now, and most of 'em are families. Fact is, we stopped in a little town that had a preacher, and I had 'em all marry up legal. That is, most of 'em. A few of the bucks and wenches followed us on foot and caught up with the wagons when we was several days out; so we do have some unattached niggers—both men and women. But I think they'll fight. Fact is, one of 'em was with me all through the war, and he is a first class fightin' man. I've had him trainin' the rest of 'em; so I think that if I can find some land, I can keep it!"

"What you gonna do with it?"

"Run cattle. I don't know anything about ranching, but I'll learn. All we ever raised on the plantation was cotton and niggers."

"Where you gonna get the cattle?" Finch wanted to know.

"Buy 'em," Humphrey said complacently. "Got enough money to buy a herd when I sold the plantation."

All three of them were quiet for a few moments. Kate brought the coffee, and they sat and drank it in silence. Finally Finch broke the silence.

"Tell you what," Finch began hesitantly. "I've got a piece of land a couple of hundred miles or so out west of here up on the Canadian River. Best cattle country in the world. It's a valley and the most beautiful place you ever saw."

"You have?" Colette exclaimed eagerly.

"I thought that was all open land." Humphrey said doubtfully.

"It is. But I've had my eye on that place for four or five years and aim to build on it. I was in Taos just last week and visited with a friend of mine, Kit Carson."

"I've heard a lot about Kit Carson," Humphrey said shortly. "He was a colonel in the Northern army."

"I know that," Finch said. "And he's a Brevet Brigadier now. But we're friends even if we were on different sides during the war. Anyway, he spent most of the war on the Texas frontier. So did I. And there isn't any politics out there. They don't mean a damned—excuse me, Colette—a darned thing when you're tryin' to save your skin or scalp."

"Like you said, Finch," Colette grinned mischievously, "they don't mean a damned thing! Go on."

"Anyhow, both of us spent most of the war fightin' renegades and outlaws and other vermin out on the plains. And now Kit is Indian Agent for southern Colorado, New Mexico, and a part of West Texas. He can call out nearly five thousand troops at any time; so the Indians pay him a bit of mind. He's friendly with most of 'em. When I was out there at Taos where he lives, he took me to visit some of the Indian chiefs, the Comanches, Arapahoes, and Kiowas and he made a deal for me. I can run cattle in my valley, and they won't bother me or my crew as long as they can camp and hunt in it. Of course, that doesn't mean I won't get raided by renegade Indians or whites—maybe even the Comancheros, and especially the Apaches. Anyway, I agreed to the terms. Even spent a night in the camp of White Horse; he's chief of the Comanches."

"You didn't!" Colette was excited, and Finch's face turned red as he remembered the Indian girl in his bedroll by the creek.

"What are you drivin' at, Finch?" Humphrey asked quietly.

"Well," Finch said slowly. "I've got the land, and with a good crew of men, we could pick up a big herd of cattle on the way out there. Nearly all the ranchers left their stock to run wild when they went off to the war. The cattle have multiplied like rabbits, and they're all over the plains and don't belong to anybody."

"You mean, use my niggers for that?" Humphrey said dubiously.

"Not to gather cattle," Finch laughed. "That would take real cowboys because some of those old mossy horns have been runnin' wild for four or five years, and they are wild as deer and mean as panthers. But if you want to spend some of your money hiring cowboys for a couple of years, I reckon your niggers could help build corrals and barns. And, of course, we would have to build houses. We can use adobe for that. Then we would need to raise some crops, both for ourselves and for the saddle stock. Your niggers would be good for that. And, of course, they'd sure come in handy when we are attacked by Indians. With all that—we just might make it."

"God-a-mighty, man! You mean go partners?" Humphrey asked unbelieving.

"I reckon I do," Finch said. "Nobody except Ma ever said I had much sense."

"I think it would be wonderful!" Colette said, her face shining. Then she sobered. "But you said when we were attacked by Indians. I thought the chiefs and your friend Kit had that settled."

"They did—as far as things can ever be settled with Indians. But you can bet that renegade Indians, and probably whites, too, would try to run us off. You would be taking a mighty big chance to throw in with me."

"But you're gonna do it anyway, huh, Finch?" Humphrey asked.

"I reckon so. Didn't figure I could do it this quick, but—" He shrugged his shoulders.

"Well," Humphrey said with finality. "You ain't the only lame brain. Nobody ever accused me of havin' any sense either. And Colette, she ain't got no sense at all, else she wouldn't have married me! We go fifty-fifty?"

"I reckon that's the way it ought to be."

The two men grasped hands in an iron grip, and Colette covered both with her strong, soft ones.

"What a beautiful day!" Colette breathed. "I've got the most wonderful feeling that this is the beginning of something big."

"How do we start?" Humphrey wanted to know.

"Well," Finch said. "First thing, I've got to return those stolen horses to Austin and resign from the Rangers! And I've still got the ranch at San Antone. Maybe I can sell it or lease it to somebody. It's just land; the cattle have been scattered for four years. But we've sure got to have a passel of cowboys, preferably those that ranched before the war and were in the army. They can shoot. Maybe I can even get one or two of my buddies in the Rangers to join us. They'd be a big help if it comes to fighting, and they can all ride. You could be rounding us up a crew while I'm in Austin."

"How do I do that?" Humphrey wanted to know.

"With that money you got. Nobody in Texas has got any money now."

"How on earth do I find 'em?"

After a moment of thought, Finch said. "Tell you what. You look for that Irish buffalo hunter and mountain man that was at the blacksmith shop today. He's an old timer, and I've got a real good hunch that he'd steer you right in hiring men—and there's plenty of 'em around that want work!"

# CHAPTER 5

It was two weeks later that Finch returned to Fort Worth. With him was a brown-skinned young Mexican man with a smiling face, glistening teeth, and a devil-may-care air. They rode to the Beatenbow camp just after sundown, and Finch was surprised at the look of permanency. Under a tarp one could still see the glowing embers of a blacksmith forge, and in the glow of several fires, a big tent could be seen among the wagons, which were neatly parked. Firewood was stacked in piles at each fire; a corral had been fashioned with stout poles, and inside it were the Beatenbow mares and mules. Tied to stout trees with strong ropes were the stud and jack. Drainage ditches had been dug, and the camp was dry. As they rode into the firelight, a huge, muscular Negro walked to meet them.

"Well, if it ain't Mars Finch!" Largo said enthusiastically. "Mars Hump sho will be glad yo is back. He and the missus is in their tent. We've already et."

"I'm glad to be back, Largo," Finch said. "This feller with me is Chico Baca."

"Hola, Largo." Chico's teeth gleamed as he smiled.

"Tell Hump that we are back, Largo." Finch said.

"Yassuh, Mars Finch. Him and Miss Colette sho will be glad."

A moment later Humphrey and Colette emerged from the tent. Humphrey strode forward and grasped Finch's outstretched hand. "God-a-mighty, Finch. I'm sure glad you are back. Was begginin' to wonder."

Finch and Chico both dismounted, and Finch introduced Chico. "Hump, this here Mexican I got with me is Chico Baca. We Rangered together. He can't ride or rope or shoot straight, but he's a singin' fool! Only way he could have stayed in the Rangers."

Chico grinned amiably and stepped forward to grasp Humphrey's hand. "Buenos noches, senor. Senor Finch he ess mucho mintoirone."

"What did he say, Finch?" Humphrey wanted to know.

"Says I'm a big liar," Finch grinned. "Don't let him fool you. He can speak English as well as we can."

Humphrey smiled tentatively and turned toward the tent. Colette was standing watching them.

"Come on out, Colette," Humphrey said. "Finch is back, and he's got a friend with him."

Colette strode forward and grasped Finch's hand firmly. Finch felt the electricity again. "Finch! We're so glad to see you back. We were beginning to worry."

"Hah!" ejaculated Chico. "You worry about Finch! He get the big head!"

"Colette," Finch smiled at her. "This little greaser is a friend of mine. Tried to find a good man to come and help us out, but I couldn't. So I had to settle for him. His name is Chico Baca."

Chico immediately offered his big sombrero and bowed deeply. "Ah, Senora! Finch did not tell me that his partner had such a hermosa esposo!"

Colette laughed delightedly. "Thank you, Chico. And Finch did not tell me that he had such a handsome amigo. Bienvenida!"

"You be careful, Chico." Finch admonished. "She speaks French, too."

All but Humphrey laughed, and he grinned awkwardly. "Come on into the tent, and let's get caught up some. I've got news."

"Me too!" Finch said as they walked toward the tent and entered. It was a big tent and apparently had everything to make one comfortable. A table was in the center, a bed, and several chairs.

"Pull up a chair," Humphrey invited. "I'll pour us a drink."

Finch and Chico removed their hats and pistols and sat at the table.

"You sit, too, Humphrey," Colette said. "I'll pour the drinks."

The men sat, and Colette put a glass before each and poured a generous helping into each. Then she sat with them.

"Well," Humphrey began. "You begin, Finch. How does it look?"

Finch was silent a moment and then began slowly. "Well," he said reluctantly. "That big feller that tried to hold you up was right about one thing—the government is gonna disband the Rangers. Says Texas can't have an armed force of any kind—but I reckon we will all keep our pistols. I got the two stolen horses back to their owner, and he leased my land. He will pay when he can. There's other news, too."

"God-a-mighty! Go on, man!" Humphrey exclaimed impatiently.

"Well," Finch said. "I hope this is good news. A feller named Wheeler and his two partners took twenty-five hundred steers to Abilene last year. Don't know what route they took, but they made it through. Dan Waggoner is goin' to try to take a herd up there next year. Oliver Loving and Charlie Goodnight are taking a herd west this year to New Mexico and then north to Colorado. Don't see how they can make it but Goodnight is a tough hombre. Chico and I have Rangered with him. Loving took a herd from Palo Pinto to Illinois about six or seven years ago, and he wintered a herd in southern Kansas in '60 and then drove up the Arkansas to Pueblo, Colorado, so he must be another tough one. But they have a lot of dry country to cross if they go straight to the territory of New Mexico, and there's a lot of Indians to contend with."

"Oh, I hope they do make it!" Colette exclaimed.

"Si, Senora," Chico smiled. "I teenk they make it. Senor Goodnight ess mucho hombre!"

"What else?" Humphrey asked quickly.

"Not much other than what we figured on," Finch said soberly. "The Indians are still raisin' hell on the plains. There's millions of buffalo out there, and thousands of cattle roamin' wild out there and free for the takin'—if you can take 'em."

"We'll take 'em!" Humphrey said confidently. "And now I've got some news for you. I've got a crew! You were right about that old buffalo hunter. He steered me right in hirin' hands. His name is Buff—at least that's what everybody calls him. And he sure was a big help in findin' the men for our crew. Knows everybody. In fact, he's goin' along with us. Says he'd like to see the fun when we start across the plains with all our niggers. He's got his own wagon and says he'll keep us in meat and pick himself up some buffalo hides on the way. Anyway. I've got fifteen men lined up, besides Buff. All but one or two fought in the war, and the best part of it is that they all have worked cattle, and one of them was with Wheeler on that drive to Abilene last year. He says that Abilene is nothing but a big camp, with a couple of saloons, a post office, and a six room hotel. But it's got the Union Pacific railroad, and they ship cattle to Kansas City. The feller that went with Wheeler is named Clem Swenson. And I think he knows cows. Said they used fifty men and more than a hundred horses on the drive."

"Whew!" Finch exclaimed. "You have been busy—and lucky!"

"I have," Humphrey said with pride in his voice.

"It all sounds good," Finch admitted. "We can start pickin' up cattle out west of Decatur, and if we can find enough cows and young stuff, and keep our scalps until we get to our place on the Canadian, we ought to be able to make a drive to Abilene in a couple of years. There isn't much profit in cattle right now, but by '68 or '69, they will be worth more."

"And by then we ought to have a good herd to take up," Humphrey said. "How far is Abilene from our ranch?"

"I'd reckon three or four hundred miles northeast," Finch said thoughtfully. "We will have to cross Wolf Creek, which won't be any trouble, and then Beaver River, which is dry most of the time, but a real panther when it rains. And the Cimarron River can be bad. I think we can miss the Medicine Lodge River. In fact, we will pass pretty close to Camp Supply and could lay over there a few days, if need be."

Humphrey said, "Clem says that a herd can travel fifteen to twenty miles a day, if necessary, but they ought to just graze their way so that they'll be fat when we get to market. Says they need to get up from their bedground without us startin' them in the mornin's and then let the hands just sort of start them grazin' in the right direction. Says we ought never to cross a river when the sun is in the cattle's eyes, talks about wagons with a 'possum' belly made of cowhide slung under the wagons so's we collect cow chips for fuel and for bedrolls and stuff. Talks about a 'hoodlum wagon', drag men, flankers, swing men, and scouts. Says every man needs eight horses. Says we can get our own meat, but we need plenty of other grub, too—well, he talked a lot, but I think he knows cattle and trail drivin'."

"Sounds like it," admitted Finch. " I reckon the niggers can manage to raise us a garden. Don't know how we can get dried fruit, but the rest sounds possible. I think you were real lucky to find a man that knows cattle. We're gonna need 'im!"

Finch and Humphrey talked long into the night. Colette listened avidly. Chico nodded and finally leaned back and slept in his chair, but was instantly alert when Humphrey and Finch rose from the table.

"We'll bunk down by the creek," Finch said, "and talk some more tomorrow. And I'll want to meet the crew."

"Sleep in our wagon if you want," Humphrey invited. "It's empty."

"Sounds good to me," Finch said. "But Chico isn't quite civilized yet, and I guess we'll just throw our bedrolls on the ground."

Chico grinned sleepily, but said nothing.

"One thing," Humphrey said. "If it won't be too much out of the way, I'd like to stop off in Decatur a bit. I understand there's quite a few people there, and shorely they must have a preacher. I'd like to get some more bucks and wenches married up legal. I'll swear that they've been poppin' out of wagons ever since we've been here. And a few have caught up on foot. Don't have any idea how many we got now. They're like a covey of quail tryin' to count 'em. And if we can get as many of 'em married as we can match up—I figure it'll save trouble."

"Fine with me." Finch said. "Anything that will save trouble, I'm all for it. We're gonna have enough trouble, anyway. But we'll have to cross the Trinity River. That could be a chore with the wagons and all."

Finch and Chico retrieved their hats and pistols and started to leave. Chico smiled at Colette and bowed again.

"Buenos Noches, Senora."

"Bon Nuit, Ami! Sleep well!"

Chico grinned again and followed Finch out of the tent.

When they were in their bedrolls, Chico said sleepily, "Senora, she ess uno bonito mujer!"

"Most beautiful woman I ever saw," Finch said glumly.

"Oh, ho!" Chico sat upright. "Like that, eh, mi amigo? Caramba!"

"Shut up, Chico," Finch growled, "and go to sleep."

\* \* \* \* \* \*

Finch and Chico were up early and had rolled their bedrolls and packed their gear as day began to break. They could see the fires of the Beatenbow camp, and they walked toward them. As they entered the firelight, a big, fat Negro woman peered at them as she stirred a pot.

"It's Mars Finch!" she exclaimed. "I seen you at that fracas at the blacksmith shop the other day, but you didn't see me. I was hidin' in my wagon! I's Kate. Been the Beatenbow cook since afore Mars Hump was borned, and that no good nigger settin' on that log is Sam. He's my husband—all legal. Mars Hump got us married by a preacher!" she said proudly as she pointed the big stirring ladle at Sam. The small, wizened little black man's face wrinkled in a toothless grin, but he said nothing.

"Mornin', Kate and Sam. Hump told me about both of you, and I'm glad to meet you," Finch said. "This here is a friend of mine, Chico Baca."

"How do, Mars Baca," Kate said. Sam nodded and grinned again.

"Howdy!" Chico said. " Is that coffee I smell?"

"Sho nuff!" Kate replied and then turned toward a wagon and spoke in a louder tone. "Ellie, bring these two gennlemen some cups."

Almost immediately a young black girl appeared. She handed Kate several cups and grinned shyly at Finch and Chico.

"This here is Ellie," Kate said. "She's mine and Sam's. Our last one up to now."

"Hello, Ellie," Finch greeted her.

"Buenos Dias, Nina." Chico grinned at her, and she again smiled shyly and stuck her finger in her mouth. Then she pointed a finger at Chico. "Is he a Indian, Ma?"

"Land sakes, no, child! Now you scat and let me finish breakfast. Yo wake everbody up and tell 'em we gonna eat in about ten minutes."

"Yes Ma'am!" Ellie turned and ran.

"This is right good coffee, Kate," Finch said appreciatively. "How old is the little one?"

"Goin' on eight or nine, I reckon," Kate said complacently. "She's most growed up. Mornin' Mars Hump."

Finch and Chico turned to see Humphrey walking up.

"Mornin, Finch and Chico. Sleep all right?"

"I always do," Chico said. "Finch, he tosses about some. I teenk his conscience bothers him."

"Mornin', Hump." Finch paid no attention to Chico. "Kate makes a good cup of coffee."

"That she does," Humphrey agreed. "She's a good cook, too. The best! Kate, pour me a couple of cups, and Finch, you and Chico come on into the tent. We'll have breakfast as soon as it's ready."

"Right soon, Mars Hump," Kate said. "Right soon. Maisie will bring yo breakfast."

Finch and Chico followed Humphrey as they carried their coffee to the tent. Colette turned from a mirror as they entered. Her face was bright as a sunrise, and her dark eyes lit with welcome. Finch's heart skipped a beat.

"Good morning, Finch and Chico!" she smiled. "How nice it will be to have breakfast with three men! I'm so glad you are back!"

"Mornin', Colette," Finch gulped.

"Buenos Dias, Senora!" Chico smiled and bowed.

"Have a seat, men, "Humphrey invited. "Maisie will have our breakfast here in a few minutes."

Finch and Chico had removed their hats upon entering the tent, and now they unbuckled their pistols and placed them on the ground at the edge of the tent.

"Why do you do that?" Colette asked, perplexed.

"Do what?" Finch said in surprise.

"Remove your guns."

"Well," Finch said. "I — I don't know. Just a custom, I guess."

"Hah, Senora!" Chico jibed. "Finch, he is tongue-tied. We remove our guns in the house because it is friendly. In here we do not need guns when we are among friends."

"But you always wear them in camp—and they are all friendly!"

"Que sera, senora," Chico shrugged. "Who knows? Finch and I have many enemies."

A worried frown creased the smooth skin of Colette's brow, and her eyes showed concern as she looked at them.

"Here's Maisie with our breakfast," Humphrey interrupted.

A tall, but voluptuous black woman entered with a big, wooden tray loaded with bacon, grits, hot biscuits, and a fresh pot of coffee. Chico inhaled the delicious aroma and sighed appreciatively.

"This is Maisie," Humphrey said. "She's Largo's wench—I mean wife."

"Hello, Maisie," Finch and Largo said in unison. Maisie only ducked her head and placed the food and dishes before them. Then she quickly left the tent. Colette intercepted the puzzled look that passed between Finch and Chico.

"Maisie has been trained that way," Colette explained. "She's really a very friendly person."

Finch frowned, and Chico shrugged as they turned to their food.

"You say grace, Humphrey," Colette said quietly.

Both Finch and Chico had to abruptly check their movement toward the food and immediately bowed their heads. To their surprise, Humphrey said a beautiful prayer. Chico crossed himself.

Humphrey raised his head and spoke to no one in particular. "I think Largo picked him a good woman," he said as he chewed. "Hope so! Largo is the best black I ever saw. Went with me through four years of war, and a good fightin' man he was. And for a blacksmith you can't beat him. Strong as a bull. He's reset the shoes on all the mules and trimmed all the mares. Even reshod Old Heck, and that ain't easy to do. And he's repaired all the wagons that need it."

"When will we get to meet the crew?" Finch wanted to know.

"Told 'em we'd meet 'em at the blacksmith shop an hour after sun up. I expect they're already there."

They finished their breakfast quickly and rose from the table. Finch and Chico buckled on their pistols. Humphrey went to a big trunk, opened it, and brought forth a long barreled pistol that looked awkward on him.

"Used a rifle mostly in the war," he explained sheepishly.

They left the tent and walked the few hundred yards to the blacksmith shop. True to Humphrey's prediction, a group of men was already there.

"Mornin', men!" Humphrey greeted them. "Is everybody here?"

"I reckon they're all here, Hump," Buff said from the back of the overhang where he sat whittling.

"Good!" Humphrey approved. "Men, this is my partner. Name of Finch, and this is his friend, Chico. Don't know all your names yet, but will soon enough. We'll be ready to pull out tomorrow, if you men can all make it."

"You've got the grub," Buff said as he spat tobacco juice. "And all of us got bedrolls; so I reckon we can pull out anytime you're ready."

"Then—sunup tomorrow!" Humphrey said with finality.

"One thing!" A man stepped forward. He had a lean, hard look about him that Finch liked.

"What is it, Clem? Finch, this is Clem Swenson that I was tellin' you about. What's the question, Clem?"

"Just who is bossin' this shindig?"

Humphrey hesitated. "Never thought about it, Clem. What do you say, Finch?"

"We ought to have one man that has the final say-so, I reckon."

"Well," Humphrey said thoughtfully. "I guess Finch knows the country best—and the Indians if we see any."

"I know the country and the Indians and the Comancheros, and a lot of other scum that are out there on the plains—and you can bet we'll see plenty of them. But I'm no boss!"

"What about you, Buff?" Humphrey asked. Buff was so startled, he swallowed his quid.

"Not me!" he sputtered. "I'm gonna be too busy huntin' an' skinnin' bufflers and keepin' y'all in meat."

"Well—" Humphrey seemed at a loss.

"Tell you what!" Finch rescued him. "Let's split it up. Clem, you're the cowman. You boss that part of it. Humphrey can take care of the wagons and the blacks. I know the country, and so does Chico. So, we'll do the scouting. When it comes to the fightin' part, maybe I'd better sort of take charge of that. When everything is all mixed up, and it will be, maybe I'd better have the say-so."

There was a general response of agreement except for one man. He was tall, gaunt, and slightly stooped. His drooping mustache seemed to accentuate his beady, close-set eyes. "There's another thing, Beatenbow," he said in a high, thin voice.

"What's that?" Humphrey asked curtly.

"I know they is a passel of niggers along, and maybe so we can abide 'em. But you didn't say nothin' about no Mexicans."

A sudden quiet fell. Chico, who had been standing beside Finch, quickly stepped a couple of paces to his right, and he said quietly. "So Senor! You do not like Mexicans! Perhaps, then, you would like to leave this one behind!"

"Maybe I would!" the man said venomously.

"Then, please, senor. Be my guest. You have a pistol, No?" Chico was smiling coldly.

Finch did not move, for he knew Chico, but Humphrey took a step forward, and Finch put a hand on his shoulder.

"Don't be a damned fool, man!" Buff hissed quickly. "That's Chico Baca. He's a Ranger, too!"

The man flinched as if hit, his face turned pasty, and he stepped a pace backward.

"What's your name, Mister?" Humphrey demanded.

"Guines. Doc Guines," the man said defiantly.

"You're fired, Guines!" Humphrey said harshly. " Now git out!"

"And what if I don't?" Guines said belligerently.

"Then, Senor," Chico said softly. "Will you please step from in front of the other men. Sometimes my pistol, she will shoot through such a thin hombre as you."

"Why you—" Suddenly the starch went out of Guines, and he turned on his heel and stalked away.

"God-a-mighty!" Humphrey whispered fervently.

"It's just as well, Hump," Finch said. "He was trouble, and Chico would have had to kill him sooner or later."

"All right, men," Humphrey said, relief in his voice. "If everything else is satisfactory with the rest of you, we'll pull out at sunup tomorrow."

With that, Finch, Humphrey, and Chico started walking back toward the Beatenbow camp.

"That damn fool!" Buff said irritably. "Chico Baca ain't as fast as Finch, but Guines never would have got his pistol out. I've heard of Chico Baca!"

# CHAPTER 6

There were fifteen wagons in line the next morning when the sun came up. The mules seemed alert and ready, and the mares tied to the wagons pawed the ground irritably. The cowboys were all waiting beside their horses.

Colette had cajoled Humphrey into letting her ride her mare. She wore trousers and rode astride. She and Humphrey rode beside the lead wagon, which was driven by Sam with Kate sitting beside him and Ellie standing behind them. Largo and Maisie's wagon brought up the rear with the breeding jack tied behind. He brayed loudly and pulled back as the wagon began to move northward toward Decatur. The men on horseback rode pell mell fashion about the wagons. Buff had the only wagon that was uncovered, and he raced completely around the caravan yelling as loudly as he could. His wagon was pulled by a span of small horses. "Mustangs," Buff had replied when Humphrey asked him what they were.

Colette felt a thrill as they pulled out of Fort Worth, and her face glowed with delight. Humphrey suddenly felt an enormous weight of responsibility and clamped his jaw stubbornly. He felt some discomfiture about Colette riding astride like a man. Not that anyone would ever mistake her for a man, Humphrey thought with a sense of pride.

Finch and Chico trotted up beside Humprey and Colette. Finch had a very difficult time keeping his eyes off Colette. As for her, she seemed quite pleased that the men looked at her appreciatively and made no effort to cover her femininity.

"We'd better take it pretty easy for the first few days," Finch said as they came alongside. "We need to break these horses in pretty slow."

"I was thinkin' that same thing," Humphrey agreed. "The way them cowboys are roustin' about, they're goin' to use up their horses in a hurry. We're gonna need extra horses. Course, they could ride some of my mares that ain't in foal, but I'd sure hate to have them do that. You reckon we could buy some extras in Decatur?"

"I expect we can," Finch replied, "and after we get out on the plains, we can catch some mustangs."

"You mean them little things like Buff is drivin'?" Humphrey said dubiously.

"Sure!"

"Why them little things?" Humphrey exclaimed. "They don't look like they could carry a grown man."

"Ho! Ho! Amigo!" Chico said merrily. "The mustang, he ess like the Mexican!. He ess a tough one!"

"That's true," Finch said in support of Chico. "In fact, those tough little critters could probably run your thoroughbreds to death."

"I sure doubt that!" Humphrey said defensively. "If they're so good, why ain't you and Chico ridin' 'em?"

"I didn't say they were good," Finch laughed. "I said they were tough. And they are. These horses Chico and I ride are called quarterhorses. They're a mixture of a lot of different breeds—thoroughbreds like your mares and stud, Arabians, Morgans, and probably a bit of mustang. They're just a great mixture of bloodlines, but they're smart, easy to handle, cat-quick; they have cow sense, and are tough, too! And you can trust 'em."

"Hey!" Humphrey said in surprise. "You sound like a Missouri horse trader, Finch!"

Both Finch and Chico chuckled, and Colette's laugh pealed like a lark singing on the morning air. Humphrey so rarely evinced humor that his rejoinder was a delight to them all.

"Guess you're right, Hump," Finch smiled sheepishly. "I reckon I just like a good horse."

"Me, too!" Chico chimed in. "Good horses ess like women—some you never forget—no offense, senora!"

"Of course not, Chico!" Colette smiled at him. "Why do you call them quarterhorses?"

"Because, senora, for a quarter of a mile they can run faster than any horse alive!" Chico replied.

"Is that the way the cowboys will catch the mustangs out on the plains?" Humphrey asked. "Just run up behind 'em on their quarterhorses and rope them?"

"Not by a long shot," Finch replied. "A mustang won't let us get in a mile of him. When we hit the plains, we will see a herd a long way off—you can see till the next day when you are on that flat country—and when we see the mustangs, we will have a couple of men start chasing them. They will ride pretty for apart so the mustangs will begin to turn one way or other; and when they do, another rider on a fresh horse will cut across country and keep the mustangs runnin' and away from water. In three or four days, if we can keep 'em in sight and keep 'em movin' without water, some will begin to straggle. Finally, with a lot of luck, we can catch some of 'em—and then the fun begins!"

"How's that?" Humphrey asked. He and Colette had been listening intently.

"Ah!" Chico said with gusto. "We start breaking eem! They keek and squeal and bite and keek and buck and roll on the ground!"

"That doesn't sound like much fun to me!" Colette said.

"Only when someone else ess doing the breaking, senora!" Chico conceded. "Then ess fun!"

"What are your mares bred to, Humphrey?" Finch asked. "I can see that a lot of 'em are heavy in foal."

"Some of 'em are bred to that jack back there—figured we'd need some more mules. And some of 'em are bred to Old Heck here!" Humphrey leaned over and patted the stallion on the neck. "And some of 'em are still open."

"Well," Finch observed. "You might do a lot worse than breed some of those good mares that are open to a mustang stud—if we can catch one."

"What about breeding a mustang mare to Old Heck?" Colette wanted to know.

"That would sure get some good colts." Finch reddened when he replied. Then he continued. "Chico and I will ride on ahead, and see if we can find a good spot to camp. We're gonna need plenty of water and a lot of grass for all this stock, but at least we won't have to worry much about Indians for a few more days."

"Need to talk to you some more about that," Humphrey said soberly. "I don't know the first thing about Indian fightin'. You will have to show me a lot of things."

"Nobody know much about Indian fighting!" Chico said grimly. "But Finch and me, we ess had our share of it—and they ess fighters!"

"That's right." Finch agreed. "Anyhow, Chico and I will fill you in all we can before we hit Indian country. Most of the cowboys have fought Indians and Yankees; so I figure they'll do all right! It's the blacks that have me worried."

"Worries me, too!" Humphrey said. "I wish I knew myself how they'll do. They've never had any responsibility, and I don't know how they'll do in a fight. But Largo sure did all right with me in the war. I'll have him talk to the rest of 'em. I just hope we don't get a bunch of people killed!"

"Well," Finch said matter of factly. "It'd be a near miracle if we crossed Indian country and all the rivers and gathered cattle and mustangs without somebody gettin' hurt. We'll just hope for the best."

"The best! Ah, amigo, eet ess good enough for Chico! Let's go find that place to camp."

With that, Finch and Chico loped ahead. Colette and Humphrey watched them for several minutes. They could hear the good natured banter between the two friends before they were out of hearing range. Chico pushed his hat back and started singing. It was a happy Mexican song, and the merry lilt carried far on the morning air.

"Well," Humphrey said. "Finch was sure right about Chico bein' a singin' fool! I don't reckon I ever heard better!"

"He does have a beautiful voice." Colette was delighted. "I hope he will sing a lot for us around the campfires."

"He will!" Humphrey said. "That is one merry Mexican."

"He and Finch are great friends, aren't they."

"They are that," Humphrey replied. "They've been through a lot together in the Rangers. Finch told me a lot about Chico before he left to go back to Austin."

"I hope they find a nice spot, close to a stream where I can bathe," Colette said wistfully.

"They probably will," Humphrey said. "They know this country. Anyhow, you can get your bath in the wagon like you always do. We still have niggers to carry warm water for you."

"I know," Colette said. "But I just like to bathe in a stream when I can."

"I don't know what is the matter with this blamed stud," Humphrey said irritably as Old Heck stamped the ground and nickered in anger. "He's been actin' the fool all mornin'."

"I know what is the matter with him," Colette said.

"What?" Humphrey frowned.

"This mare is in heat. Can't you tell?"

"Oh."

"And, Humphrey," Colette looked at him suggestively. "So am I!"

Humphrey looked at Colette in astonishment. "God-a-mighty, woman!"

"Come on. Let's get to that camp early." Colette started her mount in a lope. Humphrey shook his head and followed.

\* \* \* \* \* \*

Finch and Chico found an excellent camping spot at mid-afternoon. There was plenty of grass for the stock and a huge pecan tree near a clear running creek.

"This will do fine for tonight," Finch said. "But after we leave Decatur, we're goin' to have to pick spots that can be defended. I'm more concerned about the stock than anything else. Indians are the worst horse thieves in the world. Course, we will circle the wagons, and we can keep 'em in the circle at night, if we have to. But after we begin to gather cattle, we will have to night herd every night."

"We will, amigo!" Chico agreed. "And Chico and Finch weel have the guard duty every night, too!"

"Afraid so!" Finch said. "I doubt if any of the blacks or Humphrey, either, would know an Indian if he rode up to the wagon. Maybe we can get Buff and some of the cowhands to spell us once in a while."

"Another theeng we must theenk of, Finch," Chico said soberly, and Finch looked at Chico keenly, for he rarely called him anything but 'amigo' unless he was disturbed about something.

"What's that?"

"You know how much Indians like the mule meat! Eet's the only theeng he'd rather have than buffalo."

"I know!" Finch said grimly.

"Today we do not worry, amigo!" Chico grinned. "Plenty of time for that when we leave Decatur."

"You're right, Chico. But I do wish that Hump had some niggers that could take care of the horses. We're gonna need all the hands we have to gather those wild longhorns."

"Ah, amigo. Ess well," Chico said complacently. "Largo has been training two black muchachos. They ess been doing eet ever since they left Louisiana. They grew up weeth the mares, and they can catch any one of theem, even out on the prairie. Tonight you weel see."

"I sure hope so!" Finch said fervently. "Jinglin' horses is mighty important to all of us. We're goin' off half-cocked, anyway, and this trip could blow sky high the first night out."

"Do not worry so much, amigo!" Chico laughed. "Let Chico do some worrying for you!"

"That's all we need!" Finch said derisively. "A dozen wagons, a crazy Irishman, two dozen niggers, forty head of livestock, fifteen cow boys, a man and a woman that never saw an Indian, and a locoed Mexican to do the worryin' for us! As you say, Chico—Caramba!"

Chico's laugh was deep and pleasant. "Ess what you say, a good situation! Now, since eet weel be three or four hours before the wagons get here, I theenk thees Mexican, he weel worry under the shade of the beeg tree by the stream. If I do not worry enough for you, wake me up, and I weel worry harder!"

"Oh, hell, Chico. Go ahead and get your siesta!" Finch said with a laugh. "I guess I'm gettin' as bad as Captain Cates used to be, anyway. I'm gonna ride up the creek a ways while you get your nap. And thanks for doin' all that worryin' for me!"

"Por nada!" Chico shrugged as he dismounted and lay down; he pulled his hat over his face. "You know, amigo, I theenk we must park the Beatenbow wagon away from the others tonight. The wagon springs, they may squeak."

"Go to hell!" Finch said as he turned his horse and rode up the creek.

Chico chuckled, pulled his hat farther down over his face, took a deep breath, and was instantly asleep.

It was an hour later when Finch returned. He slowed his horse and rode as quietly as possible to within a few feet of Chico. He was not surprised to see Chico's eyes twinkling from under the hat and his pistol in his hand.

"You're sure a trustin' cuss!" Finch grinned.

"I am alive, amigo," Chico said as he sat up and replaced his pistol. "You ride all the way to Decatur?"

"What kind of a horse did Guines ride?"

"Who?"

"Guines. Doc Guines. The long, tall hombre that didn't like Mexicans."

"Oh, that one! Si, I know. He ride the pinto. I see heem leave after Hump fire heem."

"I can't be sure, but I think I saw him ridin' toward Decatur. He was a good ways off, but it looked like him. And he was ridin' a pinto."

"So!" Chico grinned. "Maybe we see heem again. Maybe he like the Mexican better thees time."

"That man is dangerous, Chico," Finch said sternly. "You watch it close when we are in town."

"Si, I watch," Chico said absently. "I theenk I hear the wagons coming."

\* \* \* \* \* \*

Finch and Chico rode toward the wagons. Humphrey and Colette loped to meet them.

"Find a place?" Humphrey asked.

"A good one for tonight," Finch answered. "Good grass and water, plenty of wood. It'll do to start with, but after we leave Decatur, we'll need some place a little different."

"How's that?" Humphrey asked curiously.

"Well," Finch removed his hat and ran his fingers through his hair. "After we leave Decatur, we will be in a sort of no man's land. We will need to camp where we can defend the wagons and the stock. But from here to Decatur will give us a chance to get organized."

"Good!" Humphrey agreed. "We had things pretty well worked out from Louisiana to Fort Worth, but I reckon things will be a lot different from now on."

"Ah, amigo," Chico chimed in with his infectious grin. "They weel be different, you weel see—but most interesting, also!"

"How in the world are we going to feed and shelter all those wild cowboys?" Colette asked seriously.

"Oh, they'll make out, Colette," Finch assured her. "They all have bedrolls and ground sheets, and probably some hardtack and jerky in their saddle bags. And they are all used at sleepin' on the ground, just as Chico and I are."

"Won't that be terribly uncomfortable?" Colette was concerned.

"We're used to it," Finch answered. "But we will have to figure out a way to feed all of 'em."

"We can manage that, all right," Humphrey said confidently. "Old Kate is the best cook in Louisiana—or Texas, or anywhere else, and we've got two or three other nigger women who can cook. But I expect we'll need to lay in a lot of extra grub when we get to Decatur."

"We will," Finch said. "We'll have plenty of fresh meat. Buff will see to that. There's buffalo, turkey, antelope, and other wild game. But we will need a lot of other stuff, too."

"And plenty of hot peppers!" Chico added his bit.

Finch paid no attention to Chico. "What I'm concerned about is all of us being organized. When Chico and I were in the Rangers, we took care of ourselves individually when we were out on a scout—but this is different. We've got a lot of stock and a lot of people to think about—especially the women and kids. It won't be easy."

"Tell you what," Humphrey said thoughtfully. "I'll have Kate and a couple of the other nigger women cook for all of us tonight in one big pot, and after supper we'll have a meetin' and assign the men to different jobs on the trip."

"I think we'd better do that. Don't you think we will need to have Clem in on the meeting, too? He's in charge of the cowhands."

"Si, and Buff, too," Chico contributed. "That old hombre ess going to furnish meat, so he say, and he has probably seen more Indians and knows more about theem than all the rest of us!"

"All right!" Humphrey agreed as he spurred his horse into a trot. "Let's get to our campground and eat; then we'll talk."

As the wagons pulled into the open space beside the creek, Finch was pleasantly surprised when Humphrey rode to the first wagon and called in a loud, authoritative voice. "All right. Just park the wagons anywhere tonight. You boys that take care of the horses know what to do. And I want all the rest of you to meet me under that big pecan tree in twenty minutes."

Sam pulled the Beatenbow wagon away from the others, and Chico winked at Finch, which he ignored.

Blacks of every description came tumbling out of the wagons as four young black men began unhitching the teams and removing the harness. In a short time they had the mules hobbled with rawhide and the mares out on good grass. One old mare was wearing a bell that clanged musically as she walked. The cowboys had ridden up to Finch, and they watched the operation with interest.

"You know," Clem Swenson said, "They do a pretty fair job of that."

"They do for a fact," Finch said with relief. "That's been worryin' me all day."

"Like I tell you, amigo. Let Chico do the worrying. Now you see—No?" Chico grinned at Finch.

"I still don't see how they're gonna catch all them mares in the mornin'," Clem said dubiously. "Course all us boys will stake our horses close to our bedrolls, and we could probably round 'em up."

"No need, senor," Chico said. "Hump, he tell me how. Two of the boys will stay with the mares until midnight, and then the other two weel take over and stay till morning."

"That still don't have 'em all caught and tied up to the wagons," Clem observed blandly.

"Senor Hump, he say the boys have been raised with the mares," Chico explained. "You see, all of theem ess still wearing their halters. In the morning, the boys catch theem and tie theem to the wagons. If one strays too far, she weel follow Hump's stud and catch the wagons. Seemple, no?"

"Simple, hell!" Clem rejoined acidly. "Them mares will booger at some critter jus' like any other horse. And I never seen nobody jinglin' horses on foot. Them two black boys ain't no jackrabbits. They're gonna have to learn to ride horses before we hit Indian country and begin gatherin' cattle."

"You tell Hump that, Clem" Finch said. "In fact, he wants you and Chico and me to meet with him after supper to arrange everything for the trip."

"That's one damn good idee and only a couple of days late at that!" Clem answered sourly. "Us boys will go off a ways and picket our horses. Be shore that stud and jackass of Hump's are tied good and tight—with a stout rope!"

"We'll do that!" Finch said as the cowboys rode off. "Be back in an hour for supper."

Finch and Chico dismounted and tied their horses to a wagon and watched as the blacks gathered under the pecan tree. Colette went inside the Beatenbow wagon. Humphrey started talking to the Negroes. Finch tried to count them but was unsuccessful. It seemed that every time he got a number, another black head would pop up. There were at least eight grown men and as many women, and a scattering of youngsters. Finch estimated the crowd at twenty-two. And once, when he turned around, he saw another black head disappear under a wagon cover. He wondered how many were still hiding in the wagons.

"You know, Chico," Finch said to his friend, "I haven't got as much sense as that jackass, or I'd never have started this! And you've got less sense than I have for comin' with me!"

"Ah, amigo!" Chico smiled his reckless grin. "Chico ess the one to do the worrying, no? It will be for us un grande viage. You weel see!"

"I hope so!" Finch said dubiously.

\* \* \* \* \* \*

After the one dish supper which Kate and some of the other women ladled into each plate, Finch, Chico, and Clem moved off to a small knoll and sat waiting for Humphrey to join them. In a short time he walked up, accompanied by Largo.

"I brought Largo," Humphrey said a bit apologetically. "He was with me during the war, and he has done some fightin'."

"Glad to have you, Largo," Finch said. "Pull up a seat."

"Where is Buff?" Chico asked.

"There he comes, now," Finch said as the big Irishman strode toward them. "He ate at his own wagon. Says he's eaten his own cookin' so long that other food doesn't taste right."

"Howdy, me lads!" Buff rumbled as he sat down and began tamping a pipe. "And now we be havin' a regular pow wow, begorra! What's up?"

"Figured maybe we'd ought to get a little better organized," Humphrey explained.

"Aye," agreed Buff. "I reckoned as much. Everybody went in seventeen different ways tonight. That won't do in Indian country!"

"What we figured!" Finch agreed. "I've been in Indian country alot, but the only thing I had to look out for was my own scalp. This time, we've got a lot more to take care of. We hoped you could help us do some plannin'."

"Aye, me lad! And maybe I can, at that," Buff admitted. "I been in Indian country some too. Spent more winters trappin' in the shinin' mountains than I care to recollect, and I been over the Santy Fee trail a couple of times with a wagon train. I spent one winter with the Kiowas. Mighty nice folks, sometimes. Furnished me a squaw an' ever thin'."

"Then you know Indian ways," Humphrey said with satisfaction.

"I reckon I do as much as a white man can know 'em. They're a different kind of critter. They don't think like a white man—" Buff glanced at Chico and Largo and added quickly, "are any other color man!"

"Well, Buff," Finch said. "How do you reckon we ought to travel after we leave Decatur?"

"Fust off," Buff puffed at his pipe and continued in his thick Irish brogue. "Fust off, we'd ort to keep a scout, or mebbe two, out ahead of the wagons quite a ways. Course, I'll be out in different directions in my waggin huntin' meat, and them little mustangs of mine can move like they had a tumble weed tied to their tails when they smell a Indian. That'll help some. But I 'spect we'd ort to have one man as a rear guard, too. Indians ain't got no manners when it comes to fightin'. They'd jus' as lief slip up behind you and cut your throat as not."

"Chico and I can take care of the scoutin' up front. And maybe Largo or one of Clem's cowhands can bring up the rear," Finch observed. "What else?"

"Waal," Buff paused a bit and frowned as he put his pipe away and cut a quid of tobacco and stuffed it in his jaw. "You shore do need drivers that can get them wagons in a circle, and do it fast. Reckon maybe they ort to practice that some."

"What else?" Humphrey asked impatiently. "I'll take care of that."

"If you ain't got plenty of rifles and ammunition, get 'em!" Buff said flatly. "And don't let no wimmin folks or younguns get far from the waggins. A Indian can hide under a buffalo chip and steal a little 'un or a woman and be gone afore you can cock a pistol. I reckon that's about all except that ever'body that's big enough to hold a rifle ort to be able to shoot straight—and that goes for the wimmin folk, too."

"I been showin' the nigger men how to shoot, Mars Hump," Largo said, then added almost apologetically, "but I didn't figger on the women doin' any. I'll take care of that."

"I didn't think of it, either, Largo," Humphrey said. "What about you, Clem? Want to add anything?"

"I reckon most of the cowboys can handle themselves all right," Clem said slowly. "Most of them was in the war, and they can shoot and ride. They've all got good guns, but they will need more ammunition. And they ain't got the money to buy it."

"We'll lay in plenty of ammunition when we get to Decatur," Humphrey assured him. "And rifles, too. Anything else?"

"A feller jus' can't figger everything in advance," Clem said defensively. "Especially with so many things we're gonna have to contend with, but there is a few things we can be sure we're gonna need."

"Like what?" Humphrey wanted to know.

"More horses for one thing. And when we start gatherin' cattle, we're gonna need a cook to keep hot coffee on all night. We're gonna have to night herd all across them plains, and that's gonna keep a lot of cowboys mighty busy, 'cause we'll be throwin' in wild cattle every day even before the herd gets trailwise. And we'll need breakfast at three or four o'clock ever' mornin'. I shore think the cook for the cowboys ort to be a man—and one that has had experience with a trail herd—but I reckon that ain't possible."

"Well, now, I don't know," Humphrey said thoughtfully. "I hear there are nearly three thousand people in Decatur, and one of 'em might be just what we need."

"That's shore be a big relief to the boys," Clem said. "Fact is, if you're willin' to hire one on, us boys will sure find 'im—if he's in Decatur!"

"Then find 'im," Humphrey said firmly.

"If we can find a cow camp cook, you reckon the cowboys could have their own chuck wagon?"

"Don't see why not!" Humphrey was puzzled. " But why would they want one?"

Clem squirmed uncomfortably before he answered. "Cowboys is apt to use a lot of rough language, especially when they're comin' in to eat, or when they're changin' the guard. And they sure ain't used to havin' women folks around."

"Doubt like hell if their language would shock any of the Beatenbow slave women—I mean nigger women—and I know it wouldn' faze Colette, but if that is what you want, we'll get it."

"The boys will be mighty pleased!" Clem said with relief. "And you can bet that if there is a cowcamp cook in Decatur, the boys will find 'im. And he'll more than pay his way 'cause you can bet we're gonna have a few stampedes, and an old time cowcamp cook will know how to get hot grub to the boys wherever they wind up."

"Stampede?" Humphrey asked quizzically. "What will cause that?"

"A lot of things," Clem answered shortly. "Indians, varmints, lightnin', somebody rattles a dish too loud, or just plain cussedness. A cow critter is the most aggravatin' animal on earth, and longhorns is the worst of the lot."

"Well," Humphrey laughed. "Guess we'd better find that cook! And I can see now that we'll need some more wagons."

"Aye. And it's been a grand pow wow we've had!" Buff rose from his sitting position on the ground. "And I reckon iver body had his say; so I reckon this Irishman will go git a wink o' sleep. Don't forgit to git a lot of 50 calibre ammunition, Hump." He walked toward his wagon.

"Anybody else want to add anything?" Humphrey asked.

"I expect we will think of a few more things between here and Decatur," Finch said as he rose from the ground. Chico, who had been dozing, was instantly alert and had his hand on his pistol.

"We'll meet again if we need to," Humphrey said. Then he turned and walked toward the creek with Largo following.

"I shore do feel a lot better," Clem sighed as Humphrey and Largo disappeared in the dusk. "I figger that Beatenbow don't know much of a damn thing about the west—but I got a hunch he'll do to ride the river with!"

"He will!" Finch said firmly.

"Si, senor Clem!" Chico smiled slowly. "Senor Hump mucho hombre! You weel see."

"See you tomorrow, men," Clem said as he too walked away.

"Well, Chico," Finch said. "I reckon we should just as well unroll our beds and get in 'em."

"I theenk so, amigo!" Chico said as he and Finch walked side by side toward their staked horses and their bedrolls. "And you see that old fellow that drives the Beatenbow wagon, he ess one smart black hombre. He park the Beatenbow wagon a long way from the others—so let the springs rattle!"

"Chico," Finch said disgustedly. "You are one boar-brained bastard! Don't you ever think of anything but screwin?"

"Ah, amigo," Chico said cheerfully as he put his hand on Finch's shoulder. "But what more ess there to theenk of but pretty senoritas, fast horses, and good guns!"

"Come to think of it, Chico—I reckon you may be right at that, even if you are a dirty-minded little greaser!" Finch laughed.

Then Chico started singing a Mexican song very softly, and Finch joined. The song ended just as they had their beds unrolled.

"Buenos Noches, amigo!" Chico said as he lay down.

"Good night, my friend," Finch replied.

# Chapter 7

The rest of the trip to Decatur was almost uneventful. Three or four times each day Buff would race his uncovered wagon toward the caravan yelling as loudly as he could. The wagons would quickly form a circle, and the men and women would take sheltered positions that allowed them to see an approaching enemy and to shoot with an unobstructed view. Humphrey timed each circling and was quite pleased to note that the maneuver took much less time and was less confused than when they had first begun. Even Buff was impressed.

"Niver been around blacks afore, meself, Hump, but begorra, it looks like you got a right smart crew on them waggins."

"They are improving, aren't they!" Humphrey said proudly. "Course, a nigger ain't smart like a white man is, but they can be trained."

"Begorra, and I ain't so sure them black folks ain't smart. They sure are learnin' in a hurry."

\* \* \* \* \* \*

Humphrey assigned one of the black women to cook for the cowboys until they got to Decatur, and he assigned two other black women to cook for other wagons of the caravan. Finch, Chico, Humphrey, and Colette were served by Kate and Sam at a table set up beside the Beatenbow wagon, which was always parked away from the others. Buff ate at his wagon, alone.

After serving the meal at the Beatenbow wagon, Kate would remove the dishes and wash them in a big pot over the campfire. Then she checked the other wagons to see that the cooks had served everyone and had tidied up the camp.

"Jus cause we's campin' out ain't no reason to be messy!" Kate admonished. "Sides, these wagons is most as good as the cabins ever one of you was borned and raised in. We is free people now, too, and we got to make Mars Hump proud of us!"

The cowboys took no part in the wagon maneuvers other than to occasionally ride their horses at full speed behind Buff's wagon while he rattled and bounced in a circle around the caravan, and Buff and the cowboys yelled like a horde of savages. Finch and Chico rode ahead and sought the best camping places, and good ones were plentiful. Indeed, it was a pleasant few days. The blacks began to emerge more visibly, and they seemed as excited as anyone to be going west. Their laughter and good natured shouts as they circled the wagons in preparation for the mock attack could be heard above the din of rattling activity. Humphrey smiled his satisfaction.

Only one incident marred the trip to Decatur. Sam drove the Beaten bow wagon, and beside him was Kate. Behind the two stood Ellie. Chico noted with a grin that her little breasts were already peeking through the thin cotton dress.

Following the Beatenbow wagon was the one that Sam, Kate, and Ellie slept in. Then came the supply wagon from which all the cooks drew rations for each meal. The others followed in no particular order except that Largo's wagon always brought up the rear.

One night after they had eaten, Humphrey saw Old Kate glance about surreptitiously and then take a plate of food to their wagon and hand it to someone inside. Humphrey's curiosity was pricked, and he walked quietly to the back of Sam and Kate's wagon and quickly shoved the cover over the end of the wagon aside.

There, sitting with his back against the sideboard of the wagon and with a plate of food in his lap was a Negro man who was trying to get a spoonful of food to his mouth with his left hand. His right arm was pulled tightly across his chest by bandages that covered his entire shoulder. Humphrey was astonished and the Negro man terrified as they looked at each other.

"God-a-mighty!" Humphrey exclaimed; then he yelled at the top of his voice. "Kate! Get your black ass back here, and be quick about it!" Kate came puffing up. "Yassuh, Mars Hump. I's here. Here I is."

"What does this mean?" Humphrey demanded angrily as he pointed to the man.

"I reckon I done wrong, Mars Hump!" Kate cried, tears rolling down her fat cheeks. "But he say if he stay in Fort Worth, they gonna hang him."

Finch, Chico, and Colette had responded to Humphrey's yell by coming to the wagon. Sam had also edged up behind Kate.

"Who is this man? And where did you find him?"

"I know who he is, Hump," Finch said quietly.

"Who?" demanded Humphrey.

"It's that nigger I shot back in Fort Worth. The one that tried to hold you up."

Humphrey looked as if he had been slapped. His face suddenly was suffused with red, and he turned on Kate furiously.

"Kate, what in hell is the meanin' of this, you black bitch?"

Colette had never seen Humphrey angry before, and it frightened her.

"Please, Mars Hump," Kate begged as great sobs wracked her fat body. "Don't be so awful mad. He come to our wagon the night Mars Finch shoot him, and he say the men gonna hang him, and he scairt. He ain't no bad man, jus' don' know what to do since he free—got nobody lak yo to look after 'im. And he hurtin' awful bad; so I doctors 'im and gives 'im somep'n to eat, and well—he jus' stay on. He got no place to go."

"Well, he damned shore ain't stayin' here!" Humphrey said angrily. "Now git out of that wagon and start high-tailin' it back to wherever you come from, nigger."

"Please, Humphrey," Colette took his arm gently. "The man is hurt and sick. Kate was just being kind—I would have done the same thing, and I think you would have too had you been in her place."

Humphrey looked at Colette and seemed to regain some composure.

"Anyway, darling, let him stay until morning," Colette pleaded.

Humphrey saw that Colette's large, dark eyes were brimming with tears. He started to say something and then clamped his jaw rigidly.

"He can stay, can't he?" Colette asked shakily. "Kate didn't mean any harm; she was just being kind to another person."

There was a long silence broken only by Kate's sobs. Finch and Chico looked at Humphrey questioningly, and Sam cringed behind Kate. The Negro in the wagon was staring emptily at his still filled plate.

"All right, Colette," Humphrey said with resignation. "He can stay if that's what you want, but he'll damn well pull his own weight. He will have a job, and he will do it! As for you, Kate," he whirled on her. "I ought to take a bull whip to you, and the next time, I will do it!"

Humphrey turned and strode angrily toward the Beatenbow wagon. Colette went over to pat the sobbing Kate on the shoulder and then followed Humphrey. Sam led Kate back toward the cooking fire. Finch and Chico stayed at the end of the wagon.

"What's your name, nigger?" Finch asked pleasantly.

The Negro looked up, surprised. "Name is Raney, Massa. Jes Raney."

"You a state policeman, like your friend said?"

"No suh. Was jus gonna be, so they said. They was gonna get us all a comm— a somepin' to make us all legal. But we never got to do that!"

"Maybe it's just as well," Finch said. "I'm glad I didn't shoot a lawman."

"I's only met 'em a couple of days afore we got to Fort Worth," the Negro said eagerly. "They say for me to come with 'em, that they was gonna be policeman. Didn't know they was goin' to try to rob nobody."

"But you didn't try to stop them, did you?"

"Why, no suh!" the Negro looked at Finch in surprise. "They was white folks."

"All right, Raney. You just be sure you behave yourself around this wagon train. You hear?"

"Yassuh, yassuh," the Negro said eagerly. "I sho do that. I sho will. An' I's mighty glad you nearly missed me when you shot them two white folks."

Finch started to speak, then turned on his heel and started walking away. Chico waited a moment. Then he removed the big hunting knife from his belt, reached in, and lifted the Negro's chin with the tip of the knife.

"Mister Finch didn't miss you, nigger. He shot you right where he aimed to. He could have shot out either one of your eyes if he wanted to—and he probably should have. Now you cause any trouble with thees wagon train, and thees Mexican greaser ess gonna stretch your black skin and throw it on Buff's wagon with hees buffalo hides!"

With that admonition, Chico nicked the Negro's chin with his knife, turned, and walked toward their picketed horses. Finch already had his boots off and his bed unrolled.

"What's been keepin' you?" Finch asked crossly.

"Oh," Chico said nonchalantly. "Raney and me just sort of got to talking. I tell heem that it was just bad luck that you heet heem at all—probably mees heem completely next time."

"Hope there isn't a next time," Finch said soberly. "But I got a bad feelin' about that nigger. I just hope Kate didn't make a mistake—and Colette, too."

"Si, amigo. I hope so too. But Kate's heart ess as big as her derriere, and that's saying a lot. And Senora Colette — her heart ess as big as Texas—so

Amigo, if they make the mistake, then Finch and Chico they weel make eet, what you say, O.K., O.K.?"

"O.K. you tongue-tangled Mex," Finch laughed. "But where did you hear that word?"

"What word?" Chico asked innocently.

"You know what word—derriere!"

"Oh, si. I hear Senora Colette use it," Chico said blandly. "Chico know what she mean. Chico one smart Mexican, No?"

"You're just a dumb greaser," Finch said affectionately. "Buenos Noches."

"Buenos Noches, mi gringo amigo!" Chico said with a smile as he rolled into his blankets. Both men were asleep almost immediately.

For the first time since they were married, Humphrey was in bed before Colette. When she crawled in beside him, he turned his back. Colette was nonplussed. She lay still for a few minutes and then sat up and removed her gown. When she lay down again, she turned on her side and pressed her taut breasts against Humphrey's back. He did not react, and she gingerly put her arm over him and took him in her hand. To her utter amazement he was flaccid. Colette began to weep silently. She had made her husband terribly angry and was remorseful.

"I just wanted to be kind, my love," she whispered. "I love you so very much."

Humphrey's stiff body seemed to relax, and he turned on his back.

"I know, Colette," he said huskily. "I just lost my temper. Makes me feel bad."

"Well, my husband. That doesn't make you feel bad, does it?" she whispered as she rubbed him gently.

"You know it doesn't, Colette. It's just that—Oh hell! I love you too, but that nigger bothers me!" He turned and took her in his arms. Colette laughed softly as he became erect.

\* \* \* \* \* \*

The only other difficulty arose when they were crossing the Trinity River. It was not a particularly bad crossing, but a driver dropped one line in the middle of the river. One of the mares stepped on it, causing the mules to turn sharply and become entangled in the harness traces. The mules were frightened and fought madly, and one of the mares broke her halter and ran back the way they had come.

Clem and the cowboys had been sitting their horses on the bank watching the wagons cross, and as the mare ran by them, one of the men adroitly dropped a loop over her head. She hit the end of the rope at full speed, but the roper had his lariat tied to the saddle horn, and most Texas cowboys did. His cowpony had whirled to face the rope and brace his legs for the shock that he had felt many times before. The mare turned a somersault when she hit the end of the rope, but immediately got to her feet, bewildered and chastened.

One of the black horse tenders ran puffing up the river bank and talked soothingly to the mare, and she submitted meekly to the halter.

"Dammit," Clem Swenson growled irritably. "I tell you them nigger horse herders has got to have horses to ride. That mare would have been halfway back to Fort Worth if Art hadn't roped her."

Humphrey, who had been watching from his wagon that was already across the river, flinched visibly when the mare was up-ended. Then he heaved a sigh of relief when she rose, apparently unharmed.

In the meantime, Finch and Chico had ridden to the rescue of the tangled team of mules. In a short time, they had the mess straightened out, but both were soaking wet.

The rest of the wagons crossed uneventfully, and Colette insisted that Finch and Chico build a fire and dry their clothing. But they refused, politely, but firmly, and the caravan proceeded on its way to Decatur.

The next day Clem rode up to Humphrey and Colette who were riding beside the lead wagon as Finch and Chico were scouting ahead.

"Hump," Clem began hesitantly.

"What, Clem?"

"Maybe it ain't none of my business," Clem said doggedly. "But again, maybe it is."

"Go on, Clem," Humphrey encouraged.

"Well, I shore do think them horse herders ought to have horses and know how to ride."

"Oh, they know how to ride," Humphrey said matter of factly. "In fact, they've been raised around horses, but I don't like them mares to be rode—and beside them boys can herd the mares on foot."

"They can now, maybe," Clem conceded. "But once we hit Indian country, them mares are most likely to get boogered by Indians or some other varmint, and the next thing you know, you'll be lookin' for a bunch of good thoroughbred mares, and some Indian bucks will be ridin' 'em."

It was a long speech for Clem, and Humphrey listened carefully. So did Colette.

"He may be right, Humphrey," Colette said anxiously.

"I am right!" Clem said with finality.

"All right, Clem," Humphrey conceded. "When we get to Decatur, I'll get them some horses and saddles, too."

"Get 'em some ropes, too."

"Ropes? Why, Clem, one of them boys couldn't rope a fence post. Doubt if they ever had a lariat in their hands."

"It ain't easy to learn to rope," Clem said. "Takes a lot of practice. But anybody jinglin' horses needs to know how."

"All right, Clem," Humphrey agreed almost reluctantly. "We will get them some horses and saddles—and ropes too, if you think it best."

"I shore do." Clem was adamant.

"Wonder if you would do me a favor, Clem?"

"Shore will if I can," Clem said placatingly.

"You reckon you and maybe some of your boys could find some suitable horses and saddles and everything you think the herders will need?"

"I'm shore of it," Clem said. "They is a lot of people in Decatur. This used to be cow country, but nobody has got any money. I reckon a feller can buy just about anything he needs."

"I'd appreciate it if you would do that, Clem," Humphrey said. "And one more thing—could you and the boys show them black boys how to rope?"

Clem started to shake his head negatively, and Humphrey, sensing that he was about to refuse, continued hurriedly. "I don't mean teach them boys to rope good. Just show them how to build a loop and throw a rope. I'll see that they practice."

"I'll do what I can," Clem said dubiously. "But we cain't make cowhands out of them nigger boys very rapid."

"You might be surprised, Clem," Humphrey said with just a tinge of pride. "Blacks seem to have a sort of natural rhythm and coordination. They've fooled me a lot of times. They may be easier than you think."

"Maybe so." Clem showed one of his rare smiles. "Anyhow, we got nothin' to lose!"

With that, Clem rode back to the cowboys, and Humphrey and Colette heard good-natured laughter as he talked to them. They surmised, correctly, that Clem was telling the cowboys that they now had to find some gentle horses and easy saddles and teach four young blacks to ride and rope.

Finch and Humphrey agreed that the caravan should take it very slowly on to Decatur in order to have more time to practice defensive maneuvers, and also to let the cowboys have a chance to help the horse herders learn to rope. Humphrey reluctantly agreed to the black boys' riding a couple of the gentle mares that were not in foal. The cowboys took turns in instructing the boys in the art of roping, and their laughter and profanity as they pursued the seemingly hopeless task was often heard. But two of the black boys proved to be particularly responsive to the task; they rapidly developed a rhythm and accuracy with the rope that won grudging approval from Clem.

Buff, in addition to his self-imposed task of staging mock attacks on the wagon train, furnished them with plenty of wild game. Deer were plentiful, and so were wild turkeys, quail, and squirrels. Kate immediately drew accolades from all the blacks and most of the cowboys for her squirrel stew.

The deer were fat from eating the plentiful acorns under the oak trees, and enough of last year's crop of pecans remained for everyone to enjoy cracking and eating them as they drove slowly along. They usually camped very early in the afternoons in order to prolong the trip where, according to Finch, Indians were very unlikely to attack. One afternoon when they had pulled up under trees beside a clear stream, Humphrey surprised Finch and Chico by removing his rifle from the wagon and killing a fat buck that was looking at them curiously from a hillside a very long shot away. When two blacks carried the deer into camp, Finch noted that it was a clean neck shot.

"Where did you learn to shoot like that, Hump?" Finch voiced his surprise.

"Oh, I can shoot a rifle most as good as anybody," Humphrey said laconically. "Been shootin' ever since I was a kid growin' up on the plantation in Louisiana. And the war didn't hurt my shootin' eye any."

"That ess very good shooting with the rifle, Senor Hump," Chico said seriously as he examined the deer. "You handle the pistol good too—no?"

"Not so good any more, Chico," Humphrey said. "Got this cranky shoulder from a musket ball at Chattanooga, but I can still use a pistol if I have to. Just takes me a little longer, and it hurts."

Finch said no more, but he was very much relieved that Humphrey was an exceptional shot with the rifle. Somehow, he had not considered him to be very adept with firearms. Another expert rifleman would almost surely come in handy when they left Decatur and hit Indian country.

Finch and Chico were scouting ahead a couple of days later and returned to the caravan to report that Decatur was only about three hours away. Finch suggested that they camp for the night at an excellent place just ahead. Everyone was delighted except the cowboys. Clem, after talking to them, announced to Humphrey that they were all riding on to Decatur that afternoon.

"All right, Clem," Humphrey agreed. "I don't know how long we will be in Decatur because we've got to take on a lot of extra supplies, but we won't be hard to find."

"We'll find you, and we will be ready to leave when you are."

"Good," Humphrey replied. "And Clem you won't forget about findin' horses and saddles and ropes for the horse herders, will you?"

"We'll find 'em, and a cow camp cook, too," Clem said confidently. "And, Hump, I'm damned if I don't believe a couple of them niggers is gonna make a liar out of me!"

"How's that?"

"Well," Clem said. "Two of them boys is already ropin' better'n I thought they ever could. Seem to sort of have a knack for it."

"They do surprise you once in a while," Humphrey agreed. "You reckon you boys might run onto a few more good wagons we could buy? And while you're at it, look for some more horses."

"Hell, yes!" Clem said firmly. "When all the men left for the war, most of 'em brought their families and belongin's into town and left them and their wagons so's they could get to the stockade in case the Indians attacked. A lot of them boys ain't comin' back, and their women folks will be glad to sell their wagons to get enough money to go on east."

"If you can find 'em, buy 'em. And pay a fair price for 'em!" Humphrey instructed.

Clem nodded approval.

"And Clem," Humphrey cleared his throat, "you reckon I ought to advance the boys a little on their wages since they're goin' to town?"

"Nope!" Clem said firmly. "Most of 'em got the price of a couple of drinks in their pockets, I imagine. And I don't want a bunch of hung over cowboys when we leave."

"All right, Clem. See you in Decatur."

Clem waved as he rode off at a gallop, followed by the cowboys.

Humphrey turned to Finch and Chico. "You boys want to go on in, too?"

"Nope!" Finch answered. "Buff will be back pretty soon, and I think we'd better get together for a last pow-wow before we get to Decatur."

"We'll talk at my wagon after supper," Humphrey said, "if that's all right with you."

"Bueno!" Chico answered for both of them.

\* \* \* \* \* \*

An almost gala ambience pervaded the camp that night. Sam built a huge fire with wood provided by Raney, he had been assigned that chore by Kate, who was doing her best to make the wounded Negro earn his keep as Humphrey had instructed.

After a huge meal of the fat venison that Humphrey had shot, all the blacks were in a jovial mood and chattered incessantly. Humphrey, Colette, Finch, and Chico had settled themselves comfortably at the Beatenbow wagon when Buff came striding in.

"Begorra, and that was some shootin' that killed that deer up on the hill today!" Buff rumbled in his thick Irish brogue. "I'd be tryin' to get a shot at him meself when he went down. Who shot 'im? You, Finch, or Chico?"

"Neither!" Colette said proudly. "It was Humphrey."

"Begorra and bedanged!" Buff exclaimed in surprise. "I reckon them two Texas Rangers'll jus' have to move over a mite! Sure and we got another rifleman amongst us!"

"That we have!" Finch agreed heartily. "And I hope we don't need him to shoot anything but deer—but that isn't likely."

"You wanted to talk, Finch." Humphrey was eager to get away from the discussion of his prowess with a rifle.

"All right, Hump," Finch agreed. "We do need to talk. We're gettin' mighty close to the jumpin' off place. The Indians are goin' to be mighty pesky once we leave Decatur. We're a sight better able to handle trouble now than we were when we left Fort Worth. The fact that the Indians haven't bothered us yet has given us time to prepare some."

"You mean Indians might have attacked us between here and Fort Worth?" Colette was perturbed. "I didn't think there were any east of Decatur!"

"The Indian, Senora, ess where he find you, and that ess usually where you least expect heem!" Chico said gravely.

"Chico is right," Finch said. "But I figured we'd get to Decatur without trouble, and we have—up to now. But, I've been through Decatur several times in the past five years chasin' outlaws and other trash. Since last spring Decatur has had more'n a dozen Indian raids. They don't usually amount to much because there is a good stockade that served as a fort during the war. Everybody gets into it when the Indians attack; so they are able to drive 'em off before they do much damage."

"The Indians actually raid a town?" Colette was incredulous.

"This is Wise County," Finch explained. "It was created about ten years ago, though the Woody brothers settled in here nearly twenty-five years ago. And the McCarrols, Calhouns, Standifers, and a few others were here, too. A man named Howell opened a store before Decatur even became the county seat. Fact is, the town was first called Taylorsville, but they changed the name after a couple of years. They built a post office and figured to stay and lots of people have. There were more than three thousand people here when the war started. Now there are only about half that many. Indians drove a lot of them away, and the men went in to the army. The Indians are mostly Comanches and Kiowas."

"Why does anyone stay?" Colette exclaimed.

"Same reason you ess out here, Senora," Chico smiled. "Sky ess so beeg, and this country, eet ess so very beautiful!"

"It is that!" agreed Finch. "And the land is rich, and there are a lot of clear, cold streams and good grass around it. Decatur is built on a hill. The courthouse is just a wooden shack, but on the very top of the hill, there is a small clearing, and they say they are goin' to put up a stone courthouse that won't be equaled by any other town in the west."

"Must be a lot of mighty strong people livin' there," observed Humphrey.

"Well, the country is beautiful!" Colette exclaimed. "The trip from Fort Worth to here has been delightful. I guess I would have stayed, too!"

"Si, Senora!" Chico smiled. "I theenk you would, too! Usted es muy correoso y bello tambien."

"What did he call me, Finch?" Colette asked with a smile.

"Said you are a locoed gringo woman," Finch grinned at Colette. "He doesn't know any better. He's just an ignorant Mexican."

"Well I think he is tres vif," Colette said pertly and smiled graciously at Chico.

"I wish everybody would speak English so's maybe I could understand part of it," Humphrey said grouchily, but there was no rancor in the words.

\* \* \* \* \* \*

The caravan pulled up to Finch as he waited atop a low, rolling hill.

"Well, there she is!" Finch waved his arm toward the cluster of buildings in the distance. Smoke could be seen coming from many chimneys.

"That's Decatur?" Humphrey asked.

"That's it."

"Looks like a pretty big town," Humphrey observed.

"It is!" Finch said. "But before the war it was a lot bigger."

"Do you suppose they have a hotel?" Colette asked eagerly. "I'd love to have a nice hot bath with plenty of water."

"And saloons?" Chico said with equal fervor. "I'd like a good hot tequila—and no water at all!"

Everyone laughed, and they rode toward the town.

"I expect maybe we'd better camp outside of town a ways," Finch said. "I've been here a time or two before when I was in the Rangers. But I've never seen a black here, so maybe we ought to sort of—"

"I know what you mean, Finch," Humphrey said. "You and Chico go on in. I'll set up camp up yonder by the creek. Then Colette and I will come in."

"Hump—" Finch began hesitantly.

"What, Finch?"

"You reckon you and Colette could—I mean—you figure on drivin' in in a wagon, don't you?"

"I reckon I know what you mean, Finch." Humphrey gave one of his rare chuckles. "We will come in the wagon, and Colette will be wearin' a dress."

"Good," Finch said with relief. "I didn't mean to—"

"I know you didn't, Finch," Humphrey interrupted. "Now you boys go on in."

"It's just that Texas is still a little wild, and there will be a lot of men on the streets, and—well, I'd hate to have trouble!"

"There will be no trouble—at least me and Colette won't cause any," Humphrey said firmly.

"Adios, Amigos, y Hola! Decatur!" Chico yelled as he spurred his horse into a run. Finch followed.

# CHAPTER 8

Finch and Chico rode abreast as they entered the town of Decatur. Each carefully scanned his side of the street, for they knew that there were some men in Texas whose reputation would be greatly enhanced if they could kill Fauntleroy Finch or Chico Baca. The street was dusty, but there was a board walk on either side. Hitching rails were in front of most of the buildings. Many of the horses in town were tied to the hitching rail in front of the saloon, some of them belonging to their own cowboys.

They dismounted in front of the general store and tied their horses.

"Let's go in and look around," Finch said. "We will probably see something we need."

"Ah!" Chico replied. "I already see something I need." He nodded toward the saloon across the street.

"You'll have plenty of time for that!" Finch said. "Besides, we know the feller that runs this store. Met him a couple of years ago when we were chasin' those brush country outlaws. Remember?"

"Si, I remember Senor Howell. He ess uno bueno hombre!"

"Chico," Finch said in exasperation, "you had better quit talkin' that Mexican lingo, especially to Colette, or Hump is gonna shoot you!"

"Senor Hump ess mi amigo," Chico said confidently. "So ess Senora Colette. They are magnifico gente. No?"

"They are," Finch agreed.

The interior of the general store was rather dim, and they stopped just outside the door. They had faced danger too many times to be careless.

"You watch!" Chico said. "I will close my eyes a minute so they will adjust to the dark when I step inside." Chico's Mexican speech and accent had miraculously disappeared.

"All right!" Finch agreed. "If anybody in there is unfriendly, drop to the floor, and I will shoot over you."

They stood for a long minute as Chico held his eyes tightly closed and Finch scanned the street carefully in each direction.

"I'm ready," Chico said and stepped through the door and to one side as he opened his eyes. A moment later he spoke in a low voice that only Finch could hear. "Come on in. Senor Howell is the only one here."

Finch stepped in and paused to let his eyes adjust to the gloom. Then he saw the man behind the counter peering at them with squinted eyes.

"Reckon I know you fellers," Howell said in a friendly tone. "Rangers, ain't you? Helped us run some redskins off a couple of years ago, didn't you?"

"Good to see you again, Mr. Howell," Finch greeted him. "We've been here a few times before, all right. I'm Finch. This here is Chico."

"Best two rifle shots I ever saw!" Howell said admiringly. "Them Indians thought they had stirred up a hornet's nest when they hit us that time."

They all shook hands warmly, and Finch looked about the store curiously.

"Looks like you've been doin' all right," Finch observed as he noted the fully stocked shelves and the various items stacked on the floor.

"Just got in a new shipment last week, and I'm sure loaded for bear!" Then Howell added morosely, "Only trouble is, nobody's got any money, now."

Finch nodded sympathetically. "Texas is pretty broke right now, but it'll come back."

"I'm gamblin' on that," Howell agreed a bit grimly. "Just hope you Rangers can get them redskins drove out of Wise county before long so's people can get back to their ranches. All the men that ain't dead will be comin' back right soon, now that the war is over. Some of 'em are already back."

"The Indians been bad?" Finch asked.

"Pretty bad," admitted Howell. "They have hit us more than a dozen times this last year. Mostly just nuisance raids, but they've done some damage too. Twelve people have been killed, and Mrs. Roberts was captured, and the two little Ball boys, and a little boy and girl that belonged to the Babbs got stole, too!"

"Sure sorry to hear that," Finch said sincerely. "Maybe now that the war is over and the men are comin' back, it'll be better."

"Maybe," Howell said glumly. "We keep lookouts each direction from town. Have to use women and old men mostly. Fact is, that's how they got Mrs. Roberts. She was out north of town on watch, and they cut her off before she could get back. Anyway, when we hear one of our scouts shoot a couple of times, we all skedaddle up to the stockade."

"It'll be different when all the men get back," Finch consoled. "How did they get the kids?"

"Nobody knows," Howell said. "They was playin' down by the creek. We found their tracks and the Indian tracks too. Figgered some bucks snuck up to 'em on foot and got 'em before they could yell."

"Any of the families gone back to their ranches yet?"

"Nope. Still too many Indians. Cattle are all gone, anyways."

"What heppened to the cattle?"

"Oh, just scattered by Indians mostly, and drifted. Must be million head between here and the New Mexico Territory that don't belong to nobody. Them old longhorns breed like flies, and they is about five generations of 'em since the war started."

"Any of 'em still branded?"

"A few old mossy horns. But anything less than five years old is as slick as a baby's bottom. I reckon ranchers will just gather as many as their land will keep and slap a brand on 'em."

"Anybody stealin' them?"

"I hear the Comancheros is drivin' some of 'em to Mexico, but I reckon that ain't what you would call stealin'. They don't belong to nobody."

Finch nodded soberly. "Tell you what, we've got a whole wagon train comin' through tomorrow. Fact is, there'll be a man and woman in today. They're from back east, and Chico and I are goin' on out west with them. They're goin' to need a lot of supplies, and they've got money."

Howell's face brightened perceptibly. "That shore sounds good. I've got a lot of goods that need sellin'."

"One thing—" Finch admonished severely. "We would appreciate it if you don't mention Indian trouble—especially about the woman and kids bein' stolen."

"You can count on that," Howell said.

"Here they come now." Chico had been prowling about the store in a manner that enabled him to keep his eye on the door. He stepped out on the boardwalk and was joined by Finch and Howell. Humphrey was driving, and Colette sat beside him on the seat and surveyed the scene before her like a queen from her throne. Her bright smile and dark eyes flashed brilliantly as she spied Finch and Chico. She waved gaily to them as the wagon approached the store. She was wearing a high necked dress which in no way diminished her breathtaking beauty.

"Lord a mercy!" breathed Howell. "That is shore a pretty lady!"

Neither Finch nor Chico replied, but Chico stepped into the dusty street to take Colette's hand as she alighted.

"Bienvenada a Decatur, Senora Colette Y Senor Humphrey!" Chico said as he removed his sombrero and bowed gallantly.

"Gracias, Chico," Colette said and smiled at him.

"This is Mr. and Mrs. Beatenbow from Louisiana," Finch introduced. "And this is Mr. Howell, Hump and Colette. He owns the store here, and he's got just about everything in it that we might need."

Humphrey and Colette shook hands with Howell, who seemed still to be stunned by Colette's beauty. He murmured something unintelligible as he took her proffered hand. Then he seemed to regain his composure.

"Right glad to see you folks. Come on inside, and I'll fix a cup of coffee."

After they had drunk a cup of very strong and bitter coffee from enameled cups, which Colette declared to be delicious, Howell invited them to inspect the goods in the store.

"Mr. Howell," Colette asked eagerly, "is there a hotel in Decatur?"

"Well, not exactly a hotel, Mrs. Beatenbow. But Mrs. Nobles has got a sort of roomin' house just down the street. Serves mighty good food, so they say."

"Does it have a bath?" Colette asked eagerly.

"Shore does," Howell said proudly. "Runs good clear creek water over some copper coils that are heated by a wood stove. You can have all the hot water you want by just buildin' a fire in that stove."

"How wonderful!" exclaimed Colette ecstatically. "I'm going there right now!"

"Now you hold on, Colette," Humphrey said firmly. "Maybe it ain't safe for a woman to walk down the street by herself, and I've got to stay here to buy horses and tack and wagons, and I don't know what all!"

"Pshaw, Mr. Beatenbow. A lady like the missus there would be safe as can be—unless we have a Indian attack, and that ain't likely today."

"And I can go by the post office, too, Humphrey," Colette said. "I know mother and father would like to have a long letter from us."

"All right, Colette," Humphrey said resignedly. "But you be careful. Indians or not!"

Colette waved gaily as she walked down the boardwalk. Howell looked at her with unfeigned admiration. Chico watched with a grin, and Finch looked with a terrible ache in the vicinity of his breastbone. Humphrey had walked back into the store.

"Maybe I better ask you something, Mr. Howell," Humphrey frowned as Howell re-entered.

"Anything you want," invited Howell.

"Well," Humphrey explained. "We are from Louisiana. Had a plantation there, but it was ruined when I got back from the war; so I sold out. And now we're headin' west. But what I'm wonderin' is—well, we got a whole bunch of niggers with us—used to be slaves on the plantation. But they're free now, and they wanted to come west with us. Do you reckon the folks here in Decatur will object to 'em? Course, we're camped outside of town, but I'd like to bring my cook in to help us pick up some extra grub, and her husband will want to come with her. I reckon some more bucks would be handy to load us out—especially if we can find some more wagons."

Howell frowned thoughtfully. "There ain't no blacks that live in Decatur," he said. "But a few years back a company of Texas Rangers come through here, and they had a nigger cook. He come in to buy grub, and nobody said anything about it. Fact is, I reckon red is the only skin color our folks would take exception to— lest, of course, he was wearin' a blue uniform."

"Good!" Humphrey was relieved. "They'll be in tomorrow, and they'll cause no trouble. I'll see to that."

\* \* \* \* \* \*

The next day Clem, Kate, and Sam accompanied Colette, Humphrey, and Chico to the store. Kate was bug eyed at the sight of all the goods packed on the shelves. Clem browsed among the riding gear and piled some saddles, coils of rope, tarps, several bridles, and extra piggin' string by the door.

"Kate, you pick us up enough grub to last a spell," Humphrey admonished. "You'll know what the niggers will need, but maybe Clem could help too. He's been on cattle drives and knows what cowboys need."

"Yassuh, Mars Hump. I's gonna get plenty for all of us'ns. If Mars Clem can help, that sho be good. Jus' so we got plenty o corn pone for the niggers."

Two hours later Clem and Kate had a pile of groceries that would fill some of the extra wagons that Clem had found and Humphrey had bought. There were sacks of corn meal, flour, beans, dried apples and apricots, canned tomatoes, bags of coffee, and plenty of molasses. Buff would furnish plenty of wild meat, including buffalo, wild turkey, deer, antelope, and even beef if necessary. Kate and Clem felt satisfied that with plenty of corn pone and sourdough biscuits, nobody would have to go hungry, and they told Humphrey so.

"Looks to me like we got everything we need," Clem said. "The boys has found us a cowcamp cook, and he's fixed him up a chuck wagon. I got some extra ridin' gear besides that for the four fairly gentle horses we got for them nigger horse herders. We've found extra horses, too. We'll need more, but we can get 'em when we hit the plains country and start pickin' up some mustangs. They're mean to break and hard on gear and men, but I reckon we'll make out."

"Be as sure as you can, Clem," Humphrey said. "According to Finch, we'll not have another chance to buy anything extra for a long time."

"All right," Clem agreed. "I'll toss in a couple more saddles, more rope, and other gear, but the hands can repair most that gets broke. Fact is, some of 'em even prefer rawhide ropes like Chico uses."

"Then let's get everything loaded, and we'll be on our way tomorrow."

\* \* \* \* \* \*

There was a general celebration that night among the Negroes, many of whom had walked into town and stared goggle-eyed at the sights. Most of them had never seen so many people in one place before. But no one molested them, and they were content to return to camp and jabber among themselves.

Chico informed Finch that he was going to the saloon and get that tequila that he had been wanting ever since he had been in town.

"All right, Chico. I figure you must have a cast-iron belly to drink that stuff and eat all those hot peppers."

"Si, amigo!" Chico grinned. "Thees Mexican, he ess tough inside and out. Want to come weeth me?"

"Nope," Finch said. "I'm gonna hang around camp tonight. I've had all the town I need the last couple of days."

"Well, adios, amigo. See you manana."

"If you get in more trouble than you can handle, you yell, and I'll come get you out!" Finch jibed jokingly.

"Ah, that weel be the day when Chico get een more trouble than he can handle," Chico jeered.

"And you be fairly sober when we get ready to leave early tomorrow!" Finch said caustically, but he knew that Chico drank very sparingly and never to excess.

"Eff I get too drunk, you tie me on my horse, amigo. Thees Mexican don't want to mees the rest of thees grand parade."

With that parting sally, he spurred his horse toward town.

It was after midnight when Finch was awakened by a shot. He was not overly concerned and had closed his eyes again when he heard a horse running swiftly. He raised up just in time to see a pinto horse running wildly by camp, and in the dim moonlight he could see the rider spurring and quirting the animal madly. For no reason that he could fathom, a cold chill ran up his spine. He instantly grabbed his hat and pulled on his clothes, belting on his pistol. He saddled his horse quickly and rode toward the saloon. As he arrived, he could hear excited and heated voices.

\* \* \* \* \* \*

Chico had tied his horse among others at the saloon hitching rack. Inside the door, he stepped to one side and surveyed the crowd thoroughly. He saw no one he knew except some of their own cowboys. After a moment's surveillance, he deemed it safe; so he walked to the bar.

"What'll it be, mister?" the barkeep asked.

"Tequila for me—and whatever mi amigos here at the bar want. I'm buying a round with thees filthy dinero," Chico said gaily as he laid money on the counter.

The men at the bar immediately responded in a friendly fashion and reordered.

"Thanks, Mexico!" one cowboy said.

"Por Nada!" Chico shrugged. "Dreenk up!"

"I'll drink to your country, Mexico!" another said jovially.

"Then you dreenk to Texas!" Chico responded proudly. "Texas! She ess my country!"

Chico downed his tequila and ordered another round for the men.

"You're shore a white man!" an imbiber toasted drunkenly.

"I ess a Mexican Texican!" Chico said gaily. "And mighty proud of it!" Chico held his glass high in his right hand. "Texas! Un grande estado!"

All eyes in the saloon were on Chico, who, standing at the bar, had his back to the door.

"Hold it, you damned greaser!" a thin, harsh voice called from the doorway.

Chico froze, his hand still holding his glass in the air. The men at the bar were completely still, and the men seated at the tables swung their eyes toward the door to see Doc Guines standing with his pistol cocked and pointing at Chico's back.

"I do hate a damned greaser!" Guines gritted viciously as he shot. Chico flinched and dropped his glass as a red blotch immediately appeared on the back of his coat, and he slid slowly to the floor.

There was complete silence for about a moment. Doc Guines quickly disappeared into the night.

"That murderin' son of a bitch!" someone shouted as several men rushed to Chico.

"Never had a chance in hell!"

There was then an immediate uproar in the saloon as the men gathered around the fallen Mexican. No one saw Finch as he strode through the door like a stalking tiger. He pushed men roughly aside until he reached Chico. He knelt beside his friend a long moment. A film had already dimmed the once sparkling dark eyes.

Chico Baca was dead.

Finch gazed into the face of his friend, and then slowly pulled Chico's eyes closed. He took a long breath and rose to his full height. His icy blue eyes were sparkling like diamonds.

"Anybody know who did it!" he asked quietly.

Several men started to speak at once, but quieted when one of them said loudly, "He was tall and had a handle bar mustache, and little pig eyes set close together. The murderin' bastard didn't give him a chance. Already had his gun out and cocked. Shot him in the back before he even gave him a chance to turn around!"

"Guines!" Finch said bitterly and started for the door just as Humphrey Beatenbow entered. Humphrey grabbed at Finch as he passed.

"What happened, Finch?" Humphrey asked urgently.

Finch did not answer but slowly and firmly removed Humphrey's hand from his arm and strode out the door.

"What happened?" Humphrey demanded of the men in the saloon.

"A Mexican got shot. In the back!" A man pointed to Chico's body. "By a damn skunk!"

Humphrey went hurriedly to Chico and knelt by him. Quiet again reigned in the saloon. Then Humphrey stood and faced the man.

"Is there an undertaker in town?" he asked of no one in particular.

"Not a real one," someone responded. "But we got a feller who takes care of things."

"Get him!" Humphrey ordered, and he too strode from the saloon.

\* \* \* \* \* \*

Colette was awake when Humphrey returned to the boarding house. When he entered the room, he lit the kerosene lamp, and Colette sat up in bed. She did not make any effort to hide her magnificent breasts that were still taut from Humphrey's lovemaking.

"What happened?" she asked anxiously. "Was it one of the blacks?"

"No."

Humphrey looked at her, and for the first time since their marriage, those cherry-tipped breasts that she so proudly and often displayed did not move him.

"Then, who—or what?" Colette demanded.

"It was Chico," Humphrey said.

"Did he shoot someone?"

"No."

"Then what?" Colette demanded angrily.

"Chico was shot!"

"Oh, no!" Colette's face paled. "Was he badly hurt?"

"Chico is dead!" Humphrey said dully.

"It can't be—oh, no!" She quickly covered herself as if to ward off a blow.

"Shot in the back by a damned coward!" Humphrey said bitterly. "Chico should have killed him in Fort Worth."

"You know who did it?"

Humphrey only nodded.

"Where is Finch?"

"He was in camp when it happened. But he came to the saloon afterward. He knows."

"Where is he now?"

"Back at camp packing up, I imagine."

"What for?"

"To find that damned yellow belly that shot Chico."

"I must go to him," Colette said, her voice cracking just a bit.

"All right, wife!" agreed Humphrey. "He won't leave before daylight anyway because he'll have to find tracks. Daylight is three hours away. I'll come to you as soon as I have the arrangements made."

"Arrangements?"

"We've got to bury Chico. There's a feller here that can build him a pine box, but I don't know whether we can find a preacher or not."

"Chico was Catholic," Colette said.

"He was?" Humphrey said in surprise.

"Yes. He told me. Most Mexicans are," Colette said as she was rapidly donning her clothes.

"I doubt if we can find a priest, but I'll try. You go to Finch. Make him wait until I get there. I want to talk to him. But you wait here till I send one of the cowboys to walk you back. I don't want you out by yourself tonight."

Humphrey left the room quietly as Colette finished dressing. She waited until there was a light tap on the door. She opened it to find one of the cowboys waiting to walk her to the place where Finch and Chico had been camped.

When Humphrey got back to the saloon, he found that a posse was being formed to capture or kill Guines. The room grew quiet as he entered.

"Any of you men know if there is a priest in town?" Humphrey asked.

There was a long silence. Finally one man spoke. "I don't think there's a preacher in town," he said, "and I'm pretty shore there ain't a priest. That's Catholic, ain't it?"

Humphrey nodded. "Chico was a Catholic. If any of you can find a preacher or a priest, I'd appreciate it. We'll bury Chico just after sunup under that big oak down where we are camped. All of us would like it if you would attend the services."

"Hell, Beatenbow, us boys is fixin' to take out after that murderin' son-of-a-bitch. He might be out of the country by daylight."

"You'd never find him tonight. He probably cut in a different direction as soon as he got out of town; so you'd be runnin' around like coon dogs that had lost the scent. I take it might friendly that you boys were goin' after 'im. But don't do it!" Humphrey ordered sternly. "Me or Finch will take care of Guines, and I promise you that! But in the meantime, we've got to get a lot of folks and cattle and horses to our ranch up on the Canadian River. That's what Chico would have wanted—and that's what we'll do."

Humphrey's tone left no doubt that he meant what he said and expected to be obeyed. He turned and walked from the saloon again. There was a babble of hushed voices as he left, but it was quite apparent that they would follow Humphrey's order.

Colette found Finch at camp just as he had finished packing his mule. His horse had already been saddled. She rushed to him and put her arms around his thin waist. "Please don't leave, Finch," she sobbed.

It was the only time that Colette had ever touched Finch that he did not feel the electric current that she generated.

"I reckon I've got to, Colette," Finch said quietly.

"I know you think so, Finch." Colette squeezed him tightly. "But, please wait and think just a bit." She was sobbing as if her heart would break. "I don't know what we will do without you and Chico, too!"

Finch seemed to come out of a dream world. He shook his head rapidly as if to clear his vision; then he put his arms around Colette just as Humphrey strode up. Neither Finch nor Colette moved, and Colette's sobs began to wane.

"You two ought to get some rest if you can," Humphrey said brusquely. "We'll bury Chico just after sunup, and then we'll pull on west."

"You mean for me to leave here when Guines is still loose!" Finch blurted his surprise.

"That's exactly what I mean!" Humphrey's voice was harsh.

Finch removed his arms from around Colette and faced Humphrey squarely. "I never wanted to kill a man before, Hump," he grated. "But Guines is too low down a varmint to let live. I've got to go after him!"

"No. You ain't!" Humphrey said firmly. "What you've got to do is get a bunch of cowboys and niggers and me and Colette through some rough Indian country and settled on our ranch."

"I haven't got to—"

"Yes, you have!" Humphrey's voice was still harsh. "You can't help Chico none by stayin' here. And I sure as hell doubt Chico would want you to let Colette go out on them plains without your help."

"But Chico is dead!" Finch could not believe what he was hearing.

"That's right!" Humphrey agreed. "And I never heard nobody complain after he was dead. And we made a deal, too. Full partners, re member? Are you a man of your word, or not?"

Finch flinched as though he had been slapped. Then his body slumped, and he suddenly sat on the ground. His shoulders shook as he bent his head down. It was the only time anyone had ever seen Fauntleroy Finch cry. He kept his face averted for a long moment, then raised it to look at Humphrey and Colette.

"I'll be ready to go on west when you are," he whispered, and the tears rolled from his blue eyes.

Neither Colette nor Humphrey said anything for a long time. Then Colette went to Finch, leaned down, and kissed his cheek and hugged him. Then she and Humphrey started walking away. They had gone a few paces when they stopped and turned. Finch was staring into space.

"Colette," Humphrey said softly. "I reckon I loved that little Mexican most as much as Finch did. And if he ever kills Guines, he'll have to see him afore I do. And one of us will see him! You can bet on that!"

Humphrey and Colette went to their wagon rather than back to the boarding house.

"You go on in and try to get a couple of hours sleep, Colette," Humphrey said. "I've got to roust out some niggers and have 'em dig a grave under that oak tree."

"Humphrey—" Colette stopped as he started away. "I'm sorry you had to do that to Finch, but I know why you did, and I love you more for it."

"He's one mucho hombre, as Chico would say—and so was Chico. We're not likely to meet their kind again. I didn't want to hurt him, and I hope he won't hold it against me."

"He won't!" Colette assured him. "I think even now he knows why you said what you did."

"I hope so!" Humphrey said fervently. "I never saw a man so tore up as him. He and Chico were as close as two men could be. I just hope he gets over it soon."

"So do I. He's such a fine person. Do you think I should go back and stay with him until morning?"

"He's not that good a friend!" Humphrey grinned for the first time since Chico's death.

"Oh, Humphrey—you know I didn't mean—"

"I know you didn't," Humphrey chuckled. "Now you get in that wagon and bed down for a couple of hours."

# Chapter 9

A large crowd of men and women gathered at the Beatenbow camp just as the sun was coming up. A wagon drove up, and in it was a pine box. Several of the Beatenbow cowboys carried the box to the open grave.

Colette and Humphrey were standing at the head of the grave. Colette looked anxiously at the crowd. Finally she spied the tall form of Finch standing alone and well back of the crowd. She tried to catch his eye, but he didn't look at her.

Neither a preacher nor a priest had been found, and Colette carried the family Bible that had been a wedding present from her mother. When the crowd gathered around the grave, she handed the Bible to Humphrey, who opened it at a place familiar to him. The men all removed their hats as he began to read the Twenty-third Psalm. When he had finished, he closed the book and handed it back to Colette. Then he spoke briefly.

"Chico Baca—" Humphrey choked up and had to clear his throat several times, "was a man! A good man and a good friend. Absolutely fearless and loyal as any man could be. And he was not only a good friend, but he had good friends. I just hope that somebody can say that about me when I check in. That's all, I reckon."

Then Humphrey prayed a prayer that amazed the crowd by its simplicity and beauty. When he finished, he donned his hat and walked away as the cowboys lowered the box and some of the blacks started shoveling dirt onto it. The hollow, thudding sounds followed the crowd as they walked away.

Humphrey stopped and turned to those following. "As many of you folks as will, come by our wagon. Kate has coffee hot."

Some of the people accepted Humphrey's invitation, and others made their way back toward town. Kate and three other black women started serving the coffee. And the crowd, as if suddenly awakened out of a slumber, began to talk with animation. Humphrey went about meeting as many of the people as he could. Colette kept watching anxiously for Finch. When the Negroes had finished filling the grave and had patted the mound down firmly, they departed. It was then that she saw Finch. He walked from behind a tree and stood for a long moment. Then his long body straightened and then slumped as if he had breathed a deep sigh, which indeed he had. Then he turned and walked purposefully to the Beatenbow wagon. Colette met him.

"You reckon I could have a cup of that coffee, too, Colette?" he asked calmly.

"I think Kate can spare another cup," Colette smiled sadly at him. "I'll bring you one."

The crowd seemed to be studiously avoiding looking in Finch's direction. When Colette brought the cup to him, she said, "Be careful. Kate makes a hot cup of coffee."

"And a good one, too." Finch smiled wanly. "Colette—"

"What, Finch?"

"I'm not much good at talking. So would you tell Hump 'much obliged' for me. For what he did for Chico today—and for what he did for me last night, too!"

"You know I will, Finch." She smiled at him and held his arm tightly with both hands. "And you have no idea how happy that will make him!"

Finch gulped the rest of his coffee. "Tell Kate the coffee was good. And now I'd better get busy. I need to see Clem and Buff and all the cowboys before we start out today. And if I know Hump, that'll be right soon now."

And with that, he walked away, his long, tiger strides making almost no noise. He did not look again at the grave, and Colette's dark eyes filled with tears as she watched his tall form disappear into the trees toward the cowboys' camp.

It was almost mid-morning when they had the wagons all lined up ready to move out. Finch and Clem rode up and down the wagon train to recheck everything. Buff drove his open wagon pulled by mustang ponies alongside and checked each wagon carefully. The drivers that had been assigned to the wagons that had been procured in Decatur seemed to be doing well. Buff nodded in approval. Largo, who still drove the last wagon with the jackass tied behind, grinned as Buff pulled alongside.

"Well, I reckon we's about ready to start out west, Mars Buff!" Largo said.

"Aye. And I reckon it's about time, too. Begorra!" Buff spat a stream of tobacco juice. "I reckon too, it's about time you quit that 'Mars Buff' talk. This here nigger ain't used to bein' called civilized names. So you better jus' call me 'Buff' like the rest of 'em do."

"I'll sho do that, Mars Buff!" Largo grinned. Buff shook his head in resignation, clucked at his mustangs, and drove away.

The train moved only a few miles west of Decatur that first day. Finch and Clem wanted to be as sure as they could that they were as prepared as possible. They had explained to Humphrey that the mares would simply have to be turned loose and driven with the rest of the remuda so they could graze their way along and thus travel more hours per day since they would not have to stop early to graze. The black horse herders were doing a good job of handling the mares, and the mounts that had been procured for them were trained to handle stock, be it horses or cows. One of the boys was tossed several times by his new horse, but he got up laughing and immediately crawled back on. The horse finally gave up and tended to business.

Humphrey had wanted to get as many more pairs of the blacks married as he could in Decatur, but there had been no preacher in town. "Not even one to hold Chico's funeral," Humphrey thought grimly.

The first night out was fairly successful. Since the cowboys had no cattle to tend, they rode with the blacks in herding the remuda. Only Humphrey's stud and the jack were tied fast to stout trees that night. When they hit the plains, they would have to be tied to a wagon.

Guards were posted in each direction from camp, and the guards and the remuda herders were relieved at midnight by other men. Before daybreak, the camp came alive, and the fires were started. Breakfast was over by sun up. The remuda was brought in, and the cowboys formed a rope corral by holding lariat ropes. The horses that had been bought in Decatur and those of the cowboys that had had that experience before were fairly easily held, for they had learned to respect a rope. But the mares were not so easily contained. One of them tried to jump the corral, whereupon the two cowboys holding the rope braced themselves and pulled hard just as she started over, catching her forelegs and flipping her. She hit the ground with her head under her, and there was an audible crack as her neck broke. She hardly moved after she hit the ground. Humphrey walked up to her and then shook his head and walked away.

"We've all got to learn," he said bleakly as he walked back to his wagon.

The two best ropers among the cowboys were Clem and Art. They uncoiled ropes and moved inside the corral. Each of the cowboys called for the horse he wanted. Either Clem or Art would adroitly drop a loop over its head. Then the horse would meekly follow as it was led outside to its rider.

The mules, however, were not so tractable. They would duck their heads under other mules or horses, making Clem and Art miss their catch repeatedly. And when they finally did catch one, he stubbornly refused to be led outside. One of the mules, a red roan, balked; the harder he was pulled, the more stubborn he became. Finally, he flopped on his side and lay in a sullen stupor. No amount of prodding did any good, and finally Humphrey told the men to leave him. Clem and Art became disgusted, mounted horses, and rode in and roped the mules, and their muscular cowponies dragged them outside where a Negro put the bridle on them. They were finally harnessed, and the train was again on its way.

Humphrey watched carefully, for he knew that he must learn quickly. In a few days they would begin to gather cattle, and that would occupy the cowboys' time. They would also have to night herd the cows. So the defense of the wagons and the horses would largely be left up to Humphrey and the blacks, for Finch would be scouting far ahead, and Buff would be hunting game.

"We'd ought to fix a possum belly on one of them wagons, Hump," Clem said as he rode up beside Humphrey just before noon.

"A what?"

"Put a tarp under one of the wagons and tie the four corners so's it makes a place where we can throw in dry buffalo and cow chips. We'll run out of timber pretty soon, and we'll need 'em for cookin' fire. And have some of the niggers cut some slender poles and put 'em in a wagon so's we can prop a tarp up when it rains out on the plains country."

"Oh!" Humphrey said. "Yeah, we'll do that when we stop for noon."

"And put somebody out to pick up them chips and toss 'em in. We'll need a lot of 'em, but they do make a hot fire. Be a good job for that nigger with the busted shoulder. He don't need but one arm to pick up chips, anyway."

"I'll do that!" The idea seemed to please Humphrey.

Two days out of Decatur, they began to see wild longhorn cattle. They were fairly well scattered, and only a few of the older ones wore brands. Humphrey asked Finch when they would start picking up a herd. Finch assured him that there would be more and bigger bunches when they got a little farther west.

Colette was still riding with Humphrey and was so engrossed in feasting her eyes on the lovely land that she was in a constant state of excitement. Trees were beginning to show the first faint tinge of green. Red, blue, pink, and yellow flowers were just peeking from their winter beds. About mid-afternoon of the third day, Colette spied Finch returning from his scout ahead, and she marveled at the grace with which he sat his sorrel gelding. It seemed that the two were welded together in fluid movement as they loped toward the wagons.

"There's Finch!" Colette exclaimed as she pointed toward him. "I'm going out to meet him."

"You be careful, Colette!" Humphrey admonished. "Keep a sharp lookout in every direction. You remember what Finch said about women and kids getting away from the wagons."

"I remember!" Colette said tartly. "But he's not far away, and the country is flat. No Indian could be hiding between here and there."

"All right," Humphrey reluctantly agreed. "But watch it! Buff swears an Indian can hide under a cow chip!"

"I'll be careful," Colette assured him as she rode away. Humphrey sighed and turned to look at the following caravan.

"Colette," Finch said sternly. "What are you doin' out here?"

"I came to meet you," she replied gaily.

"Don't do that again." Finch ordered sternly. "We are in Indian country now, and it's dangerous for you or any other woman or kids to be away from the wagons."

"I haven't seen a single Indian, or even a sign of one!" Colette replied defensively.

"That's when they are the most dangerous," Finch said. "A dozen Comanches could be hidin' between here and the wagons."

"You're joking!" Colette said.

"I'm not!" Finch said grimly. "And we've got our hands full without having to worry about you or any of the black women or kids getting away from the wagons."

"I'm sorry, Finch," she said contritely. "I won't do it again. It looked safe enough."

"Well, it wasn't. And don't you ever do it again unless Humphrey—or me is with you. The Comanches or the Comancheros either one would charge hell with a pocket knife to get hold of a woman like you."

"What about you, Finch? Would you do the same thing?" Colette's voice was teasing, but her dark, luminous eyes were fathomless as she looked at Finch's profile.

Finch did not say anything for a moment, and then quite to Colette's surprise and delight, he said in what was meant to be a jocular tone, "I reckon I wouldn't even need the pocket knife. Only trouble is that there isn't another woman like you!"

"Fauntleroy Finch, you've just been chasing Indians and outlaws too long!" Colette said facetiously.

"I reckon I have," Finch admitted. "Let's get on to the wagons."

"I'll race you!" Colette challenged.

"Nope. We don't have any horses to spare, and one of ours might step in a gopher hole."

As they loped lazily toward the wagons, Humphrey came out to meet them. How does it look?" he asked Finch.

"Looks good," Finch replied. "No sign of Indians yet, and we'll get to the Little Wichita before night. It's good place to stop. After we leave there, we can start gathering some cattle every day. They ought to be pretty well trail broke by the time we get to the Big Wichita."

"How far is that?" Humphrey wanted to know.

"A hundred miles or so to the northwest. But, it will take us a long time to get there. After the boys start gathering, we're goin' to have to do a lot of waitin' for them to gather and bunch the cattle. And once we've got a pretty good herd, some of the hands will trail it while the others range out and drive others into the herd. Gettin a fair sized herd collected and started drivin' will be the hardest part. Once we do that, the ones that are driven in will join the herd without too much trouble. Then we will have to cross the Pease River, and that may not be easy. But if we can manage that and still have a pretty good herd, and if we are lucky, we will get to the Red River valley."

"That sounds like a beautiful place," Colette exclaimed.

"It is," Finch said. "But it's close to the Indian Territory, and the Indians are almost sure to hit us there, if they don't before."

"You think they will attack?" Humphrey asked in a worried voice.

"You can bet on it!" Finch replied grimly. "I just wish there was some way to get word to White Horse that it is me that is bringing this herd through."

"Who is White Horse?" Colette asked.

"Chief of the Comanches that Kit Carson made the deal with for me," Finch said shortly. "The Comanches are the real plains Indians and the best horsemen in the world."

"Any chance of gettin' word to him?" Humphrey wanted to know.

"Don't see how!" Finch replied glumly. "If Chico—If we had another man that knew the country, I'd send him to Taos, and Kit would get word to Chief White Horse. But we haven't got anybody that's familiar with the country or that knows enough to dodge the Indians."

They rode in silence for several minutes, each lost in thought. Finally Humphrey broke the silence.

"Finch, this may be a damn fool idea, but I'll say it anyway."

"Go ahead," Finch invited. "I'd listen to any idea right now."

"Your friend Kit got anything against niggers?"

"Reckon not," Finch said frowning. "He fought for the North—remember? Why do you ask?"

"Well, just hear me out," Humphrey said. "I told you that Largo went all through the war with me. What I didn't tell you was that he is the best man I ever saw at sensing danger and avoiding it. Twice we were caught behind enemy lines, and he brought us through both times, or I wouldn't be here! Seems to me like he has a sort of animal instinct, and he can hide that big, black body of his as good as you say an Indian can. What I'm drivin' at is—if you was to describe the country to him and do the best you can to fill him in on Indian tactics—I got a feeling' that he cold make it to Taos."

Finch listened carefully as Humphrey talked. Colette didn't say anything. Finally Finch said, "You'd stand a mighty good chance of gettin' your best nigger killed."

"No more than if he stays here, according to you and Buff!" Humphrey said logically. "Besides he could ride this black stud of mine, and there ain't a Indian pony living that can outrun him! And he could travel only at night and hide out in the daytime!"

"You make it sound like sense!" Finch agreed. "When would he leave?"

"The sooner, the better!" Humphrey said. "Tonight."

"All right," Finch agreed. "All we've got to lose is one good nigger and a stud horse! I can fill 'im in with everything he needs to know in a couple of hours. Even draw him some maps. Can he read?"

"He can read maps." Humphrey said. "Learned that when he was with me in the army."

"Then as soon as we make camp this afternoon, I'll get with him and go over everything—what to tell Kit, and all. And I reckon we might as well make camp at the Little Wichita for about a week. That will give Largo a chance to get to Taos, and it'll give the boys a chance to gather a bunch of cattle."

"I'll give Old Heck a good bait of corn before he leaves, and Largo can tie a sack behind the saddle with his own grub so he can have a bait of grain every night."

"He'll need it," Finch said.

They reached the Little Wichita about mid-afternoon, and Finch took unusual pains to be sure they had a good camp that could be easily defended. He had the wagons drawn up in a fairly large circle at a point where there were no trees by the river and they could see a long distance in all directions. It would be a near miracle if they camped there a week unnoticed by Indians or renegades. Clem had the cowboys' camp close by so that they could get to the caravan for protection, and also so they could help protect the caravan.

Finch took Largo aside and explained the mission assigned him. The Negro did not change expression and listened intently. When Finch had finished, Largo asked questions that were pertinent and probing. Finch was amazed at the comprehension displayed by the Negro and began to feel much more optimistic about the success of Humphrey's plan.

"Well, Largo," Finch said. "If you don't have any more questions, you'd better get in your wagon and grab a couple of hours sleep before dark."

"Yassuh, Mars Finch," Largo grinned. "I'll sho go to my wagon and say good-by to Maisie, but I misdoubt I'll get any sleep. Maisie's gonna have her own notion about how I spends the time afore I leave."

Finch shook his head and walked back toward the Beatenbow wagon.

"Get 'em filled in?" Humphrey asked as Finch walked up.

"Yep!" Finch said. "And your boy Largo seems like mucho hombre—as Chico would say."

"He's a smart nigger!" Humphrey said almost proudly. "In fact, I'm beginnin' to think all the niggers that we've got with us are smarter than I been givin' 'em credit for bein'."

Colette had walked up as Humphrey finished speaking to Finch. She took Humphrey's arm. "Humphrey," she said solemnly, "do you think perhaps we should start calling them 'blacks' instead of 'niggers'? That sounds sort of—Oh, I don't know," she finished lamely. "It's just that 'blacks' sounds better to me, and they are free people now even if we do have a hard time remembering it."

"Well," Humphrey conceded. "I got no objection to callin' the niggers 'blacks' if that'd please you. But I'll bet you won't get Kate to call 'em that."

"I doubt if she will either, and I won't even ask her to. But the way she says it doesn't seem so—"

"I know," Humphrey agreed. "And now I'm just wonderin' which saddle to put on Old Heck for Largo to ride. Them new ones we got in Decatur would be might uncomfortable."

"Let 'im ride Chico's saddle," Finch said quietly. "And Chico's bridle, too. Nothing on his gear will rattle."

Humphrey and Colette looked at Finch in surprise.

"You don't want anything to rattle when you're goin' through Indian country at night." Finch said almost defensively.

Colette, who had been holding Humphrey's arm with both hands, released one and took Finch's arm with it. "Come on you two," she said gaily. "Kate has some coffee on." She held an arm of each as they walked to Kate's fire.

\* \* \* \* \* \*

Largo was ready to leave after dark. Humphrey had Chico's saddle on Old Heck and a bag of corn tied behind. Largo had packed a small bundle of food for himself.

"Well, you know what to do!" Humphrey said.

"Yassuh, Mars Hump," Largo agreed. "Reckon it'll be kinda like us tryin' to get back through them Yankee lines when we was in the war."

"I reckon," Humphrey agreed. "But the consequences will be a lot worse if you're caught!"

"Ain't gonna git caught, Mars Hump," Largo responded confidently. "You knows how scary this nigger is. I'll jus' run an' hide!" he grinned.

"Any more question you'd like to ask, Largo," Finch inquired.

"No suh, Mars Finch. I reckon yo done answered all I can think of."

"All right, Largo. Remember to ride only at night. Hole up in the daytime. Give Old Heck his corn cause he won't be able to graze on the way."

"I'll sho do that, Mars Hump. I sho will!"

"And," Finch added, "you remember that there are redskins out there whether you can see 'em or not."

"We'll leave here a week from tomorrow," Humphrey said. "Finch has drawed you a map of our route. Get to Taos as soon as you can, and then come back and meet us on the trail."

"I'll do that, Mars Hump," Largo agreed. "I jus hope yo all will be all right while I's gone!" Largo turned to mount Old Heck.

"One more thing, Largo," Humphrey said a bit uncertainly as he lifted his hand in an unintentional gesture as if to shake Largo's hand, but he suddenly checked the movement. "You take good care of that hoss, you heah?"

"Yassuh!" Largo grinned. "I sho'ly will."

"Please be careful, Largo!" Colette said sincerely.

"Yes'm Miss Colette. I sho'ly will!"

"Adios, amigo!" Finch said as Largo turned his horse and rode away.

Finch, Humphrey, and Colette watched as he quickly disappeared in the darkness. When they turned, they were surprised to see that Kate and Sam had walked up behind them. Tears were streaming down Kate's fat cheeks, but she said nothing.

"Don't worry, Kate," Humphrey said consolingly. "Largo will make it if any man can."

Finch was surprised at Kate's emotion. He had unconsciously supposed that blacks had very little feeling for each other. He was beginning to think that maybe he had been wrong about a lot of things concerning them.

# CHAPTER 10

The next morning dawned bright and clear. There was still a bite in the cool air, and the cooking fires shed welcome heat.

After a good breakfast, which was later than usual for they were not moving that day, Finch, Humphrey, Buff, and Clem gathered to discuss the activity for the week.

"Clem, you start the boys gathering a few cattle. Chase them a lot so they will be good tired, and try to gather them fairly close to camp, if you can," Finch said.

"All right. We'll try to pick up young stuff. Mama cows with calves, too. Seems like the older them critters is, the wilder they is."

"If we can get a small herd good and tired while we are here, they ought to handle better when we start trailin'."

"That's right," Clem agreed. "And the boys is sure gettin' restless and raunchy. I reckon that will take some of the sap out of 'em."

"Another thing or two." Buff squirted tobacco juice. "We ain't got a chance in hell of stayin' here a week without Indians findin' us. I reckon we ought to have scouts out every day, and maybe we ought to dig us some rifle pits close by. Them wagons will help, but they won't stop all of them rifle bullets!"

"All right," Humphrey agreed. "I've had some experience building revetments. I'll get some of the niggers started on 'em this mornin'."

"Another thing," Buff continued. "Clem, I shore ain't tryin' to run things, but I reckon you ought to move your camp closer in to the wagons. Be a lot safer for ever'body."

"I'll do that," Clem agreed. "Jis' hope Kate don't bang our cook over the head with a fryin' pan."

"Don't mean that close!" Buff said.

"I been wonderin'," Finch began slowly, "If we haven't been under estimating those niggers of Hump's. You reckon some of 'em could learn to ride and help with the cattle a little. They might be able to ride drag."

"That'd sure please the boys," Clem grinned. "Ain't none of 'em anxious to eat dust all the way to the Canadian."

"I dunno!" Humphrey said dubiously. "None of 'em except the horse tenders have ever been on a horse. All the other men and most of the women have just been field hands. Course, they can drive mules, but I'd have a lot of doubt about them ridin' a horse."

"Well," Buff countered gruffly, "all they been doin' on this trip is drivin' a wagon or layin' in it on a mattress and singin'."

"And screwin'," Humphrey added.

"You got any objection if we try to teach some of 'em to ride, Hump?" Finch asked. "We've got some extra horses and saddles."

"I got no objection. You, Clem?"

"Hell!" Clem responded. "I don't care who rides them hosses as long as it ain't a Indian. Hosses and cattle is color blind, anyway."

"Who's gonna show 'em how?" Humphrey wanted to know.

"That's a problem, all right," conceded Finch. "I'll be out all day scoutin', and Buff will be huntin' game."

"A couple of my boys might take on that job," Clem offered. "We didn't think them horse herders could ever learn to rope, but damned if a couple of 'em ain't pretty good, already!"

\* \* \* \* \* \*

Clem brought two of the cowboys in to camp. "This here is Choc and Bart," Clem introduced. "They'll do our hoss breakin' when we catch some mustangs. They'll show them niggers how to ride if they can. Said they'd like to see the fun, anyway!"

The two cowboys looked very young, and Humphrey had a lot of reservations when he saw them. "All right," he said. "You boys bring a couple of gentle horses, and I'll pick out two of the niggers to try out. The rest of 'em will be diggin' us some rifle pits."

The two young cowboys grinned mischievously and rode away. "Hope we don't cripple a hoss or a nigger doin' this—and especially one of our bronc riders!" Clem said as he rode after them.

An hour later several of the Negro men were busy diggin a defensive line when Choc and Bart came back leading two horses. Humphrey eyed the mounts with misgivings. One was a roan with white all the way around his eyes, which, in Humphrey's experience, meant he was very excitable and probably mean. The other was a bay horse with obvious spur marks on his shoulder.

"God-a-mighty!" Humphrey muttered to himself. "Them cowboys has brought in a couple of outlaws if I ever saw one. I reckon that's what they call fun!"

The cowboys saddled the horses without trouble, and Humphrey motioned two of the younger Negro men to come forward. He nodded for one of them to approach the horses.

"Well, now!" the young bronc rider said enthusiastically. "I bet we got us a real bronc stomper here." He grinned at the Negro. "Ridin' ain't a bit hard to do. Jus' remember to keep one laig of each side and yore mind in the middle, and you ain't got a thing to worry about."

The Negro approached the roan horse timidly. It was obvious that he was not a rider.

"I'll jus' hold 'im while you get on so's he'll go off real easy," the cowboy encouraged. "Jus' grab the saddle horn and stick one foot in the stirrup and ease up in 'im."

The Negro did as instructed, and when the cowboy noted that he was wearing flat shoes and no socks, he showed the first bit of anxiety. "Now be shore if he jumps a little, don' let your foot slip through that stirrup. It might scare 'im."

Humphrey watched the whole operation with trepidation. He was convinced that the cowboys fully intended to get the Negroes thrown. It was typical raw cowboy humor, he supposed, but he did not approve of it. Colette walked up and stood by Humphrey just as the Negro got astride. The horse stood trembling as the Negro was handed the reins and the cowboy stepped back.

The horse stood a short moment longer, then suddenly bawled, ducked his head, and jumped as high as he could; he hit the ground on stiff forelegs. The Negro's head snapped back, and he lost his wool cap as the horse jumped, but he squeezed the horn with all his strength and tightened his legs. As he did, both of his feet went through the narrow stirrups. He dropped both reins, and by sheer strength and fear was able to stay on two more jumps. Then he was flying over the horse's head. One of his feet came out of the stirrup, but the other foot was caught firmly, and the stirrup jerked him back toward the horse when he was in mid-air. Colette screamed, and Humphrey growled angrily as the Negro was dragged by the frightened horse which was kicking viciously at its dragging burden.

One of the cowboys hurriedly mounted and jerked his rope down as soon as he saw the Negro was hung in the stirrup. He was ready to throw the rope when the Negro fell free.

"Catch him!" Colette had screamed as the Negro's shoe came off and his foot came loose. The horse went bawling and pitching back toward the horse herd with the saddle stirrups flopping madly in the air.

The Negro lay for a moment without moving, and Colette ran to him. Humphrey stalked angrily toward the cowboys, who were standing abjectly, still holding the spur scarred bay.

"You two get your butts back to that cow camp!" he roared. "And tell Clem I want to see 'im right now!"

"Aw, Boss," pleaded one of them. "We was just havin' a little fun. Besides, that nigger ain't hurt much. See, he's gettin' up already."

Humphrey looked, and sure enough, the Negro was getting to his feet, assisted by Colette.

"Well, it's no credit to you two that he ain't killed!" Humphrey said angrily. "That outlaw horse was tryin' to kick his head off, and it's a wonder he didn't succeed. Now you git outta here, both of you, and tell Clem to make some tracks this way in a hurry."

The Negro man limped up to them just then. "I's sorry, Massa Hump," he said. Colette still held his arm, and he was unsteady on his feet. "I didn't do so good that time, but I'll shore do better next time."

"There ain't gonna be a next time!" Humphrey said grimly. "I'm beginning to think cowboys got less sense than niggers."

"Aw, Boss!" pleaded the younger of the two. "We shore didn't aim to get nobody hurt. I wouldn't even have put him on that horse if I had seen them flat shoes he was wearin' first."

"And don't blame Clem for us bein' damn fools!" the other added. "He told us to bring some gentle horses, but we brought a couple of the wust ones, cause they been givin' us some trouble, and we wanted to see some fun."

"Some fun!" jeered Humphrey. Then he added in a more mollified tone, "I ought to fire both of you, but I won't. I guess no real damage was done, but don't try it again!"

"You can gamble that we won't," Choc said contritely. "We been lookin' forward to this trip since Fort Worth, and we'd shore hate to miss the rest of it."

"Then take that other outlaw back and bring some gentle horses, if there are any."

"We'll do that," Choc said quickly. "I know there's a couple of old ones that are real gentle. We'll take this bay back and bring them over here."

"Why don't you ride the bay back?" Colette asked, sweetly sarcastic.

Choc had one foot in the stirrup when he heard Colette's taunt. He paused a moment, then removed his foot from the stirrup and set it on the ground. He started uncinching his saddle and pulled it off his horse and turned to Colette and Humphrey.

"Why shore," he drawled. "Don't know why I didn't think of that my own self."

Colette watched with a worried frown as Bart held the bay while Choc fitted his saddle securely. When all was in readiness, he grabbed the head stall of the bridle, pulled the horse's head around sharply, and slid smoothly into the saddle. Choc turned the head stall loose just as he crammed both feet into the stirrups. Bart slapped the horse with his hat and yelled.

Then Colette and Humphrey were treated to a show the likes of which they had never seen before. The bay was old, expert, and mean. He squealed his rage as he plunged into the air and come down with bone jarring jolts. He sunfished until Choc's offside boot could be seen under the horse's belly. Choc just kept spurring as the horse tried every trick in his ample bucking repertoire. Once he reared, and Colette was sure that he would fall backward and crush his rider. She screamed as Choc hit the horse viciously between the ears with the handle of a heavy quirt. The horse came back to earth with his forelegs spread wide apart. He was panting heavily, and sweat dripped from him. Choc let him get his breath a moment and then jerked him firmly around and spurred him hard. The bay had had enough. He trotted docilely away; Choc circled him and rode back to Colette and Humphrey.

"See!" Choc grinned. "He's as gentle as a little lamb. Jus' likes to be playful once in a while."

"I've never seen such marvelous horsemanship," Colette said admiringly. "What's you name, cowboy?"

"My name is Choc," he grinned. "And that feller over there, that scared this pore little old bay pony with his hat, is named Bart."

"Well, I must say that, if you are any example, the horses are in capable hands."

"Yes, ma'am, they are," admitted Choc as his face reddened at Colette's compliment.

"Well, go bring some gentle ones over here and see if these two boys can stay on 'em a little while," Humphrey ordered as he and Colette started walking away.

"Boss?" Bart halted them. "Would it be all right with you if we started these boys out with a surcingle?"

"What's a surcingle?"

"Just a strap around the girth of the horse and a hand hold on it. I shore hate to see a man risk a saddle with flat heeled shoes."

"Do what you think best," Humphrey said. "Just try not to get anybody hurt!"

Humphrey and Colette started walking back to the wagon. The Negro sat on the ground and watched as the two cowboys rode away.

"Phew!" sighed Choc when they were a short distance away. "We damn near got fired—you know that?"

"Shore did!" admitted Bart. "Old Beatenbow was riled up some!"

"So was his wife. But I'd ride that bay backwards to get a few more looks at her. First time I ever saw her up close. Damn near got bucked off tryin' to watch her all time. She shore is one hell of a lot of woman—didn't you notice?"

"Notice, hell! I ain't dead yet. I was lookin' at her while she was lookin' at you ride that hoss. Did he buck pretty good?"

"Couldn't tell you that! I reckon my mind was somewhere else!"

"He must have bucked up a storm, cause her face sure did change up a lot as she watched you!"

"She's got a face that a man can't forget, that's for damned shore!"

"That ain't all she's got!" Bart retorted tensely. "Don't see how Beatenbow ever got her in the first place. Now why in hell did he bring her out in this kind of country with him?"

"Well," sighed Choc. "Let's go find a couple of gentle old nags and see if we can keep them niggers on top of 'em!"

Colette and Humphrey returned to their wagon. The sun was bright and warm. They sat in chairs in the shade of their wagon and watched as the two cowboys tried to teach two blacks to ride. On the first try, the Negro that had been thrown by the outlaw horse was eager to make a good impression on his second attempt that he grabbed the surcingle, and threw his leg so enthusiastically over the back of the horse that he slipped off the other side. He quickly righted himself, however, and came back to the left side again. This time he was successful, and the cowboy handed him the reins and gave him some instructions that Colette and Humphrey could not hear.

The training session continued. The Negroes met with varying degree of success, and the cowboys alternately complimented and cajoled them. At the end of two hours, both seemed to be making progress, and each grinned broadly when he completed a circle without mishap and returned to his instructor.

"Well," Humphrey said. "Looks like them two cowboys ain't so bad after all. Anyway, this is as good a way as any to pass the time, I reckon. And we've got a lot of time to kill before we move on."

Colette didn't say anything for a moment; then she got up and went into the wagon. The sun was warm shining through the thick canvas cover. She quickly undressed and crawled into bed, pulling a sheet up to her chin. Then she called Humphrey.

"What is it, Colette?"

"Come into the wagon a minute."

"Let me watch this next nigger ride again. He's gonna lope the horse this time."

"You can see something better than a black riding a horse if you will come in here."

Humphrey sighed and clicked his whittling knife shut as he got slowly to his feet. He kept his eye on the Negro rider as he felt his way to the back of the wagon. Then he turned his face and opened the puckered canvas end of the wagon. He gasped in astonishment as Colette sat up in bed and let the sheet fall to bare her magnificent breasts. Humphrey simply stared a moment.

"I just thought that we might find a more interesting way to pass time," Colette said innocently as her lambent eyes twinkled at her husband.

Humphrey immediately jumped into the wagon and closed the opening securely. Then he crawled beside Colette who was still sitting up. Her dark eyes were enormous and filled with love and lust.

"God-a-mighty, woman!" Humphrey croaked huskily. "You're as bad as a nigger wench!"

"I'm a lot better than a Negro wench, my husband," she said lovingly. "You ought to know!"

Humphrey took her in his arms, and she lay back with a sigh, pulling him with her.

An hour later they lay in langorous ease, both lost in thought. Finally Colette said, "I was, wasn't I?"

"Was what?" Humphrey asked absently.

"Better than a black wench!"

Humphrey hugged her naked body to his. "I ain't got no idee," he said. "You know I never had no nigger wench."

"I don't know any such thing!" Colette said tartly.

"Then I reckon you'll just have to keep wonderin'!" Humphrey said. He was quite aware that Colette loved to tease him about the Negro wenches, and that she got a sort of vicarious pleasure from it. Humphrey was perfectly content to let her play her little game, which he much preferred to her knowing the real truth. Fact of the matter was—those little 'high yaller' wenches on the plantation had been more than eager partners with the "massah's" son, as had several of the white girls on adjoining plantations. But none had ever compared with Colette, and none ever could, Humphrey thought proudly.

"I'd better go see about them cowboys and niggers," Humphrey finally said. "Hope none of 'em is crippled!"

"It was a nice way to pass the time, though, wasn't it, Humphrey?"

"Cain't think of a better way!" Humphrey agreed.

"And we have a week to wait!" Colette said pointedly.

"God-a-mighty, woman!" Humphrey expostulated. "You want 'em to haul me the rest of the way in the wagon? I'm so weak now I doubt if I could crawl on a horse."

Colette's delighted laughter followed him as he closed the opening and walked toward the cowboys and Negroes. They were all sitting on the ground, and their horses were standing ground tied nearby. The horses and Negroes looked tired. As Humphrey walked to them, they all looked at him, and one of the Negroes hopped to his feet alertly.

"Wanna see me ride, Mars Hump?" he asked eagerly. "I can do it pretty good now!"

All of them grinned at the enthusiastic black.

"Go ahead and show 'im," encouraged Choc. "Take old Blue there. The surcingle is still on 'im."

The Negro grinned widely and approached the horse which pricked his ears, but did not move. The Negro gathered the reins in his left hand, grabbed the handhold on the surcingle, and nimbly hopped astride. The Negro reined the horse away from the group and drummed his heels energetically against its sides. The horse pitched half heartedly a couple of times as he broke into a lope. The Negro's laugh pealed over the camp as he clamped his legs tightly and held firmly to the surcingle. He rode the horse in a wide circle and returned to the men. His face glowed with pride.

"Well, now!" Humphrey said approvingly. "Looks to me like you're doin' a fine job!"

"They're both doin' fine!" Choc said with enthusiasm. He was anxious to atone for their first mistake in bringing the outlaw horses. "Another few days, and we are gonna have us a couple of more cowboys."

\* \* \* \* \* \*

The next two days passed uneventfully. Colette had Kate fill her tub with warm water and bathed inside the wagon each morning while they were stopped. Each afternoon she and Humphrey spent an exhilarating and exhausting hour inside the wagon and then went out to watch the cowboys instruct the Negro riders. They were amazed, as were the cowboys, at the rapid progress made by the blacks. The Negroes insisted, however, that they did not need saddles, and that surcingles would suffice for them to ride the horses forever. The cowboys did not insist.

"Reckon them niggers got a butt as hard as their head!" Bart opined.

"If they ain't now, they will have by the time they ride drag bareback and eat dust all the way to the Canadian River."

Buff camped in his wagon near the caravan, but seldom came in except to bring fresh meat. Both he and Finch left early each morning, Finch to scout and Buff to hunt. Humphrey inspected the defenses each morning and stationed blacks with rifles in strategic places. The cowboys had managed to bring in a small herd of cattle, which some of them held on a meadow close by, and the two bronc busters continued their instruction of the black riders. By the third day, five of the Negroes had grown fairly proficient in staying atop a horse, and the cowboys felt that they might indeed be useful in riding drag for the herd, thus relieving some of the cowboys for more important, and certainly more pleasant work.

About mid-morning of the fourth day the camp was surprised to see Buff's wagon careening crazily toward camp. Buff was standing in the bouncing wagon, and his long white hair was streaming, as he flayed the small mustang horses which were running swiftly with their bellies close to the ground. He wheeled his wagon up beside that of Humphrey, jumped down, and strode swiftly toward Humphrey and Colette. The whole camp came running, for it was certain that the old mountain man was excited.

"Hell to pay!" Buff said quickly. "They is a bunch of Apaches not more'n a hour from here and headin' this way!"

"How many?" Humphrey asked calmly.

"Not more'n twenty, I reckon. They's a raidin' party, war paint and all. Watched 'em in my glass. Don't make no sense, neither, Apaches is mountain Indians, and they are a long way out o' their territory. But the worst part of it is that they are led by Old Victorio!" Buff's voice was worried.

"Who is Victorio?" Colette asked in a frightened voice.

"Meanest damn Apache that ever lived!" Buff said bitterly. "I been tryin' to kill the red son-of-a-bitch for five years. He catches whites and tortures 'em—all

Apaches do! They ain't human atall! Caught a partner o' mine five year ago up in the mountains and skinned him alive, jus' a bit of hide at a time. Pulled out his fingernails and his toenails and burnt his eyes out with live coals. Most all his skin was gone when I found him. He shore did die slow and hard!"

"How ghastly!" Colette's face was pale and her voice quivered.

"Where's Finch!" Buff demanded.

"Out scouting since early mornin'," Humphrey said. "He don't usually come in till near dark."

"Well, we'd better get set for a fight!" Buff said. "Maybe so I'd better sort of take charge. Hump, you git them blacks with their rifles in them pits, and get the missus in the wagon and wrap her in a mattress. Hump, you stand in front of yore wagon as soon as they show. There's a chance in a million that they'll want to palaver, but I doubt it. Anyways, as soon as they get in rifle range, you put a bullet in front of the lead horse. If they want to talk, old Victorio will hold up his hand as a peace sign. If they start to charge, you jump behind your wagon and start shootin! Ever'body start shootin! This ain't gonna be no picnic, so be damned shore you don't miss!" Then Buff added in a calmer voice, "We got plenty o' time to git ready for 'em cause they're a ways off and ridin' slow and don't know we are here yet, but let's git set now."

"Where will you be, Buff?" Humphrey asked.

"Begorra, and I'm gonna be inside the wagon with the missus. I'll have me some peep holes so's I can see in ever direction, cause they ain't no tellin' which way they'll come from. But, begorra, me thinks old Victorio has rode into a panther's den this time! As many rifles as we got, we ought to be able to kill ever damn one o' them redskins if they charge over this open ground. Be a lot different if we was in the mountains, cause Apaches is mountain fightin' bastards. Now iver body git! And be shore that all the kids is layin' down flat in them ditches they dug!"

The blacks scattered quickly. All of the men and some of the women took rifles and ammunition and got in the rifle pits. The children all lay flat in the trench fortifications. Humphrey thought all was in order until he saw a movement in the wagon behind him. He quickly investigated and found Kate, Sam, and the wounded Negro, Raney, cowering flat on the floor of their wagon.

"Kate, what are you all doin' in here? Get yourself into them trenches."

"I's too big and fat to fit in there, Mars Hump, and yo knows it," she whimpered. "And Sam won't go lessen I does, and Raney there is too crippled."

Humphrey hesitated, undecided what to do. Then he said, "All right. Stay down flat and don't raise your heads when the shootin' starts."

Humphrey went back to his own wagon. Buff had unhitched his mustangs and headed them toward the remuda which was being held by two Negroes and two cowboys. A short distance farther away, several of the cowboys held the cattle herd.

"What in the world can we do about them?" Humphrey asked Buff as he gestured toward the herd and remuda.

"Nothin'!" Buff said flatly. "Old Victorio will hit us first cause he knows that if he can wipe us out, he can take the women, and kids, and horses when he wants. He's a smart old heathen. I'll give 'im that. But I wisht them mules wasn't in the remuda. Paches don't give a damn about cattle, but they'd rather have mule meat than buffalo."

"If there ain't more than twenty of 'em, I believe we can take 'em!" Humphrey said.

"We'll take 'em right enough!" Buff said confidently. "I'm jus' hopin' we don't get too many people killed and the remuda run off. And I shore do hope I get a shot at old Victorio. Now I'm gonna git in your waggin, Hump. I'll have a peepin' space all around and be lookin', but if you see 'em fust, you peck on the waggin, hear!"

Humphrey nodded, and Buff climbed into the wagon. He rolled the canvas up just above the sideboards so he could see in every direction. Then he rolled Colette tightly in the mattress and pushed her against the side of the wagon.

"Now you jus' stay quiet, lass, and iver thin' is gonna be all right."

A muffled sound came from the mattress, and then a deathly quiet settled on the camp. Buff peered through his peep holes constantly and hugged his big buffalo gun to his chest. Perhaps twenty minutes had passed when Buff let out a savage snarl.

"You see 'em, Buff?" Humphrey whispered anxiously.

"I reckon me Irish luck has done run out, Hump!" Buff said grimly. "Look out south of us a couple of hundred yards."

Humphrey looked and was amazed to see a band of men riding toward the camp. They were coming at a steady pace, and they were not Indians.

"Who are they?" Humphrey whispered urgently.

"Only varmint alive that's meaner than old Victorio!" Buff said bitterly. "That there is Sally Diego, damn his half-breed hide, and his bunch of Comancheros. You can tell 'im a mile away by that stovepipe hat he wears!"

"What do we do?" Humphrey asked anxiously.

"Wait! He will ride up here jus' as big as you please and try to catch you off guard and then shoot you. He don't know we're set for a fight already, and he don't know I'm in this waggin. Jus' let him ride on up close. He'll be tryin' to see how many women and kids he can steal and tryin' to figger out how much money might be about. It's gonna take guts, but you jus' stand there with your rifle across your chest!"

A muffled sound came from the mattress, but Buff mashed it firmly and then patted it reassuringly a couple of times.

The riders approached to within a few yards of the wagon. Humphrey almost shouted as he recognized the rider beside the Comanchero leader. It was Doc Guines on his pinto horse. Sally Diego held up his hand, and the men stopped.

"Hello, amigo!" Sally Diego said in what was intended to be a friendly voice.

"Howdy!" Humphrey returned the salutation.

Diego smiled and showed badly stained teeth which reminded Humphrey of a wolf.

"Looks like you got a right smart outfit here," he said.

"Good enough," Humphrey agreed.

"Mind if we look about a bit, friend? We was just passin' through when we saw you."

Humphrey started to reply, but Buff's loud voice boomed from the wagon before Humphrey could speak. "Sally Diego, ye snivelin' lowlifed son-of-a-bitch! This be Buff Larrigan talkin' to ye!"

Diego's face suddenly became wary, and he looked intently toward the sound of the voice.

"I know ye can't see me, but I can see ye, right enough. And I got me buffalo gun aimed right at yore fat belly, and me finger is itchin' on the trigger. And if ye don't call them men o' yores back that's tryin' to circle this waggin, I'm gonna blow a hole in ye that ye can stick that stove pipe hat in. Ye hear me, child!"

"Hold it, men," Diego said urgently. "Come on back here by me!" The men who had started to spread out grouped around their leader again.

"Hey!" Doc Guines said excitedly. "I know this bunch. That's the Beatenbow outfit. I killed one o' their greasers in Decatur. They got women and kids and money!"

"Right ye are, lad!" Buff said cheerfully. "And I also got a Sharp's 50 stuck in Sally's big gut, and they's a dozen more rifles pointed at the rest o' ye!"

"Hey, Sally, look!" one of the Comancheros shouted excitedly as he pointed. Buff did not shift his rifle an inch off Diego, but the rest of his men turned their heads the way the man had pointed. They saw the band of Apaches perhaps three hundred yards away and riding swiftly and silently toward them.

"Let's get out of here, men!" Sally Diego yelled as he jerked his mount cruelly about and slammed his spurs. The entire bunch of Comancheros turned to run, and as they did the Indians began their blood thirsty yells. Colette, heedless of the warnings, unrolled from the mattress and was watching the Indians' approach and the Comancheros fleeing. When the Indians were less than a hundred yards from the caravan, the leader suddenly veered his horse and started chasing the Comancheros.

"Begorra!" Buff breathed. "And maybe me luck is wi' me yet!"

Colette crawled out of the mattress, caught a movement out of the corner of her eye, and turned to see Humphrey resting his rifle on the wagon and taking careful aim at the fleeing Comancheros. Colette started to speak when the big rifle boomed. She quickly looked in the direction it had been pointing and saw a pinto horse turn a somersault. Its rider was thrown several feet. He jumped up, only to fall again as a broken leg gave way. The yelling Apaches were on him before he could rise again. Two of them slid to a stop as the others continued the chase. One of the Indians jumped from his horse and kicked the pistol away that Guines was trying to raise. Guines screamed as his arm was broken by the Indian's kick. Then he was raised by his hair and tossed across the horse that the other Indian was riding. Quickly the Indian remounted, and both Indians continued their chase with Guines flopping about as he was draped on his belly across the horse and in front of the Indian.

All the members of the caravan had been so dazed and confused by the sudden turn of events, that they emerged from their positions to watch the riders fleeing out of sight. An eerie silence enveloped the camp as the yells of the Indians grew fainter and finally faded.

It was Buff who finally broke the silence. "I ain't nivir seen nothin' like that—and I been a mountain man for thirty year," he said in awe.

"You missed Guines, Humphrey," Colette said in a small, quavering voice. "And you killed his horse."

"I wasn't shootin' at Guines," Humphrey said grimly.

"You mean you deliberately—?"

"I did!" Humphrey said almost savagely. "Figured that back shootin' Guines and Old Victorio deserved each other!" He stalked away, stiff backed, and his right shoulder drooped more than usual.

"Begorra, and you got yourself quite a man there, lass," Buff said admiringly as he watched Humphrey stride away. It was as much an accolade as Buff had ever given any man.

"Let's get out of this wagon and get some coffee," Colette said feebly. "We all need it."

"Right you are," Buff agreed. "Jus' let me git me pistol, and I'll be right wi' ye."

Colette watched and was surprised when Buff pulled a small calibre pistol from under the wagon seat.

"What are you doing with that tiny gun?" Colette asked in surprise. "Could you shoot an Indian with that?"

Buff's face showed his consternation, and he looked like a small boy that had been caught with his hand in the cookie jar. He gulped a couple of times. "Wasn't aimin' to shoot no redskin with it," he said in an embarrassed voice.

"Then why—"

"It's a bonny lass, ye be, Colette. And they was a chanct that Old Victorio would get Hump and the rest o' us, too. I was jus' makin' shore he didn't get you!"

"You mean you were going to shoot me?" Colette was aghast.

"Jus' wasn't shore Hump could bring himself to do that—even if he was still alive," Buff explained.

Colette looked faint as she stared at Buff in horror. Then she said in a quavering voice, "Let's go get a big drink of Humphrey's snake medicine instead of coffee."

"Right ye are, lass!" Buff said in a voice that was almost cheerful. "It ain't likely that any o' 'em is comin' back here, anyways."

\* \* \* \* \* \*

Finch rode into camp an hour later, his horse lathered and panting heavily. He slid to a stop and dismounted quickly. "We'd better get set!" he said urgently. "I cut Indian sign ten or twelve miles north of here."

"Aye, lad," Buff replied jovially. "They done paid us a visit—and the Comancheros, too."

"They what?" Finch said in amazement.

"That's right!" Buff's voice was jovial. He was feeling the snake medicine a bit. "Damndest thing you iver seen. Sally Diego and his bunch of varmints rode up on us and was palaverin' while they sized us up. They was still at it when the Indians come. It was old Victorio and about twenty of his braves, war paint and all. But I had seen 'em earlier and got back to camp. So we was ready for em."

"What happened?" Finch asked.

"Like I said," Buff was almost garrulous. "Damndest thing ye iver saw. When Diego and his cutthroats saw the Indians, they turned tail, and the Indians took out after 'em. We niver even had to fire a shot."

"Humphrey fired a shot!" Colette said in a thick voice.

Finch looked keely at her and then glanced at the half-empty glass in her hand.

"That feller Guines was with Diego and his Comancheros," Buff explained. "When they was runnin' from old Victorio and his redskins, Hump shot that pinto pony of his'n. Damn good shot, too. Musta been three hundred yards."

"What happened?" Finch asked, his low, pleasant voice shaking just a bit.

"Oh, nothin' much!" Buff said nonchalantly. "Guines musta broke a leg when his pony fell, and two o' them Indians stopped to give 'im a hand. He rode off on one o' their hosses. Course, he was layin' in his belly in front o' one o' the Indians."

Finch looked keenly at each of them. Humphrey and Colette both avoided his eyes, but Buff looked Finch squarely in the face and gave him a big wink.

Finch was silent for a long moment. There was no need to explain the eventual fate of Guines, if the Indians really were Apaches.

"You said it was Victorio?" Finch looked at Buff. "He's Apache, and they are mountain Indians. How do you know it was him!"

"Seen 'im through my glass." he gestured toward it. "And I seen 'im afore. He's a long ways from his home territory, but it was him for shore and sartin. I been tryin' to git a shot at the red bastard for five years. He killed a partner o' mine."

"Well, I guess—Do you reckon—" Finch was at a loss for words. "You got any more of that snake medicine, Hump?"

"I'll pour you a big glass full," Colette giggled.

# Chapter 11

Though Buff was fairly certain that neither the Indians nor the Comancheros would return that day, the camp remained on extreme alert.

"They'll be chasin' them Comancheros till dark, I'm a thinkin'!" Buff opined. "If they catch 'em they'll be one hell of a fight, and if they don't, then old Victorio is gonna want to play with Guines a bit."

"They might sneak back tonight!" Colette said fearfully.

"Nope!" Finch assured her. "Indians won't fight at night unless they have to. If they don't come back before sundown, we will be all right for today."

"I hope I never see another Indian!" Colette declared.

"Ye likely will, though, lass!" Buff said in a kindly voice. "But Finch is right. If they don't come back afore sundown, they won't come back tonight."

"We'd better have scouts out in all directions, anyway, just in case," Finch said. "You say they headed south, so I'll ride out that way for a couple of miles and spend the rest of the day."

Finch rode away. Buff went to get his mustangs and hitched them to his wagon.

"I'll jus' mosey up to that little rise north and camp so's I'll be handy. Hump, you and the lass jus' sort of rest up and don't worry no more."

When Buff had gone, Colette took Humphrey's hand and held it tightly. "This has been the most horrid day of my life!" she said. "I don't think I could live through another one like it."

"You could," Humphrey assured her matter of factly. "And we may all have to before we get to our ranch. You want to go into the wagon for a while?"

"Do you mind if we just sit out here in the sunshine the rest of the day?" Colette asked. "I am so frightened, I don't think I could even —"

"It's all right, wife!" Humphrey hugged her to him. "I'm pretty well tuckered out myself."

Humphrey and Colette sat on the sunny side of the wagon and talked of everything but the events of the day until a couple of hours before sundown when Buff came striding in.

"Finch is comin' back in," he announced. "But I don't think anythin' is wrong. He ain't in too big o' a hurry."

The three of them were standing anxiously by the Beatenbow wagon when Finch rode in.

"Two of the Indians are comin' back this way," he said. "But they are ridin' slow, and I don't figure they aim to cause us trouble."

"Hope one of 'em is old Victorio," Buff growled fiercely. "Mebbe so I'll get a shot at the old bastard yet!"

"I don't think he's one of them," Finch said. "These two look like just a couple of braves, and their horses are tired."

"Well, if they ain't more'n two of 'em, we ain't got nothin' to worry us cause Finch could knock both of 'em off their hosses afore they could touch a tomahawk!" Buff said confidently.

The two Indians appeared within minutes. They stopped several yards away, and both held up their hands, palm out.

"Their peace sign!" Buff said. "They want to palavar. Let's let 'em come on in till they git in range of Finch's pistol, anyway."

"How do we tell 'em to come in?" Humphrey asked. "I'll jus' wave 'em in," Buff said. "I savvy their hand talk some an' a bit o' their lingo, too."

Buff held up his hand, palm out, and then motioned for them to come on in. The Indians approached warily and stopped a few yards away. One of them started making hand signals and grunting their guttural language. Then they pointed to the remuda.

"What are they saying?" Humphrey asked.

"Says they got a long way to go, and they want food to take with 'em," Buff said in disgust. "But what they really want is one o' them mules to eat."

"Tell 'em no!" Humphrey said firmly.

"Wait a minute, Hump," Finch said quickly. "That may be a real good solution. They will take the mule with them. I figure the rest of the bunch have circled our camp and are headed back to the mountains. These two will lead the mule till they catch up with the others, and then they'll have a grand feast and go on their way."

"I'm thinkin' Finch is right, lad," Buff said to Humphrey. "And one mule sure ain't a lot to lose in any fracas with the Comancheros and Apaches, both."

"All right," Humphrey said reluctantly. "Tell 'em they can have one mule."

"Aye!" Buff said. "I'll tell 'em that, and I'll go git that stubborn roan one that sulled on the boys when they roped 'im the other day."

Buff again made hand signals accompanied by harsh syllables. The Indians seemed pleased and started to ride toward the remuda, but Buff stopped them with a loud grunt and more gestures.

"Now what?" Humphrey demanded.

"They was goin' after a mule," Buff said. "But I want 'em to stay here. I'll get the mule, and I don't want 'em behind my back whilst I'm doin' it. They're gonna stay right here where Finch can mind 'em with that pistol o' his, if need be!" Buff said adamantly.

Buff gestured more, and the Indians relaxed on their ponies and stared stonily ahead. Finch watched them closely. Humphrey and Colette talked sporadically, but in low tones, until Buff returned leading the roan mule. One of the Indians reached out to take the lead rope, but Buff stopped him with a hand signal and then continued with more sign language and Indian talk. The Indians apparently understood him, for they gestured and talked. One of them pointed his arm to the south and moved it in an arc from west to north. Buff seemed to be satisfied, for he handed the lead rope to one of the Indians and stepped aside, holding up his hand, palm out. The Indians rode north at a trot, leading the mule.

"What did you tell them, Buff?" Finch asked curiously.

"Didn't tell 'em nothin'," Buff said. "I was askin' 'em a question."

"What question?" Finch insisted.

"Asked 'em about the white man they took," Buff replied.

"What did they say?"

"Said he was with Victorio, and that they were all headin' north to the mountains."

\* \* \* \* \* \*

Tension gripped the camp for the next two days. Guards were constantly alert, and Finch continually rode circles around the camp. Buff did not range as far afield as usual in his quest for game, but he was able to bring in a nice fat buffalo yearling and a couple of deer.

"Aye, me lad," he said cheerfully to Humphrey as he delivered the meat. "And I reckon them Indian varmints is cleared out of the territory for the time bein'. Aint seen no fresh sign the last couple of days."

Finch rode in just as Buff was delivering this good news. "I saw one of them sneakin' up from out west of here. I think he was just a young brave tryin' to make an impression on old Victorio. He was Apache, all right. But he won't bother us any more."

Buff nodded his head in understanding. Neither Colette nor Humphrey asked any questions about the Indian, but Humphrey queried Finch.

"How soon do you think we ought to move on? Has Largo had time to reach Taos, yet?"

"He ought to get there this week if he gets there at all."

"When do you think we ought to pull out of camp here?"

Finch frowned thoughtfully. "Let's give it a couple more days. The cowboys are doin' a good job makin' riders out of those niggers, and we can sure use 'em. And if Largo gets through, he ought to get back to us by the time we get to the Big Wichita."

"How long will that take?"

"Wish I could tell you that," Finch said. "But it will all depend. If we gather a lot of cattle, it will slow us down. If the Indians hit us and we have to fight our way through, there just isn't any way to tell how long it will take us. We could make it in a few days if we didn't have any trouble."

"All right!" Humphrey agreed. "We'll give it two more days and then pull out three days from now if that suits you and Buff."

"Aye, and I'm for bein' ready," Buff replied quickly. "I got a lot of the game thinned out and scared away from near camp, here."

"Suits me," Finch said as he rode away. "See you at suppertime."

The camp began to return to its former cheerful mood. The laughs of the blacks rang through the camp again, and the children were allowed to frolic within the wagon circle. The main attraction, however, was the riding instruction that Choc and Bart were conducting. Humphrey had decreed that ten of the blacks would learn to ride; so the cowboys were quite busy with teaching, but as the Negroes progressed in their ability to ride, the bronc buster teachers began to obviously enjoy their task. They had used all of the available horses that were old and gentle and had to resort to using some of the more spirited animals. Some of the horses pitched quite briskly, but the black riders displayed a surprising tenacity and ability to cling to the hand hold of the surcingle and stay aboard. When one was occasionally thrown, he suffered the jibes and laughs of the black audience that was in constant attendance. Ironically, when one was thrown, he immediately remounted, and there developed a fierce competition among the fledgling bronc busters.

"Shore a good thing Beatenbow bought them extra horses in Decatur," opined Choc one warm afternoon. "Them niggers are takin' to ridin' like a new calf takes to his mammy's tits!"

"And some of 'em are gettin' pretty damn good," Bart agreed. "Fact is, I'm thinkin' that a few of 'em may be of some help in breakin' mustangs when we catch some. They hold on to that surcingle like a tick in a cow's ear!"

The only untoward incident occurred when one of the horses fell on its side while pitching. The black rider clung to the surcingle as the horse rose, but when he rode back to the instructor, his face reflected pain even though he was still grinning. It was quite apparent that his leg was broken, and he had to be helped from the horse.

"Now ain't this hell!" grumbled Choc. "We got a broke leg, and I reckon they ain't a doc in a hundred miles."

"Go get Clem," Bart said. "I heard him say once that he had set a broken leg."

When one of the other Negroes returned with Clem, Choc and Bart had split the trousers and had seen that the leg was bent at almost a right angle between the ankle and knee.

Humphrey and Colette had seen the incident and hurried as the crowd gathered around the unfortunate black.

"It's broke, all right," Clem stated the obvious. "But the bone ain't stickin' out through the skin. I reckon we can get it straight again, but it's gonna hurt like hell!"

Sweat was pouring from the Negro's face and he gritted his teeth but made no sound.

"Isn't there any way to make it easier?" Colette asked anxiously. "The man is in awful pain."

"No way I know of except to bash him over the head and set it afore he comes to," Clem said.

"Wait a minute!" Humphrey said quickly. "I got somethin' in the wagon that may help."

He walked quickly to the wagon and returned almost immediately with a bottle of whiskey. He knelt beside the Negro and pulled the cork from the bottle. "What's your name, nigger?" Humphrey asked solicitously.

"They call me Trey, Massa," the Negro gritted through clenched teeth.

"All right, Trey," Humphrey instructed. "You take a big drink of this, and we will wait a while to set you leg. It ought to help."

The crowd watched silently as the Negro gulped down a goodly portion of the bottle.

"We're gonna need some splints," Clem advised. "Some of you rustle around and see if you can find some good stout boards or sticks about fourteen or fifteen inches long." Three of the Negroes hurried away. "And," Clem added. "We're gonna need some wrappin' to. Anybody know where we can find some? Ought to be a couple of inches wide and as long as you can get."

"We can get some buffalo hide. Buff has got a fresh one in his wagon. We could cut some strips off of that!" Choc suggested.

"You damn fool!" Clem retorted harshly. "You want a one legged nigger? That rawhide would shrink and cut his leg plumb off."

"I know where there is something we can use," Colette volunteered. "I'll go get it."

"Feelin' any better?" Humphrey asked.

"Yassuh, massa Hump," the Negro said. "I's feelin' a little bit better now."

"Take another big slug of this," Humphrey ordered and handed him the bottle. The Negro complied.

Colette returned with strips of cloth that she had taken from one of her underskirts.

"Will this do?" she asked hopefully.

"Couldn't be better," Clem approved as he examined it. "Now where is them splints?"

Several sticks were proffered by the blacks, and Clem selected four. "Whittle them down plumb flat on one side," he ordered.

"Ain't got no knife, Massa Clem," one of the Negroes said, where upon Clem and Humphrey handed two of the Negroes their pocket knives.

While the splints were being made, Humphrey kept kneeling beside the Negro and plying him with the whiskey. "Feelin' any better, now?" he asked.

"Feelin' good, Massa. Ain't hurtin' hardly atall."

"All right," Humphrey said with satisfaction, and handed him the bottle again. "Drink the rest of this, and we'll set that leg."

The Negro took several big swallows, then a deep breath, and drained the bottle. He lay back on the ground and looked at the blue sky above.

"How's it feel now?" Humphrey asked again.

"Awful good!" the Negro grinned. "Another bottle of that, and I wouldn't care if my neck was broke!"

"All right," Humphrey said as he rose to his feet. "He's ready."

"All right, let's do it. A couple of you stout niggers get one of his arms apiece and pull 'em back over his head—and hold on tight. Don't let him slip 'cause I'm gonna have to pull like hell to get that bone back together. One of you set on his other leg, and one on his chest."

Volunteers complied with Clem's orders. Clem sat on the ground, took the ankle in both hands, and placed his booted foot in the Negro's crotch. He leaned back and pulled with all his might. Nothing happened for a moment, and Clem grew red in the face as he strained mightily. Suddenly there was a very audible snap, and the Negro uttered his first sound of pain and went limp.

"She popped back in!" Clem announced as he wiped his sweaty face with one hand while still holding the Negro's leg with the other. "He's unconscious now, so let's get it splinted and bandaged afore he wakes up."

Several of the Negroes started to move forward, but Clem stopped them. "Maybe you'd better do it, Hump," he said. "I'll tell you how as you go along."

"I'll do it," Colette said firmly. "Humphrey is too rough handed."

Clem looked at Colette in surprise, but offered no objection as she gathered the splints and bandages and knelt beside the Negro. She was able to follow Clem's instructions quite satisfactorily, and he offered only a few corrective suggestions as Colette completed the job to his satisfaction.

"Good as any doc could do, and a lot cheaper!" Clem voiced his approval as he laid the Negro's leg gently on the ground. "Some of you help him up when he comes to. And he's gonna need a crutch to get around with for a while."

They were all watchin the supine Negro. His face was peaceful and serene. Suddenly, he opened his eyes and sat up. He looked frightened when he saw all the people gathered around him. Then he looked at his leg and grinned sheepishly. "Reckon I musta fell asleep," he said contritely. "Leg don' hurt, atall, no more."

Clem shook his head in wonder. "That's one damn tough nigger!" he said as he mounted his horse and rode back toward the herd of cattle.

"Trey," Humphrey asked, "Have you got a wench—a woman?"

"Yassuh, Mars Hump. That's her right there by Miss Colette." He pointed to the rather plain, very black woman standing by Colette. "That's Lulu. She my wife, now. You had us married up back in Louisiana, remember?"

Humphrey, who still could not remember the name of all the former slaves, simply nodded and turned to Lulu. "You're goin' to have watch 'im pretty careful for a while, Lulu. Don't want 'im hurtin' that leg again before it gets well. Anybody know how long it takes a bone to heal?"

Finch, who had been watching the entire proceedings with great interest, replied, "Had one of mine broken once. Took about six weeks to heal. Don't know whether there's any difference in a nigger or not."

"I reckon we're all made about the same!" Humphrey said. "Lulu, I'm gonna whittle him a crutch out of this forked limb that somebody brought up here. I'll measure it to fit 'im. You see that he uses it."

"Yassuh, Mars Hump. I do that," Lulu replied eagerly.

"He will have to ride inside the wagon, and he needs to keep that leg stuck out straight when he ain't usin' the crutch."

Humphrey took considerable pains in whittling out and measuring the crutch, but finally he was satisfied. "All right now, a couple of you bucks lift him up careful and get him in the wagon. Don't hurt that leg!"

When Trey was safely ensconced in the wagon, he called to Humphrey.

"Massa Hump, suh?"

"What Trey?"

"My leg hurtin' again pretty bad. You reckon you got any more of that medicine?"

"You've had enough whiskey now to keep a white man drunk for a week," Humphrey replied callously. "You just lay back on that mattress. Maybe so you can even get a little sleep."

With that, Humphrey nodded to Colette. She and Finch joined him as he walked back to the Beatenbow wagon. It was almost sundown, and Kate had a table set up by the wagon. She immediately served Colette, Humphrey, and Finch some delicious buffalo steaks along with hot biscuits, gravy made with canned milk, and some of the dried apricots that she soaked and heated. They all ate hungrily and silently until Kate brought the coffee.

"Jus' wishes I had some real milk to make gravy with," she grumbled. "Ain't near as good with that canned stuff."

"Well," Finch grinned. "I reckon those longhorn cows do give milk, but I'd sure hate to try to milk one of 'em!"

Colette and Humphrey both laughed. Then all of them began to talk of the journey that would begin tomorrow.

# Chapter 12

Finch and Buff left early the next morning—Finch to scout the country ahead and Buff to hunt fresh meat.

"Begorra!" Buff grumbled "If them cowboys and niggers worked as hard as they eat, they would shore and sartin' be gettin' someplace."

Clem and the cowboys let the cattle begin grazing their way north westward as soon as they had risen of their own volition from their bedground. "You try to roust them critters out afore they're ready, and you got trouble on your hands!" stated Clem.

Humphrey was gratified that Clem had agreed to let two of the most proficient black riders trail along with the herd. Both of them disdained any suggestion that they ride a saddle and continued to employ the surcingle with its comforting hand hold.

There was no real rush about breaking camp, for the cattle would travel slowly as they grazed their way. The caravan and the remuda would travel faster. With that in mind, Humphrey spent some time directing the blacks as they filled in the unnecessary rifle pits and trenches, for he wanted to leave the campsite as nearly like they had found it as possible.

Kate carried water from the river and heated it for Colette's bath, and she also demanded that the Negro men and women take a bath in the river, which they did, half of the men going up stream while leaving the others on guard. The women and children went down stream. Humphrey immediately realized that he had an opportunity to get something done that he hadn't been able to do before.

"Colette," he said. "I haven't been able to get a good count of all the niggers since we left home. I know how many we had when we left, but a lot of bucks and wenches, too, caught up with us on foot, and they been hidin' out in the wagons. To tell the truth, I don't even recognize most of 'em cause they growed up so much while I was in the army. And I don't hardly know any of their names."

"Please call them 'blacks', Humphrey!" Colette said.

"All right—blacks," Humphrey said a bit irritably. "But anyway, now is a good time to get the right count. You count the women and kids when they go to the river and comin' back, too. I'll count the men."

"All right, my husband." Colette said tartly. "I will do as ordered."

Humphrey glanced at her a moment in perplexity, and then turned to begin counting the men.

When they had all returned, Humphrey asked, "How many?"

"Twelve women, six little ones, and Ellie," Colette replied.

"And who?" Humphrey was puzzled.

"Ellie," Colette retorted shortly. "Kate and Sam's youngest. I don't know whether to count her as a woman or a child."

"Could be either one," admitted Humphrey. "She was only about a three year old when I left for the war, but when I got back, them little tits of hers was already a pushin' out some. She must be about a nine year old by now. Them nigger women shore get grown fast."

"Humphrey Beatenbow!" Colette stormed angrily. "You quit calling them niggers. They're human just as you and I are. And Ellie is not a horse or a cow or some other animal that you would say is a three year old."

Humphrey looked at Colette in amazement. It was the first time she had ever been angry with him, and he didn't know how to respond because he was genuinely sorry that he had roused her anger and at a loss to know how he had done so.

He was silent a moment and then said uncertainly, "I guess we'd better call Ellie a woman. That's make thirteen women and six kids. I counted eighteen men. When we add in Kate and Sam and the two niggers—I mean blacks—with the herd and that crippled one in Kate's wagon, that makes—let me see now—fourteen women, twenty two men and six kids. That what you get?"

"Fifteen women and twenty-three men," Colette corrected. "You didn't count you and me."

Humphrey felt a tinge of anger but quickly smothered it. "I forgot us, I reckon. Anyways, they are thirty-six blacks, fifteen cowboys, Finch and Buff, and you and me. God-a-mighty! That's more'n fifty people. No wonder Buff is havin' a hard time keepin' us in fresh meat."

The first group of black men returned rather quickly from their bath, for the water was cold. The other men took their turn and got back to the camp at approximately the same time as the women and children.

"Now that's better," approved Kate. "Jus' cause we's campin' out ain't no reason to be dirty, leastwise not to stay that way. Now Sam, you tote some water up from the river for Raney to wash with cause he cain't get in that stream with no broke shoulder. And then me and you is gonna go and clean up our own selves."

"Now, Kate," whined Same, "Yo knows—"

"I knows yo a good fo nothin', lazy nigger," Kate interrupted. "Now yo git!"

Sam obeyed, although his reluctance was quite evident. When he returned, he set the pail inside their wagon with a bang. Kate looked as Sam walked back to the morning fire.

"Yo ain't gonna warm that water?" she scolded him.

"No I ain't!" Sam said in a tone that he rarely used. "Yo baby that nigger too much, Kate! And he's a no good if'n I ever seen one."

Kate made no reply. She had heard Sam speak in that tone of voice very few times, but she knew that, for the moment, her wizened little husband was boss of their family. It made her proud, too, for Kate, on occasion liked for Sam to order her about. "I reckon most women like their man to be bossy onc't in a while," she thought to herself.

The caravan pulled out at mid-morning. Since Largo was riding Humphrey's stud, he decided to drive his own wagon. Colette sat beside him. Humphrey glanced sideways at her many times to discern her mood, but her face was almost non-expressive for the first few miles. Then, she could not conceal her delight as her eyes devoured the countryside. The pecan and oak trees were budding; the cedars and junipers seemed to have regained a glow that they had surrendered to the cold winter. Only the mesquite and cottonwoods that were beginning to appear did not show signs of the early spring.

"Finch says that the cottonwoods and mesquite will tell us when the winter is really over," Humphrey volunteered, hoping Colette's truculent mood was gone and that she would continue the animated conversation that he was used to.

"Finch has been out this way several times, hasn't he?" Colette asked.

"That man has been most everywhere several times, seems like. Old Buff says that Finch is a legend, even in the Texas Rangers, and that he is know by reputation all over Texas and most of New Mexico territory."

"What kind of reputation?" Colette wanted to know.

"Well," Humphrey was hesitant, for he knew that Colette admired Finch, and he did not want to disillusion her. "Buff says he's a real easy-goin' feller, likes to laugh a lot, has fun, hard to make mad. He likes women, and they like him."

"I can believe that," Colette said softly. "What else did Buff say?"

Still Humphrey hesitated, then finally continued. "He says Finch ain't afraid of the devil hisself, that he's rode into trouble that a dozen men would shy away from."

"And?" Colette prodded.

"God-a-mighty, Colette," Humphrey said in exasperation. "What else do you want to hear about him?"

"Everything you know about him," Colette said.

"All right," Humphrey conceded. "Buff says he's killed more'n twenty men and that there ain't a man alive that can compare with him in shootin' a pistol or a rifle. Says Finch caught three outlaws that were supposed to be real bad ones. They thought that the three of 'em could take 'im, and they tried to draw on 'im. He killed all three of 'em before they got a shot."

"He sounds like a villain," Colette said with a little shiver. "But he certainly doesn't look or act like one."

"And he ain't!" Humphrey defended stoutly. "He's as fine a man as I ever knew. Buff swears he never killed a man that didn't need it, or one that was tryin' to kill him."

"But he's so young!" Colette protested.

"About my age," Humphrey said. "He just looks like a kid. Some people just don't show age much, and Finch is one of 'em. His hair is slippin' a little, or you'd think he was fourteen years old."

"Just once in a while his eyes look old," Colette mused, almost to herself.

"Finch ain't had no easy life," Humphrey explained. "Chico, before he got killed, told me a lot about Finch. His folks was killed when he was just a kid, and he rode the range tryin' to find some of their cattle, for a couple of years. He had to give it up, for he didn't have no help. For the last four or five years, him and Chico was in the Texas Rangers."

"But the Rangers are disbanded now, aren't they?"

"I cain't get the straight of that," Humphrey said, puzzled. "Chico said that his captain thought they were when Finch took them horses back to Austin. But he wasn't certain. So Chico and Finch resigned anyway, so's there wouldn't be no question about them. Then I heard in Decatur that they're still active. I don't know."

"I'm glad you told me about Finch," Colette said gratefully. "And even if he has killed a lot of men, I think he is a nice person."

"None finer!" Humphrey agreed. "And if he hadn't shot them two in Fort Worth, I shore wouldn't be here now. They aimed to kill me—that's for shore!. I didn't know that then—but I do now."

"Well," Colette said gratefully. "I'm glad Finch was there!"

"So am I!" Humphrey said emphatically.

"Oh, look!" Colette said excitedly. "There are two squirrels. One is chasing the other."

"Probably a she chasin' a he," Humphrey said facetiously.

Colette hit Humphrey on the shoulder playfully, and he breathed an inward sigh of relief and hoped that her strange mood had passed.

The rest of the afternoon went pleasantly with Colette her usual ebullient self and constantly pointing out something that delighted her. Finch returned to inform them that they would have to make their first dry camp that night.

"Hope you had all the water barrels filled before you left," he said. "Forgot to remind you."

"They're full," Humphrey assured him. "How far is it to water?"

"About six or seven miles farther than we ought to travel today."

"Will the horses and cow be all right?" Colette asked anxiously.

"Oh, sure," Finch assured her nonchalantly. "Those wild cattle often go that long without water. Clem thinks it will do them good anyway. Tire 'em out a bit."

"What about the horses and mules?" Humphrey was concerned. "Especially the mares?"

"We've got enough water for the mares and the mules that are pullin' the wagons, but I don't think we will need it. We'll hit Mulberry Creek about noon tomorrow. So nothin' is goin' to suffer."

"Colette will," Humphrey said jokingly. "We shore can't afford the water for her to take no bath."

"You're the one that will suffer, Humphrey Beatenbow!" she rejoined tartly. "You're the one that has to sleep with me."

Both Finch and Humphrey grinned at her spunky reply, and Finch half saluted as he loped ahead. Finch got to the place he had chosen to camp and dismounted to bask in the sun for an hour before the herd and the caravan arrived. He stared into space for several minutes, and a rare frown creased his forehead. He was troubled. Never before in his short life had he been so indecisive. The first time he had ever seen Colette Beatenbow, he had fallen hopelessly in love with her, and he was intuitive enough to realize that Colette had reciprocated his feeling to some degree. But Colette was strictly off limits to him, for she was the wife of another man. Moreover, her husband was a man he admired and liked. There was absolutely nothing spurious about Humphrey Beatenbow, and he loved his wife deeply. Finch was sure of that, and he was certain that she returned Humphrey's love, and yet—. Finch shrugged and pulled his hat off to comb his fingers through his thinning hair. "I reckon every man sees something that he just can't have," he reasoned philosophically. "Anyway, I've had my share of women."

Finch was determined to destroy his yearning for Colette, and he was equally determined to stop the tumultuous stirring of his insides every time he saw her.

That determination was quickly overcome, however, when less than an hour later he saw the Beatenbow wagon with Colette sitting so proudly beside her husband.

Their dry camp was not nearly the problem that many had feared. The laughter and banter of the blacks was not quelled in the least. The remuda was restless for a while, but as darkness fell, they were grazing, seemingly content. The cattle were a bit more restless than usual, but were not giving any indication of being unmanageable.

Old Kate prepared the usual bountiful supper for the Beatenbow wagon and set it out on the collapsible table that Largo had made. Kate seemed to be inordinately proud of that table, and Finch wondered idly why old Kate, who was usually not impressionable, had such pride in the fairly simple bit of furniture that Largo had constructed.

After supper, Finch, Colette, and Humphrey sat around the table for a while and talked as they sipped their coffee.

"No use me asking, Hump, but you've got the guards all out, haven't you?" Finch queried.

"Doubled," Humphrey assured him. "Had 'em doubled since the Indians scared us. Why? You expectin' trouble?"

"I reckon I'm always expectin' it," Finch grinned sheepishly. "Just don't want to get caught unprepared. I reckon some of that Ranger trainin' will stay with me forever."

"Well," Humphrey said, "maybe it's a good thing. You're still alive, ain't you!"

"And I'm gonna stay that way as long as I can," Finch replied firmly.

"Oh, I hope so!" Colette said softly as she reached over and put her hand on his arm, and his heart thumped crazily again.

Just then Clem rode up out of the dusk.

"You reckon we could borry a keg of water for tonight?" he asked and then added with disgust. "That damn one-eyed cowboy cook we hired in Decatur left camp with his barrel only half full this mornin'. Ain't got water enough for coffee tomorrow, and the cowboys will hang that gotch-eyed bastard if they have to do without—and I'll help 'em do it."

Everyone laughed, and even Clem grinned a bit.

"We've got plenty," Humphrey assured him. "I'll have one of the nig—blacks fill you a keg."

When Clem had departed, balancing the keg precariously on his saddle horn, old Kate waddled up. "Is yo ready fo' yo bath tonight, Miss Colette?"

"I'm not going to take one tonight, Kate," Colette said and then added facetiously, "Humphrey is afraid one of his mares might need the water, and Clem needs it for the cowboy's coffee, too."

"Well, lawsy me!" Kate shook her head incredulously as she waddled away.

"How long before we will meet Largo, do you think?" Humphrey ignored Colette's remark.

"I'm sure hopin' he'll show before we get to the Big Wichita," Finch said sincerely. "That will be two or three days from now. Fact is, I keep lookin' ahead for him and that black horse of yours all the time now, but I know it's too soon. I just hope he'll make it without any trouble."

"He'll make it, trouble or not," Humphrey said confidently.

"Let's go to bed," Finch said. "Those cattle are a little restless, and they may get us up earlier than usual in the morning."

\* \* \* \* \* \*

Finch staked a night horse securely near his bedroll, and, as usual, he was almost immediately asleep, secure in the knowledge that his night horse or his inner warning mechanism, an almost animal instinct, would awaken him if danger approached.

He slept soundly until midnight and then was instantly awake and alert. His hand automatically grasped the handle of his pistol that was always under the cover at his side when he slept. He lay still for a few moments and listened intently. He soon realized that what had awakened him was only the herd rising for their nightly stretch. He listened to them for a few moments. They were a bit more restless than usual, but the low noise of their nocturnal exercise soon abated. Finch, after looking at the starry sky, which always gave him an indefinable feeling of peace for a few minutes, turned on his side and slept again.

The cattle got to their feet earlier than usual the next morning, and Finch could see the cow camp cooking fire blinking in the pre-dawn. He could imagine the bawdy harassment that the hapless cook was enduring. He grinned, saddled his horse, and rode over. He was challenged by an armed guard as he came near the herd. After identifying himself, he rode in and spent a pleasant half hour listening to the traditional cowboy conversation and gripes, most of which were directed toward the taciturn and sour-faced cook.

Finch lingered at the cowboys' fire a few minutes until Clem came riding in. "How far to water?" he asked Finch. "Six miles, or so, I'd guess," Finch answered. "Good stream and plenty of water."

"Then we ought to make it by dinner time," Clem said. "The cattle are some restless and ready to move out."

Finch saw that Kate had a fire going; so he emptied his coffee cup and tossed out the grounds. "That was shore a good cup of coffee," he grinned at the cook only to receive a malevolent glare from the cook's one good eye.

"You might want to hold up at the creek a while," he said to Clem as he mounted his horse. "Maybe even all night. There's a good place to camp and plenty of grass. I'll stake the camp site out and then ride on north a good ways. If I remember right, there's another good stream a days' drive northwest."

Clem had his mouth full of bacon and beans, and he simply raised a hand acknowledging Finch's statement.

Old Kate had the table set up when Finch returned, and she poured him coffee. He was joined almost immediately by Colette and Humphrey. Colette's radiant face and sparkling eyes were testimony of her tremendous zest and love of life.

She greeted Finch warmly and thanked Kate as she accepted a cup of coffee. Humphrey looked sleepy and touselled.

"I've been over to the cow camp," Finch said. "Clem will start the cattle early. They're already up and grazing. He thinks they will get to water by noon. He may keep them there overnight. I'll ride on ahead and find our next camp. I think there is another creek about a day's drive on west. If there is, it would make good sense to wait over so the cattle wouldn't need to dry camp another night."

"I hope it's a good stream," Colette said.

"It is," Finch assured her. "Some groves of big cottonwoods along it, but of course they are not leafed out yet."

"Will the trees be in full leaf when we get to our ranch?" Colette asked.

"No tellin'," Finch said, a ring of pride in his voice. "Up there on the Canadian, we will have weather—not climate. Most years some of the trees start leafin' out about the middle of April, but they often get frozen back and have to start over. But the cottonwoods and the mesquites will tell us when spring has really come."

"You sound as though you like "weather"," Colette said querulously.

"I do, I reckon," admitted Finch. "And you will too. It gets cold, and it gets hot. The wind blows, and there are days when your camp smoke will rise straight up. It snows for a week, sometimes, till you horse can't get through the drifts, and sometimes it rains and a headrise comes down the river—a solid wall of water that sweeps away everything it hits. That's the reason that most of the time the river bed is real wide, but has only a small stream running in the sand."

"It sounds a little forbidding," Colette said dubiously.

"No, it isn't," Finch said quietly. "We just have to learn to live with the country because you sure can't whip it—but it's the most beautiful place I've ever seen. I think you will like it too, Colette." Finch's voice was even softer and more pleasant than usual as he described his land.

"I'll love it, Finch. I know I will if it is as charming as you say."

"It is," Finch declared a bit self-consciously. "But I reckon I do get a little carried away when I talk about it. Kit thinks so, anyway."

"I hope Largo got to Kit's and is on his way back by now," Colette said fervently.

"Largo got there," Humphrey said flatly.

"I'll ride on ahead and try to spot our next camp. I ought to get back to Mulberry Creek by the time the cattle and wagons get there," Finch said as he mounted his horse and rode away. Colette waved to him, but he did not look back as his horse loped northwest.

\* \* \* \* \* \*

When the cattle and the caravan reached Mulberry Creek at noon, there was no sign of Finch. Colette and Humphrey expressed some concern, for he was usually very accurate about his timing.

"Aye, and don' be worryin' ye pretty head about Finch, lass," Buff, who had brought in a load of fresh meat, said cheerfully. "That lad kin take care o' hisself, mind ye!"

"It's just that he's always so prompt," worried Colette.

"Aye, that he is, and ye can bet that somethin' be delayin' 'im, but he'll show up soon enough. Clem says he's gonna hold the cattle here overnight, which seems to me to be a right smart idee. It's a grand country around, lots o' game, and plenty o' fish in that creek. If you got any fishin' gear, let them niggers have it, and we oughta have a fine mess for supper, begorra. Niggers is fishin' fools, so I hear tell!"

"You hear right," Humphrey agreed. "And I got hooks a plenty in the wagon. The blacks will be mighty happy to catch some fish."

\* \* \* \* \* \*

The camp on Mulberry Creek was ideal. There were huge cottonwood trees in clusters along the lazily running, clear stream; yet the clusters were far enough apart that one could see for some distance up and down the creek, and the land around it sloped gently. Guards were able to see well in every direction, and it was unlikely that Indians could get near the camp undetected. Humphrey decided against digging fortifications. The trees would offer good protection in the event of an attack, but in any case, the wagons were drawn up in a circle.

Humphrey stopped by the wagon and surveyed the scene with a great deal of pleasure. The remuda was grazing energetically on the south side of the creek, while the herd was munching contentedly a distance up the slope on the north side. None of the animals seemed the worse for having done without water for one night. Humphrey gazed at the scene and enjoyed a sense of well-being that he had not felt before on the trip.

Kate approached the Beatenbow wagon and asked Colette, "You wants me to fix yo some warm bath water afore them niggers gets that stream all riled up a fishin' in it, Miss Colette?"

"Oh yes!" exclaimed Colette delightedly. "I think a warm bath right now would feel wonderful!"

Kate warmed the water and filled the tub in the Beatenbow wagon. As Colette was luxuriating in it, she could hear the child-like sounds of the black's merry-making.

The Negroes were delighted to be allowed to fish in the stream, but soon abandoned the fish hook and line that Humphrey supplied. They shed their shirts and waded into the stream to try to catch the fish with their hands. The stream was only waist deep. They were surprisingly successful as several of them would form a barrier with their bodies and drive the fish into niches in the bank, whereupon one or two of them would lower themselves under the water and swim into the closed off area. Almost invariably, they emerged holding a nice sized catfish triumphantly above their heads.

The women and children lined the bank to shout their encouragement, and laughed gleefully every time a fish was caught. Soon, the sack that Kate had provided began to bulge.

In the midst of the happy activity, Buff came into camp. The Negroes paid not the least bit of attention to him.

"Finch is comin' in, and he ain't by hisself," Buff informed them. "They is two men with 'im and they is travelin' slow."

"That's strange," Humphrey said. "Who you reckon could be with 'im?"

"Ain't go no idee," Buff admitted. "But they is friendly. Finch is ridin' on the left side of 'em and a little in front sometimes. If he was suspicious, he's be on the other side and a little bit behind 'em."

"Why would he do that?" Humphrey queried Buff.

"Why so's he wouldn't have nothin' to interfere between that pistol of his'n and them other fellers," Buff answered as if surprised that Humphrey would ask such a dumb question.

Colette, who had heard Buff's approach and the ensuing conversation between him and Humphrey, quickly got out of the tub, dried herself briskly, and donned clean clothing.

\* \* \* \* \* \*

Humphrey, Colette and Buff were standing by the wagon when Finch and the two men accompanying him came into view. They were too far away to recognize them immediately, but Colette quickly identified Finch because of his tall stature, and the way he sat his horse.

Kate had joined them uninvited, peering at the approaching riders intently. Suddenly a huge smile broke over her fat face, and she exclaimed excitedly. "That be Largo a-ridin' on the offside! I jus knowed he's make it back. And I's mighty happy about that!"

"How do you know it's Largo?" Humphrey asked dubiously.

"Cause I jus' knows, that's all!" Kate said confidently.

They watched as the riders came closer; they were riding very slowly, but soon the watchers were able to recognize Finch and verify Kate's assertion that one of them was Largo. The third man was an Indian brave. He was bare except for a breechclout, but he carried a rifle. Colette and Humphrey started to walk out to meet them, but Buff halted them.

"Let 'em come on in," he advised. "They've come a long ways, and they ain't no use stoppin' 'em afore they get here. Besides, that there Indian with 'em is a Comanche, and I don't talk their lingo too good."

Colette and Humphrey obeyed Buff's suggestion, and it soon became apparent why the riders were coming so slowly. Old Heck, Humphrey's big black stud, was plodding wearily along behind. His ribs were showing, and his head hung low as he evidenced every sign of exhaustion.

"Howdy, Mars Hump and Miss Colette," Largo greeted as they rode up and stopped. He was grinning broadly. "Told yo I wuz gonna make it," he said proudly. "An' I's might sorry I used yo hoss so bad, but Indians chase me a couple o' times."

"Did you see Carson?" Humphrey asked anxiously.

"Yassuh, I done tol' Mars Finch all about it."

"Who is the Indian?" Humphrey asked Finch who had not yet spoken. His pulse was slowly getting back to normal since his first sight of Colette.

"He is one of White Horse's men," Finch said. "Kit sent him back with Largo so they could ride in the daytime. His name is Big Elk."

The Indian, upon hearing his name began talking and gesturing. He pointed to the northwest several times and to Finch. Each time he gestured toward Finch, he used the term Hut se Pah se Kawe.

"What is he callin' Finch?" Humphrey turned to Buff.

"Damned if I know," Buff admitted. "Said I didn't talk Comanche lingo too good. You know what he means, Finch? Sounds like he's sayin' somethin' is cold."

Finch shifted uncomfortably in his saddle, and his face reddened as he replied. "He's callin' me Hut' se Pah suh' Kawe. That's my Comanche name, I reckon. Big Elk and I have met before, and he called me that. Seems to have sort of stuck with me."

"What does it mean?" Colette asked curiously.

"It means 'Ice Eye'," Finch said self-consciously.

Buff let out a roar of laughter. "Begorra, and I reckon Big Elk is a right smart Indian, at that." Buff continued to chuckle.

"Well, what was he sayin' about you?" Buff wanted to know. "I could get a part of it, but not all. He was sayin' somethin' about a fight."

Finch took a deep breath and explained, for he knew he had it to do. "Big Elk says he fought me before, and that I shoot pretty good. Fact is, I could have killed him once, but I didn't. I reckon he's as much of a friend as any Indian can be now, which is not much."

"What did Kit Carson say?" Humphrey directed the question to Largo.

"Mars Carson, he a mighty nice man. He give me this hoss I's ridin' and he rode back with me for a couple of days till we met a Indian he called White Horse."

"That's the chief of the Comanches," Finch informed them.

"What happened?" Humphrey asked anxiously.

"They talk mos' all day," Largo said, "and then Mars Carson tell me that everthin' is still settled and for me to tell Mars Finch he wouldn't be bothered by the Comanches, but to be leery o' the Kiowas. He said that he had heard that some o' the mountains Indians, especially the Apaches, had come down where it was warm and was raidin' on the plains some. Said we'd ort to be careful o' them!"

"Begorra, and he was damn shore right about them Apaches!" Buff interjected. "What else did he say?"

"Said White Horse would meet us when we get to the ranch, or soon after."

"That Indian gonna stay with us?" Humphrey wanted to know.

"No suh, Mars Hump. Mars Carson say he come with me to see for shore it Mars Finch a bringin' cattle and wagons, an' then he'll go back and report to White Horse."

The Indian looked at all of them a moment and then turned his horse to ride away when Colette spoke quickly to Buff.

"Tell him to wait a minute."

Buff looked at her quizzically but uttered a harsh grunt, and the Indian turned back to them.

"Kate," called Colette. "Fix this Indian a good sack of food to eat on his way back."

"Yassum, Miss Colette," Kate said and went to the chuck wagon.

Finch started to say something, but decided against it. Buff looked at Colette with a bemused expression and then shrugged.

When Kate returned with the sack of food, Colette took it from her and walked unhesitatingly to the Indian. His horse snorted and whirled as she started to hand the sack to the Indian. But the Indian was not the least unsettled by the quick movement of the horse; his copper colored body swayed with the horse as if it were a part of him. Then he pulled viciously at the rope bit in the horse's mouth, which was the only gear the Comanches used in riding. As he turned the horse back to Colette, she noted that there was blood on the horse's mouth. The Indian nudged the horse back near Colette and reached for the sack. She handed it to him timidly, but the horse stood without moving except for rolling his eyes wildly as Colette came near again.

"Comanches is the best damn horsemen alive," Buff said admiringly.

The Indian broke into a babble of talk, grunts, and gestures that Colette did not understand a bit.

"What did he say?" she asked.

Buff grinned impishly. "Didn't understand it all," he said. "But I think he said you'd make a good squaw!"

Colette knew that Buff was teasing, and she answered in the same vein. "He looks like he would make a very satisfactory buck, too."

The Indian placed the package in front of him on the horse and grunted again as he rode away. Colette waved to him, but he did not see her.

Maisie, Largo's wife, had walked toward the group when Largo returned, and she stood timidly several feet away until Largo spied her. He grinned broadly at her and winked. Humphrey saw Largo's look and turned to see the comely black girl.

"Come on up, Maisie," Humphrey invited. "Your husband is home."

The girl advanced shyly, but stopped short of coming abreast of the whites.

"Hello, Maisie!" Largo grinned. "I's back."

"Hello, Largo," she said softly. "I's glad you is back."

"What in the world are those niggers doin' in that creek?" Finch seemed to notice them for the first time. "They're actin' like a bunch of kids playin' in the mud."

"They're grabbling," Humphrey said.

"They're what?" ejaculated Finch.

"Grabbling," Humphrey repeated. "Fishin' with their hands."

"Do they ever catch one?"

"They've caught a whole sack full," Humphrey boasted. "This camp is goin' to have a fish supper, includin' the cowboys!"

"I'll be darned!" Finch was astonished.

"Begorra, and them niggers has got a lot of know how that puzzles this child," Buff said. "But I reckon them fish will shore be tasty."

After a festive meal of fried catfish, corn pone, molasses, and other tidbits whipped up by Kate, the Beatenbows and Finch discussed the successful venture that Largo had completed and the remainder of the trip as well as they could foresee it.

"I don't think we will have to make more than two or three more dry camps," Finch said. "And then for only one night. But we've got to cross the Big Wichita and the Pease River. Either one of 'em could be bad if it rains, and it's gettin' to be the time of year for that."

"How long before we get to the Wichita?" Humphrey wanted to know.

"Three or four days depending on how we travel and what good camps we can find between here and there. I found a good one today, about a good day's drive ahead. Trees, water, and grass."

"Then after we cross the Wichita, we get to the Pease River?" Humphrey questioned.

"Uh huh," Finch agreed. "But we will cross another branch of the Wichita before we get to the Pease. It's small and shouldn't give us any trouble. We ought to get to the Pease three or four days after we cross the Wichita. Then we cut a little more northwest, and we ought to make it to the Red River valley four days later."

"Oh, I'm excited about the Red River valley," Colette enthused. "I just hope it's as pretty as its name."

"It's pretty, all right," Finch assured her. "We will be just south of Red River. That's what separates Texas from the Indian territory of Oklahoma."

"We don't have to cross the Red River, though?"

"We will stay south of it, but we will travel up the valley several days. Fact is, if we don't have any Indian trouble, I think we ought to camp for several days in the valley. Wild game is plentiful. Plenty of buffalo, deer, wild turkey, quail, and just about covered up with cattle. The last time I was through there, I saw thousands of 'em, and there will be more now since spring is closer. We ought to be able to fill our herd out there. I even saw a band of mustangs there once."

"How many cattle you think we ought to try to get?"

"All Clem and the boys can handle," Finch said. "That country where we're goin' will graze a lot more cattle than we can drive into it. The biggest job for the cowhands after we get there will be to keep as many buffalo hazed out of our valley as they can."

"Can't keep 'em all out, huh?"

"Nope. Too many. Besides old White Horse likes to hunt in that valley, and I'd sure hate to have it plumb cleaned out of buffalo when he gets there."

"Will we try to catch some mustangs if we see some in the valley?"

"Doubt it," Finch answered cryptically. "We need to wait till we hit plains country for that so we can see for a long ways."

"Well," Colette interposed. "With the exception of being frightened almost to death when we met the Indians, and when Chico—when we were in Decatur—this trip has been the most marvelous thing I could imagine, even in my dreams."

"There's a lot more to come, wife," Humphrey looked at her fondly. "Some of it will be good, and some of it bad. Let's just hope that most of it is good."

"It will be!" Colette gushed excitedly. "Our ranch is finally beginning to seem real to me. Always before, it has been sort of unreal—like a dream that you never know the end of."

"Speaking of dreamin'," Finch rose, "I reckon we'd all better get in our bedrolls. And I sure am glad Largo got back without too much trouble. You got a good nigger there, Hump."

"I have, for a fact. I told you he would make it. Course, Old Heck ain't gonna be worth much for a while."

"He's already been worth his weight in beaver pelts," Finch declared. "That's some horse you have, too! Goodnight, everybody."

"Sleep good, Finch," Colette smiled at him as he left.

\* \* \* \* \* \*

Finch took the usual precautions before he stretched out his bedroll. When he was flat on his back, he cupped his hands behind his head and looked at the sky. A crescent moon was rising in the east, and the stars were bright. Finch sighed his contentment and turned on his side. Colette's soft, dark eyes seemed to be smiling at him as he went to sleep.

He had been asleep only a few minutes when he was awakened by a noise that he could not identify. It seemed to be coming from the Negroes' wagons. He listened intently for a moment. Then he heard angry voices shouting, then a scream. He surmised that there was trouble among the blacks. He had been surprised at how well they got along together, but now he supposed some of them were fighting. "Oh, well," he thought, "Humphrey will take care of the niggers in short order." Then he relaxed as things quieted down and was almost asleep again when he saw a dark shape running toward him. He sat up quickly and palmed his pistol.

"That's far enough!" he challenged as the shape kept coming toward him. He half raised the pistol, but some intuition kept him from firing. A second later, Colette, dressed in a robe, knelt beside him and grabbed his shoulder. She was completely oblivious of the fact that he had his pistol in his hand and that his shoulders were bare.

"Finch," she gasped, "Please come quick—I think something terrible has happened!"

"What—?"

"Just come!" Colette demanded. "Now!"

Her voice was filled with terror. Finch started to throw the covers back and suddenly realized he had no clothes on. He reached for his hat and slammed it on. "Colette," he said quickly, "you get on back to your wagon. I'll be there almost by the time you are!"

"Come now!" She shook his shoulders angrily.

"Dammit, Colette! I ain't got no clothes on," he protested desperately.

"I don't care if—" Colette seemed to regain a small bit of composure. "All right, but hurry!" She fled back toward her wagon.

Finch jumped into his clothes, buckled on his gun, and raced toward Colette. He was still tucking in his shirt tail when he reached the wagon. Colette was lighting a kerosene lantern with trembling fingers.

"What's wrong, Colette!" Finch demanded as he looked in the wagon.

"I don't know, she said shakily. "There was a great noise at Kate's wagon, and then all the blacks started yelling and cussing. Humphrey went to see about them, and he hasn't come back. Kate is in her wagon crying as if her heart would break. I've been afraid to go see. Will you do it, please. And hurry!" she begged.

He reached Kate's wagon in a few long, silent strides and peered inside. He could make out the huge form of Kate, only dimly. Her sobs and whimpers were like those of a wild thing that had been mortally wounded.

"Kate! What's the matter?" Finch got no answer, and he almost shouted. "Kate, dammit, what's wrong?"

The whimpering subsided for a moment, and then Kate said brokenly, "It's Ellie!" Then she wailed again.

Finch jumped into the wagon and struck a match. Ellie was lying in Kate's lap, her face swollen and bloody. One eye was completely closed, and blood ran from her mouth. Finch grabbed Kate's shoulder and shook her roughly. "What happened to her?" he demanded.

"That nigger Raney that I been takin' care of—he raped her, and he hurt her somp'n awful!"

"Where is he?" Finch demanded.

Kate didn't appear to hear him. "Wouldn't been so bad if'n he jus' raped her—that wouldn't hurt her too much — but he beat her somp'n awful!"

Kate began to sob and wail again, and Finch shook her angrily. "Where did he go? Where's Hump? Dammit, Kate, answer me!"

"Largo and Sam, they took Raney down the creek, and Mars Hump follow 'em," Kate finally managed to tell him. Finch quickly got out of the wagon and headed for the creek. Under the cottonwoods almost two hundred yards away he saw some flares. He hurried toward them.

Finch was a little short of breath when he arrived at the circle of blacks, and then he stopped and gaped in horror. Under one of the big limbs of a cottonwood, suspended by a rope around his neck, was a man. Standing near the suspended figure were Humphrey, Largo, and Sam. The suspended man seemed to move one leg feebly, and then he began to sway gently.

Finch made his way through the circle of Negroes and quickly went to Humphrey who stood looking up at the hanged man. Finch looked too and was almost ill. A part of the bandage was still around Raney's shoulder, and his eyes bulged horribly.

"What happened?" Finch demanded of Humphrey.

"Largo and Sam just hung a black hearted nigger," he said grimly.

Finch didn't have to ask why the grizzly deed had been done, but he was at a loss as to why Largo and Sam had—he shook his head as if to clear his vision.

"He's finished," Humphrey said to Largo. "You gonna cut 'im down?"

"I ain't!" Largo said emphatically. "He can hang there forever for all I cares." Then he turned, and followed by Sam, he made his way through the circle of blacks.

Humphrey stood still as the Negroes made their way back toward the wagons. When they were a distance away, Humphrey said, "I reckon we ought to bury the black bastard so's he won't stink up the country more than he already has. Let's go back to the wagon and get some shovels."

As they walked side by side in silence, Finch was still in a daze. They went to the wagon and reassured Colette, after telling her about Ellie. "We'll be gone a while," Humphrey told her. "Me and Finch got to bury that nigger."

"I'll be in Kate's wagon when you get back. Oh, the poor child! Do you think she is badly hurt?"

"No way to tell yet," Humphrey said. "Maybe by tomorrow she'll be all right."

"I have some ointment here that might help. I'll go to her right now."

"You do that, wife," Humphrey approved. "We will stop for you on the way back."

Humphrey lighted a flare, and they made their way back to the cottonwood. When the grizzly chore of digging a shallow grave and cutting the rope and dumping the dead Negro in it, and covering the grave was completed, they started making their way back to camp.

"Hump?" Finch began tentatively.

"What, Finch?"

"I reckon I'm a little mixed up about all of this. Why were Largo and Sam the ring leaders in hanging that man?"

"Cause they beat me to it!" Humphrey said grimly. "I'd a hung the son-of-a-bitch if I'd a got to him first!" he declared vehemently.

"Why didn't Largo and Sam come to get you?" Finch asked reasonably.

"I reckon they didn't think of it," Humphrey said tiredly. "And I doubt if Largo would have come for me, anyway. Wanted to take care of it hisself. You'd a done the same thing yourself if it had been your sister."

"Sister!" Finch stopped abruptly and grabbed Humphrey's shoulder. He was bewildered. "You don't mean that Ellie is Largo's sister!"

"That's exactly what I mean," Humphrey replied. "But I reckon there wasn't no way you would of knowed that."

"But Ellie is Kate's—"

"That's right," Humphrey agreed. "Largo belongs to Kate and Sam. He was their first git. Fact is, there are two or three more of Kate and Sam's in this here bunch of niggers. They're good stock."

Finch walked the rest of the way to the wagon in complete silence. He did not even stop by Kate's wagon, but stumbled his way back to his own bedroll. Humphrey's revelation explained a lot of things: why Kate was so proud of the table Largo had built, why she cried when he left for Taos, why she recognized him first when he was coming back!

Finch went to sleep hoping fervently that he would awaken to find that it had all been a bad dream.

# Chapter 13

Humphrey and Colette checked on Ellie early the next morning and found her asleep, but it was a fitful sleep, and she moaned and thrashed about. Her face was even more horribly swollen than it had been the night before.

Finch was at the Beatenbow wagon when they returned. "How is she?" he asked.

Humphrey only shook his head. "No way to tell. She's still alive, though, and she comes from tough stock. Hope she makes it!"

Colette's face was taut and drawn, and for the first time since he had known her, she did not greet Finch with a smile.

"Wish I had killed that nigger back in Fort Worth," Finch said bleakly. "Just didn't seem necessary at the time."

Neither Humphrey nor Colette replied, and Kate soon came to serve their breakfast. It was not the usual sumptuous fare that she provided, but no one commented. Kate's eyes were swollen and red from crying, and she moved slowly as if she were very tired, which she was.

Everyone seemed to be anxious to leave the camp. There was not the usual shouting and laughing among the Negroes. The teams were hitched to the wagons and ready to move out earlier than usual.

Clem rode into camp just as they were ready to leave. "What happened over here last night, anyways" he asked curiously. "The night herders said there was a hell of a ruckus down by the creek, flares and everything."

"A nigger got killed," Humphrey answered cryptically.

Clem looked at all of them keenly for a moment. "Wouldn't a been that one Finch crippled back in Forth Worth, would it?" he asked.

"It was," Humphrey said grimly.

Clem, sensing that they did not want to explain further, simply nodded his head and turned his horse about. "We already got the herd started," he said. "How far to the next water, Finch?"

"We can make it to a branch of the Big Wichita if we get a good drive today," Finch answered.

"We'll push 'em a mite," Clem said as he rode away.

A somber mood pervaded the caravan that day. Even the mules seemed eager to put Mulberry creek behind them, for they stepped out more vigorously than usual. No one looked back as they went over a rise and the creek was lost from view.

Several times during the day, Colette alighted from their wagon while Humphrey was still driving, and went back to see about Ellie. Upon her return to their wagon about mid-afternoon, she reported that Ellie had awakened but was still mute.

"It's a good sign that she woke up," Humphrey said solemnly. "Maybe if she can get a lot of rest today and eat something, she will be better tomorrow."

"She won't eat anything," Colette said dejectedly. "Kate has been trying to feed her some gruel all day, but her poor lips are so swollen, I don't think she can eat."

Humphrey started to reply and then changed his mind. He reached over and patted Colette on the leg, but it was only a gesture of reassurance. It was the first time that he had ever touched her that she had not felt a physical response.

The caravan did not stop at noon as they usually did, and they reached the tributary of the Wichita when the sun was still an hour high. The herd was close behind, and as they smelled the water, they came on in a long trot. The creek was quickly overrun with cattle, and the clicking of their long horns as they crowded in created a veritable cacophony of sound.

Clem rode in just as Finch returned from scouting. "Well, we made a good drive today, and I reckon it done them cow critters good. They're gettin' tired and easier to handle. Them two niggers ridin' drag is a big help. How far to the next water, Finch?"

"If we make as good time tomorrow as we made today, we can make it to the Pease River."

"Good!" Clem said with satisfaction. "We will. I'd like to have them cattle as tired as we can by the time we get to the valley and start gatherin' the whole herd. They're doin' right good now. Only a couple of 'em give us any real trouble, today."

"What you do with 'em?" Humphrey asked.

"The third time they broke out and started back, Buff followed 'em a good way so he wouldn't booger the herd and shot 'em," Clem answered almost absently. "We'll have beef for supper tonight."

\* \* \* \* \* \*

As was the custom, they kept the caravan and the remuda on opposite sides of the creek as a precautionary move when they camped near a stream. For the first time on the trip it rained that night. At first, it was only a gently patter, but soon there was lightning and thunder and a veritable torrent of water. Finch got out of his bedroll and quickly threw his tarp over it, donned his slicker, and hurried to the Beatenbow wagon.

"Hump!" he called urgently. "Get up and get these wagons pulled up close together side by side, and then get everyone under them!"

"God-a-mighty, Finch!" Humphrey exclaimed. "We cain't move the wagons in this rain. We can't even catch the mules!"

"Get the niggers up and let them pull 'em!" Finch yelled. "There are enough of 'em to pull one wagon at a time."

Humphrey stuck his head out of the wagon and was immediately inundated. "Why do we need to move the wagons?" he yelled as the thunder roared and he wiped water from his face.

"The cattle may run, and they could cross the creek and hit the camp!" Finch yelled.

Humphrey nodded and drew in his head. Finch quickly returned to his bedroll and saddled his night horse. When he got back to the wagons, Humphrey was rousting the Negroes out of bed. Largo was one of the first to appear followed by several of the other men in various states of undress. The lightning was almost constant now, and the rain was pouring down harder. Finch rode near Largo and yelled.

"Hook my rope to a wagon tongue, and I'll pull. You get all the men you can to push."

Largo immediately did as he was ordered, and they had the first wagon alongside the Beatenbow wagon when Humphrey appeared on Old Heck.

Finch could see him as the lightning played constantly. Humphrey waved his rope to Finch, and Finch waved for Humphrey to follow. They both hooked their ropes to a wagon, and with the Negroes pushing, they were able to get another wagon alongside fairly quickly. They got two more in the row just as a lightning bolt hit a tall cottonwood nearby. It was followed by a clap of thunder that made ears ring. Then there was a low rumble in the direction of the herd.

"Everybody get in the wagons or under 'em!" Finch yelled as loudly as he could, and then he set an example by spurring his horse to the Beatenbow wagon and crawling under it. He was immediately joined by a horde of Negroes. Mud squished as they plopped themselves down in it.

The roar of the thunder and the running cattle made conversation impossible. Finch kept listening for the cattle to hit the creek and overrun the camp. He felt sure that almost all of the Negroes were either in or under one of the wagons that were side by side. And he felt fairly sure that the cattle could not or would not overrun such an obstacle. He wondered where Humphrey was. He was confident that Colette was safely ensconced in the Beatenbow wagon, which was protected by four other wagons between it and the herd.

It seemed to Finch that he had been under the wagon a long time when he detected the sound of the herd diminishing. He breathed a sigh of relief as he realized the cattle were running parallel to the wagons and not toward camp. He quickly extricated himself from the mire and crawled out. As he stood up, he was grateful for the rain that was washing away some of the grime. He looked about and was astonished to see a rider crossing the creek from the direction of the herd. In the flare of the lightning, he recognized Humphrey. Finch ran toward him, and Old Heck shied at his flapping slicker.

"Hump, what in hell are you doin?" he yelled as loudly as he could, but Humphrey could not hear him. He rode on past, stopped at his wagon, tied Old Heck to a wheel, and crawled inside. Finch followed.

"What on earth were you doin?" Finch yelled again and suddenly realized that his voice was too loud inside the wagon. He lowered his voice, but still had almost to shout. "What were you doin' across that creek?" Finch repeated almost angrily.

"Tryin' to help the boys with the cattle," he shouted back. "But they was too far gone for me to catch 'em."

"You were what?" Finch yelled incredulously.

"Tryin' to help with the herd," Humphrey shouted. "They was too far away for me to catch 'em."

Finch started to say something, but then shook his head in amazed resignation. He heaved a great sigh of relief and sat back against the sideboard of the wagon.

Colette, who had been sitting with a quilt wrapped around her, crawled up to them. She did not try to speak, for the thunder would drown her out. The three of them sat for several minutes; then the rain began to lessen, the thunder moving to the northeast. Finally there was only a steady patter of rain on the canvas above.

"I'll light a lamp," Colette said when she could be heard.

Humphrey nodded. Finch looked as Colette struck the match. The quilt slipped off her shoulders, and Finch glimpsed one of her cherry red nipples as she lit the lamp. He felt as if a mule had kicked him in the chest. He quickly averted his eyes.

"I better go check on things," he said hoarsely and left the wagon. Humphrey followed him.

\* \* \* \* \* \*

A careful survey of the camp indicated that no damage of any consequence had been done. Kate and the other women cooks had put their cooking gear away the night before as Kate had ordered that they do when they started the trip. The mud was deep, however, and Sam had trouble building fires for the cooks. Finch rode to the lightning struck cottonwood that was still smoldering inside the bigger limbs. He threw his rope around some of them and dragged them back to camp, and soon the cooking fires were blazing cheerfully.

All of the Negroes were barefoot as they waded in the mud. Kate served breakfast inside the Beatenbow wagon, electing not to set the table in the mud.

"How is Ellie this morning?" Colette asked anxiously.

"I think she some better this mornin' Miss Colette," Kate said. "She et a bit or two of mush this mornin' but she still don' talk none. All that lightnin' and thunder last night perked her up a mite, seems like."

"I'm so glad," Colette said sympathetically. "I'll come over and see her as soon as we finish breakfast."

"She like dat," Kate said. "She always think yo de greates' lady dey is."

Colette was quiet through breakfast as Finch and Humphrey discussed the procedure for the day.

"We can get as far as the Pease River today if that creek goes down enough for us to cross pretty soon," Finch said.

"What about the cattle?" Humphrey asked.

"Clem and the boys will be with them where they stopped runnin', and they'll head 'em back this way. The cook has already packed up and pulled out. He knows the way to go, and the herd will finally catch up with him."

"You aren't even going to look for them?" Colette asked in surprise.

"No use," Finch answered without looking at her. "The cowboys will have them headed back this way by now, and Clem will be so aggravated that he'll push them to the limit. But I'm glad they ran while the herd was still small. We'll lose a lot of 'em and Clem won't waste much time gatherin' up the ones that are scattered. He knows that they can pick up all they can drive when we get to the valley. And after that run last night and a long, hard drive today, we ought to have a pretty gentle herd to build on when we get to the valley."

"He won't try to get 'em all?" Humphrey asked.

"No. He will just pick up the biggest bunch he can find and head back. Tryin' to gather all of those that scattered would take too much time, and he knows that his chuck wagon and our caravan will be headin' for the Pease. It'll be late when he gets in tonight, but I'd gamble that he makes it before midnight."

"Those poor cowboys will be starved," Colette said sympathetically.

"And the cattle will be dog tired, too," Finch agreed. "But the cowboys have had to do without before, and they can do it again. Fact is, all of them carry some hard tack and jerky in their saddle bags, anyway. What they will miss most is hot coffee."

"You figger they'll lose some cattle?" Humphrey queried.

"Sure to!" Finch answered cryptically. "If those were the only cattle we had, or could get, the boys would ride all the draws and creeks, and would bring most of 'em back to the main herd, but that would take several days, and they know we can pick up all we need further on."

"What if there ain't enough cattle in that valley?" Humphrey fretted.

"There will be," Finch said with conviction. "I've never been through there without seein' plenty of 'em. The grass is good too; so they ought to be in better shape than the ones we've got."

\* \* \* \* \* \*

The sun came out bright and hot. Steam rose from the canvas wagon tops. Finch mounted his horse and rode across the creek. He returned to inform Humphrey that they could probably cross now, but that in another hour the stream would be a lot lower. He suggested that they wait.

"Jist as well," Humphrey was unperturbed. "We got a few repairs that can be made. I'll get Largo and some of the other blacks started on 'em right now."

Humphrey directed the blacks in making some minor repairs, while Colette went to see about Ellie. She was pleasantly surprised to find that the little Negro girl seemed much improved. She even smiled a tiny bit and attempted to say something when Colette rubbed her face gently with the soothing ointment.

"She's much better, Kate," Colette said brightly.

"Sho is," Kate agreed. "That's the first time she's tried to talk, and her face ain't swole so bad. But her little pussy is tore some, an' it's gonna be awful sore for a few days. Jus' hope that rotten nigger didn't get her knocked up. I'd sho hate to have any o' his filthy blood in my family."

Colette did not answer Kate, but she was familiar with the terms that she so often heard the slaves use. She patted Ellie's shoulder and said, "You're going to be fine, Ellie. And as soon as you are feeling better, maybe you can ride on our wagon some with me when Mr. Beatenbow is riding his horse and Sam is driving for me."

Ellie smiled weakly and reached out a small hand to Colette who grasped it with one hand and patted it gently with the other. "I'll be back again soon," she promised as she took her leave.

\* \* \* \* \* \*

An hour later Finch announced that they could cross the creek at any time. The Negro horse herders quickly caught and harnessed the mules. After they were hitched, Largo went to get the jackass, that had been tethered by a long rope where he could graze, and tied him to the back of the wagon.

"I expect your wagon ought to try it first, Hump," Finch said. "I'm pretty sure we can make it all right, but maybe you ought to drive. I'll ride along, just in case."

"I think you are right," Humphrey agreed and dismounted to tie Old Heck to the back of the wagon. "Sam, you go on back and drive your own wagon. Kate and Ellie would like that anyway."

Humphrey mounted the wagon, sat beside Colette, and then paused and looked at Finch.

"You reckon Colette ought to ride a horse across? I'd shore hate for her to be in this wagon if it topples over."

Finch frowned thoughtfully for a moment. "The remuda has already crossed over down below, and we don't have an extra horse she can ride. Would Old Heck be all right, do you think?"

"He ain't no woman's horse!" Humphrey objected.

"Well, I'll ride him, and Colette can ride this one. He's easy to handle."

"Tell you what!" Humphrey solved the problem quickly. "Let Colette ride behind you. I'd feel a lot better about it that way, anyhow."

Finch started to make an objection but was interrupted by Colette. "I'll get a pair of trousers on and be with you in a minute," she said pertly as she disappeared into the wagon.

Finch felt both exhilaration and dread at the proposal of Colette's riding with him, and he did not hear a word that Humphrey said in the short interval until Colette appeared.

"He's gentle, isn't he?" Colette asked as she walked up to Finch's sorrel.

"He's gentle." Finch held out his hand and removed his left foot from the stirrup. Colette grasped his hand, placed her small foot in the stirrup, and was seated behind Finch before he knew it. She placed both arms around Finch's lank middle and locked her hands in front.

"Let's be careful," she breathed. "I've already had one bath this morning, and I don't need another."

Finch merely nodded and gulped. He was acutely aware of her arms about him and her hard breasts against his back.

"All set?" Humphrey asked.

"All set," Colette replied gaily. Finch only nodded.

Afterward Finch could remember nothing about the crossing except that Colette stayed mounted behind him until all the wagons had crossed. Largo's wagon was the last. The jackass balked at the edge of the creek and was pulled from his feet. He was under water until he was midway across; then by chance he regained his feet, only to pull back as hard as he could; he shook his head and snorted angrily.

When Colette finally dismounted and returned to the wagon, Finch's back felt naked and cold. For just an instant before she slid off his horse, Finch thought that she squeezed him just a bit harder than necessary, but he dismissed the idea immediately and turned his horse away quickly lest she, or Humphrey, noticed the bulge in his pants caused by an involuntary and unwanted erection.

"I sure don't have much sense," he thought savagely to himself.

\* \* \* \* \* \*

It was after sundown when they reached the Pease River. The cowboy chuck wagon was already there, and the cook had a fire going. There was no sign of the herd. The caravan pulled in near the river a distance upstream of the cowboy wagon. Finch felt that it would be unnecessarily dangerous to try to cross the wagons so late in the evening.

They ate supper; then Colette, Humphrey, and Finch sat in the Beatenbow wagon and talked until almost midnight. Finch had been in his bedroll only a few minutes, when, with his head close to the ground, he thought he could hear a slight rumble in the distance. He quickly donned his clothes, mounted his night horse, and rode toward the sound. He was only a few minutes away from camp when he spied the moving herd in the dim light of the half-moon and starry sky. He circled and came up to the herd from the rear and was astonished to see two black riders trailing along behind. They were still riding with out saddles.

Finch rode closer and asked where Clem was.

"Massa Clem, he ridin' point," the Negro answered in his newly learned cowboy lingo.

Finch rode well away from the herd, although they were walking laboriously as if near exhaustion, which they were.

When Finch found Clem, he rode alongside of him.

"How much further is it?" Clem asked tiredly.

"Not more'n a couple of miles," Finch said. "Your wagon and the caravan are both camped on this side of the river. It's up some, and we got in late, so I didn't want to cross tonight."

"Well, we're gonna cross these here cattle tonight!" Clem said adamantly. "I don't care if half the aggravatin' sons-o'-bitches drown. I ain't gonna let 'em stay on the same side of the river with them wagons. Besides, they is enough light with that moon tonight."

"They look too tired to run," Finch observed.

"They're damn near dead," Clem admitted. "They musta run eight or ten miles."

"Have much trouble startin' 'em back?" Finch asked conversationally.

"Not too much," Clem said glumly. "But we lost a man."

"Who?"

"Buck Favers."

"How?"

"Horse stepped in a hole."

Finch did not ask any more questions, for he knew only too well the gruesome consequences of a man and horse going down in front of a stampeding herd of frightened cattle. Finally he asked, "You want me to send some niggers back to bury him?"

"Wasn't nothing much left to bury," Clem said grimly. "What little they was we took care of the best we could. Didn't even bring his saddle back. Them damn cattle got feet like butcher knives."

They did not speak again for several minutes, each lost in his own thoughts. "Tell you one thing," Clem finally broke the silence. "Them two niggers of Beatenbow's shore was a help. The crazy bastards rode like regular cowhands, and with only them surcingles. I'm beginnin' to think a nigger ain't the dumb animal I once thought."

"They've surprised me some, too," Finch admitted.

When they neared the river, Clem asked Finch, "Reckon you could help us some to start these cattle across? Yore hoss is fresh."

"I'll help," Finch said. "Where do you want me?"

"You ride over to the other side and tell one of the wing men to drop back of 'em and then start pushn' 'em in close together. I'll do the same on this side. I'd like to have 'em in kind of a point when we get to the river. And when we do, you and me'll ride right into 'em afore they stop. Yell like hell till the first ones get in the water, and I'll do the same thing. Shoot off your pistol if you have to."

Finch nodded his understanding and loped to the other side of the herd. When they neared the river, both Clem and Finch rode their horses into the point of the leading cattle and started yelling. The leading bull hesitated only momentarily at the river bank; Clem charged his horse at him and leaned over to whack him on the back with his coiled rope as he yelled. The bull plunged in and was immediately followed by others. Clem and Finch rode alongside the leading cattle as they crossed. The cattle and horses had to swim only a short distance near the middle of the river.

In less than twenty minutes, the herd had crossed; the cowboys pushed them away from the river onto a large meadow. Most of the cattle lay down almost immediately.

Humphrey and Largo joined the cowboys as soon as they were across. "Clem," Finch said, "you and the boys go and get some hot coffee. Hump and Largo and I can night guard until you get back."

"That'd sure suit the boys," Clem said gratefully. "And me too. Jist hope that one-eyed cook has got coffee hot. If he ain't I won't even try to keep 'em from hangin' 'im."

# Chapter 14

The Big Dipper told Finch that it was after three o'clock the next morning when four of the cowboys came to relieve them. "How did they bed last night?" asked the first rider that approached.

"Like a bunch of sheep," Finch said. "Didn't even get up to stretch."

"Likely they're as give out as we are," the cowboy surmised. "Shore much obliged to you fellers for takin' our watch."

"We are still doin' fine," Humphrey said as he rode up. "Why don't you boys go on back and get some more rest."

"Nope," the cowboy answered firmly. "We got our bellies full of bacon and beans and coffee now; so we're good for the day. I don't expect them cattle to move very early, and then they're goin' to travel slow."

"All right," Finch agreed. "Just keep 'em headed northwest. We ought to reach the Red River valley in three more days—four at most."

The cowboy touched the brim of his hat as they rode away. They went only a short distance when the cowboy loped back to them. "Thought you might like to know—we found a shallow place to ford the river just down from our chuck wagon."

"How shallow?" Finch asked.

"Won't have to swim any, and the wagons ought to be able to cross without puttin' any logs on 'em to float. But it's pretty swift."

"That's good news," Finch replied with some relief, for he had been concerned that they would have to cut big cottonwood logs and fasten them to the wagons in order to keep them floating high enough to keep the gear and possessions dry.

When they returned to the caravan, they found that Sam was already building a fire and that Kate was rustling about in the supply wagon.

"I reckon there isn't much use to go to bed now," Finch said. "I think I'll ride down and check that crossing he told us about."

"All right, Finch," said Humphrey. "I'll wake Colette up. She's gonna want to know everything anyway."

"I'll go along with yo, Mars Finch, if that be all right with yo," Largo said.

Finch nodded assent, and they rode down the river. Finch noted that Largo was still riding Chico's saddle. He sighed and thought to himself that Chico would be pleased. That happy little Mexican was color-blind as far as people were concerned, and besides, Largo was a good horseman. He had probably learned that when he was in the army with Humphrey.

They found the crossing and rode across two or three times.

"Looks all right," Finch pronounced.

"It do," agreed Largo. "But we needs to keep ever thin' twixt them two big rocks a stickin' up out there. They is a big drop off if we gits very far down river of 'em."

They returned to camp to find that Kate had coffee boiling. Humphrey and Colette were sipping the steaming liquid. Colette looked as fresh as one of the wild flowers that were peeking out of their winter beds. She greeted them warmly.

"Here's yo coffee, Mars Finch." Kate handed him a cup. "Yo wants a cup, Largo?"

"Yassum, I'd sho like dat if it be all right," He looked at Humphrey.

"Of course, it's all right, Largo," Colette said quickly, and she poured a cup and handed it to him. Humphrey looked at her with a slight frown, but said nothing.

"Might as well get everybody up, I reckon," Humphrey said. "I know they're tired. Ever'body is. But if we get an early start, we can get to the next camp early this afternoon and get a good rest. The cattle are goin' to travel slow today."

"You roust them lazy niggers out, Largo!" Kate echoed Humphrey's order. "Tell 'em to get a movin'. Then yo kin come back here and set up that little table yo built for these white folks to eat on."

"Yassum!" Largo grinned and drained his cup.

Everything was in order by the time the sun was up. Finch looked across the river to see that the cattle were moving slowly northwest, grazing as they went.

"It's a good thing our next camp isn't too far," Finch smiled as he watched the herd. "That sure is one tired bunch of cattle."

"You think that crossing is all right?" Humphrey asked.

"I think so," Finch said. "Largo and I rode across it several times. We'll get Largo to ride ahead of the wagons as we cross, and I'll ride along side. The water is swift, but it's not too deep if we follow Largo. Won't get up in the wagon beds."

They pulled out and drove to the crossing. The horse herders drove the remuda across first as Finch watched carefully. A few of the horses slipped into the deep water that Largo had warned about and had to swim for a few yards, but they all got safely across.

"Now, Hump, you follow Largo with your wagon, and you ought not to have a bit of trouble."

"All right with you if Colette rides behind you again? That water is mighty swift, and some of them horses went under when they got out of line a little."

Finch started to voice an objection and assure Humphrey that it was perfectly safe when Colette interjected, "You don't mind, do you Finch? I've already got my riding pants on." She stood up to show him.

"You'd be just as safe on the wagon," Finch protested lamely.

"But I wouldn't feel as safe," Colette said as she dropped down from the wagon. Finch just gulped, removed his foot from the stirrup, and reached for Colette's hand. Finch felt a warm sensation as their hands met. Colette felt it too and paused just an instant and looked up at Finch with startled eyes; then she nimbly mounted behind him and wrapped her arms about his waist.

Largo led off, and Humphrey followed closely. His wagon crossed without incident, Colette and Finch riding alongside but to the rear. Finch did not want Humphrey to even suspect what was happening to him, but with some feral instinct, he knew that Colette was aware of it. She held on to him tightly as they crossed, and again her breasts pushed against his back, and he felt the heat go through him. Humphrey pulled his wagon away from the river in order to make room for the others. Finch stopped his horse as soon as they reached the bank and turned to watch the other wagons as they started crossing.

Colette hugged him tightly for a moment and whispered softly, "I'm sorry, Finch. I didn't realize—I mean, I didn't intend—" She was suddenly at a loss for words. "I just wish that, oh darn!" she exclaimed in exasperation and hugged him about the waist. "I won't make it happen again!" With that she quickly dismounted and walked rapidly toward her wagon.

Finch did not reply, nor did he look around as she dismounted and walked away. He breathed a sigh of relief when the last wagon had crossed and his unruly emotions were again under control.

\* \* \* \* \* \*

Old Heck had regained most of his strength and was becoming fiery again; so Humphrey saddled him. "Thought I'd ride him today. He's gettin' pretty studdy again, and Colette says she wants to ride the wagon today. Sam will drive it."

"Good!" Finch approved. "We can sure use another man today. We're gettin' farther and farther into Indian country, and we've got to be mighty careful. So if you're gonna ride anyway, why don't you scout to the northeast. Buff is hunting out to the southwest. Doubt if anything will come up from behind because the herd will be back there. But, just in case, Largo can trail behind a half mile or so. I'll scout on ahead and wait at a camping place."

Humphrey agreed, and Finch rode back to instruct Largo. Then he loped on ahead of the wagons. Colette watched with troubled eyes his tall, graceful figure that seemed to flow with the horse's movement, until he was out of sight.

"When she could no longer see him, she sighed deeply. "Oh, I wish I could talk to Mama." She was not aware that she had spoken aloud.

"What say, Miss Colette?" Sam asked curiously.

"Oh, nothing, Sam. I was just talking to myself," Colette answered almost crossly. Then she did talk to herself, but not aloud. "I wish I could talk to you, Mama, because you are so wise, and you know about men—and women too! I know that a women shouldn't love any man but her own husband. But—is it possible to love two men at the same time?" She wondered desperately, for she admitted to herself that her feeling for Fauntleroy Finch was not in the least platonic. She had first felt the animal magnetism of Finch when she saw him accost the would-be robbers in Fort Worth, and she had basked in her hidden passion, blissfully unaware that she had affected Finch as deeply. The first startling realization had come to her when she had her arms around his waist as they crossed the river. She had felt the fierce passion that flowed between them, and deep in her secret heart, she could not wish that it were not so.

The morning dragged interminably. She wanted to see Finch, and she wanted to see Humphrey. And yet, she almost dreaded to see either of them. "Oh, darn!" she thought in desperate frustration. "I wish I could handle my silly heart like Finch does his pistol."

Humphrey came back about an hour before they were to reach camp.

"No sight of any humans. Seen a lot of buffalo, and some cattle and deer. Largo come in yet?"

"I haven't seen him," Colette said. "Was the country pretty where you rode?"

"Just about like what you been comin' over," he said, and Colette was surprised that she had not even noticed the landscape as they rode. She had never failed to do so before.

"Will we reach camp soon? It's still early, isn't it?"

"About an hour, I reckon. Won't hurt us to get in early, today anyway. I don't expect the herd will get in afore dark, though. Them cattle is sure tired out."

Colette was almost surprised that Humphrey did not read her guilty feeling, and she talked animatedly as they rode, as if to shield her hidden emotions.

"There's Finch," Humphrey pointed a few minutes later. Colette had already spied him but did not mention it. She looked where Humphrey pointed and could see Finch slumped dejectedly on his horse. He looked so forlorn that Colette wanted to run to him.

"He said we'd have a good camp tonight." Humphrey was completely oblivious to Colette's inner turmoil. "Hope he's right about that."

"He always is," Colette said brightly.

Finch rode slowly toward them as they progressed and fell in beside Humphrey as they continued on their way. He did not look at Colette, and she seemed to be preoccupied with the scenery.

"Good camp?" Humphrey asked.

Finch nodded. "Just like I remembered it—a good stream of water and plenty of grass."

"Good," Humphrey replied with satisfaction.

\* \* \* \* \* \*

The camp was as good as Finch had said. A small creek flowed lazily through a clump of trees, and there was good grass all around. The camp was set up by mid-afternoon. The blacks entertained themselves by playing some sort of game in a flat area nearby. Their shouts and laughter lent a festive air to the scene.

Humphrey declared that he was going to take a nap, for he had lost a lot of sleep the night before. So had Finch, but he did not feel like sleeping.

"I'd like to take a nice, long walk," Colette said wistfully.

Humphrey and Finch voiced objection simultaneously. Finch quickly clamped his jaws shut as Humphrey repeated his statement that was garbled when he and Finch were speaking at the same time.

"Now, Colette, you know better than that," he said crossly. "Remember what Finch and Buff both said about women and kids being away from the wagons."

"Oh, I know. And I'm not going to take a walk. I just said I would like to."

"Wake me up for supper," Humphrey said as he climbed into the wagon.

There was a long silence after he went inside. Finch and Colette did not look at each other.

"I reckon I'd better go check out my bedroll," Finch said awkwardly. Colette only nodded, and Finch walked away.

Colette sat on the wagon tongue for a long time and stared into space. The sun was warm, the camp was perfect, and she should have been at peace with the world, but she was not. Finally, she stood up as if she had reached a decision.

Finch was sitting on his bedroll a hundred yards away and saw her immediately as her long, graceful legs bore her in his direction. He watched as she drew closer. She was as graceful as a young fawn, and she seemed totally unaware of her startling beauty. Finch did not move from his sitting position. She stopped only a few feet away and looked down at him with eyes as black as onyx and as smoldering as a banked camp fire. Their eyes met for a long few seconds. Then Colette asked, "May I sit with you for a while?"

Finch did not reply but slid over on his bedroll to make room for her. She sat. For several minutes there was complete silence between them, but it was not a comfortable silence. Each felt the profound poignancy of the moment. Finally, Colette broke the silence.

"Finch?" she queried tentatively.

Finch cleared his throat a couple of times before he responded hoarsely, "What, Colette?"

"Can we ever be friends again?" There was a pleading note in her voice.

"I thought we were friends," Finch said evasively.

"You know what I mean," she said evenly. "Can we ever be like we were before we crossed that river today?"

Finch was silent for some time before he replied. "I wasn't any different after we crossed that stream today than I have been ever since I saw you the first time back in Fort Worth."

"Neither was I," admitted Colette. "But I just wouldn't admit it even to myself until today when I felt you—I mean. You know what I mean!" she said almost angrily.

"I reckon I do, Colette," Finch answered. "And I know it won't work. Humphrey—"

"Humphrey Beatenbow is my husband," she said firmly. "And I love him. I've loved him since I was ten years old. He's a fine person, and I never would hurt him intentionally. I'm just a silly woman that can't make her heart behave. I guess I'm just not like other women. They seem to be able to love just one man. And I'm ashamed!" she gasped and choked back a sob. Finch reached over and covered her hand with his.

"Don't be ashamed, Colette," he said softly. "Don't ever be ashamed. It's not your fault."

"Well, it isn't yours!" she said with some fire.

"It isn't anybody's fault," Finch said sternly. "I reckon neither one of us wanted it to happen. But I feel sort of guilty every time I see you and Hump together."

"Well, let me tell you something, Mr. Fauntleroy Finch!" she said fiercely as she squeezed his hand hard. "Father always said that Mama and I were too outspoken, and that it wasn't becoming for ladies to talk the way we sometimes did. He is English, and she is French, you know. And I'm sure he would not approve in the least what I am going to say now—"

"Go ahead," Finch said huskily.

"All right," she said almost defiantly. "I would like nothing better right now than to pull off all my clothes and crawl into that bedroll with you. And I know now that I've wanted that since I first saw you—So you don't have to feel guilty in the least. And you can always have all of me except what I would like to give you most!"

"I reckon I've got that part of you I want most, Colette," Finch said warmly. "I guess I'd rather have you to—have you think of me as you do than anything you could give me."

"You really mean that, don't you, Finch?" Colette said almost in disbelief.

"Yes, I do. And that doesn't mean that I would not like to have all of you. It just means that I've got the part of you that I want most. And it makes me proud!"

Colette suddenly broke into tears and sobbed for several minutes.

"Let me answer your first question, Colette," Finch said quietly.

Colette stopped crying and looked almost fearfully at him with her large, tear filled eyes. "I don't even remember what it was," she laughed and cried at the same time.

"You asked if we could ever be friends again like we first were."

Colette nodded but said nothing.

"Well, the answer is, that I doubt it. But we can sure as hell try—and we'd better do a good job of it, or the rest of this trip won't be much fun, and it'll be pure torture when we get to our ranch."

"Oh, let's do!" Colette exclaimed as she dried her eyes. "And let's have a lot of fun the rest of the trip and after the trip is over, too."

"Well," Finch took a deep breath and said, "I feel better, anyway. And I hope you do, too."

"I do!" Colette said almost gaily. "I think I would like to run and play like the blacks are doing."

"How about taking that walk that you were wanting to take, instead?"

"Oh, I would love that!" Colette's eyes were shining again and not with tears. "But you and Humphrey said it wouldn't be safe, remember?"

"I reckon it wouldn't be too dangerous if I walk with you," Finch grinned.

"Well, come on!" Colette exclaimed eagerly as she jumped up, grabbed his hand, and pulled him to his feet.

They did take a walk up the river and talked animatedly of trivial things. Colette's long stride almost matched his. Finch said, "I expect we've gone far enough. We need to get back anyway. Buff will be coming in with meat pretty soon."

"All right, help me over this log first." Finch reached for her hand and helped her across. "Humphrey should be awake by now."

"Hope he doesn't notice anything," Finch said.

"He won't, Colette assured him. "Humphrey is not as sensitive to others as we are." And then she added teasingly, "He didn't even notice that bulge in your pants when we crossed the river today."

Finch gaped at her in astonishment. "You are a regular little devil, Colette Beatenbow. If I wasn't a gentleman, I'd slap you on that sumptuous rear of yours."

"And I would enjoy it," she laughed delightedly and ran ahead of him to the wagons.

Buff was unloading fresh game when Finch arrived. "How did the hunt go, Buff?" Finch asked in what he hoped was a normal voice.

"Got a couple of young buffler heifers and a fat deer."

"Why heifers, Buff?" Colette asked as she walked up. "Are they more tender?"

"Aye, lass, that be true. And today I could pick and choose. They was lots of game to be had."

He looked at Colette and Finch keenly, and his small blue eyes twinkled. "What you two been up to?" he asked jovially. "Look like the blarney stone kissed you, begorra."

Humphrey walked up, still yawning from his nap. "Looks like you had a good hunt today, Buff."

"Sure, and I did that. Didn't see no Indian sign either."

"Well we ought to have a good camp tonight," Humphrey said practically. "Just hope the herd gets in before too late."

"Who is that on the horse back there?" Colette pointed to a rider circling playfully on a horse back of the wagons. The rider was young and laughing. They all looked.

"God-a-mighty!" Humphrey exclaimed in awe. "That's Trey."

"The broke legged nigger?" Buff asked.

"I saw Largo boost him up on that horse a minute ago."

"It's him, all right," Buff said. "You can see that wrapped up leg a stickin' out!"

"Well," Humphrey said gruffly. "He ain't gonna get no more of my whiskey if he breaks both legs."

\* \* \* \* \* \*

Supper that night was a pleasant affair. Both Colette and Finch were more at ease than they had been. Humphrey was his usual serious self.

"Hope that herd gets here afore too late. Does Clem know whether the man that got killed in that stampede had any folks or not?"

Finch shook his head negatively. "Clem doesn't know, but one of the men found a letter in the saddlebag that wasn't plumb ruined."

"Find out, if you can," Humphrey said. "And I'll send his folks some money if he's got any folks."

"I'll do that," Finch said. "Now, I reckon I'll ride back a ways and meet the herd and help bring 'em in. You got the guards all posted?"

"Doubled as usual," Humphrey assured him.

"You all get a good night's rest," Finch said as he mounted his horse and rode in the direction of the oncoming herd.

# Chapter 15

It was after midnight when the herd arrived. Colette and Humphrey did not get up. Finch rolled into his blankets just as the caravan guards were changing. He was asleep almost instantly and did not awaken until daylight.

Breakfast was again a pleasant meal. Kate served bacon, hot biscuits, prunes, and gravy. Conversation was light and without tension between Finch and Colette.

"I'm gonna get an early start today," Finch said. "I'm afraid we may have to make another dry camp tonight."

"We managed the first one all right," Humphrey said matter of factly. "I reckon another one won't hurt. I just hope that cowboy cook fills his water barrel this morning."

"Not much chance of him forgetting again!" Finch grinned. "Those cowboys ran him ragged about it the last time."

"When do you think we will get to the Red River valley?" Colette asked.

"I think maybe we could make it the day after tomorrow if I can find water for the cattle. If not, it will slow us down again."

The cattle were grazing their way when Finch left. He felt immeasurably better since his talk with Colette and no longer harbored the heavy guilty feeling that had been plaguing him.

He kept a sharp lookout for Indians as he rode and did see a small band travelling southwest, but it did not look like a war party. Nevertheless, he hoped that they did not spot Buff who was hunting in that direction.

The first creek he came to was dry. He rode down it for a couple of miles and discovered a small pond formed by a natural dam. He judged that there was enough water in it for the remuda and the herd; so he turned back and loped up to the Beatenbow wagon. He told them what he had found and instructed Humphrey to veer his wagon just a bit to the right so he would find the pond.

"I think there's enough water in it for the remuda and herd, but it's muddy. We've got enough water on your wagon, and the niggers have all got barrels; so we will make it all right. Soon as you get there, let the horses and mules water. I'll ride on back and tell Clem."

Humphrey nodded his assent, and Colette said nothing as Finch loped away. She turned to watch him and marvelled, as always, at the astonishing grace with which he sat his horse.

"Think a lot of Finch, don't you, wife," Humphrey said.

Colette was startled by Humphrey's question, but was relieved to detect not the least trace of hidden meaning in his words.

"You know I do, darling," she said complacently. "I think we were the luckiest people who ever came out west when we met him."

"So do I," Humphrey said quietly. "For a lot of reasons. I wouldn't be alive now if he hadn't shot them two men in Fort Worth. And it was only a chance in a million that we met a man with land right in the middle of Indian country."

"We must be travelling under a lucky star!" Colette said fervently.

"We shore must be," Humphrey admitted. "And we'd never have got this far if it hadn't been for Finch. He's been doin' a lot of scoutin' and directin' the guards that we didn't even know about. And Buff has been a big help, too. I doubt if we could have found a better cowman than Clem. And the blacks have turned out even better than I thought they would." Humphrey paused. "Wife, I reckon we've got just about the best crew that ever come out west of Fort Worth."

"Oh, we have," enthused Colette. "And I can't wait to see our ranch!"

"Me neither," Humphrey said with more enthusiasm than he usually displayed.

"Humphrey?"

"What, wife?"

"I've been wanting to ask you something ever since we met the Comancheros and Indians."

"Go ahead and ask."

Colette hesitated, then blurted the question. "Did you shoot that man's horse deliberately so the Indians would catch him?"

"I did," he answered grimly. "And if the Apaches hadn't stopped and picked him up, I'd of shot him. That man hadn't the right to live after what he done to Chico. Besides, I just saved Finch the job."

"He must have met a horrible death," Colette said in a small voice.

"I shore hope so," Humphrey declared. Then he sought to divert her thoughts to more pleasant things. "I reckon this country is about as pretty as any we've seen."

"It is beautiful," conceded Colette. "But I'll bet the Red River valley and our ranch are prettier."

"I'll bet they are too, wife," Humphrey declared. "We're gonna grow with this western country."

"And we're going to have a marvelous life while we are doing it!" enthused Colette.

\* \* \* \* \* \*

The camp that night was not at all inconvenient. The remuda drank their fill, and by the time the herd got there, a lot of the mud stirred up by the horses had again sunk to the bottom. Clem let the cattle drink and then hazed them a good distance from the caravan to bed down. He then rode to the Beatenbow wagon as Finch, Colette, and Humphrey were drinking after supper coffee.

"Get down and pull up a chair, Clem" Humphrey invited.

"Don't mind if I do." Clem accepted with alacrity. "That nigger of yores does make a good cup of coffee."

"Your cook didn't forget to fill his barrel again, did he?" Finch asked with a grin, and Clem returned the grin.

"He shore didn't, and I don't reckon he ever will again, but the coffee he makes would float a horseshoe."

"Why don't you tell him to put more water in it, or less coffee?" Colette asked innocently.

"We-l-l. I tell you, Mrs. Beatenbow. Cowboy cooks jus' don't take kindly to nobody tellin' 'em how to do their job," Clem said sheepishly. "He ain't the best I ever seen, but he shore beats none at all."

"Would he quit?" Colette was incredulous.

"In a minnit!" Clem answered with conviction. "And he'd probably take the chuck wagon and a bunch of bedrolls with him."

"Well," Colette started to say something, but changed her mind. "I guess I just don't know much about cowboys."

"Finch," Clem turned from Colette. "How much farther to the valley?"

"Two easy day's drive," Finch answered, "or one real hard day."

"Then let's make it 'one hard day'," Clem said. "Most of our horses is about tuckered out. And I'd like to get there with the herd as tired as possible."

"That's fine with me," Finch agreed. "How about you, Hump?"

"We can shore make it if Clem and the cattle can," Humphrey said. "Fact is, I reckon all of us are lookin' forward to stoppin' a few days."

"All right," Finch said. "I'll ride out earlier and faster than usual in the morning, and by the time you all get there, I'll have us a good campsite staked out."

"Good," Clem said as he set his cup down firmly. Then without another word he mounted his horse and rode away.

* * * * * *

Finch rode out at dawn. A few minutes later the herd was started, and an hour later the caravan began to move.

It was the hardest day's drive of the entire trip, and many smaller calves and some of the older cows dropped by the wayside. "Let 'im be," Clem ordered. "They is plenty more in the valley, and if a calf drops out, let his mammy stay with it."

For the first time on the drive the cowboys pushed the cattle hard. The two Negro drag riders were so covered with dirt that one could not tell what color their skins were. They still rode with the surcingles.

Finch was waiting on the valley's rim when the caravan arrived. Humphrey pulled up to him and stopped.

"Well, there it is—the Red River valley." He grinned and waved his arm both east and west. Colette gasped. As far as the eye could see to the west, the grass was green, and thousands of animals of various kinds were grazing contentedly. The scene was almost unbelievably beautiful. Colette feasted her beauty-hungry eyes on it for several minutes. Humphrey said nothing as he too looked at the grand vista before them.

"It's absolutely beautiful," Colette said in a hushed voice.

"Only one place I ever saw that is prettier," Finch agreed.

"Where on earth could that be?" she asked.

"Our ranch, wife," Humphrey chuckled, and Finch laughed aloud.

"He's right, Colette," Finch still smiled. "This is only the second prettiest place in the world!"

"Then our ranch must be an Eden!" she exclaimed.

"You got us a place to camp, Finch?" Humphrey asked.

"Sure have," Finch informed him proudly. "Best place we've had all the way. Just follow the rim west a couple of miles. I tied my bandanna on a sage brush where you can drive the wagons down the rim. When you get to the bottom, go on west just a few hundred yards till you hit a small creek, and you are there. Plenty of protection. Indians can't get to us from the top, and we can see for miles up and down this valley. There is plenty of wood on the creek to last us a month, if we want it, and grass enough to graze the stock forever."

"Sure sounds good," Humphrey said. "I reckon all the stock will enjoy the rest, and we will too. And it sure looks like you were right about the cattle. There must be a million between here and sundown." Humphrey waved westward.

"They're not all cows," Finch grinned. "I saw a lot of buffalo down there, and deer, too. And I thought I got a glimpse of a mustang about five miles west of here, but I couldn't be sure. They're wilder than deer or cattle."

"What will you be doin' while we go on ahead and make camp?"

"I'll ride back and meet the herd," Finch said. "Likely they can use the help, too. And I'd like to find Buff. That Irishman could find us all right, and he would, but maybe I can save him some time."

"Hurry on to camp," Colette said eagerly. "We will be waiting for you."

"You might ought to send a scout out a mile or two each side of camp — east and west. But I don't think the Indians are in the valley yet."

"We'll do that," Humphrey said as he started moving the wagon, and Finch started back in the direction of the herd.

\* \* \* \* \* \*

The camp was everything that Finch has said. A clear, cold stream flowed from the cliff to the south of camp. Tall, slender oak trees grew in profusion along the creek, and the grass was high and thick. Wild flowers grew in abundance.

Humphrey sent a couple of scouts out the first thing, and then began directing the Negroes in setting up a semi-permanent camp.

"Might as well make the best camp we can," he told Colette. "Finch says we may be here several days."

"Humphrey, do you think it would be safe for me to walk down in the valley a little way."

Humphrey thought for a minute before he answered. "I'm shore it would, wife. Finch said that the Indians wasn't here yet. But don't go too far and come back pretty soon."

"Oh, I will!" Colette cried ecstatically as she bounded away like a frightened deer. She ran as fast as she could until she was out of breath.

She flushed a covey of quail and two turkeys. Finally she sat and gazed with awe-filled eyes at the beauty around her. The smell of wildflowers and other vegetation enfolded her. She lay back in the grass and looked at the sky and breathed deeply. Then, after a few minutes, she sat up. The sun was still more than an hour high, and as it slowly sank, she could feel and see the subtle changes in the colors that played so gently throughout the valley. She sat for a long time just drinking in the beauty of it all. When she looked westward again, she was surprised to see that the setting sun was near the horizon. With a startled leap, she regained her feet and raced toward camp. Before she arrived, she met Humphrey.

"Where on earth have you been, wife?" Humphrey asked anxiously.

"Oh, I'm so sorry, Cheri," she said contritely. "I really didn't go far, honest. But I just sat and feasted my eyes on this beautiful land."

"Well, don't do it no more!" Humphrey said almost angrily, but with obvious relief. "At least not for so long. I was afraid an Indian buck had stole you!"

"Well, one didn't!" Colette said. "And I'm still all yours, Humphrey Beatenbow, if you will still have me."

"I reckon I'll take you back," Humphrey said facetiously. "At least for a while."

Colette and Humphrey walked into camp holding hands, and to their surprise, Finch was there.

"Where is the herd?" Humphrey asked in a worried tone.

"Those cattle just about tumbled into the valley back where I met you on the rim. They smelled that green grass. And it wasn't too rough for cattle to climb down, but a wagon would have trouble making it," Finch explained. "So Clem said they would bed them down there tonight and leave their chuck wagon on top. Buff is down there, too. He's got plenty of fresh meat. We'll bring it down in the morning. We have enough to last tonight, and tomorrow he can find plenty more. But he says he's gonna stay on top to hunt. Doesn't want to frighten these critters in the valley."

"That's good," Humphrey said. "And this camp is shore all you said it was. Couldn't be better."

"But I finally caught you in a fib, Finch," Colette teased mischievously.

"How's that?"

"You said this was the second prettiest place in the world—and I know that there couldn't be one more beautiful!"

Finch just grinned, and his face looked like that of a young boy. "You just wait, Mrs. Beatenbow," he said. "In three or four weeks from now, you're gonna take that back about me fibbin'!"

Colette laughed, and the silvery sound travelled far up and down the valley.

Supper that night was a gala affair. Kate cooked one of her very best meals, and for the first time since Ellie had been hurt, Kate called her from the wagon. "Come on out here, Ellie, honey. I've got some work fo yo to do."

Ellie peeked timidly from Kate's wagon. "Come on out here, chile," Kate ordered. "Yo mammy need yo."

Colette, Humphrey, and Finch were sitting at the table, watching and listening curiously. Ellie walked hesitantly to Kate, who paid her no mind for a moment; then she handed Ellie a plate.

"Now, tonight," Kate said, "yo gonna help me serve these white folks their meal. I been doin' it all myself, and it too much fo me."

All of them were aware that Kate, in her wisdom, was trying to bring the child back to normal.

"I been a helpin' her some, Ellie," Sam said plaintively. "But this here game leg o' mine has been actin' up again." He stretched the leg and grimaced like a wounded elf. "See how bad it hurts me. Sho will ease yo pappy if'n yo'll help out yo mammy at night."

Ellie nodded uncertainly and then looked at Kate questioningly as she held the plate.

"Go, chile. Jus march right over there and set that plate in front of Miss Colette."

"Thank you, Ellie," Colette said graciously. "That looks wonderful. Your mother is a fine cook."

The little girl smiled timidly. Her face was still swollen some, but not nearly as badly as it had been. Ellie returned to the fire where Kate had two more plates ready.

"Now you jus' put these in front of Mars Hump and Mars Finch. They is hungry. I can see that."

Ellie placed the plates in front of the men. Each thanked her and acted as if there was not a thing unusual. Kate was watching carefully and smiled broadly when Ellie had completed her chore. She started busily stirring something over the fire as Ellie turned back.

"Well now, Ellie, that shore did save yo old fat mammy some steps, and yo done right good. I reckon maybe I can finish now; so yo go on back and lay down in the waggin a while. I'll bring yo supper mighty soon.

As soon as Ellie was back in her wagon, Kate brought coffee to the table.

"She is a lot better, isn't she, Kate?" Colette said.

"Yassum. I reckon she be a lot better on the outside. She healin' mighty fast on the outside, but I reckon she still hurtin' on the inside."

"Did you use the medicine I gave you?" Colette asked.

"Yassum, I shore did, and her little pussy done most healed. Didn't hurt her there much noway. Don' figger that there dirty nigger was man enough to hurt her that way. It her min' that worry me some."

"How's that?" Humphrey asked.

"She wake up cryin' in the night. Scared cryin' — not hurtin' cryin'. And she still roll and toss in her sleep a lot."

"She'll get over that right fast, Kate," Humphrey said consolingly. "And you're doin' the right thing in gettin' her to help you. Fact is, I reckon she ort to serve us all our meals now."

"But Humphrey," Colette protested, "she will have to get up so early!"

"Give her something to think about beside what happened to her."

"I think Hump is right, Colette," Finch agreed with Humphrey.

"Kate," Humphrey called loudly. "Come over here a minute." Kate waddled back to the table.

"Kate, we've took a vote, and we think Ellie does a better job than you do of servin' us, and we want her to do it all the time."

Kate smiled widely. "Yassuh Mars Hump. I sho tell her dat. She be mighty proud." Kate made her way back to the cooking fire much more sprightly than usual.

Colette looked at Humphrey and Finch thoughtfully. "I do hate to admit that men are smarter than I am," she said. "But I guess you outdid me this time."

Ellie served them breakfast the next morning. Finch and Colette complimented her again.

"You're a big girl, Ellie, and you're sure a big help to your mama," Finch said.

"You served us nicely, Ellie," Colette said. "I think you're going to be a great help to all of us."

"No reason why she wouldn't be," Humphrey said matter of factly. "She's a Beatenbow plantation black."

Somewhat to the surprise of Colette and Finch, Ellie and Kate seemed to think Humphrey's remark more complimentary than theirs, for Ellie smiled shyly, and Kate grinned broadly. Even old Sam produced a wrinkled, toothless grin.

"Did I do all right, Mamma?" Ellie asked Kate anxiously when she had removed the plates.

"Cose yo did, chile," Kate said proudly. "Yo heard what Mars Hump said, didn't yo?"

Finch and Humphrey were still sipping coffee when Clem rode into camp.

"Light and set, Clem," Humphrey said. "The coffee's still hot."

"Hopin' it would be," Clem said and looked a bit surprised when Ellie handed him a cup.

"Everything all right with the herd?" Humphrey asked.

"That's what I came to talk to you about," Clem said. "Them cattle was damn near dead when we got 'em in this valley last night, and they shore ain't in no mood to be drove further today. They're grazin' on this grass like they had bellies as big as a wagon."

"That's good, isn't it?"

"I shore think so. And while they're grazin' a lot of wild cattle is comin' in to mix with 'em. I reckon a cow is the dumbest critter on earth, and for damn shore the stubbornest, but they are mighty social. They like to bunch together."

"Nothin' wrong with that, is there?"

"Nope. And they is a lot good about it. I figger if we'll let 'em set a day or so, a lot more wild ones will start joinin' 'em, and when they do, we'll just let 'em mosey up and down this here valley till we got all we need."

"That sounds good," Humphrey said. "We ought to be able to fill out our herd pretty fast."

Clem nodded as he swished a mouthful of coffee about in his mouth. "We shore could," he finally said. "Fact is, we could probably get all we can handle by the time we come out of the west end of this here valley. But I'm thinkin' it would be a mighty smart move if we just stayed here a few days and drove 'em a few miles ever day. Maybe just up the valley and back again. It would keep the ones we drove in used to travel, and as the wild ones join the herd, they'll get a lot of practice bein' trailed. I ain't never done nothin' like that before, but it sort of makes sense. And when we hit that plains country, we shore are gonna need them critters as trail wise as we can get 'em." He looked questioningly at Finch and Humphrey.

"Makes a lot of sense to me. What do you say, Hump?"

"Clem's the cowman," Humphrey responded. "If he says so, I'm all for it."

"Besides that, it'd give us some extra time to break in some more nigger cowboys. Damn if I don't think them two that's been ridin' drag couldn't move out to flankers and do a pretty good job."

"Well," Humphrey said. "We've got a half a dozen more that would jump at the chance."

"If they can do as well as them two that's ridin' drag now, they'd shore be a help—and we could handle a bigger herd. Just wish the black bastards would ride a saddle instead of the surcingle."

"Why?" Humphrey wanted to know.

"Well, hell!" expostulated Clem. "Because—well damned if I know why. Jus' looks sort of crazy to see cowboys trailin' a herd bareback."

Finch and Humphrey both laughed. "Clem," Finch said, "we don't care what they look like as long as they do their job ridin!"

"They're doin' that, all right," Clem admitted reluctantly.

"We'll send some more down there today," Humphrey promised. "Trey had been ridin' some just for fun, anyway."

"That's the broke legged nigger, ain't it?" Clem looked at Humphrey questioningly.

"It is. But he's been gettin' Largo to help 'im up on a horse, and he's been ridin' ever day. Told 'im he wasn't gettin' no more of my whiskey even if he broke both legs."

"Well, I shore hope he don't!" Clem said. "I damn near ruptured myself a pullin' his leg back together. But he was stickin' on that horse like a horn fly on a steer; so I reckon if that there surcingle handle don't pull off, he could ride drag. Send 'im on out."

"You boys gonna stay camped where you are?" Humphrey asked.

"Might as well. We got plenty of water and grass there. And it's a good place to camp. Some of the boys was tyin' onto cookies' wagin with their ropes when I left. We'll git the chuck wagin down all right. Then, too, we'll be movin' the cattle about ever day, up and down the valley, gatherin' more wild ones, and gettin' 'em trail broke. Probably pass below your camp several times goin' up an' back."

"Sounds good, Clem," Humphrey said.

"Only thing," Clem frowned. "Our horses is jus' about plumb played out. And we ain't got enough extras. You wouldn't let the boys ride some of them thoroughbred mares of yours, would you?"

Humphrey frowned and waited several seconds to answer. Then he said firmly. "If we need 'em to get them cows to our ranch, we'll use 'em."

"I knew you'd hate to do it," Clem said sympathetically. "But when we git on that plains country, we're gonna need a lot more horses if we can't catch some mustangs."

"Let me know if you need 'em," Humphrey said rather shortly.

Clem emptied his coffee cup, mounted, and rode away without another word.

Buff drove his wagon into camp a few minutes later. "Begorra, and it looks like ye got ye selves a mighty fine place here," he said jovially.

"It's beautiful," Colette exclaimed. "The prettiest camp we've had."

"No prettier than ye be, lass!" Buff said gallantly. "I reckon it must be sump'n in the air that makes ye face shine so bright."

"Got plenty of fresh meat, Buff?" Finch asked.

"Aye," Buff affirmed. "Plenty of buffler and deer meat, too. Ought to last ye a day or two. Dropped off some at the cowboy's camp, too."

"Good," Humphrey said. "We'll help you unload."

"Begorra and that'll shore be fine!" Buff said gratefully. "Me old back is a gettin' a little stiff from all that liftin'."

Finch and Humphrey helped Buff unload the meat and suspended it by ropes high in the oaks.

"Begorra, and I'm thinkin' ye need to hang it high," Buff panted. "All sorts of varmints in this here valley."

When the chore was finished, Finch noticed the wagon was almost filled with buffalo hides. "You've about got a load, haven't you, Buff?"

"Aye, lad, and that I have. Ye reckon I could pile 'em nearby as long as ye are camped here? My little hosses would have a tough pull gettin' this waggin up that hill loaded as it is."

"Sure can!" Humphrey said. "Fact is, we got a wagon that's most empty now. I reckon we could shift things around a little and make room for 'em in it, if you want to."

"Now that would shore be fine. I'd worry some about varmints if they be on the ground."

They loaded the hides into the wagon, and Buff said, "Well, I reckon I best be goin' back out of the valley. They's more game here than ye can find upside, but I dinna want to skeer 'em a shootin'." As he spoke, Buff cut off a huge chunk of tobacco and stuffed it in his jaw.

"Wouldn't you like to have a cup of coffee before you leave, Buff?" Colette asked.

"Bless ye, lass, and that'd shore be fine. I ain't had no woman made coffee since I left the mountains."

They repaired to the Beatenbow wagon where Ellie served them coffee. "Aye, an' ye're a fine lass," Buff said to her as she handed him his cup. She smiled shyly and hurried back to Kate.

Buff blew on the cup of coffee with gusto and drained half the cup before lowering it. He had not removed his tobacco quid from his jaw. "Whew!" he said appreciatively and then raised the cup and drained it. "Now that's what I call a mighty fine cup o' coffee. You reckon I could have another one?"

Colette looked at the big Irishman in startled disbelief. "His insides must be as tough as his outside," she thought to herself.

As soon as Buff finished his second cup, he burped and said, "Well, I reckon I'd best be on my way. I got a ways to go afore I camp tonight."

With that, he mounted his wagon and started to leave, but pulled up almost immediately and turned to them. "Ye might be a mite on the lookout for the pesky redskin, I'm a thinkin'. I cut sign a few miles southwest of here yestidy. They wasn't Apache. I know their sign. And I don't think they be Comanche. Mebbe Kiowa," he said and clucked to his horses.

There was silence as Buff pulled away. His Indian talk had sobered them all.

"Let's hook some mules to the wagon that's got those buffalo hides in it and drag it a ways from camp," Finch said when Buff was out of hearing range.

"Bless you, Fauntleroy Finch," Colette said gratefully. "I can smell them now."

# Chapter 16

As soon as Buff was gone, Humphrey went to find some of the Negroes who wanted to be cowboys. He had more volunteers than he needed.

"Largo," he said, "I want you to stay here in camp. We are goin' to need you; so you pick out six of 'em that have done the most ridin' and send 'em to the cow camp."

"Kin I go, please, Mars Hump?" Trey begged. "I been doin' a lot of ridin'. Largo, he help me on my hoss, and I's as good as anybody."

"What you gonna do with that crutch you're leanin' on?" Humphrey asked testily.

"Don't need it when I's on a hoss," Trey said confidently. "Largo, he help me up, an' they ain't nothin' a gonna get me off till I gets back here."

Humphrey scowled and then said, "Just remember what I said about no more whiskey," he said grumpily. "Help him up, Largo, and pick five more of 'em."

Humphrey turned on his heel and walked back to his wagon. "Just hope we don't get no more of 'em crippled," he said as he joined Colette and Finch.

"What are you goin' to do today, Finch?"

"Thought I'd ride west a few miles and just check out the valley."

"All right. And Finch—"

"What, Hump?"

"I reckon this'll sound like a damn fool idea to you. But I'd shore like to have the blacks dig us some more fortifications around camp. I know you ain't used to fightin' Indians that way—but it worked for us in the army, and the Indian talk of Buff's has kinda got me worried. We know that they can't hit us from the rear on account of that bluff; so we know which way they got to come from, and if we was forted up, seems to me it might be a good thing."

"Hump," Finch said seriously. "I think you have a right good idea. Fact is, the pits you had dug when the Indians hit before looked like a good idea to me. And just because we haven't done something that way before sure doesn't mean it won't work. Clem never did drive a bunch of cattle up and down a trail just for practice before either—and we both thought that was a good idea."

"Good," Humphrey said with apparent relief. "I'll get 'em started right now."

"Humphrey," Colette called after him, and he stopped and turned. "Would it be all right with you if I ride with Finch today? You're going to be busy, and I'd love to see more of the valley. And Finch says the Indians are not here yet."

Humphrey looked indecisive. "What do you think Finch?"

Finch hesitated perceptibly. He and Colette had declared a moratorium on any display of emotion, but after all—!

"I doubt if there are any Indians in the canyon. But there are a lot of other varmints."

"Human varmints?"

"I reckon not," Finch grinned.

"You haven't asked Finch yet," Humphrey said in capitulation.

"May I, Finch?" Colette asked seriously. "I promise I won't be any trouble, and I'll do what you tell me to."

"All right," Finch agreed hesitantly. "Have you got a good, gentle horse that is fast.?"

"I can ride the mare."

"That won't do," Finch said firmly. "She isn't fast enough if we need to get away from somewhere in a hurry."

"All right," Humphrey interrupted. "If it's all right with Finch, you can ride his horse, and he can ride Old Heck."

"Oh, could I? I mean, would you mind, Finch?"

"I don't mind riding the stud," Finch said, "if it's all right with Hump."

"I'd feel better if you did," Humphrey said. "You'd have two of the fastest horses anywhere if you needed 'em."

Finch saddled the horses as Humphrey went about the business of directing the blacks in digging the fortifications. When the horses were saddled, Colette mounted Finch's sorrel gelding without any trouble, but Old Heck was feeling frisky and mean. Besides, he didn't like strangers to ride him. He whirled and kicked out with both hind feet. Finch dropped his foot from the stirrup to the ground and jerked the horse about. Then he kicked him hard in the belly. "Hump ought to call him 'old nick'," Finch grinned.

"Humphrey says that he really isn't mean—just full of life," Colette assured Finch.

"He's a stud," Finch said calmly. "And you can't trust one any farther than you can trust an Indian." With that he grabbed the cheek of the bridle, crammed his left foot in the stirrup, and swung aboard as he pulled the horse's neck sharply about. Old Heck stood very still for a moment. Finch fully expected him to buck, but he simply took a deep breath as if sighing and moved out sedately.

"Oh, I'm so glad I could ride with you today, Finch," Colette exclaimed her delight. "It will be dreary around camp today with Humphrey busy all the time."

"Well," cautioned Finch. "You just keep a sharp lookout for Indian sign. And don't ride over rocky places. The sun is goin' to be warm today, and the rattlers may be comin' out of the cracks to warm up."

"How horrible!" grimaced Colette. "Just to think that there are venomous creatures in this beautiful valley."

"Well, there are," Finch said dogmatically. "And snakes aren't the only ones. There are skunks, bobcats, scorpions, mean bulls that would gut a horse with one swipe of those longhorns—and a lot of others. But worst of all, there are sometimes Indians and Comancheros."

Colette shivered. "I don't see how anyone or anything could be vile in this beautiful place."

"We'll be careful," Finch assured her. "And Hump thought it was safe, or he wouldn't have let you come. Neither would I."

Colette glanced at him quickly, but returned her eyes to the beautiful valley in which they rode. The wild flowers were rife, their tantalizing aroma wafting gently on the air. Colette breathed deeply. "I expect heaven will look and feel like this," she said thoughtfully.

Finch didn't answer. Instead, he pointed out several animals and other things that he thought might interest her. She followed his oral directions as avidly as a young child, and her face glowed with delight as they rode slowly westward. There was no artifice in Colette Beatenbow, and she seemed oblivious to her staggering natural beauty.

She was a different kind of woman than Finch had ever known before. She had a magical quality in a different and intangible way. When Finch dared look in her face, he was always enraptured by the big, wide set eyes that seemed to hold a thousand dreams. Her expression, changing constantly in her delight, always seemed free, bright, and happy, like that of a young and eager child. "And she's not much more than a child," Finch thought as he looked sideways at her radiant face. Yet, withal, there was a certain earthiness and basic intuitive perception about her that Finch found both disconcerting and beguiling. A stranger might think her much older than she actually was, if he looked only at her magnificent figure—as most men did. She was an intriguing mixture of childlike eagerness, lusty maturity, and an inborn womanly wisdom that defied understanding. Finch took a deep breath and sighed as, with an effort, he pulled his mind away from her.

"Why the sigh, Finch?" Colette grinned mischievously at him. "Are you already tired?"

"Naw," Finch drawled self-consciously. "Just helpin' myself to a big chestful of this good air."

"Me too," Colette laughed as she took a deep breath and swelled out her chest. Finch winced as he saw the hard nipples of her breasts push against her thin shirt. He immediately sought to divert his attention.

"Now, about a mile ahead of us is a box canyon on the north side. Must be nearly a half-mile long with steep cliffs on both sides. There's a spring runnin' through it, and the opening into the valley must not be more than a hundred feet wide. I lay up on a cliff one time and watched some Indians drive a bunch of buffalo into it. They blocked the entrance and rode into it, and killed every one of 'em."

"How horrible," Colette said, aghast.

"Nope," he contradicted. "They needed meat, and that's how they got it. Anyway, fifty years from now, the buffalo will be gone, according to Kit Carson."

"Gone?" Colette exclaimed. "Where?"

"There are literally millions of 'em up on the plains, and they multiply fast. In a few years, there will be so many of 'em that they will destroy the grass and die out."

"I can't imagine that."

"I can't either," Finch admitted. "But Kit is a right knowin' sort of man, and I'd bet that he's been more right than wrong."

"What will the poor Indians do? Don't they depend on the buffalo for their livelihood?"

"The Indians will be gone, too," Finch said matter of factly. "Can't say I'll be sorry, either."

Colette looked searchingly at his face. "You've had some unpleasant experiences with them, haven't you?"

Finch only nodded assent and did not answer her.

"Let's go see the box canyon, Finch," she said, attempting to get his mind off the past.

"It's a couple of miles over there," Finch warned. "You're goin' to be mighty tired when we get back to camp."

"No more than you," she said firmly. "And I want to see everything I can today. I will have to stay in camp most of the time after today, I imagine."

They turned their horses north to cross the valley. When they neared the stream that ran down the center of it, Finch pulled Old Heck up abruptly and whispered urgently. "Colette!"

She stopped the sorrel and looked at Finch. "What?" she asked in a low voice.

"Don't point, but look to your left and about a mile to the west."

"What is it?" she asked.

"Mustangs!"

"O-oh!" Colette gasped. "I see them."

"Must be a hundred of 'em," Finch said. "The breeze is blowing toward us, and they haven't spotted us yet. But they will in a minute."

They both sat very still for a long moment; then they heard a faint sound that was almost like a high pitched scream, and the herd vanished like a shadow in the sun.

"Their lookout stud either saw us or smelled us," Finch explained.

"Their lookout stud?"

"Yeah, they always have a lookout—usually the biggest and strongest of the stallions. He perches himself on high ground away from the herd while they are grazing."

"It sure didn't take them long to vanish," Colette said in awe.

"They'll be five miles from here pretty quick. You still want to see the box canyon?"

"Oh yes, yes I do!" she said enthusiastically. "But I wouldn't have missed seeing the mustangs for anything!"

A few minutes later they came to the entrance of the box canyon. A stream of clear water ran from it into the meadow below.

"It's so narrow," Colette exclaimed. "And it looks rather gloomy in there."

"It isn't," Finch assured her. "Once we get through this entrance, it widens out, and the sun shines into it for most of the day. It's a right pretty place."

"How did the Indians block the entrance?"

"They just put riders here in the mouth. And they lit some flares. When the buffalo tried to get out, they yelled and waved those flares, and the buffalo turned and ran back in."

"Well, let's go on in," Colette urged.

"Maybe we had better wait here a few minutes to be sure there aren't any Indians in this valley. I'd sure hate for them to get us boxed in."

They rode into the shade of an overhang, and Finch removed his glass that he always carried in his saddlebags. He took his hat off and held it above and in front of the glass as he scanned the valley carefully for several minutes. Colette was silent. Finally, Finch lowered the glass and replaced it.

"Don't see a thing except cattle, deer, and buffalo," he said. "And they're all grazin' peacefully, which, most of the time, means that there are no Indians about."

"Why did you do that?" Colette asked curiously.

"What?" Finch was surprised.

"Pull your hat off and hold it above your glass?"

"Oh. Well, sometimes the sun hits the glass, and it sends a flash that can be seen for miles. We were in the shade, and it wasn't likely, but I like to be careful."

Finch led the way into the box canyon. As he had said, it widened, and the warm sun shone brightly on the floor of the canyon. The stream ran rollicking along over the rocks. Some large trees grew along the banks, and occasionally a deep pool of water appeared where a tree had fallen across and formed a dam.

The canyon was fairly shallow, and they reached the end of it in a few minutes.

"Kate fixed us a lunch while you and Humphrey were getting Old Heck," Colette said. "Hungry?"

Finch looked at the sky above; the sun was almost directly overhead. "About time to eat, I guess, if you've got something. I've got some jerky and hardtack in my saddle bags."

"Well, I'll bet Kate's lunch will be better," Colette said.

"I expect it will," Finch agreed. "I'll stake out the horses, and you get the lunch ready."

Finch unsaddled the horses and spread the blankets on the ground. Then he lead them a short distance away and tied both of them securely, but in reach of graze.

When he returned, he was mildly surprised to see the lunch unopened and Colette not in sight. He supposed that she had gone behind some cover to take care of an occurrence of nature, and he lay down on a saddle blanket and looked at the sky. It was a bright blue, and the sun was almost hot. He covered his face with his hat. He was dozing when he felt a movement beside him. He grasped his pistol as he yanked his hat away and half rose. Then his insides pounded like stampeding steers, and his eyes grew wide and almost frightened. For Colette was standing beside him as naked as the day she was born.

"I thought I would take a bath in the nice pool before lunch," she said in a far-away voice.

Finch could only stare in absolute incredulity. A veritable Venus!

"Colette," he gasped like a gaffed fish. "Colette, I thought we had an understanding."

"Well," Colette said as she knelt down and kissed him firmly and sweetly on the lips. "A woman can change her mind, can't she?"

Finch's mind felt like it was soaring on the wings of a hawk sailing far above as he reached for her.

* * * * * *

They rode slowly and in complete silence for several minutes as they headed toward camp. Finch finally broke the silence. "Hump is gonna shoot me right between the eyes, if he has a blue-eyed baby about nine months from now. And I won't blame him!"

"He's going to have a dark eyed one a lot sooner than that," Colette said.

"What?" Finch almost yelped. "How do you know?"

"I'm pregnant," Colette said complacently.

"You're what?" Finch was utterly flabbergasted.

"I'm pregnant," Colette repeated.

"Since when?" Finch gasped.

"Sinch Humphrey locked me in a horse stall in Louisiana about two months ago," Colette said facetiously.

"I'll be damned!" Finch never swore, but his mind was whirling. "Then why did he let you ride that horse today?"

"Because he doesn't know."

"Doesn't know!" Finch said harshly. "Why haven't you told him?"

"Because," Colette said matter of factly. "He is a man who thinks women are fragile as a snow flake, and he wouldn't have touched me again after he knew. He would be afraid of hurting me or the baby. But he wouldn't. And I'll be everything he needs for weeks, or months, yet. I won't tell him until he notices me getting fat. Women are a lot hardier than men give them credit for. At least Mama says so."

"Your mama is crazy!" Finch declared positively.

"She is French," Colette said as if that explained everything.

"I don't see how either one of us can look him in the eye again," Finch said forlornly.

"Are you sorry it happened, Finch?"

Finch pondered her question for a long moment, and then he answered her. "No, I'm not!" he said. "I know I ought to be—but I'm not. For an hour today I was happy enough to last a man a lifetime. I reckon a man can't be sorry because he was happy for a while."

"Good," Colette said, her voice indicating relief. "Neither am I. And I'm not ashamed either. I know I should be, but I'm not. I love you, Finch; but we will never have each other again. I promise you that. But just like Eve, I guess, I had to have one bite of forbidden fruit—and it was delicious!"

Neither of them spoke again for several minutes, and then Finch shook his head as if to clear his vision and looked about him as if he had just awakened from sleep. It was then that he felt the first tingle run up his spine, and the hairs on his neck prickled. He looked about keenly. His eyes squinted. Then he said in a low voice, "Colette, in just a minute I'm going to say 'go', and when I do, you spur and whip that sorrel till you reach camp. He can daylight this stud in thirty yards, but don't slow down for me. Keep going and fast."

"What on earth is wrong, Finch?" she whispered in a frightened voice.

"Indians on both sides of us. Now—Go!" he yelled and jammed the spurs in the stud.

Colette's hat flew off as the sorrel passed Old Heck, and true to Finch's prediction, he was leading by a good distance within a hundred yards. Colette looked to see Finch jerk his rifle from the scabbard, and she heard him shoot. But she obeyed his instruction and didn't slow up. In fact, the sorrel seemed to sink lower to the ground, and the trees and shrubs flew past faster than before.

She heard Finch shoot twice more, and then she heard rifles booming from the camp. The sorrel slid to a stop, and she stepped down as they tore into camp. She looked back fearfully, but Finch was still in the saddle and spurring the black stallion viciously. He slid to a stop just as Humphrey ran up to them, his rifle in one hand.

"God-a-mighty! I'm glad you're back!" he croaked. "We never seen 'em till Finch shot, but we got a couple of 'em, and they've gone to cover, I think."

"They're afoot," Finch said, "and crawlin' in that tall grass. Lucky I saw 'em before they cut us off from camp." Finch was breathing hard. "I can't see how they got down this valley without horses."

The Negroes kept up a sporadic firing, but Finch doubted that they were seeing Indians, for he was peering keenly at the places where the Indians had first been seen. Then he spied one snaking his way up the wall of the valley and snapped a shot at him. The Indian flung his bow and fell backward, just as they heard Buff's big buffalo gun boom from above. Finch looked up and saw just the poll of a horse's head, and then he understood perfectly how the Indians had got to the valley floor. They had ridden their horses to the rim, and had spied him and Colette as they rode toward camp. They had dismounted and climbed down the wall and had lain in wait to intercept them as they returned. It was fortunate that the Indians were equipped only with bows, for had they possessed rifles, he and Colette might not have been so lucky.

Finch felt more than saw a movement in the periphery of his vision. He looked quickly to see a muscular bronze body straining as the Indian extended his bow as far as it would go. Finch shot just as the Indian loosed his arrow. The Indian fell. Finch could see the arrow arch high above, and then it seemed to fall lazily into the camp.

Finch was not overly concerned because the cliff was too far away for the Indians to fire directly into the camp on a straight line; they could only arch their arrows high above and let them fall into the camp. He turned to see Colette in Humphrey's arms and her head thrown back as she looked into his face. At that instant he heard a slight swishing sound as the arrow fell and struck downward into Colette's chest. She gave a slight grunt and squeezed Humphrey spasmodically. Humphrey pulled her to him tightly. Finch ran to them and saw that the arrow had buried itself in her chest. He quickly grabbed his knife and cut the arrow close to her body.

"Mon amor," Colette said feebly into Humphrey's ear as she went limp.

Humphrey looked at Finch with terror filled eyes.

"Lay her on the ground," Finch instructed. "We've got to get that arrow out."

Humphrey laid Colette gently on her back and leaned over her. "Are you hurt bad?"

She only nodded in the affirmative. Then she turned her head to one side and spat blood in a stream. Humphrey and Finch knelt on each side of her. Her face was devoid of color, and her eyes seemed bigger and brighter than ever. She reached feebly and took each by the hand. Then with an effort she spoke in a low whispering voice. "What a lucky women I've been," she said with a ghost of a smile and squeezed their hands weakly.

"What, wife?" Humphrey leaned over her.

"I've loved two good men—and they have loved me," she whispered faintly.

"What's she saying?" Humphrey looked at Finch who only shook his head.

"Adieu, mon amor et ami!" She squeezed both hands again very feebly and then went limp.

"What did she say?" Humphrey yelled at Finch.

"I think she said 'goodby'," Finch said, his voice only a husky whisper. "She's gone, Hump!"

"God-a-mighty!" Humphrey breathed prayerfully.

Several of the Negroes had formed a ring around them as Colette lay there. Finch spied Largo and Kate. He motioned to Largo with his head, indicating for him to go to Humphrey. The big Negro took Humphrey by the hand and pulled him away. Humphrey was gasping harshly as though he could not get enough air.

Kate knelt beside Colette and looked across her body at Finch. "Miss Colette is gone, ain't she?"

Finch could only nod. Kate closed Colette's eyes gently. Finch rose and walked blindly away. He hit a tree but did not seem to notice. He only backed up a step or two and continued his walking. He stumbled back toward the way they had ridden in, impervious to the fact that Indians might still be lurking in the tall grass. Suddenly two of them jumped up and ran at him, knives drawn. He flicked his pistol and shot both of them without even breaking step. Hearing footsteps behind him, he turned to see Largo coming toward him. He held a rifle.

"Come on back, please, Mars Finch. Mars Hump is mighty tore up, and we needs somebody awful bad to tell us what to do."

Finch blinked and looked at the pistol in his hand.

"What, Largo?" he said dazedly.

"We needs yo back at camp, Mars Finch," Largo pleaded. "Sides, they is still Indians out here."

Finch nodded and started back to camp. Largo kept looking back fearfully. Once he stopped, dropped to one knee, and fired his rifle. Finch did not even look around.

He got to the camp just as Buff raced up in his wagon.

"Saw them red heathen a slippin' up on ye!" he boomed. "Tied up and injuned up on 'em from the rear. Got a couple of 'em, too, begorra! They wasn't but about a dozen of 'em. Their hosses is all gone, now. Saw 'em high tailin' it back west. Anybody hurt here in camp?"

Complete and profound silence greeted the question. Then he saw Kate and Maisie, Largo's wife, bearing the body of Colette tenderly between them and walking toward the Beatenbow wagon. Buff started to question Finch again, but his face was drained of all color, and his eyes looked like those of a trapped marten. Buff turned to Largo. "What happened, nigger?"

"They done kilt Miss Colette," Largo said.

Buff looked as if he had been slapped in the face with a beaver's tail. He quickly wrapped his lines around the brake handle and hopped down. He strode toward Humphrey, who was leaning against a tree. He approached but did not touch Humphrey. He turned back to Largo. "How did they do that?" he demanded. "They didn't have nothin' but bows and arrows!"

"Some of 'em clumb down that bluff to cut Miss Colette and Mars Finch off from camp. They had been ridin'. But the one that kilt Miss Colette shot from the cliff way up in the air, and the arrow, it come down an' hit Miss Colette."

"Any more of 'em down here in the valley?"

"Don' know, Mars Buff," Largo said. "Mars Finch, he was a walkin' out there afore I saw 'im, and he kilt two of 'em, and I run after 'im to bring 'im back, and I kilt another one. Can't say if there is any more of 'em or not. The niggers, they shot a lot. Might be they got some."

"Doubt it!" Buff said grimly, but we'd better put a couple of men on guard out that way. A bunch of raidin' Kiowas, they was, and they'll try to get their dead back after dark."

Buff walked to the Beatenbow wagon and looked inside. Kate and Maisie had put Colette's finest clothes on her and were stretching her out flat on her back. Buff looked a moment and shook his head sadly.

"A damn shame, begorra, and they kilt the pretty lass. Seems like them Kiowa varmints got a way of hittin' where it hurts most. It'll be a mighty sorry camp from here on in."

# Chapter 17

Although they did not build fires in camp that night and kept a silent vigil, they did not know when the Indians came to retrieve their dead, but the next morning, Buff, Largo, and Finch scoured the area carefully and saw where at least four bodies had been removed. They were silent as they returned to camp.

They buried Colette just after sunup under a giant oak tree growing on the hillside high above water line. Ellie, accompanied by several of the Negro women pulled armfulls of wild flowers and covered her grave.

"Need to plant some there so they'll keep a growin'," Buff said. He took a shovel and soon returned with several bunches of flowers rooted in the rich soil. He carefully planted them around the iron cross that Largo had fashioned during the night. "A bonny lass, she was," Buff said as he patted down the soil. "She loved beauty, and she shore does have a beautiful place to stay in." Buff wiped surreptitiously at his eyes with his shirt sleeve and rose.

As he approached Finch and Humphrey, they were talking in muted tones.

"I know we ort to stay a while and get the herd built up and trailin' some, but I reckon I'd like to leave this valley as soon as we can," Humphrey was saying.

"Clem says he's ready any time," Finch answered. "All the boys came up this morning for a little while. They just left a couple of the niggers to look after the cattle."

"They took a chance, then." Humphrey showed his first sign of any interest in the herd.

"Clem said that he could move the cattle any time," Finch repeated. "He says we'll have more than we can handle by the time we get to the end of the valley."

"Then let's start movin' 'em," Humphrey said tiredly. "I'd like to get 'em to that ranch as soon as we can, and then I got to go back to Louisiana."

Finch looked at him questioningly, but he offered no explanation; so Finch mounted his sorrel and rode to the cow camp. "They're already on the move," he reported back in less than an hour.

"I'll have Largo start breaking camp," Humphrey said and turned away.

By mid-morning, the fortifications that the Negroes had dug were filled in, and the mules were hitched to the wagons.

Humphrey called to Largo, and as he walked up, he said. "Finch will keep his own horse and Chico's. "I'll keep Old Heck and Colette's mare. The nigger cowboys can keep one horse apiece, and you take the rest of 'em down to the cowboy's remuda, including the mares. Tell 'em to use 'em if need be.

"Yassuh, Mars Hump," Largo said. "I starts 'em down right now. I'll git some of the other niggers to help."

"And, Largo," Humphrey called. "Turn that damn jackass loose. Maybe he'll breed us some runty mules with them mustang mares."

Largo looked at Humphrey as if he could not believe what he had heard. He shook his head and answered, "Yassuh."

"Hump," Finch cautioned. "One of those mustang stallions will kill that jack, if a panther doesn't get him first."

Humphrey grinned fleetingly for the first time since Colette and Finch had left camp the day before. "Don't worry about that jackass gettin' killed by a hoss, Finch. There ain't a more vicious fightin' animal in the world than a jack. We've had 'em kill more than one stud on the plantation. They're the toughest small animal I ever seen. And quick as a cat, too, when they want to be. I've seen one take a bite of meat out of a hoss as big as your hat. Jaws like a wild boar."

"Well, I'll be darned," Finch said. "I've just never been around one before. Don't know anything about 'em except they're stubborn—at least that one is."

"All of 'em are," Humphrey said. "Where did you Rangers get them pack mules if you didn't have no jacks?"

Finch pulled off his hat and ran his fingers through his hair. "Darned if I know," he admitted a little sheepishly. "We got 'em from ranchers about. I reckon I figgered they just grew."

"Well, they don't!" Humphrey said. "You got to cross a donkey and a horse to get a mule. That's where the mule gets his stubborness, and they can't reproduce. But we always cut the male mules when they are a year old, anyway."

"Well," Finch made a gesture of lightheartedness. "Maybe the Kiowas will get that jackass. It'll serve 'em right."

The wagons pulled out of the valley the way they had entered and would be drawn along the rim above so the drivers could keep an eye on the herd below. Finch led the wagons out, and they stopped at the top of the steep grade to let the mules blow a bit. He looked at the camp site below. Humphrey was standing beside Colette's grave with his head bared. Then he turned, jammed his hat on, and joined the caravan. Sam was driving Humphrey's wagon as they led out.

"I'll ride with you today if it's all right, Finch," Humphrey said.

"Glad to have you," Finch said. "We can see a lot of country from up here."

"How long is this valley?"

"I don't know," Finch said. "I've never been up it all the way. We will follow it twenty or thirty miles, and then leave it and cut northwest, to the Salt Fork of Red River."

"Then the cattle camp will stay only one or two more nights down in the valley?"

"Probably two more. It will depend on how they are able to add to the herd as they drive. Course we can still pick up a few when we get out on the plains, but Clem would like to get all we need while we are in here. I would, too."

"Why?"

"Several reasons, I guess," Finch said thoughtfully. "The Indians that hit us back in the valley were just a raiding party of Kiowas. Black Bull is the Kiowa chief and was one of the Indians that agreed for me to run cattle on the Canadian. That raiding party either didn't know who we are, or Black Bull didn't tell 'em to leave us alone. At least, I hope that's the case. Anyway, Kit Carson is sure goin' to give Black Bull hell."

"Why do you hope Black Bull hadn't told them braves to leave us alone."

"Because," Finch said, "that would mean that Black Bull has changed his mind, and we've got a full scale Kiowa war on our hands."

"Will they try to avenge the Indians we killed?"

"Naw," Finch said complacently. "Not unless Black Bull has gone back on his word. And I don't think that likely. They'll just figure that a few of 'em got sent to the happy hunting grounds and let it go at that."

"I sort of wish some of the other red bastards would hit us," Humphrey said grimly.

"We ought to glass the valley real careful to where we leave it," Finch warned. "If Indians saw that herd and wanted to stampede them, all they'd have to do would be hide in the grass until the herd got close, and then raise up and yell or wave some fresh cat hides at 'em, and we would lose a lot of cattle and probably a lot of cowboys, too."

Both Finch and Humphrey surveyed the valley and each rim carefully with their glasses as they rode. Nothing threatening appeared before they got to the place where Finch said they would emerge from the valley. They got off their horses and loosened the cinches and let the horses graze for a few minutes, holding the reins in one hand and hardtack and jerky in the other. As soon as they had finished eating, they cinched up and started back. They glassed the valley as carefully on their return as they had coming up.

"We ought to meet the wagons at about the right time to camp," Finch said.

Buff joined them an hour later and pulled his wagon alongside.

"Seen anything?" Finch asked.

"Got a couple of buffler calves," he said. "But nary a sign of redskins. Begorra, and it's wishin' I had. This child be hankerin' to hone Old Betsy up on a few of the red skinned varmints!" He patted his big buffalo gun fondly.

"I reckon they have left, all right," Finch said. "Hope so!"

Nothing more was said until they came in sight of the wagons, when Humphrey rode on down to tell Largo to make camp.

"I'll just unload me meat and camp nearby meself tonight," Buff said.

"I reckon we would appreciate that, Buff," Finch said gratefully.

Two hours later the herd came into view, and they were amazed at the size of it. It seemed that a veritable sea of longhorns glistened in the low sunlight. The sun shining on the multi-colored cattle reminded Finch of sunlight filtering through aspen leaves in autumn.

"Looks like Clem and the boys picked up a lot of 'em today," Humphrey said.

"They sure did!" Finch said. "I think that by the time we get to our climbing out place tomorrow, Clem will have all he can handle."

When the camp was secure, they could see the cooking fire of the cowboy camp down below. The cattle were still grazing, and four cowboys rode around them constantly. They would be relieved by four more at midnight.

Ellie served supper that night to Humphrey and Finch at the folding table, as Kate and Sam sat morosely by their fire. The entire camp was silent except for an occasional rattle of a cooking utensil. The Negroes did not laugh and banter as they usually did. Finch and Humphrey ate in complete silence, neither with any enthusiasm. When they had finished coffee, Finch stood up.

"Well, I reckon I'll turn in early tonight. I'm kinda tired."

"Finch," Humphrey said tentatively. Finch looked at him questioningly. "Mind if I bring a bedroll over and join you tonight? It's sort of—lonesome—in the wagon."

"Be glad to have you, Hump. I could use some company, myself."

Finch had his bed unrolled and his boots off by the time Humphrey had secured Old Heck for the night and approached carrying a bedroll. He unrolled the bed and pulled off his boots without speaking. When they were both in their beds and looking up at the stars, Finch broke the silence.

"The niggers are awful quiet tonight," he ventured.

"Finch?" Humphrey asked hesitantly. "Would you mind too much callin' them niggers 'blacks'?"

"Wouldn't mind, I reckon. But why, Hump?"

"Well, Colette, she said 'nigger' sounded belittlin'. She was trainin' me to call 'em 'blacks'. I guess I'd sort of like to please her if I could. Was hopin' you would, too."

"I would, Hump. I didn't know she objected to callin' a nigger a nigger. But if she didn't like it, I'll sure call 'em 'blacks' from now on."

"I still forget once in a while," Humphrey said.

"I probably will, too," Finch said. "You remind me when I do, and I'll remind you."

"Seems like she always had a funny idea about names. Never did call me 'Hump'. Everybody else did, except her and her ma, and my ma—and pa when he got made at me. Never could figger out why she wouldn't." Humphrey said absently.

"You think she objected to me calling you 'Hump'?" Finch asked anxiously.

"Not a bit! She thought an awful lot of you, Finch."

"I thought an awful lot of her, too," Finch admitted.

Both men lay with their hands cupped behind their heads, staring up at the stars.

"She's got an awful pretty place to stay in," Humphrey ventured.

"She has at that," Finch replied. "She said yesterday when we were ridin' that she imagined heaven looked and smelled a lot like that valley. I reckon now she knows."

Finch debated silently whether to tell Humphrey that Colette was carrying his child, and decided against it, for he knew that it would only add to the enormity of his loss. Finch lay staring up at the stars for several minutes more, trying to sort out the events of the past two days. Finally he sighed and turned on his side.

"Good night, Hump," he said.

"Night, Finch. Hope we can get some sleep."

"Me, too," Finch replied. But for the first time he could remember, he did not go to sleep quickly. Instead, he lived over in his thoughts that one unforgettable hour that he had spent with Colette Beatenbow in the box canyon.

When they awakened at dawn the next morning, Finch sat up, combed his fingers through his hair, and put his hat on. Humphrey was lying on his back with his fingers locked behind his head.

"You get any sleep?" Finch asked.

"Some," Humphrey said as he reached for his hat. "Guess I'm not as used to sleepin' on the ground as you are."

"Takes a little time, all right," Finch said. Then, as they were pulling on their clothes and boots, Finch continued. "Hump, when we move the cattle out of the valley, I think we ought to follow the herd pretty close with the wagons."

"Why?"

"Well, there just isn't any reason to have two groups travellin' apart. We would be a lot stronger if we were all together in an Indian attack."

"You think they will hit us again?"

"Not likely," Finch said. "Out on the plains, they are mostly Comanches, and White Horse has sent out word to them; but if they attack, it will be a big bunch of 'em, and we will be out in the open. Then, there are the Comancheros. They can be anywhere. We will need all the firepower we can get. And more of the blacks can try their hand as cowboys. Clem says that most of those that have been helpin' with the herd are doin' pretty well." Then Finch grinned. "Still hurts old Clem, though, because the blacks use surcingles. I think he would be embarrassed if cowboys from some other outfit saw 'em."

Humphrey chuckled for the first time since they had left the valley. "I notice though that he ain't sendin' 'em back to the wagons."

"He won't either," Finch said. "He can sure use the help."

\* \* \* \* \* \*

The morning that Clem and the cowboys moved out of the canyon was cloudy and smelled of rain. The wagons pulled well to one side to avoid startling the wild cattle. Finch and Humphrey sat their horses and watched the herd as they emerged.

"God-a-mighty!" Humphrey breathed in awe. "He must a gathered a million of 'em."

"He's got enough, all right," Finch agreed. "Quite a lot of buffalo mixed in with 'em though. We'll have to let them fall out as we go along. Clem sure won't let anyone go into that herd to cut 'em out."

"We've got a mighty big bunch of steers, anyway," Humphrey said.

"We don't have any steers," Finch said as Humphrey looked at him blankly. "They're all bulls, cows, and calves. If we've got a steer in the bunch, then he belonged to some rancher who cut 'im when he was a calf."

"Oh!" Humphrey responded understandingly. "Would he be branded, too!"

"Likely would be," Finch said. "We will have to put our brand on all of 'em when we get to the ranch. And we will cut most of the bulls, but save some of the best ones for breeding. And we'll ship all the steers when we make our first drive to market. But we've got a lot more cows than bulls, and that's good."

"What is our brand?" Humphrey asked curiously.

"We will have to figure out something," Finch replied. "I've been thinking about it a little. How would a HF suit you?"

"You know more about cattle than I do. What will it stand for?"

"Well," Finch said a bit self-consciously. "A connected H F could stand for Hump and Finch."

"Looks to me like it ought to be the other way around," Humphrey said. "Maybe a F H for Finch and Hump. Reckon you ought to come first."

"Nope!" Finch said. "The two letters wouldn't fit together that way. Besides, the HF can be made with a straight iron, and it won't blotch bad."

"Sounds good to me, Finch. But, if we find anything with a brand on now, we will try to find out who owns the brand and send 'im the money when we ship."

"Only right thing to do," Finch agreed. "All the brands in Wise County will be recorded at the court house in Decatur. Most of the branded cattle we will have, if any, will be from Wise County ranches."

"I'll stop by there on my way back to Louisiana," Humphrey said.

Finch looked at Humphrey again questioningly, but he was absorbed in watching the herd. Finch wondered again at Humphrey's intention to go to Louisiana, but did not question him. Humphrey would tell him in time, if he wanted to. Finch was a great believer in leaving other people alone.

When the herd had moved well away from the valley and out onto the flat country, the wagons pulled in behind them. The going was slow, and they occasionally had to stop to wait.

Clem rode back and asked them, "You gonna follow the herd with them wagins?"

"Thought it would be best," Finch said. "If the Indians hit us at all, they'll hit us hard. And the Comancheros are still around."

"Well, you thought damn right," Clem said bluntly. "And we got so many cattle we're short-handed."

"That's another reason," Finch said. "Thought if we stay behind, maybe you could break in some more black cowboys."

"Now, that is a right good idea!" Clem said with relief. "Them niggers that have been ridin' has made pretty damn good hands, even if I do hate to admit it. And havin' all the remuda together will help, too. The boys can change horses more reglar, especially if we ride some of them mares."

"Ride 'em if you need 'em," Humphrey said.

"How many of them niggers do you reckon will want to ride?"

"All of 'em except old Sam," Humphrey said with assurance. "They been pesterin' me ever since them first two started ridin'!"

"Jist wisht they would learn to use a saddle," Clem said morosely.

Humphrey chuckled and Finch grinned. "Largo will use a saddle," Humphrey said. "Fact is, he's a good enough horseman."

"Well, we're gonna need him, then," Clem said as he started to ride away; then he stopped abruptly and looked back the way they had come. "What the hell is that jackass doin' back there loose?" He pointed.

Humphrey and Finch looked too and saw the recalcitrant jack standing a safe way from the wagons.

"That son of a bitch!" Humphrey expostulated. "We turned him loose yesterday. I figgered he'd be back to Louisiana by now."

"Well, it looks like he wants to see the end of this trail, too," Finch grinned.

The jack stood and looked at them for a few moments, his long ears pointed inquisitively. Then he lowered his head and started grazing contentedly.

The camp that night was far different than they had experienced before. There was no water for the cattle, and they had to build fires with the cow chips that Raney had tossed into the possum belly of the provision wagon. Finch showed Kate how to start them, but the chips were dry, and soon he had a nice fire going with blue flames.

"It do make a right good fire, don't it?" Kate was pleasantly surprised. "Hot, too! I reckon as it'll cook our vittles, all right."

"It will," Finch assured her. "Maybe you ought to show the other cooks how to start a fire with 'em."

"Yassuh, Mars Finch. I show them niggers right now," Kate said as she waddled away.

Supper that night was a little later than usual, but Kate managed it well. Ellie served Humphrey and Finch. After the cattle were bedded down, Clem rode back to the wagons and sat down for coffee with Humphrey and Finch.

"Cattle doin' all right without water?" Finch asked as Clem sipped his coffee.

"Yeah, them long legged critters can go a long ways on the dry. But we put out a couple of extra night herders, anyway."

"Everything else all right?" Humphrey asked, for he thought he detected a slight note of hesitancy.

"Oh, Hell!" Clem said in exasperation. "I reckon so. But that one eyed bastard of a cook of ours has been belly achin' ever since we all joined up. Says he don't like to be so close associated with niggers. I told 'im that he shore didn't have to sleep with none, but he's still huffy."

"Why he ain't camped within two hundred yards of us, anyway," Humphrey said incredulously. "Even Buff is camped closer to us than that; he's camped to one side just because he likes bein' alone—not because of the blacks."

"I know that," Clem said with disgust. "That cook is just a griper and takes any excuse to bellyache. If he ain't mighty careful, I'm gonna send him off back east."

"I never knew a cow-camp cook that wasn't testy," Finch observed.

"Me neither!" Clem agreed. "But it can be over-done. How much further to water, do you think, Finch?"

"Another full day's drive, I think," Finch said. "But I'll ride out early in the morning to be sure."

"All right," Clem said. "We can go another day without too much trouble, and even two more if we have to; but them critters is a lot easier to handle when they have a bellyful of water." He emptied his coffee cup, set it down abruptly, and mounted his horse as he usually did. "Better keep that possum belly full of cow chips, Hump. Wood is mighty scarce for the next few days, I expect." He rode away without looking back.

"We ain't got that nigger that we hung anymore to pick up them cow chips. I reckon some of the kids can do it, though."

"Thought you were supposed to call 'em 'blacks'," Finch reminded Humphrey.

"And I'm goin' to, them that deserve it," Humphrey said almost aggressively. "But that nigger was a nigger! And I'm gonna call 'im one."

The cattle started moving earlier than usual the next morning, and the caravan was making preparations to follow. Finch circled the herd and rode ahead at a lazy lope. Humphrey instructed Largo to have all the Negro men to come to the front wagon. When they were assembled, he explained the need for more cowboys and asked for volunteers. All of them, with the exception of Sam, held up their hands and danced up and down to draw attention to themselves.

"All right," Humphrey said. "All of you will get your chance. Largo will bring in two or three gentle horses every morning, and then he will take you to the herd, and Clem will tell you what you are supposed to do. Just be shore you don't talk too loud, nor laugh. Sing if you want to, but do it soft and easy. That's all. Now, Largo, go bring in some horses."

"I'll need to fix some more surcingles, Mars Hump," Largo said.

"All right. Fix 'em and then go after the horses. Do we have enough bridles?"

"Yassuh," Largo said, "and saddles, too, but I reckon them niggers rather have them surcingles."

"All right, Largo," Humphrey said. "Do whatever you need to."

An hour later Largo rode to the remuda, returning with three horses. Surcingles were soon in place, and three of the Negro men rode off happily to the herd.

"Hope one of 'em don't do somethin' foolish," Humphrey said to himself as they rode off.

The day dragged. The wagons had to stop several times to keep from getting too close to the herd. The children romped beside the wagons, picking up cow and buffalo chips to toss into the possum belly. They were making a game of it, and their squeals of delight and laughter rang almost constantly. Soon the tarp suspended under the wagon sagged until it almost dragged the ground, and Humphrey had to tell them to stop.

Buff came in with fresh meat just before noon. He and Humphrey unloaded it.

"We're gonna eat in a few minutes, Buff," Humphrey said. "Want to have a bite with us?"

"Thank ye jis' the same, lad," Buff replied. "I got some vittles already in my waggin, but I'd shore take a cup o' that good coffee, begorra."

Humphrey sat with Buff as he drank two cups of the steaming coffee. Again, he had a big chew of tobacco in his jaws and did not remove it before he downed the strong brew. Humphrey just shook his head in silent admiration.

"That there is shore good coffee," Buff said as he finished the second cup. "An' now I reckon I'll be gittin' back to me waggin. Figgered I'd hunt some ahead of the herd and a little south today."

"Finch left early. He thought we would find water afore night."

"Aye," Buff said. "An' the lad was right, as usual. It's a playa lake, but I ain't niver seen it dry. Fine for the cattle and hosses, but I reckon you'd better use the barrels for cookin' and drinkin'. You got enough?"

"Plenty," affirmed Humphrey. "We could go another couple of days if we had to."

"Won't have to," Buff said. "You'll hit the lake afore dark, and they is a nice fresh stream a day's drive past that."

"Good!" Humphrey said. "You haven't seen any Indian sign, have you?"

"Nay, but I seen some Indians."

"You did!" Humphrey was alarmed.

"Nothin' to get all het up about, lad," Buff said calmly. "Only a couple of 'em, and they was still ridin' south the last I seen of 'em."

"I hope they don't circle back," Humphrey said feelingly.

"They won't," Buff said. "They was headed sommers. Could tell by the way they rode. Fact is, I'm a thinkin' ye has seen all the Indian troubles ye be seein'. Finch told me about the agreement with White Horse, and I be thinkin' he'll abide by it. He's a good Comanche."

"You know him?" Humphrey asked in surprise.

"Aye," nodded Buff. "We've met. Not on friendly terms, mind ye, but I got away with me scalp. And if he give his word to Kit and Finch, he'll keep it. Kit can be a real panther if he's crossed, and Finch could be worse. That Finch be quite a lad—ye know it."

"I'm beginnin' to think more so all the time," Humphrey agreed. "The more I learn about him, the more unbelievable he sounds."

"Well, ye can believe it all," Buff said heartily. "I been hearin' tales of the kid Ranger named Fauntleroy Finch for four or five year now. The lad is the fastest gun hand on the frontier—and the best shot. Even the Indians respect 'im. Call 'im Hut' se pah Suh' Kahe—means 'Ice Eye' in English. I niver had seen the lad afore, but I recognized 'im soon as he rode into Fort Worth."

"How did you recognize 'im?" Humphrey asked.

"Oh, I dunno. Jist a few things a mountain man like me can see that mebbe somebody else would miss. Fust thing was ye had to look twicet to even see his pistol. It's that much a part o' 'im. An' he walks like a mountain cat. And them eyes make ye think ye are lookin' into a hot cowchip fire. An' he's tall an' got hair the color of winter grass—but I reckon it be more than all o' that—jist somethin' about 'im that gives a man a feelin', specially if he's lived in the wild as long as I have."

It was the longest speech Humphrey had ever heard Buff make, and it was obvious that even the old Irish mountain man was in awe of Finch. Humphrey shook his head in bewilderment.

Buff immediately took his leave. It was soon after that Finch appeared. He rode his horse fairly slowly and circled the herd a good distance before reining in toward the wagons at the rear. Humphrey walked out to meet him.

"Find water?"

"Found it all right. It isn't running water, but it's all right for the herd and remuda. Freshwater a day's travel farther on, though. The Indians call it Pee's-su-nee, Skunk Creek. But the water is cold and good."

"I'm sure ready for that," Humphrey said with relief. "Everybody else will be too, time we get to it. Buff said just what you told me."

"He's been in?" Finch asked in surprise.

"Left just a while ago."

"Did he see any Indian sign?" Finch asked.

"Said he saw a couple of Indians, but said they was far off and ridin' south like they was goin' someplace."

"Good," Finch said. "I reckon we can rest pretty easy tonight."

# Chapter 18

The herd neared the lake late in the afternoon. The lead bulls bellowed and went forward at a trot. And, although Clem would have preferred to water the remuda first, he did not try to stop the cattle. By the time the drag men arrived, the water was muddy, and many of the cattle were standing belly deep in it.

"Let 'em drink all they can," Clem told the cowboys. The fuller they get, the easier they are to handle. We'll take the remuda over to the other side and let 'em drink."

The herd dawdled long in the water. Early flies had begun to bother them some, and they switched wet, muddy tails at them. Occasionally, a bull would make a pass at another one with his long horns, but rarely did they do much damage. Finally, they began to drift out of the lake and onto the grass. The cowboy cook had parked his wagon well to the rear and to one side of the other wagons and had started his fire.

Finch and Humphrey had circled their wagons, and Kate and the other cooks had cow chip fires going. Soon supper was ready, and Ellie served Finch and Humphrey as usual. There was still good light, and as Humphrey was eating, he looked back in the direction they had come. He stopped eating with his fork halfway to his mouth.

"Well, I'll be damned!" he exclaimed in disbelief.

"What?" Finch turned quickly to look.

Standing a good distance away with long ears erect, and staring inquisitively at the camp was the jackass.

Humphrey chuckled, Finch laughed outright, and Kate beamed. It was the first time she had heard the two of them express amusement at the same time.

"Them two is gonna be mighty good friends," she thought to herself with immense satisfaction.

"I guess he's gonna follow us all the way to the ranch," Humphrey said. "He's doin' that jist to be contrary cause he thinks we don't want him to."

"And that's a lot better than draggin' 'im behind a wagon," Finch smiled.

"That's right!"

When Finch unrolled his bed and checked the stake on Chico's horse that he was using for a night mount, Humphrey came up with his bedroll. Finch did not say anything as he unrolled his bed. He knew that Humphrey could not bear to sleep in the bed that he had shared so joyfully with Colette. Finch was thankful that he could not know the reason that he sympathized with him so acutely.

They both got more sleep that night, and Kate had coffee made by the time they had rolled their beds and staked their horses on uncropped grass. Humphrey was always very careful to tie Old Heck securely each night, for he knew what havoc the stud might play if he got loose.

"Gonna build you a pen that will hold one of them longhorn bulls when we get to the ranch," he silently promised the handsome black stallion.

As they finished breakfast, they saw Largo fitting surcingles on three other horses, and two blacks mounted. Largo gave the third a boost, for it was Trey with the broken leg. Finch and Humphrey could easily see his broad grin.

"That nigger — I mean black — is goin' to make a cowboy," Finch said. "Clem swears that a cowboy never had any sense, anyway, and Trey sure qualifies."

Humphrey chuckled. "He won't get off that horse till he gets back tonight, either, unless he falls in a hole or something."

The herd had started slowly grazing its way westward when the three Negro riders approached it from the rear. As they neared, two of the men who were riding drag came to meet them. Humphrey and Finch watched with interest. They stopped and talked a short time, and then the three riders continued toward the herd, and the two drag men rode toward the wagons. In a few minutes, both of them had dismounted near the last wagon and walked to where Humphrey and Finch were still drinking coffee. Both of them pulled off their floppy caps as they approached, and Finch recognized them as the two blacks that had been riding drag for the past few days.

"Scuse us, Mars Hump," one of them spoke hesitantly.

"All right. What is it?" Humphrey asked.

"Jis wanted to tell yo—Mars Clem said we could ride night herd tonight." Both of them grinned proudly.

"Then I reckon you two boys have been doin' a good job," Humphrey approved. "Figgered you would, or I wouldn't a let you go out there."

"Yassuh, Mars Hump. I reckon we is." They both seemed inordinately pleased at Humphrey's reply. "We jis thinks mebbe yo'd like to know."

"All right, you told me." Humphrey centered his attention on his coffee again, and the two Negroes started walking away. "Wait a minute." He stopped them, and they turned to face him again. "What names do you two go by?"

Both of them beamed. "I's Mose," the spokesman said, "and this here is Alf." He nodded his head toward the other Negro.

"All right, Mose and Alf. Now you two boys keep on doin' a good job, yuh heah?"

"Yassuh, Mars Hump. We sho gonna do dat." They both walked away as though they had been given the greatest compliment possible. And in their opinion they had.

"Hope I can remember their names," Humphrey grumbled. "I ain't never good with names, even with whites, and the blacks are a lot harder to remember."

\* \* \* \* \* \*

Finch rode out ahead of the wagons and herd. He would reach Skunk Creek early, but he wanted to check it for Indian sign. He found none and returned to the herd, cautioning the advance scout to be particularly observant, as he met him. He arrived at the wagons just before noon.

"Lookee yonder!" Humphrey chuckled and pointed his whittling knife as Finch dismounted. "That jackass has been following us all morning. Stays way back, though, and I'll bet if we was to start out that way, he would run off. Stops to graze and then trots on up to keep us in sight."

Finch grinned and combed his fingers through his hair. "Guess he got lonesome out there all by himself."

Humphrey sobered immediately. "Guess so. Want some coffee? Kate is fixin' a bite to eat, but it ain't ready yet."

The table was not set up; so Ellie served them coffee as they squatted in the shade of a wagon.

"Find anything up ahead?" Humphrey asked conversationally.

"Buffaloes, cows, and a lot of good fresh water. Won't be a hard day's drive, either."

"That's good news."

From the cowboy camp a couple of hundred yards away they heard loud, angry voices. Finch looked questioningly at Humphrey.

"Damned if I know," Humphrey said, surprised. "Them cowboys been gettin' along good, I thought. Hope they ain't crossways with each other."

Finch and Humphrey kept looking at the cowboy camp. Evidently, the cook had stopped his wagon at about the same time the caravan had halted and was preparing a noon meal, for he had a fire going.

More angry shouts could be heard. Finch and Humphrey watched with worried frowns. Soon they saw a cowboy ride rapidly away. As he rode, he uncoiled his rope. The jackass, that had been calmly grazing, suddenly raised his head as the horseman approached. When the rider neared, the jackass apparently anticipated his intention, for he whirled and ran with surprising speed. But he was too late. The cowboy's rope settled over his head, and he was brought to an abrupt stop. The cowboy immediately turned his horse and dragged the jack, bawling and stiff legged, toward the cowboy camp.

"Now what in hell!" Humphrey stared in amazement.

"No telling," Finch answered. "Cowboys do a lot of crazy things."

All activity in the caravan had stopped, and the blacks were staring in wonder as were Humphrey and Finch. Only a short time elapsed after the cowboy dragged the jackass into camp until they emerged again. Only now there was a man astride the jack; the cowboy was riding his horse behind and was leaning far over to quirt the jackass viciously and was yelling as loudly as he could. The jackass was running at a speed that amazed Finch. There was only a rope about his neck to which the man clung desperately with one hand, and he had the other gripped in the long hair of the animal. He lost his floppy hat just as they went over a rise and disappeared from sight. They heard the cowboy yell another time or two, and then he reappeared, riding sedately toward the cowboy camp.

"Now what do you reckon that was all about?" Humphrey was stunned. "Let's go see!"

"Maybe we ought not to do that, Hump," Finch cautioned. "Cowboys are pretty touchy sometimes."

"Well, I—"

"Here comes Clem now," Finch interrupted. "Maybe we will find out."

Clem rode into camp and dismounted without greeting anyone. He walked directly to Humphrey. Anger showed in his stride and the hard set of his jaw. "Beatenbow," he said without preliminary, "you got a nigger woman that can come over and cook for us?"

"I expect so," Humphrey answered. "You boys need some help?"

"We need a cook," Clem said cryptically.

"I thought you had a cook—"

Finch quickly stepped to Humphrey's side and nudged him.

"Well," Humphrey floundered. Then he called for Kate, who came waddling up hurriedly. "Kate, who is the best cook in camp?"

"Why, I is, Mars Hump!" Kate answered in surprise.

"I mean, besides you," Humphrey said almost angrily.

"Well," Kate knitted her brow in concentration. "I reckon that'd be Maisie."

"That's Largo's wench, ain't it?"

"Yassuh, Mars Hump. But yo had 'em married up legal, does yo remember?"

"I remember," Humphrey said shortly. "You go tell her to go to the cowboy camp and cook for 'em."

"Lawsy me, Mars Hump. I dunno as she—I mean Largo ain't gonna . . ."

"Kate," Humphrey interrupted her. "You go tell Maisie what I said. And tell her to have breakfast for them cowboys ever mornin' at four o'clock. Tell her she can come back over here and sleep with Largo a while every night. Now, you hear me, Kate?" Humphrey demanded sternly.

"Yassuh, yassuh, I hears yo, Mars Hump." Kate hurried away.

"Want a cup of coffee, Clem?" Humphrey asked solicitously.

Clem wavered and then succumbed. "Hell, I reckon I do." Then he grinned sheepishly. "Maybe it'll help me work this mad off."

Humphrey chuckled, and Finch grinned. "You got a good mad on, all right," Finch said jocularly. "Hump and I could see it hangin' out all the way over here."

Clem accepted the coffee from Ellie without a word and then removed his hat and squatted in the shade of the wagon. Humphrey and Finch joined him. They sat in silence for a few minutes.

"Mind if we ask what happened?" Humphrey inquired tentatively.

Clem scowled, and then a grin of pure pleasure erased the scowl. Finally he laughed uproariously. "Hell!" he said between bursts of laughter. "Nothin' much happened. That gotch-eyed cook was stirrin' up a stew for the boys. I rode in with them three niggers you sent and told 'im to give 'em a cup of coffee. And damned if he didn't just glare at me out of that one good eye of his and squirted tobacco juice in the stew and threw his spoon down. Said he wasn't cookin' for no damn niggers. Art, he was there, and he kicked that cook in the ass as hard as he could and was beatin' hell out of him when some more of the boys rode up. I think they would've hung him on the wagon tongue if I hadn't stopped 'em. So we jist sent him back to Decatur by the only transportation that nobody needed."

Finch, Clem, and Humphrey all laughed as they remembered the hapless cook holding onto the jackass for dear life.

Finally, Clem wiped the tears of laughter from his eyes. "I see that nigger woman goin' over there now," he said. "Reckon I better go show her where things is."

"She can cook all right," Humphrey assured him.

"Hell," Clem said acidly. "She won't have to be very good to be an improvement over that one-eyed bastard we been puttin' up with. Much obliged."

With that, he mounted his horse and rode back to the cowboy camp.

"What will Largo think?" Finch asked.

"Makes no difference," Humphrey said shortly. "My blacks do what I tell 'em to."

Finch thought Humphrey callous in dealing with the blacks, and he simply could not understand the respect, almost awe, accorded Humphrey by all the blacks.

They reached Skunk Creek early, and the cattle had a good drink as did the remuda. Humphrey ordered all the water barrels filled before they started supper. Kate was more silent than usual as she prepared the meal, and Ellie served it timidly.

Finch and Humphrey were getting ready to take their bedrolls out where Finch's horse was staked when Clem rode back into camp.

"Hump," he said almost jovially. "The boys had the best supper tonight they've had since we left. They're cussin' hell out of me for not runnin' that gotch-eyed cook off sooner. Jist thought I'd tell you," he said as he rode back to his camp.

Kate, who had heard him as she still worked by the campfire, muttered something. Humphrey scowled at her. "What did you say, Kate?"

"Nothing' Mars Hump. Jis talkin' to myself, I reckon," she said quickly.

"Yes, you did!" Humphrey glared accusingly. "Now, out with it! What did you say?"

"Jis hopin' Maisie be all right without much sleep," Kate explained almost fearfully. "Her gonna have a sucker an' all."

"She's knocked up?" Humphrey asked.

"Yassuh, Mars Hump, she is," Kate said, and then added almost defiantly, but with a tinge of pride in her voice. "An' she ain't the only one."

"What in hell are you drivin' at, Kate?" Humphrey was exasperated.

"Yo is gonna have two new suckers in about six months. Maybe more."

"What are you talkin' about, Kate?" Humphrey demanded.

"Me and Sam, Mars Hump. We is gonna have us a new little sucker."

"You're what?" Humphrey was incredulous. "Why Sam's too old to—"

"Yassuh, yassuh, I thought so, too," Kate interrupted Humphrey for one of the few times in her life. "I done think the sap had dreened out o that good for nothin' nigger of mine, but I reckon it ain't—it shore ain't." She looked at Sam fondly. Sam, who was sitting near the fire, just grinned his toothless grin, and wrinkles enveloped his elf-like face.

"I'll be damned!" Humphrey said in astonishment and shook his head. "Finch, let's go to bed."

After they were in their bedrolls, Finch asked Humphrey. "You reckon Kate is really goin' to have a baby?"

"I expect so," Humphrey said absently. "She knows better than to lie to me."

"But she's so old!" Finch said in wonder.

Humphrey was silent for a few minutes, and then he said, "I been figgerin'. Kate ain't so old. She's just big and fat. Makes her look old."

"How old is she?"

"Let me see," Humphrey said musingly. "Largo was her first sucker, and she dropped him when she was a twelve year old. Largo is a year or so younger than I am; so that would make Kate—let's see—" He counted silently for a moment. "Kate is somewhere around forty, I reckon."

"I'll be darned!" Finch exclaimed in amazement. "I'd have guessed her sixty, at least. How old is Sam?"

"I dunno," Humphrey said. "We bought 'im when he was full growed. Fust thing he done when he got to the plantation was knock up Kate; so my pa said. He was gonna geld 'im, but Ma talked 'im out of it. Glad she did too. They've raised us some good niggers."

"I'll bet he's at least seventy," Finch said with conviction.

"I doubt that. Fact is, I'm shore he ain't. Maybe fifty, fifty-five. The folks used 'im as a field hand for a long time. And he ain't got no teeth. Makes him look old."

"How many kids do they have?" Finch asked in awe.

"I ain't got no idee. Largo was the fust. I know that. And Ellie was their last. But they had one nearly ever year in between, I guess. I was in the army; so I don't know how many they had while I was gone. Some of their other git are with us, but I don't know which ones."

"You mean you don't even know which ones are Kate's?" Finch was incredulous.

"Oh, hell no, Finch," Humphrey said a bit impatiently. "Kate may not even know herself. After they were weaned, the mammy don't pay much attention to 'em."

"Where are the others? Their children, I mean?"

"Well, like I said, some of 'em are probably with us. We sold some of 'em, I imagine. Maybe one or two of 'em died. I don't know."

"Hump," Finch said almost disgustedly, "you talk about 'em like they were livestock."

"Well," Humphrey said defensively. "They are—at least they was till we lost the war. And good stock, too."

Finch lay staring up at the sky for several minutes; then he turned to Humphrey and rested his head on his elbow as he looked at the man beside him. Suddenly, he wasn't sure that he knew Humphrey Beatenbow at all. It was inconceivable to him that anyone could ever consider another human being as livestock. The Finch family had never owned slaves, and the little fighting that Finch had done as a civilian in the war was a result of his inborn resistance to any sort of bully, which he considered the North to be.

Finally he asked Humphrey, "Do you think the baby will really be Sam's?"

"Huh?" Humphrey grunted sleepily.

"Do you think that Sam will really be the father of Kate's child?"

Humphrey sat up in his bedroll and looked over at Finch. There was enough light from the low lying moon and the bright stars for them to see each other fairly well.

"You can bet your bottom dollar that when Kate drops that sucker, Sam is the stud," Humphrey said with absolute conviction. "Sam got her first when she was jist a little one, and he musta done a good job on her. Knocked her up fust thing and kept her knocked up most of the time after that. Kate never did look at another nigger stud, and the few of 'em that looked at her got their heads bashed in by Kate or an arm or leg broke by Sam. He ain't always been as dried up as he is now. Fact is, he was stout as a bull when he fust started workin' in the fields. He jist sort of shrunk up when Kate talked Ma and Pa into lettin' 'im help her about the house."

"That just floors me," Finch admitted.

"Kate's dam was our cook till she died, and then Kate took over. Her Ma learned her how," Humphrey said as if that explained every thing.

Finch just shook his head in bewilderment and sank back on his bedroll and stared at the stars in the sky. He went to sleep thinking of Colette and their wild hour of ecstasy in the box canyon.

# CHAPTER 19

It started raining during the night, and Finch and Humphrey had to pull their tarps over their heads. It began as a slow drizzle and continued. Clem and the cowboys waited fearfully for the lightning and thunder that usually accompanied a spring rain, but their fears were unfounded, for only the slow, soaking rain continued.

"More like a fall rain than spring." Clem said as he rode over for coffee. "And we can shore be glad of it. Lightnin' can start a cattle run."

"The herd makin' it all right?" Humphrey asked.

"They're doin' all right," Clem replied. "Ground is gettin' soft, which don't hurt nothin' but the boys horses. Makes them cattle tired is all, and they handle better that way. But the boys will have to stay in the saddle as long as it's rainin'. If it keep up tonight, all of 'em will have to ride night herd, too. They'll lose a lot of sleep, and the horses will get used up faster."

Humphrey did not reply, and Clem stood drinking the hot coffee as water ran from his slicker and hat.

"Where's Finch?"

"He rode on out early. Said he was afraid we'd have another dry camp tonight."

"Won't bother the cattle," Clem said. "They're gettin' plenty of water grazin' on the wet grass."

Then, with characteristic abruptness, Clem drained his cup, mounted his horse, and rode back to the herd.

It was still raining when Finch returned at noon. "We will have another dry camp tonight," he reported.

"Clem says the cattle will be all right, anyway," Humphrey replied. "Says they're gettin' enough water by grazin' on that wet grass."

"He's right about that. But it's sure goin' to be tough on the cowboys and horses. And I'm not sure but what we're goin' to have another dry camp after tonight. I rode quite a ways and didn't see any creeks. This rain is falling so slow that it's soaking in the ground. If it was raining harder, it would make some streams."

The rain continued throughout the day.

Finch and Humphrey constructed a shelter for Kate and the other cooks by fastening a tarp to the wagons and propping it up with the poles that Clem had ordered into one of the wagons while they were in the timber country. They ate their supper standing under the shelter.

"Clem says that if it keeps rainin' he may move a couple of the black crew to flanker and let the new ones ride drag," Humphrey said as he drank his coffee. "His cowboys are about tuckered havin' to ride day and night too in this rain."

"That's some different tune old Clem is singin' now!" Finch said. "Those blacks have sure fooled him and me, too, I guess. But I've never been around blacks much."

"Well, they have fooled me too," Humphrey said. "And I've been around 'em all my life."

The slow, drizzling rain continued for the next three days. The cowboys and horses were dead tired, although the cowboys were able to get short naps in the saddle when riding with the herd. Clem finally let two more of the blacks ride drag, and moved the black who had been riding drag to flanker. Then he moved the two blacks that had been riding flank to swing. He did so with misgivings, but he had been watching them closely, and they were doing well. They seemed to have a sort of rapport with the cattle and often could anticipate their mood as well as he could.

"Looks like we're gonna wind up with a bunch of barefooted niggers herdin' cattle with jist a surcingle around their hosses," he said grumpily.

But the blacks did not seem to mind the rain, and, although it was cold, they seemed impervious to it.

"Them damn black hides gotta be tougher than whites," one cowboy grumbled. "They ride without even a coat, and most of 'em is barefooted. Sing all the time, too."

Indeed, the blacks were having the time of their lives. Working bare from the waist up in the hot, humid fields of Louisiana had enured their skin to the weather, and their torsos were almost leather-like.

While riding drag, the first two had tied lariats to their surcingle and had practiced roping the hind feet of the laggards until they had become adept at it. As they progressed from drag, to flank, to swing, they continued their incessant practice with the rope and sang almost constantly.

They also took great pride in their ability to keep the wandering cattle from straying from the herd. It was as if their jobs, which could not be supervised by anyone, had awakened a latent sense of responsibility in them.

While the black cowboys were relieving the whites at regular intervals, Maisie kept the coffee hot and prepared food that the cowboys swore was the best they had ever had. In fact, the only thing that the white cowboys missed was any excuse to cuss the camp cook.

Late in the afternoon of the third day of continuous rain, Clem rode into the caravan camp. His face was drawn and tired and his eyes sunken. He took a cup of coffee from Ellie and stood under the tarp with Humphrey to drink it. "I'll tell you, Hump, if it wasn't for them nigger cowboys, we'd be in a hell of a fix. You reckon this rain will ever stop?"

"Buff brought some meat in this afternoon. He says the rain will stop tonight."

"Damn! That shore sounds good. And I'll bet he's right, too! That old mountain man has lived so long in the wild, he can smell weather better than a mustang."

Finch rode in from scout as Clem and Humphrey were finishing their coffee. He was wet and cold and accepted a cup of hot coffee gratefully. "Saw a little clear streak in the west," he said. "My guess is that the rain is about over."

"Buff says it'll stop tonight," Humphrey offered.

"Then you can bet on it!" Finch said confidently.

"How does it look up ahead?" Clem wanted to know.

"Plenty of good tall grass and flat country," Finch said. "Yucca is beginning to come out a bit. Lots of post oak to build fires with. Some cedars and elms, lots of cactus, cottonwoods and salt cedar close to the streams. Lots of creosote brush and sage. Some of the redbuds and primrose beginning to show a little, and I shore thought I saw a little tinge of green in a few mesquite."

"Plenty of water?" Clem was thinking of the cattle. "Plenty of good streams. We won't have to make another dry camp."

Clem shivered and shook water from his hat and slicker. "Right now a dry camp sounds mighty fine, but the livestock will shore get thirsty as soon as the rain quits and the sun comes out."

"I saw something else, too," Finch said. "Mustang tracks."

"The hell you did!" ejaculated Clem.

"Shore did," Finch affirmed. "Not more than ten miles ahead. And the tracks were fresh."

"Can we catch some?" Humphrey asked hopefully. He winced every time he saw one of the cowboys mounted on his thoroughbred mares.

"Don't see how we can do it now," Finch said. "All of the cowboys have got their hands full with the herd, and I doubt if Clem could spare any to chase mustangs."

"That's for damn sure," Clem agreed. "But we shore as hell do need some fresh horses. This deep mud the past few days has got all the horses draggin' their tails, and the boys ain't much better off."

"Well," Humphrey said with unaccustomed optimism, "Maybe things will look better if the sun comes out tomorrow."

"They shore won't look no worse," Clem said flatly. "This whole trip has gone to hell since Colette—since we left the valley, seems like." He turned, mounted his horse, and rode away without another word.

"Let's get some sleep, Hump," Finch said. "I didn't tell Clem because I'm not sure, but I trailed that herd of mustangs for a way, and if I'm right, they're in a box canyon just off the caprock, and there's plenty of grass and water. I think we might be able to let the herd stop a few days and maybe catch some of the mustangs if we can trap 'em in that canyon."

After they were in their bedrolls with their tarps pulled over their heads, Humphrey called to Finch. His voice was muffled by the tarp and rain, but he could be heard. "You really think we might catch some of them little horses, Finch?"

"I doubt it, Hump. But I'll ride out early in the morning. If they are still in that box canyon, maybe I can keep 'em bottled up till you get there."

"Largo might help," Humphrey said.

"He sure could," Finch agreed. "But he's scoutin' behind. I'd hate to take a chance with him not being there."

"Hell, Finch. We been takin' chances all the way from Fort Worth. Might as well not stop now. I'll tell Largo to send one of them young bucks back here to keep watch. He can go with you."

"All right with me, Hump. We'll leave early. Let's get some sleep." With that Finch turned on his side and was asleep.

The stars were out the next morning. Finch and Largo left camp before the cattle had risen from their beds. Largo was riding Chico's horse and saddle. They rode rapidly.

"I figure the mustangs left that canyon last night," Finch said. "But, if, by chance, that didn't, they'll leave today; so we need to get there as soon as we can."

"Yassuh, Mars Finch," Largo said. "I reckon I can stay up with yo when I's ridin' this good hoss o Mars Chico's that you let me use."

Finch did not answer, but spurred into a lope. Largo kept abreast.

"The canyon mouth is about a mile ahead," Finch said. "This ground is still wet, and we can sure tell whether they came out or not."

"How we gonna keep 'em in, if dey's still there, Mars Finch?" Largo asked.

"The mouth of that canyon isn't very wide. If they are in there, we will try to guard the entrance until the wagons and herd get here."

"And then?"

"I just dunno, Largo," Finch replied candidly. "We'll just have to figure something out, and I don't know what it will be. Maybe Clem will have some idea."

They reached the mouth of the box canyon shortly, and Finch instructed Largo to wait near the center of it while he scouted both ways. It took him only a few minutes to determine that the mustangs had not left the canyon. He rode back to Largo.

"They're still in there," he said confidently. "The tracks where they went in are almost washed out by the rain, but there are no fresh ones comin' out. They are in there all right."

"How big is that canyon, Mars Finch?"

"I don't know. I've ridden by it before, but I've never gone in it. And I didn't follow the mustangs in yesterday, cause I was afraid they would see me—or smell me."

"What do we do now, Mars Finch?"

"I wish I knew," Finch said indecisively. "We might build some fire here and try to stop them, but I'm afraid that would scare them, and a mustang would run over a cliff if he was boogered enough. I think our best bet is just to ride back and forth across the entrance and keep pretty quiet. When they see us, they'll turn back if they don't think they are being hemmed in. So let's just make out like we don't even see them, but let them see us. Maybe they'll sneak back in the canyon like any other wild animal would."

Finch was trying to conceive a plan as he talked to Largo, but his mind kept returning to another time and another place where he had spied mustangs and had entered a box canyon. He talked almost compulsively to Largo to keep his unruly mind on the task at hand.

"There is plenty of water in the stream down there in that flat for the cattle and remuda and enough grass to last a month. If we could just get those mustangs bottled up good and tight in that canyon, we could catch all we need."

Finch and Largo rode the mouth of the box canyon for hours, but did not see any mustangs. "I'll bet they've seen us, though," Finch said.

The sun was shining brightly, and it was almost hot. Finch and Largo had shed their heavy coats before noon. It was mid-afternoon when they saw the caravan and cattle plodding slowly toward them. Steam was rising from the wet canvas wagon covers, and from the wet cattle.

Finch and Largo did not leave their posts, but waited until the caravan pulled up and the herd stopped in the valley below. Humphrey rode up to Finch and Largo.

"They still in there?"

"They're in there, all right," Finch said. "Now all we have to do is figure out how to catch 'em."

"You've never caught any?" Humphrey was surprised.

"Nope. I've chased about every other kind of varmint on these plains, but never a mustang. Heard a lot of yarns about 'em, though."

"Maybe Clem will have some suggestions," Humphrey said.

"Maybe," Finch agreed. "I don't think he has ever chased any, but seems to me that I heard Bart and Choc say they had. Anyway, here comes Clem now."

As Clem rode up, they all greeted him, and Humphrey asked, "You ever caught any mustangs, Clem?"

"I aint," Clem answered. "But Bart and Choc have. They been hopin' they'd still be in that box."

"They're still in there," Finch said.

"Good," Clem answered. "I'll ride down and send Bart and Choc up. Mebbe you fellers can figger somethin' out."

Bart and Choc, the two bronc stompers who had first instructed the Negro riders, came up in a few minutes.

"You boys ever caught mustangs before?" Humphrey asked.

"We been on a couple of horse hunts," admitted Choc.

"Then how is the best way to catch 'em?"

"There ain't no best way!" Bart volunteered. "Any way we try will be rough."

"But they can be caught?" Humphrey persisted.

"Yeah. They can. But catchin' 'em is just the beginnin'. Breakin' 'em out is next."

"Well, first, how do we go about catchin' 'em?" Humphrey was impatient.

"Several ways. None of 'em easy. There was one old feller named Bob Lemon; he just went out and lived with a herd so long that they started followin' his horse. Took him a couple of months to get 'em into a corral. He was more'n half horse hisself, so I hear. Anyway, we ain't got time for that. Clem says we'll have to move the cattle in a week."

"There must be other ways," Humphrey said impatiently.

"They is. A feller can finally jist walk 'em down, but that takes time, too. And out on the plains we could chase 'em down by ridin' after 'em in relays. But that takes time, too, and we already got 'em boxed in."

"Then, how?"

"Well, the fastest way is to crease a few of 'em."

"Crease 'em?"

"Yeah, you shoot 'em jist at the top of their necks and hit their spinal cord a little bit. It sort of stuns 'em till you can get their legs tied. But you kill a lot of mustangs that way."

"Finch and I are both good with a rife," Humphrey said hopefully.

"We're not that good, Hump," Finch said. "Besides the spinal cords in horses aren't always exactly alike. I'd not like to try that."

"Well, we been talkin' about catchin' some mustangs ever since we left Decatur. Now we got a bunch hemmed up; so how the hell we gonna get 'em?"

"I reckon I saved the best and easiest way till the last," Choc said.

"Go ahead," Humphrey invited eagerly.

"Well, if we can get the mouth of the canyon plugged up some way, we can go in there and rope 'em. They'll choke down pretty quick, and we can tie their feet."

"How big is the canyon, Finch?" Choc asked.

"I don't know," admitted Finch. "I've never been in it, but I've ridden by it a couple of times."

"If it's very big, it'll make a difference."

"How's that?"

"If it's very big, we'll run a bunch of horses down tryin' to rope 'em. If it's fairly small, Art and Dee, they could rope all we need pretty quick."

"How are we goin' to be able to block the mouth of this canyon?" Finch asked.

All were silent for a few minutes. Then Humphrey volunteered, "There isn't enough timber close by to build a fence. Tell you what—you reckon we could park the wagons across the mouth of it here? We got enough wagons to do it, and we could unhitch the mules and run the tongue of one wagon under the one in front; that way it would be a solid wall of 'em."

"Might work," Choc agreed. "Providin' they ain't got a old stallion headin' 'em up. If they have, the wagons wouldn't stop 'im. I expect most of 'em will be mares and maybe a few young studs, but it's old boss stallion we will have to worry about."

They all sat in silence for a few more minutes; then Finch said, "Hump you get the wagons lined up across here. I'll take care of the stallion." Finch removed his rifle from the scabbard and turned his horse.

"What about the mules?"

"Turn 'em in here," Finch directed, "and the rest of the remuda too, all except the ones we're gonna use for herdin' the cattle and ropin' these mustangs. Probably settle the wild bunch down a little."

As Finch rode into the canyon, Humphrey started lining up the wagons. They heard a shot, and almost immediately a herd of thirty or forty mustangs appeared in a dead run toward the wagons. Everyone started yelling and waving slickers, coats, or anything else they could grab. Humphrey shot his rifle into the air a couple of times. The herd turned tail and fled back into the canyon. A few minutes later Finch reappeared. His face was grim.

"Get 'im?" Humphrey asked.

Finch nodded his head. "He was a big, pretty thing, too. I'd almost as soon shoot a man." Humphrey nodded sympathetically. He knew how much Finch loved a good horse.

"How big is the canyon?" Choc wanted to know.

"Not more than a hundred acres or so," Finch replied. "And it comes to a V at the end. A water fall comes from a bluff above when it rains hard, and it has formed a sort of sand bar below. That's the reason the mustangs are in there. They like to roll in that warm, soft sand."

Humphrey completed the task of lining up the wagons across the mouth of the canyon, and turning the mules into the canyon.

"What now?" he asked Choc.

"Well, it's late in the day, and the cattle are grazin'. I expect Clem will let 'em bed down early; they're tired after walkin' in the soft ground all day. And another night in the canyon may settle them mustangs down some, especially if them mules begin to mix with 'em."

"All right. We'll set up camp here and have a meetin' after supper. Tell Clem to bring Art and Dee and any of the others that are good ropers. Let the blacks stay with the cattle. Don't hurt them to work long hours anyway."

Choc and Bart rode back toward the herd, and Humphrey ordered Kate and the other cooks to prepare supper.

\* \* \* \* \* \*

There were perhaps a dozen men at the meeting after supper. Largo was the only black. Finch led off the discussion.

"Well, we've got a bunch of mustangs hemmed up, and we need horses. What we need to figure out is how to get 'em and then get 'em broke to ride."

"I don't know how we're gonna do it," Clem chimed in, "but it's gonna have to be done in a hell of a hurry. Them cattle gonna move in about a week. It's good grass, but it won't last forever in one spot."

"Choc, you and Bart are the mustangers," Humphrey said. "What's your recommendation?"

The two young bronc busters swelled almost perceptibly upon being asked their advice.

"Well," Choc volunteered. "Early in the mornin' Art and Dee can go in and rope a couple of 'em, and some of the rest of us will ride close by. If they don't choke down, we can heel 'em and stretch 'em out. Then tie their feet good and tight so's they will stay put till we got all we need."

"Would it help any to have more gentle horses in with 'em?" Humphrey asked.

"Sure wouldn't hurt anything," Bart said. "The more gentle ones there are, the more likely they are to mill around and not run straight out."

"Largo," Humphrey said. "Go and tell the black horse herders to bring all the mares that are carryin' colts up here and turn 'em in this canyon. Be sure to get that old bell mare."

"Yassuh, Mars Hump. I do that right now."

Other possibilities of catching the mustangs were discussed, but none proved as practicable as the one Choc had suggested. The meeting was breaking up just as the gentle, pregnant mares arrived. The men made a gap in the wagon line and turned the mares into the canyon. Clem and the cowboys went back to the herd. Finch and Humphrey unrolled their beds.

When they had stretched out, Finch said to Humphrey, "I'm not as sure about this whole thing as Choc and Bart are. I've chased mustangs a time or two just for the fun of it, and I've seen 'em jump brush and ditches that you wouldn't believe possible. I wouldn't be a bit surprised if some of 'em tried to jump plumb over the wagons."

"I'm thinkin' ye might be right, me lad." It was Buff, who had come in late with a load of game.

Both Finch and Humphrey sat up as Buff approached. "Unloaded some fresh meat at the cowboy camp, I did," Buff said. "Clem, he told me what ye be plannin'. Surprised me that them mustangs got their selves bottled up like they did. Ain't natural of 'em! But sompn' I seen today surprised me a lot more, begorra!"

"Indians?" Finch and Humphrey asked in unison.

"Worse than that, more'n likely. It was that dom jackass."

"You're jokin!"

"Fact!" Buff said. "I was takin' aim on me a nice buck deer when the damndest noise ye iver hear busted out. Sounded like a Comanche, or a painter, and a mad bull all rolled into one. I jumped so far I missed that buck by forty feet, and dom near dirtied me britches."

Finch laughed, and Humphrey guffawed. It was the first time Finch had ever heard Humphrey give a real belly laugh, and it did him good.

"Where did you see that stubborn bastard?" Humphrey asked between gasps of laughter.

"Bout a mile back. Trailin' ye like a Tennessee coon dog. Still had a little short piece of rope around his neck, too. Begorra, and I dom near shot the critter jus' for fun, but I was shakin' so bad I'd a missed him, I reckon."

Both Humphrey and Finch laughed, and Buff finally joined in. Humphrey finally sobered and resumed his usual stolid poise.

"What do you know about mustangs, Buff?" Humphrey asked.

"Not too much, me lad," Buff admitted. "I know they is the toughest little critters on the plains, and I hear breakin' one to ride or harness is about like tryin' to feed two painters outta one saucer o milk."

"What about those you drive?"

"Already broke when I got 'em. Injun broke. Wunna dast try breakin' 'em me own self. But they is good honest critters once they're gentle, providin' ye don't break their spirit."

"How do the Indians break them?"

"Never seed 'em do it, but I hear tell they catch one and tie 'im to a big log or tree for a couple of days. He fights the rope and gets skinned up bad, but learns to respect the rope. And then when he gets good and hungry and thirsty, the injun, he starts teasin' 'im with a handful of grass and a skin of water. Leaves a little on the ground and then goes off and sets. The mustang, he finally comes and takes a smell of the water and a bite of the grass. Three or four days later the injun's got a hackamore on 'im."

"Then what?"

"Then the injun jist grabs a handful of mane and hops on 'im."

"He doesn't get bucked off?" Humphrey was astonished.

"A Comanche don't get bucked off of nothin' that wears hair," Buff said with admiration. "Best horsemen in the world, anyway. But the way I hear it is them mustangs don't buck so much as they run, and the injun just sets on 'im and lets 'im run till he can't run no more. By the time he gets back to the startin' place, that little old mustang is ridin' like a old hoss and guidin' with a halter. Injuns is good hoss breakers. None better. Course, they cripple and kill a lot of 'em, but that jist means they eat good that night."

"You reckon some of my niggers could do that? The ones that have been ridin' a lot, I mean?"

"Wouldn't be atall surprised," Buff said as he spat a stream of tobacco juice and lit his pipe. "Wouldn't be surprised a bit if you could get one of them surcingles on one."

"Hm-m-" Humphrey mumbled thoughtfully.

"Jist stopped by to say 'howdy'," Buff said. And then he grinned. "Also jist happened to smell that coffee that Kate had a brewin'. See you tomorrow, maybe." Buff walked away.

"Buff may have an idea there, Finch."

"He may have, Hump. But I'm still worried about all those blacks that will be in the wagons when we are in the valley chasin' the mustangs. Especially the women and kids. Reckon you ought to caution them to run and get under a wagon if they see or hear a horse comin'?"

"I'll tell 'em to do that before we leave in the mornin'," Humphrey agreed. "Goodnight, Finch."

"Night, Hump."

# Chapter 20

Just after sunup the next morning, Clem rode over to the caravan. Art and Dee, the ropers; Choc and Bart, the bronc busters; and another cowboy that Clem called Monte were with him.

"Cattle are all up and grazin' peaceful," Clem reported. "The rest of the boys and the niggers is with 'em; so I reckon we're ready to start the fun."

"Let's drink a cup of coffee first and talk a little bit," Humphrey said.

Ellie brought all of them coffee.

"This here is damn shore good coffee," Clem said. "But it ain't much better'n what we're gettin' at our own camp now. And that ain't no slam on yore good cook Hump. That Maisie is a good 'un, too."

"Figgered she would be," Humphrey said. "How you reckon we ort to start out, Clem?"

"Well we can all ride on in and see what we got. Then the rest of us can hold back. Art and Dee can ride on in and see if they can rope a couple of 'em. But if some of 'em get past us, then the niggers ought to line up by them wagons and wave saddle blankets, dresses, or whatever they got, an' try to turn 'em."

"I told 'em that last night," Humphrey said. "And Finch and Largo will ride with us today, too. Buff is gonna circle the camp in his wagon, and that ought to be all the scout we need out for today."

"Hope so," Clem said sincerely. "But we shore do need to remember we're in Indian country."

"We will, Clem," Finch said. " I sent out four of the blacks to watch. I reckon we'll be all right for today, anyway."

"Good," Clem approved heartily.

A few minutes later they were saddled and rode into the canyon. When they came in sight of the mustangs, they were pleased to see that the mules and gentle mares had joined them. But they all turned and ran wildly as the riders approached. The riders kept pushing them, and soon they were milling about in the tight V of the box canyon. The mustangs were scrawny and thin, for they were not migratory creatures and had suffered through the harsh winter on the skimpy forage of their home range. They were a sorry looking lot when compared to the sleek thoroughbred mares mixed with them. Even the mules were larger. The mustangs were of almost every conceivable color: duns, sorrels, bays, grays, chestnuts, roans, buckskins, with a few black and dark browns mixed in.

The men just sat and looked at them for a few minutes.

"Well." It was Clem who broke the silence. "We ain't gonna catch nothin' sittin' here. Dee, you and Art ride in and see if you can put a noose on a couple of 'em. Monte, you still got that sack of piggin' string and new ropes?"

"Right here." Monted patted a sack tied to his saddle horn.

"Good," Clem said. "Give Choc and Bart a couple apiece. Now Dee, when you and Art get two of 'em caught, let 'em run this way a little ways if they will and then bust 'em on their ass. They'll fight like hell; so let 'em do it and choke 'em down as quick as you can. Soon as they are down, Choc and Bart will come in and tie their legs. An' they better do a damn good job of it, too. A mustang is dangerous till he's dead or good broke. Ready?"

The men all nodded silently. "What do we do, Clem?" Humphrey asked.

"We'll spread out across here and try to turn back anything that leaves the herd. I'll build a loop in case one of 'em gets in trouble, and Finch will keep his rifle handy."

Art and Dee approached the herd slowly. The frightened horses began to mill about restlessly. Finally, two of them broke away and tried to run past the ropers. Art and Dee slammed spurs to their roping horses, and having a good angle on them, were able to get in roping distance quickly. Each threw his rope, and the loops settled accurately over the heads of the mustangs. The roping horses set their front feet solidly for the shock that they knew was coming. One of the mustangs was flipped on his back when he hit the end of the rope, but the other only whip lashed to face his captor. The one that had fallen quickly regained his feet, and both of them began pulling back on the ropes as hard as they could. Art and Dee held the ropes taut, and their horses kept backing. The tight nooses were making it impossible for the mustangs to breathe, but they kept fighting until one of them fell heavily on his side. Choc rode quickly to him, leaped from his horse, and almost immediately had one front leg firmly secured to the two back legs. Art moved his horse a couple of steps, and Choc quickly loosed the rope about the mustang's throat. The horse lay as if dead for a moment; Dee pushed his knees into the horse's stomach forcefully. The horse gasped and then began to breathe raspingly.

In the meantime, Art and Bart had gone through the same procedure with the other mustang. Then Choc and Bart rode back to Monte for more piggin' strings as Art and Dee approached the herd again.

"That's all there is to it?" Humphrey asked in surprise as he watched the two helpless mustangs.

"Not quite," Clem grinned almost grimly. "But it's a start. We need to get at least twenty of 'em."

The next two mustangs were caught and securely tied in much the same fashion as the first two. As the ropers approached the third time, one of the young stallions broke out. It was Dee who roped him. Finch took his rifle out of the saddle scabbard. Clem cleared his rope.

"Dee's got him a stud," Clem said to Monte. "He may fight. If he does, Finch will shoot 'im. If he don't as quick as he chokes down and they get 'im tied, you go down and cut 'im."

"You mean castrate 'im?" Humphrey asked in surprise.

"Damn right!" Clem did not take his eyes off the captured stallion.

"Maybe he ain't gonna fight," Clem observed. "But if he does, Dee has got a good horse and can stay out of his way will Finch gets a shot."

"You gonna kill 'im?" Humphrey was getting his second harsh lesson in mustanging.

"Damn right we gonna kill 'im, lessen you want to go down there and take that rope off of 'im, Hump."

Humphrey just shook his head and said nothing. Finch held his rifle at ready until it became apparent that the young mustang stud was not going to charge Dee's horse, but was pulling the rope tighter and tighter about his neck until he finally flopped on his side.

Monte ran and applied the knife as soon as the horse was tied down; he threw the bloody testicles away, and Finch reholstered his rifle.

The sun was shining brightly, and little air circulated in the canyon. After they had eight mustangs on the ground and firmly secured, all the riders assembled a good distance from the herd. Art and Dee dismounted and loosened their cinches to let their panting and sweat soaked horses blow a few minutes.

"Goin' a lot better'n I figgered it would," Clem said. "But we damn shore ain't there, yet."

"Hope we don't have to shoot one!" Finch said.

"Hope not, too," Clem said. "But there's a four or five year old black stud in there that looks mean as hell. He's liable to give us trouble."

A few minutes later the roping began again, and four more mustangs were caught in short order. As Dee and Art rode toward the herd the next time, however, several of the mustangs broke from the herd. Art and Dee roped two of them, but the others, led by the black stud, evaded even the turnback men and raced toward the canyon mouth.

"Want me to shoot 'im, Clem?" Finch asked.

"Naw!" Clem answered. "The niggers and wagons will turn 'em back."

The men resumed their positions. There were plenty of mustangs left. They were watching carefully as Art and Dee approached the herd again, when they heard yells from the canyon mouth. Evidently the blacks were doing their job of turning the mustangs. But almost immediately the yells were replaced by screams and then the sound of a crash.

"Now, what the hell?" Clem glowered.

"Sounds like the mustangs ran into a wagon," Finch said. "Want me to go see?"

"Naw!" Clem said. "We'd better all stay here. Since a few of 'em got by us, the others may try it, too. We don't want to lose the whole damn bunch."

The roping continued until they had twenty of the scrawny mustangs on the ground. Clem said, "Better catch a couple of extras. We're pretty shore to cripple or kill some while we're breakin' 'em."

Two more were caught and tied. There were still several in the group of mares and mules, but everyone agreed that they had enough mustangs.

"Breakin' twenty mustangs in the next few days ain't gonna be easy," Choc opined. "And we shore don't need no more."

The sun had reached the zenith, and the day was hot.

"Let's all go get some chow, and we'll come back in a couple of hours," Clem said.

"What about the tied down mustangs?" Humphrey wanted to know.

"Let 'em lay," Clem said. Then he added facetiously, "Choc and Bart want to have 'em all rested up good when they start ridin' 'em."

As soon as the line of wagons was in sight, they immediately realized that something was amiss. The cover of one of the wagons was completely gone, and the Negroes were all gathered in a circle. None of the mustangs were in sight. The riders spurred forward.

"What happened?" Humphrey demanded as he quickly dismounted.

"Oh, Mars Hump," wailed Kate. "Sompn' terrible happened." She was wringing her hands, and tears were rolling down her cheeks.

"Well, what?" Humphrey asked angrily.

Trey hobbled up on his crutch. "A woman got hurt bad, Mars Hump."

"Hurt? A woman? Who? How?"

"Dem hosses jis come a runnin', and we all waved and yelled like yo say to, but they don' stop. The fust one, he run plumb over Dodie, Alf's wench, and jump de wagon. He done took the top offen it when he jump, and the others, dey follow 'im. I reckon one of 'em step on Dodie an' jis caved her chest plumb in."

Humphrey and Finch elbowed their way to the fallen woman. She was still alive, but her breath was coming in shallow gasps. Her dress top had been removed, revealing that her chest was caved in. She was moaning softly.

Humphrey knelt beside her. He could see the outline of a hoof. He shook his head. "Get her into a wagon and put her on a mattress," he ordered. "And one of you boys get Alf."

"He's with the herd," Clem volunteered. "Art, you go get 'im."

Dodie was moved to a wagon where she lay without moving, still moaning softly.

"Her ribs are all caved in," Humphrey said as he walked back to Finch, who was holding his horse for him.

"She dead?" Finch asked anxiously.

"Not yet," Humphrey said. "But it won't be long, I think. Here comes Alf."

Alf rode up and quickly dismounted. His horse looked strange with only a bridle and a surcingle with a coiled rope attached. Alf did not look at Humphrey or Finch, but quickly jumped into the wagon where Dodie lay.

"Wish I had shot that stud!" Finch said bitterly.

\* \* \* \* \* \*

The men moved the wagons from across the canyon mouth. Art and Dee went to get their cutting horses. Clem instructed the blacks to let any of the mustangs through when they came out of the canyon. When they returned to the herd of horses, they were still huddled in the V, and the ones that had been captured were apparently still secure.

"All right," Clem said. "Let's line up again and let Art and Dee ride in and cut the mustangs out. "We'll let them by, and hold the mares and mules in here. Them mustangs that leaves will be plumb out of the country by tonight."

Separation of the mustangs from the gentle thoroughbred mares and mules proved to be relatively easy for Art and Dee on their agile cutting horses. But they were soon drenched with sweat as the day grew hotter. The horses ridden by the turnback men also were severely tested, for occasionally a mare or a mule came out of the herd and had to be pursued rapidly until headed and turned back to the herd.

In less than two hours the task was done, however, and the men all gathered a distance away to discuss the next step.

"Let's jist let them mares and mules settle down for a couple of hours, and then bring them nigger horse herders in here and take 'em back to the remuda. They won't be no trouble, now."

All except Humphrey dismounted and loosened their cinches. He rode back to camp; when he reappeared he looked grim.

"How's Dodie?" Largo asked as he drew near.

No one spoke for a moment. Then Humphrey said, "She's bad off!"

Finch felt sick inside. He had expected the trip to be tough, but it was becoming a nightmare.

"Hate to hear that," Clem said in, for him, a gentle tone. "Do she and Alph have any little un's?" Humphrey asked Largo.

"Dodie, she got one about eight year old. A boy. Don' know if it Alph's or not, Mars Hump. Alph and Dodie was one of 'em that yo had marry up back in Loosiany."

"All right, you boys go on with the horses here. Me and Largo will get back to camp," Humphrey said.

Humphrey and Largo rode away. Clem began giving instructions to the bronc busters. Finch listened intently.

"Now, Choc, you and Bart git yore saddles ready. You'll need to shorten the cinches for them little mustangs. Art and Dee will blindfold 'em, while they are down, and then you put a halter on 'im and let 'em up. They'll stand still while they are blindfolded; so slip yore saddle on 'em real easy and cinch it tight. Get a good hold on that halter. Take a deep seat and a long rein, and we'll pull the blindfold off."

"What next?" Finch asked.

"A big, damn explosion, probly," Clem grinned. "But Choc and Bart can set 'em all right. They'll try to run first thing, but you boys spur hell out of 'em till they start buckin'. Let 'em buck till they give out. When they do, I'll ride in and pick ya up with my horse. Any questions?"

"Reckon not," Choc said. "But what are you gonna do with 'em after we buck 'em out?"

"We'll tie 'em to a tree or a log and let 'em spend the night. They'll get skinned up, or maybe crippled, but they'll learn to respect that rope. And tomorrow we'll come back and give 'em a little water and maybe a few bites or grass and ride 'em again."

"What about the ones that are still tied down?"

"Leave 'em be till we've rode all we can today, and then we'll blindfold 'em and let 'em up and tie 'em to trees, too. By tomorrow, all of 'em ought to be toned down a little."

The first two that Choc and Bart rode did almost as predicted. Choc and Bart yelled and spurred viciously until the small horses began to buck. In a few minutes the horses were exhausted and standing spraddle legged and sweating. Choc had blood running from his nose.

"Them little bastards can buck," Choc grinned as he wiped his bloody nose. "Jar hell out of a man."

The breaking continued, and they came to the gelding that Monte had castrated that morning. There was a big pool of blood under him.

"Looks like he's bled pretty bad, Clem. Reckon we ought to ride 'im?"

"Hell, yes!" Clem said. "He probly thinks he's still a stud. He'll take more tamin' than them mares. Slap a saddle on 'im!"

They blindfolded and saddled the horse which stood trembling as Choc mounted. Art pulled the blindfold; Choc rammed his spurs in the horse's shoulders and yelled. He did not attempt to run as the others had, but immediately started bucking. It was quickly apparent that Choc had his hands full. The horse bawled lustily, jumping and turning in a desperate effort to rid himself of his burden. Finch and Clem sat and watched in admiration. Suddenly, the mustang fell, and Choc's leg was caught under him.

Finch and Clem started running toward them, and Clem yelled, "Grab that saddle horn Choc and hold him down till we find out whether yore foot is out of the stirrups, or not."

As Finch and Clem ran panting to the horse and man, Finch could see that Choc had the saddle horn and was holding on grimly. The horse's feet were thrashing about, but could not get purchase on the ground as long as Choc held the saddle horn.

"Keep a holdin' that horn, Choc," Clem encouraged. "We'll get the saddle uncinched in a minute and let the bastard up. Art, you put yore rope around his neck so's you can drag 'im to a tree when he gets up."

Finch and Clem both bent over to try to get the saddle uncinched. It was tight, and they were having trouble with the latigo, when the gelding suddenly bent his neck and bared his teeth viciously. Finch reacted spontaneously and hit the horse in the mouth with his fist. He winced as he felt his knuckles meet the sharp edges of the horse's teeth.

Almost immediately Art threw his rope over the horse's head and pulled his neck taut just as Clem successfully loosened the latigo.

"Pull him out, Art. Choc, you keep the saddle atween yore laigs so if he kicks, you won't get hit in the balls."

Art's horse pulled, and the gelding got to his feet almost at once. Choc lay still for a moment with the saddle between his legs.

"You hurt any?" Clem asked solicitously.

"Naw," Choc grinned. "That hoss wasn't heavy enough to hurt my leg much. Hell! Finch is hurt worse'n I am. Look at that bloody hand. What happened to you, Finch?"

Finch looked and was surprised to see blood dripping off the fingers of his right hands. Upon closer inspection, he was amazed to see that three of the knuckles had been cut to the bone.

"What happened?" Clem said almost savagely.

"I got in a fight with a horse," Finch said facetiously. "Looks like he won, too. Hope he's got a sore tooth."

"You cut that on that mustang's teeth?" Clem asked anxiously.

"Yeah, I did. He tried to bite, and I just automatically hit him. I'm not hurt."

"I shore as hell hope not," Clem said. "But you get back to the wagons and pour some of Hump's whiskey on the cut. And then soak it in some salt water. A hoss bite can be bad!"

"I will just as soon as I help—"

"Go now!" Clem ordered. "We'll take care of the damn hosses."

"All right," Finch said and mounted his horse. He reached the caravan just in time to hear the blacks begin a low, mournful, almost feral chant. They were gathered in a circle by one of the wagons.

Humphrey came stalking out of the circle. His face was grim, and his shoulder sagged.

"What happened?" Finch asked.

"Dodie just died," Humphrey said.

"Oh."

"Let's go to my wagon," Humphrey said. "I need a drink." He got a bottle from the wagon and offered it to Finch, who took a short sip and passed the bottle back.

"What happened to your hand?"

"Oh, yeah! I got it hurt by one of those mustangs. Let me have that bottle again."

Humphrey handed him the bottle, and he poured some of the whiskey on the lacerated knuckles.

"Whew!" he whistled. "No wonder that stuff burns so much goin' down. It just set my hand on fire."

"Let me see that!" Humphrey ordered, and Finch obligingly held out his hand. "It's beginnin' to swell. I'll have Kate fix some hot, salty water, and you soak it good."

"That's what Clem said to do. But I'll fix the water. Kate will want to be with—"

"Kate will fix the water," Humphrey said crisply as he walked toward the circle of mourning blacks.

Finch shook his head in resignation. Sometimes he felt that Humphrey was a heartless stranger, and at other times he could be as compassionate as a woman. He was an enigma to Finch, though he had a profound belief that Humphrey Beatenbow was a man that could be trusted with his life. But Finch could not understand his apparent callous treatment of the blacks—nor why they seemed to adore him.

Kate brought a pan of hot, salty water, and Finch put his hand in it. The salt burned, but not as much as the whiskey.

"Yo soaks that han' good, Mars Finch," Kate admonished. "I'll set a big pail of hot water right here so's yo can heat it up if'n it start to cool."

"All right, Kate. You can go on back now," Humphrey said. "And me and Finch don't want any supper tonight. You heah?"

"I hears yo, Mars Hump," Kate said. "That right nice o' yo. I reckon them niggers gonna need me."

With that, Kate waddled hurriedly toward the circle of chanting Negroes.

"What are they goin' to do now, Hump?" Finch was puzzled.

"Gonna bury Dodie," Humphrey said, "If they can get it done afore sundown. If they can't, they'll wait till after sunup."

"Why is that?"

"No idee!" Humphrey replied. "Somethin' about their religion, I guess. They won't leave a grave open overnight, and they'll bury all her belongin's along with her."

"I'll be darned," Finch said in wonder. "Some Indians do that, too. Even bury a warrior's horse with 'im and all his weapons, too. They think he will need them in the spirit world."

"I don't know what the niggers think," Humphrey said musingly. "They've still got a lot of Africa in 'em, I guess. They believe in 'ha'nts' and ghosts and witches and spooks. And they've got witch doctors, too. I used to slip down and spy on the slaves when I was a kid. Some of the things they do are downright spooky. Makes a man think."

"You've been around 'em a lot, haven't you, Hump?"

"All my life," Humphrey said. "They got some mighty peculiar ways, but—"

Clem rode up just then and as usual dismounted without salutation. "What in hell is all the moanin' about?" he wanted to know.

"The niggers are buryin' Dodie."

"Damn! That shore is a creepy sound. Near like the blood call."

"The blood call?" Humphrey queried.

"You ain't never heard that?" Clem asked in surprise.

"Never."

"Well, an animal gets killed and spills a lot of blood, and others will smell the blood and gather around, especially cattle, and they take on somethin' fierce. Paw the ground and bawl and moan. It's plumb scary. Makes a man's hair stand up. How's the hand?"

Finch had forgotten about his wounded hand, and he removed it from the salty water, which had cooled.

"Already swole up," Clem said, "and gettin' bigger."

"I'll heat some more water," Humphrey said.

With that he got up and poured some of the water from the big pail that Kate had left. Then he stoked up the fire and set it on to reheat. Finch was mildly surprised that Humphrey did not call Kate to come do it. Then Humphrey stirred about and brought two plates of cold food. It was the first time that Finch had seen him indicate any sort of sympathy or consideration for the blacks, and he immediately suspected that Hump was not nearly as callous and unfeeling toward them as he had thought.

"Ain't much," Humphrey said apologetically. "But I reckon it'll hold us till mornin'. And we got hot coffee. Want a cup, Clem?"

"I reckon," Clem said absently as he shivered. It was not cold.

The moaning chant from the Negroes continued as they drank their coffee. Clem was silent.

"Should we go down and see if we can help?" Finch asked.

"No." Humphrey replied quickly. "They don't want no whites around when they are buryin'. They got their own way."

"That sound they make is downright spooky," Finch said.

"It is, for a fact," Humphrey agreed. "I've heard it a lot of times. Makes a man feel cold."

Clem emptied his cup, mounted his horse, and rode away without a word.

\* \* \* \* \* \*

As soon as it was dark, Finch and Humphrey were ready for bed. "Let's unroll our beds by the fire here tonight, Finch, so's I can keep that water hot. Kate won't be back here till sun up, and you need to keep that hand soakin' in hot water."

When they had their beds unrolled near the fire, Humphrey placed the pan of hot, salty water beside Finch. "You keep that hand a soakin'," he said. "I'll get up during the night and keep the water hot."

As Finch lay back and looked at the stars above and listened to the eerie sound of the moaning blacks, he could not sleep.

"Hump?" he asked tentatively.

"What, Finch?" It was obvious that Humphrey had not been asleep, either.

"Do you think there is an afterworld, like the Indians and blacks do?"

"Now why do you ask that?" Humphrey asked crossly.

"I dunno," Finch said. "It's just that—well, the Indians bury a man's horse and weapons with him so he can use 'em in the happy hunting grounds, and the blacks bury all their belongings with them—was just wonderin' what you thought."

"Makes a man think, all right," Humphrey said.

Throughout the night, the ghostly chanting continued, and Humphrey kept the water hot in the basin for Finch's hand.

As soon as day began to break, they rolled their beds and tossed them into the wagon.

"When will they stop that chanting and moaning?"

"At sunup," Humphrey said. "And then they'll go on about their business, and none of 'em will ever mention her name again. And don't you say nothin' about her either."

"Why not?"

"Because, well—hell, I don't know why not. They just don't do it, that's all. Kinda like a mare that's lost her colt, I reckon. They moan and groan a while and then go on as if nothin' ever happened."

"They're strong people."

"I ain't shore they are people. They brought a lot of superstitions over here with 'em when they came from Africa."

"Why didn't they chant and moan when Sam and Largo hung that nigger."

"I dunno. Guess they figgered he didn't deserve it. You gonna be able to ride today?"

Finch held up his hand, and his fingers looked like match sticks in a potato.

"Yeah. I'll ride. But I reckon I'd better fix me a sling for this hand. Feels like it weighs a ton."

"Damn near does," Humphrey said as he inspected the hand. "But there ain't no red streaks runnin' up yore arm so maybe you ain't gonna get blood poisoning. That's what I was afraid of. I think Colette had some salve in the wagon that will help, too."

It was the first time Finch had heard Humphrey say Colette's name since they had left the Red River valley. He remembered Humphrey's assertion that the blacks never mentioned the name of a departed one. "Whatever it is the blacks have, it sure hasn't rubbed off on Hump," he thought whimsically.

\* \* \* \* \* \*

Kate, Sam, and Ellie returned to the wagon just after sunup.

"I has yo breakfas' cooked right soon, Mars Hump," Kate said in her perfectly normal voice.

"I reckon some coffee and biscuits will do, Kate. I see Clem and the boys comin' and we need to get busy with them mustangs. But you have a good dinner fixed about noon time. You heah?"

"Yassuh, Mars Hump. I sho do dat."

Finch was not able to cinch his saddle with his swollen hand; so Humphrey did it for him. He was able to mount, however, and the sling he fashioned with his neckerchief worked well. The hand was not painful, but was terribly swollen.

"You shore can't handle a rope or a gun with that bad hand," Humphrey said.

"I can use a rifle," Finch replied. "I'll just rest it across my arm."

"You'll be shootin' left handed."

"I can do that with a rifle," Finch said.

When they checked the mustangs, they found that they were skinned and rope burned around the hocks, but were already learning how vicious the rope could be around their feet. All but the gelding had also learned to quit pulling on the rope until it choked them. The gelding had choked to death trying to free himself.

"Jist as well, I reckon," Clem said without apparent regret. "Probly would a caused trouble, anyway. If they ain't cut by the time they are two years old, they always think they are a stud. Let's git started on the rest of 'em."

"What's that?" Dee asked and pointed.

Everyone looked. Four of the Negroes were walking toward them, and each one carried a surcingle.

# Chapter 21

The horsemen stared in amazement as the Negroes approached. Finally, Clem broke the silence.

"What the hell do you niggers think you're a doin'?" he demanded. "Get yore asses back to them cattle."

"Naw suh, Mars Clem," Alf said firmly. "The cowboys, they say the' plenty to take care of the cows. We's gonna hep yo break these here mustangs."

"The hell you are—"

"Wait a minute, Clem," Finch interjected. "Let's hear 'em out."

Humphrey did not say a word, but looked keenly at the blacks, and it was to him that Alf spoke.

"Mars Hump, suh," he said doggedly. "We is been ridin' now for a while. And Mars Clem, he say we do good. Now we wants to hep break them mustangs."

"An' he got a right!" Mose spoke up. "They done kilt his wench. He got a right, ain't he, Mars Hump?"

Everyone was silent for a moment, and all looked at Humphrey who stirred restlessly in his saddle. Finally he spoke.

"All right, Alf," Humphrey said almost sorrowfully. "I reckon you got a right. We'll catch each of you one."

"Wait a damn minnit!" Clem roared angrily. "Jist who the hell is bossin' this fandango, anyway, Beatenbow?"

"Right now, I am," Humphrey said evenly. "The niggers are mine, and the mustangs don't belong to anybody yet. Dee, you and Art rope a couple of 'em."

"Now, you wait a minnit—" Clem was livid.

"Hold it, Clem!" Finch's soft voice was like a pleasant breeze. "Alf and the boys want to help. And maybe they can. And Hump agrees that Alf has a right. So do I."

Clem slumped in his saddle and took a deep breath. "All right, Beatenbow," he said surlily. "If you can spare the niggers, I reckon three or four more funerals won't slow us up much. Go ahead and rope 'em." He nodded to Art and Dee.

Two mustangs were roped and blindfolded. Bart and Choc snubbed them, while Dee and Art caught and snubbed two more. The mustangs quivered and squatted low as the surcingles were tightened. The cowboys snubbed the mustangs closely until the Negroes were astride, with the halter reins in one hand and the surcingle grip in the other.

"This may be worth losin' some mustangs and niggers!" Clem grated. "Yank them blindfolds and turn 'em loose, boys!" he yelled.

His order was immediately carried out. The small mustangs stood for a moment; then as one, they started running wildly toward the canyon mouth. The

Negroes were holding on with all their might and drumming bare heels against the sides of the mustangs. One of them lost his cap.

"Turn 'em back!" Humphrey yelled.

"Let 'em go, Hump!" Finch counselled. "As long as they're runnin' they're not goin' to buck."

"It jus' might be that them niggers is gonna stay on 'em till they ain't got no buck in 'em. But we've seen the last of them four mustangs. You can damn well bet on that," Clem said.

"We've got plenty more, Clem," Finch said. "Now let's get on with breakin' 'em. We've got a full day ahead of us. We need to start movin' on west as soon as we can."

"All right," Clem said grimly. "Art, you and Dee drag a couple of 'em out for Choc and Bart. Monte you gather up the piggin' strings and loose ropes. Me and Finch and Beatenbow will set here like we done before. I'll have my rope ready, and Finch says he can use that rifle with his left hand in case you get in trouble."

The breaking went much as it had the day before except that the mustangs did not pitch so long and hard, for they were tired and sore from fighting their tethers all night.

By noon, they had ridden six more, and they decided to quit for the morning. On their way back to the wagons, Clem said sarcastically, "Beatenbow, I reckon you might bring a pail when we come back this afternoon. Maybe some of 'em could be coaxed to drink a little. That might be of some help."

Humphrey stopped his horse, and the others turned to see what he was doing. He simply sat his horse and looked at Clem with squinted eyes. He held both shoulders erect.

"Clem," he said sternly. "Before we left, we agreed that you were to boss the cattle, and I haven't bothered you any. I am supposed to be the boss of the caravan and niggers. I reckon we sort of got our jobs mixed together this mornin' over the mustangs. You don't seem too pleased about it. Now, if you're gonna make somethin' out of it—do it now!"

Clem's jaw dropped, and Finch's eyes narrowed as he looked from Humphrey to Clem. He removed his swollen hand from its sling. The cowboys stared. Humphrey sat waiting expectantly as he and Clem eyed each other like two longhorn bulls. Clem was the first to give.

"Hell, Hump," he said contritely. "Cain't a feller git a mad on onct in a while without gettin' his ass kicked from hell to breakfast?"

"Just like to know how I stand with a man!" Humphrey said. "Far as I'm concerned, it's over. But it's up to you."

"Then it's over, boss," Clem said as he turned his horse. "I got too big a mouth, anyway."

Clem and the cowboys went to their camp for their noon meal. Kate had a good dinner fixed for Hump and Finch. Ellie served it on the table under the shade of a tarp that Kate had instructed Sam to erect.

"Lawsy me, Mars Hump," Kate said as they sat down. "Yo uns must be starved with no supper or breakfast!"

"We can eat," Humphrey admitted. "Did you see any horses and riders come out of the canyon?"

"Yassuh, Mars Hump. I shorely did. It was them four niggers on them little ponies like Mars Buff drives to his wagon. They was a runnin' like a ha'ant was after 'em!"

"Hope they don't get crippled or killed!" Humphrey said grouchily. "Finch, what was you doin' takin' you hand out of that sling when I was talkin' to Clem?"

"Just automatic, I reckon," Finch acknowledged. "Didn't realize I had till we started up again."

"Let me look at that hand again!" Humphrey ordered, and Finch held it across the table. "It ain't no bigger, and there still ain't no red streaks; so I reckon you'll live—but you shore ain't gonna hold no pistol in it for a while. We'll soak it again tonight."

"I expect you're right, Hump. But I believe the swellin' is goin' down a little. And it isn't real sore—so I think it will be all right."

"You'd be in a hell of a shape if you met up with some of your unfriendlies that Chico told me about."

"I'm hopin' I don't for a while anyway. But I can still use my rifle some."

"With your left hand!" Humphrey jeered. "Wouldn't do you too much good with enemies like you got!"

"I'll just run if I see one," Finch grinned.

Humphrey snorted his disbelief.

\* \* \* \* \* \*

The afternoon went much as had the morning with the mustangs, and before sundown Choc and Bart had ridden all except the four that the Negroes had ridden away.

Humphrey had brought two pails when they returned. He filled them and set them within reach of two tethered mustangs. They snorted and sniffed suspiciously, but apparently their thirst was too great and the smell of water too strong, for one of them finally took a short drink. Humphrey, who had been watching closely was immensely relieved. He immediately refilled the bucket from the creek and set it near another. Then he pulled an armload of grass and threw it near enough that the mustangs could reach it. During the long afternoon, Humphrey was gratified to note that each of the mustangs had drunk at least a little water.

"I reckon we might as well call it a day," Clem said as he wiped sweat from his brow. "Hump, looks like you got all of 'em to drink some. That'll keep 'em alive, and we'll ride 'em all agin tomorrow. Keepin' 'em tied to them trees is learnin' 'em to watch that rope. I figgered a couple of 'em would break a leg, but outside of that gelding that choked hisself to death, they ain't done much damage except to get some bad rope burns."

"How are we goin' to get 'em to go along with the remuda?" Humphrey asked.

"Neck 'em close to some of the cow horses, and fix the rope so's neither one of 'em will choke. That a way, they can graze some and drink, and they'll damn shore learn to lead. Besides, that's about the only way we could ever catch 'em agin."

"When do you think we can pull out?" Finch was anxious for the trip to end.

"Couple of days," Clem answered. "They'll still be mighty bronky but tien' 'em to the cowhorses will help. And we'll ride 'em as much as we can on the way.

We're gonna need 'em most hazin' them buffalo off your ranch if there are as many of 'em as you say."

"Let's go to camp," Choc said in a tired voice. "Me and Bart has had the hell beat out of us the last couple a days, and we're fagged out. Them little devils buck hard."

"You'd better rest damn fast," Clem said. "Cause you may have to ride night herd tonight. The grass is gettin' a little short, and them cattle is gettin' some restless. And we're short four nigger riders."

Both Choc and Bart groaned aloud, and Clem grinned maliciously at them.

\* \* \* \* \* \*

The sun was still an hour high as Finch and Humphrey sat at the camp table drinking coffee. Finch had his cup halfway to his mouth when he suddenly replaced it on the table.

"Look!" he said with a tinge of excitement in his voice as he pointed.

"What in the world is that?" Humphrey said as he spied what Finch was pointing at. There were three riders. Two of them were on bigger horses, and the one in the middle was on a smaller one. There were two animals trailing behind.

"I'm not sure," Finch said as he gazed with squinted eyes. "Too far off yet. But if it wasn't for that rider in the middle, I'd swear that the other two were Texas Rangers. The way those pack mules are trailin' behind them, we used to travel like that."

"They are! They're Rangers, all right!" Finch said. "And I must be crazy, but I think the one in the middle is one of the niggers on a mustang."

A short time elapsed before the riders could be seen fairly clearly.

"It is. It's Tom Murphy and Matt Jimson," Finch said in a voice as excited as he ever got. "I'd know the way those two ride anywhere!"

"God-a-mighty!" Humphrey said in awe. "That's one of the niggers on a mustang there in the middle, too."

And so it was. Finch walked eagerly toward the men. They recognized him immediately and loped forward. The Negro rider pulled his mustang sharply to one side and began flailing him with a switch that he had evidently pulled down from a tree. The mustang apparently had already begun to respond to the halter, for he veered off and began to trot slowly as the Negro pounded his ribs with his bare heels and whacked him with the switch. Humphrey walked quickly after the Negro as Tom and Matt dismounted. Finch hurried up with outstretched hand. When Matt grasped it, Finch winced, and Matt looked shocked when he saw Finch's swollen hand.

"What in the world happened to you, Finch?" he asked in alarm.

"Nothin' much. Just hurt my hand a little. Nothin' serious."

"Nothin' serious!" ejaculated Tom. "That's your gun hand!"

"I know. But it isn't bad. And it's already gettin' better. Come on in here and have a cup of coffee."

They all sat at the table, and Ellie brought coffee. Kate was bent over the cooking fire.

"Where's Hump?" Finch asked in surprise, for he had been so excited about seeing Matt and Tom that he had not noticed when Humphrey left.

"Him and Largo done gone down in the canyon," Kate replied. "Dey followin' that nigger that was ridin' that little hoss!"

"Oh!" Finch dismissed Humphrey from his mind and turned to his Ranger friends. "What brings you two out here?" Finch inquired. "Boys, it's sure enough good to see you!"

"Good to see you too, Finch," Matt grinned, and Tom smiled.

"Who are you boys after?" Finch asked again. "I know you two loafers aren't out here just for pleasure."

Both Matt and Tom sobered. Then Matt said grimly, "Well, now, maybe we are out here just for pleasure."

"Don't think I ever went on a trip that'll give me more pleasure," Tom said harshly. "And that's a fact."

Finch looked at them questioningly. It was Matt who spoke. "Word drifted down from Decatur about Chico."

"Oh!"

"Tom and me both knowed that there had to be some awful good reason that you didn't go after that killer; so we come out."

"I reckon we know now why you couldn't leave at the time. That nigger filled us in some, and we can see the rest." Tom nodded toward the caravan and herd.

"I reckon I lost my head a little that night," Finch said almost absently. "I was packed and ready to go after him when my partner knocked some sense into my head. Hurt too!" Finch said bitterly.

"Don't worry, Finch," Matt counselled. "Tom and me will git 'im if we have to go to hell and back."

"That's where you'd have to go all right," Finch said grimly. "But you won't get 'im. He's already been got."

Matt and Tom waited expectantly, and then Finch told them of the circumstances in which Humphrey had killed Doc Guine's horse to allow Old Victorio's men to capture him.

All three of them were quiet for a few moments.

"I reckon me and Tom couldn't a thought of nothin' better to do a man that would shoot Chico in the back!" Matt said at last.

"That partner of yours sounds like he's a man to ride the river with!" Tom said. "And that's a fact!"

"He is," Finch said. "You remember, I told you about him when I brought the two horses back to Austin, and Chico and I resigned from the Rangers."

"We remember," Matt said. "So does Captain Cates. Said he figured you had a responsibility you couldn't ride away from. So he sent me and Tom. Well, maybe he didn't actually send us, but when we was packed up and leavin' he says for us to get the son-of-a-bitch before we come back."

"The Rangers are still goin' then?" Finch asked. "I heard that they were bein' disbanded."

"Nobody knows for sure, even now," Tom replied. "The government is in such a damn mess that nobody seems to know anything much—which ain't too different from what it's always been!"

Finch grinned for the first time since Matt had explained their errand. "Well, tell me all the news. What have all the boys been doin'?"

"Still chasin' varmints over the country," Matt said. "Me and Tom had just got back from a scout to find some renegade Indians that burnt a ranch down close to Lampasas."

"Find 'em?" Finch asked.

Matt nodded absently. "Wasn't more'n a dozen of 'em. Kiowas."

"How did you find us?" Finch asked curiously.

"Them cattle leave a trail that'll be easy to follow a year from now," Tom said. "So we just followed it till this afternoon when—" He suddenly burst out laughing and Matt joined him. Both of them laughed until the tears ran down their faces, and they gasped for breath.

"What's so funny?" Finch wanted to know.

"Well, I'll tell ya." Matt gasped for breath. "Tom and me was ridin' along today and fixin' to find us a good place to camp for the night when all of a sudden, here comes a wild man, black as the ace of spades, a ridin' a wild mustang bareback, and yellin' and whippin' 'im ever time he hit the ground. Now we had sort of been expectin' to meet somebody unfriendly, like Sally Diego, maybe, but we shore as hell hadn't expected the devil to come a ridin' at us. I tell you, Finch," Matt gasped for breath, "I damn near swore off drinkin', and Tom, he thought he'd lost what little brains he ever had. We ain't neither one been so scared in our 'ole lives."

The two Rangers continued to laugh, and Finch joined them. They were all laughing uproariously when Humphrey walked up.

"What's so funny?" he asked.

"These two," Finch pointed at Tom and Matt. "These two big, bad Texas Rangers just got scared near to death by one pore little nigger on a runty mustang!"

Then Finch told Humphrey of the Negro riding up to Matt and Tom. Humphrey joined in the laughter. It was only the second time that Finch had ever heard him laugh heartily.

Finch had been too engrossed in the telling of the incident to remember that he hadn't introduced Humphrey. When they all stopped laughing enough that he could talk, Finch said, "Hump, meet Matt and Tom, a couple of no account Rangers that I had the bad luck to be associated with for a while. Boys, this here is my partner, Humphrey Beatenbow."

They all shook hands warmly, and Humphrey said, "I reckon this calls for somethin' stronger than coffee. I'll get some snake medicine."

He went to his wagon, returning to set a full bottle on the table. Ellie brought glasses. He poured.

Matt took a sip of his and smacked his lips in approval. "Damn near swore off this stuff today when I saw that wild nigger a ridin' out of nowhere. Shore glad now I didn't."

\* \* \* \* \* \*

The Rangers reminisced as Ellie served their supper. Humphrey felt excluded, which in fact he was. When it began to get dark, the Rangers and Finch unrolled their beds a short distance from camp and staked their horses nearby. Finch noticed that Humphrey was still at the wagon.

"Hey, Hump!" he called. "Come on and get your bed fixed. It's nearly dark."

"I'll just bunk under the wagon here tonight, Finch. You boys got a lot to talk about anyway. Besides, I've got to keep the water hot for you to soak that hand all night."

"Well, we won't say anything that isn't fit for you to hear. Come on out and unroll your bed," Finch ordered sternly.

Humphrey did not answer, but went to set a pail of water on the campfire coals.

"Thought he had a wife," Matt said in a low voice.

"He did," Finch answered. "But he lost her back in the Red River valley."

"How?"

"Indians."

The three of them were silent a moment; then Tom said bitterly, "Bet it was them damn Kiowas."

"It was," Finch agreed. "But Hump hasn't let it slow him down any. She was the most woman I ever saw, too. But Hump is a man that finishes what he starts. Come hell or high water, he's gonna get this caravan and herd to our place on the Canadian."

"That partner of yours sounds like mucho hombre, as Chico would say," Matt said sincerely.

"He sure doesn't back down from anything," Finch replied.

They saw Humphrey walking toward them with his bedroll under one arm and carrying a pan in the other.

"Where's your bedroll, Finch? I'll put this pan of hot salt water beside it so you can soak that hand."

They all stretched out on their bedrolls, and the Rangers continued their reminiscences of battles they had fought, trails they had followed, and renegades and Indians they had captured or killed.

"Never will forget that first time when me and Tom saw you and you bashed the captain over the head with your pistol," Matt chuckled. "I remember the look on his face when he come to and saw you washin' the blood out of his hair."

Humphrey lay silent, listening to the Ranger banter. He had not felt so lonely since the day Colette was killed. Finally, the Rangers slept, and Humphrey quietly got up several times to warm the water for Finch's swollen hand.

It was past midnight when an unearthly noise awakened them. The Rangers sat up immediately; each had his pistol in his hand.

"What the hell was that?" Tom wanted to know. "Sounded like a banshee."

"You Rangers better start carryin' cannons instead of them little pistols," Humphrey chuckled. "That there was a mighty dangerous animal you just heard."

"What kind?" Matt said in awe. "I ain't never heard nothin' like that before."

"That there is the Beatenbow jackass," Humphrey chuckled as the sound came again.

"Hope he doesn't start the cattle runnin'," Finch said anxiously.

"He won't," Humphrey said. "Them cattle ain't so scary as you Rangers."

"Well, I'll be damned!" Matt said in a relieved voice. "A jackass!"

"We been tryin' to get rid of im' for two weeks, Humphrey explained. "But he jist keeps followin' us. I'll go see about 'im."

"I'm gonna be a nervous wreck if I stay around this outfit very long," Matt said as he took a deep breath.

When Humphrey returned to his bedroll, the Rangers were sleeping soundly. He warmed the water in the pan and crawled into his bed. And for the first time that night, he slept.

\* \* \* \* \* \*

At dawn the next morning, the Rangers were stirring. Humphrey sat up and rubbed his eyes.

"I'm afraid I let your water get cold, Finch. I musta dozed off."

"It's all right, Hump," Finch said. "The hand is better this morning anyway. Did you find the jackass?"

"Shore did," Humphrey chuckled. "He followed one of them blacks in that was ridin' a mustang. He's in the canyon now with the rest of 'em."

"Another one got back? Good!" Finch was relieved.

"Two more of 'em," Humphrey said. "Another one came in while we was stakin' the one out. And they was makin' them little mustangs turn and trot like a cowhorse. I expect they rode 'em a long ways."

"I'll be darned," Finch said wonderingly. "That just leaves one, doesn't it?"

"Alf ain't back yet," Humphrey said. "But I won't be surprised if he shows up this mornin'."

Matt and Tom had been listening uncomprehendingly to the conversation. Finch explained, and they both shook their heads in amazement.

"You're shore gettin' some new experiences on this drive, Finch," Matt observed.

"Yeah. And some of 'em haven't been good," Finch said grimly as he remembered Colette and Chico.

\* \* \* \* \* \*

Clem rode up as they were eating breakfast. He dismounted without a word and accepted a cup of coffee from Ellie. Finch introduced Matt and Tom. Clem shook their hands perfunctorily.

"The cattle is gettin' mighty restless, and the shorter that grass gets, the worse they're gonna be," he said.

"When do you think we ought to start movin'em?" Humphrey asked.

"Today!" Clem said cryptically. Humphrey and Finch both looked at him in surprise.

"Are the mustangs ready?" Humphrey asked.

"Nope. But we can take 'em with us anyway. I'd a damn sight rather lose the mustangs than the herd. We nearly had a run last night when that jackass bawled like a painter. I'm a fixin' to shoot that bastard the first time I see 'im agin."

"Don't do it!" Humphrey said sternly. "He's followed us this far; he might as well go the rest of the way. Besides, he's in the canyon with the mustangs now."

"How'd he get there?"

"Followed one of the blacks that was ridin' a mustang."

"The hell, you say!" Clem was astonished. "You mean one of them niggers actually got back?"

"Three of 'em." Humphrey said almost proudly. "And the mustangs they were ridin' are reinin' like plowhorses."

"Well, I'll be tee-total damned!" Clem said in amazement. "I shore didn't think we'd ever see any of them mustangs again."

"You will, though," Humphrey replied. "When do you want to start?"

"I'll have the boys lead some remuda hosses up and tie the mustangs to 'em," Clem said. "Then as soon as you are ready, we will be." He mounted his horse and rode back to the herd.

"Shore a sociable cuss, ain't he!" Tom grinned.

"He won't win any contests for bein' friendly," Finch admitted. "But he's a good cowman."

"How much longer will it take us to get to the ranch?" Humphrey asked Finch.

"A week ought to do it," Finch said after a moment's consideration. "There's good water the rest of the way and mostly flat country."

"That the place you showed me that time we was chasin' them renegade Kiowas, Finch?" Matt asked.

"That's it," Finch said. "I forgot that you and Tom had seen it."

"I never saw better cow country," Tom said. "But it was covered up with buffalo when we saw it."

"Still is. But we hope to haze most of 'em out."

"Gonna take a lot of ridin'," Matt observed.

"That's why we wanted to catch some mustangs," Finch said. "You can ride 'em every day, and they don't ever seem to wear out. You boys headin' back to Austin today?"

Matt and Tom looked at each other, and Matt nodded almost imperceptibly at Finch's hand.

"Well, now, Matt said laconically. "Tom and me have talked it over and we figure if Humphrey can spare some more of this good grub we been a gettin' that we'll just traipse along with you till you get where you're goin'."

"Now wait a minute!" Finch objected. They were not fooling him a bit. "The captain is gonna need you back there. He'll skin you alive if he finds out you two loafers were just out for a joy ride."

"He'd do worse than that if he knew we left you up here with a crippled pistol hand," Matt said firmly.

"And we can furnish our own grub, if need be," Tom said. "And that's a fact."

Finch sighed in resignation. "Hump, I reckon we've got us a couple of extra hands whether we want 'em or not. Doubt if they'll be worth much, but they work cheap—if you don't count the grub they eat."

"We've got plenty of grub," Humphrey said in a voice that indicated relief. "And Kate says it's a lot of trouble to fix grub for just you and me."

\* \* \* \* \* \*

The cowboys yoked the mustangs to the cowhorses and drove them to the rest of the remuda. The task was accomplished with unexpected ease. The jackass trailed along with them. Clem stopped at the wagon.

"Hump," he said as he dismounted. "Yore gonna have a increased horse herd in about a year—or a mule herd!. I ain't got no idee what kind of critter it'll be, but that bellerin' jackass was a breedin' one o them mustang mares when we went after 'em. She was still tied to a tree, but she shore wasn't tryin' to get away nohow."

Everyone laughed, and even Clem grinned a little. "We'll go ahead and let the cattle start grazin' their way north-west. The wagons ought to be able to catch up easy enough."

"We've got a couple more hands today," Humphrey nodded toward Matt and Tom.

"I'll be ridin' scout with Finch," Matt said quickly.

"And I'll be with 'em!" Tom echoed Matt.

Finch started to object but realized that it was useless. Rangers took care of their own. "I told you they wouldn't be worth their grub," Finch said to Humphrey.

"Maybe so we can think of somethin' for them to do later." Humphrey chuckled, for he understood the situation perfectly.

Finch, Matt, and Tom were out of sight by the time the drivers had caught their mules and hitched them to the wagons. The herd was grazing steadily in the right direction. An air of excitement pervaded the caravan. Everyone knew that they were on the last leg of their journey.

Finch looked back and could not see the herd or the caravan either. "I reckon we ought to ride fifteen or twenty miles ahead and then come back and meet the herd and the caravan."

"And we'd better watch our back tracks, too," Matt said. "Indians are as thick up on the plains country as fleas on a hound dog."

"Well," Finch said mockingly. "I reckon I'll just relax and enjoy the scenery since I've got me a couple of body guards along. First time I ever had that."

"Just hope you don't need us," Tom said seriously. "But you might. I doubt if you could hold a pistol without droppin' it. That hand is still pretty bad swole up."

"Well, we might as well enjoy the ride," Matt said philosophically. "Either one of you boys know any songs?"

"Nope," Finch denied. "Wish we had that locoed Mexican with us!"

"He was a singin' fool, all right," Tom said. "And that's a fact!"

# Chapter 22

The Rangers thoroughly enjoyed the day. They saw nothing more forbidding than a lot of very flat country studded with occasional sage brush, mesquite trees, yucca, and a lot of buffalo. As they stopped to let their horses drink at a small creek lined with willows, Tom observed that the willows were beginning to show a tinge of green.

"Gives me a idee," Matt said as he rode close to a clump and cut a forked limb about the size of his thumb. He tested the limb for elasticity by squeezing the two prongs and found that they did indeed spring back to their former shape when he released his grip. He rode back to Finch and handed it to him.

"Here," he said. "Try squeezin' this with that swole up gun hand. Maybe it'll put a little stout back in it."

Finch took the stick and squeezed tentatively. He grimaced, for the pain was acute, and he could hardly hold the stick in his swollen hand. He continued to squeeze sporadically, however, and the pain seemed to diminish a bit.

"That hand ain't as big as it was yesterday," Tom said after inspecting it. "Got some wrinkles in it too. That shows the swellin' is leavin'. And that's a fact."

"It's not too bad," Finch said. "Be in good shape in a few days."

"Just hope we get a few days before you need it!" Matt said.

The rest of the day was spent in reminiscing, but each of them constantly scrutinized the country as they rode. Finch continued to squeeze the forked willow and was gratified that it pained him less each time he repeated the exercise.

When they had ridden as far as they thought necessary, they stopped and ate some hard tack and jerky before heading back.

When the caravan was in sight, they saw a horse loping lazily toward them.

"That's Hump," Finch said, grinning a bit. "He's not the most graceful horseman in the world."

"Looks like a sack of spuds on a packhorse," Tom agreed. "And that's a fact."

"Hope he can handle a gun better than he can ride," Matt said.

"He can," Finch assured him. "He isn't too much with a pistol on account of a bad shoulder he got in the war, but he's pure poison with a rifle."

"Well, that's good," Matt said. "Likely he'll need a rifle more than a pistol, anyway."

When Humphrey rode up to them, they greeted each other perfunctorily.

"What did you boys see up ahead?" he asked quickly.

"Not much of anything," Finch said. "A lot of buffalo and good grass is about all."

"What about that big lake?" Humphrey asked anxiously. "How we gonna get around that?"

The three scouts looked at Humphrey in bewilderment.

"What lake?" Matt asked, perplexed.

"That big one," Humphrey said firmly. "Right straight ahead of us. Must be five miles wide. It was in plain sight for two hours this afternoon, and then I reckon the clouds sort of made it hard to see."

"Hump," Tom said, "you been at that snake medicine of yores again. They ain't no lake ahead of us. Not in ten miles, anyway. And that's a fact."

"There is," Humphrey asserted doggedly. "I seen it just as plain—"

"Wait a minnit!" Matt said as comprehension dawned. "I reckon we're forgettin' this is the first time Hump has seen this plains country, and I guess he did see a lake."

Finch and Tom looked at Matt, non-plussed.

"What you seen, Hump, was a mirage," Matt said.

"A what?"

"A mirage."

"What in hell is a mirage?" Humphrey asked irritably.

"Well," Matt began haltingly. "I ain't sure just what it is. It's a lake, all right, I guess. But it's mebbe a awful long ways off, and the clouds, or sky, or somethin', jist sort of acts like a mirror and shines a picture of that lake right down on this flat country. Captain Cates, he called it a optical illusion—whatever that is."

Finch and Tom began to laugh, but Humphrey didn't think it funny. "I even seen some animals of some kind a drinkin' out of it," he said doggedly.

"Matt's right, Hump," Finch assured him. "It's not a real lake at all. At least not in front of our caravan. I just didn't think to tell you about the mirages. We've seen so many, I reckon we just never thought to say anything about 'em."

"Well," Humphrey did not seem convinced. "All I got to say is, this is a damn strange country. How is the hand?"

Finch held out his hand and was pleasantly surprised to see that the swelling had diminished appreciably. "It's doin' fine," Finch said. "Matt cut me a willow branch to squeeze on, and it's sure helpin' a lot." He showed Humphrey the flexible twig.

Humphrey looked at the gadget and made no comment on it. He was still a bit piqued.

Tom sensed Humphrey's mood and quickly sought to allay it. "Hell, Hump. We wasn't a laughin' at you. We was laughin' at ourselves, mostly. You ain't the first one that has been fooled by a mirage. All of us have been, too. And that's a fact."

"What did you see today?" Humphrey was still not completely mollified.

"A lot of buffalo and tall grass," Finch said. "And some real good places to stop for the night. What about the other scouts?"

"Two of 'em said they didn't see any Indian sign," Humphrey replied. "But Largo, he was scoutin' behind, and he saw a couple of Indians trailin' the herd."

"Did he get a good look at 'em?" Matt queried anxiously.

"Said he did," Humphrey replied. "I let 'im use my glass today; so I reckon he got a good look."

"What color horses were they ridin'?" Finch asked.

"Both of 'em rode gray horses."

"Any war paint on 'em?"

"Nope. They was slick."

"Good," Matt said, relieved. "If they was scoutin' for a raidin' party, they'd have paint on their faces and a hand print on the shoulder of them horses. They have any feather in their hair?"

"Each one of 'em had a feather."

"Jist one feather?"

"That's right."

"Then they were just a couple of bucks out on a hunt," Finch said calmly. "Probably Comanches, too; so we'd better put a strong guard on the remuda, tonight."

"Thought you and Kit Carson had a deal with that Comanche chief." Hump said.

"We do," laughed Finch. "And if they're Comanches, they won't attack us."

"Then why do we need to put a lot of guards on the remuda?" Humphrey asked skeptically.

"Because Comanches think stealin' horses is just plain fun," Finch said. "They don't consider it any sort of crime, and they can make off with a man's horse while he's holdin' the reins, and he'd never know it."

"And that's a fact," Tom agreed.

Humphrey just shook his head in bewilderment. "Forgot to tell ya," he said after a moment's pause. "Alf got back this mornin'. He's ridin' drag now on that mustang he rode off on."

"Must have been awful tired," Finch said.

"Said he wasn't" Humphrey replied. "Said he got off and rested a couple of hours. I don't see how he ever got back on that mustang, and he didn't say. But that critter is handlin' like a cowhorse with that hackamore and surcingle. I expect Alf broke her pretty good. Mighta been a little rough on her, though."

"Those little mustangs are tough. With two hours rest, she'll probably go all day."

"Alf says she will or else he'll leave her for coyote bait. I reckon he's gonna be a good mustang breaker."

"Looks like all four blacks will be," Finch said.

\* \* \* \* \* \*

They doubled the guard on the remuda that night, and when morning came, they were astonished to find that two of Humphrey's best mares were gone. The night guards swore that they hadn't seen or heard a thing, and that the horses were so carefully guarded that they could not have strayed.

"Comanches got 'em all right," Matt said, matter of factly.

"I'll probably see 'em again when I go to White Hores's camp—or he comes to the ranch," Finch said.

"They'll hide 'em, won't they?" Humphrey asked.

"Naw!" Finch said confidently. "Old White Horse will just think he's played a good joke on us. Figures they are fair game out here on the prairie, but he won't bother 'em when we get to our ranch. Neither will his braves. He gave his word."

"Indians is mighty strange critters!" Matt bolstered Finch's assessment of the situation.

"They shore must be!" Humphrey agreed. "How much longer till we get to the ranch, Finch?"

"Four more days," Finch said confidently.

"Well, I hope we don't lose two horses every night till we get there."

"We won't!" Finch assured him. "Matt and Tom and I will help ride guard every night till we get to the ranch."

"Who's gonna scout?"

"We are. We can get a little sleep on our horses. Won't be but three more nights, and we've done it before."

"And that's a fact!" Tom said.

\* \* \* \* \* \*

The Rangers did ride night guard on the remuda the next two nights, and they lost no more horses. On the morning of the third day, when they came in for breakfast, Humphrey asked, "Think we'll make it tomorrow?"

"We'll make it," Finch said. "We'll scout farther ahead today to see that everything is clear."

"You boys gonna be mighty tired," Humphrey opined.

"We're used to it," Matt said.

The Rangers ate breakfast quickly and mounted fresh horses. "We'll probably be late gettin' back tonight, Hump. Tell Kate to have some hot coffee on."

"She will!" Humphrey assured him. "And plenty of hot grub, too."

The Rangers rode away quickly and at a brisk pace. The sun was warm, and they saw the first heat waves rising eerily over the plains. They stopped at noon by a small creek running over a rocky bottom, but it was not lined with trees.

As they sat on some boulders eating their lunch, Tom started to put his jerky down on a warm rock and heard an ominous rattle. Matt started to yell just as the rattler coiled to strike. A pistol shot sounded; the snake's head disappeared in a bloody mass. Both Tom and Matt were stunned as they looked at Finch who was thumbing an empty out of his pistol. Complete silence reigned for a moment.

"That pistol hand must be all right," Matt observed dryly.

Finch looked at the hand curiously. "Must be," he said. "I didn't even feel it when I shot that snake. Nearly all the swelling is gone, and it doesn't hurt any. That forked stick I've been using must be powerful medicine, Tom."

"Well, I'm shore glad it is," Tom said shakily. "And that's fact." He was still a bit queasy from his narrow escape.

"It's mighty comfortin' to know you ain't crippled no more," Matt said in a relieved voice. "I got a hunch we're gonna need you today."

"What makes you think so?" Finch asked.

"I dunno," Matt admitted. "Just got a feelin' that's all."

"That's some strange!" Finch said. "I've had the same feelin' all mornin'. Thought maybe it was just cause of my sore hand."

"Well, that hand ain't so sore now that you can't use that pistol. You still got that feelin'?" Tom asked.

Finch was slow to reply and then did so reluctantly. "I've still got it."

"Then we'd damn well better look under every buffalo chip today," Matt said positively. "You got any suspicion, Tom?"

"I ain't hardly got no feelin' atall after that rattler scared hell out of me!" Tom said. "But if you two fellers got a notion, then I reckon we'd all better ride close together today and keep our eyes busy. And that's a fact."

\* \* \* \* \* \*

It was midafternoon when they saw riders approaching from the southwest.

"Who you reckon they are?" Matt asked.

Finch put his glass on them and held it for several minutes. "That's Sally Diego and four more of his Comancheros," Finch said positively. "They're comin' from the Palo Duro Canyon. That's where they hole up most of the time."

"That's quite a ways off, ain't it?" Matt said.

"Not more'n twenty or thirty miles," Finch replied. "But it's him all right. He's still wearin' that stove pipe hat."

"Well," Matt said grimly. "We've been huntin' the murderous son-of a-bitch for a long time, and we got a warrant for his arrest; so I reckon we'll ride out and take 'im. You go on with your scout, Finch."

"I'll just go along with you boys," Finch answered.

"You're not a Ranger anymore," Matt said firmly. "And it's Ranger business. Besides, that pistol hand of yours might play tricks on you next time."

"My hand is all right," Finch said firmly. "And I just rejoined the Rangers as soon as I saw who it was."

"Now, Finch, you know damned well—

"That'll do, Matt," Finch said coldly. "I'm ridin' with you boys—or by myself—Take your pick!"

"Hell, Finch, you—" Matt stopped in mid-sentence. He knew better than to argue when Finch used that tone of voice.

Typically, not one of them thought of flight or evasive tactics. They were Texas Rangers. The men riding toward them were wanted by the State of Texas. They would bring them in. Finch was riding in the middle with Tom and Matt on either side of him.

As the riders drew nearer, they stopped. Evidently one, or some of them, had guessed that the men riding so implacably toward them were not of their ilk.

"You ever seen Sally Diego?" Matt asked quietly without averting his eyes from Diego's riders. Both Finch and Tom answered in the negative.

"We wouldn't have known him for sure if he hadn't been wearin' that stovepipe hat, and he probably doesn't know us either; so we ought to be able to get in pistol range."

"What then?" Tom asked in a muted voice.

"We'll give 'em a chance to come along peaceful," Matt answered. "If it comes to shootin'—Finch, you get Diego first, the murderous bastard. Tom, you take the ones on the right. I'll shoot to the left."

No reply was forthcoming, and none was needed. When the Rangers were within a few feet of Diego and his men, they stopped.

"Buenos Dias, Senores," Diego gave them a wolfish smile.

"Sally Diego?" Matt asked.

"Si I am Sally Diego." The man sat very tall in the saddle and looked at the three Rangers with a sneer of contempt. "And who might you be, Senores?"

"Texas Rangers. And you are under arrest, Diego" Matt said calmly.

Diego's face reflected shock, but he did not hesitate even a split second. He went for his pistol as did all his men.

There was a cacophony of sound that echoed over the prairie. Sally Diego was the first man to fall, and then three of the others fell, their horses running wildly, reins flapping. One man, who had not been knocked from the saddle was spurring madly as he tried desperately to put distance between himself and the Ranger's guns.

"Go get him, Tom!" Matt yelled. "Finch and I will take care of these if need be."

"Tom is down, Matt," Finch said grimly. For the first time Matt took his eyes off the men lying on the ground.

"Look after 'im!" Matt said quickly. "I'll see if any of these can still shoot."

Finch bent over Tom who was apparently unconscious. He found the wound just as Matt walked up. "Them four Comancheros won't do no more killin'," Matt reported grimly, then added anxiously, "Is Tom hurt bad?"

"Shot plumb through," Finch said grimly. "From side to side. Looks bad."

They rolled Tom on his back and stuffed his hat under his head. Tom's eyes fluttered, and he opened them.

"Did we get 'em?" he asked feebly.

"All but one," Finch told him.

"That swole up hand musta slowed you up some, Finch," he grinned weakly.

"You hurt bad?" Matt asked.

"Shore am, Matt. Plumb bad. And that's a fact." He lapsed into unconsciousness again.

"What you reckon we ought to do, Finch?"

"Load 'im on his horse, and try to get back to camp, I guess," Finch said. "He sure won't last long out here bleedin' like that, but I doubt if he can last till we get back to the caravan."

"Well, I got some bandages in my saddle bags. Always carry 'em. Let's try to get 'im bound up some, and then we'll see if we can get 'im on a horse."

They stripped Tom's shirt and could see the bullet wounds. The slug had entered on the left side just below the rib cage, and had exited on the right side only slightly lower down. They wrapped the bandages tightly and slowed the bleeding somewhat.

"Hope he ain't bleedin' inside," Matt said glumly. "But I reckon he is."

They managed to get Tom astride his horse, and by riding beside him, they were able to keep him from tumbling off. He mumbled incoherently and rode loosely with his feet out of the stirrups.

"Can't figure it," Finch said thoughtfully. "I shot Diego twice and the man on each side of him once. A pistol must have gone off when a man was falling."

"Nope. It was my man that got 'im!" Matt said savagely. "My damn pistol didn't fire, and the man on the left was shootin' at you. That's why the bullet went in the side. He's the one that got away."

"Your pistol didn't fire?" Finch was incredulous.

"That's right!" Matt gritted. "The state furnishes us our ammunition, as you know. And lately we've been gettin' some dud shells. It ain't the first time it happened either. But you can bet your best horse that it won't happen again. From now on, I'll buy my own ammunition!"

* * * * * *

Tom was still alive when they reached the caravan. Humphrey helped get him in the Beatenbow wagon, while Kate and Sam hovered helplessly about.

"Kate!" Humphrey instructed. "You go get some of that corn that I been carryin' for Old Heck, and mash it up real good and fine; then boil it in water till it's like a good, stiff mush."

"Yassuh, Mars Hump!" Kate was relieved to be doing something.

"Let's take them bandages off and wash the wound off with whiskey," Humphrey ordered. "Then we'll put on them corn poultices that Kate is makin'. Don't know whether they'll help or not, but they can't do no harm. They put 'em on me when I got shot in the shoulder."

They complied with Humphrey's orders and then made Tom as comfortable as possible. Finch and Matt took turns sitting beside him and standing guard all night.

\* \* \* \* \* \*

Tom was still alive when they neared the Canadian River. Buff pulled up alongside the Beatenbow wagon.

"The lad still makin' it?" Buff queried.

"He's still alive," Matt said. "But that's about all."

"He'll make it, begorra!" Buff said optimistically. "Ain't nothin' tuffer'n a Texas Ranger—lessen mebbe it's a mountain man. And they ain't no one bullet in the belly a gonna put either one of 'em down for good."

"Hope you're right, Buff," Finch said glumly.

"And you tell 'im when he wakes up that the feller that done it ain't gonna shoot nobody else."

"How's that?" Finch and Matt were instantly attentive.

"Well, ye see, lads, old Buff was a hunkerin' down behind a rock by a trail down into the Palo Duro a fixin' to get me a nice buffler heifer, when a feller comes a ridin' hell for leather. So I jes riz up to say a friendly 'howdy' an' the dam fool, he ups his rifle at me without even slowin' down. So old Betsy, she says her piece, and the feller is on the ground with a hole in 'im that ye could throw a polecat through."

"Dead?"

"Deader'n last year's ron-de-voo," Buff said with satisfaction. "So I back tracks 'im and found Sally Diego, that murderin' son-of-a-bitch. Had two bullets in his face, so whoever got 'im done a fine job. The other three varmints was shot in the breastbone. So they ain't gonna steal no more wimmin and kids."

"How do you know it was Sally Diego?" Humphrey wanted to know.

"Be ye fergettin' that little fracas we had with 'im a way back on the trail, lad? The time you shot that paint pony? I saw his face real good that time, and besides his stovepipe hat was still under his head where he fell."

"Oh!" Humphrey said, suddenly remembering an incident that he had wanted to forget.

"I'd like to shake the hand of the man that got that lowdown skunk, begorra!"

"Finch got 'im!" Matt said bitterly. "And two more of'em too. Tom, he got the other one."

Buff looked a question at Matt.

"Matt's gun didn't fire," Finch explained.

"Be damned," Buff blustered. "An' I was wonderin' how that other one got away, begorra!"

"Glad you got that one, Buff," Finch said sincerely. "Likely it saved Matt a lot of ridin' and huntin'."

"And that's a fact!" Matt said grimly.

\* \* \* \* \* \*

Finch and Matt saddled their horses and rode ahead of the caravan and herd. When they reached the river, they rode across it several times to find a crossing with the least quicksand. When they were satisfied, they tore their bandannas in half, tied them to young willows about two hundred yards apart, and rode back to the caravan.

Humphrey was driving the Beatenbow wagon.

"How's Tom?" Matt asked as Humphrey stopped his team.

"Kate said he was conscious a few minutes ago, and he et a couple of bites of cold mush she had been savin' for 'im."

"That's good." Finch grinned for the first time since Tom had been shot. Matt dismounted quickly and hopped in the wagon where Tom lay. He emerged smiling broadly.

"That no-account bastard is in the wagon just a loafin' as usual!" Matt exulted. "Didn't figger you could kill 'im with a cannon, anyway! He's gonna make it!"

Matt was still smiling broadly as he mounted his horse again. "Now what, Finch? Your ranch is just across the river, ain't it?"

"That's right," Finch grinned. "You lead the wagons across between the two flags we set. Hump, you follow Matt, and if the sand starts sinkin', you beat hell out of those mules and yell till you get across. The other wagons will follow you, and when you all get to the other bank—we're home!"

Humphrey smiled broadly—a very rare occurrence. Matt broke his horse into a run and circled back to the wagon grinning idiotically. Buff pulled up alongside.

"I'll jist drive alongside ye, begorra!" he said. "Me little mustangs is used to quicksand, and they'll smell us a trail across that river like a hound dog after a coon."

Buff and Matt led off. Finch cautioned Humphrey one more time.

"Now be sure to whip the team as fast as they can go if the sand starts sinkin' some. I'll stay here and see that Clem hits the river in the right place with the herd and remuda."

Humphrey waved grandly and slapped the lines on the mules' backs as he clucked to them. Finch rode back to Clem and explained the situation.

"That quicksand is bad, but if you follow the trail of the caravan, I think you won't have too much trouble."

"We've had damn near everthin' else on this drive," Clem said slowly. "What do we do after we cross?"

"Turn 'em loose!" Finch grinned. "They're home!"

Finch rode to a small hilltop nearby where he could view the river crossing. He saw one team of mules get tangled. The wagon started sinking in the quicksand. Largo and several of the other Negroes ran to help. Matt tied his rope to the wagon tongue, but to no avail. The wagon kept sinking and had to be abandoned, but Matt and the Negroes were able to free the mules. The wagon sank slowly out of sight. Finch wondered which wagon it was and hoped fervently that it wasn't the one containing the blacksmith equipment and tools. The remuda followed the wagons, and all made it across!

Clem had the cattle in a long trot when they reached the river. All of the cowboys and six of the Negro riders were pushing them as hard as they could. The cowboys were firing their pistols, and the Negroes were whacking backsides with coiled ropes. Finch could not help but marvel at the rapid progress the Negroes had made in handling cattle. All of them still rode with surcingles, and most of them barefoot.

It took almost an hour for the herd to cross, and their trampling hooves caused water to rise in the sand; streams began to flow where there had been dry sand before.

A few of the cattle veered from the crossing path and were caught helplessly in the sand. Clem kept waving for the cowboys to continue pushing. A few of the riders shot some of the cattle that were near drowning, but Finch was surprised to see that when some of them were exhausted and simply lay on their sides, the flowing water rolled them over until they were free, whereupon they immediately rose and trotted quickly back into the herd.

The jackass, which had been trailing a safe distance behind, was the last to cross, and he bogged in the quicksand near the north bank of the river, but one of the Negro cowboys very adroitly cast his rope and the noose settled over his head. The Negro's rope was tied to his surcingle, and his horse being on firm ground, he was able to pluck the donkey out of the quicksand and drag him on his side to the bank of the river.

"Wisht he hadn't a done that," Clem complained. "I thought for a minnit maybe we had seen the last of that stubborn son-of-a bitch."

Finch, who had been watching with great interest from his vantage point on the small rise breathed a sigh of relief. But his feelings were ambivalent. He had realized a dream, but it had exacted a terrible toll! The only woman he had ever been in love with had lost her life, and his best friend had been murdered following his impossible dream. The terrible retribution that had been the last of Chico's killer, the Negro that had been hanged by Largo and Sam, the death of Dodie, the killing of Sally Diego and his henchmen, the two men killed in Fort Worth—all these thoughts raced through his mind as he sat and watched the herd spread out.

"It's all I ever thought it would be," Finch soliloquized. "But Hump and I paid a mighty high price for it!"

Finch sighed again and rode to the other side of the river where he was met by a smiling Humphrey with outstretched hand.

"Welcome home, Partner!" Humphrey smiled broadly as he and Finch clasped hands.

# CHAPTER 23

The cowboys made their camp off to one side as usual, and Finch showed Humphrey the location that he thought would make the best ranch headquarters. Humphrey was pleased, for it was on a small rise that was well away from the high water mark on the river, and it afforded a fine view of the valley.

"Wish Colette could see it," he said. "She was mighty partial to beautiful things."

"Me, too," Finch said softly.

Clem rode up and dismounted. "Well, we got 'em here, which is damn near a miracle!" he said. "What do we do now?"

"Let the cattle spread out," Finch said, "and send some of the boys around the rim of the valley so they'll know where our land is—and then start hazin' some of the buffalo out."

"All right," Clem agreed. "But we'll wait till tomorrow to start. Them cattle ain't gonna move far with all that good grass and water they got. And the boys is pretty tuckered out. So am I."

With that, he rode back to the cowboy camp. Humphrey took a deep breath and asked Finch, "Well, where do we start?"

"I can see where we ought to start, all right," Finch said. "But there's so much to do, I can't hardly see an end to it."

"Well?"

"First thing," Finch said, "we need to dig us a dugout in that bank over there to store our supplies in. Then, we need to build corrals; we can use logs for that. Then we need to build houses—a big one for the headquarters, and a bunch of small ones for the blacks, and a bunkhouse for the cowboys. We'll need a barn, too. We can use adobe for all the buildings. And we've got to slap a brand on all those cattle, and that shore won't be a picnic."

"Whoa!" Humphrey said. "You've already got a full summer's work laid out for all of us."

"I know!" Finch admitted. "But we'll be building this place for a long time to come. I'd sure like it to be permanent."

"Me, too," Humphrey said. "I'll start the niggers on the building tomorrow. You know how to make adobe?"

"I've heard how it's done," Finch said. "But I've never made any. Doesn't sound too complicated."

Buff drove up as they were talking. "Begorra!" he boomed. "And the only waggin we lost had all me buffler hides in it."

"Was that wagon that went down carryin' your buffalo hides?"

"Sure, and it were. Lost iver one of 'em, too."

"Hell, Buff I'm sure sorry to hear that!" But Humphrey breathed an inward sigh of relief, for he had been afraid that the wagon carried tools.

"Jist as well, I reckon," Buff said cheerfully. "Was wonderin' how I was gonna get 'em up to Pueblo, anyways. Me and old White Horse ain't got no treaty like him and Finch has. And that old red devil has had a mad on at me iver since I stole one o' his squaws a few year back."

"You stole his squaw!" Humphrey was incredulous.

"Only one of 'em, and jis kep' her a few days, anyway, then sent 'er back to 'im. White Horse sent word out for my scalp, the contrary old bastard. If'n he'd been a Blackfoot, nothin' would a been said of it."

Finch shook his head in resignation.

"I'll pay you for the hides," Humphrey volunteered.

"No, ye won't, laddie," Buff refused. "I already been paid a plenty, an' I got enough stashed away in me duffle for a grub stake—so don't fret none about old Buff Larrigan, begorra!"

"Well, I just like—"

"Tell ye what!" Buff interrupted. "If ye would trade me a pack mule for me waggin and team, I'd take it mighty kindly of ye. Ain't no fun tryin' to dodge Comanches when ye're drivin' a waggin. An' old White Horse's Comanches will be thicker'n flies on a dead skunk 'tween here an' Pueblo."

"Pick you out a good one, Buff," Humphrey said solemnly. "Don't know what we would a done without you. And get a pack saddle, too."

"Got one in me waggin," Buff said. "So I reckon I'll jus' pack up and move on in the mornin'."

"How far is it to Pueblo?" Finch asked.

"Not too far," Buff said vaguely. "I'll go west of the Rabbit Ears and cross over Raton pass. Stay in the timber, mostly."

"Well, eat supper with us tonight, anyway," Humphrey urged.

"Thanks, jist the same, but I reckon not. Don' want to git spiled by good cookin' afore I leave for them shinin' mountains. But I'll stop by for a cup o' coffee in the mornin' afore I leave."

With that, Buff whirled his team and drove away.

The first morning on the ranch, Humphrey and Finch were awakened by small birds and wild turkeys talking in the fast leafing cottonwoods. They rolled their bags and walked toward the river. A light blue haze seemed to hover protectively over it.

It was beginning to get light in the east. Both Finch and Humphrey had the good feeling that it was going to be a rare spring day. They gazed a while in silence, and then walked back to the wagon where Kate had breakfast ready. To their surprise Matt and Tom joined them. Tom was walking slowly, and both he and Matt were grinning widely.

"Hey!" exclaimed Finch. "Just look at what popped out of bed!"

"Finally got the lazy devil up," Matt said. "He ain't got more'n a little scratch on his belly, but he shore did take to havin' his meals served 'im in the wagon by that little nigger gal."

Both of them sat at the table. Tom eased carefully into his chair, and Finch could see that it hurt him to bend.

"Well, now. I reckon things is a lookin' up," Humphrey observed in a pleased voice. "Ellie bring us a couple more plates and lots more grub."

They had all eaten, and Matt and Tom had returned to the wagon when Buff appeared leading a loaded pack mule.

"Good mornin' to ye, lads!" he greeted jovially. "And a fine day it's gonna be fer ye to start out on, begorra!"

"That it is," Finch agreed.

"Ready for that coffee, Buff?" Humphrey invited.

"That I be!" Buff said heartily. "On this fine mornin' I reckon I'll have me an extry cup o' that good coffee too, if'n ye can spare it. Likely it'll be some time afore I taste the likes of Kate's coffee agin."

"Drink a whole pot full, if you want, Buff!" Humphrey laughed.

Buff blew lustily on the first cup and drained it. He did not remove the cud of tobacco from his jaw. Humphrey and Finch looked at each other in silent admiration of the feat. Buff handed the cup to Ellie for a refill.

"Got it all figgered out, have ye, lads?"

"Hump thinks I've got enough work already laid out to last us a year," Finch laughed.

"Begorra, an' I expect he's right, too!" Buff opined. "But I reckon I niver did see a purtier place to spend some time in—lest it was up in them shinin' blue mountains."

Buff emptied two more cups of coffee and rose. "Reckon I'll be leavin' ye, lads," he said almost sadly as he rubbed his chin gently with his forefinger. "Cain't say I iver had more fun, begorra! Wouldn't a wanted to miss it. Ye got a mighty fine bunch of niggers, Hump."

"Better than I thought," admitted Humphrey.

"Well, ye two lads watch yer topknots!" Buff said brusquely as he started leading his mule toward the river. He did not offer to shake hands.

"Watch yours!" Finch called after him.

Buff only raised a hand, but did not look around. Finch and Humphrey watched the old Irishman until he disappeared around a bend in the river. The last glimpse they had was of his long, flowing white hair.

"Well," sighed Finch. "I reckon it's time we got to work, Hump."

"Suits me," Humphrey said almost eagerly. "I'll get the niggers to cuttin' logs and buildin' a corral, first thing. I'd like to get Old Heck and that jackass penned up good so we won't have to stake 'em out."

"Good," Finch agreed. "And I'll go talk to Clem about hazin' buffalo out of the valley, and make some plans to start brandin'."

The log pens were quickly constructed, for the blacks, under the direction of Largo, worked with a will, constantly singing and laughing.

The dugout was completed, and then Finch showed Largo how to make adobe, and the Negroes fell to with seeming endless energy and vigor. The buildings began to take shape quickly.

The only time construction stopped was when Clem rode in and wanted the Negro cowboys to help with the branding, which they happily agreed to do.

The branding went fairly smoothly. As Choc and Bart roped the big cattle by the horns, Art and Dee roped the heels and stretched them out. An HF brand was burned on the left hip of each one, and most of the bulls were castrated. The

Negroes were delighted, for they loved 'them mountain oysters', and all the cooks with the exception of Kate served some every night.

Of course, the calves had to be branded, too, and one of them was the cause of the only untoward incident. Clem was applying the hot iron to the calf when it bawled lustily, and its long horned mother charged. Clem was knocked sprawling. The cow was hooking and pawing at his prostrate form when Largo hurled himself at the cow and grabbed her horns.

The cow was a powerful roan; she tossed her horns as if to rid herself of a coyote, but Largo hung on grimly. The cow started running, but finally Largo got his heel into the ground and pulled her to a stop. He looked about for help, but none was forthcoming. He hesitated only a moment, then hooked his knee around the cow's nose and grabbed one long horn with both hands. He gave a mighty heave, and the cow's neck broke as they both fell. The cow lay on her side with unmoving feet stretched out. Largo was pinned to the ground between her horns.

Some of the cowboys rushed to him as he got up and dusted himself off. Clem also got to his feet and hobbled a few steps. It was apparent that one leg was hurt. He stopped and looked at Largo with something like admiration.

"I'll tell you one thing," he said to no one in particular. "That black son-of-a-bitch is shore a white man! That damn cow would a killed me."

Everyone was so absorbed in the activity that they did not notice the incongruity of Clem's remark.

Largo made his way back to the branding fire, apparently unhurt. "You hurt bad, Mars Clem?" he asked.

"Just a bruised leg and some ribs. But I reckon I'd a been in bad shape if you hadn't got that damn cow off me. Much obliged."

Largo only grinned, and the branding continued.

That night as Finch, Humphrey, Matt and Tom were eating supper, Humphrey made his announcement. "A couple more days ought to finish up the brandin'. The building is underway, and Largo and the blacks can handle that. So I reckon I'll start back to Louisiana in the mornin'. I'd like to get back here afore cold weather."

"Gonna be a mighty long trip," Finch said. He had hoped that Humphrey had forgotten about Louisiana.

"And I ain't a lookin' forward to it none. But I got it to do!" he said firmly.

Humphrey offered no further explanation, and no one asked him a question.

"Tell you what," Matt said. "Tom and me will ride with you to Fort Worth. We need to be gettin' back to report to Captain Cates."

"Tom ain't in no shape to ride a horse!" Humphrey objected.

"He damn shore is," Matt affirmed. "He's been a ridin' a little bit ever day for a week while that brandin' was goin' on. Besides, the lazy bastard needs to get off that soft mattress and start earnin' that forty a month that Texas pays us sometimes. And I want to git back and kick somebody's ass that give me them dud shells, if I can find out who done it."

"Well, I'll shore be glad to have you boys along!" Humphrey said sincerely. "We'll leave early tomorrow mornin'." When Matt and Tom had left them, Humphrey said to Finch: "I better show you where the money is. You may need it. Some of the cowboys might quit, or somethin'."

Finch followed Humphrey to his wagon, where he took a sack from under the seat. It rattled as he moved it. He opened the sack and took a handful of coins and put them in his pocket. "Might need some on the way back," he explained. Then he handed the sack to Finch, who was astonished at its weight. Finch opened the sack and gaped as he looked at the sack that was almost filled with gold coins.

"How much money is in here, Hump?" Finch asked in awe.

"Quite a bit," Humphrey answered absently. "I been keepin' it under the wagon seat, but you may want to put it somewhere else. Tell Kate if you move it, though."

Finch nodded in dumbfounded silence.

\* \* \* \* \* \*

Finch watched them ride away the next morning, and as they disappeared down the river, he felt a sudden and almost smothering loneliness. He sighed deeply and went back to the building site. Largo seemed to have everyone busy, even the Negro women and children. Finch felt absolutely useless; so he wandered aimlessly about and then decided to inspect the wagons. He was astounded at the quantity of useable items that had been stored in them. There was furniture, several stoves—one large one and several smaller ones, plows, and other implements that would be of great use.

He felt better after checking the wagons, and then he went to the dugout. It was actually a big excavation that had been dug in the side of a hill and covered with logs, brush, and sod. The front of the dugout faced the river and was fashioned out of cottonwood logs and chinked with mud. Largo had built a strong door that could be fastened from either side; when it was open, it furnished a fine view of the river.

Finch was amazed at the great quantity of food and gear that had been stored in the large room. The ceiling was high, and Finch could stand erect even with his hat on. Bales and bags had been stacked neatly around the periphery of the room and almost to the ceiling; yet there was still a large bare space in the middle of the room. He decided that he might as well begin to get used to sleeping indoors again and moved his bedroll in.

He helped with the branding that afternoon and slept fitfully that night.

The next morning was bright and warm. Kate instructed Largo to have two of the blacks unload some plows and fix her a garden plot. Finch watched as the Negroes hitched the mules to the plow and started turning over the rich, aromatic soil. Then he saddled his horse and started riding up the valley. In less than an hour, he met White Horse and two of his braves. Tied to the Indian's saddle was a scalp that was unmistakable, and Finch recognized it immediately, for the long, white locks could have belonged to none other than Buff Larrigan. His first impulse was to start shooting, but he instantly realized that to kill White Horse would mean the end of his truce with the Comanches, and they would swarm down on the cow camp and massacre every cowboy and black.

Finch controlled his shock with a mighty effort and returned White Horse's gesture of friendship by raising his arm high with palm out. After all, White Horse had no truce with Buff, and Finch remembered that Buff had stolen one of White Horse's wives for a short time, making them sworn enemies.

There followed a broken conversation of English and Comanche between Finch and White Horse by which the Indian was able to make himself understood.

When the Indians started to leave, White Horse pointed to the northwest and said, "You come!"

"Where?" Finch asked.

"Same place. You come." The phrase was more of an order than an invitation; so Finch nodded in the affirmative.

"Three suns!" White Horse said and held up three fingers as he rode away.

Finch had lost too many friends while in the Texas Rangers to dwell too long on the death of Buff; so on the third day after the Indians' visit, he saddled his horse early and told Kate to expect him back when she saw him coming.

The Indian camp was much smaller than it had been when Finch saw it the first time, and he surmised, correctly, that only the Comanche tribe was present.

White Horse greeted him in friendly fashion and invited him into his teepee, where he lit a long, clay pipe and passed to to Finch. Finch did not smoke, but he accepted the pipe and took a long puff on it and was holding it in his mouth when three Indian women entered the teepee. They were the same ones he had seen before. The older Indian woman looked at him impassively and quickly averted her eyes. The two younger ones gazed openly at him. When the youngest and most comely one winked a large dark eye and smiled at him, Finch swallowed some of the smoke he was holding in his mouth and started coughing uncontrollably. White Horse looked at him scornfully, and the girls both giggled.

"Not used to smoking!" he gasped in explanation and had no idea whether White Horse understood, or not.

Finally, White Horse rose and motioned Finch to follow. They walked through the village, and at each teepee, they stopped. Either an Indian man or a woman, or sometimes, man, woman, and children came out of the teepee. The procedure was the same at each one. White Horse clasped Finch's shoulder and said "Hites. This Comanche Hites."

Finch was aware that the Comanche word meant 'friend', but he was relieved when the tour ended. They went back to the teepee of White Horse where the women had a bowl of food simmering on the fire. White Horse and Finch were served immediately. Remembering his first experience eating with White Horse, Finch gulped his food quickly and was finished by the time White Horse was. During the meal, Finch had studiously avoided looking at the Indian women, but he was almost sure that the small, well shaped hand that served his food was that of the youngest girl.

After eating, Finch made it known that he must return to his own camp. White Horse only grunted and rose immediately. As Finch rose, he inadvertently looked at the young Indian girl again. Her warm, dark eyes shone with a more than neighborly friendliness, and Finch would have bet his sorrel gelding that she was the one that had come to him when he spent the night in the Comanche camp. He hurriedly followed White Horse out of the teepee. White Horse gave the sign of friendship as Finch rode away, and Finch returned the gesture.

On his way back, Finch passed the Indian horse herd and noted with no surprise that Humphrey's two thoroughbred mares were in it. He grinned ruefully and continued on his way.

It was late afternoon when he reached camp, and it seemed that the buildings had grown since he left. There was a good sized garden patch plowed up, and several black children were planting seeds. Finch stopped by the garden for several minutes just to absorb the smell of the freshly turned earth. He felt better than he had since Humphrey and the Rangers had left.

Two days later, White Horse returned to the cow camp. With him were the pretty Indian girl and two braves. Finch was near the dugout, and he stared in surprise as they rode up. He held up his arm, palm out. "Ha Hites."

White Horse did not return the greeting, but began a tirade in Comanche and sign language that clearly indicated that he wanted to trade the girl for four horses. Finch demurred and pretended that he did not understand.

White Horse continued his harangue. He knew that Finch understood, and Finch knew that he knew. Finch looked at the girl. She was dressed in beautiful doe skin, and her dark eyes gleamed with excitement. She winked at him again.

Suddenly, Finch capitulated. "All right," he said abruptly. "We trade. Go get your four horses."

"Get two." White Horse grinned evilly. "Already got two."

The girl quickly dismounted and stood waiting expectantly.

The Indians left leading two more of Humphrey's prized mares. The girl simply stood and looked inquisitively at Finch. Finally, he gestured for her to follow him, and he led her to the dugout. He motioned for her to sit and went to see Kate.

"Kate," he said briskly. "You got any objection to cookin' for an Indian?"

"Lan' sakes, no, Mars Finch. Not if'n he be tame, that is. Reckon Indians gets hongry same as niggers or white folks."

"Good," Finch said. "I'll have company for supper."

"That be mighty fine, Mars Finch, mighty fine," Kate said enthusiastically. "Be easier than cookin' jis fo yo. Hope he likes white folks food."

Finch did not bother to explain that their company was not a he. He went to the wagon and got an extra bedroll. When he took it back to the dugout, he tried to converse with the girl, but was largely unsuccessful. He did find out that her name was O'oah, however, and she called him 'Finch' several times; so he felt that progress had been made.

When they went to supper, Kate did not even try to disguise her astonishment.

"Lan' sakes, Mars Finch!" she exclaimed in delight. "That be the purtiest Indian I ever did see. I's so happy yo got one. A man needs a wench, I allus tells Mars Hump."

Ellie served their food, which O'oah managed clumsily with the white man's tools, but she watched Finch closely and emulated him fairly well.

When they returned to the dugout, Finch unrolled the beds, and O'oah went outside toward the river. Finch was undressed and in bed when she returned. She ignored the bedroll that Finch had fixed for her and crawled in with him. Her body was still damp from her river bath, and she placed a small, damp hand on his chest; then Finch was absolutely sure she was the one that had shared his bed before.

The night was a replica of the one that they had spent in the Indian camp, but the next morning when Finch awakened, he felt a weight on his arm and looked down to see her classic features, touched with a slight smile and a look of absolute peace and contentment. When Finch started to remove his arm, her big, black eyes flew open for a second, and then she smiled radiantly.

As Finch rose to don his clothing, so did she, and she was unselfconscious of her beautiful, naked body as if she had been alone.

\* \* \* \* \* \*

The days passed pleasantly, and Finch was eager to return to the dugout each evening where O'oah was always waiting. And each night she greeted him warmly. One day she beckoned him to follow her, and she showed him a small pool that she had dug in the sand near the current of a creek, that was completely protected by willows and that ran to the river. She immediately shed her clothing and waded in. Her twinkling eyes and gestures invited Finch to join her, which he did, but not until he had placed his pistol within easy reach on the bank.

A few days later Finch saw White Horse, two braves, and two squaws riding toward the dugout. He walked to meet them and stopped as they neared. He held up his hand, palm out. White Horse returned the gesture and grunted, "Ha Hites."

"Trade more?" White Horse gestured toward the younger squaw and then to O'oah.

"No trade!" Finch said firmly, and O'oah stepped behind him as if to hide.

"One horse, one squaw!" He again pointed to the younger squaw and to O'oah.

"No trade," Finch said almost harshly and reached behind him with his left arm as if to protect O'oah. "Not for all your squaws and your whole horse herd," Finch said adamantly.

White Horse looked sternly at them for a moment and then smiled. "O'oah, she say we bring her or she come alone," he said. "We bring her. You keep?"

"I keep!" Finch said stoutly.

The older squaw smiled widely and tossed a big bundle to the ground. The younger squaw and the braves sat with expressionless faces.

"Hoya!" White Horse said, then turned, and they all rode away.

As soon as the Indians rode away, O'oah eagerly opened the bundle left by the older woman. It contained several garments of beautifully tanned and beaded doe skin. O'oah smiled.

\* \* \* \* \* \*

Finch took a lot of good natured joshing from the cowboys, who called him "squaw man" and other uncomplimentary names. But he paid them no mind, for he knew the kidding was in good humor and more than a little envious.

It was soon after O'oah came to Finch that Clem rode up late one evening. "The boys has got some of the buffalo rousted out of the valley, and the cattle is settled in good; so a couple of 'em want to take a trip to Pueblo. You got any money for 'em to take along?"

"What for?" Finch asked in surprise.

"They say them black wenches of Hump's is beginnin' to look so white that they figger they ought to have a doc check their eyes," Clem grinned.

Finch nodded understandingly. "Tell 'em to come by early tomorrow, and I'll have their pay ready," Finch said. "But it's an awful dangerous trip to Pueblo."

"They know that. But it ain't no more dangerous than the way they're lookin' at that nigger gal that cooks for us. She's Largo's wench."

\* \* \* \* \* \*

The two cowboys made it to Pueblo and back safely, and immediately two others asked permission to go, which was granted. The rotation of the cowboys continued throughout the summer, and only two of them failed to return. Whether they just kept riding or were slain by Indians was never known.

Finch continued language lessons for O'oah and was amazed at her progress. Within a few days they were able to carry on a broken, but understandable conversation, although it was liberally spiced with sign language. Finch was becoming more and more intrigued with the girl. When in deep concentration trying to say a white man's word, she had a habit of rubbing her chin with a forefinger. The gesture amused Finch and puzzled him at the same time, for he felt he had seen it before. But, try as he would, he could not remember where. Probably when he was in White Horse's camp, he concluded.

Finch rode out to the herd each day to spend some time with the cowboys, and then returned to headquarters to observe the building of the houses. The Negroes were putting up the headquarters house first, and under Largo's supervision, it was rising rapidly. Kate had decreed that it have two wings of four rooms each, with a large sitting room connecting the two wings, and a huge kitchen in the rear with quarters for her and Sam.

Largo was also fashioning an ingenious device in a room in each wing of the house that directed a small stream of water from a spring through a pipe in a small heating stove and on into a big tub. When a fire was lit in the stove, the water would be warmed, and when it had served its purpose, a plug could be removed to allow the tub to empty to the outside. Finch was impressed anew at the inventiveness of the blacks.

"White folks, dey likes to bathe in warm water," Kate said. "Dey skin ain't tough lak us niggers. An' dey likes lots o room, too. Still, it ain't gonna be as grand as de big house back on de plantation. Hope Mars Hump like it anyway," she added wistfully.

"He will," Finch assured her. He thought the project much too ambitious, but did not say so. In the meantime, O'oah's pool and the dugout were quite satisfactory.

\* \* \* \* \* \*

The daily bath became almost a ritual for them, and Finch looked forward to it eagerly each evening. One night, when they were eating supper, the food tasted delicious, but different.

"You are gettin' to be a better cook all the time, Kate," he complimented her.

"Warn't me, Mars Finch," Kate said. "Twere yo little Indian friend. She been comin' down ever day for a while when I's cookin'. I thinks maybe she get lonesome for somebody, even a nigger. And today she brung some plants o' some kind and puts 'em in the vittles. I don' stop her cause I know that purty little thang ain't gonna poison nobody."

Finch looked at O'oah in amazement and gestured at the food. "Good!" he said.

"Good!" O'oah repeated obediently and smiled.

"You better be careful, Kate," Finch admonished jokingly. "She's beginnin' to understand English."

"Don know about her knowin' English, Mars Finch. But I reckon she know men some!" Kate said with a wide smile.

\* \* \* \* \* \*

As the long, hot summer progressed, White Horse returned twice. Neither time was he accompanied by a squaw, but always was with several of his braves. When the big house was completed, Finch invited him in to inspect it. White Horse grunted several times, and the sound was mostly disapproving. He was particularly disdainful of the huge cook stove and of the two small wood burning stoves that Largo had installed in a room of each of the two wings of the house. His reaction to the small stream of water that had been diverted through each room was the same. Finch did not even try to explain that by building a fire in the stoves, they could run warm water into the tubs.

Kate had arranged the furniture that had been hauled all the way from Louisiana in one wing of the house that Humphrey would occupy. Largo was kept busy building furniture for the other wing. Kate was so busy and happy that Finch merely grinned and followed her orders. Humphrey would have taken her head off, Finch knew.

Finch and O'oah moved into their wing in late summer, and for the first time O'oah had a bath the white man's way. Her delighted laugh pealed through the adobe house, and old Kate and Sam smiled.

O'oah had been progressing with her English at amazing speed throughout the summer. One night as she crawled dripping from the tub, she raised her forefinger and rubbed her chin. "Begorra!" she said. "And it's a good way to be clean!"

Finch, who had been watching her, suddenly turned pale and grabbed her by the arms and shook her. "Where did you hear that word?" he demanded.

"Which word?" O'oah looked at Finch with frightened eyes.

"Begorra!" Finch said sternly. "Where did you hear it?" He shook her again.

"From my mother," O'oah almost sobbed. "Is it a bad word, Finch?"

"When did you hear it?"

"When I was little," O'oah said pleadingly. "I won't say it anymore, if it's a bad word. I never heard it before my mother used it, and I haven't heard it since. I don't know why I said it tonight."

Finch felt weak, and he suddenly sat in one of the big cottonwood chairs that Largo had fashioned.

"It isn't a bad word, O'oah!" he reassured her in a kindly voice. "It's just that a friend of mine once used it. I hadn't heard it in a long time, and it surprised me. Come sit in my lap, and let's talk a while." He motioned to her as he spoke. O'oah smiled brightly in her relief and quickly ensconced her naked body in his lap.

"How old was your mother when you heard her use that word?" Finch asked quietly.

O'oah held up both hands with all fingers outstretched, then lowered them and raised them again, one with five fingers outstretched and the other with three. "That many summers, I think," O'oah said. "I was very little."

"Was your mother the squaw of White Horse then?"

"Oh yes!" O'oah replied eagerly. "She always been squaw of White Horse."

"Always?"

"Always," O'oah said, "except a white man steal her one time, but White Horse get her back."

"What happened to the white man?"

"He run to the mountains where he come from," O'oah said. "But White Horse kill him one time."

"When?"

"O'oah don't know." She was becoming frightened at the intensity of the questions. "I hear him say so only a moon before I come to you. Did I do somethin' wrong, Finch!"

"No. You didn't do anything wrong, my little Indian squaw." Finch suddenly relaxed. "I think you just answered a lot of questions for me."

O'oah looked at him quizzically. Then Finch laughed, stood, and carried her to the bed.

\* \* \* \* \* \*

The bunk house and the Negro quarters were almost finished when the first frost came and the leaves of the cottonwoods turned into a golden canopy. Finch looked anxiously to the south every day.

"Mars Hump. He come soon now," Kate announced one morning at breakfast.

"How do you know, Kate?" Finch asked in surprise.

"Kate knows," she replied complacently. "Kate been bothered with troublesome spirits ever since Mars Hump been gone. But last night, dey don' come. Mars Hump, he be back soon."

Finch shook his head in wonder and finished his meal. He fervently hoped that Kate's voodoo spirits were right.

The next afternoon, one of the Negroes who was working on a cabin roof yelled excitedly. "Waggins! Dey a comin' and dey's a lot of 'em." He pointed to the south of the river.

Finch hurriedly got his glass and rushed to the door. He watched the wagon train for several minutes. He could see that it had a military escort. When they were almost directly across the river to the south, the wagon train stopped. A wagon and two riders separated from it. Then the caravan continued westward, and the dropouts proceeded toward ranch headquarters. Finch kept his glass on the riders.

"It's Hump, all right. Rides like a sack of oats. I'd know him as far as I could see 'im if he was on a horse. But I can't tell who's with him. Looks like a woman."

"See, Mars Finch!" Kate said excitedly. "Kate done tol' yo, Mars Hump a comin', an' he sho is. Bless his stubborn li'l heart!" And she began sobbing softly.

Finch and O'oah were standing side by side at the river's edge as Hump and his companion splashed across. Kate, Sam, Largo, and the rest of the blacks were all grouped behind them.

As they reached the river bank, Humphrey quickly dismounted and grasped Finch's outstretched hand. Then he turned to his companion. "Git down, Mandy, and meet my partner."

Finch looked up at the woman and gaped stupidly. He could have sworn that he was looking into the eyes of Colette until she removed her hat to loose long, ash blonde hair that cascaded almost to her waist. She dismounted in one fluid movement and proffered a shapely hand.

"Finch," Hump said, "this here is my wife, Maureen. We call her Mandy."

Finch took her hand almost fearfully. Her hand was soft and warm, but her grip was strong and her smile radiant.

"I'm glad to meet you at last, Finch," Mandy said sincerely. "Hump has been telling me about you ever since we left Louisiana."

Finch held her hand and stared into her face. He sighed inwardly with relief that no electricity flowed between them. There was only friendly warmth.

"I'm glad to meet you, too, Mandy," Finch gulped. "I hope you will excuse my starin' at you. It's just that you reminded me of someone I used to know."

"Does remind you of Colette, don't she!" Humphrey said calmly. "Got a right to. She's Colette's aunt."

Finch shook his head as if he had just awakened.

"Hey!" he said. "I was so surprised I near forgot everything." Then he reached out and took O'oah by the arm and pulled her forward. "I've got a wife too, Hump and Mandy. This is O'oah!"

It was Humphrey's turn to gape. O'oah was obviously an Indian and would have been recognized as such even without the doeskin garment she was wearing. But Humphrey was up to it. He held out his hand; and, though O'oah had never been introduced to anyone before, she had seen Mandy take Finch's hand. She took Humprey's hand.

"Well, Finch," Humphrey said gallantly. "You shore pick 'em purty."

O'oah did not understand all Humphrey said, but she knew that it was complimentary, and she smiled shyly at him.

"Mandy, come on an' meet Finch's wife. He musta stole 'er while I was gone."

"Didn't steal her!" Finch grinned. "Traded four of your good mares for her."

"Well, you shore got a bargain—Mandy this here is—"

But Mandy did not wait. She went to O'oah and hugged her. "I'm Mandy," she said, "and if you are Finch's wife, he is a lucky man. You are very beautiful."

"Mars Hump, Mars Hump!" Kate's wailing voice broke in. She had been ignored long enough. "I jis knowed you was a comin' back soon. Tol' Mars Finch jis yestiddy!"

Humphrey looked from Mandy and O'oah to the group of Negroes. He stode forward and hugged Kate's huge frame that was made even bigger by her obvious pregnancy. Kate sobbed loudly as Humphrey released her and went to Sam. He threw his arm around Sam's shoulder and stuck his right hand out to Largo. Largo looked startled, but took Humphrey's hand; they gripped strongly. It was the first time Humphrey Beatenbow had ever taken the hand of a Negro.

\* \* \* \* \* \*

After all the greetings were over, Humphrey, Finch, and their wives went into the big house. Kate followed discreetly but could not contain her enthusiasm when they started inspecting the rooms. She took charge, and Humphrey did not object.

Maureen was pleased with the arrangement and told Kate so. Kate beamed.

After supper that night, Finch, Humphrey, O'oah, and Maureen moved into the big center room. A fire burned cheerfully in the huge fireplace. The weather was not really cold enough to justify a fire, but Kate had instructed Sam to light it, for she wanted to show off as much as possible for Humphrey. Ellie served coffee.

"Well," Finch sighed as he relaxed in a big chair. "How was your trip, Hump?"

"A little rough goin' down," Humphrey admitted. "A few Indians. I'd never have made it without your Ranger friends."

"Anybody get hurt?"

"Tom got an arrow in his shoulder, but it was high up. Didn't amount to anything."

"Tom is gonna have to learn to duck!" Finch grinned. "But he's been shot before. He'll make it!"

"How have things been goin' on the ranch?"

"Good, mostly," Finch said. "We got all the cattle branded and the bulls cut. The cows are droppin' a few calves, too. You saw most of the buildings. Largo has been doin' a good job of bossin' the blacks, and they've been workin' all day every day. And it's been hot!"

"They're used to workin' hard," Humphrey said.

"That's about all, I guess." Finch hesitated a moment. "The cowboys have been takin' turns goin' up to Pueblo. Two of 'em didn't come back. Don't know whether it was Indians or not. Hope they just decided to keep ridin'. I paid 'em wages out of your money sack."

"Out of our money sack," Humphrey corrected.

"Anyway, we've been doin' pretty well up here. A prairie fire scared us pretty bad. It came from the southwest and would have wiped us out if the river hadn't stopped it, but it drove a lot of buffalo into our valley."

"I reckon things are shapin' up then," Humphrey said with satisfaction.

"One bit of bad news!" Finch said reluctantly.

"What's that?"

"When White Horse came to see us, he had Buff's scalp tied to his bridle."

"How do you know?" Humphrey asked.

"I reckon I couln't mistake that long, white hair of his," Finch said bitterly. "And there wasn't a thing I could do about it. White Horse didn't have any treaty with Buff, and besides, if I had shot White Horse, the whole Comanche tribe would have wiped us out."

"Put you in a mighty tough spot!" Humphrey commiserated. "I thought a lot of that old Irishman, and I know you did, too. But you did the right thing."

"Get your business settled in Louisiana?" Finch was anxious to get away from the subject of Buff.

Humphrey nodded absently. "Wasn't much to it. Just had to face up to a man."

Finch did not question him further. "Well, I'm glad you're back. It's been a long time."

"Took me a while to get Mandy to come back with me. Had to go all the way to New Orleans to get her. And then we had to wait for a wagon train comin' west. A man would be crazy to come out here with a woman jist by hisself. Lost one wife to the Indians. Didn't want to lose another one."

"You said she's Colette's aunt?"

"She is. She's Colette's Ma's sister—half sister, that is. They got the same ma, but different pa's. Mandy's pa is a big Swede with some Cherokee blood in him. She gets that yeller hair from him."

"Well," Finch said. "You shore been lucky twice. She's most as pretty as Colette."

"She's only four years older, too. That still makes her younger than me. She lost her man in the war. Since we're speakin' of women, where did you get O'oah? And what does her name mean in English?"

"White Horse brought her here," Finch said. "I think the crafty old devil knew we had been together before. And we had. O'oah means 'little owl'."

Humphrey looked a question at Finch, but got no reply. Then they both looked at Mandy and O'oah, who were talking animatedly as they sat on a long seat in front of the fireplace.

"Can't get over how much Mandy looks like Colette," Finch mused as he looked at them.

"She does, for a fact," Humphrey said. "That little Indian of yours shore is a purty one, too. I'm crazy to even think of it, but she reminds me of Buff Larrigan some—the way she rubs her finger across her chin. We stopped by Colette's grave back in the Red River valley, and them flowers that Buff planted was growin' fine. Surprised me."

"I'll tell you about Buff, sometime," Finch said. "Right now it's gettin' on to bed time."

They rose and walked to Mandy and O'oah.

"Well, how do you like your new home, Mrs. Beatenbow?" Finch said lightly as the women rose.

"I think it's delightful." Mandy smiled beautifully. "And you are a lucky man, too, Finch. I've never seen a more beautiful woman than O'oah. She speaks English well, too, and I know we will be great friends." Mandy put her arm around O'oah's shoulder.

"Well, Finch," Humphrey beamed. "I reckon we are all set for a long stay out here west of Fort Worth. What we need now is jist to start populatin' this here country." Humphrey looked at Mandy fondly. She blushed.

"That's a fact, Hump," Finch grinned. "Time we were gettin' started."

Both of the women giggled and looked embarrassed.

"This shore calls for a drink!" Humphrey said enthusiastically. "Kate!" he yelled.

Kate immediately appeared, a wide smile splitting her dark face.

"Bring us some likker and four glasses."

Kate quickly reappeared. When the liquor was poured, Humphrey raised his glass.

"Here's to the HF brand, the two purtiest women in the world, and the two luckiest men!"

"I'll drink to that!" Finch responded.

Just as they raised their glasses in response to Humphrey's toast, an eerie, unearthly sound rent the moonlight night. It began as a low rumble and ended in a shrill, screaming pitch that echoed and re-echoed up and down the Canadian River. The Beatenbow jackas was roaring his defiance to the big, wild, beautiful world!

# PART 2

## MESQUITE ROOTS GROW DEEP

# Chapter 1

Kit Carson died May 28, 1868. The news reached the HF Ranch four days later.

It was Kit who, two years before his death, had managed to persuade the Kiowa and Comanche tribes to allow his good friend Finch to run cattle in the great valley just north of the Canadian River.

Of the fifteen cowboys who had accompanied Humphrey and Finch on their trek west, few remained. One was gored to death by a longhorn bull; another drowned when a headrise came down the river; two disappeared while on a trip to Pueblo—their fate was unknown. Others were killed by Indians. Those cowboys were replaced by riders who came looking for work or adventure. Clem Swenson, the cattle foreman, needed at least fifteen hands to keep most of the buffalo out of the valley and to tend the burgeoning herd of longhorns.

For almost two years the HF herd had increased dramatically. Now the men were preparing for the long trail drive to Abilene, Kansas, with 3100 head of the older steers. Finch and Humphrey were sitting their horses under a big cottonwood discussing the coming drive when the rider from Taos brought the news of Kit's death.

"Who killed him?" Finch asked quietly.

"Nobody. Heart attack."

"Oh!"

"What will it mean for us, Finch?" Humphrey wanted to know.

"I wish I knew!" Finch replied. "The Indians acting up any?" Finch posed the question to the Taos rider.

"Not yet. And maybe they won't," the rider replied, "but the fact that Kit could call out four or five thousand troops at any time was bound to have had some effect on them Indians. Especially the Kiowas. I expect the Comanches under White Horse will stay hitched, but the Kiowas and old Black Bull are mighty unpredictable, especially now that Kit is dead."

"Much obliged for letting us know," Finch said.

"Figgered I ought," the rider responded. "You folks are here with women folk and kids and all them niggers, too."

"Well," Humphrey sighed, "Rest your saddle a bit. We'll go up to the house and have a cup of coffee."

"Thanks just the same," the rider refused. "They is some more folks on south and east that ought to know about Kit." With that, he rode away.

Finch and Humphrey were silent for a few minutes after the rider left. Humphrey's hawk-like features were grim, which was not unusual, for Humphrey Beatenbow was a person who lived within himself and only rarely revealed his true feelings. Finch, however, had an open, smiling face that reflected his feelings like a mirror—except when he was confronted with danger.

The two men were very different in many ways. The bearded Humphrey looked years older than he actually was; his brown, goldflecked eyes rarely showed emotion. Finch, with his tawny hair, and sparkling blue eyes that could turn as cold as chunks of ice, but were usually twinkling with pleasure, actually looked much younger than he was.

Finch would avoid confrontation when possible, but when faced with the unavoidable, used his pistol with unbelievable speed and accuracy. Humphrey, to the contrary, would not take one unnecessary step to avoid trouble.

Although their partnership had been launched because of simple need, their relationship had developed from a strictly practical, business-like association into respect and confidence in each other, and finally, although never expressed, into a deep relationship that approached brotherly love. For all their differences, they were, in a strange, inexplicable way, very much alike. No man who ever saw the two together doubted that both were strong men who were very much at home in their time and place.

"What do you think, Finch?" Humphrey finally broke the silence.

"I don't know what to think," Finch said candidly. "I've got a feeling that White Horse will honor his agreement with Kit, but I don't know about Black Bull and his Kiowas. Then, there is Gray Eagle and his Arapahos to think about. Fact is, we've been sitting right in the middle of a hornet's nest for the past two years."

"Well, we haven't been bothered much," Humphrey said. "A couple of raids by some renegade Indians and one by Comancheros that didn't do us much damage."

"Yeah, thanks to those good adobe buildings that the blacks built, and them learnin' to shoot rifles. The Indians didn't know what to think when they circled headquarters and rifles started spitting at 'em out of every slot on the roof. But it was the Comancheros that got the worst of it."

"They shouldn't a rode up in a bunch when they came." Humphrey was not sympathetic. "Them women and kid-stealin' bastards had it comin'!"

"Anyway, the Indians carried off their dead, but we had to start a cemetery to take care of the Comancheros!"

"Well." Humphrey took a long breath. "We can't look back now. Carson couldn't have died at a worse time for us."

"Guess he didn't have much choice!" Finch replied curtly. He knew that Humphrey always had a grudge against Kit for having served in the Union army.

"I reckon not," Humphrey replied, unconcerned. "But I shore don't know about tryin' to drive 3100 head of longhorns to Abilene without knowin' more about what the Indians will do."

"I guess I'd better go break the news about Kit to Clem and the hands. I'll tell Clem to come up to the house. We'd best talk a bit. After all, Clem is gonna have the responsibility for the herd."

"All right," agreed Humphrey. "I'll tell Largo to come, too."

Largo, the son of old Kate, had accompanied Humphrey through four years of war and had come west with him. Now, Largo was the boss of the blacks, an excellent blacksmith, a worker of wood, and a fierce fighting man when necessary.

Humphrey Beatenbow depended greatly on the advice of the huge, muscular Negro, but would have admitted that to no man—especially Largo or Finch.

\* \* \* \* \* \*

The meeting was held in the big room of the headquarters building about mid-afternoon. Clem sat at the table and drank coffee with Finch and Humphrey. Largo came in and unobtrusively sat on the floor in a dark corner of the room.

Finch opened. "We may have a real big problem, and we may not have one at all. That depends on the Indians. They may continue to abide by their agreement with Kit, and they may not. I think White Horse will stay put—but I'm not sure about Black Bull and Gray Eagle."

"Well," Humphrey spoke up, "we've held on for two years and been raided a few times. We've held our own and better. I don't see no reason that can't keep up."

"Depends, Hump," Clem replied. "If all them damn redskins hit us at once, we'd be in for a hell of a fight, and probably lose it. We've lost some cowboys in the last two years as it is."

"We know that, Clem," Finch interjected, "and we lost some blacks here at headquarters when that renegade bunch of Kiowas and the Comancheros hit us. What we're tryin' to figure out today is the best move to make. Do we start the trail herd to Abilene tomorrow or wait a while?"

"Well, that feller named Gregg that come by last year said Abilene was a payin' good prices for cattle since they got that Northern Pacific Railroad. And then, that Colonel Hitt and Charley Gross that come to see us a couple of months ago said the same thing. They figgered after we get acrost the Oklahoma strip, then we ort to have pretty good sailin' the rest of the way. There is a sort of halfway trail after we get east of here a long ways. I was with Wheeler when he took a herd to Abilene in '65."

"I know you've been to Abilene," Humphrey said. "You went up the Chisholm trail, but we won't hit it for a couple of hundred miles, according to that map you drawed, and it'll be new country until we hit it."

"That's right. But it damn shore won't be no picnic even after we hit the trail—if we get that far," the ever pessimistic Clem rejoined.

"What's Abilene like?"

"Not much when I was there. A few shacks and a lot of saloons. Course, they got the railroad now! That's the important thing! And, they have a shippin' yard with Fairbanks scales now. And they're buildin' a hotel, too!"

"Well." Humphrey's face and voice were grim. "I took their word for it, and I give 'em mine that we would deliver 3100 steers there this summer; so I reckon we got it to do. I don't figger they would lie to a man."

"Mebbe not!" Clem was skeptical. "But Hitt and Gross was jus' drummin' up business. I doubt if either one of 'em ever drove a steer."

"I doubt it, too," Humphrey agreed. "But we got 3100 six-and eight-year old steers and a few cows and calves boxed up in a big draw. They're all road-branded and ready to go as soon as we give the word."

"That's just it!" Finch said. "We aren't sure about all the cowboys leavin' the ranch with the Indian situation so uncertain."

"Well, we been takin' on hands ever since word reached Fort Worth and Decatur that we was makin' a drive. They been droppin' out of caravans goin' west on that branch of the Santa Fe trail jus' south of the river. Mostly, they been comin' in pairs—but a few singles—and some of 'em even come acrost the Indian country alone. We got about thirty men now, and that's a bunkhouse full. The old hands know how to shoot and ride, and most of the new ones look all right. Fact is, a couple of 'em look like gun hands. And they is about eight or ten niggers that is good enough cowboys, if'n they'd jus' trade them damn surcingles for saddles! I'd like to have a few of 'em on the drive. They ain't got much sense, which is shore a good recommendation for a cowboy!"

"We may need all of 'em," Finch said. "If all the Indians hit us at one time, we'd be in real trouble!"

"Thought your wife was that Comanche chief's daughter," Clem said.

There was an almost imperceptible pause on Finch's part. He did not reply to Clem directly.

"I don't think White Horse will hit us. It's the Kiowas and Arapahos that worry me."

"Well, God-a-mighty!" Humphrey said. "We could hold the whole tribe off with all the cowboys and blacks we got!"

"I think so, too," Finch replied. "But, if we start the herd next week as we intended, that means at least fifteen cowboys will be gone from here."

"We'd still have a small army," Humphrey argued. "All the nigger men and most of the women have learned to shoot pretty good."

Humphrey had trouble calling his former slaves 'blacks' as his first wife Colette had wanted, and now, his wife Mandy chided him about the same thing. Humphrey often forgot his intention to honor their wishes. Besides, he was eager to start the drive.

"Give the word, and we'll start tomorrow," Clem said. "Tell you what, though. Them shippin' cattle is in good shape for water and feed in that big draw where we're holdin' 'em. They can stay there for a few days. How would it suit everbody to wait a little bit? The Indians ort to do somethin' by that time if they're goin' to. Fact is, I'd jus' as soon have all the extra hands ridin' our boundary line, anyway. I'd shore hate to come back and have all our other cattle gone."

"Makes sense to me," Humphrey agreed.

"That's fine with me, too," Finch said.

"I'll get the boys together tonight and tell 'em that we're a fixin' to wait a while. They're gonna be aggravated as hell, though. Waitin' is mighty hard work—especially for a cowboy," Clem said and then added almost apologetically. "Meanin' no offense, Hump, but I reckon it'd make sense for Finch to stay here at the ranch too, instead of you."

Humphrey looked at Clem in surprise. "Why do you say that?"

"Well." Clem was hesitant. "Finch knows Indians better'n you do, and he can shoot a hell of a lot better'n you—or anybody else—can. Shanker Stone ort to stay too; outside of Finch, I ain't never seen nobody as good with a gun as he is. With Finch and Shanker and twelve or fourteen hands left here at the ranch, I reckon the women folks and kids might be safer."

Humphrey mulled Clem's statement over for a moment, and then to the surprise of both Clem and Finch, said, "Makes sense, Clem." Then he looked at Finch. "What do you think, Finch?"

"I'll go or stay," Finch said quietly.

"Good!" Humphrey said. "I reckon I'd feel better about the ranch if you stayed."

"Then it's settled." Clem rose abruptly and departed. He didn't want any of them to change his mind.

When Clem had left, Finch and Humphrey looked at each other.

"I reckon everbody's satisfied," Humphrey said. Then he spied Largo sitting in the dark corner. "What do you think, Largo?"

"Why do Mars Clem object to them nigger cowboys usin' surcingles?"

Humphrey and Finch both laughed.

"It's just a new thing to him, and he's afraid that other cow outfits will laugh at him for usin' the blacks a bareback."

"Whisht he'd take some of 'em on de drive. They's done a good job roustin' buffalo outta the valley. And some of 'em is even better ropin' than the cowboys."

\* \* \* \* \* \*

When Clem left the headquarters house, he walked to the corrals, hooked his elbows over the top rail, and for a time watched the horses in the corral as he mentally went over the roster of hands. They were a nondescript bunch of men; yet they had much in common. Clem felt that he had assembled a good crew. Some of the men had come west from Fort Worth with Humphrey and Finch as they had brought their caravan across Indian country, gathering ownerless cattle as they came. Others, upon hearing that the HF ranch had survived for two years in the middle of hostile Indian country and that its owners were planning a drive to Abilene, Kansas, come warm weather, had latched on to a caravan that was coming west and had dropped off there.

Most of the men were young, and all were looking for adventure, excitement, and jobs. The prospect of working for the HF ranch in a situation so fraught with inherent danger and uncertainty appealed to their free spirits and combative natures. Then, too, they had all heard of the two men who ran the ranch. The reputations of Finch and Humphrey had probably been embellished around many campfires, but no man who had ever known them would deny that Fauntleroy Finch had no equal in the use of firearms, and that Humphrey Beatenbow had never been known to take a backward step when he started a project—big or small.

A few of the men had actually crossed Indian country alone and had ridden up to the ranch and asked for jobs. Two of the older men who rode in were technically deserters from the Confederate army, although they did not consider themselves so; for they had joined A. W. Terrell's cavalry regiment. When the order came in 1863 to unhorse the regiment, they, along with eighty-nine other men, simply rode away. Some of them joined other cavalry units, and some went home. They had signed up to fight on horseback, and, said one, "Be damned if I'm gonna git off my hoss just to get shot at!"

Two men had ridden for the short-lived Pony Express. Others were of various backgrounds, but all were good horsemen, and proficient with firearms. Clem was impressed with their ability to cross Indian country and hired most of them immediately. He rarely turned one away, but when he did, the man was almost certainly wearing a faded blue coat or talked with a northern accent.

One thing that Humphrey Beatenbow and Clem Swenson had in common was their hatred for the North. Both felt, with what they deemed proper justification, that the North was the cause of all their past misfortunes, and they had no intention of fraternizing with the "sons-o-bitches" unless absolutely necessary.

One hand that Clem was particularly glad to get was a half-breed Mexican called Tonio, who could speak most of the Indian dialects and was a tracker of some reputation.

Then there was "Gabby". Clem swore that if you asked him a question, he would tell you a hell of a lot more than you wanted to know.

Shanker Stone was a slender, talkative young man who was light on his feet and easy of movement. Clem had seen him shoot the head off a rattlesnake once and had been impressed. But Shanker was not a troublemaker. In fact, his happy disposition reminded Clem of Finch. So Clem did not feel any resentment or reservation about Shanker. Besides, he was a good cattleman and probably had a good deal more schooling than the others. Clem was convinced that Shanker should stay at the ranch while the others were away on the drive. But he guessed Shanker wouldn't like it.

One of the other men who fancied himself expert with firearms was a dour young man who wore two pistols tied down and was constantly practicing his fast draw. Clem groaned inwardly as he watched and surmised that Finch could have shot both pistols off his hips before he could have touched them. He had introduced himself as 'Mac.' "But them that knows me best calls me 'Swifty,'" he had added. The man did seem to know cattle, however, and he said that he had been on some cow hunts and a couple of drives in south Texas. Clem hired him.

Dutch Horst did not appeal to Clem in the least. He used obscenities almost constantly, his teeth were unclean, and his eyes were big and bulged almost as if he were choking. Clem was inclined to send him on his way, but he did need help for the drive, and the man said he knew cattle. Clem never asked a man for his name, and usually they gave only one—which was good enough. But Franz Horst had given himself two names and said that he was from Beaumont, which answered another question that Clem never asked. He didn't care where a man was from as long as he was not a Yankee and did his work. And Clem was convinced, albeit erroneously, that he could smell a Yankee a hundred yards away. Franz Horst was, in fact, a Southerner who had gone to the North to join the Union army, where he had stayed only a very short time, being highly resentful of authority and the lack of any sort of female companionship. With the likelihood that both shortcomings would continue for an interminable length of time, he had deserted the Northern army. And now he was wanted for desertion, rape, and murder. He felt that the HF Ranch in the midst of Indian country (and with an alias for himself) was a safe place for him to be until the army forgot about him.

Then there was Tiny. It was the only name he gave, and none other was needed. He was a huge man who veered off from a caravan going west. He was riding a mule that was almost as tall as one of the ranch thoroughbred mares. "Need a big animal to carry all this blubber," he explained in a soft, musical voice. He had fierce-looking eyebrows and wore a bristling moustache, but his eyes were friendly and softly smiling. His entire demeanor spoke of gentleness and friendliness. He had been in the Confederate navy during the war and for several years before the war, he said. In fact, Tiny was almost fifty years old and had returned from the war to find his wife dead of cholera and his two children, both girls, married.

Clem was immediately taken with Tiny and hired him on the spot.

But the brightest acquisition in the entire hiring process was Brandy Wine. At least, that was what he said his name was, and he was by far the most amazing person Clem had ever seen. He was probably no more than thirteen or fourteen years old, but had either outgrown or never possessed the awkwardness of youth. His small, slender body was muscular and sinewy, and he moved with the grace of a cat. His complexion was smoothly tanned, his hair was a sandy brown, his teeth were white and even, and his sparkling blue eyes held lurking saints and devils. His limitless energy created a minor whirlwind wherever he went, and his irresistible laugh pealed frequently, causing all who heard it, with the exception of Franz Horst, to smile. Even Ellie smiled, as she had rarely done since the trip west.

There really wasn't any good reason for Clem to hire Brandy, but, as Clem blithely explained, "I got as much right to be a damn fool as anybody, I reckon."

It was almost sundown when Brandy had first ridden to the ranch where Clem and several of the cowhands were standing in front of the bunkhouse. Brandy rode up to them on a small mustang of a dirty yellow color. The horse was cow-hocked and bog spavined; he had a head like a clawhammer, and a large ring of white completely circled his eyes. Both of his front legs seemed to come out of the same hole. Clem and the rest of the boys gaped in amazement. It was beyond a doubt the most completely homely horse that any of them had ever seen. Yet his rigging was new, and the cowboys recognized it as costly. Brandy also carried a pistol and a rifle—both empty. The pistol hung in its holster almost at the center of his back, and the rifle dangled loosely from a saddle strap.

Not a man spoke as Brandy rode up to them.

"I be looking for the head lad, if he's about." Brandy spoke first.

The men seemed to come out of a trance.

"I'm ramroddin' this here outfit, if that's what you mean," Clem finally answered.

"That's what I mean, old chap," Brandy said. "I heard that some chaps out this way were hiring lads to take some cows up north somewhere."

"You know anything about cattle?" Clem asked unbelievingly.

"All I know is that the ones I've seen in Texas are dirty on one end and dangerous on the other."

Clem looked blank for a moment and then burst out laughing. "That's the best description I ever heard of one of the aggravatin' damn critters," he admitted.

The other cowboys joined in the laughter and eagerly awaited further conversation between Clem and the youngster. The accent was completely new to all of them except Tiny, who recognized it as British. The cowboys were intrigued.

"Well, now," Clem said in a voice to indicate that he was ready to discuss serious business. "Since you know about all there is worth knowin' about a steer, how else do you reckon you'd be able to make a hand on a trail drive?"

"I know horses," Brandy said quietly.

"You know horses?" Clem was flabbergasted. The cowboys roared their mirth.

Brandy's face flushed, but when the laughter subsided, he continued stoutly. "I bloody well do know horses. Since I was a tot, I've been working with horses every day of my life."

"Then, why—where—how did you get that one you're ridin'?"

"I fished Punkin out of a bog on the Trinity River, and he's been with me since. And a fine horse he is, too!"

"You call that a horse?" Franz Horst jibed contemptuously.

"They call you a man, don't they, old chap!" Brandy shot back.

Horst growled angrily and started to move forward, but Tiny's big hand was immediately placed on his shoulder. Tiny's great bulk was not blubber, but was solid muscle, as the cowboys had long since discovered; so Horst subsided. The cowboys again roared in laughter, but this time they were laughing at Horst, who spat an obscenity and stalked angrily away.

Clem, who had laughed more since Brandy rode up than he had in the past two years, gasped, "Well, now, I guess that the HF shore ort to have at least one man that knows somethin' about horses, so I reckon you're hired."

"Splendid, my dear chap. I'd surely like to have a go at it."

"You got a handle?" Clem asked.

"A wot?"

"A handle. A name."

"Oh. Of course. Sorry and all that. I forgot to introduce myself. My name is Brandy. Brandy Wine."

\* \* \* \* \* \*

Brandy had in fact, been a stable lad in one of the foremost racing stables in England since he was nine years old. When he had been there four years, he was deemed capable of accompanying one of his charges on a boat across the channel to France, where the horse ran dead last in one of the premier races of the year. And Brandy, having heard of the Wild West in America, where his beloved animal, the horse, ran wild and free, sent his horse home with another lad and got a job as cabin boy on a ship sailing to America.

When the ship landed at Houston, he collected passage wages and set off on foot to the top of the Texas map he had managed to secure. Weeks on the trail wore out his shoes, but not his spirit. And he had indeed found the little yellow mustang in a bog in the Trinity River. It took almost the entire day and part of one night for him to pull brush and weeds, and to tug to get the forlorn creature out, but he finally managed it. For two days, he pulled grass and fed the horse until it was able to stand and walk on steady legs. It followed him into Fort Worth where he bought tack for the horse, and guns for himself. Supplied with some grain for his horse and food for himself, he headed west of Fort Worth. Only the boy and his horse knew how they had survived Indian country and arrived at the HF. But they had.

Brandy quickly became the favorite of the entire ranch, including the Negro men and women, but excluding Dutch Horst. Brandy's love of horses was soon apparent, and the horses responded to him in a manner that perplexed the cowboys. Even the old, spoiled horses succumbed to his method, and none ever bucked with him; many of them would neigh a welcome when he came in sight of the remuda.

\* \* \* \* \* \*

While the cowboys rode the vast expanse of the HF to take care of any problems with the cattle, Brandy was getting acquainted with the horses that would be in his charge on the drive.

"Every horse has a personality, just like a human," Brandy confided to Clem, who was introducing him to his various duties on the trail.

"These here might be a mite different, Brandy," Clem said mildly. "They're mostly mustangs, and they prob'ly got more longhorn blood in 'em than human blood." It had been so long since Clem had attempted levity that he was awkward in the attempt. And for some strange reason, he tried not to cuss when he was around the youngster.

"I'm sure you are right, Mr. Clem," Brandy said politely. "But Punkin seems to respond to gentle treatment. So if you don't really mind my doing so, I suppose I'll have a try at the rest of them."

"Brandy, they'll be more'n a hundred mules and horses in that remuda!"

"I know that, Mr. Clem," Brandy replied. "But—"

"All right!" Clem capitulated. "Handle 'em any way you want. Jus' be shore they're available at daybreak and noon and night so's the cowboys can have a change of horses when they want 'em. An' when you stop 'em for the night, be dam—be sure you ain't close to no woods or hills or anything where one can hide out, lessen you have to spend a couple of days lookin' for 'em. We ain't gonna have no horses to spare."

"I understand, sir, and I'll do my best—"

"An' herdin' the remuda ain't the only job you're gonna have, neither."

Brandy looked at Clem questioningly.

"We'll have a possum belly under the chuck waggin—"

"A possum belly, sir?"

"Oh, hell, Brandy!" Clem's exasperation finally got the best of him. "It's a big buffalo hide stretched out under the chuck waggin, and you got to keep it filled with prairie coal—"

"Prairie coal?"

"Dammit, Brandy—buffalo chips! Don't you know nothin'?"

"Very little, I'm afraid, sir," Brandy said contritely.

"Well, anyways, you'd ort to throw dry buffalo chips in it, if we hit flat country where they ain't no wood."

"I'll do that, sir."

Clem had to clamp his jaw to prevent himself from telling Brandy not to call him 'sir'. "If we're in country where there's wood, you'll need to drag wood up to the fire with your horse. An' sometimes, you might even help wash and dry dishes, though I doubt if that's likely on this drive; we're gonna have a couple of women doin' the cookin', and another to help out, too. But you'll need to catch their mules, and harness 'em up and unharness 'em. Maybe even grind coffee. Fact is, Brandy, the horse jingler, he does jus' about ever dam—ever thing there is to around camp."

"You mean we're going to have ladies to do the cooking?" Brandy was big-eyed.

"Not ladies," Clem said testily. "Nigger wenches. An' they's a little nigger boy about your age that's gonna help you out, too. He's pretty good with horses, and I reckon even a jingler has got to sleep some."

"Oh, good!" Brandy enthused. "I shall enjoy a companion!"

Clem clicked his knife shut with which he had been whittling, shook his head in complete wonderment, and went into the bunkhouse.

\* \* \* \* \* \*

Clem, upon remembering these past events, grinned, which was unusual for him. Then, with a shrug of resignation, he dropped his arm from the corral fence and walked resolutely toward the bunkhouse.

He had few reservations about the crew he had hired. They were all good riders, and with the exception of Brandy, they could shoot. They would give a good account of themselves if it came to Indian trouble—or any other kind! He did have some doubt about Horst, but discounted it as a personal dislike for the man.

He sent word for all the hands who were not on guard duty to meet in the bunkhouse after supper. He did not relish the chore of telling the men the drive was delayed. "Damn the job of foreman, anyway!"

# Chapter 2

When the cowboys were all gathered in the bunkhouse after supper, Clem addressed them. "Men," he began almost belligerently, "we ain't gonna start the drive tomorrow. Mebbe so not for three or four days." There was an audible groan, but Clem continued. "You old hands know what we'll be doin', and you men that has rode in just to make the drive will have plenty to keep you busy here on the ranch. We got to hold the trail herd where it is, and keep a sharp eye out for Indians—and mebbe have a full scale Indian fight on our hands. I'll let you know when we're ready to start the drive to Abilene."

"I got a question." It was a young cowboy that had come from Fort Worth when he had heard that the HF was making a drive.

"All right!" Clem answered shortly. "What is it?"

"I understood that Finch had a treaty with the Indians that would let him run cattle here without trouble."

"He did! And mebbe still does. But it was Kit Carson that got the treaty for 'im. Now that Kit is dead, there ain't no tellin' what the Indians will do. Everbody thought it best to wait and see."

"Hell!" Swifty said with disgust plainly in his voice. "I thought Hump and Finch was tough customers. Anyway, that's the way I heard it over in Fort Worth. Heard Finch was somepn' special with a pistol, too!"

Clem eyed Swifty grimly for a long moment. Finally, he said quietly, "They're tough enough. You damn shore don't want to find that out for yourself."

"Hah!" Swifty snorted disdainfully. Clem simply looked at him, but did not respond.

"Anybody else got any questions?"

Another new cowboy raised his hand. Clem nodded to him.

"When do we get paid?"

"When we sell the herd in Abilene. You won't need none afore that. Fact is, you won't have none comin' till we get to Abilene, anyway. You signed on to drive there, and you'll damn well do that—or pull your stakes."

"Is there a trail that we'll follow?" another wanted to know.

"There will be after we make the first drive, but there ain't none now—not for the first couple of hundred miles or so, anyway."

"Then how do we get there?"

"We're already north of the Canadian, and we don't have to cross it; so we drive north and hit the Oklahoma strip, which is pretty damn wild, so they say, and I'm a-thinkin' we ain't got a chance in hell of crossin' it without Indian trouble. Not this year, anyway!"

Clem was drawing a rough map with his spur on the hard clay floor as he talked. The men crowded around to see.

"We'll have to cross the Beaver and the Cimarron. Then, we can cut across north of Camp Supply, which is on the north fork of the Canadian. Then we hit Medicine Lodge River and Salt Plains River, and a lot of others. We'll have to cross a lot of streams, which is good, cause that means we'll have water for the cattle. A hundred miles or so south of Abilene we'll hit the Chisholm trail. I was up it in '65, and it's a pretty fair cattle trail, but it was jus' a waggin road at first, made by a half-breed trader who drove his waggin from Abilene to Fort Worth. He died a few months back, so I hear. Dan Waggoner took a herd to Abilene last year. Accordin' to Colonel Hitt and Charley Gross, that come by here a while back, several drives will be made this year. Joe McCoy that was here last year said they was buildin' a six-story hotel in Abilene. They's a lot of whores already there, and the town is pretty wide open. Hump give his word that we'd deliver 3100 steers to McCoy this summer; so I reckon, come hell, high water, or the whole damn Indian nation, that's what we'll do. Hump ain't no man to go back on his word!"

This was greeted by enthusiastic yells and whistles from the cowboys.

"They say that Ellison from Caldwell Company, Bill Butler, and J. L. McCaleb are makin' drives this year, so we're gonna hafta be careful that we don't get no herds mixed."

"Well, we got a road brand on ours that you can read from a hundred yards away; so I reckon they won't be hard to find in a mix-up," one enthusiastic cowboy observed.

"Mebbe not hard to find," Clem said sarcastically, "but findin' 'em ain't gettin' 'em back in one herd. A cow critter is the orneriest animal on four laigs, and they damn shore ain't gonna bunch up jus' to please us."

"You bossin' the drive, Clem?"

"Yep. I am. Hump will go along to take care of business, but you'll take your orders from me. They won't interfere."

"Thought Finch was gonna go."

"He was. But now since the Indian scare is on, Hump is goin' and leave Finch here."

"Why will he do that?"

"Cause Hump can't shoot as fast and as straight as Finch can. Nobody can! An' Finch knows Indians."

"Hah!" Again, the derisive sound came from Swifty. "What about them outlaws I keep hearin' about that's up in Kansas?"

"If we're lucky, we won't see any of 'em!" Clem replied. "Mebbe some herd cutters, but I figger we can handle that. Quantrell was killed a couple of years ago over in Missouri. But the James boys and Cole and Jim Younger are still raisin' hell. They mostly pick on banks, but I shore wouldn't want to meet up with 'em after Hump collects for the herd. He won't take pay except in gold. That's why I wisht Finch was goin' along."

"Hell!" expostulated Swifty, "Finch ain't the only one that's good with a pistol. I wouldn't mind meetin' up with some of them fellers, my own self!"

"Yeah!" Clem's voice betrayed his disgust. "You'd probly try to braid a mule's tail, too—and get hell kicked out of you!"

Swifty's face flushed, but he did not respond.

"All right. This here meetin's over. Shanker, you take Swifty with you and ride the north rim of the valley. Mebbe so, he can learn you somethin' about shootin' a pistol."

Clem and Shanker grinned at each other. Swifty looked puzzled.

Several of the older hands looked at Swifty keenly, and two or three of them shook their heads in resignation. Clem eyed him almost sympathetically, then shrugged his shoulders.

"That's all," he said. "I'll let you know when we're ready to trail."

\* \* \* \* \* \*

That night, for one of the very few times in his life, Finch did not go to sleep quickly. Instead, he cupped his hands behind his head and lay staring into the night. His lovely wife, O'oah, lay, love-spent and relaxed as a kitten, beside him. The moon shone through the window just enough for him to make out her classic face that still held a small, satisfied smile. Her hair, black as a crow's wing, lay in a tangled disarray on her pillow. And her arm was across his chest, as it was every night when she went to sleep.

Quietly, Finch eased from the bed. O'oah had awakened at Finch's first slight move, her eyes wide and dark as the night, but she gave no indication of being aware as Finch donned his shirt and trousers, then slipped his feet into soft moccasins that O'oah had made for him. He took his rifle and went soundlessly from the room. He mounted the stairway that led to the roof of the big adobe house and walked silently around the waist high parapet that went entirely around the edge of the roof.

From his vantage point, he could see the entire headquarters of the ranch, the row of Negro cottages, Largo's blacksmith shop, and the wellhouse. To the north were the barns and corrals that held the horses the cowboys would ride the next morning, and near them were the two sturdy, round pens that held the ranch stud and jackass.

Finch grinned as he looked at them. The stud pawed the ground in anger as the jackass chewed with complete composure on a bit of hay. Those two were important, for the jackass had sired all of the mules on the ranch, many of them out of the fine thoroughbred mares that Humphrey had brought from Louisiana, and the stud was being used on the mustang mares that they had captured. Some fine-looking quarter-horse-type colts were the result.

Suddenly, memories poured in on Finch as he gazed about the moonlit scene. He remembered the first time he had met Humphrey Beatenbow, and the terrible thump of his insides when he first laid eyes on Colette—the most beautiful woman he had ever seen—and Humphrey Beatenbow's wife!

He remembered Chico Baca, the kind of friend every man should have, but few ever did. He remembered the death Colette and their arrival here, which to Finch was the most beautiful place on earth! He grinned as he remembered the delight and surprise of old Kate when he had brought O'oah home.

"Laws-a-mercy!" Old Kate had exclaimed. "That be the purtiest Indian I ever did see!"

Finch was almost certain that O'oah had been sired by Buff Larrigan, an old mountain man. It happened that Buff was in Fort Worth when Finch and Humphrey had formed their partnership and had volunteered to go west with them. Buff had been a great source of optimism on the trek, and had furnished the camp with plenty of game. It was during the trip that he had confided to Finch that he had stolen one of White Horse's wives and had kept her for a while before sending her back to White Horse, who had sworn vengeance upon Buff.

"Contrary old bastard!" Buff had complained to Finch as they rode together one day. "If'n it had been a Blackfoot, nothin' would a been said about it. Anyways, I expect old White Horse has got a young 'un that he didn't sire, and I got a hunch he knows it."

Finch had that same hunch, for an occasional gesture, a fleeting look, and O'oah's joyous outlook on life reminded Finch of the old Irishman.

But White Horse had exacted his avowed vengeance, for only a few days after Buff had left the HF ranch and headed back to his beloved mountains, White Horse had ridden down to see Finch. Tied to his saddle was the unmistakable, snow-white hair of Buff's scalp. Finch's first reaction had been to shoot White Horse dead, which he could easily have done. But in a flash, he realized that if he did, the entire Comanche nation would descend on the ranch and massacre every man, woman and child, white and black. He stayed his hand.

Finch shook his head violently as if to clear it of the memories that had flooded his mind. He walked once again around the roof parapet. The ranch lay calm and serene in the Texas moonlight. Finch sighed and returned to his room. O'oah was still awake, but did not say anything. As Finch eased himself silently into bed, she reached for him and cuddled her lovely naked body close to him.

\* \* \* \* \* \*

Waiting for the drive to begin was borne by the men with varying degrees of patience. Finch, with animal-like stoicism, gave no indication of restlessness. Humphrey paced and muttered and was cryptic in conversation.

The Negroes were kept busy about the headquarters. Humphrey had heard of a new device to put on the back of a chuckwagon that made a lot of sense to him, and he started Largo to building one. Finch came upon Humphrey and Largo while they were discussing the innovation.

"Ever seen one of 'em?" Humphrey asked Finch.

"No, but I've heard about it. I rangered with Charlie Goodnight, and he told me how he was gonna build a chuck box on the end of a wagon that would hold most of the staple foods. You could raise a lid and cover it, and then let the lid down and prop it up to make a table to work on. Sounded like sense to me."

"It is," Humphrey agreed. "One of the cowboys that come in told me that Goodnight had already built one. And it worked fine, too."

"I'll bet it did, if Charlie Goodnight had anything to do with it," Finch smiled.

"You know, Finch," Humphrey said musingly as he propped one foot up on the wagon tongue, "I never knew what a rough life cowboys do lead until we came out from Fort Worth. I thought the war was rough—and it was. But life on the plantation was mighty easy livin'. It never did occur to me until we came out here that men live rough all the time. I aim to make it easier if I can."

"We get used to it, Hump," Finch said almost defensively. "Besides, here on the HF the cowboys have a good life. A bunkhouse most nights, and three meals nearly every day. That's a lot more than they were used to. Of course, when I was in the Rangers, I roughed it pretty much. But since we got here—I'd be gettin' soft if it wasn't for O'oah."

"She keeps you a goin', don't she?" Humphrey chuckled. "I reckon everybody on the ranch knows about them all night rides you all take out on the flat country."

"O'oah likes the wind and the rain, too. She likes to be out in it. Says it makes her feel closer to the land. I reckon I feel the same way," Finch grinned sheepishly.

"Well, there ain't a cowboy on the HF that wouldn't give his best horse to be in your boots. Anyway," Humphrey continued, "I don't figger a trail drive needs to be so damn tough as everybody's been makin' it. That's the reason I'm a makin' this here chuck-wagon the way I am. I know most folks use oxen and maybe a cart for the chuckwagon, but I aim for the HF to do things a little better than some. That's why we're gonna use mules and pull two wagons. One of em's gonna be a hospital wagon, and the other the chuckwagon." Then to Largo, Humphrey posed a question. "You think that new-fangled chuck box will be all right, Largo?"

"Ought to work real good, Mars Hump," Largo grinned, "when I gits it fixed good."

"Our cowboys are gonna be mighty spoiled on this trip," Humphrey said in a jocular tone. "I figger most of 'em are part human anyway! Gonna take a nigger wench, maybe two of 'em to cook, and we'll have four mules to pull this fancy chuckwagon."

"What wench you gonna take," Mars Hump?" Largo asked anxiously.

"Not sure yet," Humphrey replied. "Your wife, Maisie, did a good job for the cowboys on the way out from Fort Worth."

"Yassuh, Mars Hump. She did," Largo admitted." But we got two little 'uns now. They be mighty vexatious to take on a trail drive."

"Won't take 'em," Humphrey replied absently as he continued to look over the new chuck box. "The oldest one is already weaned, and the youngest mighty nigh ready. Leave 'em with Kate. She can take care of 'em."

"But, Mars Hump. . ." Largo's voice was protesting.

"Now that'll do, Largo!" Humphrey said sternly. "Nigger kids—I mean black kids—got no use for their own dam once they're weaned, and you know it."

"Yassuh, Mars Hump," Largo replied dispiritedly.

Finch wondered for the thousandth time how Humphrey could be so callous to his former slaves. And what puzzled him more was why they all regarded him so highly.

\* \* \* \* \* \*

Maisie and Largo had both been petulant when Humphrey called Maisie from her quarters.

"You got any thoughts about what other women we ort to take, Maisie?"

Maisie considered for a moment before replying. "I reckon Liza be all right for dat, Mars Hump," she replied.

Liza was one of the two black women on the ranch that had no permanent man. Actually, Maisie knew that some of the HF cowboys had been visiting Liza's cabin at night for some time.

"Ain't she that light-skinned wench that lives down on the south side of the quarters? I thought they was two of 'em."

"They is, Mars Hump. But I reckon that Rhody that lives with Liza hadn't ort to go on no long trail drive."

"Why not?" Humphrey demanded.

"Well, Mars Hump—I reckon she done knocked up a little bit."

"Knocked up?" Humphrey demanded angrily. "She ain't got no buck, and I told all of 'em—"

"I reckon it ain't no nigger buck that got 'er knocked up, Mars Hump."

"You mean—"

"Yassuh. Some of de cowboys—dey be comin' to—"

Humphrey was silent for a long moment, then set his jaw stubbornly and walked away.

# Chapter 3

Even with the specter of an Indian raid hovering, only a few guards were posted around the ranch at night, for Indians rarely attacked in darkness, and before the sun came up each morning, the men were saddled and riding the canyon rim. While they once had ridden singly, they now rode in pairs.

The buffalo had been thinned out to the point that Finch, to ensure that enough were left for the Indians to hunt as he had promised White Horse, had instructed the cowboys to discontinue driving them out of the valley. Consequently, the cowboys had only to doctor an occasional cow or calf or assist one of the young heifers in giving birth. Yet, with all the activities and hard work and the ever present prospect of danger and excitement, the cowboys were becoming impatient. The wanted to see Abilene!

\* \* \* \* \* \*

While the drive was delayed, Clem kept the cowboys so busy riding during the day that they had little time to fret, but when they gathered at the bunk house at night, many became quarrelsome and impatient.

Nothing seemed to bother Tiny, however. His soft, musical voice and his calm, friendly demeanor were a quelling influence. He and Brandy Wine became almost inseparable.

Swifty practiced his fast draw every night. Gabby talked incessantly.

"You say 'how are you?' to that blabber-mouthed bastard, and you done said too much," one cowboy opined. Yet, all the cowboys stood the interminable monologue with good nature and paid no attention to Gabby.

Tonio lay on his bunk and did not enter into the conversation unless directly addressed. Dutch Horst seemed intent on picking a quarrel.

"Don't see why in hell we ain't on our way," he grumbled. "They already drove cattle all the way up to Montana." Although the delay had been only three days, Horst was irritable at the wait.

Shanker Stone was not impressed by Horst. "Yeah! I know, but Johnson had a bunch of soldiers with 'em most of the way."

"Thought they impeached 'im!" Clem said, surprised.

"That's what I heard, too," Shanker replied. "But that was just the House of Representatives. The Senate cleared 'im. I don't know what the hell 'impeach' means—but anyway, they didn't fire 'im!"

"Well, Throckmorton was elected governor a couple of years ago. Sheridan fired 'im, and then Sherman appointed Pease as governor last year."

"Hell!" sneered Horst. "Them politicians ain't got sense enough to pour water out of a boot, noways. One of them high muck-a-mucks up in Washington even bought Alaska last year. Paid $7,000,000 for it."

"Alaska!" Clem was disbelieving. "What I hear, that's all ice and snow up there and damn shore won't graze no cattle!"

"Maybe, sometime, we will be glad Alaska is part of the United States," came Tiny's pleasant voice. "Might find gold or something up there."

"If they don't, Tiny and I can go up there and have us a ruddy good snowball fight," Brandy's cheerful, immature voice chimed in.

The cowboys laughed, and the tension and frustration in the bunkhouse vanished.

\* \* \* \* \* \*

It took three days to finish the chuckbox. Finch rode almost constantly. He hoped that the Indians would continue to honor their agreement, but he rode on the alert.

In any case, it gave him a fine excuse to ride his fox-eared sorrel gelding through the lush grass of the valley. Finch had named his favorite horse Rafter for some obscure reason that he could not remember, but he did remember quite vividly that Colette had been riding him the day she was killed by an Indian arrow. Humphrey had encouraged her to ride with Finch that day, and Finch had agreed provided she rode Rafter, for he was the fastest horse Finch had ever ridden. There was nothing on the HF that could come near him in a race.

After three days of waiting, Finch met Humphrey. They rode side by side to look at the mottled herd of longhorns that would trail to Abilene.

Most of the longhorn's ancestors had come from Spain; some had crossed the Atlantic with Columbus. The Spaniards in Mexico had stocked their ranches, and some had trailed northward with Coronado and other explorers. Inevitably, some were lost, strayed, or abandoned. They roamed the plains country, and being a belligerent and virile breed, they had multiplied until in many places in south Texas they had become a nuisance and were slaughtered for their hides. For four centuries they had survived, however, and they had mixed with other breeds so extensively that they were simply a breed of their own—tough, dangerous, and aggressive.

Finch and Humphrey sat in companionable silence that neither found uncomfortable.

"How's the chuckwagon comin' along?" Finch finally asked.

"It's finished. You know that fellow Goodnight had a right good idea."

"He's quite a man, all right."

"You know 'im pretty well, huh?"

"Nope. Was in the Rangers at the same time, but not the same company. He must have been hell on wheels in a fight, though, from what I hear. But his partner, Loving, was killed last year over in New Mexico. Indians."

Humphrey nodded his understanding.

"Well, Maisie is shore gonna enjoy that chuck box. She's already got it packed almost full— and the wagon, too."

"Gonna take her on the drive, huh?"

"Aim to. She's a good cook. May take Ellie, too. She'd be a help around camp. And Maisie might like some female company."

"She's awful young to be away that long, isn't she?"

"Naw!" Humphrey's attention was on the herd. "She's a twelve-year-old, I think. Lots of 'em have suckers by the time they're that age, but seems like she's scared of men since that black bastard raped her a couple of years ago when we was comin' west."

"I don't blame her," Finch said feelingly, remembering her battered face.

"The grass holding out all right here in the draw?"

"It's gettin' a little short but ought to hold them until we can leave."

Finch had been riding hard for three days and had seen nothing unusual or threatening; he now posed a question to Humphrey.

"Could you be ready to start in a couple of days?"

"Well, God-a-mighty!" Humphrey said with a sigh of relief. "I reckon we can. Everbody will shore be glad. The cowboys are all so damn fidgety they're beginnin' to quarrel among themselves."

"I guess they haven't got a lot of Indian blood in 'em or they'd know how to wait," Finch said.

"I guess not—except maybe for Tonio, but they got nearly ever other kind of blood in 'em. There's some Mex blood in some of 'em, a lot of Irish, some English and French. Wouldn't doubt that some of 'em got a drop or two of nigger blood in 'em."

"You don't believe that!" Finch was startled.

"Maybe not—but I damn shore wouldn't doubt it any. When you come to think of it, you're married to a Indian, even if she is pretty. And Mandy and Colette are so mixed up, I never did quite get the straight of it."

"You told us that Mandy was Colette's aunt," Finch said. "And that puzzled me. Mandy doesn't look much older than Colette did."

"She ain't!" Humphrey confirmed. "She's only four years older than Colette was, which still makes her a few years younger than me."

"I don't see how that could be!" Finch said.

"Oh, hell!" Humphrey said with some exasperation. "They're all mixed up just like the rest of us. Mandy's ma and Colette's grandma was the same woman, and she had a passel of kids, but they was sired by two different men. Her first man was a Frenchman. He got killed after Colette's ma was born. And then Colette's grandma got married again to a Swede, and several years later Mandy was born. That's where she gets that yellow hair."

"I see," Finch said. But he was confused.

"I shore as hell doubt if you do," Humphrey said with annoyance. "Doubt if anybody could— the way I told it—doubt if I do! All I know is that I'd a married Mandy if she was part Chinaman." Humphrey was disgusted with himself, for he was not an articulate man, except when quoting the Bible.

"I sure don't blame you!" Finch laughed heartily. "She is a beauty."

"Well, I was mighty pleased when me and Mandy got back from Louisiana and found you all married up. Mandy was too. She thinks that little squaw of yours is somethin' special."

"So do I!" Finch said fervently.

"Fact is," Humphrey returned, "we're sort of like them long-horns there. Got jus' about ever kind of blood in us."

"Maybe so." Finch enjoyed arguing pleasurably with Humphrey as long as the subject was not serious. "I reckon we are a lot like these longhorns that have a lot of different strains in 'em. But I'll bet that none of the cowboys ever bedded a nigger wench. I know I haven't, and I wouldn't!"

Humphrey looked at Finch closely. "Maybe not," he conceded, "but Maisie says some cowboys been sneakin' down to that nigger cabin where them two high yeller wenches that ain't married to no buck is livin'."

"You don't mean. . ."

"I do mean," Humphrey rejoined strongly. "Prob'ly goin' on ever since the new hands started comin' in. Did even back on our plantation in Louisiana."

"Well, why didn't you put a stop to it?"

"God-a-mighty, Finch! It wasn't none of my business. Besides, you ain't gonna keep men nor animals from breedin'—that's what Kate says, and she's damn shore right about that. Fact is, by the time we've all been on these plains as long as them longhorns have, I doubt if you can tell a white man or a nigger or a Indian apart, we'll be so mixed up."

"Well, the longhorns have been here nearly four hundred years; so I reckon we haven't got anything to worry about. In the meantime, I'm sure not goin' to get in bed with any black wench."

Humphrey opened his mouth to reply, but evidently thought better of it. He closed his jaws firmly and shook his head in wonder at Finch's naivete.

"Let's get back to headquarters," he said.

Finch, in perplexity, turned his horse to follow Humphrey. He wondered if he could ever really get to know Humphrey Beatenbow. He had just the same as admitted that he had taken Negro wenches, and at the same time, he gave every indication that he considered them like cattle. The Beatenbows had branded their slaves when Humphrey was a youngster. Even now, Kate and Sam wore their brands on their left shoulders, and both were inordinately proud of it and showed it to anyone at the least excuse. And now Humphrey philosophized that eventually all races would be melded into one. Finch gave up trying to figure it out and nudged his horse up beside Humphrey's.

"Can you be ready to pull out in two days?" Finch asked.

"We can," Humphrey said matter-of-factly. "The chuckbox is finished, and the niggers killed a couple of hogs last week out of that litter that old sow had—the one we traded a good steer for, from that caravan passin' by. Good thing we did that, too. Kate's been makin' soap, and we got some bacon cured out. We ort to be in good shape for grub—at least part of the way."

"Kate's makin's soap? How does she do that?"

"I dunno!" Humphrey answered absently. "Uses ashes and lard and other stuff. She's been makin' it for years back on the plantation, but we ain't had no lard before up here. And it's gonna come in mighty handy to grease the hubs."

"Kate can do a lot more than just cook, can't she!"

"Yep. She had to back in Louisiana. She's got plenty of neat's-foot oil too by boilin' the feet and shin bones of cattle that Clem has had the boys pickin' up from dead carcasses the past month or so. All the cowboys have got their tack oiled up good. We'll have some along to oil wet gear if we need it."

"I guess we ought to raise her wages," Finch said admiringly. "How much do we pay the blacks, anyway?"

Humphrey looked at Finch in surprise. "Haven't paid 'em anything yet. Don't know what they'd do with it out here, anyway. Why do you ask?"

"Just wondered," Finch said. "They've sure made the difference in us being able to stay out here."

"Doubt that!" Humphrey said a bit shortly. "We'd a stayed. I'll admit, though, they have made things easier. Fact is, I may take a few of the black cowboys on the drive."

"They'll do a good job," Finch said. "Of course, Clem will fume 'cause they won't use saddles."

Humphrey chuckled. "Let 'im fume. I ain't fixin' to tell them niggers they got to use saddles jus' to please Clem. I'll bet he's most thirty-five years old and gettin' crotchety as an old longhorn bull, anyway."

"How many blacks you figure on takin'?"

"Don't know yet. I'm takin' Maisie to do the cookin'—course, that's causin' Largo to pout, and I may leave 'im here. Ellie will go and help Maisie about the wagon. Gonna take one or two of them single wenches that the cowboys been visitin' so regular here lately."

"Why?" Finch was amazed.

"Why, God-a-mighty, Finch! To drive the hospital wagon and haul the bedrolls. We'll put a mattress in it for her to sleep on."

Finch gulped but made no objection to Humphrey's outrageous plan. He could see some of the cowboys sneaking into the 'hospital' wagon at night.

"This is goin' to be the damndest trail drive Texas ever saw!" Finch thought as he spurred Rafter into a lope.

# Chapter 4

The day before the drive was to begin was fraught with excitement and anticipation.

Each man assigned to the drive had at least one pistol and a rifle, which he oiled and cleaned carefully. Most of the men carried a calibre 44 Winchester rifle and the Remington 44 army revolver.

All the men were veterans of outdoor life. They wore heavy cotton drawers and woolen undershirts. A few had an extra pair of boots which they would stash inside their bedroll. Their socks were thick cotton or wool, and their trousers were made of thick, soft woolen material. Texas weather, they knew, was capricious. Each carried a good pocket knife and whetstone. Most also carried a large skinning knife attached to their belts. In their "possibles" bag, many carried a bundle of buckskin, needles or a small awl, thread or a few shreds of dried sinew, beeswax, some extra buttons, and perhaps a pencil and some paper.

Each item was carefully checked. The cowboys were grateful that their bedrolls and extra gear would be carried in a wagon, thus relieving them of a burdensome bulk tied behind their saddles.

As soon as each man was satisfied that his gear was the best he could manage, he rolled into his bunk to get a good night's sleep, for they knew it might be a long time before they got another.

\* \* \* \* \* \*

The morning of July 4, 1868, opened the day with a gaudy and beautiful red sunrise that spread warm fingers of light across the plains and valleys of northwest Texas.

The cowboys were ready.

Maisie, the statuesque and handsome wife of Largo, sat perched on the chuckwagon seat, holding the lines of the mules hitched to it. Beside her sat her husband's young sister, Ellie, who was several shades lighter than Maisie. Even at twelve years of age, she showed a voluptuous maturity, though her large, dark eyes held shadows of sadness that had been there for more than two years.

The cowboys who were going on the drive were all mounted on their best horses and were gathered near the big barn to await the arrival of Clem, who would give the word to go.

Clem, Finch, and Humphrey were engaged in serious conversation on the gallery of the ranch headquarters. They had apparently finished their talk, for Clem, as was characteristic of him, turned abruptly away from Finch and Humphrey and mounted his horse to ride to the cowboys.

Mandy and O'oah stood in the doorway leading from the gallery to the living room. Mandy held a baby in her arms, and another clung to her apron. O'oah stood beside Mandy. Both were tall, both were beautiful. Mandy's dark eyes shone with compassion, love, and patience, while O'oah's eyes sparkled with merriment, excitement, and an almost feral fire that defied description.

Humphrey, who was not a demonstrative man, turned to his wife, but did not approach her. He had said his goodbye the night before.

"Take care of things, wife," he said brusquely. "Let Finch know if you need anything. If he's not around, Shanker Stone will be."

Mandy nodded, but tears welled up in her dark, luminous eyes as Humphrey turned to Finch and stuck out his hand.

"Take care of 'em, Finch!" Humphrey's voice was a bit hoarse.

"Do the best I can," Finch agreed.

"Well. . ." Humphrey cleared his throat and seemed to be at a loss for words. He mounted his horse and rode after Clem.

Finch and the two women watched the cowboys as they rode toward the herd being held by men who would remain on the ranch. Finch counted fifteen men besides Clem and Humphrey, which meant that approximately that many would be left behind. The drivers were all talking excitedly about the delights they expected to find in Abilene. The Beatenbow jackass brayed plaintively as he watched the cowboys and wagons depart, and he began pacing his round pen and pawing angrily.

The drive had begun auspiciously. The cattle, which had been held in a draw that led away from the valley ranch, were allowed to begin grazing their way eastward. The herd consisted of 3121 head. Thirty-one hundred were longhorn steers ranging from four to ten years of age. Many of them were huge animals, standing seventeen hands, with horn spans of six to eight feet, and weighing 800 to 1800 pounds. They were long legged, narrow-hipped, and high shouldered. The older ones had a hump at the base of the neck and hair over their faces. All of them were belligerent and wild. They were of every conceivable animal color.

The twenty-one cattle, in addition to the steers, were ten cows and eleven calves; one of the cows had twins. Clem had included the cows and calves, for he knew that in the event of a stampede--which he anticipated—the cows, upon becoming separated from their calves, would stop and begin to bawl, which would have a dampening effect on the running steers.

The drive was expected to take at least a month, if all went well; but Clem, ever the pessimist, said, "We'll be damn lucky to git to Abilene with a thousand cattle, and back to the ranch before snow flies."

Maisie's chuckwagon followed the men, and behind her was the 'hospital' wagon, as Humphrey called it, driven by a light-skinned black woman, who, Humphrey said, could take care of the aches and pains of the cowboys. Finch suspected that Humphrey knew the woman driving the hospital wagon would do more than take care of the aches and pains of the men. He had made no objection, but he had a lot of reservations, especially since four of the cowboys accompanying the herd were black. There was Alf, who could rope anything that moved or stood still; there was Trey, the ranch horsebreaker; Shanks, one of the small black boys, who had been assigned to help Brandy with the remuda; and, of course, there was Largo.

All the blacks, except Largo, rode with surcingles. Largo still rode the saddle of Chico Baca.

Finch, Mandy, and O'oah watched from the gallery as the herd moved eastward.

"They may have a dry camp tonight," Finch said to the two women. "But that will suit Clem just fine because tired cattle trail better."

"You mean they won't have any water at all?" Mandy asked.

"Oh, the men will have plenty. There is a barrel of good water on the chuckwagon. But the cows and horses will have to miss a drink."

"Will it hurt them?"

"Not a bit. Clem figures it'll do 'em all good. Besides, they'll hit a branch of Wolf Creek tomorrow, and those steers will gorge themselves with water and be a lot easier to handle."

"How long do you think the drive will take?"

"No telling. They'll hit the Oklahoma strip in three or four days; if they make it across the strip without trouble, they could be in Abilene by this time next month."

"What kind of trouble will they have crossing the Oklahoma strip?"

Finch did not answer Mandy. "Think I'll just saddle up and scout around the valley today. We don't have as many cowboys on the ranch now, and we'll need to keep a good lookout all the time."

"I'll come, too," O'oah said gaily.

"You stay here." Finch's voice was kind but firm. "Maybe Mandy can use some help with the young ones."

Both O'oah and Mandy were immediately aware that Finch was concerned with Mandy's loneliness, but O'oah could not understand why he should be. Indian men rode away often and at will on dangerous missions, and their women were proud and happy to see them go. Mandy, however, did understand and appreciated Finch's concern and consideration; her dark eyes spoke a silent "thank you" to Finch. It was the first time that Mandy had ever looked at her husband's tall, blond partner and had seen him as the powerful, virile, and compassionate human being that he was.

"I'll be back before night," Finch said. "If you need anything, remember to fire two shots and then wait a second and fire a third. There'll be a rider in earshot, and he'll relay it all the way around the valley, like we practiced so many times."

"We'll remember," Mandy said solemnly. "And you be careful, too."

"Now, you two behave yourselves." Finch grinned at them as he turned his horse and rode away. Mandy waved at Finch's back, as O'oah looked at her with puzzled eyes.

Finch rode the rim of their valley ranch on one of the regular ranch horses; he left his favorite horse, Rafter, in the corral with a good bait of feed.

When he returned in the afternoon, he ate rather hurriedly and then saddled Rafter. O'oah looked after him with puzzled eyes and a bit of pique as he rode in the direction the trail herd had taken.

\* \* \* \* \* \*

When the herd had strung out and were grazing slowly eastward, Humphrey rode up to Clem and observed that it looked as if the herd was going to be fairly tractable.

"Yeah," Clem agreed dourly. "They'll be good till a grass-hopper or some other terrible critter scares the stupid bastards, and they'll scatter to hell and gone."

"Hope not!" Humphrey said. "Take a lot of time to put that many together again, and I aim to sell 3100 head in Abilene."

"Be damn lucky to get there with a thousand!"

"We'll get there with 3100," Humphrey said firmly. "Ain't no reason not to."

Clem peered at his boss with narrowed eyes as they rode along together, and he sighed inwardly as he remembered Humphrey Beatenbow's reputation for completing what he started. Many admired his determination. Clem was often irritated at what he considered Humphrey's bull-headedness.

"They's prob'ly a thousand reasons between here and Abilene, but we'll keep the aggravatin' sons-of-bitches close to the river for a couple of days where the sand is fairly deep. Make a few of 'em footsore, but it'll tire 'em out. They'll trail better when they're tired, but it'll slow 'em down some. Doubt if we'll make ten miles today. I didn't scout out ahead today, 'cause we're so close to the ranch, but I'll have it to do from now on."

"I'll tell Maisie to find a good campin' spot and stop about an hour afore sundown," Humphrey said as he started to ride away. "She knows the kind we want."

"She done a good enough job comin' out from Fort Worth a couple of years ago—and she's a damn good cook, but I shore don't think you ort to let 'er drive that wagon ahead of the herd."

"Why not?" Humphrey asked in surprise.

"Well, hell, Hump! I reckon you ain't noticed it, but Maisie is one damn good lookin' woman, even if she is black, and that little gal that you got helpin' her would put any Abilene whore in the shade with that figger of hers—even if she ain't but twelve or fourteen years old."

"Well, God-a-mighty, Clem. You know Ellie was raped by that nigger that we hung on our way out. She ain't looked at a man since. Seems scared of 'em."

"Mebbe so," Clem agreed. "But that don't mean that men won't look at her, especially an Indian! She's got a figger most grown women ain't got. An' that nigger wench you got drivin' the hospital waggin ain't no slouch, either. We're gonna be damned lucky to keep some of the cowboys out of that hospital waggin at night."

"Ain't gonna try to keep 'em out. Fact is, a few of 'em been visitin' her cabin at night afore we left the ranch. I've knowed that for a month. She's one of the wenches that ain't bot a buck—that's one reason I brought 'her along. But they won't bother Ellie none. Largo will see to that!"

"You mean you brought that nigger woman along, knowin' that some of the cowboys been screwin' her?" Clem exclaimed in astonishment.

"Well, God-a-mighty, Clem. Men and women will breed—no matter what their color. And I reckon we can all be glad of that, else you and me wouldn't be on this drive—nor anybody else."

"Well!" Clem's voice indicated resignation and disapproval. "I hope you know what you're doin', but I jus' hope it don't cause no trouble. With stampedes, floods, rivers, Indians, and a few other things to worry about, we shore don't need no trouble over a nigger woman!"

"There won't be," Humphrey said shortly. "I'll see to that!"

"Well, you can be damned shore I ain't crawlin' in that hospital waggin at night," Clem vowed stoutly as he rode away.

Humphrey chuckled, for he knew Clem to be a woman-hater, although not even Humphrey knew anything of Clem's life before he joined the westward drive from Fort Worth two years before.

As the cattle grazed their way along the sandy north side of the Canadian River, they flushed quail, coyotes, rabbits, turkey, and prairie chickens out of the sage brush, salt cedar, and wild plum thickets. The cottonwoods were in full leaf, and the yucca were beginning to drop their blooms. The colorful sumac grew in abundance among the hackberry and black locust trees. The ripening sunflowers bent their heads toward the warm sun, and meadow larks sent their happy songs soaring on the clear morning air. Blue jays screeched their raucous protest at being disturbed by the passing herd.

The drive continued without incident. At noon, Maisie pulled the chuckwagon off to one side and prepared a meal. The cowboys took turns coming in to eat, although the herd continued peacefully grazing its way.

When Humphrey rode in to eat, he instructed Maisie to drop behind the herd with the chuckwagon.

"What fo', Mars Hump?" Maisie wanted to know. "If'n I's ahead, I can have the grub cooked by the time the herd an' the cowboys catch up."

"There will be Indians, 'specially when we hit the Oklahoma strip. Clem thinks you and Ellie ort not to be ridin' in front." Humphrey was looking at Maisie as he spoke. He had never really looked at the two women before, except as he would look at a promising young filly or at a strong, well-conformed broodmare. And he was somehow shaken as he suddenly realized that they were indeed women; as he eyed the mature, voluptuous figure of Maisie and the appealing physique of the younger girl, he silently agreed with Clem. Both of them had an animal-like indifference to their bodies; an earthy, almost tangible aura of the female was in their every movement.

"When yo want us to start follerin' de herd, Mars Hump?" Maisie asked.

"Today!" Humphrey said curtly. "Soon as you pack up again. Just drop behind the herd. And tell that gal drivin' the hospital wagon to do the same thing. What's her name, anyway?"

"Liza her name, Mars Hump."

"All right. Tell Liza to drop back with you."

"Yassuh, Mars Hump. I do dat. But I reckon them cowboys gonna have to wait a little longer fo dey grub."

"Let 'em wait!" Humphrey growled. "Won't hurt 'em, and, anyways, that'll be better than losin' a cook."

"Losin' a cook? Now, Mars Hump, yo knows me and Ellie ain't gonna go nowheres."

"Maybe not," Humphrey admitted. "But Clem thinks the Indians might like to have a couple of extra squaws—and I can't say I doubt it."

Maisie was shocked. "Why, Mars Hump. Yo knows I ain't gonna have nothin' to do with no Indian, and Ellie she too little. . ."

"Ellie ain't too little!" Humphrey rejoined angrily. "And the Indians we're likely to meet won't ask your leave to do what they want."

"Well, Largo will take care of Ellie and me," Maisie said stoutly. "He always has ever since yo had us marry up back in Louisiana."

"Dammit, Maisie, you do like I said," Humphrey shouted. "Clem was shore right about you two—you're both women, even if you are black, and so is that gal drivin' that hospital wagon. And I reckon a Indian ain't put off none by skin color!"

"Well. I ain't worried," Maisie said complacently. "Largo, he take care o' us!"

"God-a-mighty!" Humphrey breathed prayerfully. "Hope nothin' happens to 'em. Ain't shore I should a brought 'em along."

Maisie pulled the chuckwagon off to one side and sat watching stoically as the herd grazed past her wagon. She was joined shortly by the hospital wagon driven by the other black woman.

"What fo' yo stop, Maisie?" she wanted to know.

"Mars Hump, he say fo us to foller along behind the herd, Liza. He say maybe Indians run off with us, if'n we drive up ahead."

Liza giggled. "Ain't sho that would be so terrible bad, Maisie. I seen some of them red men that looks like they be mighty good pesterin'."

"Now yo jis do like Mars Hump say, Liza," Maisie said firmly. "Ain't no what fo about it! 'Sides, I knows yo been pleasurin' some o' them cowboys that been comin' to yo cabin at night—an' yo better not let Mars Hump catch yo at no shenanigans."

Liza got down from her wagon, stretched, and yawned. Her full figure was everything that Clem had cautioned Humphrey about.

"I misdoubts that Mars Hump don' already know I been havin' some cowboy company at night," she said archly. "Doubt if'n he's be too put out if'n some of 'em comes to get doctored up at the hospital waggin while we's trailin' either. Mars Hump, he likely know a lot more'n he let on about."

Ellie eyed Liza with big, startled eyes; Maisie looked at her sternly, but said nothing.

When the herd had drifted slowly past, the wagons fell in behind and stayed there until Clem called a halt for the night. There was good grass, though the land was still sandy with a stream running from the north into the river. It was a good place to camp.

Maisie pulled her wagon onto a firm patch of grass, and she and Ellie went about gathering dead branches of sage and mesquite to build a supper fire. Liza was unhitching her team when Brandy Wine rode up.

"I'll unhitch the mules and turn 'em in with the remuda," Brandy said gaily. "You ladies just go on about your business."

"I be thankin' yo, Mars Brandy," Maisie said. "I reckon I jus' ain't much around mules, nohow."

"Mules are almost human, just like horses," Brandy said. "Maybe a bit more stubborn, but they are jolly good workers, if you treat them right."

Ellie looked at Brandy with round, adoring eyes as he unhitched the mules of both wagons and hazed them toward the remuda.

"That Mars Brandy! He sompin', ain't he!" Liza observed. "He sho do talk funny, though."

"That's 'cause he's from England, Largo says," Maisie said.

"Where's England?" Liza asked.

"I dunno," Maisie answered. "Acrost the ocean sommers, Largo says."

"Largo says!" Liza sneered. "Don' yo know nothin' but what that big buck nigger of yo's tells yo!"

"I knows that if'n yo don't help us gather this firewood and cook some supper, I's gonna tell Mars Hump we don' need yo no mo—and it ain't no long walk back to the ranch."

Liza started to reply, but evidently thought better of it. She had her own ideas about what her "hospital" duties were going to be, and she didn't want to miss the drive; but she knew that Maisie and Largo had a lot of influence with Humphrey, and she wasn't going to take chances. She started gathering firewood.

\* \* \* \* \* \*

Clem had assigned some of the cowboys to the first night shift of herding, and the others were gathered around the cooking fire eating beans, beef, sourdough bread, and prickly pear jelly out of tin plates and drinking strong coffee made of freshly ground coffee beans. It was a good meal, and they were hungry and well-pleased that the first day of the drive had gone so smoothly. The ribald humor so characteristic of cowboys at chow was not inhibited by the three black women who served the food, for the cowboys had been around the blacks so much that they scarcely noticed them. The black cowboys took their turn at chow and at work with the rest of them, and the white cowboys paid no more attention to them than to the other whites.

The supper fire had died down to embers as a magnificent, colorful sunset closed another beautiful Texas day.

Tiny had just begun to play a mournful tune on his harmonica, and most of the cowboys were lolling on their saddle blankets when Clem suddenly rose and looked toward the west. Tiny's harmonica stilled. Outlined against the last faint light of the western sky was a rider. He sat very still. A wolf howled in the distance. Humphrey, Clem, and the cowboys all reached quietly for their guns.

"Hello, the camp!" called the rider.

Humphrey recognized the voice.

"Hello, yourself!" he called out cheerfully. The rider was Finch. The entire camp relaxed again, and grins were on the faces of most of the cowboys as Finch rode up and dismounted. He was riding Rafter.

"Thought you were stayin' back at the ranch to look after things," Humphrey said with feigned severity.

"I am," Finch smiled. "But you all didn't hardly get out of the front yard on this first day. Just thought I'd ride out to see why."

"Well, Clem, he thought we'd ort to stay close to the river the first couple of days where the sand is deep, so's the cattle will get tired out some and maybe trail better."

"That's right," Clem chimed in. "Them long-legged bastards can outwalk a camel, and they shore handle a lot easier when they got a little of the sap took out of 'em. Besides, we're headin' northeast toward the Chisholm trail, so we ain't losin' no ground."

"How come you left the ranch, Finch?" Humphrey frowned a bit. "Any trouble?"

"Nope. Everything is fine, and you know that Indians won't attack at night; so I thought I'd just ride out and see how the day went. Wasn't more than ten miles, anyway."

"Well, everything went fine. Things keep goin' this way, we'll be in Abilene in thirty days."

"Well, they damn shore won't keep goin' this a way!" Clem, the pessimist, chimed in. "We'll be lucky to get there afore snow!"

Everyone but Clem laughed, and the banter began again, but Tiny didn't start playing his harmonica. Suddenly, he held up his hand, and the camp quieted. The howl of wolves sent a veritable crescendo of feral sound over the land, and they all listened intently.

"They make a lot purtier music than I ever could," Tiny said quietly. No one disagreed.

Finally, Finch rose to go. "I'll be getting back to the ranch. Likely won't see you boys again before you get back from Abilene."

He nodded to Humphrey as he walked away, and Humphrey followed him.

"Got your night horse staked out?" Finch asked.

"Right over there." Humphrey nodded his head.

"Get 'im," Finch said.

"What for?"

"I want to swap horses," Finch said.

"You what!"

"I'm gonna swap horses with you," Finch said.

"What the hell for? You know you wouldn't take a thousand dollars for that Rafter horse of yours."

"That's right!" Finch agreed. "I've never ridden a faster horse, nor one that had as much sense as he has. That's why I want to swap."

"But, why. . ."

"Look, Hump. There isn't another horse in Texas, or Kansas either, that could catch Rafter, and it stands to reason that you'll need a fast horse worse than I will. So I'm gonna trade 'im to you till you get back."

"God-a-mighty, Finch!" Humphrey was overwhelmed. "A man don't give his best horse away. Not unless it's mighty important."

"I do!" Finch said. "And it's important."

"Well—well. . ." Humphrey was at a loss for words. He knew how much Rafter meant to Finch.

"Besides," Finch said brusquely. "Largo is still riding Chico's horse. With him and Rafter, you will have the two fastest horses anywhere."

"We've got some of our thoroughbred geldings," Humphrey said lamely.

"They're good for a long race, all right," Finch conceded. "But you're not likely to need a fast horse for a long distance. And you know that a thoroughbred isn't any match for a quarterhorse in a short race—especially one like Rafter." He uncinched his saddle and turned it on the pommel as he put it on the ground. "Now where is your night horse?"

Humphrey shook his head and walked away. A couple of minutes later he returned leading a very ordinary looking horse. Without a word he handed the lead shank to Finch, who took it, looped the end over the neck of the horse, and removed the halter. Then he removed the bridle from Rafter and put it on

Humphrey's horse. He had to let the bridle out a couple of notches until it fit, for Rafter's head, for all his muscular build, was small and dainty.

When Finch had his saddle cinched on Humphrey's horse, he slipped the halter on Rafter and patted him on the neck. His hand lingered a moment, and then he handed the lead rope to Humphrey. Then, without another word, he mounted, sat for a moment, then leaned over and shook Humphrey's hand. He didn't look back as he rode away. Rafter looked after him quizzically.

Humphrey stared at the dim shape of Finch as darkness hid him from sight. Then he shook his head as if to clear his vision.

God-a-mighty!" he breathed fervently.

As Humphrey led Rafter to his stake, he passed near enough to the fire that the cowboys recognized Rafter.

"What the hell!" Clem ejaculated.

"Looks like Hump just swapped for himself a pretty good horse," Tiny opined.

"Pretty good!" Clem exclaimed. "They ain't a horse in this country that can hold a candle to that sorrel of Finch's. Ever cowboy on the HF has tried to buy Rafter off'n Finch, and Indians has tried to steal 'im a dozen times. But Finch watched 'im like a hawk. An' I shore can't blame 'im. That Rafter horse was sired by Old Billy and out of a mare called Paisano. Finch got 'im from one of his Ranger buddies named Fleming. An' all them Old Billy horses is somethin' special, but I ain't never seen one that can equal that Rafter horse. Never would a thought Finch would part with 'im."

"He wouldn't for money, maybe," Tiny's soft voice almost whispered. "But I expect he would part with him for a friend. He must think an awful lot of Hump."

"He shore as hell must!" Clem said. "I reckon I been underrating them two all along. Never figgered they thought too much of each other."

"Some men just don't talk much, but feel awful deep," Tiny said.

"I reckon you're right, Tiny," Clem said with a sigh. "I'll start scoutin' ahead tomorrow; so now I'm fixin' to get a couple hours of sleep. The rest of you fellers better do that, too. We'll all have to relieve the night herders at midnight."

With that, Clem rolled in his blankets and was soon asleep. The rest of the men quietly followed suit.

\* \* \* \* \* \*

The Beatenbow jackass had watched with mounting excitement as the wagons and trail herd moved eastward out of sight. He circled his strong, round pen continuously until dark. Then, with a mighty effort, he ran and leaped at the top rail. He was able to get his front feet over, and then he clawed furiously with his back hooves until he raised his small body high enough to topple over. He hit the ground on the outside with a loud whoosh of exhaled breath, but clambered quickly to his feet and took the trail at a fast trot. He had his nose close to the ground, smelling the trail, until he topped a small rise and saw the familiar sight of the longhorn herd, the wagons, and campfire. He pricked his long ears and stood for a few moments, and then with a sigh of relief lowered his head and began to graze contentedly.

The moon came from behind a cloud; wolves howled as the embers of the campfire began to lose their glow. And the first day of the drive passed peacefully into eternity.

# CHAPTER 5

During the next couple of days, the herd proved to be cranky and obstreperous, for a strong southwest wind had begun to blow, forcing the steers to travel almost directly away from it. For centuries, they had learned to survive and prosper while enduring blizzards, wolves, drought, and Indians; and their primitive nature dictated that they graze into the wind in order to scent danger.

They were a tough and belligerent breed with an apparently permanent antagonism toward the world. They could easily walk fifteen or twenty miles a day and go for two or three days without water and suffer no ill effects.

All the cowboys knew that the southwest wind might continue for days, for it was a windswept country, and for long periods of time the constant push of the southwesters would bend the tall grass almost flat. They also knew that so long as the wind blew at their backs, the steers would be irritable, even with each other. Bull fights were common among longhorns, but rarely ended in the death of either combatant. Steers fought less frequently than bulls, but, nevertheless, would occasionally fight; when two of them locked horns, it behooved whoever was near to give them a wide berth, for when one of them was whipped, he would suddenly turn tail and run with amazing speed; anything that was in his escape route was in grave peril.

The men had to repeatedly prod some of the steers which persisted in turning their heads into the wind. The men accomplished this task by folding a long length of their ropes, and, riding precariously near the animal, hitting it across the face just as hard as they could.

"Aggravatin'est damn critters alive!" Clem complained as he rode up to Humphrey. "I'll be glad when the wind stops blowin' so hard. Mebbe they'll travel a little better."

"Hope so!" Humphrey agreed. "But the wind don't pay much attention to what we want up here on the plains."

"That's for damn shore!" Clem growled. "I saw a big bull up clost to the point that had a brand on, too."

"What?" Humphrey said in surprise. "I don't see how we could a missed seein' 'im when we gathered for the drive."

"Didn't." Clem said cryptically. "He's a big brindle bastard with hair growed all over his face and a big dewlap. Got horns eight feet across. Must be fourteen or sixteen years old. He's been hidin' out along the river for a long time and joined the herd sometime last night—or slipped out of some bushes somewheres and mixed in with the herd."

"You say he's got a brand on?"

"Yep. Hard to see with that long hair, but I'm pretty shore it's a brand."

They rode along in silence for a few minutes; then Humphrey spoke.

"Why don't we have some of the boys cut 'im out of the herd and let Alf rope 'im and see what we can find out."

"Already told 'em to do that. There's a couple of 'em cuttin' 'im out right now." Clem pointed ahead where two cowboys were doing their best to drive the bull a distance from the herd. Humphrey and Clem loped toward them.

"Ugly son-of-a-bitch, ain't he!" Clem observed as they rode up. The bull was a monstrous specimen, mean of eye and furious at being molested.

"Where's Alf?" Humphrey asked.

"Here he comes now." Clem nodded toward an approaching rider. He had a blanket strapped firmly under his surcingle, and the long, snake-like, rawhide rope tied to it. "Wish them black bastards would ride a saddle like humans!" Clem fumed.

"Largo rides a saddle," Humphrey said.

"Yeah!" agreed Clem. "But he can't throw a rope like Alf. That nigger can make that rope act like he had a long, black finger."

Alf grinned as he rode up. "Yo be wantin' me, Mars Hump?"

"Want you to rope that bull," Clem answered for Humphrey. "You'll have to build a loop the size of a barn door to get it over them horns. An' be damn shore that surcingle is plenty tight. That bull will go sixteen hundred pounds."

"Yassuh!" Alf grinned. "It's tight, but I won't have to build no big loop. I jus' build a little loop an' throw this here rope over one horn an' his haid."

"Jus' be damn shore you got 'im where he can't get loose!" Clem said. "Soon as you got 'im good, try to move 'im about a little bit so one of the boys can rope his heels. You'll prob'ly jus' have to circle around 'im 'cause you damn shore can't drag 'im. He'll weigh a lot more'n that runty mustang you're ridin!"

"Yassuh! I do dat, Mars Clem." Alf grinned and loosed his rope. He built a loop not much bigger than his floppy hat as he rode toward the bull. Before Clem or Humphrey thought he was nearly close enough, he flashed a muscular arm, and the long, black rawhide rope sailed unerringly and neatly encircled one of the long horns and the muzzle and throat of the bull. Alf quickly wheeled his horse as the bull charged, laughing delightedly as his wiry mustang outran the irate monster. Clem started to yell for one of the men who had been driving the steers to rope the back legs, but he saw that they were too far away for a quick catch; so he downed his own rope and quickly gathered both of the bull's hind feet in his loop. Both Clem and Alf knew what to do. They turned in opposite directions; when their ropes tightened, Alf's mustang grunted as both front feet left the ground, and Clem's saddle groaned as his bigger horse pulled with his belly close to the ground.

The bull strove mightily, but the two horses were too much for him. As his hind feet were pulled together and the horses strained, he fell heavily on his side with a grunt that could be heard a hundred yards away. Humphrey rode up and quickly dismounted.

"Take your piggin' string and tie them two back feet together—an' tie 'em tight. But be shore to make a bow knot so we can tie a rope to the end of it and untie it, when we get ready to turn 'im loose. That big bastard could gut a horse or a man either if he was to accidentally git up."

Humphrey complied and had completed his task when two other riders came up.

"Swifty," Clem ordered, "you put your rope on his front feet and pull 'em tight. Tiny, you come set my horse and keep my rope tight. The horse would prob'ly keep it tight anyway, but me and Hump want to look at a brand he's wearin', and we damn shore don't want 'im to git up with us afoot."

"Where's the brand?" Humphrey asked.

"High up on his shoulder there." Clem pointed with his opened knife. "I'll cut some of the long hair off, and we'll see if we can read it. Notice he's got a swallow fork in his ear, too. Somebody musta been savin' 'im for a herd bull."

Clem made a fairly quick work of cutting the long hair away from the brand with his sharp knife.

"It's a brand, all right. Old. And it was burned deep." Clem traced the brand with his fingers. "I make it out to be a wine glass. What do you think?"

"I expect you're right, Clem. You know more about brands than I do, but I saw one like it when I examined the brand books in Decatur when I went back to Louisiana a couple of years ago."

"Whose brand?"

"Don't remember, but we can find out when we send pay back for 'im."

"Ort to do that all right, if we can get the big bastard to Abilene and sell 'im," Clem said solemnly. "But you won't be payin' for a bull, 'cause I'm makin' a steer out of 'im right now."

With that comment, Clem pushed the bull's testicles up into his stomach, grabbed the huge scrotum, and severed it completely up near the bull's belly; then he reached in and found the withdrawn testicles and pulled them as far out as he could. The bull roared and moaned his anger and helplessness as Clem severed the cords and threw the testicles away.

"Well," Humphrey observed. "Now we've got 3101 steers."

"All right, men," Clem said as he stood up. "One of you throw me Hump's rope; I'll tie the end of it to the piggin' string on his back feet. Swifty, you hold them front feet good and tight with your rope. Tiny, you keep holdin' them back feet tight till I get on my horse, and then you get on yours. Alf, as soon as everbody is ready, you git down and git your rope off of 'im. We'll hold 'im stretched out good till you're back on your horse. Then me and Swifty will give 'im slack, and Hump will pull his piggin' string loose; he'll stretch them loops and git up."

Everyone did as instructed; the longhorn rose from the ground and glared angrily as he charged the nearest horse, which was Humphrey's.

"Run like hell, Hump!" Clem yelled as he unsheathed his pistol. Swifty, who always wore two guns, also pulled one of his. He was just a shade faster than Clem, but no one noticed, and Humphrey did not need instructions from Clem! He was spurring viciously as he outdistanced the brute. When he was safely ahead, the newly made steer stopped, glared about, and then trotted with long, swinging strides toward the herd.

All the men were relieved when the job was done. They had been so absorbed in what they were doing that they had not noticed that the wind had died down.

"Hey!" Clem exclaimed. "The wind has let up. Maybe now we can cover some ground."

As he spoke, there was a slight and much cooler breeze wafting in from the northwest.

"Doubt if the weather is through yet," Tiny said softly. "That northwest wind could bring some rain. If I was on a ship, I'd begin to batten down."

"Doubt it," Clem said. "This here is pretty damn dry country most of the time. We ain't a hell of a long ways from the Oklahoma strip, and we're liable to have more'n weather to worry about there."

\* \* \* \* \* \*

The herd travelled fairly well the rest of the day; about midafternoon it turned sultry hot. Sweat poured from the horses and the faces of the white cowboys. Only the longhorns and black cowboys seemed to be unaffected. The blacks removed their shirts and let the hot sun pour down on their skin, reminding them of the plantation in Louisiana, which not long before had been their home.

"Them damn niggers ain't got no human feelin's a-tall," Clem observed sourly to Humphrey. "They don't pay no more attention to the damn weather than a animal."

Humphrey winced at Clem's observation, for in spite of his enigmatic personality, he was a deeply religious man, and he felt any aspersion cast on the weather was to profane his God who made it.

"They are human, I reckon," Humphrey replied in a voice that, for him, was soft. "I'll admit, though, that three or four years ago I had a lot of doubt about 'em. Figgered 'em for livestock, mostly."

"They still are!" Clem said firmly.

"Doubt it!" Humphrey's rejoinder was almost curt. "Fact is, they are a lot like them longhorns. We've bred 'em up till they're bigger and stouter than most whites—and tougher, too. I reckon when they've been around as long as them longhorns, they'll be so mixed up with white and red and brown blood, that you can't tell which is what—except maybe so that mixed breed will still be tougher and bigger."

Clem looked at Humphrey in amazement. "You don't rightly believe that, do you, Hump?"

Humphrey was silent for a long moment. "Reckon I do. Finch says them longhorns been in this country four hundred years. A lot of things can change in that length of time."

"Well, I'll be damned!" a perplexed Clem muttered as he rode away.

Later in the day a cloud seemed to grow out of the earth in the west. The sun went down behind the cloud.

The next morning, the sun came up and splashed red rays across the land. Birds seemed to be flying higher and faster, a coyote howled at mid-morning, and the cattle were restless and grazed faster, but many of them turned their heads to the northwest. The day was clear, however, and the cloud that had been in the west the night before had disappeared.

It was mid-morning when Tonio, the half-breed, rode back to Humphrey. "We're gonna have a bad storm, boss," he said shortly and turned away before Humphrey could question him.

Humphrey circled the herd and rode up to Clem, who was on point. "Tonio says we're gonna have a bad storm."

"Well," Clem said. "That half-breed may be able to track a snake over a flat rock and talk Indian lingo, but he damn shore can't predict West Texas weather. Nobody can!"

"I don't know about that!" Humphrey replied. "You remember that old mountain man, Buff Larrigan, He could tell when a storm was comin' or when the rain would stop. Saved us a lot of trouble, too."

"Maybe so," Clem conceded. "I remember Buff all right. But Tonio ain't no Buff Larrigan."

"Maybe not," said Humphrey. "But this morning things feel different, somehow. The sage brush smells real rank where the steers have walked on it, and there was a ring around the moon last night, and there's a ring around the sun today."

Humphrey had been surprised at Clem's lack of his usual pessimism, but he figured that Clem was simply reluctant to admit that the half-breed, Tonio, could anticipate the weather, although he knew, as did all the others that a bad storm could play havoc with a herd.

Clem looked up at the sun, shading his eyes with his hat as he did so. "That ain't no ring around the sun. Ain't nothin' but dust in the air," he opined. "Jus' makes it look funny."

Humphrey started to reply, then shook his head slightly and rode back toward the wagons, which were following a couple of hundred yards behind the herd.

"Maisie," Humphrey said as he rode alongside the chuckwagon that she was driving. "Tonio says we're gonna have a storm; so you be sure that all the grub is fixed so it won't get wet. And if a storm does hit, you get down and unhitch the mules and tie 'em to the wagon, if you have time."

"Yassuh, Mars Hump. I do dat. I's got a feelin' too 'bout dis weather," Maisie said.

"Tell that nigger woman drivin' the hospital wagon to do the same thing," Humphrey instructed. "Them mules ain't got much sense, and they might run away if real bad weather comes in. We shore don't want to lose the wagons."

"Yassuh, Mars Hump. I tell Liza, and I see she do what yo say."

Humphrey nodded and rode back toward the herd. Just before he reached the drag men, he stopped his horse and cocked his head to one side. There could be no doubt about it! He heard the unmistakable roar and screech of the ranch jackass! That animal could not possibly have gotten out of his pen—not unless someone had turned him out. But. . .

Humphrey shook his head in bewilderment and then grinned fiendishly as he remembered how that primitive, feral sound had once caused the old mountain man, Buff Larrigan, to flinch so badly that he had missed by forty feet a deer that he should have killed with his eyes shut. And Humphrey remembered how the same eerie sound had caused two Texas Rangers who were visiting their camp overnight to sit up in their bedrolls, wide-eyed and pistols palmed. It surely looked as if the drive was beginning to show some signs of life!

\* \* \* \* \* \*

Late that afternoon, an almost complete calm settled over the land. The dust from the herd rose straight up. Flies and gnats began to torment men and horses, and when the horses switched their tails to rid themselves of the pests, their tails stuck to their sides. Soon huge cumulonimbus clouds began to form in the north;

they were dense and towered high in the sky. They began to darken, and then were almost black. Even Clem began to look with some degree of uneasiness. An icy wind blew, and within minutes the towering, black cloud began to move visibly toward the herd. It was travelling fast, which meant that the storm would probably be severe, but of short duration.

A flash of lightning and a clap of thunder preceded the first drops of cold rain. All of the cowboys loosed their slickers, which they always had tied behind their saddles.

Clem loped back and pulled up beside Humphrey, donning his slicker. "Looks like that half- breed guessed right. It's gonna storm, all right."

"What will the steers do?" Humphrey asked anxiously.

"No tellin'!" Clem said sourly. "The stupid bastards may jus' hump up and take it—and then again, they may run to hell and gone. Tonio may be able to guess the weather, but he damn shore can't tell what a longhorn will do!"

"Anything we can do?" Humphrey asked.

"Not a damn thing! The herd has stopped and turned their backs to the storm, and all the cowboys is ridin' 'round the herd singin' like a bunch of caterwaulin' cats, hopin' the steers will pay some attention to 'em and keep their minds off the storm. Most of 'em, except Tiny, got a voice like a constipated bull frog, which will likely scare the steers worse than the storm. You got the wagons ready for it?"

"I think so, but I'll ride back and check." Humphrey turned his horse and rode to the wagons just as Brandy Wine dismounted from Punkin. The rain suddenly became a downpour.

"You ladies get in the wagons!" Brandy yelled. "I'll unhitch the mules and tie them to the wagons."

As Brandy quickly began to unhitch the mules, the first few small hailstones began to fall. Humphrey, seeing that things were as well in hand as possible, turned and rode quickly toward a tree- lined creek nearby. He was riding Rafter, and he didn't want anything to happen to that horse!

By the time Brandy had all the mules safely tethered to the wagons, the hailstones had grown to alarming proportions. The sky was almost jet black, and the storm was roaring in rage. The hailstones had lost their symmetrical shapes and were simply rough chucks of ice.

Maisie and Ellie were inside the wagons under a quilt, as was Liza in the wagon behind them.

"How come Mars Brandy calls us 'ladies'?" Ellie almost had to shout at Maisie.

"Cause he's a gennelmun," Maisie replied. "An' he don' think of us as niggers, that's why."

Just then, a big chuck of ice tore through the canvas wagon top and hit with a resounding thud near Maisie's head. Brandy opened the puckered end of the wagon cover and yelled, but the two women did not hear him; so he hopped in and pulled the quilt from Maisie's head. "Get under the wagon!" he yelled. "And hurry!"

Maisie heard, and followed his advice with alacrity. Ellie, however, had the quilt wrapped so tightly around her head that she did not hear. When he tried to unroll her, the hail, wind, and rain blasted with such force that nothing could be heard. Brandy pulled the quilt over his head too and crawled under it beside Ellie.

The storm lasted for an hour and then passed as quickly as it had arrived. The steers had simply bowed their backs to the storm and had borne it with the stoicism of any wild thing that had been caught by the caprice of nature. Many of them were bleeding from cuts made by the huge, sharp stones of ice, and all were badly bruised. One of the small calves had been killed, and several horns had been broken off the steers.

Most of the cowboys had fared better, for those that had been unable to find shelter had pulled their saddles off and had covered themselves with them, and although their legs protruded, they were able to cover their heads and shoulders, thus averting injury other than bruised legs and buttocks.

The Negro cowboys, however, had not fared so well, for except for Largo they rode with surcingles, and although they removed the blankets and covered themselves, they were not nearly so well protected as those who had saddles. Alf sustained a badly cut forehead, and Trey had a swollen jaw.

In their haste to seek shelter from the vicious hailstones, rain, and incessant lightning, not a single cowboy had witnessed the foxfire that had caused balls of light to sit on the tips of the long horns of the cattle and which outlined their horses' ears. Thus, they were robbed of a yarn that they had heard around many a campfire, and one that they would have loved to tell, if they ever finished the drive.

As the cowboys emerged from their shelters, they again saddled their horses and began to follow the steers, which had begun grazing as if nothing had happened, even though the ground was covered with hailstones. It was late for the cattle to be moving, but they had missed a couple of hours' grazing time and seemed bent on making up for it. The sun shone brightly on the freshly washed land and the scattered hailstones.

Humphrey and Clem had both escaped without injury, for they had found a small bluff for protection. As the storm abated, they were able to talk to each other.

"That there was some storm!" Clem opined when he could be heard. "Damndest noise I ever heard. "I'd aswore that one clap of thunder sounded jus' like that jackass back at the ranch."

"That jackass ain't back at the ranch," Humphrey said. "And you did hear 'im. I did, too. I even saw 'im for a second afore he hid behind a bush."

"You what!" Clem was incredulous.

"I saw 'im," Humphrey repeated.

"Well, how in hell did that long-eared bastard git out of his pen?"

"I don't know," Humphrey admitted. "But he shore did, and he's followin' us."

"Why, that son-of-a-bitch!" sputtered Clem. "I'm shore as hell gonna shoot 'im this time like I damn near done a dozen times when we was comin' out west from Fort Worth."

"Don't do it, Clem," Humphrey said firmly. "I want some more good mules out of our thoroughbred mares."

"But. . ." Clem stopped as Largo rode up to them.

"Yo all right, Mars Hump?" Largo asked anxiously, and then thought to add, "an' yo, too, Mars Clem?"

"We're all right," Humphrey said as he noticed a red slash on the side of Largo's face. "How are the rest of the men?"

"Most of 'em is all right, I guess, Mars Hump." Largo's face showed dismay. "All, but Mars Newt. He got kilt!"

"Killed?" Humphrey exclaimed. "How?"

"Lightnin', I reckon, Mars Hump. His hoss got kilt, too, and they's jus' piled up an' smellin' lak burnt hair."

Humphrey, Clem, and Largo rode quickly to the fallen man. As they came close, they stopped and were quiet for a moment. Newt was still astride his fallen horse, and the spur of his boot glistened in the bright sun.

"It was lightnin', all right," Clem said. "He'd ort to of got off that horse and pulled his spurs off, too."

They all sat silently for a few moments more, and then Humphrey sighed deeply. "What was his full name, Clem?"

"Never heard 'im say," Clem answered quietly. "Said his name was Newt. I never asked 'im the rest of it."

"Well," Humphrey said with resignation, "we can't do anything for 'im now. If the cooks are all right, we'll let everybody eat supper and then have his funeral and let one man take 'im back to the ranch and bury 'im in the HF graveyard."

"Might as well bury 'im right here," Clem said.

"He was a HF man," Humphrey said as if that settled the matter.

Largo started riding toward the wagons. He was worried about Maisie and Ellie.

"Largo!" Humphrey said, and Largo turned his horse back toward them. "One of them small calves was killed by the hail. Get it and butcher it out. Tell Maisie to fix everbody a good steak supper. Be shore to take it away from the herd and down wind so they won't smell blood."

"I'll be damned!" Clem muttered as Humphrey and Largo rode away. "Hump is learnin' a little bit about longhorns. I reckon he's heard of the blood cry." Then he added to himself, "I reckon I'll jus' stay here with Newt till they get back."

\* \* \* \* \* \*

After a supper of beef, beans, and sourdough biscuits, Humphrey ordered two of the men to take a tarp and wrap Newt's body and bring it to the camp. When they had done so, Clem, who was pale and looked a bit sick, accompanied them. All of the men that Clem felt were not necessary to watch the cattle gathered around the tarp-wrapped body. They were a somber and quiet group; although most of them had witnessed death many times, they had rarely before been in the presence of death that had been caused by other than an act of man.

The three Negro women stood with bared heads, and the cowboys removed their hats as Humphrey took a worn Bible from his saddle bag and then preached a short, but beautiful and touching service.

When it was done, they located Newt's body over a pack mule and secured it firmly.

"Tell the blacks to dig 'im a grave as soon as you get there," Humphrey ordered. "Tell Finch what happened. No use to bother anybody else."

One of the men who had ridden most with Newt nodded, mounted his horse, and took the reins of the pack mule. The rest of the men were silent as he rode away.

"All right, men." It was Clem who broke the silence. "We've done all we can do. Now, everbody get back to work."

As the cowboys began catching their night horses, Clem said to Humphrey, "Looks like we'll be a couple of men short the rest of the way."

"No, we won't," Humphrey replied. "That cowboy will get to the ranch in a full day's ride. Then Finch will send another man back with 'im to take Newt's place. They'll catch up with us in a couple of days."

"That'll leave 'em a man short at the ranch. Besides, how do you know Finch will send another man back with 'im?"

"Because I know Finch," Humphrey said matter-of-factly.

\* \* \* \* \* \*

Two of the night herders who had attended the funeral were riding silently side-by-side toward the herd when one of them suddenly spoke.

"Well, I shore didn't know the boss was a preacher."

"He ain't no preacher, but he's shore as hell a religious man."

"Religious!" the rider exclaimed. "I hear 'im sayin' 'God-a-mighty' all the time."

"Maybe so," the other rejoined. "But he ain't a cussin'. That's just somethin' he says to say what he wants to say."

The other rider shook his head in bewilderment. "You mean that Humphrey Beatenbow is a religious man and still raises these damn contrary longhorn cattle."

"That's what I mean," the other replied doggedly.

"Well," rejoined the other. "I shore do find that mighty damn peculiar!"

The two cowboys separated and began their monotonous riding around the bedded down herd.

# CHAPTER 6

Finch had been scouting the flat country around the periphery of the valley ranch all day and was relieved that he had seen no Indian sign. He wondered idly where White Horse was. The Comanche chief had not visited the ranch since Kit Carson's death. Finch had ridden to the Comanche camp northwest of the ranch a few days after the news of Kit's death had reached them, only to find it deserted, and from the sign he read, the camp had been unused for some time.

Finch had no bitterness toward Indians. In fact, he secretly sympathized with them and often envied their wild, free life and complete lack of white man's morals. Finch wondered if White Horse knew that Buff Larrigan had impregnated his number one wife while he held her captive, and White Horse had too much pride to admit it. Finch suspected that was true. In any case, Finch was grateful, for O'oah had been his wife for two years; and her wild nature and loving disposition had paid Finch handsomely for the thoroughbred mares he had swapped for her.

Finch was remembering that first night he had spent in the camp of White Horse, when he had taken his bedroll down by a creek near White Horse's teepee, and where O'oah had come to him in the night. His pleasant reverie of the exhilarating time was abruptly terminated when his horse stopped and pricked his ears.

Finch, instantly alert, looked where his horse was looking, to see a rider leading a pack mule. He sighed in relief as he recognized the rider's garb as that of a white man. He veered his horse and loped toward the rider. A few yards away, he slowed to a walk, but the rider made no suspicious moves. On coming closer, Finch recognized the man as Jody, one of the ranch hands who had gone on the trail drive.

"Howdy, Jody," Finch greeted. "Thought you were on the drive."

"Was," Jody said quietly. "And will be again in a couple of days. Hump told me to bring Newt back to the ranch here." He nodded toward the pack mule. Finch would have recognized the body of a man even if two boots had not been showing beneath the tarp.

"Newt? He was your saddle partner, wasn't he?"

"A good 'un, too," Jody said tensely. "Hated to lose him."

"What happened?"

"Lightning."

Finch nodded in understanding and then shook his head in sympathy.

"Hump said to bury him in the HF graveyard. He said to see you. I'm thinkin' he didn't want nobody else to know—the women folks and kids, I mean."

It was getting dusky dark, and the headquarters of the ranch were only a couple of miles away. Finch thought for a moment.

"All right," he said. "I'll lope on ahead and get a couple of the blacks to diggin' a grave. You come on in and put your horse and mule in the barn and go to the bunkhouse and eat. I'll eat too so the women won't think anything is wrong. Then I'll come down to the barn, and we'll bury 'im."

Jody nodded his agreement, and Finch rode away.

Two hours later Finch came to the barn with a lighted lantern. Jody was waiting. They walked a hundred yards up a gentle slope to the graveyard. The waning moon gave only a faint light, but they could hear the sound of digging, and they walked toward it. Two muscular blacks were throwing dirt from a grave.

"You boys about through?" Finch inquired.

"Mos' done, Mars Finch." One of the blacks straightened up and mopped sweat from his face. "I's six foot tall, and we is about that far down."

"Then that's far enough," Finch said. "You boys rest up a few minutes, and we'll be back."

Newt's body was still tied atop the packmule when Finch and Jody entered the barn. Jody took the lead rope, and they walked back up the hill.

When the body had been lowered and the grave filled in, the men stood silently for a moment.

"I reckon we ought to say something," Finch said a bit lamely.

"Hump already preached 'im a good funeral," Jody said. "Reckon I never heard no better one."

"Hump can say a good funeral, all right," Finch said almost proudly. "He buried the best friend I ever had back in Decatur, name of Chico Baca. But seems like maybe we ought to say something now, too."

"Well," Jody replied. "I reckon we can just say 'so long.' He was a damn good saddle partner." Jody started walking away. Finch walked with him.

"What was his whole name? I'll have a marker put up for 'im."

"Just Newt, I reckon," Jody said tiredly. "He never give another one, and they wasn't no letters or anything on 'im to tell us no different."

"How long since you slept, Jody?"

"Couple of nights, I reckon," Jody said. "Why?"

"You go to the bunkhouse and roll into a bunk."

"Nope. Got to get back to the herd."

"You'll get back quicker if you do what I tell you. Besides, I've got to find another man and get 'im rigged up to go on the drive. That'll take some time, but I'll have a man ready and some fresh horses at daylight. Now you go get to sleep."

Jody hesitated. "Well, all right. But if you're gonna send somebody to take Newt's place, he'd better be a hell of a good man."

\* \* \* \* \* \*

Jody and another rider caught the herd two days later.

"This here is Hank." Jody introduced the new man to Humphrey and Clem. "Finch, he said to tell you a couple more riders had dropped off at the ranch, and they didn't need Hank."

"Knew Finch would send somebody," Humphrey said matter-of-factly. "Glad to have you, Hank. We can use the help."

"That's for damned shore," growled Clem. He wondered at the depth of understanding between Humphrey and Finch. There was never the camarderie between the two men that usually indicated a close relationship, but Clem had the very definite feeling that there was a closeness between the two that defied his understanding. "We'll be in the Oklahoma strip tomorrow, which is jus' a couple of steps from hell, so I hear. And we got to cross the North Canadian and the Cimarron on our way across the strip."

\* \* \* \* \* \*

There were no physical markings to indicate the boundary between Texas and the Oklahoma strip, but as the herd grazed across the line, there seemed to be a strange and inexplicably wild aura about the land that permeated the mind of the most insensitive cowboy. Even the steers seemed to look wilder and more primitive.

"We must be in the Oklahoma strip," observed Humphrey as Clem rode up to him.

"How do you figger that?" Clem asked curiously.

"Don't know," Humphrey replied. "Just a feelin' I got."

"Me, too," Clem admitted. "Damndest thing. Don't make no sense. But the hair of my neck riz up a ways back, and I figgered we had crossed into the strip."

"How long will it take us to cross it?"

"No tellin'. Ain't but about thirty miles wide, but we'll angle acrost it goin' east so's to hit the Chisholm trail about the time we get to the Kansas line."

"Flat country all the way?"

"Damned if I know," Clem said sourly. "But we got the North Canadian and the Cimarron to cross before we get out of the strip."

"They could cause some trouble if they are up, couldn't they?"

"Shore as hell could, especially after that big rain and hail we had—but we could wait out a swole up river. It's the damn Indians I'm worried about."

"Joe McCoy warned us that we might meet up with some in the strip, and in Kansas, too." Humphrey didn't seem worried. "Said we might meet some herd cutters, too, but he said that they were mostly harmless."

"Yeah!" Clem rejoined cynically. "But you remember that Joe McCoy and that there Colonel and Charley Gross was a-tryin' to get ranchers to drive cattle to Abilene. That McCoy feller gets a bonus from the railroad for ever' car that ships out, so I hear."

"I figgered that," Humphrey said. "But they were able to get to our ranch from Abilene; so I don't see no reason why we can't get to Abilene from the ranch."

"Well, hell, Hump! They wasn't drivin' three thousand ignorant animals in front of 'em either, and they wasn't slowed down by no waggins and women. It's pretty damn easy to talk brave if you ain't got nothin' to be scared about."

"You think we have somethin' to be scared about, Clem?" Humphrey asked a bit anxiously.

"Damn right, I do!" Clem's answer was firm. "And I'm scared, too! There ain't a chance in hell that we'll make it to Abilene without a lot of river trouble and Indians and herd cutters, too. Damn right, I'm scared! Them Indians been on the peck ever since that Sand Creek massacre back in '64. An' I reckon you can't blame the red bastards much at that!"

"Maybe not," Humphrey agreed. "But, back in '65, all the tribes in these parts agreed to go on reservations, according to the treaty of the Little Arkansas."

"I know that," Clem said almost savagely. "But it wasn't a year later till they was raidin' and raisin' hell again—burnin' waggin trains, killin' settlers, and stealin' ever'thing in sight with four legs- -and some on two legs. Fact is, they burned Council Grove, Kansas, to the ground less than six months ago!"

"God-a-mighty, Clem!" Humphrey was aghast. "I didn't know that! Who told you that?"

"I dunno," Clem said absently. "Some rider that slept in the bunkhouse when he was on his way west. They stop by pretty often, and we get a lot of news that a way."

"I wish you'd a told me." Humphrey's voice was tinged with anger.

"I did tell Finch." Clem was unperturbed by Humphrey's tone. "But I reckon he figgered it wasn't no use to tell all the folks up at the big house. Prob'ly jus' worry the women folks!"

"You'd ought to told me!" Humphrey's voice was harsh. "You know Finch! He wouldn't be afraid of the devil if he had a pitchfork in both hands."

"Oh, hell, Hump!" Clem was becoming irritated. "You wouldn't a been scared, either. An' you know it! Besides, it wouldn't a made a damn bit of difference if you had been. I learned a long time ago that it wasn't no use to argue with you when you set out to do somethin', and you was hell- bent on makin' this drive."

"I reckon I was—and I am." Humphrey was a bit mollified. "And I guess you got cause to be jittery about the Indians, but we'll make it to Abilene," he said with conviction.

"Oh, hell! 'Course we'll make it!" Clem said with a deep sigh. "I reckon Council Grove wasn't no real big place, anyways. Besides, we got the men and the guns to go through a whole Indian nation. It's jus' that I wisht it could be done peaceable. Them longhorns is a big enough pain in the neck, without worryin' about Indians, herd cutters and such."

"Well," Humphrey rejoined philosophically. "As long as men are on this earth, you can bet they'll be doin' two things."

"What's that?" Clem was surprised at Humphrey's apparent acceptance of the whole thing.

"Breedin' and fightin'!" Humphrey answered laconically.

"Well—I'll be damned!" Clem looked at Humphrey for a moment in amazement, then reined his horse aside and loped toward the herd.

\* \* \* \* \* \*

The drive continued without incident for the rest of the day, which was steamy hot. They camped for the night on green grass near a clear stream. Maisie had a good supper waiting when the night herders came in just before sundown, so they could begin their night shift on a full belly.

The cowboys, who were usually jocular and verbose at the evening meal, were inexplicably quiet and reserved. The eerie feel of no man's land seemed to have muted their characteristic raillery. The cattle were grazing peacefully, and the sun was still an hour high when one of the men said, "Uh, oh!" and pointed with his spoon.

Everyone looked where he pointed to see three Indians riding toward them from the west. Humphrey, who was eating, said quietly to the cowboy beside him, "Go get Tonio. We may need somebody who can talk Indian lingo. Better get Clem, too."

Without a word, the man placed his tin plate on the ground beside him, walked to his horse nearby, and rode toward the grazing herd.

The Indians were walking their horses slowly toward the chuckwagon. As they neared, every one of the cowboys felt for his pistol, but did not otherwise move or say anything. Maisie motioned for Ellie and Liza to get in the wagon, and they complied quickly. Maisie stood her ground. The three Indians rode within a few yards of the fire and stopped. Humphrey stood up.

The Indians were all braves, but wore no war paint. The biggest one, who was apparently their leader, held up his hand, palm out, and jabbered a few unintelligible grunts. Humphrey replied in English that he did not understand their lingo. That seemed to anger the Indian who had been speaking, for he drew himself up and smashed a fist against his chest and continued his harangue. He was a magnificent specimen, obviously very tall, though he was astride a horse. The muscles of his huge chest and flat belly rippled as he gesticulated with his arms. He had not finished his speech when Tonio and Clem rode up. The big Indian looked keenly at Tonio and then directed his speech to him.

"What does he say, Tonio?" Clem asked.

"Says he wants beef," Tonio replied. "They are Cheyennes."

"Well, tell 'im he can't have any," Humphrey said firmly.

Tonio relayed the message to the Indians. The answer apparently infuriated the leader, for he again hit his breast with his fist and pointed to the grazing herd and shouted.

"He says you got many cows, and his father is Chief Yellow Wolf. This is their land, and they want beef."

"Well, he can't have 'em," Clem said doggedly. "An' tell 'im we don't give a damn who his daddy is!"

Tonio translated. The Indian's face diffused in rage; he started swinging his arm about when he spied Maisie standing near the cooking fire. Suddenly he stopped his gesturing and jabbering and looked piercingly at the tall, handsome Negro woman. Every eye in camp followed the Indian's gaze. Her statuesque figure and long, slender legs showed quite plainly through her thin cotton dress as the soft wind blew it gently against her body. But it was her face that held every man spellbound as they watched her. Her nostrils flared as she unflinchingly returned the stare of the Indian.

Clem felt a cold chill up his back as he looked at her face. "Damned if she don't look wilder than them Indians!" he thought silently.

Humphrey was puzzled and shaken as he looked at the face of the Negro woman he had known for so long, but did not really know at all. And he suddenly felt as though he were in a primeval African jungle looking at a queen of some ancient and feral tribe.

Suddenly, the big Indian started jabbering again and pointed at Maisie.

"What now?" Humphrey had to clear his throat before he could speak.

"He says. . ." Tonio hesitated.

"Go on, man. What does he say?"

"He says if he can't have cows, he will take the black squaw."

Humphrey, Clem, and the cowboys were dumbfounded, and complete silence fell. Maisie, who had heard the exchange, drew herself up even more proudly, and her face and dark eyes plainly spoke their silent contempt as she looked disdainfully at the handsome brave.

"Tell 'im no" It was Maisie who broke the silence. "I's already got me a man!"

Better not say it to 'im jus' exactly the way she said it, Tonio," Clem whispered urgently.

"Where is Largo, anyway?" Humphrey asked almost crossly.

"He's with the herd," Clem answered. "Tonio, you jus' tell 'im that the squaw ain't available."

Tonio spoke for several seconds, but the Indian did not seem to hear. He still stared unflinchingly at Maisie. Then, without removing his eyes from her, he spoke in his guttural language again.

"Says he'll let you keep your cattle, but he will take the squaw!" Tonio translated.

Several of the cowboys who had been on herd had seen the Indians approach camp and had quietly left the cattle to graze and had ridden around until they approached the Indians from the rear. Each one had his rifle out and across his arm. Clem had seen them as the Indians had been concentrating on Maisie. When Tonio relayed the Indian's demand, Clem felt secure with the cowboys now behind the Indians.

"Tell 'im to go to hell!" Clem said harshly. "He don't get no beef, and he don't get no squaw!"

In the quiet that followed, there were the very distinct clicks of cocking rifles behind the Indians that their keen ears interpreted correctly. Tonio translated Clem's reply verbatim.

The Indians did not look around, but did move their eyes from Maisie to Humphrey, whom they had recognized as the head man of the whites. The big Indian seemed to relax on his horse a bit and spoke directly to Humphrey. Humphrey waited for Tonio to translate.

"He says he trade four horses for squaw. You keep beef."

"Tell 'im no," Humphrey said firmly. "No squaw. No beef!"

When Tonio translated, the Indian's rage was apparent to all. He jabbered for a long time and gestured wildly.

"He say he Big Moose, son of Yellow Wolf, and what he want, he get. Say he get her now, or he get her later, and cows, too—and he say some other stuff, too, that there's no need for me to say to you." Tonio spoke to Humphrey.

Big Moose shook his fist at them, turned his horse and rode away, followed by the other two. They did not look aside as they passed between four of the cowboys who held cocked rifles.

"You boys that have finished supper better get on your night shift. I reckon the other boys will be hungry," Humphrey said matter-of-factly.

The last thing that the Indians heard as they rode away was the raucous bray of the Beatenbow jackass.

# CHAPTER 7

All hands were especially alert for Indians the next day, but none appeared. The only incident to break the monotony of the drive occurred when Alf roped a two-year-old buffalo heifer that had ventured near the herd. Her curiosity had been rewarded by Alf's chasing her for a couple of hundred yards and then deftly tossing the noose of his long rawhide rope around her neck.

It was the first time Alf had roped a buffalo, though he had roped many of the longhorns and even an occasional antelope or other wild animal. He had been able to successfully deal with his prey before, for they would continue to run even after the rope was around their necks. Alf would simply flip his rope across their back and veer his horse in the opposite direction. When his horse and the quarry came to the end of the rope, there was a great jar, but the animal would be thrown heavily on his back and stunned, whereupon Alf would quickly alight from his horse, tie the animal, or kill it, depending on the reason that he had roped it.

But the buffalo was quite different. She did not run when she felt the noose tighten about her neck. Instead, she turned and started chasing Alf's horse. He ducked and dodged for several minutes, but found it impossible to trip the animal that would not run from him. Finally, one of the cowboys came to his rescue and roped the buffalo's hind feet and stretched her out. Alf alighted from his horse, which kept the rope taut, and cut the throat of the buffalo.

"Well, we can have buffalo steak for supper tonight," the cowboy observed.

"Yassuh, I reckon we kin." Alf was panting from his exertions of the past few minutes. "Fust time I ever roped no buffalo, and I ain't gonna do dat no mo!"

The cowboys joshed Alf about his penchant for roping everything in sight. Nevertheless, they had all enjoyed Alf's predicament, for it furnished some relief from the monotony of the drive. It also furnished some good buffalo meat for supper.

As they neared the North Canadian River, Clem rode ahead to check the water level, and to see that no ducks or geese were on the river which might fly and stampede the herd. He returned at mid-afternoon to report that the river was very high, and that he thought it best to hold the herd at least until the next day so that the crossing would be less hazardous.

"We might be able to make it," he reported. "But there's a high bank on the north side, and the cattle will have to leave the river through a narrow gap in the bank. So we stand a good chance of the crazy bastards gettin' into a mill in the river and losin' a bunch of 'em."

"You think we can cross tomorrow?"

"Likely can," Clem answered. "High water goes down pretty fast in this country, and we've got good graze for 'em here. Only thing that worries me is them redskins a comin' back."

"We can handle 'em, Clem," Humphrey said confidently.

"We could," Clem agreed, "providin' they don't come back with a whole passel of warriors. I think mebbe we'd ort to let 'em have that nigger woman."

"You know we couldn't do that, Clem!" Humphrey said testily. "She's a Beatenbow nigger!"

"Oh, hell, I know that, Hump. I was jus' a talkin'!"

"Fact is," Humphrey half-heartedly tried to mollify Clem, "if they'd a wanted that Liza wench that's drivin' the hospital wagon, I might have let 'em have her."

"Like hell!" Clem showed one of his very rare grins. "You know damn well you ain't gonna give up nothin' without a fight!"

Humphrey returned Clem's grin. "Might as well let the cattle spread out, I reckon. But I expect we'd better tell the hands to be ready—just in case."

"Won't have to tell 'em!" Clem said. "They're all damn near as scared as I am, and that's a plenty!"

\* \* \* \* \* \*

The cattle scattered, and the men loose-herded them to keep any from straying too far. Several of the cowboys had dismounted and loosened their cinches and were lying on the ground enjoying the warm sunshine. Some had even removed their boots.

"This stop is gonna do Gabby more good than it will them steers," Clem said to Humphrey.

"How's that?"

"He's got a carbunkle the size of a hen egg on his rear end," Clem grinned evilly. "Do the loud-mouthed bastard good, too. He ain't been talkin' so damn much the past couple of days."

"How long has he had it?" Humphrey asked curiously.

"No idee," Clem said absently. "But he's been ridin' standin' up in his stirrups since yesterday."

"Well, tell 'im to come on in to the hospital wagon, and we'll try to do somethin' about it."

"Hell, Hump, Gabby don't need screwin'—he jus' needs for that thing to bust open, and then he'll be all right."

"Send 'im in, anyway!" Humphrey said.

Clem shook his head and loped toward Gabby's horse, which was standing hip-shot while Gabby lay on the ground on his stomach. A few minutes later, Gabby rode up to the wagons, standing in his stirrups so that his rump did not touch the cantle of his saddle.

"Git down, Gabby, and let these nigger women have a look at that carbuncle Clem says you got."

Gabby looked astonished, and for the first time since Humphrey had known him, he seemed speechless.

"Well, git down," Humphrey commanded.

"But, Hump. . ." Gabby faltered. "That there carbuncle is on my—it's back of my—it's where no woman had ort to be doctorin' it."

"Yours won't be the first rump these wenches have seen. More'n likely some of 'em was white, too. Now git off that horse."

Gabby dismounted and a few minutes later was lying on his stomach in the hospital wagon with his pants pulled down.

"It ain't quite ripe yet," Maisie observed. "That core ain't riz up enough to git a holt of it, but I think maybe we can fix it. I done a lot of 'em back in Louisiana. Not on white folks, though, but I reckon they ain't much different from us."

Maisie heated water to the boiling and poured it into a small mouth jar. When she deemed the jar hot enough, she emptied the hot water and immediately placed the mouth of the jar over the angry looking boil on Gabby's rump. Gabby yelped at the first application, but soon realized that the process was not really painful; so he relaxed as Maisie applied the hot jar a few more times. As the jar cooled, it created a suction over the boil, which was actually pleasant for Gabby.

Maisie removed the jar again and looked closely at the boil. The white core stood out like a white maggot in the inflamed area. Ellie and Liza looked at Maisie inquiringly.

"Now, Ellie," Maisie instructed, "you go an' git a long hair out'n one of them mule's tails, an' yo be careful how yo does it. Don' git kicked."

Ellie returned with the long hair and handed it to Maisie, who made a loop in it and bent down close to the boil. She carefully encircled the core with the hair and tried to pull it tight around the white, evil-looking thing. At last she was successful. She tied the hair firmly and then gave a short yank. The core came out, and the boil erupted pus and blood. Gabby groaned, but it was a groan of relief.

"Thinks we got mos' of the corruption out, Mars Gabby," Maisie said. "Now I jus' go and git some calomel we got in my waggin. Mars Hump, he brought it to doctor saddle-galled horses' backs, but I reckon it do right good on yo, anyway." A few minutes later, Gabby rode back toward the herd; he was sitting down in his saddle and talking incessantly. "Hump's got the best damn doctors in the Indian nation back there in them wagons," he gloated to every cowboy he saw.

The cowboys just grinned and nodded as they rode away, and Gabby continued the description of his stay in the hospital wagon. All the men knew that Gabby would continue to talk whether they listened or not.

\* \* \* \* \* \*

No Indians appeared the rest of the day, and the next morning Clem reported that the river had gone down enough that the cattle could safely cross it.

"They'll have to swim some jus' before they git to the climbin' out place, but the sun won't be in their eyes; so the stupid bastards ort to drive as good as they ever will. We're gonna have to string 'em out then so's they'll be only three or four abreast. That gap in the north bank ain't much wider'n a wagon, and we shore don't want to have 'em start millin' in that deep water."

"Can the wagons make it all right?"

"We're gonna have to raft 'em," Clem said. "But I reckon they'll make it."

"Raft 'em?"

"Yeah. There's plenty of big, dead cottonwood trees along the river. I'll have some of the boys drag 'em up and cut 'em the right length. We'll tie 'em under the wagons and on each side, too. They'll float."

"You sure?" Humphrey was worried about the chuck in Maisie's wagon.

"Hell, no! I ain't shore!" Clem growled. "I ain't shore of nothin'—but we've done it before, and it worked."

Humphrey watched as several of the cowboys dragged big, dead cottonwood logs up to the wagons. Clem instructed the men as they chopped the dry, light logs into various lengths and tied them under and on each side of both wagons. Finally, he was satisfied, and the sweaty, puffing cowboys who had been wielding the axes sighed in relief and mounted their horses.

"I reckon that'll do it," Clem said. "Now I expect we'd better git a couple of men to drive 'em acrost. Them nigger women ain't the best mule skinners I ever seen."

"Largo can drive the chuckwagon," Humphrey volunteered. "And I'll drive the other one myself."

"All right. I'll have the boys start stringin' the steers out in a long line. The waggins can cross last. I'll tell Brandy to take the remuda over first."

Brandy and the black youth that was his helper pushed the remuda toward the river. When they neared the wagons, Clem rode to meet Brandy and explain the crossing.

"They need to be strung out, Brandy," Clem said in an unusually pleasant voice. "They got to go up the other side and through that narrow gap in the north bank. They'll have to swim for a few yards close to the other side."

"That will be no problem, sir," Brandy said in his immature voice. "I'll ride Punkin in the lead, and the others will follow. Shanks can bring up the rear end."

Clem nodded his head. He was intrigued with the young English lad and had long since learned that Brandy could handle the remuda better than any man he ever saw. He did wonder, however, how Brandy and Punkin would make out when they hit deep water. He had no doubt that they would manage, though, for the little, homely mustang that Brandy had ridden into the HF headquarters followed him about like a faithful dog. The little horse even grazed near Brandy's bedroll at night and greeted him each morning with a soft whinney. Clem knew that Punkin would jump off a cliff if Brandy asked him to. Moreover, the entire remuda had very subtly been persuaded to follow the two as they grazed along the trail a few yards away from the steers.

Largo had taken a seat beside Maisie and Ellie on the chuck-wagon as Brandy rode into the shallow water near the river edge and was followed by the remuda. Punkin didn't hesitate in the least, and Brandy pointed him toward the exit gap. They were more than half-way across when they hit the deep water. Punkin was surprised and straightway plunged all the way under. Brandy held on, and he, too, sank completely out of sight.

Ellie, who had been watching intently, her dark eyes shining with pride, screamed as Brandy disappeared beneath the water. All hands stopped their activity for a moment until both Brandy and Punkin came to the surface. There was an audible sigh of relief as the little mustang followed Brandy's guiding straight to the gap and climbed out. The rest of the remuda followed and soon were high and dry on the north bank.

The cowboys ordinarily would have removed their boots and pants to hold them above the water when they had to swim a river, but with the Negro women present, they were reluctant to do so. Clem did not say anything to them. He didn't remove his pants, either.

The cowboys had managed to string the herd out in a thin line for almost a mile. Then some of them formed a V that led to the river, and the other men began pushing the steers into the mouth of the funnel formed by men and horses. As the cattle approached the river, the cowboys crowded them until only three or four could enter the river at one time. The lead steer was a bit reluctant, but when a cowboy whacked him across the rump with a coiled rope, he jumped into the water. He was followed by other steers moving no more than three or four abreast. Two cowboys in the river near the north bank successfully guided the steers to the sloping, but narrow, exit.

The crossing continued with success that surprised and pleased all the men. It took almost an hour to cross. There was a high clay bank just above the sloped exit. Many of the steers, when passing it, would bellow furiously and thrust their long horns in the soft soil as if polishing them.

"Why do they do that, Clem?" Humphrey asked curiously as he and Clem both sat their horses on the south side of the river, from where they could easily see across the narrow stream.

"Damned if I know," Clem admitted. "Never seen 'em do it afore, but a ignorant longhorn don't need no damn reason to do somethin' stupid."

Largo was holding the lines of the chuckwagon's mule team when the last steers climbed out on the north side. Humphrey had one foot on the wheel hub of the other wagon in preparation to mount when Clem said, "Now who the hell you reckon that is?"

He nodded toward the north bank of the river. Humphrey set his foot back on the ground and followed Clem's gaze; he saw three men riding toward the river exit. They rode in a group, but were still too far away to tell much about them except that they were not Indians.

"They're not our men," Humphrey said. "One of 'em is ridin' an Appaloosa, and we don't have one in our remuda."

"I reckon we'd best git on over there," Clem said.

"Yo wants me to go over first, Mars Hump?" Largo asked.

"You lead out, Largo. And be shore you don't let them mules get crossways in that river. Take your whip and keep their minds on what they're doin'."

"First time I ever knew a bastard mule had a mind," Clem said in an attempt at humor. He was worried.

"Yassuh!" Largo grinned at Humphrey and popped a long whip loudly over the mules' backs as he splashed them into the shallow water at the river's edge. It was the first time the mules had heard the snap of a whip on the drive, for Maisie had always held the lines. But they remembered the lash from many previous experiences; so they hit their collars with vigor. Humphrey quickly mounted and moved the other wagon forward. Clem brought up the rear.

Largo kept yelling and popping his whip, and the mules splashed through the shallow water at a trot. When they hit deep water and lost footing, the first two mules tried to veer, but Largo brought the whip down on their rumps viciously and made the hair fly. The mules straightened out, and Clem, who had uncoiled his rope, sighed in relief as the wagons floated without incident across the deep water.

The mules had to strain mightily as they pulled the wagons up the steep exit, but the solid footing inspired them to pull with a will. Both wagons and Clem had just topped out on the exit slope when the three strange riders arrived to meet them. Both Humphrey and Largo quickly handed the lines to the Negro women, climbed from the wagons and mounted their horses, which had been tied behind.

The three men were waiting patiently a few yards away. They did not speak until Clem and Humphrey rode up to them.

"Howdy!" Clem greeted the men civilly. "You fellers lookin' for a job?"

Humphrey said nothing, nor did he nod his head. There was something about the trio that triggered caution.

"We ain't lookin' for no job," the man who was evidently their leader said. "But I reckon we got a lot of work to do anyways."

"How's that?" Clem said warily, for he, too, had sensed that something was amiss.

"We're gonna cut this here herd."

Humphrey and Clem looked closely at the three men. They were a scroungy looking lot, and each wore two pistols and had a rifle in his scabbard. Clem started to speak, but Humphrey beat him to it.

"You ain't gonna cut this herd!" he said firmly.

"Yep. We're gonna!" The leader, who had a fiery red beard, grinned evilly. "A lot of us been losin' cattle lately. Likely they're some of 'em mixed up in your herd."

"We've got 3100 head of steers and ten cows and ten calves in this herd," Clem said tightly. "Ever one of 'em is wearin' a HF brand on the hip and our road brand on the side. You can count 'em if you want. But you can't cut none out!"

"Oh, yes, we can," the leader said. "We got our credentials right here." He removed a folded paper from his vest pocket and waved it vaguely before he stuffed it back in his pocket.

"Mister!" It was Humphrey who spoke again. "I don't know what credentials you got, and I shore don't care. These are HF cattle, and we've got fifteen cowboys, plus me and Clem here, that says you ain't cuttin' this herd."

"Be a lot easier if'n you'd be agreeable," the leader said in a tone that he felt indicated that his demand was reasonable.

"Agreeable or not—you're not gonna cut this herd!"

The leader rejoined angrily, "We'll cut it today, or else we'll cut it tomorrow when we come back with more men," he threatened.

"Come back with an army if you want!" Humphrey was becoming angry. "But you ain't cuttin' this herd. Now you fellers git outta here!"

The leader started to say something else when one of his men said in a low voice, "Maybe we'd better wait, Red. We got company comin'."

The leader looked around to see four or five of the HF cowboys riding toward them.

"All right, Dammit!" he snarled as he jerked his horse viciously. "But shore as hell, we'll be back tomorrow with plenty of men to do the job!"

\* \* \* \* \* \*

All hands kept a sharp lookout the rest of the day, but saw nothing more threatening than a few small bunches of Indians, who gave the herd a wide berth. Clem called an early stop in a meadow with a good stream of water and ample grass.

Maisie had time to fix a good supper of buffalo steaks, beans, which the cowboys called "pecos strawberries," and dried apple pie. To give the meal an extra special touch, she scrambled some turkey eggs that had been robbed from a nest by one of the men that day. Ellie, who was ladling out the food in the tin plates as the cowboys passed in line, put an extra spoon of scrambled eggs in Brandy's plate and smiled shyly at him.

The day crew were still riding listlessly around the grazing cattle as the night crew, full of good food and sipping freshly ground Arbuckle coffee, lounged around the chuckwagon. A few of them were playing poker, using beans for chips.

It was a good time of day. The sun was still a couple of hours high, and the day was warm. It had been an easy drive and an uneventful one since crossing the North Canadian and meeting the herd cutters. The cowboys all knew that the serenity wouldn't last, but they were all content to take their ease and leisure where, and when, they could.

It was Humphrey who saw the two riders approaching from the east. Their easy manner of riding and their garb tickled a remote corner of Humphrey's memory.

"Riders comin'," he said to no one in particular, for every man was already aware of them and eyeing them closely as they rode near.

"Light and set!" Humphrey invited as the men stopped their horses a short distance away. "The coffee's hot."

"Was hopin' it would be," the taller of the two men said as he dismounted. It was then that Humphrey's memory clicked.

"Hey!" he said in genuinely pleased surprise. "Ain't you Matt Jimson?"

"Was hopin' you'd know me, Hump," Matt grinned. "It's been a while since me and you and Tom took that trip from your ranch to Fort Worth."

Humphrey strode rapidly to Matt and shook his hand eagerly. "Don't know anybody I'd rather see than you, Matt. Where's Tom?"

"Aw, that slowpoke bastard didn't dodge quick enough, and a damn rustler got 'im about a year ago," Matt said somberly. "Where's Finch?"

"He's back at the ranch keepin' an eye on things while we're gone. I'm shore sorry to hear about Tom."

"He was a mighty good man, and I ain't likely to forget that. Seems like, though, that he was just always gettin' in the way of a bullet or arrow. You remember he got shot through the belly by one of Sally Diego's men when we was with you a couple of years ago. And then he got a arrow in the shoulder when we was on the way from your ranch back to Fort Worth. I reckon his luck just finally plumb run out. But he was packin' a mighty lot of lead when he went down the last time. Took a bunch of riffraff with 'im when he went, too!"

There was silence for a moment. Humphrey knew that Matt and Tom had been inseparable when they were in the Rangers and that their relationship had been as strong as that of brothers. Matt recovered from his reverie before Humphrey did.

"Hey!" he said brusquely. "I reckon I'm forgettin' my manners! This here is Cap Fallon. He ain't much better than old Tom, but you have to take what they give you in the Rangers."

Cap Fallon grinned as he stepped forward and heartily shook Humphrey's hand. "Matt has told me about you, Hump—and Finch, too. I been wantin' to meet Finch," he said eagerly and then added a bit lamely, "and you, too, Hump."

Humphrey turned to the men who were eyeing the newcomers curiously. "Men," he said proudly, "I want you to meet Matt Jimson. He and his partner rode part way from Fort Worth with us when we was comin' out west, when Finch was laid up with a sore pistol hand. And then, him and his partner shore saved my skin once when I was a goin' back to Louisiana on some business, and Matt and Tom rode from the ranch to Fort Worth with me."

The men all grunted some sort of acknowledgement, and all of them stood up.

"And this here is his saddle partner now, Cap Fallon."

There was a general hubbub of talk and handshaking as Maisie and Ellie brought the visitors hot coffee. Matt and Cap looked questioningly at the Negro women, but only said their 'how do's.'

"Hey, Hump," Matt wanted to know as Maisie and Ellie went back inside the chuckwagon, "wasn't that the little nigger gal that took care of Tom when he was gut shot? Ellie was her name."

"That's Ellie, all right," Humphrey agreed. "I reckon she's growed up some since you saw 'er."

"Shore has!" Matt agreed. "Looks like a grown woman now, with a figger that most of 'em ain't got."

"Well, she's right at a twelve year old now, I reckon. Time she growed up," Humphrey said absently.

"Boy! Old Tom would sure be pleased. He thought a awful lot of that little nigger gal. I remember she had been raped and was most scared to death of a man."

"Still is," Humphrey said disinterestedly.

"She ain't afraid of Brandy!" one of the cowboys chimed in.

"Hell! Nobody's scared of Brandy," Clem said with a rare grin. "He ain't nothin' but a kid."

Everyone settled back down, for it was another hour before the first shift of night herders would relieve the day men. They all listened with intense interest as Humphrey and Matt talked of their experiences together.

"I reckon you and Finch has fooled most everybody," Matt said. "Nobody figured you all could run a big ranch right in the middle of Indian country."

"Well, we've made it for a couple of years, anyhow," Humphrey said. "We figger to keep it up. This is our first drive. Most of the hands that was with us when we came out from Fort Worth is back at the ranch with Finch. Finch married old White Horse's daughter. Did you know that?"

"Married her!" Matt exclaimed. "Hell, no. I didn't know it! Somehow, I never did figure Finch would get married. A squaw man!" Matt grinned as he said it.

"And one of the most beautiful women you ever saw, too," Humphrey responded. "Speaks good English."

"I'll be damned!" Matt said in wonder. "I'd shore like to see that lucky bastard again. Fastest man with a gun that ever was! Wasn't a Ranger or anybody else on the frontier could match 'im."

Swifty, who was among the men present, shifted impatiently and touched one of his two guns as he looked sourly at Matt.

"Well, he hasn't lost any of his speed," Humphrey said complacently. "So you're still Rangerin', Matt?"

"Yep. Reckon I'll keep on till I move too slow sometime, like Tom done. And it ain't gettin' no easier either. The damn Indians, killers, and herd cutters seems like are worse than ever since that Medicine Lodge treaty."

"We had a visit from some herd cutters this morning," Humphrey said.

"You what!" Matt yelped in surprise.

"They met us at the river. Three of 'em. Said they was gonna cut our herd."

"They didn't, did they?" Tom asked anxiously.

"No," Humphrey replied firmly. "And they ain't gonna, neither, but they said they was comin' back tomorrow with more men."

"Good!" Matt said enthusiastically. "We got a detachment camped about two miles down river, and we'd shore like to make their acquaintance. What did they look like? Anything special about 'em?"

"I reckon not. Looked mean as hell. One of 'em was a big man with red hair and beard that one of the others called 'Red.'"

"Red Roark!" Matt slapped his knee in satisfaction. "I've got papers on 'im and probably the others, too. Come on, Cap. Let's get back to camp. The boys need to know that they got a little fun a comin' to 'em. It's been a pretty dry trip up to now."

When Matt and Cap had mounted their horses, Matt turned to Humphrey and said, "When you see 'em comin' tomorrow, let 'em come on in. We'll be a watchin'!"

"We'll let 'em come in," Humphrey said grimly. "But I ain't makin' no promises about lettin' 'em ride out again."

"You don't need to," Matt grinned. "Us Rangers will take care of that!"

Matt and Cap rode away and left a babble of excited cowboy voices behind.

# Chapter 8

It was dusky dark when the night crew went to relieve the men who had been herding the steers. The cattle, content with a full belly, had sought spots of tall, dry grass on which to bed down, and as many as could find a small knoll or hill to lie on so that they could have a better view and also catch any cool breeze that they could. As each lay down, he knelt on his front knees and then lowered himself gently, until finally plopping with a big grunt, and then holding his breath a moment before letting out a long contented sigh.

The Beatenbow jackass topped a small rise nearby and looked with apparent satisfaction at the scene below. He began to graze contentedly.

As the men gathered around the cooking fire and Maisie and Ellie served each plate as they passed in line, the men were talking excitedly about the herd cutters and the Rangers' visit. To a man, they were looking forward to the next day and the promise of excitement.

"Tomorrow may be as good as Abilene," one cowboy said gleefully. "Maybe so we'll have us a scrap."

"I'm kinda hopin' we do," another rejoined. "This here trail drivin' can be pretty damn dull."

"Wonder where they got the name 'Abilene'?" another asked incongruously. "I never heard no Indian word like that. Must mean somethin'."

"It comes from the Bible." It was Humphrey who answered the query. "From Luke. Third chapter, I think. I hear that a woman named it."

"I'll be dam—darned," the puncher said almost in awe. "You read the Bible, Hump?"

"Lots of times," Humphrey affirmed. "Some mighty good sense in it, too."

There was a short silence as the men all looked at Humphrey.

"Well, what does 'Abilene' mean, then?"

"Don't rightly know." Humphrey dismissed the subject.

"Well, what about 'Kansas'?" the inquisitive puncher persisted. "Where did that come from?"

"'Kansas' is Indian lingo." It was Tonio, the half-breed interpreter who replied. "It's Kiowa. Means 'People of the South Wind'."

"Oh, hell! Who cares what 'Abilene' or 'Kansas' either one means?" a disgruntled Dutch Horst said bitingly. He was tired of the mental gymnastics. "Abilene, Kansas, means good likker and bad women as far as I'm concerned, and maybe so a chance to buck the tiger some."

"Well," Humphrey observed levelly, "we may not all get to sample the pleasures of Abilene. We've still got some Indians and herd cutters to deal with afore we get there."

"Hah!" sneered Horst. "Them Indians nor herd cutters neither don't scare me none."

"Well, they damn shore ort to scare you!" Clem had been silent all through the banter around the fire. "They shore as hell scare me."

"If a feller is a scared to die, then he ort not to be out in this country!" Horst said acidly.

"A lot of men ain't afraid to die!" Clem's anger at Horst's insinuation was apparent. "But some people don't give a damn whether they live or die—especially Indians. And you had better damn well be scared of that kind of a man!"

Brandy, who had been taking in the conversation avidly, sensed that trouble was near.

"Hey, Tiny," his youthful voice piped up, "why don't you play us a few tunes on that mouth organ of yours?"

"Aye, lad. I'm thinkin' that's a good idea." Tiny's musical voice quickly eased the tension.

As Tiny began to play some mournful tunes, the wolves began to howl, but he continued to play as the men, one or two at a time, sought their bedrolls.

\* \* \* \* \* \*

At three o'clock in the morning, the night herders came in to wake their relief. They leaned over their sleeping replacement and whispered until he finally roused. They knew better than to touch a sleeping man, for they might get a pistol slug in the belly from a cowboy who thought he was being attacked.

When the replacement was awake, he usually raised up and yawned. The first thing he reached for was his hat, and then, if he had removed his pants, which he did not always do, he pulled them on. Next, came his boots which, barring expected trouble, he did almost always remove. Before pulling each boot on, however, he carefully turned it upside down and pounded the heel with the palm of his hand in order to remove any insect, mouse, or other varmint that had crawled in for safety and warmth. Last, came his pistol, which he had kept beside him in his bedroll. When it was buckled on, he walked to the cooking fire and gulped a cup of hot coffee. Then he mounted his night horse and rode slowly toward the herd, ready for the next several hours in the saddle.

If the sky was clear, the cowboy looked for the Big Dipper, for it was his timepiece. He rode his monotonous rounds of the herd until the day began to break. Then the cattle started rising from their bedground. As they heaved themselves up, first getting their back feet on the ground and then rising laboriously to their front feet, they usually emitted a grunt as they came erect, and then stretched much as a man did upon rising from his bedroll.

The steers began to graze slowly, and the men gently, but firmly, pushed them in the direction they were to travel that day. Usually, the cattle were all up and moving before the riders who had come on during the night were relieved. When they gave way to their relief man, they rode toward camp for a breakfast, which usually consisted of beans and, occasionally, bacon or buffalo meat. They washed it down with cups of steaming coffee and went to catch another horse to ride until noon. Then, they would change horses again.

The days were long and hot now, and many of the cowboys developed the knack of sleeping as they rode. If it were important that they stay awake and alert, many of them would rub tobacco in their eyes when they felt they could no longer stay awake. It was Clem who had always admonished the cowboys to "get your sleep in the wintertime, for you damn shore ain't gonna get none on the trail."

The long trail drive was essentially monotonous and routine. As the cowboys followed the slow-moving herd, they all dreamed of the delights that they would find at the end of the trail. In the meantime, they passed the time in various ways. Swifty continuously practiced his fast draw, Gabby talked incessantly whether anyone was near or not, Tonio studied the tracks of the steers, horses, or any wild animal spore that they passed. Alf tossed his long, snake-like rope at everything within his range as he rode along. Each cowboy had a favorite way to make the time pass more pleasantly. Many of them would take a run at the Beatenbow jackass, which would occasionally come near as if daring the cowboys. They would chase him for a short ways, and though they probably could have roped him, it was enough to see the long-eared little animal run and kick up his heels as he sped away. Invariably, the cowboys got a laugh out of his antics. Even Brandy could not coax the stubborn little creature to let him lay a hand on him.

The day after meeting the herd cutters, however, the cowboys had no trouble staying awake. They had no doubt that the cutters would make good their threat to return, and the presence of the nearby Rangers added another dimension to their controlled excitement.

The morning passed peacefully enough, and the cowboys went in relays to eat their noon meal. There was an air of tension, broken only by the occasional high pitched laugh of Brandy, who pushed the remuda well away, but parallel to the grazing herd. The cowboys often wondered what he found to laugh about, but his shrill merriment was contagious, and invariably, every cowboy, including Clem, grinned when he heard it. Only Dutch Horst scowled.

It was near mid-afternoon when the herd cutters appeared on a rise just ahead. There were more than a dozen of them, and they rode straight into the face of the herd, stopping it. Then, they rode in a group to one side and back to where Clem and Humphrey were sitting side-by-side on their horses. Several of the cowboys abandoned their assigned positions and rode toward them.

"Well," Red greeted Humphrey and Clem, "told you we'd be back today with enough men to cut this herd, and here we are!" He grinned evilly.

"You're here all right," agreed Humphrey. "But you ain't gonna cut this herd!"

The men with Red sat their horses indolently. They were looking forward to taking a good bunch of cattle back with them, and they had no doubt that they would be able to do so.

"We're gonna cut it, all right!" Red answered. "You're the one that will decide whether we do it peaceable or not."

Red's men grinned at their leader's statement.

"I've already decided," Humphrey said grimly. "You ain't gonna cut this herd, peaceable or unpeaceable!"

"Now Dammit!" Red's face was becoming as florid as his beard and hair. "You know we got the men and the guns. There just ain't no use bein' a damn fool and gettin' killed over a few cows!"

Clem, who had spied the Rangers riding up a draw toward them, said, "It jus' might be that you fellers has bit off more'n you can chaw this time!"

"The hell we have!" Red was furious. "We got a plenty. . ." He suddenly broke off as he, too, spied the detachment of Rangers emerging from the draw. He looked at them, and his brow furrowed. He was puzzled.

The Rangers rode up and stopped.

"Havin' trouble, Hump?" Matt Jimson queried pleasantly.

"Not yet!" Humphrey replied. "Looks like maybe we're goin' to, though. These here men say they're gonna cut our herd. I say they ain't!"

"You say right, Hump," Matt agreed. His Rangers had drawn up beside him in a line.

"Now just who in hell are you?" Red sneered.

"Who I am ain't important, I reckon," Matt answered levelly. "But what I am is important!"

"Then what are you?"

"I'm a Texas Ranger," Matt replied. "And these are my men."

"You're a little out of your territory, ain't you mister? This here's the Oklahoma strip."

"We didn't see no signs that said so," Matt said conversationally. "And it wouldn't make any difference if we had. Herd cutters is herd cutters, wherever they are, and we aim to see that no herd cutters operate anywhere that we can reach 'em. You ain't gonna cut this herd."

"Like hell we ain't. . ."

Red's words were drowned out by a pistol shot. The man to the right of Red had grabbed for his pistol and had been abruptly shot out of his saddle. Smoke curled from Matt's gun.

There was dead silence for a moment. Swifty had ridden up and had seen the man go for his pistol and had immediately grabbed his. It was only half way out of his holster when the man fell. Swifty looked about quickly to see if anyone had seen his move, but they were all looking at the herd cutters. Swifty quickly pushed his pistol back in its holster.

"Maybe you didn't hear me, Red," Matt said pleasantly. "I said you wasn't gonna cut this herd. Looks like one of your gun hands didn't believe it."

Red was considering his answer when Matt removed a small black book from his shirt pocket with his left hand. "Fact is, Red, I got papers for you and several of your men that I can recognize from the posters that was sent and descriptions that was give us. So, I reckon we'll just take all of you in."

"Like hell. . ." Red began to bluster.

Matt replaced his pistol in its holster and looked at Red questioningly. The challenge was painfully clear.

"Men," Matt paid no attention to Red, "you all know what to do," he said to his detachment. "Some of you begin on the right, and the others on the left. And don't leave a man standin'."

The Rangers all grinned delightedly, but none pulled his pistol. "We know what to do, Matt," one of his men answered him, "and I reckon we're itchin' to do it."

"Now you wait just a damn minute!" Red blustered. "You can't. . ."

"We'll wait," Matt interrupted him, "but not for a whole minute. You either drop your pistols in five seconds or start tryin' to shoot em!" Matt's voice was steely now. The other Rangers watched attentively but did not touch their pistols. They would give the cutters a chance—such as it was.

"We'd better do it, Red," a voice behind him said. "Them Texas Rangers is tough. I've run into 'em before."

The man's words were followed by the sound of his gun being dropped on the ground. It was followed by others. Finally, Red was the only man who still had his pistol in his holster.

"Well, Red," Matt said as he cupped both hands over his saddle horn. "What will it be? Back to Texas with us or here in the Oklahoma strip forever?"

Red seemed to come out of a trance. He looked around at his disarmed men and quickly unbelted his own gunbelt and dropped it.

"Now, all you others," Matt directed, "drop all your gunbelts and your rifles, too. And if any of you boys feel lucky while you're doin' it, I reckon my men ain't had much fun today, so..."

There was immediate action among the herd cutters as their pistol belts and rifles were dropped to the ground.

"Now, you men ride away from them guns," Matt instructed. "Cap, you and a couple of the other boys move these scum off to one side and search 'em. They're treacherous bastards, so be careful while you're doin' it. Maybe so some of 'em got a hideout gun."

Immediately, three or four other guns were thrown on the ground as the herd cutters moved away from their dropped guns.

"Hump, I shore hate to put you out, but you reckon you could haul all them guns up to Abilene and turn 'em over to the marshal up there? Name's Tom Smith. He's a friend of mine and a good man if you don't give 'im no trouble."

"We'll haul 'em up there and turn 'em over to 'im," Humphrey agreed. "Want me to tell 'im anything?"

"Just tell 'im you're a friend of mine and a partner of Finch. He'll understand."

"I'll do that," Humphrey agreed. "And I'm much obliged to you and your men. We would of been in some trouble if you hadn't showed up."

"You'd a handled it," Matt said confidently. "You ain't got a shovel or two in your wagon, have you?"

"We have."

"Reckon we could borry 'em so's we can bury that fast gun hand?" Matt nodded at the man on the ground.

"I'll have a couple of my boys dig a hole," Humphrey said.

Largo and one of the white punchers started digging a grave. The ground was fairly soft, and the job progressed rapidly.

"Cap," Matt said to his saddle partner, "move them bastards off a ways and make 'em set on the ground. Let a couple of the boys guard 'em, and the rest of you come back to Hump's wagon. Maybe so we can talk his cook out of a cup of coffee."

"You can do more'n that, Matt," Humphrey answered graciously. "I'll have Maisie whip you boys up a good batch of grub."

"Thanks just the same, Hump," Matt said. "But coffee will do us, I reckon. We need to get started back soon as we get that feller buried."

"We can take care of that, Matt."

"I know you can, Hump," Matt grinned. "But fact is, I been tellin' the boys about your cook and that purty little nigger gal that nursed old Tom so good, and they been wantin' to see 'er."

Humphrey's rare guffaw surprised everybody. "Well, come on," he said grandly. "Maisie will be mighty proud to make that coffee, and Ellie, she'll be glad to serve it to you. Got another nigger woman in that back wagon, but she don't do much around camp."

"I'll have the boys change up guards so's they can all get some coffee," Matt said.

The Rangers and some of the cowboys whose presence was not absolutely necessary with the herd gathered around the chuckwagon and began to talk fast and friendly as Maisie brought the coffee to a boil. Swifty looked surreptitiously at Matt and then at his gun.

When the coffee was ready, Ellie passed a cup of the strong, steaming brew to each man, who thanked her politely.

"Now, you see, men," Matt said triumphantly. "Didn't I tell you why ole Tom was so slow gettin' over that gunshot, with Ellie nursin' 'im? Purty as a new calf, ain't she—even if she is a little on the dark side."

Ellie hung her head in embarrassment as the men loudly and fervently agreed with Matt. It was just then that Brandy walked up. Matt saw him first and then almost choked on his coffee as he spied the ugly little lemon-colored mustang following Brandy like a friendly pup. It was Clem who recovered quickly enough to introduce Brandy.

"Matt," he said solemnly, "this here is our horse jingler, Brandy Wine—and they don't come no better."

Brandy evidently felt that he should explain his absence from the remuda, for he addressed Clem first.

"Shanks is with the remuda, Mr. Clem," he said. "He can handle them quite well until I'm back, I'm sure."

"Shore, he can," Clem said graciously. "Brandy, this here feller is Matt Jimson, a Texas Ranger that pulled us out of a hole a few minutes ago."

"Yes, sir," Brandy agreed. "I saw the whole thing." He stepped up to Matt and proffered his small hand. "And I'd like to say that you handled the situation jolly well, Mr. Ranger."

Matt was so taken aback that he found it difficult to answer, but he engulfed the small hand in his big brown one. "I'm right glad to meet you, Brandy," Matt said weakly. "These other fellers here that you don't already know are my ridin' partners."

Brandy solemnly shook hands with all the Rangers, and then said. "Well, I just wanted you to know that I thought all of you acted magnificently, and all o' that! Now, I suppose I'd better get back on my job, what?"

The Rangers were all staring at Brandy, and the cowboys were grinning at their amazement.

"You've got time for a cup of coffee, Brandy," Humphrey said.

Brandy looked questioningly at Clem, who nodded agreement.

"Well, if it won't be too much trouble for the ladies, I'll jolly well have one," Brandy replied.

Maisie poured a cup of the strong liquid and then added a half-cup of water before she handed it to Ellie. Ellie took the cup to Brandy. She flashed him an eloquent look of pride as she turned away.

"Well, I'll say one thing, for damn shore," Cap Fallon ejaculated. "You shore was right about Finch and Hump doin' things in style. I never saw no trail herd with its own female cooks, and a hoss jingler that speaks French!"

All the men laughed. There was an air of friendliness, respect, and camaraderie around the cooking fire.

* * * * * *

Largo and the white cowboy walked up as the men finished their coffee.

"We got it dug, Mars Hump," Largo said. "I reckon he's ready to go in. What yo wants us to do now?"

He looked at Matt, who shrugged.

"Wrap 'im in his slicker and roll 'im in, and cover 'im up," Matt said. "Unless you want to do something more, Hump?" Matt had heard Finch tell of Humphrey's preaching Chico Baca's funeral.

"I reckon we'd all best be lookin' after the cattle," Humphrey said gruffly.

Largo and the cowboy were still shoveling dirt when the cowboys rode away, the wagons pulled out, and the Rangers herded their sulking charges over a small hill and disappeared.

# CHAPTER 9

The next day proved to be uneventful, but the cowboys were still filled with excitement from the herd cutters' attempt to steal some of their cattle and the fortuitous appearance of the Texas Rangers.

"Damn!" exclaimed one of the cowboys as he and another rode beside each other. "I wish that there red-headed bastard had had the guts to go for his pistol!"

"The Rangers was a wishin' the same thing," replied the other. "You could tell they was just askin' for a fight, else they would a pulled their pistols when Matt did. They was just hopin' to tempt them herd cutters into tryin' to shoot it out!"

"Well, if the rest of them Rangers is as fast as Matt with their pistols, wouldn't many of the low-lifed bastards a got away."

"Some of 'em probably faster than Matt," the other replied. "I've heard Finch talk about 'em. And I doubt if any of them herd cutters would a got off without lead in 'em. They had the Rangers outnumbered all right, but while they were palaverin' I saw Clem and a couple more of our boys slip behind a wagon and take their rifles with 'em. And Hump, he had that big ten gauge shotgun of his that's loaded with buckshot—and he had the hammers back on both barrels."

"The hell he did!" exclaimed the other. "You know, I got a feelin' that Hump Beatenbow ain't nobody to fool around with."

"And I got a feelin' you're right. Clem ain't no pussycat neither."

"Well, if it comes to a bad fight with outlaws or Indians either, I reckon we can get our part of it."

"Reckon so. Say, ain't we just about even with that army supply camp?"

"Ought to be. It sits right where Wolf Creek and the North Canadian come together. We crossed Wolf Creek a couple of days before we hit the Canadian; so I guess right now we're just about due north of the camp, accordin' to Clem."

"They call it Camp Supply, don't they?"

"That's what I hear. But there ain't nobody drove cattle this way before; so nobody is shore of anything."

"Well, I'm damn shore of one thing," the other said firmly.

"What's that?"

"It shore as hell gits mighty dull lookin' at a longhorn's rear end everday."

"Well," the other laughed heartily, "I reckon Brandy was right when he said a longhorn was dirty on one end and dangerous on the other!"

"He was at that! But, when we get to Abilene, I'm gonna turn my wolf loose and let 'im howl like a catamount, if it gives the governor of Texas the trots."

"Hey! Just who the hell is governor of Texas, anyway?"

"Damn if I know. Last I heard a feller named Throckmorton was elected, but that damn Yankee general Sheridan fired 'im."

"Fired 'im! I didn't know you could fire a man that's been elected."

"Me neither. But Sheridan is the Yankee commander of the Texas district; so's I reckon he can do most anything he wants. But Sherman outranks Sheridan, and he appointed a feller named Pease. And then Pease got in a squabble with some other Yankee general and quit; so now I don't know who in hell is the governor."

"Oh, well," the other cowboy replied without showing much interest. "I reckon it don't make much difference anyway. Them politicians ain't gonna pay much attention to the Panhandle of Texas, anyway."

"And we can be damn glad of that!" the other cowboy said with satisfaction.

\* \* \* \* \* \*

It was a long day's drive to the next creek and good grass, but the herd was finally bedded down in a place to Clem's satisfaction. After supper, several of the cowboys, along with Humphrey and Clem, sat by the fire and drank coffee.

"Ain't we fairly close to that army stopover they call Camp Supply?" Humphrey asked.

"I reckon," Clem replied glumly. "It ort not to be more'n a few miles south of here. Jus' wisht I knew this country better. It ain't no fun to foller a bunch of ignorant cattle when you know the country, and it's sure as hell worse when you're goin' over strange land."

"You've been over the Chisholm trail, ain't you?"

"Yeah, onct. But that was three years ago, and we won't come to it for several more days, even with good luck."

"Where did you get that name, anyway?"

"Aw—some half-breed by that name drove his wagon from Kansas to Fort Worth several times, and his tracks made a trail you could foller."

"Half-breed?"

"Yeah. His daddy was a Scotchman, and his ma a full-blooded Cherokee, so they say. Fact is, he died jus' a few months back. He was jus' a trader. He wasn't no cowman."

"What killed 'im?"

"I dunno," Clem said disinterestedly. "Some cowboy that stopped by the ranch said he died early this year—March, I think it was. He was all swole up when he died. They figgered it was poison of some kind."

"Clem," Humphrey said tentatively, "we're mighty short of grub and plumb out of bacon. You reckon if we rode down to that camp, they would let us have some?"

"I dunno," Clem perked up, "but I doubt it like hell. That there's a Yankee army camp anyway, and I wouldn't ask the sons-o-bitches for grub if I was starvin' to death."

"Well, I would." Tiny's soft voice carried to all the men lounging around the fire. Everyone looked at him questioningly. "I'll ride down that way, if you'd like for me to, Hump. I've got a brother that I haven't heard from in two years or so. And I might get some news of him."

"A brother?" Clem was surprised.

"Yes. His regiment was part of the 11th Corp under General Meade."

"You mean you had a brother in the Union Army?" Clem was disbelieving.

"Yes." Tiny's answer was terse.

"And you was in the southern army?"

"I was in the Confederate Navy," Tiny corrected him gently.

"Well, I'll be damned!" Clem expostulated. "If I had kin folks in the Union Army, I shore as hell wouldn't claim 'em."

"I would." Tiny's voice was still soft and almost wistful. "He was a good brother. When the war started, he said he thought the North was in the right. I didn't agree with him. So we shook hands and parted. I fought for the South, and he fought for the North. I think either one of us would have been ashamed of the other if we hadn't fought for what we believed in."

Tiny's speech was followed by a long silence. Humphrey, Clem, and all the cowboys stared into the fire. Finally, Clem broke the silence.

"I reckon I never thought about it in jus' that way, Tiny." Clem's voice was softer than any of the men had ever heard it. "It jus' never did occur to me that—well, hell! I reckon some good men did fight for the North. At least, they was fightin' bastards. Anyways, I never meant nothin' bad about your brother when I said what I did." Clem finished lamely and was astonished that he suddenly felt some sort of compassion for the damn Yankees.

"Tiny," Humphrey said gruffly, "you reckon you could ride down there and maybe get us some supplies if they've got some extra?"

"I'd be glad to try, Hump. But, of course, I sure can't promise anything. Just because my brother fought for the Yankees doesn't mean that I'm on good terms with all of them. We were just doin' what we thought was right for us at the time."

"I'm beginnin' to see a little bit of your thinkin', Tiny. Never did before. I reckon you'd ought to take a pack animal just in case—and I've got some money in Maisie's wagon."

"Be all right if I take Brandy with me?"

Humphrey and Clem both looked at Tiny in surprise. "Shore," Humphrey finally said. "Take 'im if you want. Can't see what good he'd be, though."

\* \* \* \* \* \*

Tiny and Brandy rode away from camp a few minutes later. Tiny was on his big mule. Brandy was riding Punkin, and they led a pack horse. All the men watched them out of sight.

"That soft-talkin' bastard makes a man think some." Clem was regaining his lost prejudice. "And I ain't for damn shore that's a good thing!"

Tiny and Brandy returned before daylight. The cooking fire was embers. The Beatenbow jackass, standing a safe distance away, perked his long ears and watched curiously as Tiny and Brandy dismounted and began unloading the packhorse. They moved about as quietly as they could, but Maisie heard them and climbed from her bed in the chuckwagon.

"What yo got there, Mars Tiny?" Maisie asked.

"Extra grub," Tiny answered. "Got several big slabs of sow belly, too."

"Well, Mars Hump and the men be mighty glad o dat," Maisie said with satisfaction. "We was plumb out of hog meat. Didn't hardly have none to start with."

Ellie, having heard their voices, climbed sleepy-eyed out of the wagon. She saw Brandy and sidled toward him. She wore only a thin night dress, and her voluptuous young figure showed quite plainly as she passed in front of the smoldering embers of the cooking fire.

"Well, we've got plenty now," Tiny said. "And we can thank Brandy for that."

Ellie looked at Brandy with big, adoring eyes, but said nothing.

"Well, yo uns go on and get a mite o sleep," Maisie said. "Yo mus' be awful sleepy, bein' up all night. Me and Ellie will unload all this and store it up in the chuckwagon. The men will be stirrin' in a few minutes and a wantin' breakfast anyway. They is hot coffee now."

"Yo can crawl in my bed if'n yo wants, Mars Brandy," Ellie said shyly to the sleepy-eyed youngster. "It already warm, and I's got to help Maisie with breakfast, anyhow, so I won't be usin' it no more tonight."

Tiny walked to the fire and dipped a tin cup in the pot of hot coffee suspended over it. Brandy hesitated only a minute and climbed into the wagon.

\* \* \* \* \* \*

The men who were going on day shift stood around the fire and drank coffee as Maisie finished cooking breakfast. The aroma of freshly fried bacon permeated the air just before dawn.

"Damn, that shore smells good," one of the men said as he rubbed his hands briskly. "Thought we was plumb out of bacon."

"We was." Humphrey walked up to the fire as the man spoke. "I reckon Tiny and Brandy talked them soldiers out of some over at Camp Supply."

Maisie was serving the fragrant bacon and a big spoonful of beans to each man as they passed by. They picked their sourdough biscuits out of the big Dutch oven, and most of them sat cross-legged on the ground to eat.

"Man, that shore does taste good, Hump," one of the men said jocularly. "You can tell Tiny and Brandy we gonna recommend for you to raise their wages!"

"Tell 'em yourself," Humphrey said happily. "Here they come now."

Tiny strode into the firelight as Brandy crawled out of the chuckwagon, rubbing his eyes. Clem looked at him thoughtfully, and then a twinkle lit his eyes. It seemed that Brandy was finally melting the hard shell of the cocoon that Clem had built around himself.

"Well," Clem said, "they damn shore put in a good night's work."

"Brandy did. I mostly just visited," Tiny said enigmatically as he reached into his pocket and handed Humphrey the money he had been given to pay for the provisions.

"You mean they didn't even charge you for all the grub?" Humphrey asked.

"Nope," Tiny said. "Fact is, when they learned we were from Texas, they said they wasn't furnishing any grub for Johnnie Rebs."

"Well, then how. . ."

"It wasn't too complicated," Tiny replied. "I asked if any of them knew my brother, and some of them had heard of him, but didn't know him personally. So, while we were visiting, Brandy, he spied their storehouse on the way in. He said he was sleepy and left. When I got through with my talkin', Brandy had borrowed the grub and had our horse loaded. Good thing he was little, too. He had to crawl through a window that I couldn't a got my big rump through."

The men all laughed uproariously, and one of them touselled Brandy's hair and said, "Best damn horse and grub jingler on the trail."

"They know anything about your brother, Tiny?" Humphrey asked.

There was a long silence. Finally, Tiny said, "He didn't make it. Killed in the battle of Shiloh."

Clem flinched as if struck. He had fought in that battle—but, of course, there wasn't a chance in a million that. . . Clem threw the coffee grounds in his cup to the ground almost viciously.

"All right, men," he said grimly, "let's go relieve them night herders. Likely they're mighty hungry."

With that, Clem walked away from the fire, caught his horse, and rode toward the herd. The other men followed him silently. Tiny was a favorite of all of them, except Dutch Horst, and they all shared his loss.

\* \* \* \* \* \*

The next few days were largely routine dullness, with the exception of one skirmish with Indians, which the cowboys had beaten off with little trouble and no loss of life. Only one of the men had been wounded, but even that was superficial, and the Negro women bandaged it neatly after washing it with some of Humphrey's medicinal whiskey.

A few days later Clem announced that they should hit the Chisholm trail sometime the next day. "I jus' hope we don't run into no other herds. I hear that they's a lot of 'em goin' up this year."

The Chisholm trail was fairly distinct. Old wagon ruts that had been cut deep in wet weather were still visible, and the grass showed quite plainly that a herd had gone up the trail recently.

"They came through a week ago, I expect," Tonio reported after riding around a few minutes.

"How do you figger that?" Clem wanted to know.

"It has rained since they passed," Tonio replied. "Their droppings are all spread out and old. Insects been in 'em. There is a lot of coyote and wolf tracks on top of the cow tracks, and I found a dead steer that has been et completely. That takes a while—even for wolves and coyotes."

"Good," Clem said approvingly. "Jus' hope they ain't none close behind us. I was over that trail onct back in '65. They's a good place to stop for the night on the Salt Fork of the Arkansas."

Clem was right about the place to hold the herd overnight. The grass was good even though it showed signs of grazing. The river, contrary to its name of Salt Fork, was sweet and cold. It was also shallow and proved no problem in crossing; Clem, ever the pessimist, insisted that they cross as soon as they reached it.

"Can't never tell when a rise will come down and flood ever damn thing in sight," he said.

The herd crossed the river and drank their fill as they did so, and were grazing peacefully on the short, but plentiful, grass.

The first night shift of cowboys were eating their supper when a rider appeared. He was headed south and apparently in a hurry.

"Light and set," Humphrey invited as the rider came up.

"I'll shore take a cup of coffee," the rider said gratefully. "But, I reckon I'd best not take time to eat"

"Why not?" Clem felt the rider's urgency.

"The Indians is raisin' hell all over Kansas," he said. "And they is three or four more herds behind you that need to know that."

"What's got 'em so damn stirred up?" Clem wanted to know.

"I reckon nobody down this way has heard about it. That's the reason I need to get on my way. That damn Sherman, he give Sheridan orders to drive the redskins out of Kansas, and he said to kill all the red bastards that didn't run."

"Then I reckon we got a long road from here on in," Clem said grimly.

"Maybe not!" the rider said. "They're mostly all scattered out west of here, and soldiers is chasin' 'em. But there's still little bunches of 'em all the way up the trail."

"Any herds ahead of us?" Clem asked.

"I saw one herd a ways on north. Feller named Little was trail boss. Joe McCoy said Bill Butler and John Meyers, and maybe a couple more, had drives behind you."

"How about water and stoppin' places on north?"

"You won't have no problem if you stay west of the Arkansas. I come that way, and they's a lot of streams that run into the river. Water won't be no trouble."

"Grass?"

"Grazed some right close to the river," the rider said. "But you can spread out to one side a ways, and they is plenty."

"Sounds fine, except for the damn Indians," Clem growled.

"Well, since you already know about 'em, I expect you can handle 'em all right. Maybe so you'd ought to send a few men out in front of the herd a ways. There ain't no big bunches that I saw; so I expect the biggest danger would be if they tried to start a stampede."

"And I reckon you're right, mister," Clem agreed. "And we're obliged to you for lettin' us know. Anything we can do for you afore you leave?"

"Well," the rider seemed a little reluctant. "This here coffee put me in pretty good shape—but if you've got a fairly good horse you could trade me, I'd sure appreciate it. I been ridin' mine pretty hard, and he's most give out."

"We'll trade you a horse," Humphrey said matter-of-factly. "And a couple of our men will get 'im and change your saddle while you eat a bite."

"That would sure be a help," the rider said gratefully.

"And Maisie," Humphrey spoke to the Negro who was standing by her cooking fire, "you fix this man a packet of food that he can tie to his saddle."

"Well, that's a lot more than I expected. And I'm mighty obliged. You're sure white folks!"

The words were not out of the rider's mouth when he saw Maisie and Ellie standing by the fire. Liza had joined them, and Largo and Alf were seated on the ground. The rider immediately recognized his blunder and sought to correct it. "What I mean is—what outfit is this, anyway?"

"This is the HF herd. We're ranchin' over on the Canadian River in the Texas Panhandle. That there," Clem nodded his head at Humphrey, "is Hump Beatenbow. Him and a feller named Fauntleroy Finch is the ramrods."

"Finch? Was he a Texas Ranger once?"

"Yep."

"I've heard of 'im. Must be hell on wheels with a pistol. But I didn't know anybody was runnin' cattle that far west. That's right in the middle of Indian country."

"We've been runnin' 'em for two years now," Humphrey said firmly. "And we aim to keep on."

"Well, good luck to you fellers," the rider said as he swallowed a last bite of food, accepted a packet from Maisie, and mounted his horse. He stuffed the food packet in his saddle bag and looked at Maisie. "Thank you, ma—thank you!" he stammered.

Then, as he started to ride away, he grinned at all the men. "Redskins ain't all you got to worry about!" he said facetiously.

"How's that?" Humphrey asked quickly.

"Abilene!" the rider said as if that explained everything. "It's a jumpin' like a cricket in a hot skillet. And they got a marshall that's a regular cyclone if he's riled, but nice enough if you leave 'im alone. He's a big Irishman named Tom Smith."

"Any other good news you can tell us about?" Clem said sarcastically.

"Well," the rider hesitated again, "I ought not to be wastin' so much time, but you folks been awful nice to me. They's a patent medicine peddler that comes through about once a month. His medicine is good enough. Got enough alcohol in it to make a jackrabbit chase a coyote. But his big deal is to talk some cowboys that come in with a new herd into a horse race. He's got a sway-backed grulla horse that pulls his buggy, and he'll match 'im against anything on four legs. But he's got a ace up his sleeve, though. He stakes a dead ringer for that grulla outside of town and switches the day of the race. Got hair on the sides of that ringer clipped off so's it looks like he's been between the traces, but he ain't. And the damn critter can fly. That peddler's broke more cowboys than the card tables."

The rider waved as he rode away.

"Well, now," observed one cowboy, "if'n we can jist git through them Indians, I shore ain't gonna bother that marshall none, but I got me a pretty fast horse my ownself, and I reckon I might jist double my wages."

A huge grin split Largo's black face, and his teeth gleamed in the firelight. "And Mars Hump, he got that Rafter hoss o Mars Finch's!"

# Chapter 10

Excitement permeated the air the next morning as the herd began grazing its way toward Abilene. The cowboys felt that they were on the last lap of their long journey, for they knew that in a week or ten days, barring bad trouble, they would reach their destination.

Brandy drove the remuda into the rope corral that the cowboys fashioned by holding lariat ropes between them. When the horses were all inside, Brandy dismounted, took a lead shank from his saddle, and walked up to a big, bay horse, put the rope around his neck, and started leading him toward the periphery of the circle. A couple of the men looked on inquisitively, but lowered the rope between them so the bay could walk over it.

"Hey, kid! What the hell you doin'! That there's my horse!" Dutch Horst's voice boomed loudly enough for everyone in camp to hear.

Brandy didn't answer, but kept leading the horse toward the wagons. Dutch intercepted him before he got there. Humphrey, Tiny, and Clem, having heard Horst's threatening yell, walked toward Brandy and Horst.

"I said what the hell you doin' with my horse?" Horst's angry voice rose again as he reached out and took hold of the lead strap. Brandy did not relinquish his hold.

"The poor chap has a bad sore on his back," Brandy replied. "I'm going to doctor it."

"The hell you are!" Horst yelled. "This is my horse, kid, and you leave 'im alone, you hear!"

With that, Horst jerked the rope viciously, and Brandy's slight body was yanked from the ground; he fell in a heap. Brandy's spirit was not subdued, however, by his ignominious tumble, and he looked up at Horst angrily. He had not relinquished his hold on the lead strap.

"The horse jolly well has a bad sore on his back and shouldn't be ridden. I'm going to doctor it."

"I'll damn well take care of my own horses, kid!" Horst sneered angrily. "If they need doctorin', I'm the one who'll do it!"

"Then, why don't you?" Brandy's thin voice rose in anger. "It should have been taken care of a week ago, by the looks of it. Horses have feelings, too, you know!"

Rage suffused Horst's face, and his eyes bugged out even farther than usual as he took a step toward Brandy and raised a big boot to kick the fallen youngster. It was Tiny who interposed his big bulk between Brandy and Horst. Horst stopped short, his foot still in mid-air.

"You kick the lad, and I'll break the leg that did it!" Tiny's voice had lost its musical quality.

"And then I'm damn shore a fixin' to put a bullet through the same leg!" It was Clem who was standing behind Horst with his pistol drawn.

A look of consternation and amazement was on Horst's face. He slowly lowered his foot to the ground. He looked at Tiny with hatred in his bulging eyes. Tiny stood firmly. There was no emotion that crossed his face, but the gentle, friendly twinkle was gone from his eyes. Horst turned to face Clem, whose pistol was pointed squarely in his belly.

"Well," Horst blustered, "that horse is mine, and the damn kid had no right to mess with 'im!"

"He had every right to." It was Humphrey's voice. He was standing beside Clem. "Besides, that ain't your horse. It's a HF horse, and it's Brandy's job to take care of 'im. Now you go wash out that saddle blanket good and clean and catch another horse. And if you sore up his back, you can walk the rest of the way to Abilene."

Horst looked at Humphrey, Clem, and Tiny in turn, and then realizing that he was hopelessly outmatched, spat an obscenity and grabbed his saddle blanket as he walked toward the river.

Neither Clem nor Tiny said a word, but each went to get his saddle and choose a horse from the remuda.

"Brandy," Humphrey said in a kindly voice, "you take the bay and doctor 'im. There's some calomel in the hospital wagon."

"I'll do that, Mr. Humphrey," Brandy said as he rose and brushed grass and twigs from his clothing. He had a nasty gash on one cheek where he had fallen on a sharp stick. "And I surely do appreciate. . ."

"Before you do that, though," Humphrey interrupted, for it always embarrassed him when anyone expressed gratitude to him, "grab a good, dry blanket and throw it down there by Horst's saddle. And when you're through doctorin' the horse, turn 'im out and don't bring 'im in again until his back heals up."

"Yes, sir, Mr. Humphrey. Is it all right if I get one of the ladies to clean out this little scratch on my cheek, too?"

"That'll be all right," Humphrey replied with a twinkle in his eyes.

\* \* \* \* \* \*

The herd trailed well as they grazed northward and parallel to the river, which was a beautiful stream lined with elm trees, salt cedars, a few ash-colored trees, and huge cottonwoods. Many of the cowboys veered off from the herd to get a cool drink of water and take advantage of a few minutes in the shade, for the day was hot.

At noon, when Maisie had pulled off to one side to fix the noon meal, a small band of Indians approached. They were in view for a few minutes before they arrived, however, so Humphrey, Clem, Tonio, and several of the cowboys were at the wagon when they arrived. They were a scraggly lot and did not look menacing. However, they kept looking to the north as if expecting someone.

The leader of the Indians spoke in a guttural tongue which no one but Tonio could understand.

"What does he say, Tonio?" Humphrey asked.

"They're Osage," Tonio replied. "Says they want tobacco and beef."

Humphrey did not use tobacco, but he had stored some in the hospital wagon in case some of the cowboys ran short, for he knew that they became irritable and short-tempered when they did.

"Liza!" Humphrey yelled. The Negro woman stuck her head out the back of the covered wagon. "Get a few sacks of tobacco out of that box under the seat and bring 'em out here."

Liza was not enthusiastic about leaving her wagon when the Indians were present, but she did so. She carried the tobacco to Humphrey and gave it to him.

"Tonio," Humphrey instructed, "tell 'em they can have some tobacco." Humphrey held it up for them to see. "But, tell 'em they can't have any beef."

Tonio translated. The Indians talked among themselves for a few minutes.

"What are they sayin', Tonio?"

"Most of 'em want to take the tobacco and leave," Tonio replied. "They think a bunch of soldiers is chasin' 'im."

"They're likely right about that," Clem said. "I figger that the feller that stopped by and told us about Sheridan runnin' 'em out of Kansas knew what he was talkin' about."

The Indians argued for a few more minutes and finally seemed to reach a decision. The leader spoke to Tonio.

"He says give 'em more tobacco, and they will leave the herd alone."

"Tell 'im he don't get no more tobacco, and he better leave the herd alone!"

Tonio translated. The Indians argued a bit more, but finally accepted the tobacco and rode on south.

"Hope they ain't more no worse than that between here and Abilene," Clem said with relief.

Less than an hour after the Indians passed, a detachment of soldiers came by. Humphrey and Clem rode out to meet them. They were led by a corporal who wanted to know if they had seen any Indians.

"Six of 'em came by about an hour ago," Humphrey replied.

"Did they stop?"

"Yes."

"Give you any trouble?"

"They wanted tobacco and beef," Humphrey said.

"You didn't give them any, did you?"

"Give 'em some tobacco," Humphrey admitted.

"The army wouldn't like that, mister," the corporal said sharply.

"God-a-mighty, man!" Humphrey responded in irritation. We're a drivin' a trail herd, and I reckon we don't much care what the army likes or don't like!"

"That's for damn shore!" Clem chimed in.

The corporal started to counter Clem's sharp reply with one of his own when he suddenly remembered his orders not to antagonize civilians.

"We just want information," he finally said in a more moderate tone.

"Well, you got it," Humphrey replied testily. "Six Indians. They was headin' south about a hour ago. We give 'em some tobacco. Now you got your information, and we've got a herd of steers to look after." With that, Humphrey turned his horse and rode toward the herd.

Clem stood his ground and waited expectantly.

"What kind of Indians were they?" The corporal made no move to call Humphrey back.

"One of our men that talks Indian lingo said they was Osage."

"Seems like every damn Indian tribe there ever was is in Kansas, now," the corporal said with a tinge of bitterness.

"What's the army so damn fired up about, anyway?" Clem asked. "Feller come by our camp last night and said Sherman had told Sheridan to clean the Indians out of Kansas."

"That's right!" the corporal said. "We got orders to run 'em across the Oklahoma line or shoot ever one of the red bastards. And we're just hopin' they don't run!"

"You're bloodthirsty as hell, ain't you!" Clem said sarcastically.

"It ain't that!" The corporal was nettled. "But a lot of folks are tryin' to start ranches in Kansas now, and they can't do it if they got to watch their cattle and horse herds ever day and night to keep the thievin' redskins from runnin' 'em off!"

"Well." Clem simply had to get in a dig at the Yankees. "You boys has bit off a mighty big chaw—so has Sherman and Sheridan."

The truth of Clem's statement nettled the corporal further, and he retorted angrily. "We'll chew what we bit off, mister! Don't you worry none about that! And you might be a little more respectful of Sherman and Sheridan, too, by puttin' General before their names!"

"Well, well!" Clem needled in mock surprise. "I mebbe so forgot my manners. But I reckon you did, too, corporal. The feller that jus' left here was a colonel—in the Southern army!"

With that parting shot, Clem wheeled his horse and loped toward the herd. The corporal stared after him a minute, shook his head slightly, and then he and his men rode on south.

\* \* \* \* \* \*

The herd kept travelling well, and the cowboys were taking their ease as they rode in the warm Kansas sunshine. Alf, who was one of the men assigned to ride ahead of the herd, was moseying his still half-wild mustang along near the river and playing with his long, well-oiled rawhide rope as he did in every spare moment that he could. He always kept it securely tied to the surcingle that he used instead of a saddle, much to Clem's disgust. As he rode along, he kept a sharp lookout for Indians, which in no way kept him from spying rocks, sticks, or anything else that he could dab his rope on. In his hands, it seemed that the rawhide took on a life of itself and went unerringly to the object that Alf aimed at. He chuckled with satisfaction after each perfect cast.

As he started to cross a small ditch covered with weeds, a big raccoon came boiling out of it, and after taking one look at the varmint that had disturbed him, took off at full speed for the river. Alf howled in glee as he gave chase. But just as he started to throw his rope, the coon reached a big dead cottonwood and started scrambling rapidly up it. Alf watched until the coon had climbed to a height that he deemed safe and perched on a dead limb. He looked at Alf with dark white-ringed eyes. Alf grinned delightedly, and his long rope flew like an arrow, the small loop settling snugly around the coon's neck.

Alf howled in delight and yanked the rope as hard as he could. The big boar coon felt himself flying through the air until he landed on what he thought was another limb, but which was, in fact, Alf's head. The coon dug his claws in. Alf screamed and dropped his reins, fighting frantically to dislodge the coon. The mustang, frightened by Alf's yell and the sudden loosening of his reins, bawled lustily and started pitching. Alf, with both hands trying to rid himself of the coon, was unceremoniously tossed in the air. He hit the ground hard and raised up just in time to see the mustang running and bawling straight toward the front of the herd, with the coon hitting the ground and bouncing as he was dragged at the end of the long rope.

Alf watched as if mesmerized until the horse and the frightening apparition that he was dragging ran straight for the lead steer, which turned tail and ran. He was accompanied by a tidal wave of frightened longhorns.

"Oh, no!" Alf wailed and beat the ground with his fist.

\* \* \* \* \* \*

The cowboys who were riding swing veered farther to one side; the mass of cattle grew wider as they turned and ran. The drag men could hear the bedlam and spurred their horses out of the way as if their lives depended on it—which they did.

In less than two minutes, Humphrey, Clem, and fifteen cowboys were looking at the dust made by the steers they had followed and cared for for so many days. Immediately following them was Alf's mustang, still running and pulling his bouncing burden.

"God-a-mighty!" Humphrey gasped as he rode up to Clem. "What happened?"

"I got no idee!" Clem was so flabbergasted he forgot to cuss. "I ain't never seen cattle run like that afore," he said in awe.

"Did Indians scare 'em?"

"Something damn shore did!" Clem was regaining some of his crust. "I seen cattle run afore, but I never saw 'em jus' up and leave the country like a cat with his tail on fire afore. What the hell was that thing a chasin' 'em? Looked like a big panther with a long tail and a skunk tied to it. Them damn cattle will be back in the Oklahoma strip afore sundown!"

"Well, let's see if anybody else is hurt," Humphrey said.

"You mean somebody was hurt?" Clem asked anxiously.

"Aw, not much," Humphrey said. "I just got a scratch on my leg when I rode over and tried to turn 'em."

Clem looked down to see Humphrey's blood-soaked pant leg.

"You tried to turn 'em?" Clem gasped in amazement. "Hump, them cattle wouldn't a turned if they had been a forty foot bluff in front of 'em!"

"I know that, now," Humphrey agreed. "I reckon I didn't even think about it. Just thought I ort to do something!"

"Well, we're gonna be damn lucky if we ain't got a bunch of men killed, and the wagons wrecked!" Clem declared.

"The wagons were well off to one side," Humphrey said. "And the remuda, too. So I reckon all we lost is a herd of steers."

The cowboys had all been riding toward Humphrey and Clem; as they approached, Clem counted and was relieved to see that all were present except Alf.

"Any of you boys hurt?" Clem asked. He got no response and assumed, correctly, that the answer was negative. Absolute astonishment and fear was on their faces.

"Well, we're damn lucky at that," Clem said. "If we didn't lose nobody but that nigger Alf, we shore as hell are gettin' off lighter than we got any right to expect."

"We didn't lose Alf." Tiny's soft voice carried to them all. "Here he comes. But he's limping and looks like he may be hurt."

The cowboys all waited as Alf limped up to them. His face was bloody from the coon's claws.

"You all right, Alf?" Humphrey asked anxiously.

"Yassuh, Mars Hump," he said in a quavering voice. "But I reckon I done messed things up some."

He immediately had the attention of all the men.

"What in hell happened, Alf?" Clem demanded. "Do you know?"

"Yassuh, Mars Clem. I knows."

"Then, Dammit, man, what happened?"

"Well, Mars Hump, you see I. . ." His voice was pleading.

"Go on, Alf!" Humphrey demanded.

"There was this coon—he jump up right under my hoss—an' he run. . ." Alf gulped and stopped again.

"Go on, Alf!" Humphrey commanded harshly.

"Well, he run and clumb up a tree an'—an' I ropes 'im. . ."

"Go on!"

"Well, Mars Hump. . ." Alf was almost crying. "I jis give that rope a jerk, and de coon he come a tumblin' outer that tree and lights right on my head! I thinks maybe I yelled or sompin, an' I drops my reins, and my hoss, he pitch me off, and then he jis run as fast as he can with that coon a bouncin' along behind 'im—an' he runs smack into de front of de herd."

There was a long silence. Not a man spoke or moved. Alf hung his head.

"God-a-mighty!" breathed Humphrey.

"Mars Hump," Alf looked up abjectly.

"What, Alf?"

"I ain't gonna do dat no mo!"

\* \* \* \* \* \*

Humphrey went to the wagon to have his leg doctored, accompanied by Alf, who also needed some repairs. They both limped. Maisie and Ellie had just finished pouring whiskey in the gash on Humphrey's leg, and Liza was doctoring Alf, when Brandy rode up on Punkin.

"What happened, Mister Humphrey?" Brandy inquired. His eyes were big and round, and he looked scared.

"The cattle run," Humphrey said tersely.

"Yes, sir, I saw that," Brandy said in a small voice. "The remuda got excited, too, but Shanks and I got them settled down, and now they're grazing peacefully.

I came to see what happened. Shanks can handle them well enough, I'm sure. I hope it was all right for me to leave the remuda for a few minutes."

"That's fine, Brandy."

"What happened, Mr. Humphrey?"

Humphrey started to reply and then checked himself; a small twinkle lit his eyes, and he grinned ruefully.

"Nothin much, Brandy. Alf—he roped a coon!"

\* \* \* \* \* \*

Clem and the cowboys followed the fleeing herd for more than five miles. When they topped a rise, they were dismayed to see below them a milling and restless herd of cattle much bigger than the one they had been driving.

"Hell to pay, now!" Clem said in despair. "The crazy bastards has run into another herd!"

The cowboys stopped in a group and gazed in awe. They could not quite comprehend the catastrophe that had befallen. They sat silently and grimly and watched as a rider from the enlarged herd rode toward them.

As the rider neared, Clem said, "I'll do the talkin'." There was desperation, resignation, and a tinge of fear in his voice.

As the rider came up, however, he was grinning. Clem pulled his horse a few steps forward to meet him.

"You drivin' a bunch of cow critters that can outrun a race horse! They got an HF on their left hip and a road brand you can see for a mile." The man grinned. Clem's relief was almost palpable.

"We was," Clem agreed. "Till a damn spook scared hell out of 'em about five miles back."

"Name's Skeet Dawkins." The man proffered his hand, and Clem grasped it eagerly. "I'm trail boss for Bill Butler. We got nearly three thousand in our herd—hell of a lot more, now." He grinned again. "When them cattle come over that hill, I could of swore they was runnin' from a prairie fire. I mean, they was in a full run, and their eyes was wild as hell, and their horns were rattlin' like a hail storm. Thought for a minute our herd might run. But I got some good boys, and they got 'em millin' quick. So now they'll all be so give out they won't be hard to handle for a week."

"That millin' will take more meat off'n them crazy bastards than the run did," Clem said.

"Shore will," Skeet agreed. "But it won't make a lot of difference to us. Bill—that is, Bill Butler—is gonna hold 'em out west of Abilene on good grass till cool weather. Feller named McCoy from Abilene come down last winter and said he figgered that would be the best time to sell."

"That was Joe McCoy, I reckon," Clem said. "He come by our ranch last year, too."

"Say!" Skeet exclaimed. "You ain't from that ranch on the Canadian up in the Panhandle of Texas, are you?"

"That's us," Clem admitted. "That HF brand stands for Humphrey Beatenbow and Fauntleroy Finch."

"Joe told us about you fellers," Skeet said admiringly. "Must take a lot of nerve to run cattle right in the middle of Indian country like that."

"It don't take nerve," Clem said. "The only requirement that I can figger out is not to have no brains a-tall."

Skeet laughed good-naturedly. "Well, anyway, I hear you boys have got a good spread out there."

"We have. And this was our first shipment, too. Now, we're in one hell of a mess!"

"What on earth scared them so bad?" Skeet asked with concern. "We could hear them horns a-poppin' a long time before they got here. You're lucky they run all together and didn't break up into bunches."

"I reckon we are lucky," Clem admitted. "It was one of our damned nigger cowhands that scared 'em!" Clem said with disgust in his voice. "The son-of-a-bitch rides with just a surcingle around his horse, but he's got a sixty-foot rawhide rope that he can rope a bird with. He seen a coon run up a tree and roped 'im and jerked 'im down. But the damn thing landed on his head, and his pony bucked 'im off and ran back into the herd with that coon a bouncin' forty feet in the air."

Skeet let out a roar of laughter and slapped his chaps-covered knee. "Don't blame them steers," he said. "I reckon I might a run, too. I'll bet the boys took the hide off that nigger!"

Clem removed his hat and scratched his head. "Funny thing," he said, incredulity in his voice. "Wasn't a man said anything to 'im. I didn't. And Hump—he's one of the owners—jus' asked 'im what happened. I figger that if any one of us had started to say what we thought, we'd a killed the black bastard!"

"Did you lose any men?"

"Nope. Couple of 'em crippled some, but not bad. Hump, he had some fool notion about tryin' to turn 'em and rode in to try it, and got a horn in his leg. And the nigger has got some deep cuts where that coon clawed and a sore leg from gettin' bucked off."

"Well, you're mighty lucky," Skeet said. "Fact is, them cattle run into the only thing that could a stopped 'em without hurtin' a lot of 'em."

"That's for damn sure!" Clem agreed. "But it's gonna take a month to get 'em all separated."

"It won't look too bad in the mornin'," Skeet said, nodding toward the herd. "The boys have got nearly all of 'em out of that mill, and most of 'em are startin' to graze. They'll bed down good after that run. We can start separatin' 'em tomorrow. Your road brand is easy to see, so we won't have any trouble with identification."

"How many men you got, Skeet?"

"Fifteen, countin' me," Skeet said. "We started out with sixteen, but a couple of 'em went to town when we passed Austin and didn't come back; then we picked up a couple of good men out west of Fort Worth. Both of 'em were in the Rangers. But we lost a man when we was crossin' Red River."

"River flooded?"

"Headrise hit us when we had about half the cattle across. Split the herd. We lost a good cowboy and a couple of hundred steers."

"Tough!" Clem said. He and Skeet were both quiet for a few minutes. Skeet was reliving that awful scene of the big cottonwood tree hitting the cowboy and his horse, their desperate fight to escape, and his own futile attempt to rescue them. Clem broke the silence. "How'd you get the rest of 'em across?"

"Four or five men were already across; so they held the part of the herd that was on the north side of the river, and the rest of us held ours on the south side. We crossed over without much trouble the next day and got the herd together again."

"You shore as hell can't tell what's gonna happen on a trail drive," Clem said. "But you can bet it'll be something you don't expect."

"That's a fact," admitted Skeet. "Just like that nigger a ropin' that coon and stampeding your herd! Pure accident. Wasn't nobody's fault."

"Well," Clem said with a mighty sigh of relief. "I'm jus' shore glad you ain't mad as hell. Some men would be!"

"Could happen to me—or anybody."

"Skeet," Clem was quickly regaining his crotchety, tactless self. "If this is Butler's herd, why ain't he along? How come you're the trail boss?"

"'Cause I've got Bill Butler a thinkin' I'm the best damn cowman alive!" Skeet's grin robbed the remark of any hint of braggadocio. "Just like you got Hump fooled."

"Them two men you picked up. Rangers, you say?"

"Yep," answered Skeet. "And you can believe 'em, too; they handle a pistol like it was an extra finger."

"Then they might know Finch. He was a Ranger, too."

"I've heard 'em talk about a Ranger named Finch. But they never used his other name—must not be the same man, though. They talk about the Ranger they knew that was a happy-go-lucky young feller, but hell-on-wheels with a pistol, or any other kind of a gun. They say he's killed more than twenty men. Ain't scared of the devil himself!"

"That's Fauntleroy Rinch," Clem said positively. "Him and Hump Beatenbow is partners."

"He with you?"

"Nope. He stayed at the ranch. Expectin' Indian trouble."

"Oh," Skeet said understandingly. "Well, I'll tell you what! I got plenty of men, and them cattle ain't gonna try to go nowhere tonight. Yours are give out from that run, and ours have been on this trail all the way from Karnes County, and they're most as gentle as milk pen calves by now."

"Karnes County?" Clem asked in surprise. "Then you must a been on the trail a long time. That ain't far from San Antone—joins Goliad County, don't it?"

"That's right. We been on the trail since March, and them steers are gettin' mighty tame, else I expect they would have run when your herd hit 'em."

"That's one hell of a drive," Clem said in admiration. "Must be close to a thousand miles."

"I reckon so," Skeet said. "We been takin' our time, though. Stopped a few times to let 'em graze on good grass to put on some weight. Our boys been takin' it mighty easy. So why don't you and your boys go on back to your chuckwagon and get a good night's sleep, and we'll all start workin' like hell tomorrow. We're gonna need to separate soon so's the grass won't give out."

"Hell, Skeet, I. . ." Clem stammered, for expression of gratitude was very difficult for him. "That's shore as hell white of you—I mean you think your men can handle 'em all right?"

"I know we can." Skeet grinned and stuck out his hand again. "See you in the mornin'. Early!"

"You damn shore will," Clem agreed. As he rode back to his men, he thought to himself, "That son-of-a-bitch got a heart bigger than that damn coon Alf roped."

\* \* \* \* \* \*

Clem and the cowboys returned just at sundown. Maisie had supper ready.

"Well?" Humphrey looked at Clem questioningly.

"Couldn't be much worse!" Clem growled. "We followed the ignorant bastards about five miles and then found 'em. They had run into Bill Butler's herd. Now we got about six thousand brainless varmints all mixed up. We'll be a month separatin' 'em if we ever do. But Butler's trail boss will damn shore do to ride the river with. Said for us to come down in the mornin'. They'll ride herd tonight."

"You mean you left the whole HF herd with a man you didn't even know?" Humphrey was incredulous.

"Now why the hell not?" Clem said angrily. "He's got good men, and he shore as hell ain't gonna steal 'em. He shore as hell couldn't get far with both of them herds all mixed up afore we could catch 'im. Besides, he's Bill Butler's man, an' I'd bet my hat on 'im!"

Humphrey grunted but was not pleased that almost half of his earthly property had been left with strangers.

There was a babble of conversation. It was the first time that all the cowboys had been together since they left the ranch, and for them it was sort of like a reunion.

"Well," philosophized Humphrey to the astonishment of all, "we ain't got no cattle to worry about tonight, so we all ought to get a good night's sleep."

The others agreed, but made no moves to go to their bedrolls. They were anxious to talk.

"Never seen anything like that before," one cherubic-faced cowboy said almost reverently.

"Ain't likely you ever will again," another volunteered. "Cattle don't run like them done today—not unless they got a mighty good reason to."

"I reckon they had a good reason!" another chimed in. "That mustang of Alf's a draggin' that coon and him hittin' the ground ever forty foot would of scared most folks. Would me!"

Alf, who had been hiding in the shadows of the cook fire, determined that the cowboys bore no animosity toward him and began to inch into the firelight.

Humphrey and Clem sat on the periphery of the firelight and discussed the procedure they must take on the morrow. Maisie and Ellie kept all the coffee cups filled.

"It couldn't be much worse," Clem said to Humphrey. "All our cattle mixed up with Bill's, and that's a pure damn mess. He's got three thousand or more, and so have we. "They're a mixin' together like long lost kinfolks. It's gonna take a lot of time and sweat to separate 'em. But that there foreman of his is shore a mighty fine feller. Wasn't even mad."

"How long do you figger for the outside?" Humphrey queried.

"A week might do it!" Clem replied glumly. "But likely ten days would be more like it."

"You think we can get all of our cattle back?" Humphrey asked.

Clem shook his head moodily and then replied, "I reckon mebbe we can get most of 'em back—but there ain't no way we can keep from losin' some."

"We started from the HF with 3100 head of steers," Humphrey said adamantly. "I figger to get to Abilene with 3100 head!"

"You're forgettin' about the ten cows and calves," Clem reminded. "An' that maverick bull we cut when we was only a few days out."

"I ain't forgettin'," Humphrey said firmly. "I ain't so set on gettin' them to the shippin' place as I might be. Them cows and calves can make it on their own. But I'm gonna deliver 3100 head of steers like I told Joe McCoy I would. He wasn't expectin' no cows and calves, and I reckon they'll be all right if we cut 'em out tomorrow and let 'em graze."

"What about that bull—that steer that was cut afore we left the Oklahoma territory?"

"We'll sell 'im," Humphrey said firmly. "And whatever we get for 'im, I'll send back to Decatur. That's where his brand come from, I think."

"Prob'ly!" Clem agreed. "But first we got a hell of a job separatin' our HF cattle from Bill Butler's steers. An' that damn shore ain't gonna be no picnic!"

The Beatenbow jackass, still maintaining his safe distance from camp, loosed his unearthly bray just as the men were rolling into the bedrolls.

"I'm gonna shoot that damn jackass yet! Sounds like he's tickled to death!" Clem growled. The other men just grinned and soon were asleep.

# CHAPTER 11

The HF cowboys left camp before daylight the next morning, each with an extra horse.

"Brandy," Clem instructed, "you mosey the remuda along behind us. We'll all be needin' fresh horses by dinner-time. Cuttin' cattle is pure hell on horses."

"What about the wagons?" Humphrey wanted to know.

"We'd best have the nigger women bring 'em on down, too," Clem said. "Ain't no tellin' how long it's gonna take to get them herds separated."

"I'll drive the hospital wagon myself," Humphrey said. "This here leg of mine is as stiff as a poker this mornin'."

"You poured some whiskey in that gash, didn't you?" Clem asked anxiously.

"Yeah," Humphrey answered. "It ain't much of a wound. Just bruised, mostly."

"It's a wonder you got any laigs," Clem said grouchily. "Tryin' to turn a bunch of runnin' longhorns by yourself was a damn fool thing to do."

"I know that now," Humphrey replied mildly. "You go ahead. We'll be there, and the cooks will have dinner ready when it's time."

Clem nodded and loped after the cowboys. He, too, led an extra horse.

\* \* \* \* \* \*

Some of the Butler cowboys were just finishing breakfast when the HF men rode up; the night herders were still riding slowly around the herd.

"Light and set," Skeet greeted them with his infectious grin. "Likely another cup of coffee won't hurt you before we begin. "We've got a long day ahead of us."

"That's for damn shore!" Clem agreed as he accepted a tin cup of hot, strong coffee. "Men and horses both gonna be tuckered by the time the day is over. And it still ain't light enough to see brands very good."

The Butler cowboys who were not on duty welcomed the HF men as if they were long lost friends. In fact, both crews had become just a bit weary of their own company, and they welcomed the conversation of new men.

There were no black cowboys at the Butler breakfast. Trey and Alf stood back almost out of the firelight. Largo had stayed to help with moving the camp. It was the camp cook who noticed Alf and Trey.

"What the hell is the matter with you two cowboys?" he growled fiercely. "Don't you want some coffee?"

"Yassuh—I mean nosuh, masta," Trey said nervously. "But we is black."

"I don't give a damn if you're pokeydot!" the cook growled. "Anybody that's been a followin' cow critters as long as you two ain't too damn good to drink my coffee."

The cook limped toward the wagon and picked up two tin cups. His awkward walk indicated that he was a broken down old cowboy who could not resist the lure of the trail and had become a camp cook in order to lead the life he loved, even in such lowly status.

"No suh," Alf grinned. "We was jus'. . ."

The cook limped back to the fire, filled the cups, and held them out to Alf and Trey. "Now drink this here coffee," he demanded, "or I'm gonna pour it out on the ground."

"Yassuh!" Alf grinned widely. "I reckon that cup of coffee gonna taste mighty good!"

"Ort to," the cook agreed, "It's been a simmerin' since last night, and I been buildin' to it ever couple of hours or so."

Alf and Trey took the coffee gratefully. They did not want the coffee nearly as much as they wanted to be accepted as part of the crew, and they knew that the crotchety old cook's action had accomplished that. They both grinned as they reached for the cups.

Clem and Skeet drew off to one side to discuss the strategy for the day.

"The river is real shallow here," Skeet said. "If it's all right with you, we'll cut out all of our cattle and push them across the river. There's good grass over there, and they won't be hard to hold. We can push your cattle on over west a ways, and we'd ort not to have any trouble holdin' 'em when we get 'em all split up. You can push yours up one side of the river, and we'll take ours up the other side."

"Sounds as good as any," Clem agreed. "How long you figger it's gonna take us?"

"No tellin'," Skeet said mildly. "Maybe a week—maybe ten days. Depends on how good your cowboys are and whether they got good cuttin' horses or not."

"The boys can ride good enough, and our horses are all right, too."

"So are mine," Skeet said. "But it's gonna be mighty hard on horses—and men, too."

"Well, all the boys brought an extry horse, and we've got a whole remuda a comin' this way. Ort to be here afore dinner time."

"Then I reckon we'd best get at it," Skeet said. "it's nearly light enough to see."

"One thing!" Clem said.

Skeet looked at Clem questioningly.

"We got another nigger cowboy besides them two over there a drinkin' your coffee."

"Well?"

"An' we got another nigger kid that helps our wrangler. An' our wrangler ain't hardly old enough to wean—but he's the best damn horse jingler I ever saw. Some kind of foreigner, I reckon. Talks funny. Awful polite."

"Sounds like you got a pretty good crew, yourself," Skeet said.

"That ain't all," Clem gulped. He was determined that Skeet hear him out. "We got three nigger women with us," he finished almost defiantly.

"Women!" It was Skeet's turn to be surprised. "What in hell you got nigger women on a trail drive for?"

"One of 'em is our cook," Clem said resignedly. "An' a damn good one, too. She pitched in when we run a gotch-eyed camp cook off when we was comin' out west from Fort Worth. Another one, a young one, is one of the nigger cowboy's little sister. She helps out with the cookin' and stuff. Then we got one that drives the 'hospital' wagon—as Hump calls it. She washes saddle blankets, and hauls bedrolls, and does a lot of other things." Clem didn't say what he suspected the 'other things' were. "Hump, he had 'im a plantation back in Louisiana, and he brought a whole passel of niggers with 'im when he come west. The rest of 'em are still back at the ranch."

"Well?" Skeet's brow wrinkled.

"Well." Clem squirmed in his saddle uncomfortably. "You reckon your men gonna take it all right? Us with them niggers and all—especially with them nigger cowboys?"

"Oh, hell," Clem! Skeet said, a tinge of disgust in his voice. "My men don't give a damn who they're workin' with so long as they do their share. Can them nigger cowboys ride and rope?"

There was a long silence. Finally, Clem took a long breath. "To tell you the truth, Skeet, I ain't never seen nobody that could rope like that nigger that roped the coon and stampeded our herd. He never had a rope in his hand till we bought him one in Decatur on the way out. Now, he makes his own with rawhide, and he can make the damn thing do everything but talk. That's Alf. The other one is called Trey. And I ain't never seen him throwed off a horse, yet. In fact, one fell with 'im and broke his leg. An' he jus' stayed on an' kept on ridin' 'im when he got up. I damn near ruptured myself a settin' his leg."

"Then my men shore won't mind working with 'em," Skeet said.

"Only thing is. . ."

Skeet waited.

"Both of 'em rides with a damn surcingle. They won't use a saddle."

"A surcingle?" Skeet was incredulous. "How can they rope and hold anything with a surcingle?"

"Oh, they got a loop fixed to tie their rope to. An' damned if I don't believe a horse can hold or drag more with that surcingle than he can with a rope tied to the saddle horn."

Skeet thought for a minute, then said thoughtfully. "You know, that sort of makes sense, all right."

"Mebbe so," Clem said ruefully. "But I still wish the crazy bastards would ride a saddle like humans."

Skeet laughed heartily. "What do you care, Clem! So long as they can do the job?"

"Well—hell!" Clem looked embarrassed. "It jus' don't look right for a cowboy to be a ridin' with jus' a rope around his horse's belly. Anyway, Largo, he's the other nigger, rides a saddle and is a damn good hand with cattle or anything else. Went all through the war with Hump when he was still a slave."

"Well," Skeet grinned widely. "All I got to say is that it shore looks to me like the HF outfit travels in style! Now, let's get to work."

"We shore as hell got plenty of it to do," Clem said. He was relieved. The whole Butler crew seemed friendlier and happier than any trail crew was likely to be.

\* \* \* \* \* \*

The cattle were loose-herded on the west side of the river, and about half of the cowboys held them in a scattered pattern, while the other half rode in and began to separate them.

The Butler cattle, having been trailed so long, were easiest to handle, and soon a good-sized bunch of them had been pushed across the shallow river and were grazing contentedly on the other side. The HF cattle were pushed farther west as they were separated from the mixed herd. Soon there were actually three herds—the mixed herd in the middle, the Butler cattle across the river, and a smaller herd of HF cattle farther west.

The cattle were easily recognizable, for in addition to their regular brands, each herd carried a distinct road brand. The ear marks were harder to distinguish, however.

"Be a little easier to tell 'em apart if their ear marks were a little different," Skeet observed.

"Shore would," Clem agreed. "That overslope that your cattle has and the swallowfork that ours has is hard to tell apart, 'specially with them both on the left ear and some hair growed out over 'em."

"We'll manage," Skeet said optimistically.

"Oh, hell, yes!" Clem said. "But I wish Hump had let me cut a dewlap on ours when I wanted to. But he wouldn't. Said it hurt their looks, which didn't make no sense at all. I don't see how you could make a damned longhorn any uglier than it already is."

"You're right, Clem," Skeet agreed. "But the money they'll bring in Abilene will be mighty pretty. And we'll get 'em separated all right."

"I reckon," Clem said. "But with a dewlap, you can see that long floppy skin a hangin' down in front of their forelegs for a mile. Looks like a big, limber pecker."

"It does at that," Skeet laughed. "There is a man down in Refugio County that marks his cattle that way. I've seen 'im do it, and it doesn't hurt hardly any because that dewlap is just a big fold of loose skin. They don't bleed any more than an ear mark."

"Well," Clem said, "I wasn't interested in not hurtin' the long-legged bastards as I was in bein' able to tell which was ours."

"We're doing all right, anyway," Skeet said mildly. "Your bunch, and ours too, is growin' right fast."

The separation of the herds was indeed going better than any of them had expected. And a lot of progress had been made when the HF wagons arrived before noon. They were parked on a small hill a good distance from the working men. Brandy and Shanks held the remuda even farther away.

When the wagons were parked, Humphrey instructed the women to start fixing the noon meal. He mounted Rafter. He could not bend his sore leg; so he had to ride with one foot out of the stirrup. Rafter was an easy travelling horse, but it was still painful for Humphrey to ride. Largo mounted the horse that had once belonged to Chico Baca.

As Humphrey and Largo neared the herd, Skeet and Clem rode out to meet them. Clem was surprised that Humphrey was riding Rafter, for he usually kept him just for his night horse. But Clem said nothing; he introduced Humphrey and Skeet, who shook hands.

"This here is Largo." Clem nodded toward the Negro. And to his great surprise, Skeet kneed his horse over close to Largo and stuck out his hand.

"Hello, Largo," Skeet smiled. "Clem has told me about you. Says you're a handy man to have around. I'm glad to meet you."

Largo was startled, but hesitated only a fraction of a second and reached out his big black hand to meet Skeet's. "Yassuh, Mars Skeet. I's glad to meet yo, too." He could think of nothing more to say.

"Well, how's it goin'?" Humphrey asked.

"Better'n we expected by a hell of a lot," Clem said. "Skeet's cattle is as gentle as a bunch of kittens and drive easy. The cutters has changed horses once, and when they git tired out, then the boys that is loose herdin' the three bunches will swap out with 'em. Their horses ain't tired out from jus' walkin' an' standin' mostly. We may not even need our remuda today."

"From the looks of the two horses you fellers are ridin', the HF must have a mighty fine remuda," Skeet said admiringly. "I reckon I never seen two better lookin' quarterhorses than the ones you're ridin'."

"You ain't likely to, neither," Clem chimed in. "That horse that Hump is ridin' is Rafter. He was sired by Old Billy out of a mare called Paisano. Ain't a horse in the country can hold a candle to 'im. An' the one Largo is ridin' used to belong to Chico Baca that got killed."

"Rafter belongs to my partner, Finch." Humphrey explained. "He just loaned 'im to me to make the drive with. He got 'im from one of his Ranger friends, name of Fleming."

"Those Old Billy horses are known all over south Texas. That stud stands at Leesville, which is in Gonzales County, not but a little ways north of our ranch in Karnes County. I'd give a summer's wages to own one of his colts. Your partner must think a awful lot of you!" Skeet said as he eyed Rafter admiringly.

Humphrey was relieved that he did not have to reply, for one of the Butler men rode up just at that time. "Hey, Skeet," he said, "I found a steer in there that ain't got no road brand nor earmark either."

"What color?" Clem asked quickly.

"A big brindle with a dark spot on his face and a white front leg. Looks pretty old and mean."

"Oh, hell!" Clem said. "That's the stray bull that we found in the Canadian River breaks when we was only two or three days out. We roped 'im and cut 'im and throwed 'im in with ours. Hump says he'll send the money back to Decatur, which is prob'ly where he come from. Musta been hidin' out for ten years. He's sixteen or seventeen years old, and mean as hell."

"Tell one of the HF men to haze 'im into their herd," Skeet instructed.

The Butler cowboy turned his horse and trotted away.

"Tell you what!" Humphrey spoke up. "Maisie and Ellie will have some dinner ready when it's time; so why don't I jus' ride back and tell 'er to fix dinner for both crews."

"Whoa, now, Hump!" Skeet objected affably. "That could just cause a sure enough ruckus. Our cook might just think we was desertin' 'im for better grub, which it probably would be. But I shore don't want him to quit."

"Hadn't thought of that!" Humphrey was contrite. "I jus' thought your men might like a change."

"And you're right, too. They would." Skeet thought for a minute and then said, "Tell you what—I'll go down to our camp and tell our cook the boys have been braggin' on him so much that your hands want to try his grub. That way, your men can come down to our camp for dinner, and my men can eat at your camp. That way, they'll both have a change, but your men will shore be gettin' the worst of it!"

"Good!" Humphrey agreed. "I'll go tell Maisie. She'll likely want to put on a little extry with company comin'." With that, Humphrey rode back toward his camp. His stiff leg stuck straight down, and his left shoulder slumped badly as a result of the musket ball he had carried since the battle of Cedar Creek. It still pained him occasionally.

"What yo wants me to do, Mars Clem?" Largo asked.

"Might jus' as well start helpin' the boys loose herd," Clem said. The situation was so well in hand that he did not want to alter it.

\* \* \* \* \* \*

Word was passed that the HF hands would eat dinner at the Butler camp, and that the Butler men would eat at the HF camp. The news was greeted with approval of all concerned, and when the sun was at its zenith, a group of the Butler cowboys rode toward the HF wagons. Clem and Skeet were sitting their horses and chatting when the men passed. Clem looked at them and almost fell off his horse. He recovered in a moment, but his face was flushed as he turned to Skeet.

"Dammit, Skeet," he said angrily, "you didn't tell me that!"

"Tell you what?"

"That you had some nigger cowboys!"

"Oh," Skeet answered equably, "that was Bill and Levi Perryman."

"They're niggers!" Clem said accusingly.

"Good hands, too!" Skeet said. "Reckon I just didn't think to tell you what color they was. They're brothers."

# CHAPTER 12

Separating the herds progressed rapidly, and all the cowboys were having a hilarious time doing it. The entire Butler crew seemed to have absorbed the genial nature and friendly attitude of their trail boss. They yelled at each other in derision when one let a steer that he was cutting from the herd get past him. It was all in good fun, and no one took offense. In truth, the cowboys were enjoying the furious activity after the boring days of trailing the slow moving herds.

The cowboys from the different camps seemed to be pairing up with another from the opposite camp. It seemed to make no difference to the men whether their new partners were black or white, and the good nature of the men from the Butler camp seemed to be permeating the HF camp. Only Dutch Horst remained surly and noncommunicative. He paired, not with a black cowboy, but with one of the youngest of the Butler men who joshed him continuously and seemed impervious to his glowering scowls and growls of anger. The young cowboy just laughed good-naturedly.

"Hope that young feller don't push that damn Dutchman too much," Clem said to Skeet. "That big bastard always seems to be lookin' for a excuse to bash somebody's head in."

"I hope so, too," Skeet said. "'Cause if he tried that, you'd be short a hand the rest of the way. That 'young feller' is one of them Texas Rangers that joined us out west of Fort Worth."

Clem looked at Skeet in surprise and then grinned in sheer delight. "I reckon I won't worry no more about it then," he said cheerfully. "We could make it the rest of the way with one less man, anyway."

Humphrey, whose swollen leg had made it necessary for him to remain in camp, fretted in the shade of a tarp that had been propped up beside the hospital wagon. Liza applied a hot towel and liniment to his swollen leg every few minutes. He was glad to see Clem and Skeet riding his way.

"How's the leg, Hump?" Clem asked as they rode up.

"Hurts," Humphrey answered cryptically. "How's the cattle job comin' along?"

"Fine," Skeet smiled. "We're gonna have 'em all separated in another full day, and my boys are gonna be sorta disappointed, I think. They've been enjoying the company of your hands and especially the grub they've been eatin' at your chuckwagon."

"Ever body's surprised as hell," Clem said. "'Specially me. I never thought it would go so fast. But Skeet's got a bunch of mighty good cowhands."

"Not any better than yours," Skeet rejoined. "I've never seen a better man than that nigger, Trey, at separatin' a steer from a herd and movin' it out. Seems like he knows what the critter is goin' to do before it does. And his horses stick their noses down to the ground and move about like a hound dog trailin' a coon."

"Well, he's broke enough horses in the past couple of years—he ort to be good at it. If'n he'd jus' ride a saddle, I'd say he was a pretty good hand," Clem admitted.

Both Skeet and Humphrey laughed, and Skeet said, "What do you care what he rides, Clem, so long as he gets the job done? I shore wouldn't! But it looks to me like he'd get bunions on his butt from ridin' bareback."

"Hell!" Clem snorted. "More'n likely his horses has got sores on their backs cause of his rump. It's as hard as his head."

"Hey, Hump," Skeet said, "That there is some contraption you got on the back of your wagon. Never seen one like it before. You make it?"

"Naw!" Humphrey replied. "Heard tell of one that Charlie Goodnight made; so I had Largo build it for me."

"Well, it's shore a dandy," Skeet replied. "I'm gonna tell Bill Butler about it, if I ever get back to Karnes County. Maybe so he'll have one built before we come up next year."

"You really think we'll get the herds separated by tomorrow?"

"Looks like it," Skeet said. "We've got some sore-footed horses that are slowin' the boys down some, but I believe we'll make it."

"An' that's about a week sooner than we could expect," Clem said.

"Say you got sore-footed horses?" Humphrey asked Skeet.

"Yeah. About six or seven of 'em."

"How come?" Humphrey asked. "We haven't had hardly any wet ground."

"Oh," Skeet said off-handedly, "we haven't got anybody that can do much of a job shoein' a horse. So most of the men just sort of nail 'em on and hope for the best."

Clem started to reply, but Humphrey beat him to it. "Skeet, we've got the best horseshoer in Texas or anyplace else. Largo can put 'em on, and they stay put. Don't sore 'em up, either."

"Well, you're lucky to have 'im along," Skeet said.

"What I was drivin' at," Humphrey said, "is that if you'd bring 'em over here, Largo he's got a anvil and tools in the hospital wagon, and he could put 'em on for you. As good as the cattle are workin', you could do without him workin' the herd."

"That's mighty neighborly of you, Hump," Skeet said sincerely, "but the truth is that most of 'em that are sore-footed are mighty bronky. That's one reason the boys couldn't put 'em on good. And we have one big grulla that we just have to throw plumb down to put shoes on 'im, and you shore can't get much of a fit that way."

"Won't make a damn bit of difference to Largo." Clem beat Humphrey to the reply. "That nigger is most as big as a horse and nearly as stout."

"He's the only man that can shoe a big stud that we keep at the ranch," Humphrey added. "Why don't you bring yours over and let 'im have a try at it?"

Skeet was obviously wavering. He did need the sore-footed horses.

"I'll go tell Largo to come to the wagons," Clem said as he turned his horse abruptly and rode away.

"Well," Skeet capitulated, "I'll go and bring some of 'em over here and see how he makes out. It'd be a big help, all right!"

\* \* \* \* \* \*

An hour later Skeet had brought six horses to the HF camp and tied them to nearby bushes. One was a big grulla with white-rimmed eyes. Largo had unloaded his anvil and other tools and tied a leather apron around his waist. He was heating some horseshoes in the embers of Maisie's cooking fire.

"Now, Largo," Skeet admonished, "some of these horses are pretty rank. In fact, all of 'em are. So you be mighty careful and don't let one of 'em hurt you—especially that big grulla. He'll give you trouble; so just throw 'im down and put 'em on as best you can."

"Yassuh, Mars Skeet," Largo grinned. "I do de best I kin, an' I won't git hurt. I shoes all our horses. 'Sides, I gets Brandy to help me."

"Brandy!" Skeet was incredulous.

"Yassuh. He's our horse jingler."

"I saw 'im," Skeet said. "He's just a kid. He ain't big enough to. . ."

"He's big enough!" Humphrey chimed in. "He don't try to outstout 'em—just holds their lead rope and talks to 'em. Clem swears he's half horse himself!"

Skeet just shook his head and rode back to the herd.

The separation of the steers continued throughout the hot afternoon. When the sun was still two hours high, the herd of mixed steers was no bigger than the HF herd grazing to the west or the Butler herd across the river.

The riders circling the mixed herd had little to do except push a steer back into the herd occasionally. Tiny sang softly in his melodious voice. Swifty practiced his fast draw with both pistols. When he jerked at his guns as he was meeting one of the Butler hands, he was appalled and frightened to find himself looking into the business end of a big pistol.

"What's that for?" He didn't point his pistols, for they had not cleared his holster.

"What I was wonderin'," the cowboy said levelly. "You went for your guns. Why?"

"Why?" Swifty asked incredulously. "I was practicin'," he said. "Do it all the time."

"Well, don't do it no more when you're ridin' up to me!" the young cowboy said. Then he grinned. "You shore might scare a feller plumb to death!" He reholstered his pistol and rode on.

Skeet had seen the incident and grinned. The cowboy that had so badly outshone Swifty was the other former Texas Ranger that had joined them.

\* \* \* \* \* \*

Two hours before sundown, it was decided to stop cutting the steers and to let them graze peacefully so that they would be well filled to bed down for the night. The cowboys pulled away from the mixed herd. Many of them got off their horses and sat on the ground. Clem and Skeet rode toward the HF wagons. As they neared, they could see five of the six horses that Skeet had brought to be shod; they were still tied to bushes.

"Looks like Largo took on too much," opined Skeet. "I was afraid he had. Those are bronky horses."

As they drew a bit nearer, Clem held up his hand. "Let's wait a minute," he said. "They're a shoein' that grulla now, an' we might spook 'im if we ride up too close."

They stopped their horses. Skeet was amazed to see the big grulla horse standing patiently. Brandy was holding his lead strap. With their horses standing still, Skeet and Clem could hear Brandy talking quietly and soothingly to the horse. Largo was bending over and had one forefoot lifted.

As Skeet and Clem watched, Largo set the foot gently on the ground and stood up. He then picked up another horseshoe and placed his hand on the horse's neck, running it gently down the length of the horse's side and up on his hips. Then, without raising his hand from the hip, Largo began to move it slowly and gently down the horse's back leg. As he reached the hock, the horse started to move, but Brandy exerted gentle pressure on the lead shank and continued his soft, almost musical, talk to the horse. Largo moved very slowly as he bent over and took hold of the long hairs on the fetlock. The horse stood still as Largo lifted. It was a moment before the horse gave way, and Largo had exerted most of his massive strength to get him to do so. When the leg was up a ways, Largo moved slowly under it until the leg was stretched backward and rested across Largo's hip and side. With snail-like movements Largo took the shoe that he had already fitted from his back pocket and placed it on the hoof. Then, with very light taps he began to nail on the shoe. The horse again started to move. Brandy put gentle pressure on the lead strap again and rubbed the horse on the forehead rather firmly, still talking in his low, soothing voice. Largo made no move to change his position and soon was hammering harder. The horse stood still. In moments, Largo had the shoe nails clinched, and the job was done. He let the leg down gently, rubbed the horse all the way up his leg, then down his back, and finally to his neck.

"All done, Mister Largo?" Brandy asked in his childish voice.

Largo simply grinned and mopped sweat from his face.

Skeet and Clem were still sitting their horses quietly. Skeet said, almost in awe, "I wouldn't a believed that if I hadn't seen it. Not sure I do even now."

It was Clem's turn to smile. "I hate like hell to say anything good about a nigger, but that one is the best damn horseshoer I ever seen. He's mighty near as stout as a horse. And Brandy—I think he puts some kind of spell over 'em. Anyway, between both of 'em, I ain't seen one that they couldn't shoe."

"I'd double that man's wages if Hump would let me have 'im."

"Doubt if Hump would part with 'im," Clem said. "He owns his ma and his wife, and a couple of his kids, too. That's his wife and little sister that's doin' our cookin'."

"Owns 'em?" Skeet looked at Clem in surprise. "They ain't slaves any more, Clem."

"I reckon they ain't, accordin' to the law, maybe," Clem admitted. "But Hump owns 'em, anyway. They was all slaves on his plantation back in Louisiana, and they come out with 'im 'cause they wanted to. He shore didn't make 'em do it. And he still treats 'em like slaves. An' every one of the crazy bastards thinks he's the biggest man alive. Damned if I know how he does it!"

"Well," Skeet said, "let's ride on up. Hope he doesn't have any more trouble with the others than he had with the grulla."

"Likely he won't—seein' as how he's already got shoes on the rest of 'em," Clem grinned again. It seemed that the good nature and camaraderie of the Butler crew was infecting him.

"Surely not," Skeet said dubiously.

But the other horses were shod, and Largo grinned widely when Skeet expressed his amazement and gratitude.

"Wasn't no trouble a'tall, Mars Skeet," he said. "'Sides, I had Brandy to help me."

"Don't see how you do it, Brandy," Skeet said seriously. "You shore got a way with horses!"

"And you have some jolly good horses, Mister Skeet," Brandy said. "All they want is someone to be kind to them. They're just like people."

Skeet shook his head and rode over to where Humphrey was sitting with his leg propped up under the shade of the tarp.

"You got a couple of shore enough good hands there, Hump."

"They'll do," Humphrey said gruffly.

"Well," Skeet said, "looks like we'll be all done by this time tomorrow. Especially now since we got these horses shod."

"Took less than half the time I figgered," Clem said.

"You say we'll be through by this time tomorrow?" Humphrey asked.

"Shore will," Skeet confirmed.

Humphrey thought for a few minutes, his brow wrinkled. "Tell you what," he finally said. "I ain't been no help a'tall with this gimpy leg and wouldn't a been much help if I hadn't been stove up. But I been walkin' some today, and the swellin' is goin' down. So by tomorrow I'll be able to get around good. So—what do you say we celebrate a little bit tomorrow night. I'll have Largo butcher one of the calves. You and your night herders come over early, and I'll have the cooks fix us up some special grub. Then, when the night crew goes on, the rest of the crew can eat. It'll give your cook a rest."

"That sounds awful good, Hump," Skeet said. "But you remember what I said about our cook. He's not the best in the world, but I'd sure not want to lose 'im."

"If you do, I'll loan you one of the wenches till you get to Abilene. But I got an idee that I can keep 'im from quittin'."

"How's that?"

"I'll send Brandy over to talk to 'im and invite 'im to come over, too."

"You know, that just might work," Skeet laughed. "Let me know how you make out."

Skeet and Clem rode back toward the herd, and Humphrey sent Ellie to get Brandy.

"Did you want me, Mister Humphrey?" Brandy asked.

"I've got a job for you," Humphrey said. "And it may not be as easy as tamin' them wild horses."

"I'll jolly well do the best I can, Mister Humphrey."

Humphrey went into detail as to how he wanted Brandy to approach the Butler cook. Brandy listened intently and nodded his head in understanding.

"Do everything you can to convince 'im—except lie to 'im—don't never do that!"

"No, sir, I wouldn't do that to him or any other man," Brandy said seriously. "I just wonder, sir, if you would mind if I took Ellie with me to see him?"

Surprise showed on Humphrey's face. "I reckon I wouldn't mind—but I can't see why you'd want to."

"Well, sir," Brandy said soberly, "it's just that I think sometimes a lady can persuade a person when a man can't."

Humphrey smothered a smile by wiping his hand over his face. "Then, I reckon you'd best take 'er with you."

"We'll jolly well give it a bonny good try, sir," Brandy said as he went to get Ellie.

\* \* \* \* \* \*

The herd was separated earlier the next day than even Skeet had predicted. By mid-afternoon, the job was done. Humphrey insisted that Clem do a count of their cattle, which he did and reported back that they were three head short. Humphrey was greatly disturbed.

"Well, where are they?" he demanded.

"Hell, Hump!" Clem's exasperation was apparent. "We could a missed 'em in the cut and they're with the Butler herd. Or they could a cut off from the herd during the run, or any one of a thousand other damned things. We're lucky as hell we didn't lose three hundred, much less three."

"Well, we're gonna have to find 'em," Humphrey said adamantly.

Clem started an angry retort, but clamped his jaw tightly and rode off. "Bullheaded bastard," he muttered silently.

Maisie was going about fixing the huge supper with her usual serene competence. Ellie was flitting about, giggling excitedly. Liza, in whom one of the Butler black cowboys had shown obvious interest, was obeying Maisie's orders promptly and with a willingness she had not shown before.

Humphrey had sent Largo a couple of miles down river with his 10-gauge shotgun to see if he could find any game to supplement their meal, and he had returned with three big turkeys and a sack full of prairie chickens and quail. He also reported seeing a band of Indians, which brought Humphrey back to the stern reality that they were still in Indian country.

"God-a-mighty! How big a bunch?" he asked Largo anxiously.

"'Bout twenty or thirty, I think, Mars Hump. Couldn't get no real good count on 'em cause I's hidin' down under a bank on the river."

"They'd have a might hard time doin' us much damage, us with two crews," Humphrey said. "But I'd shore as hell hate to have 'em scatter these herds again, or the remuda. You didn't see anything of them three steers we're a missin', did you?"

"Naw, suh, Mars Hump," Largo said. "But I seed some tracks along de river. Looked like they was six or eight went on down."

"Then we'll find 'em tomorrow," Humphrey said firmly.

\* \* \* \* \* \*

The supper was a huge success. Maisie had outdone herself and had seriously depleted her larder, but she knew that Humphrey wanted her to prepare the most sumptuous meal possible, and she had. The turkeys and other birds that Largo had bagged added an extra special touch.

Shanks came in with the night herders to eat on the first shift, which was unusual for Brandy. He usually ate first so that he could be sure the remuda was well situated for the night. Shanks felt that he needed to explain.

"Mars Brandy, he tole me to come eat first tonight, Mars Hump," he told Humphrey almost fearfully. "Said he wanted to eat with the last shift so he could see a friend of his'n."

"That's all right, Shanks," Humphrey assured him. "We got plenty of company a comin' tonight."

The men from both crews who were going on the first night shift lined up, and Ellie served each plate with extra large helpings. All the cowboys ate voraciously and bragged extravagantly on the food. When they had finished, they took an extra cup of coffee, and threw their tin plates and other eating utensils in the wreck pan, which was boiling merrily over the fire. They finished their extra cup of coffee quickly and tossed their cups after their plates. Ellie and Liza stirred the water which had been made sudsy with lye soap and then fished the eating gear out, rinsed it in another pot of cold water, and placed it on the chuckwagon table lid. Thus, they were ready for the next shift when they started coming in.

It was almost sundown when the second shift had lined up and was being served. Clem and Skeet were the last in line. Humphrey had not eaten and was wondering where Brandy was when he saw Skeet look toward his own camp as a surprised grin split his face. Humphrey followed his gaze to see Brandy and a long, gaunt older man who seemed to have difficulty walking as they approached. As they came near the fire, Brandy took the old man gently by the arm and guided him toward Humphrey.

"Mister Humphrey," Brandy said formally, "this is Mister Cook."

Humphrey stuck out his hand, and the tall, gaunt man met it with a firm grasp. "Name's Taylor," the man said. "Told this here button that my name was cook, 'cause that's what I do for the Butler crew." He ruffled Brandy's hair with a gnarled hand.

"Well, Mr. Taylor," Humphrey said sincerely, "we're mighty glad you could come over and eat with us."

"So am I," Taylor replied. "I know why them lyin' cowboys been swappin' chuckwagons to eat, and I don't blame 'em. Said it was because they'd been braggin' on my cookin'—but they was lyin'."

The old fellow's grin was contagious; both Clem and Skeet smiled, and the cowboys, too, smiled and whispered. Humphrey returned Taylor's grin.

"Well, anyway, we're shore glad to have you, Mr. Taylor."

"Call me Cookie," Taylor said. "I ain't much on long-handled names, myself. And I reckon you're Hump."

"That's right," Humphrey said jovially.

"Well, I'm shore glad to be here, too," Cookie said as he sniffed the aroma emanating from the cooking fire. "I'm jist as hungry for some good grub as them damn, crazy cowboys that was afeared I'd quit if I thought they didn't like my cookin'. Hell, I don't like it my own self. But I ain't always been a cook—been up the trail a few times myself till I got too stove up to ride!"

The cook's salty remarks brought gleeful comments from the cowboys. Skeet and Clem both laughed loudly.

"Come on, Cookie," Skeet insisted. "You get in line ahead of me and Clem. You, too, Brandy."

Humphrey motioned to them, and they lined up in front of Skeet and Clem. As Ellie was filling their plates, Skeet whispered to Clem, "You know, I may not be as smart as I thought I was."

"That's for damn shore," Clem grinned, and then their plates, too, were filled.

A full moon eased quietly into the sky as the sun set and the cowboys finished their supper and filled coffee cups to sit around the cooking fire. Tall tales were bandied about, mostly having to do with horses or men they had known.

"I'd shore like to meet that partner of yours, Hump," one of the young ex-Rangers said. "I've heard some mighty tall tales about him. I reckon they can't all be true, but if only half of 'em is, then he must be a special sort of man that ain't got any equal with a pistol."

"You can believe all you've heard," Humphrey said brusquely. "And I expect you ain't heard all of 'em, either. I doubt if any other man in the world can handle firearms like him."

"Hey!" Clem sought to turn the conversation. "Tiny, why don't you whip us out a tune on that there mouth organ of yours!"

"Glad to," Tiny said and removed the instrument from his pocket, hit it a couple of times on the palm of his hand, and began to play the sad and lonely songs of the range.

As Tiny played, the moon rose higher in the sky, and the wolves began their mournful accompaniment to the music.

A lone Indian rode slowly to the top of a nearby hill where he could look down upon the camp. His horse showed every sign of near exhaustion, and the Indian's back was covered with dried blood from a suppurating bullet wound high on his shoulder.

The Indian sat for several minutes and surveyed the scene before him. The night was still, and he could hear Tiny's harmonica and the howl of the wolves. Finally, he turned his horse and rode slowly southward. His shoulders slumped.

The Beatenbow jackass peered from his hiding place behind a bush and watched with his long ears pointed inquisitively as the Indian disappeared.

# Chapter 13

The HF herd started grazing slowly northward early the next morning. Skeet said that he was going to hold the Butler herd for a couple of days on the good grass on the east side of the river.

"Give 'em a chance to put a little taller on that they lost in the mixup," he explained. "Besides, we are not in a big hurry, and it'll put some distance between our herds."

"That's a good idee," Clem agreed. "An' I shore do hope ours don't run back this a way no more."

"Likely they won't," Skeet said. "We're not too far from Abilene now, and your cattle are pretty tired. Tell Alf not to rope no more coons, though."

"I'll see to that!" Humphrey declared.

"Well," Clem said, "I reckon I'd best be scoutin' out ahead for a few miles to see if I can find a good camp spot and be shore there ain't no hostiles up ahead."

With that Clem turned his horse to circle around the herd and go ahead of it. He had gone only a short distance when he pulled up and turned back to face Skeet and Humphrey.

"Skeet. . ." Clem began uncertainly. He had had little practice in what he wanted to do. "Skeet—I jus' wanted to say—oh, hell—much obliged!"

He turned and loped his horse away.

"Old Clem has some trouble a talkin' sometimes, don't he!" Skeet grinned.

Humphrey nodded. "He does, for a fact. But he's a mighty good cowman."

"One of the best," Skeet said. "I've got a hunch that he's got a lot of country and maybe some bad memories behind 'im."

"I expect you're right, Skeet," Humphrey said. "Don't know anything about his past except that he was in the war. He joined us when we were in Fort Worth a headin' west."

"Well, you're lucky to have 'im!"

"I shore agree with that," Humphrey said brusquely. "And I reckon we're mighty lucky that it was your herd that we run into, too!" With that, Humphrey stuck out his hand. Skeet grinned as he and Humphrey shook; then they both turned their horses and rode to their own herds.

Clem rode several miles ahead of the herd, as he usually did, and found several small streams that ran into the Arkansas River from the west, but he wanted to put as much distance between the herds that day as possible; so he passed up three likely looking campsites and found another that was a bit far for a day's drive, but decided to use it. He turned and rode back toward the herd. A couple of hours later, he rode to the top of a hill and could see the herd strung out for almost a mile. He waved his hat and was quickly answered by a wave from one of the point men. He turned his horse and started back toward the campsite he had chosen. As he rode, he kept feeling that something was not quite the same with the herd. He stopped his horse and wrinkled his brow in concentration. Then he rode to the top of the hill again. He counted several times to make certain. There were only twelve men with the herd—there should have been fourteen.

"Now, what the hell!" he growled, but rode on toward the spot he had chosen for the night. The stream was good, clear water, and a large meadow was lush with tall grass. It would be a good place to stop.

The camp was a good one, and the steers were tired from a long drive that day. They grazed for a shorter time than usual and bedded down early. The men who were to take the first night shift had eaten and were finishing a last cup of coffee. Clem, who had been making a last check of the herd and counting the men, rode to the chuckwagon. A quick survey told him that Largo and Tonio were missing.

He addressed Humphrey, who, still nursing his sore leg, was seated on a bedroll with his back against a wagon wheel. "Hump, where the hell is Largo and Tonio?"

"I sent 'em back to find the three steers that are missin'."

"You what?" Clem was incredulous.

"Largo said he saw cattle tracks goin' south when I sent 'im out to hunt for game for supper last night. I figger maybe three of 'em were ours."

"That's the damnedest thing I ever heard of!" Clem exploded. "A few head of steers more or less ain't gonna make a hell of a lot of difference."

"Makes a difference to me," Humphrey said equably. "I give my word to Colonel Hitt that I'd deliver Joe McCoy 3100 head of steers, and I aim to do it."

"Well, hell, Hump!" Clem was almost pleading. "Hitt and McCoy won't hold you to the exact number. No man would."

"Just the same," Humphrey said grimly. "I give 'im my word, and a man that don't keep his word ain't no man a'tall."

"But, you're riskin' the lives of two men," Clem argued reasonably. His attitude had inexplicably but noticeably mellowed toward Negroes since they had done such a good job separating the herd, and Skeet's high regard for them as cowboys. "Nobody would expect you to do that."

"I would," Humphrey said firmly. "Besides, Largo ain't no pilgrim. You remember he rode all the way from Mulberry Creek in Texas to Taos to tell Kit Carson that it was our herd a comin' so's the Indians wouldn't bother us. He damn near killed my stud a runnin' from Indians that chased 'im a few times. And Tonio can track a fish through water and talks a dozen Indian lingoes. So I figger it ain't so big a risk as might be."

"We've still got them cows and their calves that I throwed into the herd a thinkin' they might help out if we had a stampede—not that it done a damn bit of good. But I figger they ort to make up for three or four steers," Clem said in the forlorn hope of persuading Humphrey.

"Well, cows ain't steers!" Humphrey said. "Besides, we ain't far from Abilene."

Clem started to make a biting reply but stopped himself short, clamped his jaws, shook his head hopelessly, and rode back to the herd.

\* \* \* \* \* \*

Three days later, just after they had stopped for the night, Largo and Tonio returned. They were gaunt from lack of sleep and exhaustion, but in front of them were six steers that seemed to be in worse shape than they were. The steers managed a tired trot as they entered the grazing herd.

When Clem saw them his jaw dropped in astonishment. Word quickly spread to all the men.

Largo and Tonio, realizing their responsibility had ended when the strays entered the herd, rode straight for the chuckwagon where Brandy had a good fire going. Humphrey was sitting on a bedroll as they approached.

"Found 'em, huh?" he greeted Largo. "Figgered you would."

"Yassuh, Mars Hump." Largo managed a tired grin. "We finds 'em all right. An' three more 'sides. Didn't figger it was no use to leave 'em for the Indians; so we brought them, too."

"Where in hell did you find 'em?" It was Clem who had ridden up.

"Quite a ways on south of where we was," Largo said. "Dey had left de river and was travelin' on some mighty rocky ground and flat country when we come up to 'em."

"Don't see how the hell you found 'em if they left the river," Clem said doggedly.

Largo said, "Tonio, he track 'em. He say some of 'em is ours when he see de tracks."

"How could he do that?"

"Oh, Senor Clem," Tonio said nonchalantly, "I see one track with a short front toe. I'd seen it before; so I know he ess ours."

"You mean you recognized the track of one of our steers?" Clem was disbelieving.

"Si. I know the tracks of many of our steers. Not all—but many. The track to Tonio ess like the brand to you."

"Well, I'll be damned!" Clem's amazement was almost ludicrous.

"Told you they'd bring 'em back," Humphrey said matter-of-factly. "What I sent 'em out to do."

Clem stared at Humphrey for a moment and then at Tonio and Largo. Without a word, he turned his horse and rode away.

"Hope you boys didn't run too much taller off them steers," Humphrey said grumpily. "What was the brand of them three extrys that you brought in?"

"Tonio say two of 'em is wearin' a turkey track brand, and the other one, he ain't got no brand," Largo answered.

"He got a track that shows a wore down heel on the left back foot," Tonio said.

"Well, that ain't no brand! But anyways, you boys done a good job. Figgered you would."

Largo smiled at the great compliment, as did Tonio.

"De nada," Tonio shrugged.

"I guess you boys could use some coffee and a bite of grub, too."

"We sho could, Mars Hump," Largo agreed. "We ain't et in two days."

Humphrey started to call Maisie, but as he turned his head to summon her, he saw her standing only a few feet away. Her dark face glowed with pride as she looked at Largo.

"Maisie," Humphrey directed, "bring Largo and Tonio a cup of coffee and fix 'em up a big batch of grub."

"I sho do dat, Mars Hump," she said. Then she spoke softly to Largo. "I's glad yo is back, Largo."

"I's glad to be back, Maisie," Largo said.

"Git that coffee fixed, Maisie," Humphrey said gruffly. "These men are hungry."

As Largo and Tonio were eating, Brandy came from behind the chuckwagon. "I'm glad you are back, too, Mister Largo, and you too, Mister Tonio." His young voice expressed the sincerity felt by all.

\* \* \* \* \* \*

When Clem came in to eat after the first night shift had taken over the herd, he announced that he had seen a nester when he had scouted ahead that morning.

"Feller named Hersey. Said he had a pretty fair crop an' a few cattle," Clem said. "But the Indians raided 'im and ruined his crop, burned his shack, and run his cattle off, but him and his wife and kids got away, and now he's lookin' for his cows. He hasn't found any, but he said that Abilene is only about three days' drive on up the river—four at most."

The announcement was greeted with enthusiastic yells from the cowboys, followed by bawdy exclamations of what they were going to do when they got there.

"Jus' remember what Matt Jimson said about that tough marshall they got," Humphrey warned. "And there was talk that he wasn't gonna allow no guns to be carried in town."

"Well, that marshall don't bother me none," Swifty bragged. "And they ain't no man gonna take my guns offen me—marshall or not!"

"Hear he ain't much for gun play." Humphrey looked sternly at Swifty. "But he's mighty tough with his fists. Name's Tom Smith. Maybe you ort to remember that, Swifty."

"Hah!" Swifty snorted disdainfully.

\* \* \* \* \* \*

The next day the drive took on new life. The steers, after a good night's rest, grazed faster than usual, and the cowboys laughed and jested. Some of them swore they could smell whiskey fumes on the light breeze wafting gently from the north.

They covered fourteen miles that day, which was farther than usual. Clem, as was his custom, rode out to scout ahead and had found an excellent camping spot. That night the riders were still excited and talked enthusiastically of their imminent arrival at the western cattle metropolis.

Humphrey was non-communicative, and Clem was characteristically gloomy.

"We ain't there yet," Clem cautioned. "An' we're jus' damn lucky we didn't have to cross the Wichita River and Deer Creek, an' a lot of streams like Skeet's herd had to do, but we still got a few to cross. Cow Skin Creek and the Ninnescah River could still be bad."

But nothing could dampen the spirits of the lusty cowboys. Many of them, though in their bedrolls, were still awake and dreaming of the end of their grand adventure when it was time for them to take their night shift.

Clem rode out earlier than usual the next day. He had chosen his biggest and best horse to ride. He did not return until late. Humphrey had stopped the herd and set up camp for the night.

Clem was obviously tired when he rode into camp. He unsaddled and turned his exhausted horse into the remuda before he strode to the campfire. He took a cup of coffee from Maisie without a word. The cowboys looked at him expectantly, but none dared question him, for they knew his snappish disposition, especially when he was tired. Humphrey finally broke the silence.

"How'd it go, Clem?"

"All right," Clem said after taking another swig of coffee. "I rode all the way into Abilene."

There was an excited murmur among the cowboys.

"How far?" Humphrey asked.

"Couple of days. Short drives, at that. I saw Joe McCoy. He said to tell you he would meet us tomorrow at a little creek about five miles south of town."

"Good!" Humphrey said appreciatively. "Did you tell 'im we had 3100 head of steers?"

"Yeah!" Clem replied almost bitterly. "An' I told 'im we had three or four extry steers, and a few cows and calves."

"How big is Abilene?" an excited cowboy asked eagerly. "Any saloons?"

"It ain't no metropolis," Clem answered shortly. "Anyways, you'll see it in a couple of days."

"What time will Joe be there?" Humphrey asked.

"Said he'd be waitin' at the creek. There's a good campsite there."

\* \* \* \* \* \*

The cowboys urged the steers to graze a bit faster the next day, and true to his word, Joe McCoy and Colonel Hitt were waiting. They exchanged warm greeting with Humphrey.

"Well, you're a man of your word, Hump," McCoy observed.

"I aim to be," Humphrey said firmly. "How's the cattle market?"

"Good," McCoy replied. "There are buyers from four states in Abilene. My advice is to veer your herd a bit to the west and camp on Mud Creek tomorrow night. I'll bring the buyers out the next day and let them bid on your herd."

The cowboys fired a cacophony of questions at McCoy.

"Now hold up, men!" admonished Humphrey. "Me and Joe has some talkin' to do, and you'll git to ask 'im all the questions you want to at supper tonight."

\* \* \* \* \* \*

Being so near Abilene, Clem felt relatively safe in assigning a minimum guard for the first night shift, for he knew that all the men were anxious to question Joe McCoy about Abilene. The cowboys waited until the most important function, supper, was over and then gathered around the fire with their coffee cups.

"How big is it?" one cowboy asked excitedly.

"Well," McCoy said, "it isn't any Kansas City yet, but you won't have any trouble finding entertainment. I've just finished a three-story hotel. I call it 'Drovers' Cottage.' It's got a bar, card tables, a pool hall, and a place to eat."

"Whoopee!" one exhilarated cowboy yelled.

"What about women?" Dutch Horst demanded.

"Figured you might want to know," smiled McCoy. "The women are all on Texas Street. They got several houses there, and the women are available and willing, if you've got the price."

"Oh, boy! I know where most of my money is goin'," a young cowboy said.

"Well, you'll have plenty of choice," McCoy said. "There is every kind there—old, young, white, red, Mexican. Even got one Chink girl and one black."

A cowboy rubbed his palms and grinned in anticipation.

"The card games straight?"

"I can't vouch for that," McCoy said after a pause. "But Tom Smith, he's our marshall, sure does try to keep them that way."

"Well, if they are straight, I figure to own Abilene in about a week."

"Any permanent settlers there, Mr. McCoy?" It was Tiny's musical voice.

"Some," McCoy said. "More than you'd expect, I imagine. And we've even got a Baptist church."

"We heard about that. Sure sounds like a growin' town."

"It is," McCoy agreed. "But most of the entertainment that you boys are looking for is on Texas Street and south of it."

"Why is that?" Humphrey asked curiously.

"Well." McCoy hesitated. He seemed reluctant to explain. "Dan Waggoner and W. M. Childress drove the first herds up last year right after we got the Kansas Pacific and the shipping pens built. And Jim Ellison and J. L. McCaleb have already brought in herds this year. So have J. J. Myers and Ad McGehee. Bill Butler ought to be here in a few days."

"Bill Butler's herd will," Clem chimed in. "We run into his outfit a ways back." He did not realize the ambiguity of his statement.

"Well," McCoy continued doggedly, "after a long trail drive, the boys all seem to like to blow off a lot of steam, and there are plenty of places to do it. There's plenty of whore houses. Then, there's the Alamo, the Bull's Head, The Peach, and the Old Fruit. They're all saloons and gambling halls. The Alamo is on Texas Street."

"It damn well ort to be!"

"Anyway, they've all got bad-sounding pianos, and a few have guitar and fiddle players, and all of 'em have girls for any purpose, day and night. So Tom Smith—he's our marshall—figured it'd be best to keep the drovers south or on Texas Street."

"Marshall, hell!" Swifty cut in. "He ain't gonna keep me from goin' where I want!"

"I don't know!" McCoy shook his head dubiously. "He's a mighty tough Irishman, used to be a New York cop. And he was in the Bear Creek, Wyoming fracas. He's a pretty tough lawman!"

"Sounds like a mighty good town to me!" another cowboy chimed in.

"Now, I hope you don't think Abilene is all saloons and whore houses." Colonel Hitt spoke for the first time. "We've got a church and a school house. And we've got a bank, a post office, and a deed office, too. And there's a blacksmith shop and. . ."

"I think you've told us enough," Humphrey interposed. "We'll push the cattle a little west of town to Mud Creek, like you said. And we'll expect you out with some buyers the day after we get there."

"You're not havin' much Indian trouble now, are you?" Clem wanted to know.

"Some," admitted McCoy, "but not a lot. A bunch of Cheyennes raided a nester, name of Hersey, out west of town a few days ago. Ruined his crops, burned his house, and run off his cattle, but he didn't have much to begin with. He saved his wife and kids. I expect you have heard that Sherman has ordered Sheridan to drive all the Indians out of Kansas or kill 'em! And the soldiers are sure trying to carry out his orders. And then General Custer attacked a village of Cheyennes down in Oklahoma a few days ago and killed 'em all, including Black Kettle!"

"Killed 'em all?"

"Well, I did hear that he took a good-looking Cheyenne girl along with him for company on the way back. But, as many men as you have, I don't think Indians will bother you any."

Clem clamped his jaw rigidly when McCoy told of the Black Kettle massacre.

"Tell you what, Hump," McCoy said, "why don't you saddle up and go into town with me tonight. I've got an extra room in my hotel. We can have a drink and a late supper, and I'll introduce you to the buyers. And we'll all go out to your herd when they get to Mud Creek."

Humphrey hesitated. He'd had a lot of trail chow! His leg was still sore. But he declined. "We got to count the cattle when we get to Mud Creek," he said.

Clem did not look up, nor did he look after McCoy and Hitt as they rode away. He stared vacantly into the campfire for a few minutes and then threw his coffee cup as hard as he could into the flames.

"That son-of-a-bitch!"

"Who?" Tiny's voice was startled.

"That damned Custer!" Clem said viciously. "I saw that fancy blond-headed bastard onct during the war. Had a good head drawed on 'im, too. But somebody shot his horse out from under 'im jus' as I pulled the trigger, and I plain damn missed 'im!"

"Wish you hadn't!" a cowboy veteran of the war said sincerely.

"So do I!" Clem said raspingly. "An' if I ever get another shot at the struttin' murderin' bastard, I won't miss—war or not!"

# CHAPTER 14

The camp on Mud Creek was not ideal, for the grass was shorter where other herds had been held; but it was adequate, and the steers were fat.

"It ain't the best camp we ever had," Clem said sourly, "but anyway, the water is good."

"And it's close to town!" one of the cowboys enthused.

Humphrey nodded his head to Clem, indicating that he wanted to talk to him privately. They walked a few yards from the chuckwagon and stopped under the shade of a cottonwood.

"Clem," Humphrey began a bit hesitantly, "you're in charge of this drive, and you've done a mighty good job of it, but I wonder if you'd do me a favor?"

Clem looked at Humphrey suspiciously. "Will if I can."

"Would you mind tellin' all the hands to stay in camp tonight? Let all of 'em ride night herd! We've got the cattle this far, and I shore don't want to lose any of 'em now. Besides, we've got to get a good count of 'em before McCoy gets out here with them buyers tomorrow."

A muscle jerked in Clem's jaws as he clamped them tight. Humphrey's determination to deliver 3100 steers to McCoy, as he had promised Hitt he would, seemed downright ridiculous to Clem. Nobody was going to haggle over a few steers, more or less.

"All right, Hump," he said with resignation. "I'll try to give all the men jobs that will keep 'em out of town tonight—but it won't be easy for 'em. It's been a long drive, and Abilene is only about a mile away."

"I know it is," Humphrey said apologetically, "but I'll close the deal tomorrow, if I can. And then pay the men off, and they can tear up Abilene for all I care—except for the loadin' pens and them Fairbanks scales McCoy says they got," Humphrey finished with what he considered a bit of humor. "Besides, we're gonna need all of 'em for the count in the mornin'."

"All right, Hump," Clem agreed. "But the longer you hold 'em out of town, the wilder they're gonna be when they get there."

\* \* \* \* \* \*

Clem assigned all fourteen cowboys to herding that night, seven of them circling the herd one direction and seven in the other.

"An' I don't want even a jackrabbit into or out of that herd tonight," Clem said grimly.

Most of the cowboys expressed their disapproval in emphatic and profane terms. Never before on the drive had all the hands ridden night herd at one time except in the stormiest weather. But Tiny only smiled slightly, for he recognized the strategy. Largo did not even change expression, for Mars Hump, he knew, had given the order. Brandy and Shanks were with the remuda, and it made no difference to them, for they had not planned to go into town anyway.

The whistle of a whippoorwill came from the woods along Mud Creek as the cattle began to sink to their knees for a night's rest. From the distant hills, coyotes and wolves sent their mournful yowls up to the half-moon that shone down on the bedded steers chewing their cuds contentedly. The mass of longhorns shining in the pale moonlight was an awesome sight. The bray of the illusive jackass only added to the eerie mystique of the night.

As the last of the grumbling cowboys left the campfire to discharge their assigned duties for the night, Clem grinned maliciously and retired to his bedroll to get his first night of uninterrupted sleep since the drive began, for he knew that the herd was secure.

About midnight the steers rose slowly, stretched and yawned, some even browsed a bit, and then lay down again.

\* \* \* \* \* \*

As the herd began to rise the next morning, the sleepy cowboys loosened the circle they had been riding, but did not move the cattle in any direction. As the cattle began to graze, Clem rode out and gave the order for half the men to go to breakfast and then come back and relieve the others. A quick check told him that one cowboy was missing.

"Where the hell is Swifty?" he demanded, but got no reply until he addressed Tiny directly. "Where is he, Tiny?" Clem asked savagely.

"I'm not sure, Clem." Tiny's voice was soft, but tinged with weariness. It had been a long night. "We were riding in different directions around the herd. I passed him several times before midnight, but not later."

"That swaggerin' son-of-a-bitch!" Clem exploded. "He rode into town—that's what! An' he's damn shore gonna get his wages cut, too. In fact, he may not even get any wages!"

None of the men responded, and Clem instructed them on their assigned jobs while counting the steers.

"You men squeeze them steers between me and Tonio," Clem said. "An' do it slow. This is our last count, and it damn well better be right."

Humphrey heard Clem's order and nodded his approval.

The count went smoothly, and when the last steer had passed between Clem and Tonio, they compared notes. Clem had tied a knot in his piggin' string as each one hundred passed, and Tonio had shifted a handful of small stones from one hand to the other. They agreed that there were 3104 steers, 10 cows, and 5 calves.

"That tallies," Clem said with satisfaction. "We left with 3100 steers, 10 cows, and 11 calves. We picked up that old bull on the Canadian that we cut, and Tonio and Largo brought in three extra steers when Hump sent 'em back down the Arkansas to find them three that we was missin'. We still got the ten cows we started out with, hail killed one calf, and we butchered five. So that tallies out—which is damn near a miracle!"

Humphrey nodded his satisfaction, but said nothing.

McCoy and John T. Alexander, who was reputed to be the biggest cattle buyer in the world, appeared almost as soon as the count was completed. Humphrey told them the count.

"There's three extra steers in there that I'd like to sell if you can use 'em," Humphrey said to Alexander.

"I'm sure that the three extras will be fine," Alexander said. "A few, more or less, won't make any difference, if we can make a deal."

"Does to me," Humphrey said.

"Thought you said there was four extra steers?" McCoy queried.

"There is," Humphrey said. "But only three of 'em is wearin' brands. I'll sell 'em and send the money to their owners, or take it to 'em—or their families. Their brands are almost shore to be registered in Wise County."

"What about the extra steer and the cows and calves?" Alexander asked.

"I got another plan for them." Humphrey did not elaborate.

The buyer rode slowly among the steers as Humphrey, Clem and McCoy watched from a short distance away.

"Give 'im a chance to look without nobody a botherin' 'im," Clem said.

"Well," McCoy said, "you ought to get a good price on 'em, Hump. They are fatter than most herds that have come up."

"Where does that farmer live that got his place burned by Indians and the cattle run off?" Humphrey asked McCoy abruptly.

"You mean the one that I was telling you about? Hersey?"

"That's the one," Humphrey said. "Clem met up with 'im when he was lookin' for some of his cattle on the Arkansas down south a ways."

"He doesn't live far from here," McCoy said, puzzled. "About five miles almost due west. He's dug himself a sort of cave out there and covered it with brush and sod and moved his family back out there. Why?"

"Clem," Humphrey did not answer McCoy's question directly, "have two or three of the boys cut out them cows and calves and that one steer that hasn't got a brand and drive 'em out there."

"What!" Clem almost yelped, and McCoy looked at Humphrey in astonishment.

"Drive 'em out there," Humphrey repeated, "and leave 'em."

"I'll be damned!" Clem said. "What do you want the boys to tell 'im?"

"Tell 'im—oh, hell, I don't know. Jus' tell 'im that we found some extry cattle and figgered they might be his."

"What about the HF brands on them cows?"

"Tell 'im to put his own brand on 'em," Humphrey said. "And tell 'im if a HF cowboy ever stops by for 'im to give 'im a good feed."

Clem rode away mumbling to himself. "I shore as hell can't figger Hump out. Doubt if he can figger himself out!"

"Well, Hump," McCoy said sincerely, "that was a mighty fine thing to do. It'll sure help him get started again. You're a real Texan!"

"Not yet, I ain't, not yet!" Humphrey replied. "But I'm workin' on it. My partner, Finch, is a real Texan—roots as deep as a mesquite tree."

"Well," McCoy said jocularly, "I think you'll do until a real one comes along."

"Here comes that buyer." Humphrey was anxious to change the subject.

As the buyer rode up to Humphrey and McCoy, they all talked for a few minutes. Then Humphrey waved for Clem to join them.

"Clem," Humphrey said, "I reckon we're about ready to close the deal. This feller has offered a fair price, and I aim to take it. You come with us, and we'll ride into town and close the deal."

"You won't need me," Clem objected.

"I might," Humphrey said. "You tell ever one of them cowboys to stay with the herd till we come back, and then you come on into town with us."

\* \* \* \* \* \*

Humphrey, Clem, McCoy and the cattle buyer went to the palatial Alamo Saloon to finalize the deal. Humphrey declined to sell the remuda, which was unusual, for most of the men who trailed cattle to Abilene also sold all their horses except the ones they would ride back.

"Horses are too hard to come by out in our country," Humphrey explained. "Have to catch and break mustangs mostly."

"Well, I saw some pretty good quarterhorses in your remuda and some fine mules."

"Yeah, we've got a few. And I've got some good thoroughbred mares and a good stud and jack; so maybe we'll have more. But right now we need all we have."

"Hump," Clem said when they had finished talking and had ordered a drink to seal the deal. "You fellers don't need me here. I'd like to look the town over a mite while you all are doin' your business."

"I got a job for you, Clem," Humphrey said.

"How's that?"

"I want you to find Swifty and pay 'im off and tell 'im not to come back to camp." Humphrey dug in his pocket and pulled out some gold coins.

"He's ridin' a HF horse," Clem protested. "At least, he was last night, and I reckon he rode it into town."

"All right. Let 'im have his saddle, and you take his horse out to the edge of town. The horse will go back to our remuda."

"All right, Hump," Clem agreed. "But I'm a fixin' to short 'im one day's wages, and we ort not to pay 'im at all."

"Do what you want, Clem," Humphrey said. "When you've fired 'im, come back here. We ort to be through by then."

Clem left the saloon with long, determined strides. While he was gone, the men discussed the method of payment for the herd. McCoy suggested that Humphrey take enough in gold to pay the hands and provide the necessary supplies to run the ranch for a year, and to take the rest in a draft drawn on Donald Lawson and Co. of New York City.

"I want it all in gold," Humphrey said firmly.

"But, Hump," McCoy said reasonably, "those drafts are as good as gold, and you would be taking a big chance carrying gold back through Indian country. You'll be back again next year, and things will be a lot more settled by then. Besides, the Younger and James boys are still on the loose."

The buyer said nothing but looked at Humphrey in surprise. They could not accept the fact that a man would carry that much gold into Indian and outlaw country.

"I'll take my chances," Humphrey said. "I don't doubt that the drafts are good, but I want it in gold. That's the way we did business on our plantation back in Louisiana, and I reckon it's a good enough way for me to business out here."

While the buyer and McCoy were trying to dissuade the adamant Humphrey, Clem burst through the saloon doors and strode up to the table where they were sitting.

"Find Swifty?" Humphrey asked.

"I found 'im!" Clem said savagely. "But the swaggerin' bastard run into that town marshall, Tom Smith, last night, and I reckon Swifty wasn't as swift with them two guns of his as he's been tryin' to make us think he was."

"Did Tom kill him?" McCoy asked quickly.

"Naw!" Clem said. "Jus' busted hell out of his jaw. The doc has got 'im over in a shack that they call a hospital. Says he's gonna have to send 'im to Kansas City to get his jaw fixed up proper."

"Did you give 'im his pay?" Humphrey asked.

"Left it with the doc," Clem said. "Swifty, he was still dead to the world. That marshall shore must pack a hell of a punch. Swifty's jaw was so whop-sided, his teeth didn't even meet."

Clem had hardly finished speaking when a man wearing a badge came through the bat wing doors and quickly stepped to one side. As his eyes adjusted to the dim light, he spied the men sitting at the table and started walking toward them.

"That's Tom Smith," McCoy said almost urgently.

The marshall strode to their table. He was almost six feet tall and lithe and muscular.

"Did one of you fellers come in with a herd yesterday?"

"I did," Humphrey said.

"Then, I reckon it's your man that I had a little run-in with last night."

McCoy quickly introduced Humphrey and the marshall. Both men nodded, but neither proffered his hand.

"What happened?" Humphrey asked.

"Nothing much," Smith said. "Your man was raisin' hell, and I told him that he'd be welcome in Abilene so long as he stayed south of Texas Street."

"Then what?"

"He said that no damn lawman was gonna tell him where he could or couldn't go, and he went for his guns. He was wearing two of 'em."

"I reckon we know the rest of it," Humphrey said. "I'll pay whatever fine you put on 'im. He was workin' for me until Clem here paid 'im off a few minutes ago. So I'll make good any damages he done."

"He didn't do any damage," Smith said. "Just shot off his pistols a few times, and we haven't passed any law against that yet."

"Sit down, Tom," McCoy urged. "Maybe you can help us talk Beatenbow out of trying to take his herd money in gold and carrying it back to his ranch through Indian and outlaw country."

Tom Smith looked at Humphrey keenly and then pulled up a chair.

"I'll be gettin' back to the herd," Clem said, but no one heard him or paid any attention as he left.

"Where is your ranch, Mr. Beatenbow?" Smith asked.

"On the Canadian River out in west Texas," Humphrey answered. "Not far from the New Mexico line."

"You wouldn't be one of the men that Kit Carson talked the Indians into letting you run cattle on their land, would you?"

"My partner and me," Humphrey answered.

"Is your partner named Fauntleroy Finch, by any chance?"

"He is," Humphrey said. "Fact is, it was him that Carson made the deal with the Indians for. They had Rangered together some."

"I've heard of him," Smith said. "And from what I hear, I hope that if I ever meet him, it will be on friendly terms."

"Likely will be," Humphrey replied. "Finch shore ain't one to hunt trouble. And we met a friend of his on the trail, a feller name of Matt Jimson. He was in charge of a detachment of Rangers that helped us out when a bunch of herd cutters stopped us. Fact is, I've got a whole bunch of rifles and pistols in the wagon that Matt said to turn over to you."

The marshall grinned with pleasure at the name of Matt. "How is Matt?" he asked eagerly.

"Tom," McCoy broke in; he didn't want a change in subject of discussion, "don't you agree that it would be foolish to try to take all that gold back with him, with the Indians raising hell and the Younger and James boys still on the loose?"

"Foolish or not," Humphrey replied firmly, "I want my pay in gold. And you needn't worry— I'll get it back to the ranch."

Smith's steely gray eyes looked into Humphrey's brown flecked ones and his hawklike face. Humphrey looked back at him; their eyes met and held for several seconds. The two men seemed to recognize in each other a kindred spirit.

"I expect Mr. Beatenbow will get his gold home all right, Joe," Smith said, and a wisp of a smile touched his eyes.

"All right!" McCoy threw up his hands in defeat. "I've got enough gold in my safe over at the bank. I'll take the drafts, and Hump can have his gold."

"One other thing," Humphrey said, "I want to sell the cattle range delivery. My boys have had a long, hard trip, and they're ready to come to town."

"That can easily be arranged," Alexander said. "There are enough broke cowboys in town that I can have enough men out there in a couple of hours to take over the herd."

"I'll have my men paid off and ready to turn the herd over to you," Humphrey said in a tone that indicated the deal was done. "Let's go."

With that, the men rose from their chairs. Humphrey and Smith simultaneously thrust out their hands.

"Sorry I had to rough up one of your men, Beatenbow."

"You done what you had to do, Marshall. Besides, he ain't a HF man no more. We fired 'im."

\* \* \* \* \* \*

Humphrey, McCoy and the cattle buyer went to the bank where McCoy opened the huge safe to exhibit an enormous pile of double eagles. He took a draft drawn on Donald Lawson and Co. of New York and signed by Alexander.

"All right, Hump," McCoy said, "we'll count out your herd money. How are you going to carry it? It's going to weigh a ton!"

"I'll jus' take enough with me to pay the hands right now, and I'll send a wagon in for the rest when I'm ready to leave."

"All right," McCoy agreed. "I'll give you a receipt for what you leave in the safe."

"No need," Humphrey said. "We both know how much it is, and you'll have to open the safe when I bring a wagon in for it anyway."

McCoy and Alexander looked at Humphrey in surprise, but said nothing. Both assumed, correctly, that Humphrey Beatenbow would get all the money that was coming to him.

\* \* \* \* \* \*

Two hours later Humphrey had paid off all hands and had added enough for a couple of drinks each. The crew that Alexander had hired to take over the cattle arrived, and the HF cowboys headed for town.

\* \* \* \* \* \*

An old timer years later described the entry of the HF cowboys as a cyclone coming from straight west. They were yelling, shooting, and riding abreast down Texas Street. When they came to the end, they wheeled their horses and rode back again. People raced from the saloons and stores to watch as the apparently wild and savage men raced by. Cowboys, who had been in the saloons, were now standing in front; they joined in the yelling and shooting. The few merchants shook their heads. There were no women or children in sight.

When the cowboys reached the end of the street where they had first entered town, their horses were panting, their pistols were empty, and they were ready to taste the flavor of the town. They pulled up in front of Twin Livery Stables and turned their horses over to Ed Gaylord, who owned the new establishment that could care for more than a hundred horses.

Most of the men headed for Seely's store to buy new clothing, and then to the public bath and barber shop. In due time they all emerged wearing new hats, bandannas, and other clothing that was available. Some had even bought new boots. They were a clean and wholesome bunch of young cowboys that descended on the Alamo Saloon to take the first drink after a long dry spell and to try their luck at Monte and Faro. The bartender was waiting, and he had plenty of refreshment cooled by ice cut from the Republican River the winter before. And the first drink was always on the house.

Dutch Horst had not taken time to make himself presentable. He headed straight way south of Texas Street where the prostitutes plied their trade promiscuously in hastily constructed bawdy houses, and some even in crude shacks. Gabby had not lingered either, and he was downing his fourth drink when the rest of the crew entered the Alamo.

"What'll it be, gents?" a cherubic-faced bartender asked genially.

"Just set it on the bar, partner, and we'll drink it all," one of the cowboys yelled as they all set a foot on the brass rail. And we're buying for the house." The cowboys had removed neither hat, guns, nor spurs.

Most of the men in the saloon arose eagerly and joined the HF hands at the bar. The dance hall girls also converged on the cowboys as the brass band, which played night and day in the Alamo, struck up a loud and lively tune.

One of the young HF cowboys, with a drink in his hand and a buxom blonde's arm around his neck, turned to the professional gamblers still sitting at their tables with the bank in its alcove at the opposite end of the hundred-foot building.

"Here's to Texas!" he yelled. "And to the lanky, longhorn bastards that we followed up here to this wonderful place!"

"To hell with Texas!" a big man in flat-heeled boots jeered.

"That's a insult!" an HF cowboy said as he dived at the man.

There ensued a brawl that was the talk of Abilene for weeks. The professional gamblers simply moved their chairs and tables to the periphery of the big room, the dancing girls screamed and yelled, and the bandsmen moved their instruments. They watched as the melee rose to a crescendo. All the cowboys were fighting, and it seemed to make no difference who the adversary was. Luckily, no one pulled a pistol, and the spectators looked on more with amusement than fright.

Suddenly, there was a pistol shot, and the fighting abruptly ceased. Standing just inside the bat wing doors was Tom Smith. Beside him stood Humphrey Beatenbow.

"God-a-mighty!" Humphrey breathed. "What happened?"

"Just a friendly little ruckus," the barkeep grinned as he rose from his hiding place behind the bar. "Nobody got shot. Didn't even bust the place up much."

"I'll stand good for damages," Humphrey said grimly. "Most of 'em was HF men. My name is Humphrey Beatenbow."

"Aw, that's all right, Mr. Beatenbow," the barkeep said. "Just a busted chair or two, and likely they'll buy enough likker to pay for that!" He started setting bottles and glasses on the bar.

The yelling cowboys rushed up and started eagerly to take advantage of the invitation.

Humphrey and the marshall watched as they lined up at the bar. Smith holstered his pistol, and Humphrey shook his head in resignation. They turned and left the saloon together. As they walked down the street, there was a strange similarity about them. Both were broad of back, and although the marshall was a couple of inches taller, no one would have noticed. There was an aura of implacability about them.

# CHAPTER 15

Early the next morning the HF cowboys began to filter out into the bright sun and dusty street. Some were walking unsteadily from the Devil's Half-acre south of Texas Street. Others emerged from the saloons and gambling halls. Most of them were carrying monumental hangovers, some had black eyes and skinned faces, and all of them were considerably lighter in the pocketbook. More than half of the cowboys gathered near the livery stables and were discussing their first night in Abilene.

"What I need," one hungover cowboy said morosely, "is a big batch of them Pecos strawberries and a big slab of beef and about a gallon of the Arbuckle coffee that Brandy grinds up every day."

There was a general agreement among the others. They had had enough of city life for a few hours at least.

As they started toward the livery stable, the sound of a shot came from a saloon. A man, whom they recognized as one of their own, ran through the bat wing doors and jumped on a horse that had been standing hip-shot at a hitching rail in front of the saloon. The last that they saw of him, he was spurring the horse madly, his long hair flying in the wind, and he wore neither hat nor coat. He did not look back as he left Abilene heading south.

The HF cowboys ran the short distance to the saloon and rushed in with guns drawn.

"What happened?" one demanded of the bartender.

"Something a long time overdue," the barkeep said grimly as he nodded at a body on the floor. "That there is—was—Chance Dawes, a crooked gambler. He thought that cowboy was drunk, and he was. But he wasn't too drunk to catch a crooked deal and called 'im on it."

"What happened then?" the cowboy demanded.

"Then Chance, he made another mistake and pulled a derringer on that cowboy and got shot for his trouble."

"Ain't no law agin a man protectin' hisself, is they?" another HF man demanded belligerently.

"Oh, hell, no!" the barkeep said. "And I can swear it was self-defense. So can any of the others in here that saw it." He nodded toward the few men who were still playing cards.

"That's right," one man agreed. "I saw it."

"Tom Smith has been onto Chance for quite a while, I think. He won't do nothin' about it, maybe give that cowboy some more shells."

"That cowboy," an HF man said grimly, "is already two miles out of town and ridin' fast on somebody else's horse and saddle."

"He shore as hell ought not to of done that!" the barkeep exclaimed. "That's horse stealin'!"

All the men rushed outside to see whose horse was missing.

"Hey!" a freckled-faced cowboy yelled. "That was my horse!"

"We'll pay for 'im," the HF cowboys chorused.

"Now wait a minute," the man, obviously a puncher, grinned. "That damn Chance cleaned me a couple of nights ago, and I couldn't catch 'im at it. Besides, I just remembered—I traded my horse and saddle for his horse and saddle just before he left town. Even trade."

The cowboys all looked at him for a moment and then began to laugh. "Well, you may get skinned again. His horse is in the livery stable, and he ain't much. But he's got a good saddle."

"Shore he has," the cowboy agreed. "That saddle was what made me want to trade. We're all even."

The HF men gathered around him, slapped him on the back and shook his hand.

"You'd make a good HF hand!" one of them said enthusiastically.

"Well, you are a man short, I reckon, and I'm lookin' for a job. My outfit left a few days ago. I still had a little money."

There was a general hubbub as the cowboys talked excitedly, until one of them yelled and pointed down the street.

"What the hell is that?"

They all looked down the dusty street and gaped, for approaching was a gaudily-decorated surrey being pulled by a grulla horse. As it neared the group of cowboys, they saw lettering on its side: DR. SHANDOW'S ELIXIR. Below the sign in smaller letters: "guaranteed to cure most of the ills of man—including cholera and frostbite."

The gawking cowboys stood transfixed until the surrey pulled up to them.

"Good morning, my friends." A big, rotund man with a checkered vest, a gaudy watch chain across his bulging belly, and a top hat greeted them cheerily. His eyes were beady, and his small mouth with its fat lips, constantly wet, sent spatters of saliva as he spoke, reminding one of a large fish with a small mouth. The man rose from the surrey seat, removed his hat, and bowed deeply.

"I assume," he said, "that I am addressing cow drivers from down south?"

"You're talkin' to a bunch of damn fools," a disgruntled cowboy with a skinned cheek and dark-rimmed eyes answered.

"Ah, yes!" the drummer replied magnanimously. "I can see that you are somewhat fatigued as a result of plying the long and arduous efforts of your manly trade! And I assure you I have just the thing that will revitalize and renew you, my men!"

He turned his head and yelled down into the surrey. "Copo! Bring us a bottle of that wonderful elixir that we brought, just in case we met some unfortunate soul such as this man."

A big, bald-headed brute of a man hopped out of the surrey and landed on his feet as light as a cat. He was holding a bottle which he handed to the drummer, who had also dismounted. He took the bottle from Copo and turned to the men.

"Gentlemen," he said pompously, "I am Dr. Shandows, and in this bottle is an elixir that is a panacea for all the ills of men. I hope you won't think me unduly braggadoccio when I say that it took me years to develop the precise mixture of this wonderful medicinal miracle."

There was a general mumbling among the cowboys, and one or two started to move away.

"But wait, my friends!" the doctor said loudly. "As proof of my rather grandiose statements, I would like to offer a free bottle to that terribly fatigued young man over there."

He handed the bottle to the dilapidated cowboy with the skinned cheek. The cowboy hesitated a moment, then said, "What the hell! I can't feel no worse that I do now!" He uncorked the bottle and took a long drink. He removed the bottle from his mouth, coughed a couple of times, and raised the bottle again. When he removed it again, he held it up and looked at it appreciatively. "Damned if I don't think we got something here. This stuff would make a man kick a polecat!"

The rest of the cowboys surged forward eagerly, but were blocked from the surrey by the huge Copo.

"Now, just be patient, men," the doctor advised. "I can see that you are all weary and trail worn. But there is enough for all! Of course, there must be a slight charge, which I assure you, is much less than it costs me to bring it to you."

The cowboys immediately started digging in their pockets. The few who were completely broke borrowed from their buddies, and soon all of them had a bottle of the concoction that was almost pure alcohol.

An hour later, the entire crew were much drunker than they had been the night before, and true to the good doctor's predictions, their weariness seemed to vanish as the supply diminished.

"Now, gentlemen," the huckster said loudly, "I can see that my wonderful elixir has had its usual gratifying and rejuvenating results. And since we are almost depleted of our supply, I suggest that we seek some other form of entertainment. Do you have any suggestions?"

A volley of raucous voices answered him. "Women! Faro! Roulette! A footrace!"

The man held up his hand to silence them. "Since you are men who ride, I would like to suggest a horse race. The sport of kings!"

The men howled their approval.

"I'll race my horse against anything that wears hair!" a drunken cowboy yelled.

"Me, too!" another yelled drunkenly. "I ain't never seen nothin' that could outrun my old bay hoss!"

The doctor raised his hand again, and the cowboys quieted.

"It seems to me, gentlemen," he said suavely, "that it would hardly be sporting for you to run against each other. I shall make a proposal."

The cowboys agreed loudly and enthusiastically.

"You can see the poor creature that is pulling my surrey," he said almost sadly. "I doubt if he can run very fast—but I don't know. I have never raced him. But you men have been so cordial and friendly that I suggest that we match him against a horse of your choosing. Just pick any one you like out of your horse herd, and let's meet later today in front of The Alamo. We will complete arrangements and run this afternoon. Of course, I could not conceivably expect to win—

but one can only try. I might even cover a small wager or two if any of you gentlemen would like to make it more interesting."

There was general approval; the cowboys went to the livery stables and saddled their horses. The freckled-faced cowhand, whose horse had been ridden away by the fleeing HF hand who had shot the gambler, was shown the horse that he said he had traded for. He saddled up.

When they started to leave, several of the HF men insisted that he come to camp with them.

"We got the best damn cook in Texas," one cowboy said. "And the coffee is always hot."

The freckled-faced puncher grinned his acceptance. "They call me Freck," he said.

\* \* \* \* \* \*

They were still more drunk than sober when they reached the chuckwagon. Maisie and Ellie poured them strong coffee, and they drank it eagerly. Most of them ate only a few bites and then went to their bedrolls. It had been a long night; even now it was only mid-morning. It was hours before the horse race.

When Humphrey returned to camp just before noon, he looked at the sleeping men and then at Largo, who, along with the other Negroes, had not gone to town.

"They all drunk?" Humphrey asked rhetorically.

"Yassuh, they is," Largo said.

"I reckon they had it comin' to 'em," Humphrey said idly. "Had a few myself with McCoy and that marshall down in McCoy's fancy hotel."

"Mars Hump?" Largo questioned cautiously. "Yo thinks maybe it be all right if me and Maisie went into town? We ain't never seen no towns except Fort Worth and Decatur."

Humphrey thought for a moment. "I'm pretty shore it would be all right, Largo," he said. "The town is mostly asleep this time of day. Besides, I saw a couple of blacks in town anyway. I'll give you some money to take with you."

"Let 'im take Ellie and Liza, too," Clem said as he rode up. He was sober. "Be all right if Alf and Trey went with 'im, too. Fact is, I'll ride in with 'em and then come back."

Clem was completely oblivious to the fact that many of his long-held prejudices had been shattered on the trail drive. First, Tiny had made him realize that maybe some good men had fought for the North when he explained why he had fought for the South and his brother for the North. And Skeet Dawkins' unreserved acceptance of the black cowboys and his admiration of their skills, caused Clem to admit, though tacitly, that the Negroes had done their share, and more, of the hard and dangerous work on the trail—especially in separating the mixed herd of cattle.

As Clem and the Negroes rode toward Abilene, Hump muttered under his breath, "Old Clem has done a big turn-around! He wouldn't a been seen dead in town with a nigger afore this drive."

\* \* \* \* \* \*

An hour later Clem rode back, his face flushed with anger.

"You know what them crazy bastards done?" he demanded of Humphrey, who had something of a hangover, too.

"No tellin'," he answered without much interest.

"They done went and matched 'em a horse race!" Clem said savagely.

"Ain't nothin' wrong with that that I can see," Humphrey said grumpily.

"Wrong with it!" Clem yelled at Humphrey. "You remember that feller a tellin' us about that damn drummer that matches his buggy horse agin the other feller, and then he's got a ringer staked out that he's got the hair clipped off the sides so's it'll look like he's been pullin' a wagon? Both of 'em grullas look like twins; but accordin' to that feller, they ain't nothin' can outrun that ringer he's got."

"Well, let 'em run," Humphrey said grumpily as he sipped strong coffee.

"But they're gonna bet on that race!"

"Let 'em bet. I doubt if them cowboys got $20 amongst 'em, anyway. An' that drummer shorely ain't got much."

Clem started to answer, but mounted his horse and started riding back toward town.

"Hey, Clem!" Humphrey hailed him. "When they gonna run that race?"

"A couple of hours afore sundown," Clem answered, "if them drunk bastards are sober enough to saddle a horse and find Abilene."

Humphrey just grunted, rolled under the shade of a wagon, and went to sleep.

\* \* \* \* \* \*

The groggy cowboys began to emerge from their bedrolls about noon. They immediately began to converge on the cook fire where Maisie had left a huge pot of coffee to stay hot. They were a sorry looking lot of young men, and Humphrey, who also roused, looked no better.

The cowboys began discussing the horse race that was to be run and which horse and rider they would select to challenge the grulla. Humphrey sat and scowled. The cowboys finally decided on the horse and rider they would use, and then all of them saddled up and rode to town.

Humphrey emerged from his shady spot under the wagon and drank coffee. He also ate some of the cold beans and sourdough bread that Maisie had left over from supper the night before. He was surprised when Brandy rode into camp on Punkin.

"What you doin' here, Brandy?"

"Why, I just came in to have a bit to eat, Mr. Beatenbow," Brandy said in surprise.

"Oh!" Humphrey said, rubbing his hands through his hair and over his face. His head throbbed. "God-a-mighty!" he breathed deeply. "I forgot you and Shanks was still out here with the remuda. They ain't much to eat neither, 'cause I let all the niggers—the blacks—go into town. I reckon Maisie forgot about you all, too, so there ain't much to eat."

"That's perfectly all right, Mr. Humphrey," Brandy assured him. "The ladies need a rest just the same as the men, I'm sure. I'll find plenty and take some out to Shanks, too."

Humphrey shook his head and watched as Brandy filled a big pan with beans and biscuits.

"You tell the ladies that we can jolly well manage for the evening meal, too, if they would like to stay in town," Brandy said as he mounted Punkin and rode back toward the remuda.

Humphrey puttered aimlessly around camp for an hour or two and then saddled a horse and rode into town. Most of the horses were at the hitching rail in front of The Alamo. So was the peddler's surrey. Humphrey tied his own horse and stepped through the bat-wing doors, only to stop abruptly and stare in amazement.

The peddler was standing on the marble top of the bar. Also piled on the bar on each side of him were pistols, spurs, chaps, and every other kind of cowboy regalia.

"All right, gentlemen," he said, his small, puffy lips spattering saliva as he spoke. "The wagering will continue for only a few minutes more. If any of you have anything of value to wager, please step forward. All bets will be covered. Sam will put your name down in his book, and you can come and collect what is due you after your fine horse outruns that poor old buggy horse of mine."

Humphrey spied Clem standing a bit apart from the crowd. As he caught his eye, he nodded for Clem to join him, which he did.

"What's goin' on?" Humphrey asked, almost goggle-eyed.

"Them damn, crazy cowboys is fixin' to get skinned outta their hides," Clem said grimly.

"What's all the stuff on the bar?"

"Damn near everything but their long britches," Clem said. "That fat bastard give all of 'em a bottle of that elixir of his, which is damn near pure alcohol, and then started takin' all bets. And them locoed sons-of-bitches started puttin' up their guns, and spurs, and damn near everything else they could use for money."

"They're crazy," Humphrey said flatly.

"You're shore as hell right about that, Hump," Clem said tightly. "You remember that feller that warned us about the peddler and his grulla horse that nothin' could outrun!"

"I remember," Humphrey said. He paused for several seconds and then said, "Clem, don't you let 'em start that race until you see me, you heah?"

Clem looked at Humphrey in surprise, but simply nodded. Humphrey turned quickly, went to his horse, and rode rapidly to camp. He did not stop at the wagons, but rode directly to the remuda, which was grazing contentedly. Brandy and Shanks were both lying by their horses on opposite sides of the horse herd. Humphrey rode directly to Brandy.

"Brandy, did you ever ride a race horse?" Humphrey asked without preliminaries.

"No sir, not in a regular race," Brandy answered in surprise, "but I've jolly well exercised and galloped a few back in—back when I was working at a racing stable."

"That's good enough," Humphrey said. "Go and fetch Rafter."

Again Brandy looked at Humphrey in surprise, but said nothing. He did as Humphrey asked. When he led Rafter up, he said, "He's a fine looking horse, isn't he? I never saw better, even in England."

Humphrey was so preoccupied that he did not even hear Brandy as he inadvertently let slip the name of his native country.

"You think you could ride Rafter bareback and him runnin' full speed?" Humphrey asked.

"I'm sure of it, sir," Brandy said confidently. "And I'd jolly well enjoy doing it."

"All right," Humphrey said. And then he gave Brandy detailed instructions and rode back to town.

He found Clem still in the Alamo, though betting had ceased. The cowboys had bet their all, and Sam, the barkeep, had it all down in his book. Humphrey explained to Clem what he had done. A smile of pure delight erased the malefic frown on Clem's grim face.

The drummer again called for attention. "All right, gentlemen," he said pompously. "The race will start in just exactly one hour." He removed the big, gold watch from his vest, pushed the stem, and cover snapped open. "The race will begin just the other side of the stock yards, and will be run right down Texas Street to the Sweet Alice saloon. That's about five hundred yards, and I doubt if my pore old buggy horse can make it that far, but sport is sport, and I'm a sporting man!"

"Clem," Humphrey said urgently. "Brandy and Rafter are waitin' just south of the yards. You go down and wait with 'em. When that feller gets to the startin' place, you go with Brandy. See that he gets an even break at the start."

"You can damn well bet on it!" Clem said eagerly and left hurriedly.

\* \* \* \* \* \*

Copo, the drummer's major-domo, was standing at the starting place. He was holding the lead shank of the grulla horse that very much resembled the horse that had been pulling the surrey, but Clem's practiced horseman's eye told him that the horse was indeed a ringer. Mounted on the grulla was a weasel-like little man, with small beady eyes, who looked at Rafter keenly as Clem and Brandy rode up. A look of consternation approaching fear crossed his face. Copo did not change expression. He would not have distinguished a racehorse from a mule.

"All right," Clem said in a business-like way. "They said to start when we was ready. You boys all set?"

Copo nodded and unsnapped the lead shank on the grulla. Brandy rode Rafter up beside him. The grulla pawed the ground nervously. Rafter seemed to be half asleep. The small man on the grulla tightened his legs on the light saddle he was riding. Brandy wrapped one hand in Rafter's mane and smiled.

"We'll start at the drop of a hat." Clem looked at Copo. "Yours or mine?"

Copo said nothing, but suddenly reached up and removed his derby hat and slammed it on the ground.

Rafter and the grulla each gave a mighty leap that sent clods of dirt high in the air.

After three jumps, it was no horse race! Rafter took a half length lead and was stretching it when dust obscured Clem's vision.

\* \* \* \* \* \*

All of the spectators were lined up on either side of the street in front of the Sweet Alice, where a finish line had been marked across the dusty street. The drummer was smiling broadly as he was positioned exactly at the finish line.

As the horses came into view, the drummer's smile faded; a look of incredulity replaced it, then fear and anger. The sorrel gelding was leading by a good three lengths and widening the gap.

"Stop it!" he yelled furiously. "Stop it! Stop it! Stop it! Spittle was spraying from his perch- like mouth, and he was squealing in fury and fear, like a trapped rat.

But no one heard, for they were all yelling and cheering.

Just before Rafter crossed the finish line, the drummer grabbed a spectator's rifle, aimed, and fired. As Rafter's nose crossed the finish line, his rear end went into the air as he flipped. Brandy was still on him when his back hit the ground. Rafter quickly got to his feet, but one foreleg was dangling, and a white bone protruded from his sorrel hide just below the knee. Brandy lay where he had fallen.

There was a moment of almost complete silence, and then angry yells went up. Two of the cowboy spectators wrestled the fat drummer to the ground. One of the cowboys was beating him in the face when Marshall Tom Smith stopped him.

"Never mind, cowboy," the marshall said grimly, "the law will take care of him!"

"Law, hell!" the cowboy shouted. "The fat son-of-a-bitch just shot a good horse and maybe killed a boy!"

The marshall quickly tied the drummer's hands and led him away. When the drummer resisted, Smith said, "You want me to turn you loose?"

The drummer heard the angry roar of the crowd and went quite willingly with the marshall.

As soon as Rafter had fallen and Brandy lay still in the dusty street, Humphrey, Clem, and Tiny ran to him. As they knelt beside him, he was mumbling. It was a language that was foreign to Humphrey and Clem.

"Wonder what he's sayin'?" Humphrey asked anxiously.

Tiny held his head close to Brandy's lips. "He's confessing his sins," Tiny said huskily and wiped a tear from his eye with a sleeve.

"What for?" Clem asked.

"He's dying," Tiny said.

"God-a-mighty!" Humphrey said prayerfully.

"He ain't dead yet," Clem said with forced optimism.

"The Lord is King. The Lord is King. The Lord is King." Brandy's voice could be heard and understood by all three men. Then he took a deep breath, and it came out slowly.

"He's dead now," Tiny said vacantly.

Humphrey and Clem stared at the childish face for a moment.

"Don't see what that little feller had to confess," Humphrey said brokenly.

Clem was the first to stand, then Humphrey. The crowd that had gathered around them melted. Humphrey looked and saw Rafter standing dejectedly on three legs a short distance away. He walked to the horse, saw the splintered bone projecting from the cannon. He patted the horse gently and then shot him between his gentle, intelligent eyes.

# Chapter 16

Humphrey, Tiny, and Clem wrapped Brandy's body in a blanket. Several of the cowboys stood by helplessly. When they had finished, Tiny mounted his big mule.

"Hand him up to me," Tiny said. "I'll carry him back to camp."

Humphrey and Clem rode on either side of Tiny as he carried the small form. They rode slowly; when they reached camp, Tiny handed the body tenderly to Clem and Humphrey.

The Negroes were back in camp when they arrived. When told what had happened, Ellie screamed and ran to the wagon. She crawled into the possum belly and cried as if her heart were broken.

"That little nigger gal thought a lot of 'im," Clem observed solemnly. "Reckon all of us did."

"I reckon we'd ort to go through his things and try to find out who he was," Clem said.

Tiny brought Brandy's saddle, and in the pockets they found a letter with a return address: Rabbi and Mrs. Bernard Weinberger. They also found a well-worn copy of the Torah.

Humphrey looked at the book quizzically and shook his head. "It's in some other language," he said. "I can't read it."

"It's the Torah," Tiny said. "I carry one in my saddle pocket."

"What's that?" Clem asked.

"The book of instructions for Jews," Tiny replied quietly.

"Brandy was a Jew?"

Tiny nodded his head in the affirmative. "So am I."

Neither Humphrey nor Clem said anything for a moment. Then Humphrey said almost pleadingly to Tiny. "Then maybe you can help us out with the buryin'."

"I'd like to do the best we can for him," agreed Tiny.

"Tell us how."

"First, his body ought to be cleaned thoroughly and then dressed in a white linen shroud."

"Maisie can wash 'im," Humphrey said, "unless you think he wouldn't want a nigger woman to do that."

"I doubt that Brandy would mind," Tiny smiled faintly. "He was not one to be prejudiced against any race or color."

"Then what?"

"To do it right, we ought to have a wooden coffin to bury him in."

"Largo can build that, even if we have to tear down the chuckbox for the lumber."

"I'll get the lumber," Clem said grimly.

"What next?"

"He should not be left alone before he is buried, but not left where people can view him. He needs to be remembered as he was when he was alive."

"I'll see to that," Humphrey said.

"The Jewish day begins at sundown," Tiny said, "and the burial should not be postponed any longer than necessary."

"It's nearly dark now. You reckon right after sunup would be all right?" Humphrey was out of his depth. "I'll have Alf and Trey dig 'im a good grave while Largo is buildin' the coffin."

"Sunrise will be fine," Tiny said, "and I'll sit with him tonight so he' won't be alone."

"Clem and me will sit with you soon as we get back from town. Clem, he'll bring back plenty of lumber, and I'll find some white cloth to make him a shroud. Don't know where I'll find any linen in Abilene, though."

"I'm sure that any white cloth would be adequate. We Jews have had to improvise before."

"We'll shore do our damn—I mean we'll do our best."

"Brandy would be pleased," Tiny said. "Judaism teaches that all people have a share in eternal life. I know that he thought a great deal of you and Mr. Beatenbow." It was the first time Tiny had referred to Humphrey as anything but "Hump."

"There's only one other thing that needs to be done, but I guess it is not possible."

"What's that?" Humphrey asked.

"He should be buried in an all Jewish cemetery, but I don't see how that can be done."

"I do," Humphrey said firmly. "We'll dig his grave on that little knoll north of camp. After he's buried, we'll put a good stout fence around it. He'll be the only one in it, and I reckon that would be a all Jewish cemetery."

Tiny thought a moment and then smiled. "I think it would be," he said.

The raucous bellow of the Beatenbow jackass sounded muted and mournful that night.

\* \* \* \* \* \*

Clem and Humphrey left for town after Humphrey had instructed Alf and Trey where to dig. It was almost midnight when they returned. Humphrey had a roll of white canvas cloth, and Clem was pulling the drummer's surrey with his lariat rope tied to the tongue.

"Reckon this will do?" Humphrey handed the bolt of cloth to Tiny.

"Yes," Tiny said. "Maisie has his body cleaned, and I'll wrap it now." He took the roll and walked toward the wagon.

Clem had secured a large hammer from Largo's tools and was taking the surrey apart. Largo watched anxiously.

"Ort to be enough good wood in this thing to make 'im a good coffin," Clem said to Largo.

"Yassuh, Mars Clem. They ort to be," Largo agreed and began to assemble the boards that Clem was removing from the surrey.

\* \* \* \* \* \*

The HF cowboys, deeply sobered by the tragic turn of events, had gone back to The Alamo Saloon to collect their bets. Copo objected that the race had not been fair and that all bets were off. A cowboy hit him over the head with a pistol. He slumped to the floor, and the barkeep began paying off the cowboys.

The payoff took a long time, and the cowboys drank to pass the time, but strangely, the liquor did not seem to affect them. The conversation was desultory and muted. They had all collected their bets, which made them richer than they had ever been before. When Clem appeared, his face was drawn and haggard.

"Boys," he said loudly, and his voice carried over the big room which was unusually quiet. "We're a gonna bury Brandy jus' after sunup tomorrow right north of camp. I reckon everbody that wants to come would be welcome."

Clem left immediately and rejoined Tiny and Humphrey, who were sitting beside the sturdy coffin that Largo had built.

Before sunup, the cowboys started drifting in. Maisie had a pot of coffee, of which they all partook, but none accepted the food that she offered.

When the sun was a few minutes above the horizon, Tiny said, "I guess it's time."

Humphrey, Clem, Tiny and Largo picked up the casket and carried it with ease to the open grave, which had been guarded throughout the night by Alf and Trey. They set the casket beside the grave. Tiny stood at the head of the grave, opened the Torah, and read several passages in Yiddish, and then said, "Brandy was my friend—and a friend of all men. He was especially fond of Mr. Beatenbow, and I think Brandy would be pleased if he said a few words."

Humphrey cleared his throat several times, then opened the Bible that he had been carrying and read the 23rd Psalm. Then, he spoke eloquently for a few moments. He finished by saying, "Tiny tells me that Judaism teaches that all people have a share in eternal life. So maybe we'll get to see Brandy again."

Dutch Horst, who had been standing behind Tiny, said in a loud whisper, "You mean that little bastard was a Jew! Ain't no wonder I never did like 'im."

Tiny wheeled, and his massive arm moved like a striking bear. Horst knocked three cowboys down as he fell backward. The cowboys got up, brushed themselves off, and turned back toward the grave. Horst lay unmoving. He was bleeding from the mouth, and some of his front teeth were missing.

The grave was filled, and Largo, Trey and Alf were erecting the strong fence around it as the cowboys started drifting away. Humphrey and Clem stopped and looked down at Horst, who was beginning to stir. A minute later he was on his feet.

"Horst," Humphrey said grimly, "you're fired!"

"You can't fire me, Beatenbow. It was Clem that hired me, and he's the one that's gonna fire me, if anybody does."

"Well, I hired Clem," Humphrey said, "and now I'm firin' 'im, so that gives me the authority to fire you!"

Horst said nothing, but glared at both men malevolently. He started walking away.

"That's a HF horse you're ridin', Horst," Clem said harshly. "Unsaddle 'im and turn 'im loose."

"Just how in the hell do you expect me to get back to town, anyway? Walk and carry my saddle?"

"Damn right, I do!" Clem said savagely.

"You ain't got the right to fire me," Horst said almost triumphantly. "Beatenbow just fired you."

"And I just hired 'im again," Humphrey said. "Now you git! And don't never let me catch you even close to the HF again!"

Horst looked at Humphrey's hawklike face that was almost cruel at the moment and at Clem's flushed and angry countenance. He started to say something, but then spat an obscenity and turned. Several of the cowboys rode past him carrying his saddle on his back as he plodded toward town. None of them spoke to him or offered help in any way.

The cowboys returned to the Alamo to discuss the events of the day, but a pall seemed to lie over the entire town. Even Hell's Half-acre below Texas Street was quieter than usual. The prostitutes plied their trade openly, but they did their slowest day of business since coming to Abilene. Being philosophical about it all, most of them took the lull in stride, knowing that as long as the cowboys were in town and had money, their business would flourish again, perhaps with renewed vigor.

The Alamo Saloon had many customers, though not the usual overflowing number. The HF cowboys were gathered in a small group in one corner of the big room.

"I say we ought to break the bastard out of jail and hang 'im," one cowboy said seriously.

"I'd be all for that if it wasn't for that damn marshall, Tom Smith," another replied. "But he's bad medicine. Any fool can see that."

"When are we gonna start back? I'm sick of this damn town."

"Back where?" another replied. "We only signed on for the drive. Doubt if Hump and Clem are gonna need us any longer."

"Well, they're damn shore gonna need somebody if they aim to tote all that money back across most of Kansas and the Oklahoma strip."

And so the evening passed. The cowboys played Faro, roulette and poker. And, although they had plenty of money, their play was lethargic, and they refused all offers from the professional gamblers or the men from other outfits to join a game.

Humphrey, Clem, and Tiny stayed in camp.

"I reckon we'd might as well start back pretty soon," Humphrey said absently. "Finch and the women may be wonderin' about us."

"Sooner the better as far as I'm concerned," Clem said.

"Hump," Tiny began hesitantly, "would you mind a lot if I didn't get back with you?"

"I'd shore like to have you, Tiny," Humphrey said solemnly, "but you don't owe the HF nothin'. You've done your part—and more. What you got in mind?"

"To tell you the truth, Hump, I miss the sea," Tiny said. "I sailed it for twenty years, and I'd like to go back."

"Clem told me you was in the Southern navy. I didn't even know we had one. What did you do?"

"Oh," Tiny said vaguely, "nothing much. I was on the Merrimac. They called it the Virginia after the war started. We ran supplies to the South and were doing pretty well until we hooked up with the Monitor. She had steel, and we had wood. They banged us up pretty bad. After that, we got some smaller ships and brought supplies down the Mississippi."

"Hell, I didn't know nothin' about that, Tiny!" Clem said, almost in disbelief.

"Well, whatever we did, it wasn't enough, for the North whipped us pretty good."

"That's for damn shore!" Clem agreed. "But they ain't no war on now, so what will you do?"

"They're shipping a lot of cattle from Indianola now to New Orleans. And from a lot of other Texas ports, too. Even shipping some of them to Cuba. I think with what I've learned about cattle on this trip, and what I already know about sailing—maybe I could make a hand again."

"I don't doubt that a bit, Tiny," Humphrey said. "You'd make a hand anywheres. And I reckon I can understand your hankerin' for the sea—onct in a while I sorta get a itch for our old plantation over in Louisiana."

"You'll never leave Texas, Hump, and you know it!" Clem said jestingly.

"You're right, Clem," Humphrey smiled. "I reckon my roots already got too deep!"

"You said you had a brother in the northern army that night you and Brandy raided Camp Supply?"

The implicit question was one that Clem would never have asked under ordinary conditions.

"That's right, Clem," Tiny admitted. "My whole name is Theodore Salamon, and my brother, Ed, was in Meade's Army of the Patomac."

"Well, Tiny," Hump felt that he ought to direct the conversation in another direction. "Like I said, you don't owe the HF nothin'. So, if you want to go back to sea again, we will wish you luck!"

"That's for shore!" Clem added.

"How will you get back down there, Tiny?" Humphrey was curious.

"Some of the hands that came up with a herd a few weeks ago are leaving the day after tomorrow. They'll go through Decatur and Fort Worth. From there on, I should make it by myself pretty easy. Most of the Indians have been run out of that part of Texas."

At the mention of Decatur, Humphrey's interest quickened. "You'll be goin' through Decatur, you say?"

"That's what the boys said," Tiny agreed.

"Tell you what!" Humphrey said with more animation than he had shown since Brandy was killed. "The brands of them three extry steers that we got up here with are almost shore to have come from Wise County. Decatur is the county seat. I'd take it as a mighty big favor if you could look 'em up and get the money to their owners or some of their kin. Fact is, I'll pay you wages till you get there."

"I'll do the best I can to find them, Hump. But you won't pay me any wages. I'll get the money to them; if I can't, I'll send it back to you—or bring it if I have to."

Humphrey immediately went to Maisie's chuckwagon and pulled a bag of coins from under the seat. He was counting it out to Tiny when Tom Smith and another man rode up.

"Howdy, Marshall," Humphrey greeted him. "Light and set. We got coffee."

"Thank you, just the same, Beatenbow, but I reckon not. Joe and me has got to ride on north a ways to bring a feller that killed a man a while back," Smith replied. "Just wanted to tell you that I'm sorry about what happened in my town."

"What you gonna do with that drummer?" Clem demanded.

"We've got him locked in what passes for our jail. I'll hold him until the next circuit judge comes along. Don't know what to charge him with, though. He didn't shoot the boy. Anyway, I'm gonna be gone three or four days, and likely you'll be gone before I get back."

"Figgerin' on leavin' tomorrow," Humphrey said.

"Glad to hear it," Smith said. He and his partner rode off a few yards, stopped, and turned.

"Hump!" It was the first time Tom Smith had called Humphrey anything but Beatenbow. "Tell them cowboys of yours to be shore not to give that jailer of mine any whiskey. He's a drinkin' fool and would be dead to the world before you know it, and my prisoner might escape."

With that the marshall and his partner rode north. Humphrey, Clem, and Tiny looked at each other; understanding immediately dawned on them. Tom Smith had just issued his approval of frontier justice!

"Clem," Humphrey said quickly, "you ride into town and tell all the boys that they're back on the HF payroll, and I want 'em out here at camp by sundown."

"They'll be here," Clem said grimly.

At sundown eight cowboys had made it back to camp.

"Where is the rest of 'em?" Humphrey demanded.

"Well," Clem said, "you know that Swifty got busted up, and a couple of our boys took 'im on into Kansas City to get doctored up. Said they wanted to see the big town, anyways. And then, there was Kinky that shot that crooked gambler and then run off. Where the other two are, I ain't got no idee. Prob'ly drunk in some whorehouse."

"Well, we've got enough, anyway," Humphrey declared. "It's gettin' on to dark now, and here's what I want you to do." Then he described in detail what each man was to do.

"Now, let's git at it!" he said grimly.

\* \* \* \* \* \*

An hour later, Gabby showed up at the makeshift jail with two quarts of whiskey. He feigned drinking out of one bottle and held the other in his hand. He seemed to be surprised when he opened the door to see a cell door and a guard in front of it. Gabby hadn't got his name for nothing, and before the guard could even question him, Gabby had talked so fast that the jailer's ears were ringing. Gabby walked unsteadily around the small room, talking all the while. He looked at the bottle in his other hand as if surprised and then held it out to the jailer. The jailer licked his lips, but shook his head. Gabby continued to walk and talk. At each turn, he held out the bottle to the jailer. Finally, the jailer succumbed and accepted the full bottle. He yanked the cork out with his teeth and took a small sip. A beatific smile crossed his face, and he took a bigger one. In less than an hour, the bottle was empty, and the jailer was snoring on the floor. Gabby quickly went to the door, flung it open, and waved his floppy hat.

Almost immediately, Humphrey, Clem and Tiny entered. Clem quickly located the keys and opened the cell door. The drummer opened his eyes; when he saw the three men, they filled with horror. He knew that he was staring death in the face. He started screaming. His hands were still tied. Clem quickly tore a strip of cloth from the dirty pillow and stuffed it in the drummer's mouth and tied it securely.

As Clem and Tiny took the drummer by each arm and dragged him across the street, they were followed by Gabby, who had his pistol drawn, and by Humphrey, who carried his 10-gauge shotgun at the ready.

As they entered the saloon, there was absolute quiet. Around the periphery of the room stood eight HF cowboys with pistols drawn.

"Men," Humphrey announced, "most of you in here saw what happened yesterday. I ain't gonna say much about it, but a good horse got killed, and that's worse than stealin' a horse—and that's a hangin' offense. Ain't no use to mention the fine young man that got killed because of it. Now, here is the man that done it. I aim to give 'im a fair trial—for killin' a good horse—which is worse than stealin' one, a lot worse. Now I need a jury."

The terrified drummer squirmed, and squeaks could be heard coming from his gagged mouth.

"Now, how many of you fellers are willin' to serve on a jury?"

Immediately every cowboy in the saloon raised his hand. The gamblers simply looked on in fascination. Copo, who had been sitting in the back of the room, rose to his great height and started toward his boss. For the second time, he was bashed over the head with a pistol. He lay quietly.

"All right," Humphrey said, "I counted twelve hands in the air, and that's a legal jury. Does anybody want to defend the man?"

No one spoke.

"Then the prosecution will ask for a show of hands for them that thinks this here horse-killer ort to be hung," Humphrey said pontifically.

Every cowboy again raised his hand. One of the HF hands threw a rope over a ceiling beam. At the end of the rope was a noose, already prepared. Clem and Tiny pulled the drummer to the bar and lifted him on it. Clem held the man while Tiny crawled up on the bar, jerked the drummer upright, and placed the noose around his neck.

"Pull that rope tight," Clem directed. Immediately, several of the HF cowboys did so.

Clem also climbed up on the marble-topped bar beside the trembling drummer. Tiny held him firmly on his other side. Clem jerked the gag roughly from his mouth. The man's small fat lips worked spasmodically, and spittle sprayed forth, but no words.

"All right," Clem said, "you boys take up the slack." Then he and Tiny threw the drummer in the air, and the cowboys brought the rope taut and tied it securely to the bar rail.

The drummer's feet danced rapidly for a few seconds, then slowed, and finally stopped. Humphrey, Clem, and Tiny watched until they were sure the man was dead. Then Humphrey laid a handful of coins on the bar.

"That's for messin' up your nice saloon with a lot of filth, Sam," Humphrey spoke to the barkeep. Then he turned to the room. "Now, all you HF men that wants to go back to Texas, be in camp at daylight."

Humphrey and Clem walked out into the street where they paused for a moment.

"Clem," Humphrey said, "you go back to camp and be gettin' everything ready to go. Then, come back here before daylight with the hospital wagon. And bring Largo with you. I'll be in front of the bank with Joe McCoy, and we'll load the gold."

"All right, Hump," Clem agreed, "but you know you're takin' a hell of a chance a takin' all that gold back home."

"We'll get it there," Humphrey said grimly, and with that, he started walking down Texas Street. Clem watched with interest until Humphrey entered one of the whorehouses that fronted the street.

A look of amazement and surprise crossed Clem's face.

"That there hangin' musta hurt old Hump more'n I thought," he muttered grimly and shook his head.

# CHAPTER 17

Clem and Largo drove the hospital wagon to the front of the bank well before daylight. Humphrey and McCoy were waiting.

Clem had Hump's big double-barrelled 10-gauge and stood watch as the other three men loaded the heavy sacks of gold. When it was finished, Largo took the reins, and Clem sat on the seat beside him with the shotgun.

When they reached camp, the mules were hitched to the chuckwagon, but Maisie and Ellie were still doling out food to the cowboys.

"We'll eat," Clem said. "I put Trey to help Shanks with the remuda today. We can all trade off on doin' that because we'll be travelin' a lot faster."

"And not near as far," Humphrey agreed. "I aim to cut across country. There ain't no reason to follow the Chisholm trail again goin' back. We won't have no cattle to bother with."

"Some rough country, though," observed Clem.

"We'll make it," Humphrey replied doggedly.

The men had eaten and were ready to go. Humphrey had all the gold loaded in the chuckwagon under the seat and had transferred many of the heavier tools to the hospital wagon. When they were ready to pull out, Liza had not appeared.

"Where in hell is Liza?" Humphrey yelled.

"Uh, Mars Hump. . ." Largo began hesitantly.

"Well, what is it?" Humphrey demanded.

"Well, Mars Hump, it lak dis. . ." Largo was reverting to the slave mode of speech that he had been slowly overcoming.

"Out with it, Largo!" Humphrey was becoming angry.

"Well, Mars Hump," Largo gulped, "Liza she went into town las' night, an' I look fo' 'er mos' all night. Finally found 'er in one of dem hoah houses, an' she say she ain't a gonna go back. She havin' mo fun den evah in 'er life, and gettin' paid fo it, too." Largo hung his head.

"God-a-mighty!" Humphrey said in disbelief. Then he quickly recovered. "Well, tell Maisie to drive the hospital wagon, and I'll drive the chuckwagon."

\* \* \* \* \* \*

The sun was just coming up when they left, headed southwest. The four mules pulling the chuckwagon moved out briskly, and the hospital wagon followed closely. The cowboys rode pell-mell. Some helped with the remuda; some rode side-by-side, talking. Later in the morning a few of them stopped in the shade of a tree to grab a wink of sleep, knowing that they could catch the wagons easily. And they were still close enough to Abilene that the Indian menace was not acute.

They crossed rolling hills most of the morning. The country-side was not awe-inspiring, but there were a few cottonwood and elm trees, and the grass was tall. They hit some fairly flat country before reaching the Solomon River where they nooned. If they had been driving cattle, they would have made camp, but with only the remuda to contend with, they were covering miles, and Humphrey was in a hurry. They stopped for the night at Mulberry Creek. There were low mountains in the distance, but there were no trees on them. The water was sufficient for remuda and camp.

There was not the usual raillery about the campfire that night. It was a somber group of young men who were returning to the HF.

Freck, the man who had swapped his horse to the cowboy who had absconded after shooting the gambler, broke a long silence.

"What you reckon ever happened to the little runt that was a ridin' the ringer grulla horse that got outrun so bad?"

"Last I saw of 'im, he was a beatin' hell outta that horse and still a goin' west. He didn't even look back."

"I expect he's all the way to Colorado by now."

"If he ain't, he soon will be. I'd gamble on that!"

\* \* \* \* \* \*

The next night they camped at the Smoky Hill River. The four mules pulling the heavy chuck wagon were becoming gaunt. But they left the next morning early. They travelled over rolling hills, and there were some natural lakes. They had stopped to water the mules and the remuda when they saw four riders approaching. Humphrey mounted the chuckwagon seat and laid his shotgun in his lap.

"Howdy," one of the men greeted as they rode up.

"Howdy," acknowledged Humphrey.

"You fellers seen any Indians about?"

"Not since we left Abilene," Humphrey said.

The cowboys had all ridden up and were looking keenly at the four men. Tonio's eyes widened in recognition as he looked at them, and he loosened his pistol in the scabbard.

"Take a herd to Abilene?"

"That's right—3100 head of steers," Humphrey said almost proudly.

"Get a good price for 'em?"

"We sold 'em!" Humphrey said shortly.

"They tell me that they pay by draft. That right?"

"They didn't pay us with no draft," Humphrey answered.

"Looks like your chuckwagon is pretty well loaded," the leader observed.

"It is," Humphrey said evenly as he picked up the shotgun in his lap. "And it's gonna be just as heavy when we get back to the HF back in Texas!" he added pointedly. There were two very audible clicks as he cocked his 10-gauge.

The leader looked at Humphrey keenly for a moment and then laughed. "I expect it will be," the leader grinned. "Hope you left a little of that gold in the bank that McCoy keeps his safe in."

"They is some left, I reckon," Humphrey said.

"Well, you fellers have a good trip back to Texas!" the leader of the men said with a grin, and the four of them turned their horses and rode away.

Tonio rode quickly to Humphrey's wagon. "You know who those men were, Hump?" Tonio's English was quite good.

"Nope," admitted Humphrey, "and I don't give a damn."

"That was the James boys and Cole Younger. They robbed a bank over in Russelville a few months ago."

"Thought they worked over in Missouri. That's what Hitt said."

"They do," Tonio answered. "And Jesse, he was the little one, got shot up some over in Kentucky a couple of years ago—but they ride most everywhere."

"They wasn't gonna ride any place no more if Hump had a turned that cannon of his on 'em, and they knowed it!" Clem said.

All of the cowboys joined in the laughter, but they were, nevertheless, relieved when the outlaws were out of sight.

"They knew we was carryin' gold," one man said incredulously. "Why didn't Hump just tell 'em he got paid with a draft?"

"Hell!" Clem growled, "Humphrey Beatenbow don't even know how to tell a lie!"

\* \* \* \* \* \*

The next day they crossed the Ninnescah River. The water was low, but adequate, and they continued after watering the horses and mules and refilling the kegs on the sides of the wagons. During the afternoon, they hit flat country, which enabled them to travel faster. One bunch of Indians was sighted; but it was a small bunch, and seeing the number of men accompanying the wagons and remuda, they turned and rode away.

They camped that night on Elm Creek. Clem told Humphrey that he was mounting guard all night over the remuda and wagons.

Much to the surprise of everyone, the Beatenbow jackass walked near the camp that night. He had an Indian arrow through the thick crest of his neck, and he held his head low and was the picture of dejection. He stood absolutely still as several of the men approached him.

"That's a Kiowa arrow," Tonio said.

"Missed his windpipe and jugular," Clem observed, "else the little bastard would be a roastin' over a Kiowa fire tonight."

Clem and Tonio walked up to the jackass, which stood meekly as they examined the arrow. Clem severed the shaft with his sharp knife. He and Tonio pulled. The arrow came out easily. The jackass raised his head tentatively and apparently felt no pain, for he immediately perked his long ears, uttered a short bray, wheeled, and kicked. One of the small hooves caught Clem on the shin. Clem cussed the jackass as he ran, kicking up his heels and breaking wind, until he was out of sight.

Clem limped back to the campfire still swearing vengeance on the jackass. But he was not too hurt or angry to remember his responsibilities as trail boss.

"This country is still full of Indians," he warned Humphrey. "An' we got to be careful. Besides, them damn crazy cowboys is mostly over the boozy headaches by now; so it won't hurt 'em to stay awake some at night. I'll change shifts at midnight."

The cowboys quickly forgot the impertinent jackass.

"You're the boss, Clem," Humphrey said. Clem looked at him and shook his head slightly. Humphrey was not an easy man to figure out, but all of the men could feel his urgency to get back to the ranch.

"Can't see why he'd go to a whorehouse in Abilene when he's got such a pretty woman at home," Clem thought to himself. "Says he's religious, too! Must be he's sort of half and half!"

\* \* \* \* \* \*

All the cowboys stood their guard over the camp that night. There was no grumbling. They, too, seemed to be anxious to get back to the ranch, for Humphrey had promised all of them steady jobs if they wanted them. Ordinarily, trail crews got a month's pay in advance and rode down the Chisholm trail to a vague destination.

"I figger that there good Texas air is gonna do me more good than that bottled brimstone that there peddler give us!" one of them observed.

"Me, too!" answered another. "When we get to the Texas border, I'm gonna step across it and then lean back and holler jus' as loud as I can!"

They had no trouble crossing Medicine River or Cedar Creek. In fact, the rivers and streams posed few problems for them. It was late summer, almost early fall, and few real thunderstorms were expected. Then, too, if a river should be high, it would be a fairly easy job to raft the wagons across, and the remuda could swim most currents with ease.

The next couple of days they saw a few more Indians, but none threatened to attack. There were several natural ponds on the way, and a few canyons that they had to go around. Obviously, their route was not a trail. They were cutting across untravelled country. There were pretty valleys, a few small evergreens, oak thickets, and some hackberry trees. When they reached the Cimarron River, the men felt their trip was almost over. Just to be as sure as possible that a headrise did not cut them off, Clem directed that they cross the Cimarron late in the day and camp on the south side even if it was in the Oklahoma strip.

"Them red bastards ain't gonna raid us with all the men we got," Clem said confidently. "Likely they was done for when Sherman told Sheridan to drive 'em out of Kansas or kill 'em. They ain't gonna give nobody no trouble now! Besides, we ain't more'n three or four days from home."

\* \* \* \* \* \*

But Clem was wrong! The next day the most brutal fight that any of them had ever seen took place between Largo, the former slave, and Big Moose, son of a Cheyenne chief!

It was also the day the Indians raided the HF Ranch!

\* \* \* \* \* \*

The Indians hit the HF at mid-morning: the worst possible time for the ranch. Many of the black women were taking advantage of the warm, sunny day to hang laundry on bushes near the river, while others were picking plums in the thickets that grew profusely nearby. Many of the older black children were playing in the yard. And among the younger ones was Mandy's oldest, a little girl.

They seemed to erupt from the slight cover of the river, and their demonic screams and eerie appearance in their war paint and regalia were more than enough to send a shock of terror through all who heard.

Finch was in the big storage half-dugout. When he first heard the fiendish yells, he grabbed his rifle, ran to the house, and up the inside staircase to the roof. He was chilled at the scene below. Most of the Negro men were running to the relative safety of the buildings where they armed themselves with rifles and climbed to the top of the buildings, where the parapet around the edges of the roof afforded some protection and afforded them a good firing position.

Finch quickly assessed the situation. Several of the black women and children had already been felled by the Indians. One Indian brave was chasing a young black boy; he was yelling gleefully as he leaned forward on his horse and raised his club to strike. Finch shot before the Indian could land the blow. The terrorized child ran screaming toward shelter, and the Indian's pony galloped away.

During his younger years on the family ranch near San Antonio and later in the Texas Rangers, Finch had acquired many of the emotional reactions of a wild animal. He never showed fear, and only rarely did he evidence anger, but he was never careless. He looked at the scene below him without apparent emotion. Then he saw something that caused the shadow of primitive caution that always lay deep in his blue eyes to be replaced by sheer terror. The little black children that had been playing in the yard were running toward the Negro quarters. Mandy's daughter was running as fast as she could toward the headquarters house. In full pursuit and yelling like banshees were several Indian braves. Then, from the corner of his eye, Finch saw a feminine figure, long black hair flying, running with unbelievable speed toward the child. It was O'oah!

The terrified Finch did not take time to run down the stairs, but quickly mounted the parapet and dropped to the ground. As he fell, his rifle was jarred loose, but he quickly rose and ran after O'oah. He had not reached her when an Indian leaned from his horse and smashed her skull. She fell across the body of Mandy's screaming child. Finch shot the Indian twice; as the Indian fell, Finch continued to fire at others with the three remaining bullets in his pistol. An Indian fell at each shot. When the hammer clicked on an empty cylinder, he threw the gun at a yelling Indian and continued to run toward O'oah and Mandy's child. He was just bending over them when a wisp of blond hair floated from his head and wafted on the slight breeze.

Mandy and O'oah had each been in their wing of the headquarters when they first heard the yelling. O'oah knew immediately! Mandy, who was having her leisurely morning bath was, at first, puzzled and then horrified. She jumped from the tub, drew a robe around her body, and ran to the window just in time to see O'oah felled by the Indian and to see Finch crumple. She screamed and started to run to them when old Kate grabbed her around the waist with big, fat arms as strong as ropes.

"Not now, Miss Mandy," Kate said harshly. "We done been hurt enough."

Mandy continued to struggle for a moment and then sagged helplessly in Kate's arms.

The Indians were riding their horses pell mell among the buildings, yelling and shooting. But, now, most of the blacks had now gained the safety of their quarters and were beginning to take a toll of the Indians. The firing from the buildings became so intense that the Indians began to pull away and started their traditional circling attack. Riderless Indian ponies were galloping wildly away.

Then came a shot from the direction of the barn. One of the cowboys, hopefully more than one, had heard the shots and had ridden to join the fight.

A movement up the valley caught the attention of Shanker Stone, for he had fired the shot from the barn. He was appalled to see the Comanche Chief White Horse and a party of braves riding swiftly toward the battle site. Shanker's optimism turned to dismay. He had thought the fighting was almost over, for Indians did not relish paying such a high price for victory. But now, with White Horse and his fierce Comanches joining the Kiowas, the situation looked black indeed!

But Shanker's dismay quickly turned to elation when it became apparent that White Horse and his warriors were attacking—not the ranch—but the Kiowas!

The fight lasted only a short time after the arrival of White Horse and his braves. The Kiowas fled, pursued by a large contingent of the Comanches. White Horse, mounted on one of the prized thoroughbred mares he had stolen when Finch and Humphrey were making their drive from Fort Worth, rode back to the spot where O'oah and Finch had fallen.

Mandy's little girl crawled from under the body of O'oah, her face streaked and dirty. She ran to the house where her mother gathered her into her arms and held on as if she would never let go.

White Horse, accompanied by three of his braves, sat, his face impassive, for several moments as he looked down at O'oah. Then he grunted something, and one of the braves dis-mounted and lifted the body of O'oah. White Horse took her in his arms and rode toward Mandy and her children who had gathered on the ranch gallery when the fighting was over. He pulled his horse up for a moment as he passed the body of Finch and then rode on.

White Horse stopped his horse a few feet away; his eyes seemed focused above Mandy's face.

"O'oah go home!" he said sadly. "Finch he still Comanche hites—he stay. He live. Kiowa dishonor Indian promise. We go."

"Uddah," Mandy whispered as he rode away. She turned to old Kate, and Sam,

"Kate," Mandy said with urgency, "you and Sam come with me. Finch may still be alive."

With that, she ran to him and lifted his bloody blond head. He was still breathing, and Mandy could see the long path of the bullet along the side of his head. The white bone of his skull showed obscenely.

Kate gazed about fearfully, but saw only bodies of several blacks. The Indians had vanished.

Mandy and Kate each took an arm, and Sam took Finch's legs, who for all his slender build, was surprisingly heavy. In short order, they had him deposited on the bed that he and O'oah had shared so blissfully in their wing of the headquarters house.

Kate bathed Finch's head and poured some whiskey in the wound, which made him groan in pain.

"Well, he ain't dead, nohow," Kate said with obvious relief. "Dat bullet, it don' break his skull, jis whomp his brain about some. I thinks Mars Finch be all right come mornin', or maybe several mornin's."

"Oh! Do you really think so, Kate?" Mandy asked. Her dark eyes were filled with tears as she looked at the fat old Negress hopefully.

"Yassum, Miss Mandy. I ain't felt no troublesome spirits in dis room. I thinks he be all right. Maybe a day or so afore he gits his head clear agin, though."

"Oh, I do hope so!" Mandy said fervently. "Poor O'oah!"

"Now, Miss Mandy, yo goes and sees about yo young uns. Sam, he gonna build me a fire to heat some water. I get his clothes off and give Mars Finch a bath all over. Then, maybe he rest some."

Mandy raised her eyebrows at Kate. "A bath all over?"

"Yassum. He needs it. Sides, this ole nigger gal seed a lot o nekkid men afore. Ain't gonna bother me none, and Mars Finch, he ain't gonna know nothin' about it, nowhow."

Mandy said nothing, but left the room quietly and went to the Beatenbow wing of the house where she found her children playing and completely oblivious to the tragedy that had occurred so close to them.

\* \* \* \* \* \*

Kate bandaged Finch's head. Sam built a fire to heat the bath water. Kate began gently removing Finch's clothes. His boots were hardest, and she had to get Sam to help, but the rest of the garments were easily removed. Kate hung his pistol, belt, and hat on the bed post, for she knew those were the first items he would look for when he woke up—if he woke up.

Sam had gone back to the kitchen when Kate started bathing Finch. She washed his chest and stomach thoroughly and began her ministration farther down, whereupon Finch immediately became erect.

"Reckon Mars Finch bigger dan mos' nigger bucks," Kate mumbled matter-of-factly. "Ain't no wonder dat pretty lil O'oah always look so satisfied."

\* \* \* \* \* \*

Finch did not regain consciousness that day. Kate bathed his face with a cold cloth every few minutes, and Mandy came to check on him regularly.

"He ain't no different," Kate told Mandy that afternoon. "I reckon it jis gonna take some time for 'im to come about. He awful restless, though, and he gonna be some tore up when he knows about the pretty lil Indian wife o his'n!"

"I know he is," Mandy said sadly. "I just wish there were some way we could make it easier for him!"

"Well, there ain't, I reckon," Old Kate replied grimly, but philosophically. "I reckon we all gonna die when our time comes. An' Miss O'oah was mighty happy afore she died. I reckon that's better'n a lot of us can say."

"You're not happy, Kate?" Mandy asked in surprise.

"Reckon I ain't never thought about it one way or another," Kate replied. "Allus thinks I is mighty lucky to be a Beatenbow nigger. An' Sam, he a mighty good man fo me. An' we mos' allus had plenty to eat. Reckon us niggers cain't ask for much more—."

"But—" Mandy interrupted but could think of no reply. She shut her mouth grimly and shook her head slightly before she continued. "If Finch wakes up, please come and let me know." Mandy placed a soft hand on Finch's shoulder as she left the room.

\* \* \* \* \* \*

Kate went to the Beatenbow wing of the house just before Mandy was ready to retire for the night. She knocked timidly on the bedroom door. Mandy quickly opened it and looked questioningly at Kate.

"Mars Finch, he still a breathin'," Kate said. "Fact is, I reckon they ain't nothin' wrong with 'im ceptin' that clout on de haid. But he mighty restless, and he keep bumpin' dem covers up lak he de Beatenbow jackass. He mighty restless, Mars Finch is."

"Do you think that if I went to him, it would help calm his down?"

"I reckon it might help some. Leastwise, it won't hurt nothin'. I jis wisht Miss O'oah wuz here."

"So do I, Kate," Mandy said. "But the children will be asleep in a few minutes, and I'll come to him. Will you be in the kitchen?"

"Yassum. Reckon me an' Sam, we stay in there tonight, jis in case."

"Good," Mandy approved. "I'll be along in just a few minutes."

As old Kate waddled back to the kitchen, she mumbled under her breath. "If'n he a nigger buck, I know how to calm 'im down. Any nigger wench would! An' I'd do it, too, if'n I wasn't afeared he'd wake up whilst I's doin' it."

\* \* \* \* \* \*

When Mandy came to the kitchen, she was still dressed in a night robe, and her hair was pulled back and tied, though her blond tresses still reached to her hips. Kate and Same looked at her and then averted their eyes.

"What should I do, Kate? Just sit by his bed?"

"Yassum. I reckon that be about all anybody can do. I put a pan of cool water by his bed and a rag. Yo might jis sorta wipe his face a little onct in a while. He sweatin' some. Wouldn't hurt none if yo jis sorta held his hand some, too."

"I'll do that, Kate. And thank you. You and Sam can get some sleep now, if you like. I'll stay with him."

"No ma'am," Kate replied firmly. "We both jis set here tonight, but we won't come into Mars Finch's room lessen yo call us. Might bother 'im even if we think he don' know nothin'."

Mandy shut the door softly behind her and tiptoed to the bedside. Finch was pale, and the blood had seeped through the bandage. There were small beads of sweat on his face, and she wiped them away tenderly with a cool damp rag. Then she sat beside the bed to wait.

Finch groaned and moved about. Mandy rose quickly to do she knew not what. Then she was a bit startled to see the covers over his goin rise and fall. She knew that what Kate had meant when she referred to the Beatenbow jackass. Finch was certainly not disabled as far as his body was concerned.

The male body was no mystery to Mandy, for she had been married for a year to a young soldier who was killed in the war, and for the past two years she had been married to Humphrey Beatenbow. Her first husband had been a raunchy youngster who delighted in Mandy's beautiful body and used every technique in his limited repertoire to give her pleasure, and she had delighted in it. Humphrey was an almost complete antithesis of her first husband. Though he was a strong and virile man who made love to her often, he seemed to think their lovemaking was for the pleasure of the man only, and he had often rebuffed Mandy gently when she attempted a deviation from what he considered normal. In fact, Humphrey would have been astonished to know that the sensuous woman to whom he was married often felt frustrated and unfulfilled when he had completed his perfunctory lovemaking.

Mandy felt a surge of guilt as she mentally compared her two husbands while she watched Finch closely. She bathed his face every few minutes. Then she pulled the quilt down just a bit to wipe the cool rag across his muscular chest. When she did, he groaned softly, and Mandy's eyes were drawn as if by a magnet to the bulge in the quilt that seemed to throb and pulse.

She looked quickly at the bedroom door and remembered that Kate had said that neither she nor Sam would come unless called. She wondered if—. Gently, she moved the quilt farther down and sponged his flat, rock-hard belly with the cool rag. He groaned again and squirmed as if in pain. She moved the quilt lower and gasped as she saw his penis erect and throbbing; she was mesmerized. Without conscious intent, she reached and took the big organ in her soft warm hand. Immediately, it ejected a stream of grayish-white semen. Mandy shut her eyes tightly and squeezed. Finch groaned again but without pain that Mandy could detect.

Mandy took the cool cloth and cleaned Finch thoroughly. She was astonished that she had to cleanse him almost to his chin. When she was through, she looked quickly at his face, which was still drawn but not as tense. His penis had not diminished. Again, she looked at his face and the long, muscular body. Her eyes were gentle as a moonrise, and her lips as soft as down as she bent over him.

\* \* \* \* \* \*

An hour later Mandy walked quietly out of the room. Kate and Sam were still sitting by the kitchen stove. Sam was snoring softly. Kate looked up as Mandy entered.

"I think he's better now," Mandy said calmly, although she did not look directly at Kate. "He seems more relaxed, and he isn't groaning anymore."

"Dat good!" Kate said approvingly. "Now yo go gets yo some sleep. I stay right by his bed all night."

"All right," Mandy agreed, "but please call me if he gets restless again."

"I sho do dat, Miss Mandy. Now yo run along."

Kate took her position beside Finch's bed and was surprised to see that his face was relaxed and that a trace of a peaceful smile was on his lips. She checked the water pan that had obviously been recently refilled, and she saw that the damp cloth was rinsed and spread on the bedstead. Kate pulled the covers down and smiled in surprised delight. Finch was as flacid as a tired gelding.

"Reckon us nigger wenches ain't the only ones as knows more'n one way to pleasure a man," she chuckled.

\* \* \* \* \* \*

Finch lay unconscious for three days. Kate cared for him continuously, and Mandy came to soothe him each night. But it was finally Mandy's scream that pierced the fog engulfing Finch's brain and immediately exploded the darkness that had held him helpless for three days. He was instantly alert and sat up in bed. He shook his head and blinked several times. The scream came again, and he threw back the covers. Suddenly, he realized that he was naked. He looked about quickly. His clothing was stacked neatly on a bedside table, and his pistol and gunbelt hung on the bedpost. He grabbed his hat and slapped it on his head, only to be foiled by the thick bandage. It was the first time he realized that he had been hurt. He threw the hat on the floor and donned his pants as rapidly as he could. He slapped the gunbelt around his waist after quickly determining that his pistol was fully loaded.

The scream came again. Barefoot and shirtless, he made his way quickly out of the room and toward the sound. His long strides were silent as he opened the door to the big room that connected the Beatenbow and Finch living quarters.

The light was dim, for the walls were thick and the windows small. But Finch's eyes adjusted quickly. They beheld a sight that made his scalp prickle. Leaning against the wall by the fireplace stood Dutch Horst. His left arm was around Mandy's throat as he held her close to him, and beneath her arm he held a cocked pistol aimed at Finch. Mandy's blouse had been torn completely away, and her breasts stood taut and cherry-tipped as her blond head was pulled backward in the iron grip of Horst's arm. The tableau was frozen. Not a movement or a sound!

It was Horst who broke the silence.

"Well, if it ain't the fast gun, hisself!" he sneered and grinned evilly, showing his discolored teeth. "I reckon now I'll just see if you're faster'n a bullet!"

"Let her go!" Finch demanded.

"Well, now!" Horst said. "I reckon I may do that—after I've broke 'er in good a few days down the trail. Reckon, though, I'll just try 'er out a little first to see whether she's worth takin' along or not."

Mandy made a sound and struggled as Horst tightened his arm around her throat.

"You can't get away with it, Horst," Finch said quietly. "You're already a dead man."

"Now, look who's talkin'! I got my gun in your belly, and in just about a minute, I'm gonna put a 44 slug in that long, lean gut of yours. May just cripple you and tie you up good so's you can watch a real man in action. I reckon this bitch may beg me to let 'er come along with me when that pretty ass of hers knows what a real man is like."

"Beatenbow will kill you, Horst." Finch's blue eyes were shooting sparks, but his voice was steady.

"I reckon not," Horst replied almost gaily. "He's three or four days behind me, and when he gets here, he's gonna be mighty busy takin' care of his kids and buryin' a lot of niggers and cowboys—and maybe this bitch of a wife of his and her kids, if she don't take to me."

Finch had never felt so helpless. He knew that Horst, with his pistol cocked, would get off a shot. He weighed his chances. He knew that he could get off at least one shot even with Horst's bullet in him. The trouble was that Mandy's body shielded that of Horst, except for his head. And, wounded, Finch might flinch just enough to miss his mark.

"I reckon I'll just put a bullet in that shootin' arm of yours first," Horst gloated, "and then—."

There was a sound as the outside door of the room opened. Horst did not move his body, but his eyes flicked for a fraction of a second, and with blurring speed Finch's arm moved. One of Hurst's bulging eyes disappeared, and the back of his head seemed to explode as blood, bone, and brains spattered the wall around the bullet buried in the adobe behind him. His arm fell from Mandy as the sound of the shot died, and his pistol dropped to the floor. It did not fire. Mandy stood for a moment, as did Finch. Mandy's eyes were huge, dark pools of terror as she made her way unsteadily toward Finch, completely unaware of her bare breasts. She put her arms around Finch and held him tightly as she pressed against his naked chest. Her smooth, taut breasts triggered a reaction in him that made him ashamed. Nevertheless, he put his arms about her and held her protectively, and then glanced at the outside door from whence the diversion had come. Shanker Stone stood in the doorway, his pistol drawn, his eyes wide and his mouth agape.

"Is everything all right?" Shanker gulped.

"It is now," Finch said tightly.

"I saw 'im ride in," Shanker said. "Was just saddlin' a fresh horse down at the barn. He just didn't look right, somehow."

"He wasn't," Finch said, his arms still around Mandy and her head buried in his shoulder. Her long, blond hair cascaded down her bare back. "I'd take it as a favor if you'd get him outside before the kids see him!"

"I'll do that," Shanker said and proceeded to lift the heavy body of Horst by the shoulders and drag it outside.

Finch and Mandy stood unmoving until Shanker had closed the door.

"Where's O'oah?" Finch whispered hoarsely.

Mandy did not answer but squeezed Finch tighter and shook her head. He felt her warm tears as they rolled down his bare chest.

Finch knew immediately, and he flinched as though he had been hit.

"Where are your children?" he asked in a steady voice.

"In their bedroom." Mandy's voice was muffled against his chest.

"They all right?"

Mandy nodded mutely.

"Then, everything is all right now," Finch said grimly. "Go to them."

For the first time, Mandy raised her face and looked at Finch. "Everything isn't all right!" she said brokenly. "Several of the Negro children and women are dead, and some of the cowboys and black men, too. And O'oah—."

"Never mind," Finch said softly. "Hump will be back in a few days, and everything will be all right again."

"It won't be all right!" Mandy said fiercely. "Things will never be all right again! This is cruel land, and I hate it!"

"It's not the land that's cruel," Finch said consolingly. "We're just a few years ahead of our time out here. And we're a long ways west of Louisiana."

"Sometimes I think this land is west of everywhere!" Mandy said bitterly.

"This land is good!" Finch answered. "You'll love it again. Now go to your children." Finch tightened his arms about her for a second and then took her shoulders and turned her toward the children's bedroom.

"Mandy!" She stopped, but did not turn toward Finch. "Was it White Horse?" he asked fearfully.

"No," Mandy said in a small voice. "It was the Kiowas. It was White Horse who saved us."

Finch took a deep breath and made his way back to his quarters.

# Chapter 18

Just as the two wagons and the cowboys were ready to pull away from the Cimarron the next morning, they saw a bunch of Indians approaching from the west. Humphrey immediately climbed to the seat of the chuckwagon and laid his shotgun in his lap. Largo, who had been tending the remuda since midnight, was in Maisie's wagon asleep. Nearby, cowboys loosened their pistols and saw that their rifles were ready and at hand in their saddle scabbards.

As the Indians neared, it was easy to recognize the magnificent physique of Big Moose. He rode just to the right and slightly behind another Indian who was bedecked with colorful feathers and other finery of an Indian chief. Big Moose carried a long spear with a tassel of hair attached. Behind them were perhaps a dozen other Indians, four of them leading unsaddled horses.

Clem recognized them first. "It's that damn redskin that tried to steal Largo's wench on the way up," he informed Humphrey and the cowboys. "Calls hisself 'Big Moose.'"

"Well, he's shore named right!" one cowboy drawled. "I never saw a bigger Indian in my life."

"That's a chief ridin' in front," Clem said a bit anxiously. "Must be Yellow Wolf. He said that his daddy was a chief named Yellow Wolf."

"They're Cheyenne," Tonio said.

All the cowboys who had been riding some distance away from the wagons began unobtrusively to veer their mounts toward the approaching Indians. Each felt for the reassuring presence of his pistol as he did so.

The Indians came within a few feet. The chief stopped his horse and held up his hand, palm out, and said, "How!"

Humphrey and Clem returned the gesture, but the cowboys kept their hands near their pistols.

The chief began speaking in an Indian tongue, which no one but Tonio could understand.

"He say Indian and white man good friends," Tonio translated.

"I shore as hell doubt that!" Clem growled. "But tell 'im 'good' jus' the same."

Maisie, who was seated on the hospital wagon behind the chuck-wagon had recognized the huge Indian immediately, and her nostrils flared like a wild mustang that had scented danger.

The Indian chief resumed his guttural speech for several moments.

"What does he say?" Clem demanded of Tonio. Humphrey had quietly eased back the two hammers of his shotgun.

"Says his son, Big Moose, want black squaw. Says they will trade horses for her. Says Indians are friends!"

"Like hell!" Clem said through clinched teeth. "Tell 'im we ain't got no squaw to trade."

Tonio translated. It was Big Moose who responded in a tirade of Indian lingo as he pointed to Maisie, who sat on the wagon seat as proudly as a queen. When the Indian pointed at her, she simply averted her eyes, sat a bit straighter, and stared fixedly toward the western horizon.

The shouting had awakened Largo. He lay for a moment until he heard voices raised in anger. He wore only the short, loose trousers that he slept in. He was bare from the waist up and was barefoot. He slipped quietly out of the rear end of the wagon and moved alongside it away from the view of the Indians. He waited until he heard Clem say angrily, "Tell the stupid bastard that the black squaw already has a man and don' want no other one!"

Tonio interpreted. The big Indian responded with a tirade that sounded abusive. The chief and the other Indians remained stoically cold of face.

"He says," Tonio reported, "that Big Moose wants the black squaw, and he's gonna get her. Says she may have another man, but he is a better one; and he'll trade for her—or fight for her!"

It was then that Largo stepped into view. The Indians looked at him: Big Moose with contempt, Yellow Wolf with shrewd, measuring eyes. The other Indians showed no emotion, but simply sat their horses quietly. Clem saw Largo as he came into the view of the Indians.

"Tonio," Clem said with a bit of relief in his voice. "Tell 'em that this is the black squaw's man." He pointed to Largo.

Tonio dutifully translated, and Big Moose directed his speech to Largo. Largo stood, uncomprehendingly, looking from the Indian, to Clem, to Humphrey.

"What he sayin', Mars Tonio?" Largo asked in bewilderment.

"He wants to trade the four horses that they are leading for Maisie. Says they are good horses."

"But we's got plenty of horses," Largo said.

"He knows that," Clem grated. "He jus' wants your squaw."

"Well," Largo said, "I reckon she's my wench, an' I keeps 'er. Can you tell 'im that, Mars Tonio?"

"I can tell him that," Tonio assured Largo, "but I don't know whether he'll believe it or not," he added with a sardonic grin.

Tonio translated to Big Moose, who reacted as if he had been stung by a bee. He began a furious harangue that ended with his throwing his spear viciously. It sank deep into the ground at Largo's feet and stood quivering upright until Largo placed a hand on it. The big Indian barked a few more guttural words at Largo.

"What he say, Mars Tonio?" Largo's voice was querulous.

"He says he fight you for the squaw!"

Largo's face showed surprise, and then something like defiance. He looked at Humphrey, who still sat on the wagon seat.

"What I do, Mars Hump?" he asked pleadingly.

"She's your wench, Largo," Humphrey said without apparent sympathy. "That Indian offered four horses for 'er. I reckon you can take 'im up on that—or you can fight 'im."

"Is it all right with yo if'n I fights 'im, Mars Hump?"

"You'd be a damn pore Beatenbow black if you didn't," Humphrey said sourly.

Largo grinned and looked at Tonio. "Tell 'im I fight!"

Tonio translated. Big Moose immediately threw his leg over his horse's neck and hopped to the ground. He had a big knife in his hand.

"Hey, Largo!" Clem yelled as he tossed his own knife to Largo, who caught it deftly.

The two big savages faced each other for a moment, then lunged. It sounded like two longhorn steers coming together as their muscular bodies met. Each grabbed the knife hand of the other, and they stood straining for several seconds. Sweat popped out on Largo's brow. It was Largo who shoved first, and they parted. As they circled each other warily, each looked for a minute opening that might give him an advantage. Largo lunged. Big Moose stepped back to evade the lightning-like blow of the knife. As he did so, he stepped on a round stone and fell backward, but as he fell, he threw his knife at Largo. But from his position on the ground, his usual unerring skill failed him, and the knife struck Largo high on the shoulder. It hit just below the collar bone and sank to the hilt. The long blade penetrated the black skin on Largo's back. The Negro looked with surprise at the knife in his shoulder. He quickly grabbed the handle and yanked the knife out. Blood flowed. Largo threw the Indian's knife to the ground, and then, in anger and with little skill, he threw his own knife at the Indian and missed him completely.

The Indian gave a yell of triumph, leaped to his feet, and rushed Largo, who met him half-way. The two wrapped their arms around each other and strained. Their mighty muscles, powered by desperation, bulged like great ropes. It was quickly apparent that Largo was the stronger of the two. Big Moose loosed one arm and reached for Largo's face. He stuck one huge thumb in Largo's eye and squeezed with all his might. The eye popped out like a cork from a jug. Largo's scream was shrill and feral. He gave a mighty hug around the Indian's waist and butted him in the face. The crack of bone was audible. The Indian's legs went limp, and Largo let him fall. The Indian had uttered no sound, but glanced about and spied a knife, which, because of his useless legs, he had to crawl toward.

Largo's eye was dangling grotesquely on his cheek by a gray cord, but apparently he could still see out of the other, for as the Indian reached for the knife, Largo leaped and delivered a kick to the side of the neck with a thud that sounded like a side of beef being dropped on a chopping block. The Indian dropped, and his head lay almost perpendicular to his body. It was obvious that his neck was broken, for not one of his great muscles moved.

The men, who had been watching the fight as if transfixed, immediately removed their pistols from their scabbards and covered the other Indians. Humphrey lifted his double-barrel and pointed it at Yellow Wolf, who, too, had been watching closely; no emotion crossed his face. There was silence for a moment; then Humphrey spoke. His voice betrayed his feeling.

"Tonio," he said, "tell Yellow Wolf and his men to take Big Moose and light out, else I'm gonna put both barrels of this shotgun right in his belly."

Humphrey did not remove his eyes from the Indian chief, and the shotgun did not waver as Tonio translated. Yellow Wolf sat for a moment and then spoke to the Indians. Two of them immediately dismounted and loaded the body of Big Moose on his horse. Then, without a word or sign, the chief turned and rode away, followed by the other Indians. Four of them were leading the horses they had come to trade, and another led the horse that carried the son of Yellow Wolf.

Not a man in camp spoke for a moment as they watched the Indians depart. It was Maisie who broke the silence. She jumped from the wagon and ran to Largo.

"Yo is hurt, Largo," she said almost in a whimper.

"Yes, I is, Maisie," Largo said and raised a hand to the eye dangling on his cheek.

The cowboys holstered their pistols. Humphrey uncocked his shotgun and crawled down from the wagon. He walked up to Largo, who was standing mutely. Maisie had her arms around his waist and was sobbing. Humphrey looked at Largo critically.

"Well," he said, "the shoulder wound ain't much but a scratch. But the eye is bad. I reckon we'd best cut that cord it's a hangin' by."

"Oh, no suh!" pleaded Largo. "Please, Mars Hump, don' cut me no mo'!"

"It's the only way, Largo," Humphrey said sympathetically. "We can cut the cord and then sew that eye up."

Maisie leaned back and looked at Largo. Her face reflected his pain.

"Wait, Mars Hump," she said quickly. "Maybe we can put his eye back in. I saw it pop out, and dey's jus' a little hole there that it fits into. We could poke it back in there."

"Wouldn't work," Humphrey said gruffly.

"Oh, please, Mars Hump!" Maisie's voice was pleading. "Please jus' let me try!"

"All right," Humphrey agreed. "It won't do no good. But try if you want."

Ellie helped Maisie spread a quilt in the shade of a wagon, and Largo lay on it. His eye rolled to the side of his face. Humphrey brought a bottle of whiskey from the chuckwagon and handed it to Maisie.

"Have 'im drink most of this and then wash his eye and the socket out real good. That's gonna hurt like hell!"

"Yassuh, Mars Hump," Largo said. "It hurt now!"

"It'll hurt worse," Humphrey said unsympathetically as he walked away.

Maisie held the bottle to Largo's lips, and he drank deeply.

"Still hurt?" Maisie asked. Largo nodded, and Maisie held the bottle to his mouth again. The procedure continued for a few minutes. Then Maisie raised her voice to ask, "Mars Hump, you got any more of that whiskey? Largo, he drunk all the bottle, and it still hurt 'im."

"God-a-mighty!" Humphrey said almost in awe. "A full bottle of that would kill a white man if he drank it as fast as Largo did, and it didn't even faze 'im!"

Humphrey brought another bottle and knelt down beside Maisie and Largo. Ellie knelt uncertainly beside Maisie.

"Let 'im drink till he passes out," Humphrey said to Maisie, "and then you can work on 'im."

"Thanks, Mars Hump," Largo said. His voice was still clear.

Humphrey did not leave. Maisie continued to ply Largo with the whiskey. After a long gulp which half emptied the second bottle, Largo went limp, and his head rolled to one side.

"He daid, Mars Hump?" Ellie almost screamed her fright.

"He's not dead," Humphrey said. "Just passed out. Now, Maisie, you wash that socket out good with whiskey and wash that cord and eyeball good with it, too, afore you try to stuff that eye back in. Don't want 'im a gettin' no corruption on top of everything else."

Humphrey watched as Maisie followed his instructions, and he made an occasional suggestion. Maisie gently performed her ministrations, but was frustrated when the eyeball kept popping out of the socket.

"Ellie," Humphrey directed, "you get a needle and thread out of Maisie's sewin' box and bring it."

Ellie complied quickly. Humphrey directed that the thread and needle be immersed in the whiskey before it was used. Humphrey washed his hand in the fiery liquid.

"Now, Maisie, I'm a gonna push his eye back in and hold it there, and you start a sewin' his eyelid so's it'll hold it."

"Yo thinks that'll work, Mars Hump?" Maisie's voice was desperate.

"If it don't, I've wasted some good whiskey," Humphrey replied.

With great tenderness and infinite skill, Maisie sewed Largo's eyelid shut. She shuddered each time the needle perforated the lid. When she was done, she snipped the thread and looked at Humphrey.

"What now, Mars Hump?" she asked quaveringly.

"Might as well look at his shoulder while he's out, I reckon," he said.

They poured whiskey on the wound where the Indian's knife had penetrated Largo's shoulder.

"It ain't bad," Humphrey said. "If he don't get corruption in it, it ort to be all right."

"Yo means he can see again?" Maisie asked eagerly.

"Doubt like hell if he'll ever see out of that eye again," Humphrey said after a pause. "But I've seen animals recover from some wounds that I didn't think they could. So, we'll just have to wait and see."

"I specs he's gonna be all right," Ellie said optimistically.

"Well, he's shore as hell gonna have a terrible headache when he wakes up, with that gouged-out eye and all my whiskey he drank!"

With that, Humphrey went to his wagon and returned with another bottle. "I'll have some of the men load 'im on that mattress in yore wagon, Maisie," Humphrey said as he handed the bottle to her. "You give 'im some of this when he wakes up and gets to hurtin' too bad."

As Humphrey went back to the chuckwagon, a couple of the men, who had been following the Indians to see that they did not turn back returned. Humphrey told them to load Largo in the hospital wagon, which they did. Humphrey looked and was surprised that the sun said it was only mid-morning. He felt that it had already been a long day.

"Where are the rest of the boys?" Humphrey asked the two who had loaded Largo.

"Some of 'em still follerin' the Indians, and some of 'em driftin' on up ahead with the remuda."

"All right," Humphrey said. "We've gotten a late start, but I figure to be across the North Canadian by supper time. Tell the boys we won't stop for dinner."

\* \* \* \* \* \*

At approximately the time Maisie and Humphrey were plying their crude surgical treatment to Largo, Shanker Stone was facing another problem back at the HF Ranch. He had dragged the heavy body of Dutch Horst from the headquarters, but he was at a loss as to what to do with it. The body could easily be buried, but the horse and saddle posed a greater problem. The horse was almost surely stolen, and Horst's big saddle would be recognized by the cowboys. Finally, he reached a decision. He went to the mess hall where a Negro man was preparing the noon meal for the cowboys.

"Go and see if you can find a strange horse around the place. He'll have a saddle on."

The Negro complied and soon returned leading a big, Roman-nosed horse. The saddle was still on him, and the cinch was tight. Shanker and the Negro were extended to load Horst's big body across the saddle.

"Now, there ain't nothin' wrong with this here feller," Shanker assured the Negro. "Maybe so he had a mite too much to drink, but I don't want you to tell anybody that you ever saw 'im, you heah?"

"Yassuh, Mars Shanker," the Negro said. "I sho ain't gonna tell nobody."

"And that means nobody!" Shanker grabbed the Negro by his flimsy shirt and pulled his face close. "If I ever hear that a strange man was on this place today, I'm gonna know who told it, and I'm gonna nail yore black hide to a cottonwood tree!" Shanker said menacingly.

"Yassuh, Mars Shanker. I ain't gonna tell nobody never!" The Negro walked hurriedly away. He was frightened, but he was not fooled a bit. He knew that the man was dead, but he sure wasn't going to tell anyone!

Shanker saw Horst's hat lying on the ground; he picked it up and crammed it firmly under the saddle skirt. Then he led the horse carrying the body on a circuitous route behind the headquarters buildings, out of sight of the Negro quarters, then to the river and down it to the east for almost a mile. At a sharp bank about four feet high, he stopped and peered over. The water was clear and running only about an inch deep, but under that water, Shanker knew, lay a bottomless pit of quicksand.

He secured all the gear firmly on Horst's horse and led him to the bank. Shanker tied the reins over the horse's neck and pulled a long roweled spur from one of Horst's boots.

"It's a tough way to go, partner." Shanker patted the horse's neck. "And I can't say you're goin' in good company, but I can't think of no other way."

With that, Shanker jabbed the spur in the horse's flank. The horse, surprised and pained, jumped from the bank into the river, only to sink to his belly in the quicksand. He struggled for a moment or two as the quicksand sucked at him. He turned his head toward Shanker, who shot him in the forehead.

"A lot better'n sinkin' gradual, partner," Shanker said regretfully.

Shanker sat on the bank as he watched the horse and Horst's body sink slowly out of sight. He got up and walked to the bank. The water was again flowing smoothly over the sand. Shanker started to leave when he realized that he still held Horst's spur in his hand. He threw it into the river and watched as the heavy metal object quickly sank.

Shanker Stone turned and walked away, secure in the knowledge that the mysterious Canadian River that held a million secrets in its bosom would never reveal a trace of its latest acquisition.

\* \* \* \* \* \*

Three days later, the returning trail drivers arrived. Finch met them at the corrals. All the mules were gaunt and showed the effects of their fast travel and heavy load. The cowboys quickly unsaddled and headed for the bunkhouses. Alf and Trey penned enough of the remuda horses to furnish mounts and turned the rest out in the lush meadow to graze. The Beatenbow stud neighed his welcome. And the jackass, which had followed the wagons to Abilene and back, trotted sedately to his strong, round pen and entered meekly when the gate was opened for him.

Finch, wearing his hat far to one side because of his bandaged head, strode with his long, smooth stride to the stud corral where Humphrey stood with one foot on a rail, looking at the stud. He heard Finch approach and turned to him. They shook hands.

"Have a good trip?" Finch asked.

"I reckon as good as we could expect," Humphrey replied. "We got there with the 3100 head that I promised we would. What happened to you?"

"Got shot," Finch answered cryptically. "The Indians hit us a few days ago."

Humphrey looked quickly at the headquarters house where Mandy and the children were standing on the gallery. "Anybody else hurt?" he asked anxiously.

"Several of the blacks were killed, some of them kids. And O'oah—." Finch choked.

"What happened to O'oah?" Humphrey demanded.

"She got killed, too."

"God-a-mighty!" Humphrey breathed. "It wasn't White Horse's Comanches, was it?"

"No," Finch said. "Kiowas, so they told me, and it was White Horse that ran 'em off."

"They told you?" Humphrey asked incredulously.

"I got knocked out by a bullet, but wasn't hurt much. Laid up for a couple of days and didn't remember what happened. Mandy told me," Finch explained.

Humphrey wanted very much to say consoling words to his friend and partner, but could think of nothing. He noticed Finch looking intently at the remuda. Humphrey knew what he was looking for.

"Rafter. . ." he began, uncertain how to break the news to Finch. He cleared his throat and continued. "Rafter, he got his leg broke bad, and I shot 'im."

Finch simply nodded. "How did it happen?"

Humphrey wanted to tell Finch something that would make him feel better, but words failed him; so he simply told Finch how it had all happened. He did not try to lighten his own complicity in the tragedy that ended with the peddler going beserk and shooting Rafter, breaking his leg, and the death of Brandy.

"That grulla horse couldn't a caught Rafter if they had run till sundown," Humphrey said proudly. "He was a leadin' that grulla by four lengths when he fell over the finish line."

"He was a good horse," Finch said. "Best one I ever saw. Shore do hate it about Brandy. What happened to the peddler?"

"We hung 'im," Humphrey said simply.

Finch only nodded his approval. "Well, I reckon things got to be paid for in one way or another," he said. "And I'm not blaming you any, Hump. I'd a done the same thing, myself. Mandy said to tell you to come on up to the house. The coffee is hot."

Humphrey breathed a great sigh of relief as he and Finch turned to walk toward the headquarters house. Finch noticed Maisie and Ellie holding Largo by each arm as they led him to their quarters in the Negro section.

"What's the matter with Largo?" Finch asked.

"Got his eye gouged out in a fight with a Indian buck," Humphrey said tersely.

"Oh," Finch said vacantly. "I didn't figure there was any Indian that could whip Largo."

"He didn't whip Largo."

Finch looked at Humphrey keenly and noticed the grim set of his hawk-like features. He knew that Humphrey had said all he was going to for the moment.

"I'll just stop by his cabin and see how he's feelin'," Finch said and turned to follow the Negroes. He was glad to find an excuse to avoid the meeting between Humphrey and Mandy.

Finch knocked on the door of Largo's cabin; a Negroid feminine voice bade him enter. Largo was lying on the bed. Beside the bed was a bottle of whiskey less than half-full.

"How you feelin', Largo?" Finch asked solicitously.

"Porely, Mars Finch, porely," Largo replied weakly. "But that there whiskey that Mars Hump give me help some."

"I'll send you down some more," Finch said.

"I'll be thankin' yo, Mars Finch," Largo said as he closed his one good eye.

Finch turned to Maisie and Ellie. "What happened?"

Maisie told him the details of the fight, omitting only that it was she that they were fighting over. She also told him of the doctoring that she and Humphrey and Ellie had applied.

"I've never heard of anything like that before," Finch said in amazement. "Do you think he can ever see out of that eye?"

"De good Lawd only knows dat," Maisie said calmly. "But I ain't never felt no troublesome spirits in dis house since we got here."

Finch shook his head and departed after admonishing Maisie to send for him if she needed help. As he walked toward the mess hall, he remembered that Ellie had seemed much more mature than when they had started the drive. "I guess the blacks do mature mighty fast," he mused to himself as he entered the mess hall. Shanker Stone was drinking coffee. Finch sat across the table from him, and the cook poured coffee.

"You got rid of Horst, all right?" Finch asked.

"Yeah. I got rid of 'im," Shanker agreed.

"Hope that his horse goes back where he come from," Finch said. "I'd hate to have a stolen horse on the HF."

Then Shanker told Finch of the method he had used to dispose of Horst, his horse and saddle.

"That was mighty thoughtful of you, Shanker," Finch agreed. "I'd hate to have 'im buried in our own graveyard, even if we have got Comancheros, Indians, Mexicans, and niggers buried up there, along with some of the HF hands. I reckon he was the worst of the lot."

Shanker only nodded and started to take another swig of coffee, but his hand shook so badly that he spilled some of it, and he set it back on the table without tasting it.

"Don't feel bad about what you did, Shanker," Finch said soothingly. "I'd have done the same thing if I'd had sense enough to think of it."

"Hell!" Shanker burst out. "I don't feel bad about buryin' that evil bastard in the quicksand. Hated to shoot the horse, though."

"Then, what are you so nervous about?" Finch persisted. "You're shakin' like a cottonwood leaf."

"Finch!" Shanker took a deep breath. "You're lookin' at one of the biggest damn fools you ever saw!"

Finch removed his hat and laid it on the table. The white bandage around his head made his tanned face look darker.

"Want to tell about it?" Finch invited.

"No," Shanker said firmly. "But I'm gonna, anyway. You know I always fancied myself pretty damn rapid with a pistol—."

"A lot of other people think so, too," Finch said.

"I saw that whole thing up there at the headquarters, the day you shot Horst. That son-of-a-bitch had a pistol cocked and pointed right in your belly. He jus' shifted his eyes when I opened that door, and you drawed and shot his eye out afore he could pull a trigger."

"I reckon I am uncommonly fast with a pistol," Finch admitted.

"Fast, hell!" expostulated Shanker. "Up till I saw that, I couldn't help but wonder if I was as fast as you—after hearin' all them stories about you in the Rangers. And I got to admit that the damn, crazy idee kept naggin' at my mind to find out—and if I had, I'd might as well have jumped into that quicksand with Horst."

Finch laughed for the first time since O'oah had been killed. "Well, don't worry about that, Shanker. I guess every man needs to know how good he is. But you and I will never know which one is the fastest, for I shore won't ever fight you."

"You damn shore won't!" Shanker grinned ruefully. "I already know which one of us is fastest! I doubt like hell that any man alive can match you with a pistol!"

# Chapter 19

Life on the HF continued much as it had before the trail drive to Abilene. Humphrey hired all the extra hands that had made the drive, on a permanent basis. He was not convinced that the Indians would not attack again, particularly in view of the fact that Sheridan was pushing the Indians south out of Kansas. Besides, they now had plenty of money to pay wages, and some of the cowboys and blacks had been killed in the raid.

The cowboys rode the ranch daily, and guards were posted at night. The most noticeable changes were in Finch and Ellie. Finch was no longer his laughing, carefree self, and his blue eyes had lost their twinkle. The loss of O'oah had affected him deeply, and he could not rid his mind of the misty memories of the times he dreamed that she came to his room for several nights after she had been killed, and of the gentle ministrations that she had performed on his body that had resulted in the most exquisite sensation he had ever experienced.

Finch knew that his foggy hallucinations were the result of the rifle bullet that had left him unconscious for four nights, but he could not rid his mind of the fantastic illusion as he went to bed each night. As a result, he moved his bed to the big, cave-like storehouse that had been built in the side of a hill when they first came to the ranch and where he and O'oah had spent their first nights as man and wife. It was with great relief that he slept soundly there, and no dreams of ecstasy intruded upon his rest.

Humphrey and Mandy had objected to Finch's moving, but he had prevailed, and Mandy had agreed for two of their children to sleep in Finch's bed in the Finch wing of the big house. Finch still took his meals with Humphrey and Mandy.

"Wish you would talk to Finch, wife," Humphrey said to Mandy after they had gone to bed the night Finch moved his bed to the storehouse. "I'd do it myself, but I jus' can't think of the right words to say, and I hate to see 'im hurt and not be able to help 'im."

Mandy lay silently beside Humphrey for a few moments; then she rolled over and kissed him on the cheek. "I know you love Finch, my husband," she said softly. "We all do. And I will talk to him if you think it would help."

"It shore won't hurt anything," Humphrey said, relieved. "He's been mopin' around like a dogie calf since we got back. Ain't like hisself at all."

"When do you want me to talk to him?"

Humphrey was silent for a few moments. "Wait till tomorrow night," he said. "After he's gone to that cave where he sleeps. Nobody will bother you there, and maybe he'll talk some, and it'll help. Does me."

Mandy said nothing more, and soon Humphrey was asleep, but she lay awake for hours staring into the darkness.

\* \* \* \* \* \*

The day after their return, Humphrey instructed some of the Negroes to bring the sacks of gold coins to the kitchen and give them to Kate.

"Kate," Humphrey said, "you hide that gold like you always did on the plantation back in Louisiana, and then tell me where you hid it. Tell Finch, too, but don't tell nobody else. He was quiet for a moment, and then added, "Maybe so you'd better tell Mandy, too."

"Yassuh, Mars Hump," Kate agreed. "I hide it good, and I don' tell nobody but you and Mars Finch and Miss Mandy."

Ellie, who had been in the kitchen, heard the conversation and said, "I'll help you, mama."

"No, yo won't!" Kate glared at Ellie fiercely. "Didn't yo hear Mars Hump when he say nobody gonna know but him and Mars Finch and Miss Mandy?"

"It's awful heavy," Ellie said as she left the kitchen and walked toward the Negro quarters.

"Mars Hump," Kate began hesitantly, "does yo—.?"

"Does I what?" Humphrey barked at her.

"Does yo know what has come over Ellie? I's her ma, an' I'd ort to know if'n anybody do— but I don'. An' she been different since she got back. Don' seem to be afeared o no man no mo lak she was ever since that no-count nigger rape 'er when we was on our way out west from Fort Worth."

"I reckon I ain't noticed much difference in 'er," Humphrey admitted. "She's growed up some, and her tits are gettin' bigger, but all yore git growed up fast. An' she's a twelve-year-old now."

"Yassuh, I reckon yo right, Mars Hump," Kate said with resignation. "But she do seem sort of different, somehow."

"Well, she seemed like she liked that little horse wrangler, Brandy, a lot. The one that got killed. Bawled like a lost calf the day he died. But he was a white man!"

\* \* \* \* \* \*

At supper the night after Humphrey's request that Mandy talk with Finch, she kept up a lively conversation. Humphrey was his usual silent self. Finch tried valiantly and vainly to enter into the conversation, but failed miserably. He excused himself early and went to his storehouse bedroom.

He was sitting on the side of his bed with his boots off, reading the label on a tin can by the light of a kerosene lantern when there was a knock on the storeroom door. He unlatched the door from the inside and opened it. Mandy stood there, her magnificent blond hair loosened and framing her beautiful face.

"May I come in?" she asked timidly.

"Why—I reckon so." Finch was taken aback. He opened the door and moved to one side. Mandy stepped in, pulled the door shut, and latched it. Finch looked a question at her.

"Just so we won't be disturbed," she smiled. "I want to talk to you, Finch. And I don't want to be interrupted."

"Why—why—sure," Finch managed to stammer.

There was only one chair in the dugout, and Finch pulled it up for her. He sat on the bed.

"Something I can help about, Mandy?"

"Yes," she said firmly. "You can laugh and smile again. I know that losing O'oah was a terrible blow to you. But sorrow can be overcome. I lost my first husband in the war, you know."

"I know you did, Mandy," Finch said gently. "And you've made Hump a wonderful wife since then, too!"

"Then you can find your way back, too!" Mandy said encouragingly. "You know that O'oah would have wanted you to!"

"It isn't O'oah altogether that's bothering me," Finch said lamely.

"Then, what is it?" Mandy probed. "Surely you aren't bothered by that vile creature that you killed when he was attacking me! Oh, please! I hope not!" Mandy had unconsciously reached over and covered one of Finch's hands that was resting on his knee.

"No. Of course not, Mandy," Finch said. "I've killed men before. A lot of them. And I can't say I like doing it, but it hasn't worried my mind any. And I reckon Horst less than any of them."

"Then what is it?" Mandy insisted. "Something is!"

Without conscious awareness of what he was doing, Finch suddenly began to tell Mandy of the dreams that he had had when lying unconscious the days after he had been shot, of his delusion that O'oah came to him each night, and of the exhilarating moments he had experienced.

"Of course, I know now that it wasn't O'oah, for I remember seeing that Kiowa sink his axe in her head. And I started running toward her. But that is all I remember. I know that she didn't come to me when I was unconscious, for she was dead. But I still remembered those dreams, or whatever you call them, every time I slept in that bed. I reckon that bothered me some." Finch finished his speech almost defiantly, for he was sure that Mandy would think him still out of his mind.

"Poor Finch," Mandy said softly. "That is what has been bothering you!"

"I guess you think I'm still crazy," Finch said.

Mandy looked at him for several moments. She squeezed his hand gently, and a tear rolled from her dark, luminous eyes.

"You are not crazy, Finch," she said gently. "You just have your women mixed up. It was I who came to you each night. And it was I who did what was necessary to get you to relax and sleep."

"You!" Finch was absolutely shocked.

"Yes. And I would do it again, if you needed someone as badly as you did then. Humphrey and I both love you, Finch."

Finch sat with a dazed look on his face as Mandy went to the door and unlatched it. Before she opened the door, she turned to him again.

"So you see, Finch, you aren't crazy at all!" Mandy smiled at him. "And there is something else, too!"

"What?" Finch gasped.

"I enjoyed doing it," Mandy said as she left and closed the door behind her.

\* \* \* \* \* \*

At breakfast the next morning there was no tension between Finch and Mandy, although Finch did cast a grateful look at her. She replied by smiling warmly at him.

"Finch and I had a nice, long talk last night," Mandy said to Humphrey.

"Good!" Humphrey said as he helped his plate to more bacon. "Finch, Kate has got that gold hid, and she'll show you and Mandy where it is. Ain't likely the Indians or nothin' else will get us all at one time; so we ort to have enough to run this place for some time."

"We sure should," Finch agreed. "And I expect we'd better make another drive next year."

"I reckon," Humphrey said. "Think you could manage the next one?"

"I can sure give it a try. I think the Indians will be better settled by then, and in the meantime we've got plenty of rifles to take care of things, anyway, with all the extra hands you brought back from Abilene."

"I rode the pasture yesterday," Humphrey said. "Seems like ever cow we got had twins while I was gone."

"I hope not," Finch said facetiously. "Too many twin calves can get a rancher hung for rustlin'."

They all laughed and enjoyed another cup of coffee.

\* \* \* \* \* \*

Early signs of a bad winter began to appear in October. The horses and cattle began putting on long hair, coyotes howled at mid-day, and high flying geese and other birds that summered in the north began their southern migration.

One night as they were eating supper, Kate came in to serve them.

"Reckon we's gonna have a mighty cold winter," she opined. "I done got troublesome spirits a sayin' it gonna be a bad one, and Sam's rumatiz is botherin' 'im sompin awful already."

"Where is Ellie?" Mandy asked, for it was usually she who served them.

"Ellie ain't feelin' too good today, I reckon. I tells 'er to go to baid."

When Kate left the room, Humphrey frowned and said, "A real bad winter could shore hurt us. Wisht we had some farm land so's we could grow some feed on it."

"Maybe the winter won't be bad," Mandy said optimistically.

"You don't really believe all that voodoo stuff the niggers talk about, do you, Hump?" Finch asked.

Humphrey didn't say anything for a moment. Then he spoke seriously. "Maybe I don't believe in it. But I got more sense than not to pay some attention to it. Them niggers are a lot closer to the natural run of things than we maybe think. You got to remember that it ain't been long since they was animals, too."

\* \* \* \* \* \*

True to Kate's prediction, winter came early. In late October a heavy snow fell, driven by a mighty north wind. The cowboys, in addition to their daily duty of riding the rim of the valley, had the extra chore of rescuing cows and calves from snowdrifts. But, as all of them knew, the Indians were loath to travel in cold weather; so danger of an attack was somewhat abated.

It was in October, too, that Humphrey finally noticed that Ellie was pregnant. Mandy and Finch had noted it sometime before and had passed knowing glances. Humphrey's fork was half-way to his mouth when he looked at Ellie one morning at breakfast. He lowered the uneaten food to his plate.

"Ellie," he said harshly, "are you knocked up?"

"Yassuh, Mars Hump. I is," she confessed with no sign of self-consciousness.

"Kate!" Humphrey roared as Ellie scooted from the dining room into the kitchen. Kate appeared.

"Yassuh, Mars Hump. Here I is. Yo be wantin' sompin?"

"Damn right I am," Humphrey glowered. "Ellie says she's knocked up."

"Yassuh, Mars Hump. She is. I's knowed it for a time now."

"Well, who in hell is her buck?" Humphrey roared.

"Don' know, Mars Hump," Kate replied calmly. "I ain't ask 'er."

"Then, ask her, Dammit. She's yore git."

"I knows dat, Mars Hump," Kate agreed, "but I's a nigger, and so's she, and we don' go a pokin' into other's doins! We got our ways."

"God-a-mighty!" Humphrey ejaculated. Mandy and Finch smiled at each other.

\* \* \* \* \* \*

The rest of the winter proved to be as cold and harsh as a west Texas winter can be. A big snow fell in mid-March, only to be followed by clear days and bright moonlight nights that reflected diamonds in the snow. One evening, Kate failed to appear in the kitchen, and Ellie was absent, too.

"Where in hell is that lazy nigger Kate?" Humphrey demanded.

"She's probably down at the Negro quarters," Mandy said calmly. "Some of them may be ill. I expect there's a pot of coffee on the stove. I'll pour you and Finch some, and then I'll cook your supper."

Humphrey scowled as he accepted the coffee, but said nothing. Finch said, "thank you," and looked at Mandy. They smiled conspiratorially.

It was dark, and the full moon was high overhead when Humphrey and Finch finished supper and were drinking another cup of coffee. Mandy had just begun washing the dishes when Sam, Kate's elf-like husband, came into the kitchen. He had on a heavy coat, and his feet and head were swathed in rags. Only his beady black eyes showed.

Mandy watched him as he unwrapped. She knew that it was miserably cold outside.

"Where is Kate?" Mandy asked gently as the old Negro walked up behind the stove to warm.

"She down at Ellie's cabin." Sam grinned his toothless grin. "She say tell yo all she mighty vexed up about not gittin' yo supper, but Ellie had her sucker jis a while ago, and Kate, she thinks she be needed."

Mandy hurried to the dining room to tell Humphrey and Finch. Finch immediately rose and started donning heavy clothing.

"Where you goin'?" Humphrey asked.

"Gonna go see Ellie's baby," Finch said.

"So am I," Mandy echoed Finch.

"What for?" Humphrey said gruffly. "Them niggers can drop a sucker in a snowbank, and they'll both be all right."

"Oh, Humphrey," Mandy said in exasperation. "Quit calling them 'niggers' and the babies 'suckers.' Now come on and go with us. You know it will make Ellie feel good—and Kate, too."

"Mandy, you're beginnin' to sound more like Colette ever day," Humphrey grumbled. But he, too, rose and began donning heavy clothes.

"I ought to sound like Colette," Mandy said to Humphrey. "I was her aunt, remember?"

"I remember," Humphrey said and followed them out the door to Ellie's cabin.

Inside the cabin a kerosene lamp furnished a yellow light that enabled them to see Ellie lying on the bed holding a bundle in her arms. She smiled weakly, and a huge grin split Kate's face.

"We's awful glad yo come, Mars Hump," Kate said. "An' yo, too, Miss Mandy and Mars Finch. Come on over and look at Ellie's sucker."

"He ain't no sucker. He's a baby!" Ellie's voice was weak, but clear.

Kate took the kerosene lamp from the shelf and held it above Ellie and the baby. Ellie pulled the wraps back for them to see a red, wizened face and a small pate of reddish brown hair.

"He awful pretty, ain't he," Ellie said proudly.

"He certainly is," Mandy agreed, and Finch echoed her compliment. Humphrey said nothing and had not bent as far over the bed as Finch and Mandy.

"What is his name?" Mandy asked the age-old question of a new mother.

"His name be Brandy," Ellie said proudly. "Brandy Beatenbow!"

Humphrey's face flushed with anger. He was outraged that a Negro would have the temerity to name a sucker 'Beatenbow.' He started to protest when Finch laid a hand on his shoulder.

"Brandy must have been a fine man," Mandy said soothingly.

"Yassum, he was," Ellie agreed. "I reckon he a mite young for a white man to sire a baby— but he done it a lot of times to me. An' he called all of us nigger women, 'ladies,' too."

"I'm sure he will be a fine young man," Mandy said.

"Yassum. He gonna be," Ellie said. "I gonna raise 'im so's Brandy be proud of 'im."

Humphrey, Mandy and Finch left the cabin and walked out into the deep snow. The full moon shone down, and crystals of ice in the air glistened in its glow. Humphrey stopped for a minute and looked up at the moon. Mandy took Humphrey's arm, and Finch put an arm over his shoulder.

"Things change, Hump," Finch said kindly.

"God-a-mighty!" Humphrey responded in defeat, prayer, and hope.

As they started on toward the house, there began a low, roaring bray that rose to an eerie, unearthly sound and ended in a shrill, screaming pitch that echoed and resounded up and down the Canadian River. The Beatenbow jackass was roaring his approval of the beautiful night, and the big, wild, wonderful world!

# Where The Wind Lives

# Chapter 1

Finch was returning from the camp of his Comanche friend White Horse that warm spring morning in 1870. He sat loosely and gracefully in the saddle as he rode his horse onto a rocky promontory overlooking the great valley that was the HF ranch.

He breathed a sigh of pure pleasure as he viewed the scene before him. The warm wind felt good as it pushed gently at his long, wiry body. His superb physical condition had not been sapped by the eager young Indian maiden that had sought his blankets the night before. One of the wives of White Horse? One of his daughters? There was no way to tell! All that Finch knew, or cared about, was that she had been a welcome and enthusiastic bed partner.

Finch was a celibate man only by necessity. It had been a year since his wife O'oah had been killed by Kiowas. He had soon found that the long ride to the Comanche camp paid off in many ways, for he forged a stronger friendship with White Horse, and, invariably, he was visited in the dead of night by an Indian girl. Different ones, he knew, though he had never seen one of them. They were, however, all adroit, eager, and insatiable.

Finch was convinced that Mandy knew the purpose of his visits to the camp of White Horse. Although one wing of the adobe ranch house had been built for him, and he and his lovely half-Indian wife O'oah had shared it blissfully until she was killed, Finch had moved back into the large half-dugout, which the former slaves had built first. He still took his meals with Humphrey and Mandy in the big house dining room.

During the meals, Mandy would talk pleasantly and softly, and her musical voice was pleasing to the ear, as her blond hair and big, dark eyes and creamy complexion were to the eye. She was also utterly female and intuitively recognized the lusty male drives of Finch. When he became a bit restless or preoccupied, she invariably sensed his need.

"Why don't you go visit White Horse?" Mandy would suggest. "We need to keep our relations with the Indians as friendly as possible, and I know that White Horse regards you almost as his own son."

"I expect I ought," Finch replied. "I haven't been up there in a couple of weeks."

"That's a long ride," Humphrey said almost grouchily.

Mandy and Finch looked at each other; a mysterious and esoteric message was sent and received.

"I can make it in a day," Finch said. "I'll ride Gato. He's fresh and ready for a long ride."

Gato had been Chico Baca's horse. After Chico was murdered on their drive out of Fort Worth, and after Rafter, the fastest and most durable horse that Finch had ever owned, had been killed on the trail drive to Abilene, Finch had started riding Gato.

When returning from his trips to the Indian camp, Finch always rode down through the big valley on the north side of the Canadian River. He feasted his eyes on the scene below him for a few moments and then reined Gato to the trail that led to the valley floor. As he approached the bottom of the valley, a huge covey of quail flushed and made Gato shy and jump sideways. Finch swayed lithely with the motion; when Gato landed a few feet from where he had launched himself, he stood stiffly for a moment and pricked his small ears toward the flurry of sound that was receding as the quail flew away. Finch laughed and leaned over to pat the horse on the shoulder.

"Scare a fellow to death, won't they, old boy!" Finch said soothingly. Gato relaxed, and they continued their way down the valley.

It was several miles to the headquarters, and Finch was prepared to enjoy every bit of it. Once he had seen a sentry riding along the valley rim, but the rider did not see Finch, for he was scanning the prairies for any sign of an approaching band of Indians; Finch had also seen a big lobo wolf that was eating a newborn calf, and which he shot almost automatically; and once he caught a flash of tawny hide as a big puma disappeared into a gully. Now, longhorns stared belligerently as he passed. There was no fear in their eyes as they looked at the man and horse. A few of the bulls pawed great clods of earth and issued an obvious challenge, which Finch ignored. Antelope were plentiful; a few deer paused in their browsing to look curiously at him.

Finch was as relaxed as he ever was, although he constantly scanned ahead and to either side for signs of danger. When he was within a mile of headquarters, he took a trail to the top again and rode to the hill above the cluster of buildings. The light morning breeze had died, and Finch could hear the song of a meadow lark, which he thought was the sweetest sound in nature. He observed the headquarters house, the long bunkhouse, the small cabins that were the Negro quarters, the huge barn, and the corrals. Finch felt a sense of pride and accomplishment, as he always did when seeing the place that looked so peaceful, though, in reality, it was situated in the very midst of hostile Indian country.

Mandy had been looking out the window anticipating Finch's return and his invariable stop on the hill to survey the scene below. Her dark, expressive eyes shone with an unfathomable light as she looked at his tall figure sitting so erectly on his horse.

"Oh, I do hope he found someone who was good to him," she thought silently.

Mandy knew a great deal about Finch's libido, though Finch was not aware of her knowledge. For he had lain unconscious for four days when an Indian bullet had grazed his skull. Humphrey had been on a trail drive, and Mandy had helped Old Kate nurse Finch day and night. And although his mind was swathed in darkness, the rest of his strong, slender body was functional. And Mandy had discovered that there was a portion of his anatomy that would delight any woman. She subconsciously envied the Indian maiden, whoever she was, who had shared his blanket the night before.

Humphrey, who was standing in the hallway of the barn, spied Finch at the same time Mandy did, but his reaction was quite different. "Would-a been a hell of a lot easier for 'im to walk a hundred yards down to the nigger quarters last night," he grumbled under his breath. "A black wench is just as good as an Indian woman—maybe better!"

Humphrey's thought stemmed from his experience on the plantation back in Louisiana when the blacks were still slaves. But Finch and Mandy would have been astounded at Humphrey's observation. They had blithely assumed that he thought Finch's visits to the camp of White Horse were just what they purported to be: to continue their good relations with the Comanches. Neither Mandy nor Finch had any inkling that the prosaic, unimaginative Humphrey had discerned the real reason for the visits.

But the pragmatic Humphrey had been born and raised on the Beatenbow plantation, which had been renowned for the quality of mules and slaves it bred. Copulation by animals and humans was no novelty to him. He fully agreed with old Kate, the jolly, fat Negress who had been the Beatenbow cook since before he was born and who was often heard to say, "Humans and animals is gonna breed. It de nature o 'em, and ain't nobody gonna change dat!"

* * * * * *

Finch rode down to the barn a few minutes later and was unsaddling Gato when Humphrey walked up.

"Have a good trip?" Humphrey was being sociable.

"Yep," Finch agreed.

"Think White Horse and his Comanches are still gonna keep their word to Kit, even if he's been dead nearly two years?"

"I'm sure of it," Finch replied. "At least, I'm as sure as anybody can be about Indians," Finch modified his statement.

"I reckon nobody can be absolutely sure of the red bastards," Humphrey replied gruffly. He had harbored a hatred of the red man almost as great as his hatred of Yankees, ever since they had killed his first wife on the trek west of Fort Worth.

"I expect you're right," Finch agreed. "But it doesn't hurt anything to pay a friendly visit to them once in a while."

"Let's go to the house." Humphrey changed the subject abruptly. "I expect Kate has got dinner near ready—and Mandy, she'll be wantin' to know how you made out."

Kate had the noon meal almost ready; first she served coffee in the dining room to Mandy, Humphrey, and Finch. As they waited for the food, they sipped the black coffee, and Mandy queried Finch eagerly about his visit. Her big, dark eyes shone with pleasure as she looked at Finch and vicariously shared his pleasures of the night before.

Finch spent the afternoon lazing about the headquarters, which was unusual, for it was his custom to scout several miles each day, and always in a different direction, so that he might pick up any sign of an unusually large group of Indians who might be a force that would menace the ranch. But the night in the Indian camp and the long ride back to headquarters had left him with a pleasant feeling of lassitude, and he was content to laze about the ranch.

He wandered down to the Negro quarters and was greeted by wide grins from the black women, many of whom were taking advantage of the warm day to hang laundry. The black children howled with glee as they spotted him and ran forward to grab his hand or hang around one of his long legs. Finch was their favorite white man, for they were in awe of the stern, hawk-faced Humphrey; yet they knew that all the grown-up blacks adored 'Mars Hump',even though he paid little attention to them. Finch tousseled some of the kinky heads and picked up a couple of the smallest children and held them in his arms as he walked past several of the cabins. He wished that he had some candy to give them and wondered absently if any of them had ever tasted sweets other than a 'sugar tit', which was nothing but sugar tied in a small wad of a rag.

Humphrey was directing several of the Negro men in mending some corrals and in cleaning the big loft of the barn in preparation for a new crop of prairie hay which they would reap in the fall. The number of blacks who were available for labor was dwindling, however, for some had been killed, and more of them were becoming adept at riding and hazing buffalo out of the valley. Clem, the ranch foreman continued to be disgusted that the blacks still preferred the surcingle to a saddle when they were riding.

After supper, Finch sought his bed earlier than usual. He entered the big half-dugout which served as a storage place and where he had slept while the blacks were building the head-quarters house during the months that Humphrey had returned to Louisiana. It was also the place where O'oah had first lived with him.

The headquarters had been completed by the blacks under the direction of Largo during the months of Humphrey's absence. When he had returned with Mandy, his new bride, they had insisted that Finch and O'oah move into the wing of the big house that had been designated for them. Since O'oah had died, however, Finch was uncomfortable with the memories of O'oah that seemed to linger in the bedroom that they had shared so blissfully, and he had moved back to the storage dugout. His bed was simply a roll of blankets, but the place was warm in winter and cool in summer. Finch always felt that a friendly cocoon had wrapped him every time he entered it. That night he stretched his long length on his bedroll, gave a contented sigh, and was asleep in seconds.

Finch slept soundly until just before daylight, and then, as he always did, awakened rested, bright-eyed, and ready for the day. He leisurely dressed and walked the short distance to the big house. He unbuckled his gun belt and hung it on the handsome hall tree that had been fashioned by Largo.

Humphrey was already sitting at the table drinking coffee when he entered the dining room.

"Mornin', Hump!" Finch greeted him.

Humphrey returned the greeting with a non-intelligible grunt, as he always did. Humphrey was not at his best before breakfast.

Finch pulled up a chair, and old Kate quickly appeared with coffee. The two men drank their coffee in silence for a few minutes before Mandy entered the room. She wore a robe, and her golden hair was loose and fell to her waist. Her dark eyes sparkled with love of life and zest for living. Finch quickly rose and pulled out a chair and marvelled at her sparkle, radiance, and beauty. Humphrey returned her cheerful greeting as he had to Finch.

Mandy chatted gaily as old Kate set food on the table. Finch was ravenously hungry, as he always was at breakfast. Humphrey took big bites and swallowed with a minimum of chewing, a habit he had acquired when serving four years in the Confederate army. Mandy picked at her food and sipped coffee.

The meal was not completed when a scream that sounded neither animal nor human, but was carried on waves of agony, pain, and terror penetrated the thick adobe walls of the ranch house.

Finch and Humphrey looked at each other for a second as if stunned. Mandy paled.

"God-a-mighty!" Humphrey breathed in awe. "What was that?"

Finch rose quickly and in a few long strides was in the hallway. He was buckling his pistol around his waist as he rushed outside. Humphrey followed closely with his rifle in his hand. The fact that neither men had a hat on gave mute testimony to the impact of the terrifying sound.

The scream came again, and with it a high-pitched squeal. Though it was still not quite sunup, they could see two animals in furious motion near the round pens of Old Heck, the ranch stallion, and the Beatenbow jackass.

Cowboys came pouring from the bunkhouse in various states of dress, but all had firearms in their hands. The Negro quarters were also being emptied of Negro men, who also had guns. All of them ran toward the tumultuous activity. Finch was the first to arrive and was appalled to see that the strong pens which had held the stud and the jackass were wide open. The stud and the jackass, who had hated each other for years, were finally locked in mortal combat.

"What the hell happened?" Clem panted as he ran up.

"Somebody opened them gates!"

"Go get me a blacksnake!" Humphrey ordered one of the blacks. The man ran toward the barn.

The cowboys and Negroes were throwing hats, articles of clothing, and everything else they could lay their hands on in a futile effort to distract the maddened animals.

A Negro ran back from the barn with the long bullwhip and handed it to Humphrey, who uncoiled it and started walking toward the gladiators, whipping it violently as he came near. Finch palmed his pistol. Clem shoved a shell into the chamber of his rifle, for both knew Humphrey's reputation of never taking a backward step when faced by man or beast, and Finch and Clem were both prepared to kill the struggling animals if Humphrey walked into range of their flailing hooves.

The sight was awe-inspiring. The stud was big and muscular, the jackass small and dainty. But both were imbued with a festering hatred that had finally had the opportunity to vent itself.

Although the stud was bigger and stronger, the jackass was quicker and apparently possessed a primitive instinct for combat. The stud held his head low to the ground and stalked the jackass like a huge serpent, while the jackass darted in and out like a sparrow attacking a hawk; he would whirl and kick too fast for the eye to follow. Humphrey kept walking in on them, slashing as hard as he could with the bull whip that popped like a pistol shot when it found its mark. When the tip of the whip hit the eye of the stud, temporarily blinding him, he paused for a fraction of a second. The jackass took advantage by darting in, and with the speed of a striking rattler, grabbed a large chunk of hide and meat in his iron-strong jaws. He wheeled away, taking a strip of bloody hide more than a foot long. The stud screamed again in agony and reared in the air, whereupon the jackass darted in to whirl and kick viciously with both back feet.

The breaking bone was audible, even in the din of battle. The stud fell backward, but regained his feet immediately, only to have one hind leg flop obscenely as the bone protruded from it, and he fell to the ground again.

The jackass apparently knew that the fight was over, for he fled from the yelling men and the punishing whip and ran back to his round pen, cowering there.

"Who in hell opened them gates?" Clem demanded belligerently of the cowboys. He got no answer.

"I was on watch atop the bunkhouse last night," one offered. "I was a-watchin' close, and I never saw nothin' move.!"

"God-a-mighty!" Humphrey groaned. "The most valuable animal on the place!"

There was only one remedy to the condition of the stud, and all knew it. Clem shot him with his rifle and started walking purposefully toward the jackass's pen.

"What are you doin', Clem?" Humphrey yelled.

"I'm gonna kill that damn jackass!" Clem answered grimly. "The son-of-a-bitch has had it a- comin' for a long time!"

"Don't do that!" Humphrey ordered sternly. "God-a-mighty, man! Losin' the stud is bad enough, and if we lose the jackass, we'll be a-havin' to work longhorns to our wagons instead of mules!"

Clem hesitated, and then his shoulders slumped in defeat as he turned reluctantly.

"Well, I reckon we'll be ridin' pure mustangs now since we ain't got that stud to cross on them little mares. Old Heck was a-gettin' some good colts out of 'em, too."

"And there ain't another stud other than a damn, runty mustang in two hundred miles of here!"

# Chapter 2

Mandy had been looking out the window, but could not see the corrals from her vantage point. She flinched and turned pale when she heard the rifle shot that mercifully ended the life of the stallion.

"What happened? What was it?" she asked anxiously as Humphrey and Finch came back into the house. Both men had touselled hair, for they had rushed outside without their hats, a very rare thing for them to do.

"Just a horse fight," Humphrey replied.

"But all that noise! And I heard a shot!" Mandy persisted.

"It was the stud and the jack," Humphrey said in a tired voice. "They've always hated each other, and they finally got together."

"Which—what—?"

"Old Heck got his leg broke." Finch sought to soften the blow. "Clem put 'im out of his misery."

"You mean—?"

"He's dead," Humphrey said harshly. "And that means we're in mighty bad shape to raise any more horses that's fit to ride."

"We'll need another stud mighty bad," Finch agreed. "We shore won't be able to improve our remuda with what we have."

"Couldn't come at a worse time, either," Humphrey said glumly.

"Finish your breakfast," admonished Mandy. "It isn't the end of the world."

"You're right," Humphrey agreed. "But if this here ranch is ever gonna amount to anything, we've got to improve our stock, just like we did on the plantation back in Louisiana."

"Well, we've still got the jackass, and we've got some mighty fine mules by him out of the thoroughbred mares."

"I ain't too shore about that jackass," Humphrey said. "Old Heck got some pretty good kicks in on 'im, and his side looked like it was puffed up pretty bad. Got some ribs broke, more'n likely."

"If he's hurt bad, we are goin' to be in a mighty poor way for raisin' livestock except for longhorn steers," Finch agreed.

"Maybe you can capture a mustang stud and breed it to the thoroughbred mares," Mandy suggested helpfully.

"We've had a few mares get bred to mustangs when they was runnin' out in the valley. The colts don't do any better than the pure mustangs. Maybe a little bigger is all."

"Wonder how those two gates got opened," Finch mused aloud.

"I don't know," Humphrey said dourly. "But I've got Tonio a-sniffin' out trails, and you know he can trail a catfish through water. So I'm hopin' he'll find out who did it."

Tonio was a real enigma—a half-breed Indian and Mexican, who spoke several Indian dialects, as well as perfect Spanish and faultless English, when he wished, and he was unsurpassed as a tracker. He had shown up at the ranch two years earlier. His horse was exhausted, and so was he. No one asked him questions, and he volunteered no information about himself.

"It was an Indian that opened those gates, and Tonio will find their sign. You can bet on it," Finch said. "I expect that there were some hiding out in the willows enjoying the whole thing."

"I hope you're right, Finch," Humphrey said grimly. "I know damn well one of the blacks didn't do it. They'd know what they had a-comin'. I just hope Tonio don't find out that one of the cowboys done it. I'd hate to lose Old Heck and a cowboy too."

"You'd fire him?" Mandy was big-eyed, and she looked at her husband almost fearfully, for his anger was never far beneath the surface.

"I wouldn't fire 'im," Humphrey said cryptically.

"But—you said—"

"I'd hang 'im!" Humphrey said harshly and got up from the table and stomped out the door.

Mandy's face was pale as she looked at Finch. "He wouldn't—he wouldn't!" Mandy pleaded with Finch.

"It was an Indian," Finch said, evading her eyes. "I'd bet my saddle on it!"

\* \* \* \* \* \*

They never did learn who turned the animals together. Tonio swore he could find no sign at all. It was the first time he had ever failed. For days, the conversation in the bunkhouse at night centered around the fight and the possible miscreant who had made it possible by opening the gates. But they never found out, much to the relief of Finch, for he suspected that some fun-loving cowboy, who had no idea of the disaster that he would perpetrate, had done it. Finch also thought that Tonio knew the truth, for in the two years that Tonio had been with the ranch, he had never failed to follow a trail—no matter how dim or old. But Tonio had also learned that Humphrey Beatenbow was iron-willed and had a very stern idea of justice. Tonio did not want to see one of his friends hanged.

\* \* \* \* \* \*

Finch and Humphrey talked over the problem at length. Many of the mares would be foaling soon, and there was branding to do, and the increased Indian activity in springtime made it necessary for them to increase the number of scouts and sentries.

"Wish that Gato horse that used to belong to Chico was a stud," Finch said glumly.

"So do I," Humphrey said. "He's one of the best I ever saw—except that Rafter horse of yours that I let get killed up in Abilene."

"You didn't have a thing to do with that, Hump. And you know it," Finch said patiently. He knew that Humphrey had always felt guilty about the great quarter horse that Finch had owned and loaned to Humphrey to make the trail drive. Finch had always done his best to erase any feeling of guilt that Humphrey had, but he knew that his pragmatic partner would never quite be able to forgive himself, even though he was not at fault.

"Well, anyway," Humphrey said as if he hadn't heard Finch. "When we get the brandin' done, and the damn redskins get a little spring sap out of their systems so's we won't have to ride guard so heavy, I'll take a few of the boys and go back east this summer to get us a stud. I'd shore like to get a good one, too. Back in Louisiana, the Beatenbow plantation raised the best horses and mules and niggers, too, in the whole country. I'd like to do the same out west here."

"Well, we won't be raising niggers here!" Finch said.

"That's for shore," Humphrey said. "And you just watch and see if them blacks don't start a- gettin' weaker, too. When a white man can't put a good buck to a nigger wench that will cross good, the strain is gonna get weak."

"Where you gonna look for a stud?"

Humphrey didn't even hear Finch. He was concentrating on a subject that he knew something about and that he was interested in.

"And we need to get us some of them short horned cattle and bring in here. Cross 'em up with these longhorns, and you'd get a mighty fine cow critter, I'm a-thinkin".

Finch was amazed. It had never occurred to him that longhorns would mix with any other kind, and he doubted that they would.

"They'd probably gore a short horned cow to death if you put 'er in with 'em."

"Nope!" Humphrey said firmly. "If she's in heat and a-standin' on four feet, one of them longhorn bulls will breed 'er."

"I don't know!" Finch shook his head doubtfully. "Anyway, we're gonna need a stud before summer. Some of those mares are going to start dropping foals in a few weeks, and they ought to be bred back pretty quick, most of 'em on foal heat."

"Well," Humphrey said, "I don't know what we can do about it. I shore don't think we can spare the men now—do you?"

"No, I don't," Finch agreed. But Humphrey had given him an idea, and he was quick to act on it. "We could spare ME, though," he said.

"You!" Humphrey said. "You couldn't ride across that Indian country by yourself. No stud is worth that!"

'I've done it before," Finch said.

"Gettin' a new stud can wait." Humphrey said. "It ain't worth gettin' killed over! Anyways, there may be a caravan pass by a-goin' back east pretty soon. and one of us could ride with it."

"Most of 'em are going west, Hump," Finch argued mildly. "That branch of the Santa Fe trail south of the river isn't the main route, and when a caravan does go by on it, they don't usually come back this way. Besides, if I can find a good stud and maybe a few good mares to bring back, I can hire men to help. There's a lot of men in south Texas that are looking for work."

"Just the same—we'll wait," Humphrey said in a voice almost like that he used when ordering the blacks around.

The easy-going Finch would have acceded to Humphrey's suggestion, but his tone had been such that it nettled him.

"I'll leave tomorrow night," he said tersely and walked away.

Humphrey realized immediately that he had crossed that invisible line that was anathema to Finch, for he would not be bossed by any man. But Humphrey Beatenbow was a man who did not know how to apologize, and he did the best he could.

"Where you figger to find one?" Humphrey asked as he hurried to walk beside Finch.

"Down by Austin, I reckon," Finch said. "Old Billy may be still standing down there if he's alive. He was the sire of Rafter. I might be able to find a young stud by 'im. If I could, he'd be better than Old Heck."

"Rafter was the best horse I ever saw," admitted Humphrey. "If we had a stud as good as he was a gelding, we'd be in good shape."

"It's possible," Finch said. "That old stud was still alive when I left the Rangers in '65; so he could have some colts around four or five years old by now."

"What dam was Rafter out of?" Humphrey was beginning to show interest. "I'm a thinkin' that the mare is about as important as the stud. Anyways, that's how we figgered back on the plantation, and we shore raised some good niggers and horses, too."

"Rafter's dam was a mare called Paisano, but she was old when he was born, and I doubt if she's still alive. Even if we could find a stud that's a full brother to Rafter, I expect he'd cost us a pot full of double eagles."

"Well," Humphrey said almost eagerly, "we got a-plenty of double eagles from that drive we made to Abilene—and I doubt if anybody ever paid too much for a real fine animal."

"I'll take enough to buy a stud and a few mares," Finch said. He was relieved that Humphrey had tacitly agreed to his making the trip, for Finch did not doubt his ability to cross the Indian infested plains alone as much as he doubted his ability to stay at the ranch with Mandy and maintain a comradely association while Humphrey was gone two or three months to look for a stud.

\* \* \* \* \* \*

Humphrey had old Kate draw up a bucket of gold double eagles she had hidden in the well that had been dug in the kitchen floor and that had been covered ingeniously so that no matter how diligently the house was searched, it would be highly unlikely that anyone could possibly find the gold. They had originally dug the well to be sure that they would not run short of water during a prolonged Indian attack. One had also been dug in the bunkhouse and in the Negro quarters; and, although the water was brackish from being so close to the river, it lay near the surface, so the wells were not deep.

When Kate removed the well cover and drew the gold to the top, Humphrey began counting double eagles. It was a small fortune and enough to meet ranch expenses for several years. Finch got his saddle bags, and Humphrey began to stuff them with gold.

"That's way too much, Hump," Finch protested.

"You can't pay too much for good stock," Humphrey said firmly. "And if you can find some mares, you're goin' to have to hire men, too. And I shore wouldn't want nobody to think that the HF was a-runnin' short of money."

Humphrey continued to stuff the saddle bags. Finch knew that his action was in partial atonement for the death of Rafter; so he protested no further.

# CHAPTER 3

Finch waited until the dark of the moon to leave. Just at dusky dark, Mandy and Humphrey walked with him to where his horse and pack mule were tethered. Mandy squeezed his arm in silent farewell, and Humphrey thrust out his hand.

"You take care of yourself," he said gruffly. "Too big a job for me to run this outfit all by myself."

Finch gripped Humphrey's hand and laid his hand gently on Mandy's shoulder, then turned and stepped into his saddle on the good gelding Gato.

Mandy and Humphrey could see his arm but dimly as he raised it in farewell and rode silently into the night. Only the soft footfalls of his horse and pack mule could be heard, for all metal, including the gold coins in his saddle bags, had been secured so that they would not rattle as he rode, and his saddle had been well-oiled to be sure that no squeak or sound betrayed his presence as he crossed the Indian country to the southeast.

It was Finch's intention to ride only at night and to hide out during daylight hours, for, although White Horse was his friend, he knew that other Comanches and the Kiowas and Cheyennes resented intrusion into their country. For that matter, his truce, even with White Horse, was good only so long as he remained in the valley. And even the unfathomable Indian mind of White Horse might take an erratic turn at any moment.

Finch sighed as he rode to the edge of the river and then turned east. The darkness was almost total, and he could see only the dim bulk of the big cottonwood trees and salt cedars as he let his horse pick his way. He had absolute confidence in the horse, for he had been ridden by his merry Mexican friend Chico when they served together in the Texas Rangers. When his own horse Rafter had been killed, Finch had begun to ride Chico's horse. Now, the horse that Chico had called 'Poco Gato', which in Spanish meant 'Little Cat', was ten years old. Finch had thought it a very inappropriate name for a handsome, sorrel quarter horse of Steel Dust breeding, and he had chided Chico about it. Chico had only laughed.

Finch grinned in the darkness as he thought of Chico. Had his eyes been visible, one would have seen the merry twinkle that was usually present in his blue eyes, but few men who had seen him faced with dangerous and seemingly insurmountable odds doubted that blue sparks literally shone from those eyes.

As Gato picked his way through the brush near the river's edge, Finch could see the small stream of water flowing near the north bank, and as he became more accustomed to the darkness, he could vaguely make out some familiar spots. At one place he paused near a sharp bank of the river only a few feet high. He knew that just below that bank lay one of the most treacherous and greedy pools of quicksand on the river. Once, Shanker Stone had buried a man there. It was an incident that Finch did not like to remember nor dwell upon, for he had killed the man that Shanker had buried.

Finch let his horse go at a quicker pace as he left the place and continued his ride. A mile farther eastward, he knew that there was a fairly safe crossing, and he trusted the river-wise Gato to take him safely across.

As light began to show in the east, Finch rode down to McClellan Creek and let his horse and pack mule drink; then he rode a mile to the south and stopped in a small draw, well concealed by brush, but with good grass. He unsaddled and picketed Gato and the mule. Then he unrolled a blanket and placed it where there would be a shadow when the sun rose and where he could see his horse and pack mule, for he knew that they would alert him to any approach by animal or man.

He removed his pistol, checked it thoroughly, and placed it on the blanket. He wiped his rifle clean and placed it alongside the pistol. Then he stretched his long length on the blanket and was instantly asleep.

At mid-afternoon, Finch awakened and was immediately alert, his pistol in his hand. He did not move, but looked at his horse and mule. Both of them had their ears erect and were looking westward toward the head of the draw. Finch had not removed his boots. He quickly slipped his pistol in its holster, took his rifle, and strode quietly in the direction the animals were looking. Taking advantage of every bit of cover, he crept to the top of the draw, peered over the rim, and saw a party of perhaps twenty Indians riding westward. Finch lowered his head and crept back to his bed. Quickly, he rolled his blanket, and in less than two minutes he was saddled and packed. He tied Gato to a sturdy juniper bush and again walked to the rim and peered over. The Indians were still travelling westward and apparently would continue to do so.

Finch breathed a sigh of relief, went back, and mounted his horse. He rode slowly and as quietly as possible. The pack mule followed meekly.

A half hour later, after taking advantage of all available cover, Finch felt that he was relatively safe and rode out onto flat country. The sun was still an hour high, and he could see for miles. He saw nothing but a few buffalo grazing contentedly.

\* \* \* \* \* \*

Finch rode off the caprock that night, and when day began to break, he was nearing the Salt Fork of Red River. Just as the sun came up, he saw a rider coming toward him. It was a white man, and as he came closer, Finch saw that he was very tall; he wore a black, flat-crowned hat pulled low over his eyes. Feral instinct told Finch that the man was dangerous, but friendly. They veered their horses toward each other, stopped a few paces apart, and sat silently as each measured the other. The stranger had piercing black eyes and dark stubble; his hat was fastened below his chin with a leather string. He was riding a good horse, but had no pack animal. He wore a faded blue army coat. His wooden handled pistol rested in a well-worn holster, and Finch knew immediately that the man could, and would, use it—probably with great speed and effectiveness. The tall man apparently recognized the same qualities in Finch.

"Howdy," Finch grinned.

"Howdy," the stranger answered cryptically.

"They call me Finch," Finch introduced himself.

"They call me Tell. I'm friendly if you are."

"Same here," Finch said.

The man relaxed, and his leonine grace as he sat his horse reminded Finch of a big panther.

"Going west?" Finch asked in his quiet, friendly voice.

"Aimin' to," the man answered. "You a-comin' from that direction?"

"From the Canadian River. Headed for Austin."

"I'm goin' out to Mora. You seen any Indians out that way?"

"One little bunch. About twenty. They were riding west."

"Give you a chase?"

"Nope. I hid from 'em and was mighty glad to do it," Finch answered candidly. "Looked like Kiowas, but I didn't ride close enough to make sure."

"That's sensible," the tall man agreed and answered Finch's grin with a fleeting one of his own. "I had a tussle with a little bunch south of Salt Fork. I out-run 'em."

"You've got the horse to do it, looks like," Finch said.

"Yep. Lost my pack animal, though. I reckon them Indians will be bloated on mule meat tonight."

"I've got some extra grub in my pack," Finch offered.

"Thanks just the same," the man replied. "But I reckon I'll make do. I've lived off the land afore."

"Me too," Finch said.

There was a long silence. Apparently the conversation had run its course.

"Well, I reckon I'll be movin' on. Mora is a long ways from here."

"So is Austin," Finch agreed. "Seems to me I've heard the name Tell before."

"I've heard the name Finch, too."

The dark visaged stranger and Finch grinned at each other. With that, each man lifted his right hand in farewell. Neither looked back as he rode away.

\* \* \* \* \* \*

Finch rode eastward along the Salt Fork of Red River. The river bed was wide and showed signs of fierce headrises that had pushed debris toward the sea. There were big cottonwood trees and salt cedars along the banks. There were also a great many plum bushes that were laden with fruit that would be ripe in July.

In an unusually wide strip of river bed, Finch spied a small island. Evidently the river split and flowed around the island, for there were several big cottonwood trees on it, and it was covered with brush. He headed toward it. The stream was small, and he did not find any quicksand in crossing. Ascending the steep, sandy side of the island, Finch was pleasantly surprised to see a small meadow of lush grass below. He immediately rode to it, unsaddled, and picketed his horse. As he spread his blanket under one of the cottonwood trees, he flushed a covey of quail, which made him start, and he was a bit surprised and chagrined to find his pistol in his hand.

Finch awakened at mid-day. He lay listening for a few moments before rising. He heard only the call of a meadowlark, the cooing of a dove, the barking of a squirrel, and the pleasant sound of his horse and mule cropping grass. It was a quiet and pleasant time, and for a few minutes Finch simply lay and enjoyed the world. Suddenly, he felt a sense of freedom that he had not felt since he left the

Texas Rangers. He had absolutely no one to care for except himself; until that moment he had not known how much responsibility he had felt since joining Humphrey and establishing the ranch. Subconsciously, he had felt that, somehow, the safety of Mandy and her children, the blacks, and even Humphrey had depended upon him. Now, for a while at least, he was free of all of that, even though he missed it.

Suddenly, he came to a decision. He would go by Fort Worth on his way to Austin. It was in Fort Worth that he had first met Humphrey Beatenbow and had fallen in love with the most beautiful woman he had ever seen. She had been Humphrey's first wife—Colette!

Having made the decision, Finch immediately rose, went to his pack, and took from it a small bag of grain that he had saved. He divided it between Gato and the mule.

After climbing to the highest spot on the island and seeing no sign of Indians, he returned and built a small fire of very dry wood that would emit very little smoke. He ate the first hot meal since he had left the Canadian.

The decision to go by Fort Worth had lain dormant since he had left the ranch, and needed only the thought of Colette to trigger it into reality. Finch knew the country well; he would follow the Salt Fork for a few miles and then cut south to the Prairie Dog Town Fork and follow that until it reached the main Red River which formed the line between Texas and the Oklahoma Territory. Along the river also lay the beautiful valley where Colette Beatenbow's grave lay. He would keep to the river for several days and then cut south to the Trinity River and follow it to Fort Worth. He would also ride in daylight. Even if he did see Indians, he knew that Gato could outrun them. If he had to sacrifice his pack mule, it would be well worth it.

He visited Colette's grave and was grateful that the wildflowers planted by Buff Larrigan were in bloom. It was a peaceful spot, and Finch sat by her grave for almost an hour. His mind was almost completely blank. It seemed that only a great emptiness engulfed him.

Finally, he arose, tightened the cinch on Gato, and mounted. He sat for a moment and removed his hat. He felt that he ought to say something—and the thought made him feel foolish. He replaced his hat and started to ride away. Then he stopped and turned again to the lonely grave.

"Goodbye, Colette," he said softly.

\* \* \* \* \* \*

When Finch reached Fort Worth a few days later, he was pleasantly surprised at the growth and apparent prosperity. When he had last seen it, most of the buildings around the square were vacant, and many of the homes were, too. There had been only two hundred and fifty inhabitants at that time, for the men had gone to war, and a pall seemed to hang over the almost deserted village. Even the stone courthouse of Tarrant County had been only partially finished, and no work had been in progress. There had been no saloon or rooming house. There had been a flour mill and a cobbler's shop. But the hub of activity had been the blacksmith shop, which faced the square, with an open front and a protruding canopy covered with brush and supported by cedar posts, that reached the street.

Finch remembered that blacksmith shop only too well, for it was there that he and Humphrey had faced three impostors, two white and one Negro, posing as lawmen, who demanded that they be allowed to search Humphrey's caravan. Humphrey refused, and a fight ensued in which Finch, with the uncanny speed and accuracy that had made him a legend in the Rangers, shot and killed the two white men, and intentionally, only wounded the Negro.

Finch did not like to remember that particular part of his stop in Fort Worth, but his feelings were mixed—for that was the first time he had ever seen Colette Beatenbow!

He rode a few hundred yards from the square to a huge pecan tree on Clear Creek where he unpacked his mule and staked him to graze. Then he remounted and rode back to town. As he rode around the square, he was pleasantly surprised to see that the stone courthouse was completed. Most of the buildings were now occupied. There were several saloons and even a three story hotel. But the center of activity still seemed to be the blacksmith shop where several men lounged in the shade of the overhang. On impulse, Finch decided to ride over to it. The same dour smith that had been there in '65 was still at work. Finch dismounted, several of the loungers grunted salutations.

"Howdy, everybody," Finch grinned.

"You needin' somepin'?" the smithy asked.

"Thought I'd get you to reset the shoes on my horse if you've got the time."

"In a hurry?"

"I'd like to pull out sometime tomorrow," Finch said.

"Bring 'im in early in the mornin'," the smithy said slowly. "I got this here waggin wheel to fix afore night."

"Any particular time?"

"Sunup."

"I'll be here," Finch said.

"We got a mighty fine Hotel here now, stranger. That is, if'n you got the dollar it takes and you're tired of your own cookin'."

"I just might try that," Finch answered in a friendly tone. "I've come a long ways, and I'm not the best cook in the world, either. The last time I was in Fort Worth, I camped under that big pecan tree down there on Clear Creek. Fact is, my mule is staked out down there now."

When Finch mentioned that he had been there before, the smithy paused, looked keenly at him for a long moment, nodded his head, and resumed pounding the red hot iron.

Finch staked his horse on good grass near the big tree and turned his pack mule loose, for he knew that the mule would stay with his horse. He shouldered his saddle bags, which were very heavy with the gold he was carrying. But Finch was exceptionally strong, for all of his slender build, and he carried them easily. He took his rifle in his right hand and walked back toward the blacksmith shop.

"Think I'll try that hotel," he said.

"You'll shore get your money's worth, if you got any," a man with only one arm offered. "Ma Higgins bakes a mighty good pie, and them beds is mighty soft. I slept there one night when I first got back from the war."

"I left my saddle and pack down by the creek. Don't reckon anybody will bother 'em, do you?"

"We got some sorry son-of-bitches here in town," the man with the empty sleeve said. "But I reckon none of 'em is lowdown enough to steal a man's saddle and grub!"

"Good," Finch said as he again shouldered his saddle bags and headed for the hotel.

In the group of men in the shade of the overhang were two who were shifty eyed and non- communicative. They were strangers to the rest of the men, and their keen eyes noted the heft of the saddle bags, even though Finch carried them easily.

\* \* \* \* \* \*

Finch was at the blacksmith shop at sunup the next morning. The smithy had his forge going energetically. Finch dismounted, unsaddled his horse, and handed the reins to the smithy, who, in a no nonsense manner, pulled the shoes off Gato, rasped his hooves, and replaced the shoes in less than an hour.

"Ain't the same horse you was ridin' when you stopped here in '65," the smithy said as he let the last leg to the ground.

"I'm surprised that you remember!" Finch said in amazement.

"Ain't likely to forget that fracas that took place right here in front of my shop," the smithy said in, what was for him, a friendly tone. "Ain't never seen the likes of you a-killin' them two renegade whites and shootin' that no-good nigger in the shoulder."

Finch was at a loss to reply. Finally he said, "I'd appreciate it if you'd forget that shooting. But I'm glad you remember my horse."

"What happened to 'im?"

"He got killed."

"Oh!" The smithy went back to his forge.

\* \* \* \* \* \*

An hour later, Finch, followed by his pack mule, rode out of Fort Worth in the direction of Austin. The smithy paused in his work long enough to see him disappear in the trees near the Trinity River, and ten minutes later he saw the two rough looking strangers, who had been under his canopy when Finch rode in the day before, follow him. The smithy shook his head, seemingly in resignation, and continued to pound red-hot metal.

The smithy had mended a broken iron stirrup, shod two horses, and fixed a loose wagon wheel when he saw the two strangers return, except that now one of them was leading a horse with the body of the other one draped over it. The rider rode up to the shop.

"You got a buryin' ground here?" the rider asked harshly.

"Just outside of town north," the smithy answered. "They is a man here who takes care of the buryin' if you got the price."

"I got the damned price. Where can I find 'im?" the man growled.

"What happened?" The smithy was only human, after all, and he could not contain his curiosity.

"Damndest thing I ever saw," the man said as if he still could not believe it. "Rafe and me was a-fixin' to lighten the load in that feller's saddle bags, and we rode around in front of 'im. Rafe, he had his pistol out and a-pointin' at 'im when he rode up to where we was a-waitin'. Then that feller—he jus' shot Rafe out'n the saddle and had his pistol a-pointin' right betwixt my eyes afore I could even lay a hand on my pistol."

"You stupid bastard!" the smithy growled. "That there feller you tried to hold up was Fauntleroy Finch—fastest man with a pistol that ever lived. He was a Texas Ranger before he was good growed."

"Then why in hell didn't you let us know?" the man demanded.

"I reckon you found out without me a-tellin' you," the smithy said with a hint of satisfaction in his voice as the man started riding away leading the body-laden horse.

"Crazy bastards!" the smithy mumbled as he began pounding a red-hot piece of iron. "Bracin' that feller! They'd might jus' as well a-got off their horses and tried to snap it out with a rattlesnake!"

# Chapter 4

There was a slow drizzle falling the day Finch rode into Austin. The streets were soggy, and Gato's feet made a squishing sound as he walked. The small clapboard Ranger office was still where he remembered it, and he rode to it. The windows were shuttered, and weeds grew around it. It looked as though it had not been used in some time. Finch hailed a raincoated stranger walking down the boardwalk.

"Hey, mister! Can you tell me where the Ranger Headquarters is now?"

The man looked at Finch from under his dripping hat brim. "Ain't sure there IS a headquarters now. But Captain Cates, he's a-stayin' in that there red building down that-a-way. Can't miss it—only red one on the block." The man pointed.

Finch nodded and rode in the direction indicated. He tied his horse to the rail in front and dismounted. He stamped mud from his feet and shook water from his hat and slicker as he stood on the wooden steps; then he knocked.

"Come on in," a voice that Finch recognized called.

He opened the door to see Captain Cates' small figure seated behind a big, scarred, wooden desk. He looked ten years older than when Finch had last seen him, and he wore spectacles. He also held a big pistol in his hand, pointed directly at Finch.

Cates looked over his spectacles, and a wide smile lit his face.

"Fauntleroy Finch!" he ejaculated in pleased surprise. "Damned if it ain't you. Come on in this house and sit!" He removed his glasses and rose as he extended his hand. They shook briefly and heartily.

"Don't know nobody I'd rather see than you, boy!" the captain said as he slapped his hand on Finch's shoulder.

"Sure good to see you, too, Captain," Finch said sincerely.

"I'll pour us some coffee," Cates said and proceeded to do so. Finch noticed that he limped badly as he went for the coffee.

When Finch had removed his slicker and hat and had hung them on a nail, he joined Cates and sat at the table. Both blew on the strong, hot coffee and took a sip.

"Good coffee," Finch approved. "You've changed your headquarters."

"A lot of things have changed since you was here," Cates said glumly. "The government is in a big, damn mess, as usual. They've cut the Rangers down to near nothin'. We don't get paid half the time, and they don't even furnish us ammunition any more. Have to buy our own. Let's see—you left here in '65—right?"

"Right."

"Well, Throckmorton was elected governor that year, but Sheridan fired 'im about the middle of '67, and then Pease was appointed governor by Sherman, and then Pease resigned over some damn argument, and Davis was elected governor last year—no tellin' how long he'll last! But he's sure a- raisin' hell while he's at it. They got a law passed that let 'em have what they call a 'State Police', which ain't nothin' but a bunch of legalized killers and thieves. About half of 'em are niggers—even got some nigger officers. Folks hereabout are mighty put out!"

"Don't see how that can last long!"

"It won't. But the Rangers will. We've been a-goin' for thirty five years, and I been with 'em for fifteen. I aim to be a Ranger for the rest of my life—I don't give a damn who them carpet baggers elect governor."

Well," Finch said, "it sure looks like the government is still in a mess!"

"You sure must be a long ways out of town if you haven't heard about it!"

"We are," Finch said. "We're running cattle up on the Canadian River—not far from the New Mexico Territory, and even closer to the Oklahoma Strip."

"That's right in the middle of Indian country, ain't it?"

"Sure is," Finch agreed. "But Kit Carson got us a truce with most of the tribes, and we haven't been raided but two or three times by the Indians, and once by Comancheros! What about the Rangers?"

"Oh, hell!" Cates said in disgust. "We're still Rangers, all right, but the damn politicians call us 'State Police'. Don't make no difference to us what they call us as long as they pay us our forty a month—which they do some of the time."

"Things still bad out west?"

"Worse than ever! Horse thieves, cattle rustlers, Indian raids, Comancheros—you name it, and you'll find the vermin still operatin'. We're losin' a lot of men now."

"I heard about Tom."

"There's been a lot more killed."

"What about Matt?"

The captain grinned. "That lazy bastard is still a-goin' strong. Got a wild hair last year and said he was gonna quit, but I made 'im a sergeant. So he stayed."

"My partner Hump said that Matt and his detachment pulled 'im out of a bad scrape with herd cutters when he was on a trail drive to Abilene."

"Heard about that. Fact is, Matt and the boys brought that whole mangy crew all the way back down here. That Red Roark was a mean son-of-a-bitch, but he got off without no prison time. One of Matt's boys picked a fight with 'im and shot 'im, though."

"Where is Matt?"

"He's got three or four detachments camped along the river just north of town. Some of 'em went out after some rustlers last week. Ought to be back about now."

"Well, I reckon I'll ride out that way and see if I know anybody." Finch rose.

"What brings you back, Finch?"

"I'm looking for some good horses by Old Billy and maybe Steel Dust."

"Well, you may be in luck. Old Billy is still standin' over at Leesville in Gonzales County. You had one of his colts when you was with us, didn't you?"

"Yep. Best horse I ever had. Got 'im from Fleming. He still in the Rangers?"

"Nope."

"Killed?" Finch asked.

"Quit. Said he was gonna raise horses. I hear he's still got that Old Billy horse, too."

"I sure hope so," Finch said seriously. "I'd like to take some of his colts back with me."

"Well, Old Billy colts are still something special—especially out of that Paisano mare. Cost you a year's wages to buy one, though."

"Thought that old mare was too old to have colts."

"Well, she ain't. I heard she had another one last year and is in foal again."

"Any Steel Dust colts around?"

"I hear some of the boys has got one or two. They'd know more about 'em than I do. I ain't been doin' no ridin' for the past couple of years."

"What happened?"

"Oh, nothin' much! We was chasin' some damn horse thieves, and one of the lucky bastards put a bullet in my leg. Busted the bone up bad, and I was laid up for about six months—but I'm fine now—just can't set a horse like I used to."

"Well," Finch drained his coffee cup. "I reckon I'll ride out and see the boys."

"If Matt is back, tell 'im to come in. I got a job for some of the boys to do. They just sent word that there was a big bunch of Indians a-raisin' hell out in Concho County."

"I'll tell 'im," Finch said as he took his leave.

\* \* \* \* \* \*

Finch rode up the Colorado River for almost half an hour before he smelled wood smoke. The river was muddy and rolled along sluggishly. As he topped a small rise, Finch could see smoke curling lazily from three fires, which meant that probably the entire company of thirty men were in camp, for they usually had one mess for ten men and took turns cooking. As he rode nearer, he was surprised that he was not challenged, but he supposed that being near headquarters, they felt secure. Usually, they had at least six or eight men guarding the horses. He was pleased that the camp was drab and colorless. The only bright spots were the three smoldering cooking fires, but there was no flash of metal of any kind, and the varied uniforms of the Rangers were chosen to blend with the background.

The soft ground muffled the sound of his horse's feet, and he was close to camp when he was finally discovered by a young Ranger who was lolling under a blanket stretched between stakes to provide a dry spot. The Ranger was reading a book and looked up to see Finch approaching. He yelled as he quickly palmed his pistol.

A general movement rippled through the camp as each Ranger pulled his pistol, but quickly Matt Jimson yelled, "Hey! That's Finch! I'd know that lanky bastard's hide in a tannin' yard!"

There was a rush of men to meet Finch as he rode in. Matt reached him first and grabbed his hand. "Hey! What are you doin' way down here, you slow poke bastard?" he said fondly.

"Looking for some no-account Rangers to scare hell out of while they were all asleep," Finch grinned as he clasped Matt's hand. "I mighty near took a shot at that iron kettle on the fire just to wake everybody up, but I was afraid I might scare somebody plumb to death!"

"Git down, man! Git down! Boy, it's good to see you!"

Finch dismounted and shook hands with all the men. Almost all of them were young and smiled excitedly. A few of them Finch recognized as having been in the Rangers when he was. The ones who had joined since he had been gone had heard of the fabulous derring-do of the legendary Fauntleroy Finch and were eager to meet him.

Coffee was poured, and the entire company moved under the canopy of oak trees to shield them from the misty rain that was still falling. They sat on saddles or blankets and looked at Finch expectantly.

"Well, dammit, Finch—start a-talkin'. What are you doin' down this way, anyhow? Did the Indians wipe you out up there on the Canadian?"

"Nope." Finch grinned. "We're still going strong up there. I came back down here to get some of those 'Old Billy' horses, if I can find some—and maybe some 'Steel Dust' bred horses, too, if I can find 'em."

"I remember you had one. Old Rafter. Still got 'im?"

"Nope. He got killed."

"Indians?"

"Not Indians," Finch said.

Then he explained how Humphrey had matched Rafter with a villainous itinerant peddler's horse when he took a herd to Abilene two years before. The ranch cowboys had been celebrating and were suckered into a horse race by the avaricious peddler, who had a race horse hidden out. The cowboys had bet everything they owned on a fairly fast bay in the remuda. Humphrey knew that the boys were going to lose everything, for he had heard of the ruse practiced by the peddler. He sent Clem to camp to get Rafter and to bring Brandy, their young horse herder, to ride him. The race took place, and Rafter was leading the peddler's horse by four lengths as they neared the finish line. The peddler went berserk, yelled, and grabbed a bystander's rifle. He shot just as Rafter crossed the finish line, breaking the horse's leg and causing him to cartwheel and crush Brandy beneath him. Brandy was killed, and Humphrey had to shoot Rafter, who had a bone protruding just below the right knee.

There was a long silence when Finch finished. The Rangers felt more sympathy over the death of a good horse than they did over the death of a bad man.

"Hump ort to of hung that son-of-a-bitch!" one of the Rangers grated.

"He did," Finch said grimly.

There was another long silence. It was Matt who broke it.

"That horse you're ridin'—it was Chico Baca's horse, wasn't it?"

"Yes," Finch said. "And he's a good one, too. Not quite as fast as Rafter, but still one of the best. We've got some good thoroughbred mares on the ranch that Hump brought from Louisiana, but our stud got killed. We've been mostly breeding the mares to the Beatenbow jackass and raising some good mules. But we'd like to start a good horse herd, and I figured a young stallion by Old Billy would sure fit the bill. And maybe some Steel Dust mares, too."

"Well, you're in luck," Matt said. "Fleming quit the Rangers a couple of years ago, and now he's standin' Old Billy over at Leesville in Gonzales County."

"I bought Rafter from Fleming," Finch said.

"Old Billy's colts are known all over south Texas. Especially the ones out of that old Paisano mare—but they'll cost you a year's wages."

"I'll try to get some, anyway," Finch said. "How far is it to Leesville?"

"It ain't only two or three days' ride from here. Just about due south. I'll ride down that way with you. I got a hankerin' to see Gonzales County and do some horse tradin', too."

"Oh!" Finch said. "Captain Cates said for you to ride in. The Indians are acting up over in Concho County."

"I'll ride in," Matt sighed. "I reckon my hankerin' to see Gonzales County is gonna have to wait a while. Anyway, Fleming can probably help you find some good horses."

Matt changed the subject. "You know, I still get my hackles up when I think of how Chico got shot in the back by that damn murderin' skunk, Doc Guines."

"Well, he paid for it," Finch said grimly.

"How's that?" a young Ranger wanted to know.

"Hump Beatenbow, that's Finch's partner, was in a good spot one day. Old Victorio and a bunch of his Apaches was a chasin' a feller on a pinto horse. It was Guines, no mistake! Hump just shot his horse out from under 'im, and let the Apaches have 'im. I expect that afore he finally died, he wisht a lot of times that me and Tom had caught 'im. We was huntin' 'im at the time. At least we would a-hung 'im without pullin' his skin off first."

"Man!" a young Ranger exclaimed. "That partner of yours must be quite a man, Finch."

"He is," Finch agreed.

\* \* \* \* \* \*

Matt's face was grim when he returned and announced that he would be ready to go to Gonzales County at any time. Finch was puzzled but did not question him.

"Let's pull out early tomorrow," Finch said.

"That's mighty good with me. But first I got to pick out a detachment to go out to Concho County." Matt's voice was harsh. Finch looked at him questioningly, but said nothing; and Matt volunteered no information.

Matt called for volunteers to go to Concho County to take care of the Indian trouble there. To many Rangers raised their hands. Matt picked nine of the youngest and one of the most experienced men to form a detachment. They packed their horses while the cooks prepared supper, which consisted of beef, beans, molasses, canned tomatoes, and coffee.

"You boys that are goin' out to Concho County better eat a-plenty, cause you damn shore won't have time to cook no Pecos strawberries while you're gone," Matt said jokingly. But, somehow, Finch felt that Matt was not as light hearted as he pretended.

The men just grinned, finished their meal quickly, and each took a small sack to the chuck wagon and packed jerky, left-over Dutch oven biscuits, and some dried fruit in it. They stuffed the food in their saddle bags, rechecked their guns and ammunition, and mounted.

"You fellers don't git in no more trouble than you can handle while we're gone. Hate to come back and have some of you a-missin'—especially the cooks," the oldest Ranger, who was possibly twenty-two years old, said jocularly.

His admonition was greeted with grins from those who would remain behind.

The detachment rode away amid good natured insults shouted at their retreating backs by the envious men left behind.

"How far to Concho?" Finch asked.

"Three or four days," Matt answered absently. "Maybe less. They'll ride fast."

"That the reason they didn't take pack mules?"

"That's one reason," Matt said with a tinge of bitterness in his voice. "Another reason is that there will be a hell of a fight when they get there, and they'd just lose some good pack mules. A whole company should have gone out there."

"Why didn't they?"

"Oh, hell!" Matt said with disgust. "The damn government has gone plumb crazy. Davis has cut us to the bone, and what's left of us don't get paid half the time. Besides, there is more hell raisin' in Texas now than ever."

"Captain Cates said things were in a big mess," Finch said.

"Well, what's left of them boys I sent out there will be back in a week or ten days. I'm near glad I won't be here when them that makes it does get back."

"The captain said you had been losing a lot of men the last year or so."

"Well, the captain was damn shore right about that!"

"How come you won't be here when they get back?"

"Hey, Finch! You're forgettin' somethin'—we're a gonna go a-horse tradin' down in Gonzales County tomorrow! Remember? And the best horses may be a long ways apart. Besides—I figure I got a long vacation a-comin'. I been gettin' shot for damn night eight years now."

\* \* \* \* \* \*

When the camp had settled down after the detachment rode away and the cooks had finished cleaning the pots and pans, it was almost dark. Matt assigned four men to take first guard on the horse herd, and two more to ride to high places that overlooked camp to act as guards.

"Ain't a chance in a thousand we'd have trouble this close to town," Matt said by way of explanation. "But I ain't got to be as old as I am by bein' careless."

The men who were still in camp gathered around the biggest fire. The rain had stopped, but most of them brought a blanket or other object to sit on. Many of them brought a tin cup of hot coffee. A few smoked pipes or rolled cigarettes.

The talk was animated as the young Rangers recounted recent adventures, but they were most anxious to hear of the feats of the fabulous Ranger that they had heard so much about! The man who had no equal with firearms—the youngster who loved to laugh and play and had killed more than twenty men in face to face gun battles—the legendary Fauntleroy Finch!

Finch, though not particularly articulate, managed to steer the conversation away from any of the experiences he had had during his four years as a Ranger.

The men quickly sensed that Finch was reluctant, even embarrassed, to be the topic of conversation; so they soon turned their reminiscing to good horses, bad men, and recent Indian and outlaw forays in which they had been involved. Finch listened avidly to the campfire conversation and felt a sense of camaraderie and belonging that he had, unconsciously, been missing since he had left the Rangers.

It was almost midnight when the first man sought his bedroll. Others followed at intervals. Finally, only Finch and Matt were left.

"I tell you, Finch—there just ain't no better men nowhere than in the Texas Rangers," Matt said with something like regret in his voice.

"You're right about that, Matt," Finch agreed. "And most of 'em aren't old enough to be away from home!"

"Most of 'em older than you was when you joined up. I was in the office that day when you come in. Remember?"

"I remember," Finch said. "You and Tom were there."

"Old Tom! That slow-poke bastard took four horse thieves with 'im before he went down. They counted eight bullet holes in 'im, so I hear. I wasn't there."

There was a long silence as Finch and Matt gazed into the fire.

"Well," Matt said finally. "I reckon we'd best roll up. We need to get an early start tomorrow. You have to trade real slow to get a fast horse—especially an Old Billy colt."

# Chapter 5

Finch and Matt left camp early the next morning. Each of them felt like a young colt just turned out to pasture, for they were headed south of Austin where they were not likely to meet hostiles, red or white, and their mission was one of pure pleasure.

"Any man that don't enjoy horse tradin' just don't know what fun is!"

Somehow Finch felt that Matt's enthusiasm was forced.

"That's shore right," Finch agreed as their horses took the trail briskly. "I just hope we can find enough of those Old Billy and Steel Dust horses to make the trip worthwhile."

"We'll find 'em," Matt said with conviction. "It may take us a long time to do it, but there's quite a few of 'em scattered around Gonzales and Karnes County, and some in DeWitt and Lavaca counties, too. Fact is, they're pretty much scattered all over south Texas. That old stud must be a powerful breeder. I just hope you got enough money to buy what you want—they're gonna cost like hell!"

"And I just hope that we don't stay so long that Captain Cates takes the hide off of you when we get back," Finch said.

There was a long silence. Matt's face suddenly sobered. Finch looked at him curiously.

"Finch—"

"What, Matt?"

"I wasn't gonna tell you this till we got back—but I reckon maybe I ort to."

"Tell me what?"

"Finch—I—I—well dammit! I resigned from the Rangers."

"You what!" Finch almost gulped in disbelief.

"I resigned from the Rangers," Matt repeated doggedly.

"When?"

"Yesterday when I went in to see the captain."

"What on earth for?" Finch was incredulous.

"Oh, hell, Finch," Matt almost groaned. "The captain ain't been hisself since he got that leg busted all to hell and he can't ride a horse no more. I don't mean he's scared—or anything like that— but he just ain't like he used to be. When I went in yesterday and he told me about them Indians a-raisin' hell out in Concho, I told 'im I'd take a couple of detachments out there and take care of things."

"And—?" Finch encouraged.

"Well, he told me to send one detachment and for me to stay close to headquarters. Now, I ain't no more anxious to get killed than the next man, but that one detachment ain't got a chance in hell of roustin' them Indians without losin' most of the men. Maybe so, if I had gone, we could of saved some."

"Well—" Finch started to say something, but Matt held up his hand to silence him.

"Fact is, I started to quit once before for just about the same kind of reason, but he talked me out of it—even made me a sergeant. So—like a damn fool, I stayed, and the captain has been a-keepin' me out of the worst of the fights. That's the reason I wasn't with Tom when he got shot by them horse thieves. I reckon the captain thinks I'm too old to be a Ranger no more."

"Maybe he—"

"Maybe—hell!" Matt interrupted. "Maybe I am too old! I'm a-pushin' thirty, and I been in the Rangers nearly ten years—so maybe that's long enough."

"You've been lucky!" Finch said.

"I've been careful," Matt corrected. "And I'm good with guns. Not as good as you are—but pretty damn good! And the captain says he's gonna make me a Lieutenant now—and I damn shore don't aim to spend the rest of my life a-pencillin' out papers and a-orderin' supplies and such—"

"Matt!" Finch said placatingly. "I don't blame you for quitting. I would have done the same thing."

"I'm mighty glad to hear you say that, Finch." Matt heaved a big sigh of relief. "Anyway, now you know why it don't make a hell of a lot of difference what the captain thinks or don't think."

"I shore do!" Finch agreed heartily. "But I reckon the captain was doing what he thought best."

"Course he was," Matt said firmly. "They don't come no better than that little stiff-legged bastard. But we just don't dance to the same tune no more."

"Well, ex-Ranger Matt," Finch sought to lighten the mood. "I'll ease your mind about one other thing! I've got plenty of money to buy horses with." Finch patted the saddle bag. "All in gold, too. Hump took a herd up to Abilene in '68 and made 'em pay 'im in double eagles. Hump don't hold with paper money. When he got home, he had old Kate, our cook, hide the money and then tell just him and me and his wife Mandy where it is. Hump near stuffed my bags full when I left the ranch. I think he still feels bad about losing Rafter."

"Yeah, I remember Hump a-takin' that herd up to Abilene. Fact is, me and some of the boys sort of sided Hump when some herd cutters was a-botherin' 'im."

"That's right," Finch said. "Hump told about that. You shot one of the herd cutters, didn't you?"

"Ort to of shot the whole damn bunch—especially that Red Roark—he was the stud. We give 'im ever chance in the world to draw, but after I shot that one feller, the rest of 'em didn't seem to have no hankerin' for more—which shore disappointed the boys."

"Whatever happened to 'em?"

"Oh, we brought all of 'em in," Matt said almost absently. "But the damn government turned 'em loose. Said we was actin' illegal since we found 'em in Indian Territory!"

"The government must be in a mess!" Finch said seriously.

"It is for damn shore that!" Matt said. "But anyway, one of the boys picked a fight with Red Roark and shot 'im, and the rest of 'em left these parts. Probably still stealin' cattle along the Chisholm trail."

"Well, we've got horses to buy and time and money to do it with," Finch said almost gaily. Their conversation had seemed to lighten the mood of both men

"Hey, Finch," Matt suggested. "Let's go by San Antone. Won't take a lot longer, and we might find some excitement!"

"I shore wouldn't mind a little excitement!" Finch grinned.

\* \* \* \* \* \*

They camped a couple of miles north of San Antonio and slept until the sun was up the next morning. They picketed their horses on fresh grass and went about preparing and eating breakfast in a leisurely manner.

Two Mexican men stopped by their camp before they were ready to leave. Finch was careful to keep his eyes on them as Matt looked about to be sure there were no others. It quickly became apparent that the men were friendly, however, and they seemed to be excited. Neither spoke English, but both Finch and Matt could use their language well enough to understand most of their rapid fire lingo.

Their excitement stemmed from the fact that there was going to be a horse riding match in San Antonio that afternoon and a dance in the plaza that night. The Mexicans laughed heartily at Finch and Matt's clumsy use of Spanish.

"Hasta la vista," one of them smiled as they rode away.

"Adios," Finch called after them.

"Well," Matt said as the men disappeared into the scrub oaks and junipers. "Looks like I was right about some excitement in good old San Antone!"

"Looks like it!" Finch said. "Let's get on into town."

As they approached the plaza, they could see wagons, horses, carts, and other means of transportation converging on the center of town from streets resembling wagon wheel spokes coming to a focus on the plaza.

There was a hotel near the hub, and they went in. Finch asked for two rooms on the ground floor. They were available. They were directed to a stable where they could put up their horses and pack mule.

"What did you get two rooms for?" Matt asked curiously.

"Oh!" Finch said nonchalantly. "Just a habit I picked up from Chico Baca."

"Well, all I got to say is—you shore must have plenty of money in them saddle bags."

"I have," Finch grinned. "And we may need both of the rooms real bad. Chico and I did."

Finch did not explain further, but he had been to San Antonio before, and he knew that the senoritas were extremely friendly. Finch was a natural man, and it had been a long time since he had had a woman other than a Comanche maiden.

When they had unpacked their gear and hidden Finch's saddle bags in what they deemed to be a safe place, they walked out on the streets. The Alamo was visible from the plaza, and its simple beauty affected both Finch and Matt more deeply than they would have admitted.

"You know, Finch," Matt said as he nodded toward the small mission, "them fellers that was in that fracas there about thirty-five years ago had 'em one hell of a fight."

"I know!" Finch said. "Neither one of us was born then, but I reckon we've heard plenty about it."

"I expect folks will talk about that one for a long time!"

They encountered many men, as they walked along, and learned that the riding match would be held at an arena about a mile west of the plaza.

"Gonna be a big crowd there," a man said proudly. "Men been bringin' in their women and kids all day. And I hear that some tame Comanches is a-comin' to take part in the ridin' match."

"There ain't no such thing as a tame Comanche," Matt said flatly.

"Some of 'em aren't so bad," Finch said, thinking of his friend White Horse. "And they're the best riders I ever saw."

"Just the same, I'll keep my eye on 'em if they're there," Matt said, evidently not convinced that any Indian was a tame one.

\* \* \* \* \* \*

After eating in the hotel, Finch and Matt went to the stable and saddled their horses, for they had no intention of walking a mile to see anything. Their pack mule brayed plaintively as they rode away.

They reached the arena, which was simply a fairly flat and unfenced area that had been cleared of rocks and brush. Completely encircling it were wagons, horses, mules, and other contrivances which would accommodate a solid ring of people. There were women, old and young, and children of every size and color. Finch was startled to see a group of Indians sitting their horses side by side at the edge of the field.

"They're Comanches, all right," Finch said as he stopped his horse and looked keenly at them. "If they ride, the whites are sure going to have their hands full to beat them."

"Ort to shoot ever damn one of the murderin' bastards," Matt said harshly.

They rode near the end of the arena and found a vacant spot where they could ride their horses up to the circle. It was just opposite the Indians.

They sat for a few moments waiting for the action to begin. The day was hot, and Finch pulled off his hat to wipe sweat from his brow. They heard a loud exclamation from an Indian and then a general babble among them. One of the braves kept pointing at Finch and Matt, repeating the words "Hut 'se Pah Suh Kahwe."

"What the hell you reckon he's a-sayin'? And why is he pointin' at us?"

"They're Comanches, all right," Finch said, and a note of grimness crept into his voice. "And I reckon I've met that one that's pointing at us, before."

"You know 'im?" Matt was amazed.

"I don't know 'im, but I reckon he knows me," Finch said. "That word that he was yelling was my Comanche name."

"Your Comanche name!"

"Yes. I didn't ask for it, but I was in a fight with some one time, and they gave me the name. The Comanches have called me that ever since."

"Well, what the hell does it mean?"

"It means 'Ice Eye'," Finch said self-consciously.

"I'll be damned!" Matt was agape. Then he laughed. "I reckon they named you right," he said gleefully. "Wish I could remember what it was so I could call you that."

Finch simply grinned and made no comment.

\* \* \* \* \* \*

The action was ready to begin. A spear was placed in the center of the arena, and the starter, who was a white man, sat his horse at the end of the arena, which was perhaps a hundred yards long. A young cowboy rode out, and the starter said something to him; he nodded. The starter dropped his hat, and the cowboy's horse leaped as if stung. He raced madly down the center of the arena, and when in position, the cowboy leaned down and picked up the spear. He did not slacken the pace of his horse until he reached the end of the arena, where he whirled about and raced back; he replaced the spear in the same spot it had been before. The crowd cheered wildly.

The next contestant was one of the Comanches, who rode a wild looking mustang to the starter. His face was impassive as the starter spoke to him. The Indian gave no indication that he had heard; so the starter dropped his hat. The Indian repeated to perfection the same routine that had been set by the cowboy. However, the Comanche rode bareback with only a rope in his horse's mouth for a bridle. The crowd cheered again—perhaps not so spontaneously as for the cowboy, but they were people who appreciated horsemanship, whoever performed it.

The same event continued until three cowboys and three Indians had participated. There was not one bobble on the part of any rider. Most of the people had never seen such horsemanship and continued to applaud. It seemed to make no difference now whether it was Indian or white who rode.

The lance was then replaced by a glove and the same feat performed. Finally, one of the cowboys missed the glove, and a moan followed by derisive jeers swept the crowd. The red-faced cowboy rode out of the arena.

Next, two obviously untamed mustangs were dragged into the arena and tied to stakes driven deep into the ground. A cowboy carried his saddle near one, which fought madly, but could do little with his head tied so closely to the ground. He tried to strike the cowboy with his front feet, but could not. The cowboy took a large scarf from his neck and quickly whipped it over the horse's eyes. Blinded, the horse stood still, but trembled, as the cowboy put his saddle on and cinched it tight.

While the cowboy was saddling his horse, one of the Indians had approached the other. The Indian stood stoically and watched impassively as the cowboy mounted a pulled the slip knot that bound the mustang to the stake; then he jerked the blindfold from the horse's eyes and yelled. As he did so, the Indian, in a movement too quick to see, slashed the rope of his mustang with a knife, grabbed a mane hold, and jumped astride. Both horses took off at a hard run, and both the cowboy and the Indian were yelling. The crowd parted hurriedly as the horses ran through it. The cowboy and Indian were last seen as their horses raced madly across the prairie

Both the cowboy and Indian returned in an hour, their horses lathered and exhausted. In the meantime, other riders performed the same feat, but had not returned.

So passed the long afternoon. When Finch and Matt got back to the hotel, they were more than glad to take advantage of the bathtub afforded by the hotel. After supper, they were ready for the Fandango.

People were already dancing, and many of the older ranch women were performing like girls half their age. There were also a lot of very pretty Mexican girls available, and Finch and Matt each quickly claimed one.

Finch had not danced for a long time, but his natural rhythm and sensuous coordination soon had an admiring group cloistered around him and his vivacious partner. They danced to many of the Mexican tunes and to such gringo tunes as the "Buck and Wing," the "Kentucky Heel Tap," and the "Arkansas Hoedown." Finch was adept at all of them.

Finally, one of his partners, a sparkling-eyed, almond skinned beauty, whispered in his ear. Even Finch's limited Spanish could understand the provocative invitation. They melted into the crowd and minutes later were in Finch's room.

An hour later Finch was exhausted. The pretty senorita had proved to be an enthusiastic and adept bed partner; yet when Finch lay back and looked at the ceiling, he felt an unaccountable sense of restlessness. Inexplicably, he thought of Mandy Beatenbow, although he knew that she would understand, for she had always sensed his male needs and had encouraged him to visit his Comanche friend White Horse. And with her fine womanly intuition, she knew when Finch returned to the ranch, that he had been with an Indian girl. Her warm, dark eyes always held a mysterious and knowing smile for him when he returned.

The girl beside Finch had fallen asleep with one shapely leg draped over him and her hair across his chest. She snored gently.

A loud knock on the door and a yell intercepted Finch's reverie. He immediately palmed his pistol which he always kept under his pillow. The girl beside him quickly sat up in bed, making no effort to hide her nakedness. The yell came again, and her eyes widened and filled with terror.

"Mi esposo!" she whispered in terror and quickly dived under the covers and lay trembling.

"Your what?" Finch whispered urgently.

The girl did not answer, but curled into a tight ball and yanked the covers more securely about her.

In that instant, Fauntleroy Finch—legendary Texas Ranger, the fastest and most accurate shot on the Texas frontier, sitting upright with his pistol in his hand—felt a chill of sheer terror, for he knew that it would be impossible for him to shoot the man if he broke through the door.

"Why didn't you tell me you were married?" Finch gritted as he quickly jumped from the bed and grabbed his clothes.

The loud knocking and yelling continued as Finch, with his clothes under his arm, his holster belt around his neck, his boots in one hand and his pistol in the other, began to scramble out the small window. He had one foot on the ground when the yelling and banging suddenly ceased. Finch started running toward the stables.

Matt, who had been watching Finch closely, for he was well aware of the fiery Mexican temperament, saw Finch and his girl disappear into the crowd. He lost sight of them and looked anxiously about the plaza. Suddenly he knew! He rushed into the hotel and down the hallway as a big, mustachioed Mexican was pounding on Finch's door and yelling curses in Spanish.

Matt didn't need an explanation, and he didn't hesitate. He slapped the big Mexican on the side of the head with his pistol. The man fell without a sound. Matt pulled his room key from his pocket; evidently one key fitted all rooms, for the door opened easily, and Matt rushed in. He glanced at the bed and then ran to the open window to see Finch, naked as the day he was born, running toward the stables.

Matt took time to let out a roar of glee, and then turned to the bed and pushed the covers off. The girl lay wide-eyed and terror stricken as Matt looked at her lovely, naked body.

"Hell! I shore can't blame Finch none!" he said appreciatively. "But you'd ort to of told 'im you was married! You could get somebody killed, woman—and damn near did!"

With that, Matt turned to the man he had clubbed with his pistol. He was still unconscious; Matt dragged him into the room, tore a sheet in strips, and bound and gagged him. Then he turned to the girl, who was now sitting on the side of the bed.

"Now, Lady," Matt grated, "you just sit an hour before you turn 'im loose, you hear?"

The girl stared in incomprehension.

"Una hora!" Matt said and pointed to the trussed up man. "Una hora! Comprende?"

The girl nodded her understanding, and Matt looked quickly about the room to be sure Finch had left nothing; then he went to his own room, grabbed his things, and headed for the stables.

Finch was dressed and had his horse saddled and the mule packed when Matt arrived.

"Get your horse saddled—and hurry!" Finch demanded.

Matt bridled his horse and then lay down on the stable floor and howled his glee.

"What's the matter with you?" Finch demanded urgently. "Let's hurry!"

"I was just—" Matt held his stomach and roared with laughter. "I was just a-thinkin' about you a-runnin' like a scared rabbit and dressed in your birthday suit, with your pistol in one hand and your boots in the other, and your clothes tucked under your arm," Matt gasped.

"Well, dammit! Get your horse saddled, and I'll tell you about it," Finch growled.

"I already know about it!" Matt gasped between gales of laughter. "It was me that bashed that hombre that was a-tryin' to knock your door down."

Finch looked at Matt blankly. "If it was you, then you know why I'm in a hurry!" he said fiercely.

"I damn shore do!" Matt kept laughing as he saddled his horse, and they rode away from San Antonio.

When they had travelled an hour as fast as their mule could follow, they stopped for a breather.

"You know, Matt," Finch said in a querulous voice, "that's the first time I've ever been really scared in my life—and it isn't a good feeling!"

"Scared?" Matt said. "Hell, Finch, you could of shot the hombre's eye out afore he got two steps into that room."

"I could," admitted Finch. "But I wouldn't! Not when I was in bed with his wife!"

"If you hadn't, he'd a killed you," Matt said soberly.

"I reckon he would have," Finch answered. "And he'd a had a cause to—that girl didn't tell me she was married."

"Just wait till the boys hear about that!" Matt howled in glee again.

"Let's go, you locoed bastard!" Finch managed a sickly grin.

# Chapter 6

The trip to Leesville was a pleasant one. Neither Finch nor Matt was in a hurry. Their horses picked their way leisurely through the brush country. Both men wore tapaderos on their stirrups, and both wore chaps. The little pack mule was very adroit in avoiding brush that would scrape his pack; he would occasionally stop to get a few tufts of grass, and then trot to catch up. They camped early each night. The second day out, a young white tailed deer jumped up almost under their horses' feet. The horses shied violently. Finch shot the deer before it had taken two jumps.

"Don't seem like that easy livin' you been a-doin' up on the Canadian has hurt your pistol shooting none!" Matt said admiringly as he examined the deer and saw that Finch's shot had broken its neck.

"I reckon not," Finch admitted. "But some fresh deer meat will go mighty good tonight."

"It will at that," Matt admitted.

\* \* \* \* \* \*

They reached Leesville about mid-afternoon. Fleming greeted them enthusiastically, for they had all been together in the Rangers, at one time. He quickly invited Finch and Matt to unsaddle and come into the shack near the barns and corrals, where Old Billy was kept.

Finch wanted to see the renowned stallion before doing anything else, however, and Fleming obliged.

Old Billy's appearance would have been disappointing to many, for there was a ring of bare hide around his neck where no hair grew, and his feet looked as though he had been foundered. But the classic lines of his conformation were very evident to a real horseman. The short back, sloping shoulders, bulging gaskin muscles, dainty head, and wide-set, intelligent eyes told their own story.

"Don't look like much, does he?" Fleming voiced the unspoken thoughts of Finch and Matt.

"He does look a little ragged," Finch admitted.

"He's got a right," Fleming said almost proudly. "They kept 'im chained to a tree for a few years during the war. He had a hole tromped out that you could bury a steer in, and his hooves had growed out till I had to chop 'em off with a axe and a saw afore he could walk good again."

"Why did they keep 'im chained up?" Finch was incredulous.

"Weren't nobody's fault," Fleming said. "There wasn't nobody but women folks to take care of 'im, and he was awful raunchy when he was younger. The women would just throw 'im some hay and maybe some grain ever day. How they fetched water to 'im, I don't know! It's a wonder he lived through it, but he shore did, and I'm mighty glad of it."

"A lot of people are. I sure am. I had one of his colts—best horse I ever had."

"I ort to remember!" Fleming said. "I sold 'im to you when we was both in the Rangers. Called 'im 'Rafter'. You still got 'im?"

"Nope," Finch replied.

"What happened to 'im? You sell 'im?"

"He got killed."

"Oh." Fleming sensed that Finch did not want to talk about it. "I thought I recognized that horse you was ridin' when you came up. I reckon I've seen 'im afore someplace."

"He was Chico Baca's horse," Finch replied.

"That's right!" Fleming said with satisfaction. "Called 'im 'Poco Gato', didn't he?"

"That's right," Finch said in surprise. "Don't see how you could remember his name!"

"Hell!" Fleming said. "When you're around horses as much as I am, you remember them and their names better than you do people. Even remember their breeding—that Poco Gato that Chico rode was Steel Dust bred."

"Right again!" Finch exclaimed. "I don't see how you do it!"

"All horses are different," explained Fleming. "They all got their peculiar ways and looks— just like people. And most of 'em are a hell of a lot better'n some people I've knowed."

"That's for shore," Matt chimed in.

"Heard about what happened to Chico," Fleming said soberly. "That was one good Mexican, and he shore enjoyed livin'!"

"Well, his killer didn't enjoy livin' very long!" Finch said with satisfaction.

"Heard what happened," Fleming said. "That partner of yours must be pure hell to cross."

"He is," Finch said.

"Hey, Fleming!" Matt joined in again. "You said somethin' about coffee."

"Well, hell!" Fleming said as if coming out of a trance. "All this palaverin' we been a-doin' has made me forget my manners. Come on in the house!"

"The 'house' was little more than a shack, but it did have a small stove and some bunks around the walls. In a short time they were drinking strong, hot coffee at a wooden table that boasted no cover of any kind.

After they had all taken a few tentative sips of the strong brew, Fleming asked, "Well, what brings you two lazy devils down into this neck of the woods?"

"Looking for some Old Billy horses," Finch answered.

Fleming sat thoughtfully for a moment and then said, "Well, there's quite a few scattered about here in Gonzales County, and some down in Karnes County that I know of. But they're hard to find and a hell of a lot harder to come by. Maybe so they're over-rated—I don't know—but folks ask a hell of a price for 'em. Fact is, I'm a-gettin' a $10.00 stud fee on Old Billy now, and he's a-makin' me money, too. He's still a powerful breedin' bastard—even if he is old!"

"How old is he?"

"Don't rightly know!" Fleming said after a moment of silent deliberation. "But he's smooth mouthed. Has been for a long time."

"I'd shore like to get a young stud sired by him, and out of that old Paisano mare," Finch said longingly. "Our ranch stud got killed a while back, and we shore do need another one."

"Well, I've got one," Fleming said proudly. "Just a four year old, and bred like you said. But I reckon you'd have to shoot me in both laigs to lead 'im off from here. I'm a-savin' 'im to take Old Billy's place."

"Any Steel Dust mares around?"

"They ain't so hard to find," Fleming said. "And they ain't so hard to come by neither."

"Can you tell us where to look?"

"Hell!" Fleming said. "I'll do better'n that. I'll go with you. I got a no account hand that'll be comin' in about dark, and he can take care of things while we're gone. I figure you two greenhorns gonna need somebody to keep them horse traders from a-sendin' you back bare assed!"

\* \* \* \* \* \*

The hand that Fleming had mentioned came in just at dark. Fleming introduced him only as 'Chip'. Fleming explained to him that he would be gone for a while and gave him instructions to follow in his absence.

"How long you gonna be gone?" It was the first time Chip had spoken; he had a deep, almost guttural voice.

"Damned if I know," Fleming said gaily. "When you're a-traipsin' around with a couple of ignorant orphans a-tryin' to keep 'em from gettin' skinned out of their britches by some smart horse traders, it ain't no tellin' how long it's gonna take!"

Chip nodded and began to prepare supper. After they had eaten, Chip washed the dishes, and the three former Rangers relived their many, dangerous, reckless, daring, and occasionally foolhardy escapades on the Texas frontier, until far into the night.

\* \* \* \* \* \*

The next four days were spent in scouring the county for horses. Fleming seemed to know every rancher and horse in the country and how to find them.

They rode by the Bill Butler ranch in Karnes County where Skeet Dawkins, the foreman, greeted them pleasantly and with a wide grin. When Fleming introduced him to Finch and Matt, he looked at Finch keenly for a moment.

"You wouldn't have a partner by the name of Hump and a foreman named Clem, would you?" he asked Finch

"Sure have." Finch was puzzled. He had not ever seen Skeet before. He was sure of that.

When Finch admitted knowing Humphrey and Clem, Skeet burst out laughing.

"What's so funny?" Finch asked.

"They ever tell you about that nigger that roped the coon out of a tree, and his horse a- throwin' him off and draggin' that coon right through the herd that they was drivin' to Abilene a couple of years ago?"

"They told me." Finch returned Skeet's grin.

"Well!" Skeet laughed heartily. "That herd was about three miles in front of one of ours. I never saw a bunch of critters so wild-eyed and scairt as they come right into our herd. Damndest stampede I ever saw, and if they hadn't hit our herd, I reckon they'd still be a-runnin'."

"What happened?" Fleming asked eagerly.

"Not much," admitted Skeet. "Our herd was trail-wise and tired out. We'd been on the road for nearly two months. When that herd hit ours, there was a hell of a bashin' of horns, but the boys somehow got 'em to millin' and they finally settled down. Took us several days to get 'em separated, though."

Everyone had a good laugh, and then Skeet added, "We shore got a lot of good chow that your nigger women cooked, out of it, though. And we got some bronky horses shod by that nigger buck that could damn near out-stout a horse. But you know the damndest thing—they had a young feller that was a-jinglin' horses for 'em, and he held them broncs while that nigger shod 'em. Talked to 'em, he said! They didn't even move. He shore as hell knew horse talk!"

"He did, for a fact!" Finch agreed. "And I never saw one that he and Largo couldn't shoe."

"Well, it was a big help to us, anyway.—You're a long ways from home, ain't you, Finch? I remember Clem sayin' that you was right up at the tip of Texas on the Canadian River."

"We still are. We're down here looking for some horses. Our stud got killed, and we're trying to breed up our remuda."

"Well, Fleming is shore the horseman in these parts. But, I remember that Hump was ridin' a mighty good horse. Said he was by Old Billy out of that Paisano mare. Said his partner loaned 'im to 'im."

"I loaned 'im to Hump, all right," Finch said.

"That horse you ridin' now looks a lot like the one that big nigger was ridin'."

"He is," Finch said. "He used to belong to a partner of mine."

"You buy 'im?"

"Nope. Partner got killed."

There was a short silence. "You still got that horse Hump was ridin'?"

"Nope. He got killed, too—and so did that young horse herder that held those broncs of yours for Largo to shoe."

"That's tough!" Skeet commiserated, but he did not ask further questions about the boy or the horse. Death was all too common on the frontier, and they did not dwell on it. It was Skeet who broke the somber mood that had settled on the group.

"Well," he grinned. "Old Clem was damn shore a good cowman, but he seemed nigh mortified to tell me that they had some nigger cowhands, and then got mad as hell at me when I forgot to mention that we had some of our own."

"That's Clem, all right," Finch laughed. "He still can't abide the nigger cowboys usin' a surcingle."

"That big nigger horse shoer rode a saddle. You still got him?"

"He's still on the ranch. Got an eye gouged out in a fight with an Indian, though."

"Damn!" Skeet said sympathetically. "You boys must be a-ridin' a rough string up where you are!"

"Hey!" Fleming broke in. "We come to look at some horses—remember? Not to listen to you two jaybirds a-squawkin' at each other all day."

"Well, we've got some, and you know it," Skeet said. "Don't know if any of 'em is for sale or not. I'll have to ask Butler."

\* \* \* \* \* \*

Bill Butler agreed to sell two mares to Finch, but asked an outrageous price. Fleming tried to dissuade Finch, but one of the mares was a real beauty—sorrel with flaxen mane and tail, and gentle as a friendly pup. Finch could envision Mandy Beatenbow on her! The other mare was a good bay with one stocking. Both were Steel Dust breeding.

When they left leading the two mares, Fleming didn't say a word until they were out of earshot of Skeet and Butler; then he exploded.

"Dammit, Finch," he blustered. "You must have a lot more money than you got sense. If you'd a-let me jaw for a hour or so, I could a-got them mares for half what you paid for 'em!"

Finch just grinned.

\* \* \* \* \* \*

A week later, they had found three more mares that Finch liked and bought. But they never were able to find a stallion that suited him. They had made a big circle through Gonzales, Lavaca, Karnes, and DeWitt counties, and had finally ended up near Fleming's place in Leesville.

"Let's go by the place and get a good meal and some coffee that ain't full of wood ashes," Fleming suggested. "Maybe so I'll think of somebody else that's got a stud that would suit your damn, finicky taste, Finch."

As they rode up to Fleming's barn and corrals, Old Billy gazed at them incuriously. But in a run built of sturdy logs, there was a horse that neighed and pawed the ground angrily as they came near.

"You been a-hidin' one out on us, Fleming?" Finch joked.

"Naw," Fleming said absently. "That's the four year old that I was a-tellin' you about. He was in a stall when you come by. He's out of Paisano by Old Billy. I figger on usin' 'im to replace Old Billy when the time comes."

"Let's take a look at 'im."

They rode up to the strong log fence. Sitting their horses, they could see over quite easily. Finch gave a quiet gasp, for before him was the most magnificent stallion he had ever seen. A light sorrel, deep of chest, bulging muscles, short back, neatly sloped shoulders, and a small, dainty head. His eyes were wide-set and intelligent, but his temperament at the moment was explosive. He seemed to know that he was making an impression, for he pitched, bucked, and ran around the small paddock with blazing speed. Finch was sure that he would injure himself.

"Is he always like that?" he asked Fleming.

"Ever time I turn 'im out of his stall," admitted Fleming with pride.

"I'd shore as hell hate to try to ride 'im," Matt said.

"Several of the boys has tried to ride 'im," Fleming said. "But he ain't been rode, yet. Let's go get that coffee."

Finch was quiet as they sat and drank coffee. Matt and Fleming carried on a running conversation. Finally Matt said, "Finch, you all talked out? You shore been doin' a lot of it in the past few days."

Finch ignored Matt. "Fleming," he said, "how much would it take to buy that horse out there?"

Fleming looked at Finch in surprise. "I told you, Finch—you'd have to shoot me in both laigs to lead that horse away from here. He just ain't for sale!"

"I'll give you two thousand for 'im!"

"God-a-mighty, Finch!" Fleming was awe-struck. "You just shot me in one leg—but he ain't for sale."

"Then I'll shoot you in both legs!" Finch grinned. "Five thousand. In double eagles. I got 'em in my saddle bags."

Fleming gulped and turned pale. "Hell, Finch! You ain't got that kind of money. Nobody in Texas has!"

"I have," Finch said firmly.

"Finch—dammit! That's more money than a cowboy can make in ten years!" Fleming almost yelled.

"Yep. And you'd have to breed five hundred mares at $10.00 a stand to make that much."

"Finch—" Fleming stood up and threw his coffee out the door in disgust. "Finch, you long- legged bastard, I reckon you just shot me in the other laig. Ain't you got no mercy a-tall?"

\* \* \* \* \* \*

The next morning, they fitted the stallion with a stout rope halter. Fleming led him outside the barn. "He leads good enough," he said. "I been handlin' 'im since he was a little 'un, but he shore as hell ain't broke to ride."

"We've got a nigger cowhand that can ride 'im," Finch said with conviction.

"He one of them that uses a surcingle?"

"Yep."

"Shore as hell hate to see a nigger on that horse, but he ain't mine no more."

Finch took the stallion's lead rope and dallied around his saddle horn. Matt tied two of the mares beside him.

"You're a-gonna have a hell of a bash-up if'n one of them mares comes into heat," Fleming said with a touch of satisfaction in his voice.

"We'll make it," Finch said firmly. "And you might be on the lookout for some shorthorn cattle. Maybe so we'll be back in a couple of years for some. Hump's got the idea that mixing them with longhorns might get a better cow brute."

"Now, that's a damn crazy idea!" Fleming ejaculated. "Ain't no self-respectin' short horn that would breed with a ugly longhorn, no way."

"You got a name for this old plug stud horse that you damn near robbed us to pay for?"

"I been callin' 'im 'Hawk'," Fleming said. "And I ain't none proud of sellin' the best horse I ever saw, even if it does make me the richest damn fool in Gonzales County!"

\* \* \* \* \* \*

Finch and Matt camped that night several miles from Fleming's place. It took more time than usual, for in addition to caring for their own horses, they had to find good graze for the five mares and Hawk. Finch was very particular to tie the stud securely. The pack mule was turned loose, for they knew he would stay near the horses.

After they had eaten and were drinking coffee as they sat with their backs to a small tree, Matt asked, "Which way you figger on goin' back, Finch?"

"Been thinking on that," Finch admitted. "I figure to go just about due north to Austin and then cut northwest straight through. Don't figure to go by Santone going back."

"Shore don't blame you for that!" Matt grinned.

Finch flushed, but ignored the insinuation.

"Well, you're shore gonna have your hand full a-takin' six horses across them plains by yourself," Matt said. "You gonna have to cross the Colorado, the Lampasas, the Concho, and the Brazos, and no tellin' how many more rivers and creeks, afore you get to the Canadian. And you best remember that them damn Indians is worse than ever out on the plains country."

"I know that," Finch admitted. "But horses will cross rivers better than cattle. Besides, I don't figure on doin' it by myself."

"You don't?" Matt said in surprise. "Who's a-gonna help you?"

"You are."

Matt stared in astonishment. "Me?"

"Yes, you!" Finch said. "You don't have a job now, and I'm offering you one. Forty a month and found."

Matt stared into the fire a long time and threw a chunk of wood into it, making the sparks fly. "Hell!" he said with a shrug. "Might just as well, I guess. I got no folks except way back in Tennessee someplace. And I shore as hell ain't gonna go back to the Rangers."

"You'll take the job, huh?" Finch asked eagerly.

"Hell, yes, boss!" Matt grinned. "I've been a-wantin' to see that place of yours again, anyway. When me and old Tom was with you, when you drove that herd in, I thought it was the purtiest place I ever saw."

"I remember that all too well," Finch said. "It was a rough trip, and I doubt if we'd a-made it if you and Tom hadn't shown up to help us out on the last part of the drive."

"Wasn't no hell of a lot of help," Matt said grimly. "We had to haul old Tom flat on his back in a waggin the last few days after he got shot by old Sally Diego's man. Didn't think he'd ever get well, but he did."

"You reckon we could find another man or two to help us out? Leading six extra horses is a mighty big chore for just two men."

"Maybe we can when we get to Austin," Matt said. "We'll go by the Ranger camp and see if they know of anybody, and I expect they will. A lot of men are needin' work since the war. Besides, I need to tell them Ranger boys to stay clear of San Antone, cause I saw a feller get into a mighty dangerous situation down there." Matt grinned at Finch.

"Go to hell!" Finch said. "You'll keep your big mouth buttoned up. I'm your boss, now. Remember?"

"I remember," Matt answered in mock servility. "But I can see right now that you're gonna be pure hell to work for! Just hope I don't talk in my sleep."

\* \* \* \* \* \*

They were able to hire two more men in Austin. One of them was a youngster with a chubby face and crossed eyes, the other a grizzled oldster with a long, drooping moustache, who smoked a pipe. But both had good mounts, and their guns looked as if they had been used.

"What do they call you fellas?" Finch asked.

"My name is Terrence," the younger said, and then he paused, his face flushed. "But they been a-callin' me 'Gotcheye' ever since I was a kid. I guess maybe you'd better call me that. Likely, I wouldn't know who you meant if you called me by my real name."

Finch felt a pang of sympathy for the youngster.

"Call me Pete," the oldster said without taking his pipe from his mouth.

They loaded on some extra food and a sack of grain for the horses, for they knew that grain-fed horses might come in mighty handy, especially if they had a long chase with Indians.

As they left Austin, each of the extra men led two mares. Matt led one mare, and Finch led Hawk. "I'd like to have Matt as loose as possible in case we meet some unfriendlies," Finch explained. "He's good with his guns, and we may need 'em fast."

"Well, hell, boss," protested Gotch-eye. "I'm good with guns, too. Just cause I'm gotch-eyed don't mean I can't shoot straight."

"Figgered you might be," Finch consoled him. "But Matt and I have ridden together before, and we pretty well know what the other one will do."

The youngster was somewhat mollified, but he seemed still to be a little disgruntled as they left Austin. He felt that Finch had cast an aspersion on his crossed eyes, but that was the farthest thing from Finch's mind. He knew that a cross-eyed man had to overcome a lot of doubt about his ability to see and shoot straight. He figured the young man had done so, or he would not be wanting to cross Indian and outlaw country with all the impediments they carried. As far as the older man was concerned, Finch had no misgivings. He looked like an old Lobo wolf that had survived many a tough battle.

# Chapter 7

The first few days of the return trip passed without serious incident. The Brazos River was high; all the horses crossed easily, but the pack mule went under water when a limb swept by him. The pack was soaked and most of the grub ruined, but the grain for the horses was not damaged.

They rode as fast as they felt their mounts could sustain the pace, and they fed them grain each night. The mares were broken to ride; so they were able to switch mounts occasionally, which spared the horses a great deal. The only problem was that one of the mares came into heat, and Hawk started acting studdish. Finch had to ride Gato and keep the young stallion tied close. Even so, he would bite viciously at Gato's neck, and Finch had to hit him across the nose several times with the butt end of his quirt. The steady Gato went about his business and seemed to ignore the fiery young stud.

When they hit the Red River, they were on the Texas side, but near the Oklahoma Territory. The river was high and rolling. Big logs and a lot of brush were being swept seaward; they deemed it prudent to camp for the night, although it was only mid-afternoon. They picketed the horses on good grass, gave each a ration of grain, and built a fire to cook supper. They made no pretense of trying to hide their presence, for the open country made it impossible to do so.

They had finished eating supper and were sipping coffee, when Pete grunted and pointed with his pipe. The rest of them looked and saw three Indians on horses. The distance was too far to tell much about them, and they were probably within the bounds of the Indian Territory.

"Indians, all right," Finch said. "Can't tell from here what kind."

"Kiowa," Pete said laconically.

"Hope to hell they stay where they're supposed to," Matt said somberly.

"They won't," Pete said cryptically.

"How do you figure that?" Finch asked.

"They've seen us and our horses, and they know we can't cross the Red tonight. So by tomorrow, they'll have a good sized bunch and jump us some place up ahead."

It was the longest speech that Pete had made, and they all listened carefully.

"How do you know that?" Matt asked curiously.

"Cause I know Injuns," Pete replied. He said nothing more. He didn't need to.

While they were drinking coffee, they kept a constant eye on the Indians, who sat their horses for half an hour and then rode back to the east.

"Best we keep two or three men a-watchin' the horses tonight instead of just one like we been a-doin'," Pete said as he puffed complacently on his pipe.

Then, there ensued a discussion as to the best way to deal with the Indians the next day if they came back with reinforcements.

"There's quite a few breaks in this here country," Matt said. "I figger we'd best just run like hell till we get to a rough spot or a buffalo waller, and then just get off and start a-shootin'. With as many guns as we got, we can hold off quite a passel of 'em."

"Won't work!" Pete didn't miss a puff on his pipe.

"Why not?" Matt asked.

"Cause we can't find a place deep enough to hide our horses, too, and the red bastards would just shoot 'em all and leave us afoot, and then they could pick us off—or starve us out."

"We could get a lot of 'em before they could do that," Finch said. "Especially if they're just using bows and arrows."

We could take some of 'em," Pete admitted. "Mebbe most of 'em, but we couldn't get 'em all. Besides, they got rifles."

"How do you know that?"

"Saw the sun flash on one whilst they were a-settin' over there."

"Then what do you figure is best?" Finch asked.

"They'll come at us in a bunch," Pete said. "Just as we're a-goin' up a rise. They allus do. What we're gonna have to do is ride right at 'em a-shootin' as fast as we can. Prob'ly surprise the red bastards some. Mebbe so, they'll scatter. And we might even pick off a few as we go through 'em, but when they split, we'll just keep a-ridin' like our tails are a-fire, and we got a chance of out- runnin' 'em. Their horses ain't as good as ours, and they ain't grain fed."

"You sound as though you've had some dealings with 'em before," Finch said.

"I've fit the red heathen afore, alright. Mighty nigh since I was no older than Gotch-eye there."

"Well, it makes sense—sort of," Matt said. "I just wish Finch didn't have to be bothered with that damn stud. He could wipe a dozen of 'em out of their saddles afore the rest of us could get a shot at 'em."

"Turn the damn stud loose!"

It was the first time Gotch-eye had spoken. He looked scared, and Finch surmised that he had not fought Indians before. Neither Matt nor Pete echoed Gotch-eye's idea, for they knew it was useless. Finch just looked at Gotch-eye and turned away.

\* \* \* \* \* \*

All four of the men stayed awake that night, and they were heartened when the river began to subside rapidly about midnight. Before daylight, they had their mule packed, and their horses saddled, and the mares and stud in tow.

"I think we can make it now," Finch said as he eyed the red, clay laden water.

They did. And by the time the sun was up, they were miles away, for Finch was setting a rapid pace.

There was no conversation, for each man was diligently searching the country around them. Gotch-eye carried his rifle in his arms, though it was awkward trying to lead his mares and keep a rifle at the ready at the same time.

It was mid-afternoon when Matt finally opined, "If'n we don't kill these horses we're a-ridin', we may make it yet. The Salt Fork of the Red River ain't but about a mile on up ahead."

The words were hardly out of his mouth when the Indians hit. There were probably thirty of them, and they erupted out of a small draw just ahead of them.

"Let's go!" Finch yelled and jabbed his spurs into Gato's side as he unsheathed his rifle in one fluid movement and got off a shot. An Indian fell from his horse. Finch dropped two more before the others joined in the shooting.

As Pete had predicted, the Indians seemed surprised that the white men were charging instead of running. They pulled up momentarily as the white men and their horses cut through them. Everyone was shooting. Several of the Indian horses were down, and some were riderless. Finch had begun to use his pistol as they were close in, and his uncanny ability with it emptied saddles. The legendary Ranger, Fauntleroy Finch, was no fireside yarn!

They were nearing the Salt Fork of the Red when the Indians had regrouped and given chase.

"Follow me!" Finch yelled as he spurred down the sloping bank and across the narrow stream of water. A hundred yards ahead was the island where he had camped on the way down. There was a small meadow in its center, and plum bushes grew in thickets on the sand dunes that encircled the meadow.

In less than a minute all of the men were on the island. They quickly jumped off their horses, ran to the top of the sand dunes, and peered through the plum thickets. Finch was the last one up, for he had taken the time to tie the stud securely to a giant cottonwood that was near the center of the meadow.

The Indians had reached the edge of the river and were riding their horses into the water when the men began firing. The distance was not more than a hundred yards. Finch fired three times that sounded almost as one shot. Matt, Pete, and Gotch-eye joined in. Almost instantly, riderless Indian horses began galloping wildly away. Another barrage from the men, and only two Indians were still on horses. They stopped, whirled, and started running away.

"Hold your fire!" Finch yelled.

Matt and Pete obeyed, but Gotch-eye had his sights lined on the broad back of a retreating Indian, and he pulled the trigger. The Indian fell into the water.

"Dammit!" Finch yelled. "That'll do. Now quit shooting!"

An eerie silence descended on the little island as the men watched alertly, lest another band of Indians should appear. The day was very still and hot. The silence was finally broken by the comforting sound of horses cropping grass in the meadow below.

Then came another shot. It was Pete. "Saw one of them red bastards a-crawlin' outen the water," he explained. "Had a rifle, too."

"You must have eagle eyes!" Matt said. "I didn't see nothin'."

"I can see," Pete admitted. "And that there red-skin ain't a-gonna crawl up on us and shoot nobody."

"Anybody get hurt?" Finch asked.

"I got a scratch," Matt said. "Nothin' bad."

"Didn't touch me," Pete answered.

Gotch-eye did not answer.

"Gotch-eye!" Finch asked more loudly. "Are you all right?"

Still no answer. Finch made his way through the plum bushes to where he thought Gotch-eye should be. He stopped abruptly and looked down at Gotch-eye, who lay flat on his back, eyes that were already filming over staring lifelessly into the hot summer sky. Gotch-eye had been mortally wounded, and his last shot had killed an Indian as his dying act.

"He's here," Finch called grimly. "He's dead. Shot plumb through, looks like."

Matt and Pete joined Finch. They all looked at the dead youngster; then they silently walked away. They gathered on the highest sand dune to look about again.

"You think they'll come back, Pete?" Finch asked.

"No tellin' about a Indian. My thinkin' is that bunch was all they was in this particular part of the country—but then again—they may be a million of them red bastards hidin' behind a sage brush and a-lookin' at us right now."

"I met a man just north of here a ways as I was coming down. Said his name was Tell and that he had been chased when he was south of the river by a bunch about that size. He outran 'em, but lost his pack mule."

"Well," Matt said, "he ain't the only one that lost a pack mule!"

"We lost ours?" Finch asked quickly.

"First thing," Matt said. "He went down before we got through them Indians."

"Well," Pete said with grim satisfaction, "they ain't enough of them red varmints left to eat all of 'im at one sittin'. Hope he gives the bastards a bellyache, anyway."

Finch sighed. "We've got a job right now of burying Gotch-eye. You know anything about 'im, Pete?"

"Nope."

"Pete, you stay up here and keep watch. Matt and I will bury 'im."

"Got a shovel?" Pete asked.

Finch and Matt just looked at each other.

"Take this." Pete flipped a huge knife with a long, wide blade at Finch's feet. "Works pretty good."

Finch picked up the knife and stuck it under his pistol belt. Then, he and Matt dragged Gotch-eye to another big cottonwood and started digging. No air reached the depression, and both men were sweating profusely before they thought the job was done, even though the sandy ground made easy digging.

When they carried Gotch-eye to the grave, they searched his pockets, but found no identification of any kind.

"The cottonwood will make him a good tombstone," Finch said. "But wolves will sure dig 'im up if we don't put something besides sand on top of 'im, and there aren't any big rocks in the river."

"They is some big, dead cottonwood logs we can drag up," Matt offered.

"Let's get our horses," Finch said.

When they walked to the meadow to get their horses, Finch saw that Gato was lying down, the saddle still on him. When Finch approached, Gato nickered weakly, and Finch saw that blood was coming from his mouth and anus. He rushed to the horse to find that he was also bleeding from a wound just behind the saddle fender.

Matt had mounted and ridden to Finch. "What's wrong?"

"The red sons-of-bitches gut shot 'im!" Finch said grimly. "I felt 'im flinch when we rode through the Indians, but I didn't think about it. He was sure one hell of a horse to run all that way with a bullet through his body. The sons-of-bitches!" Finch said bitterly.

"He's done for, all right," Matt said. "Ain't but one thing left to do."

"I know that!" Finch said harshly as he eased his pistol from the holster and walked to Gato's head. The horse raised his ears and looked inquiringly at Finch. Something like a sob shook Finch.

"You do it, Matt!" Finch said brokenly. "I just haven't got the guts for it!" Finch walked away toward Gotch-eye's grave.

"I'll be damned!" Matt thought in startled surprise. "He's killed more'n twenty white men, and he ain't got guts enough to shoot a horse! I will be damned!"

Matt shot the horse and rode after Finch. He roped a big, dead log and dragged it to the grave. Both men struggled to get it in place.

"We'll need a couple more," Finch said. "If we put a good heavy one on each side of this one, I don't see how anything could get to 'im."

Matt dragged up two more logs, which were finally fitted to their satisfaction. Both men were sweating. Finch pulled off his hat and mopped his brow.

"Well, I reckon we ought to say something over 'im. Wish Hump was here. He can shore preach a good funeral."

"Well, he ain't," Matt said practically. "So let's just say 'so long' and get the hell out of here!"

Finch nodded and put his hat on. Then they went to retrieve Finch's saddle from the dead Gato. It took some tugging, but they managed it.

"Well," Matt said. "we got one less horse and one less man to go the rest of the way. You gonna ride Gotch-eye's horse?"

"No. I'm gonna ride that stud," Finch said grimly.

"You're what?" Matt yelped in surprise.

"I'm gonna ride that stud," Finch replied firmly.

"Hell, Finch! You ain't no bronc rider, and you heard Fleming say that he had throwed ever body that ever tried to ride 'im."

"I may not be a bronc rider," Finch admitted. "But that stud doesn't know it. Besides, the sand is dry here, and I'm not in any mind to humor 'im anyway. If I hadn't been leading 'im, Poco Gato might not have got killed."

"But, Finch, you know damned well—"

"Now, that'll do!" Finch said, and there was steel in his voice. Matt had heard him use the phrase before, and he knew that the time for decision was past.

"I'll snub 'im up tight," Matt said. "And maybe you can get your saddle on 'im."

Thirty minutes later, men and horses were dripping sweat, but Finch's saddle was cinched firmly on Hawk's back. Finch stepped back and took a deep breath; then he tied his spurs firmly with a piggin' string and fastened his pistol securely in the holster.

He took another deep breath, put his foot in the stirrup, and swung aboard. He held the horn tightly and rared back in the saddle as he took the reins in his left hand.

"Turn 'im loose, Matt!" Finch gritted.

Matt quickly tossed the halter lead rope to Finch. There was only a second of hesitation before Hawk realized he was not snubbed to the other horse. Then he whirled and jumped.

Matt could not believe his eyes. Hawk jumped higher than he had ever seen a horse jump and screamed his rage as Finch jabbed savagely with his spurs.

Pete came running. "What the hell is a-goin' on?" he demanded. "Sounded like a gut-shot panther!"

Matt said nothing, but just nodded at Finch and the wildly bucking horse. Hawk tried every trick. He ran through the plum thickets to the sand dunes and then headed to the river. Finch sat on him as if glued and jabbed the squealing stud at every jump. When they hit the river bottom, the horse began breaking westward. Matt and Pete watched in awed silence for a while.

"Ain't no use for you to tell about that little set-to, Matt—'cause folks would think you was a damn liar. I ain't never saw no buckin' horse like that afore!"

"Me neither," Matt said feelingly. "And I ain't even shore I believe it myself!"

\* \* \* \* \* \*

An hour later, Finch returned. Hawk was lathered all over and gasping for breath, but he was obeying the reins. Finch's face was pale and drawn with pain. Blood still dripped from his nose and smeared his face.

"Let's get started!" Finch said as he rode up. His voice was shaky.

"All right," Matt said. "I reckon Pete and me can lead the mares and Gotch-eye's horse. We'll tie 'em head and tail."

And so they did. Indeed, they looked more like a pack train than trailing horsemen as they left the north bank of the Salt Fork.

When it began to get dark, Matt kept looking expectantly at Finch, thinking that he would call a halt. Finally he said, "Hey, Finch, you reckon we ain't travelled far enough for one day?"

"I know we have," Finch said. "But all of a sudden, when this horse was bucking up that river bed with me, I got a fierce notion that something isn't right at the ranch. It's not more than seventy or eighty miles straight across, and you fellers can trade off horses by riding one of the mares and Gotch-eye's horse. We can make it up on the caprock by midnight and get to the ranch by dark tomorrow."

"What are you gonna ride?" Matt said testily.

"Me? I'm gonna ride what I'm on."

"You'll kill that stud," Matt admonished. Pete was silent.

"No, I won't." Finch managed a feeble grin. "He's just now getting his second wind."

Matt just shook his head in resignation, got down, and changed his saddle to another horse. Pete did likewise.

A quarter moon gave a dim light as they topped out on the caprock at midnight; they stopped to let their horses breathe. For the first time since he had mounted Hawk at the Salt Fork, Finch stepped off of him. He did so with a quick, fluid movement, but kept the halter rope wrapped tightly around his hand. Hawk did not budge, and Finch loosened the cinch.

When they had rested for less than half an hour, Finch handed Matt Hawk's lead shank.

"Maybe you'd better snub 'im up again, Matt," he said as he tightened the cinch. Matt said nothing, but tightened his own cinch and mounted. He dallied Hawk's lead rope around his saddle horn. Finch mounted, but the stud did not move.

"Turn 'im loose," Finch said.

Matt unwound the rope and carefully handed it to Finch, then backed his horse away. Finch nudged Hawk gently with his spurs, and the horse stepped out briskly.

"I'll be damned!" Matt whispered. "I've heard that them Old Billy horses has got a lot of sense. "I reckon now I'll believe it!"

Finch led the way; Matt and Pete followed. They rested their horses twice more. Both times, when Finch dismounted, Hawk stood still without being snubbed.

They came to the Canadian River just at sundown and rode westward toward the ranch headquarters. It was just getting dusky dark when they were within a quarter of a mile, and Finch heard the Beatenbow jackass. It was not his usual raucous emission of sound, but somehow sounded forlorn. A low, moaning sound wafted through the trees on the riverbank. It sounded like lost souls crying out in lonely, agonized torment.

"What the hell is that?" It was the first time Pete had spoken all day. "The hair just riz right up on my neck—an' I ain't too damn easy to scare."

"I don't know," Finch said tightly. "But something is wrong, and I've known it since we left the Salt Fork."

With that, Finch nudged Hawk into a fast trot. Matt and Pete followed. All of them felt for the reassuring presence of their pistols.

# Chapter 8

Finch seemed to come out of a trance. The news of Humphrey's death had stunned him.

"Clem, these fellers with me are Matt Jimson and Pete. They helped me bring some horses back."

"I've met Clem," Matt said.

Clem looked closely at Matt. "Yeah," he said. "I remember Matt. He shot a damn herd cutter out of the saddle afore nobody else could touch a gun, when Hump and me was a-takin' that herd to Abilene a couple of years ago."

"I'd better go see Mandy," Finch said reluctantly. "But I shore am not looking forward to it."

"I don't blame you!" Clem said. "I'd a-ruther walked into a den of rattlers than go tell 'er today—but I had it to do. She just flinched like I'd hit 'er with a quirt, when I told 'er. But she didn't say a word—just looked at me out of them big black eyes like she was a-starin' at a hant or somethin', and turned 'er head, and set down in that rockin' chair they got in front of the fireplace. Likely that's where she's still at."

"Matt, you and Pete find yourself a bed here in the bunkhouse. I'll see you in the morning."

Finch walked slowly toward the big house. His shoulders slumped with an almost overpowering weariness. When he mounted the steps and gained the gallery, he stopped, took a deep breath, and then knocked on the door. No invitation to enter was forthcoming; so he opened the door quietly. The room was almost totally dark, but when his eyes adjusted, he could see a form in the rocking chair. He walked quietly across the big room that he knew so well and lit a lamp that sat on a table near a window. Then he turned and walked to Mandy and placed his hand on her shoulder.

"It's Finch, Mandy," he said softly.

There was a moment of quiet, and then a soft voice said, "I know. I recognized your footsteps."

Finch was at a total loss for words that might console her. He had never felt so helpless in his life.

"Are you all right?" he finally asked.

Mandy took a deep breath and straightened her shoulders as she rose from the chair and looked at Finch.

"I'm all right," she said in a quiet, steady voice.

As she looked at Finch, her dark eyes were big and round. Finch felt that he was drowning in their depths.

"I heard about Hump," Finch said lamely.

"I knew you had," Mandy said in a voice that somehow conveyed her sympathy for Finch.

"He was a good man."

"He was," Mandy said. "And he was a good husband and father. And I know that you loved him—and so did I, but—Finch, I was never in love with him. I haven't even been able to cry!"

There was nothing hypocritical about Mandy.

"You were a wonderful wife to him," Finch consoled.

"I was the best I could be," Mandy replied. "And he gave me three wonderful children, and I'll be forever grateful to him for that. But instead of just loving him, I wish I could have been in love with him. I know now that I just wanted to follow a dream with him. Does that make me a bad woman, Finch?" she asked almost pleadingly.

"If it does, that makes two of us!" Finch said. "I loved O'oah, but I wasn't in love with her, either. I loved the way she walked and talked and laughed and enjoyed living, but I reckon I never was in love with her. There is a difference, I know, and I wanted to be in love with her, but I never could."

"You were in love with Colette, weren't you, Finch?"

Finch did not reply for a moment, and then he said, "I reckon we can't make our minds do just what we want. I know I can't."

"I'll have to leave here now and take the children," Mandy said almost in a whisper.

"Why?" Finch felt as if the world had stopped for a moment.

"A widow with three children couldn't possibly live in this land," she said sadly.

"Well—" Finch could think of nothing more to say for a moment. "Are the kids all right?"

"They're fine," Mandy said. "I don't think that they fully realize what happened. I moved them from your wing of the house back into their own beds."

"But, why?"

"I was hoping that you would move your things from the dugout and stay in your own quarters again—at least until I leave. I'd feel much safer." There was a tiny note of fear and pleading in her voice.

"All right," Finch agreed. "When do you want me to move back?"

"Tonight," Mandy said firmly. "I was expecting you today. Old Kate said that the spirits told her you were coming."

\* \* \* \* \* \*

Finch moved his bed back into his wing of the house that night. He did not go back to the big room to talk to Mandy again, but he rolled and tossed most of the night, and several times he got out of bed to stare out his windows which faced the west. For the first time in his young life, he felt inadequate to face the future.

The next morning, there was a knock at his door. He opened it to see Mandy standing there. Her face looked drawn and tired, but very beautiful.

"Breakfast is ready," she said.

"I'll eat with the hands," Finch said.

"No, Finch, please," she pleaded. "I cooked breakfast myself. Kate and Sam are both at the Negro quarters, and—I don't want to eat alone."

"All right," Finch agreed. "I'll be in as soon as I wash up."

Mandy left, and Finch joined her at the breakfast table a few minutes later. The sun was not yet up, and the eerie, moaning sound still came from the Negro quarters. The children were still asleep.

"You get any sleep last night?" Finch asked.

"A little, I think," Mandy said. "Did you?"

"Some."

The conversation remained stilted and erratic until the sun pushed its way into their world. There was a sudden change in something, just as the first warm finger of sunlight came into the east window. It took a moment for them to realize what it was. They looked at each other blankly.

Then Finch grinned feebly. "It's the blacks—they've quit that awful yowlin."

"That's it!" Mandy exclaimed. "I'm glad! That unearthly moaning and chanting made this the lonesomest place in the world."

"Hump told me once that the blacks took on something terrible all night when someone was— when they lost—"

"I know." Mandy rescued him. "But for them, it's over now. They'll go back to their normal activities."

Just then, Old Kate entered the room. Her eyes were red and swollen. "Lawsy me," she said, but the old spirit was not in her voice. "Mars Finch, we is sho nuff glad yo is back! Tole Miss Mandy jist yestidy yo'd be here mighty soon. The spirits been a-talkin' to me."

"I'm glad to be back, Kate," Finch said. "Wish I could have made it sooner."

Kate did not miss the significance of Finch's remark. "Wouldn't a-made a smidge o difference in what happened, Mars Finch. What gonna be gonna be!"

"You may clear the table and fix breakfast for the children, Kate," Mandy said. "I'll get them up and dressed."

"Yassum," Kate answered. "I was a hopin' I'd be back in time to fix yo breakfast, too, but I couldn't leave afore the sun riz."

"We had a good breakfast, anyway, Kate." Finch wanted to console the old Negress.

"Yassuh, Mars Finch," old Kate said. "I reckon yo did! Miss Mandy—she a mighty good cook."

"She is," Finch agreed. Then to Mandy he said. "I'll go out and get things moving again, if I can."

"Oh!" Mandy exclaimed. "I forgot. Did you get the horses?"

"I got 'em," Finch grinned. "The best stallion I ever saw. He's by Old Billy out of Paisano, which makes 'im a full brother to Rafter."

"Oh, I'm so glad!" Mandy's face lit up for the first time since Finch had been back. "I know that Humphrey would be happy for you, too! It always bothered him that Rafter was killed when you let him use him on the trail drive."

"I know it did," Finch said. "That was one reason I went after some more— that, and the fact that the jackass killed Old Heck and left us without a stud. But I brought some more horses. Five mares, all Old Billy and Steel Dust breeding. I picked one especially for you. A young Steel Dust sorrel with a flaxen mane and tail."

"Finch! You didn't!" Mandy's face showed a trace of her former animation. "How on earth could you bring all of them back all alone?"

"I picked up a couple of good hands in Austin," Finch explained.

"Good," Mandy said. "You may need more help here on the ranch now. Do you think they will stay?"

"One of them didn't make it all the way back. We ran into some Indians."

Mandy looked at Finch's face and did not question him further. She had become enured against men's sudden and violent death, and she knew that Finch did not like to talk of it.

"I'll come back after I see the boys. I expect Clem and Shanker will have things going all right, but I'll just go see. Then, I'll take you down to the corral to see your mare and the new stallion."

"Good," Mandy said.

Finch found most of the men gathered around the corrals looking over the mares and admiring Hawk.

"Finch," Clem said as Finch walked up. "That there is the best damn piece of horse flesh I ever saw. The son-of-a-bitch looks like he could paw the moon!"

"He damn near can." It was Matt who replied. "Finch ort to know. He hadn't been rode till we had us a brush with some Indians, and Poco Gato got killed. Finch, he topped 'im off for the first time."

"Did he buck?"

"I'm a-tellin' you, man—that horse—"

"Remember what I said, Matt." Pete broke his usual silence. "They ain't no use to tell folks about that, cause they're gonna think you're a damn liar."

"Well—" Matt started to speak again and then simply said, "Yeah. He bucked some."

Clem finally ordered the men away from the corrals so they could relieve the valley rim- riders that had been on night shift.

After all of them had gone and a few night riders had come in, Finch went to the house to get Mandy. She came with a hint of enthusiasm in her dark eyes. She gasped in delight when Finch pointed out her mare.

"She's beautiful, Finch," Mandy said. And then after a pause, "I almost wish I could stay here just so I could ride her. Is she gentle?"

"As a pup!" Finch said and crawled over the corral bars and led the mare by the mane up to Mandy, who rubbed her velvet nose. The mare lifted her lip in delight. Mandy laughed.

After they had petted the mare for a few minutes, Finch said, "Come on. I'll show you the stud."

The corral bars on the stud pen were so high that Mandy had to look through them. Hawk seemed to know that someone special was eyeing him, for he bucked and pitched and ran around the corral at top speed.

"That's the most magnificent horse I ever saw, Finch," Mandy said. "And you'd never know that he just ended a long trip last night. He acts like a colt."

"He's just showing off," Finch said and grinned. "Fact is, I rode 'im all the way from the Salt Fork of Red River, all the way to the ranch without unsaddling."

"That's a long way, isn't it?"

"It shore is," Finch said. "We won't ever have to worry about him having bottom."

"His sides are all bloody," Mandy said. "What caused that?"

Finch did not reply for a moment. Then he said, "He didn't want to be rode at first."

"Oh." Mandy understood and involuntarily looked at Finch's spurs, which still had blood on them

As they started back to the house, they walked quietly side by side for a distance. Then Mandy stopped and took Finch's arm.

"Finch, will you take me by Humphrey's grave? The men wouldn't let me see him after—they buried him before they told me. Clem just brought me his hat. I hung it on a peg by the fireplace."

"I'll take you, Mandy," Finch said tightly.

They did not speak as they walked the few hundred yards to the ranch graveyard. The pile of fresh dirt was quite evident; it was at the foot of the biggest tree in the cemetery. They walked to it and stood silently for a few minutes. Finch removed his hat.

"Some people thought he was a hard man," Mandy whispered. "And I guess he was in some things—but I think he was a good man."

"He was one hell of a man!" Finch said grimly. "They didn't come any better."

As they walked away, Mandy bent her head but did not cry. Finch looked at the graves as they wound through them.

Some of them were for Comancheros who had raided the ranch; crude wooden crosses had been carelessly nailed together to form a cross; many were falling over and deteriorating. Others were for blacks who had died or been killed on the ranch, and Largo had laboriously chiseled their names on sandstone that he had hauled from a distance down the river. Others were for ranch hands that had been killed, and Largo, always aware of the lower status of blacks, had erected larger stones for them. Finch wondered idly what he would do for Humphrey.

When they reached the house, Mandy's three children were playing in the yard. The oldest, a girl who bore a startling resemblance to her mother, except that she had black hair, ran to Finch, grabbed him around the legs, and then reached up for Finch to take her in his arms, which he did and was rewarded with a kiss and a hug.

"Hey, Mandy," Finch said in mock concern. "You're gonna have to quit kissing strange men. You're nearly three years old now!"

The youngster giggled and hugged Finch tighter. Her mother smiled wanly.

"I guess we're going to have to change her name, or mine, one. She's getting so big, people will begin to get us mixed up."

"Well, I reckon that won't be much of a problem," Finch grinned in the good natured exchange. "If she keep growing and stays as pretty as now, they'll pretty soon be calling you 'Granny'."

Mandy hit him playfully on the arm, and then called to the two young boys. "Tom, you and Ed come on into the house; the sun is getting hot."

"Aw, maw!" Tom, who was two years old, protested. Ed, who was a year younger, could not walk yet; so Kate came out, picked him up, took Tom's arm, and went into the house.

"Mars Tom!" she scolded lovingly. "Yo dassen't talk to yo mamma like dat. When she tell yo sompin'—yo do it—hear?"

Kate had made coffee, which she served to Mandy and Finch in the big room.

"Well," sighed Mandy. "I guess I'd better be making plans to go back east. I don't know what else I can do!"

"I reckon people do what they have to do," Finch said glumly. "I know it'd be mighty hard for you to stay here now, but—Well, anyway, we've still got plenty of money from that trail drive for you to take with you. We'll probably make another one every year or two. So you won't have to worry about money. I'll send it along as it comes in."

"But, Finch—"

"Anyway," Finch interrupted. He didn't like to think of her leaving. "You can't leave until a caravan with a military escort comes by going east—and most of 'em are still going west—so I reckon you don't need to hurry up too much."

"You'll stay here on the ranch, Finch?" Mandy asked querulously.

"Till I die of old age," Finch replied firmly.

"Oh, I do hope so!" Mandy said fervently. Finch looked at her with a touch of a puzzled frown. "What I mean is—" Mandy said with a bit of a smile, "that I do hope you die of old age. Nobody has since we've been here. They have all been killed in some way or another. This is a fearful country, Finch," she said almost fiercely. "I never know who will come back when they leave in the morning. I don't want that for you, Finch." Mandy laid her hand on his. "Please tell me you will be careful."

"Yes, ma'am!" Finch sought to lighten the mood. "I'll be the carefullest man you ever saw— and you may be surprised when you come back in a few years. We may be part civilized when you do!"

"Oh, Finch!" Mandy exclaimed and pressed his hand as tears welled in her eyes. She rose abruptly and walked hurriedly to her room.

# CHAPTER 9

The effects of Humphrey's death were almost immediate and widespread. The Negroes became morose, and some were almost unmanageable. A few of the men refused to work until the huge fists of Largo persuaded them to do so. Even as they did the assigned chores, however, they were surly and ill-tempered with each other.

"We ain't got Mars Hump no mo to take care of us!" one of them lamented

But it was old Kate who seemed to be absolutely devastated. Her once ponderous bulk began to shrink, and soon her face and arms were a sea of deep wrinkles. She finally was so emaciated that she resembled her elf-like husband, Sam. No longer was her booming laugh or her loving chiding of the children heard. She served Finch and Mandy's meals in silence.

Gloom pervaded the entire Negro quarters. They no longer sang and chatted as they worked, and the compound at night was almost silent.

The cowboys, however, were largely unaffected. They had seen too much of death to dwell on it. Matt and Pete both agreed to stay on and work, which pleased Finch mightily. He and Matt had not been close friends, but they had shared many experiences while in the Rangers, which seemed to create a bond between them. But to Finch's disgust, Matt refused to share quarters with him in his wing of the house.

"Why not?" Finch had argued.

"Cause I ain't nothin' but a cowhand, now," Matt said firmly. "I'll just stay in the bunkhouse with the rest of them pore damn saddle straddlers. Likely they'd think I was a-tryin' to get in good with the boss if I bunked up in the big house." Matt's grin robbed his remarks of any sting, however.

"You never tried to 'get in good' with anybody in your life, Matt Jimson—and you know it! You're just afraid you might get to be part civilized," Finch rejoined.

"That's for damn shore a fact," Matt said. "Besides, I ain't et with no womenfolks in so long, I can't remember which hand you're supposed to eat with."

Finch laughed. "Well, go ahead and eat that lousy grub if you want to. I'll be thinking of you every morning while I'm eating a good breakfast."

"And lookin' at one hell of a pretty woman!" Matt added.

"Pete is gonna stay with us, too." Finch changed the subject. "I figured he'd saddle his horse as soon as he rested up a little."

"Funny thing about that old bastard," Matt said musingly. "I figgered the same way as you did, but he seems to be as satisfied as a new calf a-suckin' his maw's titty. Don't hardly say nothin', but he eats like a boar hawg and then just sets on his bunk and sucks on that old pipe of his. Seems sort of peaceful with him in the bunkhouse. Good hand with cattle, too!"

"I'm glad he's staying," Finch said. "I'll bet he had a hell of a past!"

"Well," Matt said cheerfully. "if he stays on this ranch, he may have a hell of a future, too. I hear that Largo is havin' some trouble with the niggers."

"Largo can handle the blacks," Finch said confidently. "It's the Indians that have got me to thinking some. Hump was beginning to get a sort of reputation with them. Especially the Kiowas. News travels fast among the tribes, and they knew that Hump wouldn't back off from a fight. And they've heard about his shooting Doc Guines horse so the Apaches could catch 'im. That's the sort of thing the Indians understand."

"What about the Comanches?" Matt asked. "I hear they're the big tribe up here."

"I don't think the Comanches will bother us," Finch said. "Their chief is White Horse, and he's the main one that Kit Carson got to agree to let me run cattle here. Besides, I was married to one of his daughters. And I've visited 'im a lot of times since she got killed by the Kiowas. I think Chief White Horse is my friend."

"Then you're damn hard up for friends!" Matt said firmly.

Finch laughed again. "I expect you're right. But White Horse is as much of a friend as an Indian can be to a white man."

"That ain't no hell of a lot," Matt said. "Well, I reckon I'd better saddle up. Clem has got me on the night shift a-rim-ridin' tonight."

\* \* \* \* \* \*

Two weeks after Humphrey's death, four of the Negro men disappeared. Clem sent Tonio after them.

Tonio, half-Indian and half-Mexican, was the best tracker any of them had ever seen. But his background was a complete mystery, and his demeanor did not invite questions.

"He'll find 'em!" Clem said.

Tonio returned two days later and reported that the Negroes had travelled rapidly to the west and had caught a caravan going that way. They had managed to join it.

"Let 'em go," Clem said. "The pore bastards will prob'ly come back in a few days, anyway."

"Dey won't come back. Dey knows better'n dat!" Largo said dogmatically, and the fierce gleam in his good eye convinced Clem that what he said was true. They had rather face a mad longhorn bull than Largo's wrath.

A few mornings later, old Kate did not wake up. They buried her in the ranch graveyard, and only days later her husband Sam rested beside her. Largo and his wife Maisie moved into the kitchen quarters, and Maisie assumed the duties of cooking and taking care of Mandy's children. The handsome Negress was as capable as old Kate.

Maisie was unrestrainedly proud of her huge, muscular husband, who had had his eye gouged out in a fight with an Indian who wanted Maisie for his squaw. Largo had killed the Indian.

"He de best nigger on de ranch, even if he ain't got but one good eye," Maisie said stoutly, and none of the Negro men would disagree with her—nor would any of the Negro women whom Largo occasionally visited surreptitiously at night after Maisie was asleep.

Other changes were taking place, too. Clem, the woman-hating foreman, had Largo build him an adobe cabin well away from the bunkhouse. "Tired of sleepin' in there with them snorin' bastards!" he exclaimed. But a few days later, Ellie, the pretty light-skinned youngest daughter of old Kate, moved in with him.

Ellie's little son, only a year old, had been sired by Brandy Wine, the young English Jew who had been killed while riding Rafter in the race in Abilene. Nobody had thought anything about the two of them being together so much, although Ellie, at twelve years of age, was a well-developed female. Humphrey had been annoyed when he learned that she was pregnant, and he had been infuriated when she had the temerity to name her little bastard Brandy Beatenbow.

"Them damn niggers is a-sayin' some pretty bad things about Ellie and her kid down on the row," Clem explained. "She cain't help it cause her skin is so light and her kid's hair is sort of rusty color."

It had amazed everyone, including Finch and Mandy, that Clem had taken the girl in. But Finch and Mandy were too sensitive to others to say anything about it, and the men were afraid to. Nobody knew whether the relationship was parental or conjugal.

Finch knew what Humphrey would have said: "Well, God-a-mighty! It ain't none of our business as long as they work like they're supposed to."

Clem echoed Finch's thought when he said, "It ain't nobody's damn business but mine, and I'll shoot any son-of-a-bitch that says anything about it!"

Nobody said anything—at least not to Clem.

\* \* \* \* \* \*

The ranch work went on as usual. The guards rode the canyon rim day and night, but no Indians appeared for several days. Then White Horse rode down with two of his braves. The cowboys knew him, for he had often visited the ranch when his daughter O'oah had been married to Finch. He had visited a few times since.

Finch was riding Hawk when White Horse came. The Indian scarcely looked at Finch, for his eyes were on the handsome stallion.

"Your haite', he die?" White Horse finally said, but his eyes were still on Hawk.

"Got run over by a bunch of steers," Finch answered. He knew that White Horse could understand English fairly well. Since O'oah had taught him, Finch could handle the Comanche language enough to converse with White Horse.

Finch and White Horse talked for several minutes. Though the Indians' conversation was oblique, Finch finally got a strong impression that White Horse had come to warn him of a Kiowa attack.

"Ha Hites!" White Horse said as he rode away. "Finch still Comanche Hites!"

"Goodbye, friend!" Finch saluted him as he left.

White Horse had not mentioned the horse that Finch rode, nor had he given any evidence of interest other than his constant looking at the animal.

As soon as the Indian had gone, Matt, who had been watching from the bunkhouse window, rushed out to Finch.

"You've played hell now!" Matt said angrily.

Finch just looked at Matt uncomprehendingly.

"Why didn't you put that damn stud in a stall so that Indian couldn't see 'im? You had plenty of time to do it!"

"Why?"

"Why? Hell!" Matt blustered. "Showin' a horse like that to a Comanche is just like danglin' a sugar tit in front of a nigger kid. A damn Comanche would kill a dozen men or trade every squaw he's got for that horse—and you know it."

"He won't steal 'im as long as I keep 'im in this valley, and I aim to do that," Finch said confidently. "Besides, I think what he really came for was to tell me that the Kiowas are going to hit us."

"When?" Matt's anger subsided immediately, and anxiety was apparent in his voice.

"He didn't say," Finch answered. "You know Indians, they talk in riddles, but I'm thinking that we'd better get set for a big one," he said calmly.

"I'll go tell Clem and Shanker and the rest of the boys." Matt started hurrying away.

"Tell Largo, too," Finch called to his back. "The blacks—all that are still here anyway—can use rifles, even the women. They've done it before."

"I'll shore as hell tell 'em to be ready!" Matt had stopped and half-turned.

"I think we've got some time," Finch said. "I've got a feeling they'll hit us about sunup. But get everybody ready, and be sure to put all the horses inside the barn."

"What are you gonna do with Hawk?"

"I'm going to put 'im in that big dugout I used to sleep in," Finch said. "And I'm going to fasten the door mighty tight."

\* \* \* \* \* \*

Finch pointed his rifle in the air and fired two shots. He counted to three and fired one more. It was answered by the nearest daytime rim-rider. Then Finch heard another answer from farther along the river. The riders were responding to the pre-arranged signal, and someone came in on a lathered horse. He was followed at intervals by the other riders, and soon all hands were present. They quickly put their horses away and headed toward the buildings carrying their unsheathed rifles.

Parapets with rifle slits had been erected around the top of all the buildings except the one that Clem had had the blacks build for him and Ellie. There were also inside stairs in each abode so that those inside could climb up without being seen.

Soon, all the cowboys had gathered pistols and ammunition, and had taken their places on roofs behind the parapets. Clem brought Ellie and her baby to the big house and left them in the kitchen quarters with Maisie. Finch sent for Matt and Shanker Stone to come to the headquarters house. Mandy and her children were behind the thick walls of her bedroom. Largo joined Finch, Matt, and Shanker on the roof. They were ready.

It was still an hour before sunset. Finch did not expect an attack before dawn, for he knew that the Indians did not like to fight at night, but he had been fooled by Indians before, and he was taking no chances.

They spent a long night on the roof. There was a half moon, but visibility was still poor, for as always, a blue haze hung over the river.

Maisie served all of them hot coffee, and she, herself, had chosen a rifle slit and laid a rifle near it.

"Shore glad I ain't down at the bunkhouse with them pore cowboys," Matt grinned in the darkness as Maisie served them hot coffee. "Likely, they're just a-shiverin' away without no good coffee to drink."

"They'll get coffee!" Clem said flatly. "Ain't no damned red-skins a-gonna keep the boys away from that sheep dip they drink and call coffee."

\* \* \* \* \* \*

The waiting was filled with tension, probably more so because they were not sure an attack was imminent. Some of the men dozed, while others had whispered conversations. Pete puffed contentedly on his pipe. Tonio sat stoically with his back propped against the wall and stared into the night.

It was Pete who saw them first as it was just breaking day.

"Where?" whispered a man urgently.

"Comin' through them salt cedars about a quarter of a mile down river."

All of the men peered intently, but saw nothing.

"You shore, Pete?"

"I'm shore."

"Then you must have eyes like an eagle. I can't see a damn thing."

"I can see, all right," Pete said. "They're a-comin', and it looks like a big bunch. Them bushes is a-movin' for a long ways."

There was an endless wait, and the silence was almost complete. Even the ranch animals were quiet.

Pete had laid aside his pipe and was watching with squinted eyes.

"Them smart bastards is a-layin' a circle around us," Pete said.

"Indians don't fight that-a-way," Clem said. "They rush up and start a-circlin' and shootin' and raisin' hell!"

"Indians fight any way they can to win," Pete said. "And this bunch must be led by a mighty smart chief. They're a-tyin' their horses in the bushes."

"I see one, I think," someone whispered excitedly.

Day was fast breaking, and the men were able to see shadowy forms almost all the way around the headquarters. The Indians had left their horses in the river bushes, the better to hide themselves, and they were masters of concealment. The anxious cowboys could spot one as he sped from one tiny bit of cover to another, where he would stop and blend so naturally with the object that he was invisible.

"Hey!" Pete said as his eyes darted from one to another. "Them ain't Kiowas. They're Cheyennes."

"How the hell do you know?" someone demanded in fright stimulated anger.

"I can see," Pete said laconically.

A moment later, an Indian rose from behind a small sage brush and then fell backward. The sound of Pete's big buffalo gun echoed and re-echoed up and down the river.

"Well, that's one of the red bastards we don't have to worry about," someone said grimly.

\* \* \* \* \* \*

Finch and Matt, atop the headquarters house, had already realized that the Indians were Cheyennes and that they were attempting to circle the buildings on foot. Quickly, after Pete had fired, Finch also fired, and another Indian fell from behind a clump of grass that didn't look big enough to hide a rabbit.

"The Cheyennes any worse than the Kiowas?" Shanker Stone asked.

"They damn shore ain't no easier!" Clem rejoined. "Their chief is Yellow Wolf. It was his boy, Big Moose, that Largo killed in that fight up on the Cimarron when Big Moose tried to steal Maisie for his squaw!"

"Then, if Yellow Wolf knows Largo is still here, we got one hell of a fight on our hands. May be a thousand of the red devils out there."

"We can hold 'em off!" Finch declared. "We've got water and food and plenty of guns. They won't be willing to pay the price of rushing us. It's the horses I'm worried about!"

"We got five men in that barn loft, and all the horses in the barn," Clem said. "And they ain't gonna steal none. That's for damn shore."

"I don't think so either," Finch said. "But if they try to get into the barn and get some men killed, they're gonna shoot flaming arrows into it, and those cottonwood logs are going to burn mighty fast."

All of them were silent for several minutes. Then Largo asked, "When yo thinks they gonna try to do dat, Mars Finch?"

"Not today," Finch said. "Maybe tomorrow. They're going to try to weaken our defenses first."

"What can we do about it?"

There was another long silence, and then Finch said, "I wish we could get word to the men out there to turn the horses out, and for them to join the boys on the bunkhouse roof—or in here."

"Yo say dey wait to tomorrow?" Largo queried.

"I'd bet on it."

"Den tonight I slips down dere and tells de boys, and we turn all de horses out and come back here on de roof."

"You'll damn well get killed, too!" Clem said sourly.

"No suh!" Largo said firmly. "I wait till after dark and afore de moon comes up, and I slips down dere. Me and Mars Hump done dat a lot o times durin' de war."

"He's right," Finch said. "I've heard Hump say a lot of times that Largo could sneak into a den of skunks and come out without a stink."

"Dammit, Finch," Matt objected. "That'll leave us afoot, and we'd shore as hell be in a fix then."

"We'll be afoot anyway if the Indians burn that barn, and we'd lose some men besides."

"Well, how in hell will we catch 'em again, if we turn 'em out?"

"I've got Hawk in that dugout, and the Indians couldn't burn that anyway because of the dirt on top of the roof, and the door is locked good. A longhorn bull couldn't bust it in. The horses won't stray far from this range, and some of the mares we brought back from south Texas are easy to catch. I can round up some of 'em on Hawk, but it will take a while!"

"If we waltz through this here little fandango," Clem said curtly.

The Indians had started firing, but were not effective. Each time a man peered through a rifle slot and saw a suspicious object, he shot at it. Very few shots were wide of the mark. Most of the time, an Indian fell, but the others returned a barrage of fire that thumped ineffectively into thick adobe walls of the ranch buildings.

"What about that jackass, Finch?" Matt asked. "He's right out in the open in that round pen of his."

"Let the Indians have the son-of-a-bitch!" Clem said almost enthusiastically. "I been a-wantin' to shoot that bawlin' bastard ever since we come west from Fort Worth. He'd prob'ly give all of 'em a good bellyache when they eat 'im!"

"I've been wondering about that, too." Finch paid no attention to Clem. "I just can't figure out anything. Just hope we can hold 'em so far off they can't get 'im."

"Even if we can hold 'em back, they'd shoot 'im," Matt said.

Finch had no answer for that. Ellie, who was serving them coffee at the time said, "Mars Finch, you won't pay me no mind if I says somepin', will you?"

"Of course not, Ellie," Finch said kindly to the timid black girl.

"Well—Mars Finch—yo know dat cabin me and Mars Clem and Brandy been a-stayin' in— well, it ain't got nobody in it now. And if yo locked 'im up in dat, I sho clean up de mess."

"Now, just a damn minute!" Clem objected. "I ain't gonna have no animal in that cabin— especially that jackass!"

"Ellie, that's a great idea!" Finch said. "If we could get 'im in there, I think he would be safe enough."

"I gets 'im in dere tonight, Mars Finch," Largo said confidently.

"You reckon you would have a chance to sneak by the bunkhouse and tell Tonio to join us up here?" Finch asked Largo.

"Yassuh, I thinks so, Mars Finch," Largo said. "I tell de men in de barn to go the bunkhouse, and dey can tell 'im."

"I can see why Hump placed store by you, Largo!" Finch said gratefully. Largo swelled with pride.

# Chapter 10

In the few dark hours before the moon made its appearance, Largo started making ready to go to the barn. Matt also was stuffing his pockets with ammunition.

"Anybody got a good big knife?" Matt asked. "Mine ain't the best, and it's liable to be close work and too dark to shoot if we run into any of them damn Cheyennes between here and the barn."

"Matt!" Finch exclaimed. "What do you think you're doing?"

"I'm a-fixin' to go with Largo," Matt said adamantly. From his tone of voice, Finch knew it was useless to argue with him. It was Largo who posed the opposition.

"Mars Matt, suh,—yo reckon maybe so I hadn't better go by myself. This old black hide of mine be mighty hard to see in de dark."

"I know that, Largo," Matt said. "But you can't see in front and back, too, especially with that—"

Matt didn't finish the sentence, but all were acutely aware that he was referring to Largo's bad eye.

"Here's my knife." Clem handed the weapon to Matt hilt first. "Sharp as a razor and damn near as big as a butcher knife. Hope you come back with a lot of red Indian blood on it."

Ten minutes later, Largo and Matt made their way cautiously down the inside stairway and out the front door of the headquarters house. They disappeared in the direction of the barn.

Maisie, Ellie, and Mandy all appeared on the roof to wait, too.

It seemed an interminable time to those waiting, but it was in reality only a few minutes when they heard a rush of horses' hooves. Then there was some sporadic firing. In less than thirty minutes, Largo made his way silently back to the roof to join the others. He was followed almost immediately by Tonio.

"All the men made it to the bunkhouse," Tonio said; then he sat and leaned his back to the parapet.

"Where's Matt?" Finch asked anxiously.

"He a-puttin' dat jackass in Mars Clem's cabin," Largo answered apologetically.

"You were gonna do that, Largo!" Finch said angrily.

"I know dat, Mars Finch." Largo almost whined. "An I was a gonna—but Mars Matt, he tole me to get Tonio in case de men in de barn don't get to the bunkhouse—an' yo knows I got to do what Mars Matt say. He white!"

"All right, Largo," Finch said. "You did what you thought you had to do. Did you have any trouble?"

"Yassuh. Some."

"What?"

"Three o dem Indians jump us jis afore we gets dere. Ain't no shootin'. Mars Matt and me had knives, and dey did, too. I reckon Mars Matt was right about dis bad eye o mine. I misdoubted I'd a-seen 'em. But Mars Matt did."

"Anybody hurt?"

"We kilt two o de Indians. De other, he run off. I gets a mite of a scratch on de arm. Don' know if Mars Matt do or not. It too dark to see."

The 'mite of a scratch' on Largo's arms was a deep cut across the forearm almost six inches long, which gaped widely and showed the pink flesh beneath the black skin.

"Go get 'im some whiskey, Ellie," Finch ordered. "Wash that cut and give 'im a slug so he won't hurt so bad. Won't take as much as it did when his eye was gouged out. Maisie, you sew that thing together.'

"Let's take him downstairs," Mandy said. "The light will be better, and we can wash the blood off."

"All right," Finch agreed. "But you'd better hurry. We're going to need all the firepower we have before long, I'm afraid. And all you women stay downstairs this time."

In less than half an hour, Largo returned. He reeked of the strong liquor that old Kate always brewed and kept for Hump and Finch. Neither knew the ingredients of the powerful concoction, and Finch felt a momentary tinge of regret when he realized that old Kate's secret had probably died with her. But, unknown to him, Maisie had learned the brewing secret from Kate, and there would never be a shortage of libation on the ranch as long as she was there.

\* \* \* \* \* \*

The waiting continued, and the tension mounted. The moon finally rose to lend but little light to the landscape. Matt still had not returned at sunrise, but the firing on both sides was intensified. An Indian bullet spattered adobe in Clem's eye; he swore furiously and swiped at the tears running down his cheeks with his bandanna.

About noon an Indian strode toward the headquarters. He walked erect and held a white patch of animal hide at the end of a long willow pole. Nobody fired on him, and when he came close enough, he yelled in Indian language. Tonio stood up.

"What does he say, Tonio?" Finch asked the unlikely half-breed linguist.

"He says they want the big black man and his squaw, and they go away."

"It's Yellow Wolf, all right," Finch said grimly. "Tell him to go to hell!" he instructed Tonio.

Tonio and the Indian talked for several minutes in the Cheyenne language.

"He says big black man kill Yellow Wolf's son. They want him. They will wait for two moons, if they have to."

"Tell 'im he can wait till hell freezes over," Finch instructed. "But we're going to be killing his braves every day that they stay."

Tonio and the Indian conversed again.

"He says they will wait," Tonio translated.

"Tell 'im that a caravan with a military escort will be by here before two moons."

Again, the unintelligible conversation ensued. The Indian finally yelled angrily, threw his pole on the ground, and started walking away. Immediately there was a shot, and Tonio fell. He had been exposed above the waist while standing, and evidently, throwing the pole on the ground was a signal of diplomatic failure. As soon as the shot was fired at Tonio, there was a barrage of shots from the buildings. The Indian messenger was literally shot to pieces.

Finch rushed to Tonio, who lay on his back, holding his hand over a bleeding shoulder.

"You hurt bad?" Finch asked tensely.

"I think not," Tonio said. His dark eyes were unblinking. "Maybe, though, we ought to plug up this shoulder and use some whiskey to wash it out."

"I'll take care of him," a soft, feminine voice said. Everyone turned to see Mandy Beatenbow.

"Mandy!" Finch yelled. "What are you doing back up here? I told all you women to stay downstairs."

"I came to help if I can," she said evenly. "And it looks like I can, too. We have clean dressings and whiskey in the house."

"What about your kids?" Clem demanded.

"Ellie is taking care of them. Come with me, Tonio." Mandy turned and went back down the stairs.

"Yes, ma'am," Tonio said and followed her.

A long silence followed their departure. Finally, Largo said in a very humble voice, "Mars Finch?"

"What, Largo?"

"Mars Finch." Largo's voice cracked a bit. "I goes down dere, yo wants me to—but I don' take Maisie with me!"

All of them looked at the huge Negro in pure astonishment.

"Don't be a damn fool, Largo!" Finch said and added with finality, "Nobody is going out there. You hear?"

"Yassuh, Mars Finch." Largo let out a great sign of relief. "I hears. And thankee!"

\* \* \* \* \* \*

After Largo's astounding sacrifice offer, the men kept peeping through the rifle slots; occasionally one would aim and fire quickly and then duck behind the parapet.

"They're losin' a lot of Indians," Shanker Stone observed after having completed what he deemed to be a successful shot.

"They'll lose a lot more," Finch said grimly. "I just hope we don't lose anybody."

Although Finch nor any of the others knew it, they had already lost two of the blacks. One of the small Negro girls, taking advantage of her mother's diverted attention, darted out a cabin door and was running down a brush lined trail toward the river when an Indian brave jumped out and grabbed her. He threw her over his shoulder and ran. The little girl screamed and kicked, and her mother turned to see through the door that was still ajar. She groaned and ran desperately after the child. She had barely reached the trail when another Indian stepped from behind a bush and crushed her head with a stone axe.

A few minutes later Finch got a whiff of freshly brewed coffee and turned to see Mandy standing at the top of the inside stairway with a big pot. Her head was above the ceiling of the house, but well below the parapet. Finch started to reprimand her, but when her large, black eyes met his, he got the distinct impression that a reprimand would get a cool reception. He shrugged his shoulders in defeat and thought ruefully that he just never would understand women.

Every few minutes thereafter, one of the women would appear with coffee or food. The men took turns shooting and eating.

"I thought that Yellow Wolf and the Cheyennes was one of the tribes that Kit made the agreement with to let you run cattle here," Clem said.

"He was," Finch answered. "In fact, Kit was married to a Cheyenne woman once, by the name of Rai-Du."

"Well, Yellow Wolf is shore as hell a treacherous son-of-a-bitch!"

"He's not trying to run us out of the valley," Finch explained. "He just wants Largo and Maisie because Largo killed Big Moose when he tried to take Maisie away from 'im."

"I saw that fight," Clem said. "And I'm damned if it wasn't the goriest one I ever did see. I reckon I can't blame you for not givin' 'em up."

"Do you really think there will be a caravan goin' by on that Santa Fe trail, Finch?" Shanker Stone asked.

"I do," Finch answered firmly. "There's been one every month or so ever since we've been here. And most of 'em have a military escort."

"Well, I wish they'd hurry," Shanker said. "I'm about tired of shootin' Indians."

"We'll wait till winter if we have to," Finch avowed. "We've got food and water and plenty of ammunition. And if a caravan doesn't scare 'em off pretty soon, there's shore going to be a lot of Cheyenne squaws without a man."

There came two shots and a pause, and then one more, from the bunkhouse roof. It was a signal that they had used since founding the ranch, to call the men in. Finch peered through a rifle slot at the bunkhouse where a rifle was sticking out above the parapet; whoever was holding it was jabbing the barrel to the southeast as rapidly as possible.

"Let me get my glass!" Finch said with a trace of excitement. "Looks like the boys may be seeing something." He hurried down the stairs and quickly reappeared with the long monocular glass. He focused it in the general direction of the jabbing rifle barrel.

Everyone watched anxiously as he scanned the prairie south and east of the river.

"It's a caravan!" Finch said. "Not too big, but there are a lot of riders. I'm almost sure it's a military escort."

"Damn, damn, damn!" Clem ejaculated. "I shore do hope you're right."

"Well, they can't get here before tomorrow. They're a long way off."

"You reckon them Indians can see 'em?"

"No. We have the height, and unless they have a scout out that way, they won't know about them."

"Wisht they would get here tonight," Clem said fervently. "I shore don't like to be this close to them red bastards, even if we have got a good spot."

"I had intended to take Largo and go try to find Matt tonight, but now I reckon I'll wait and hope we don't lose any men before they get here," Finch said.

"How do you reckon them boys on top of the bunkhouse saw 'em? They ain't got no glass."

"It was Pete," Finch said confidently. "That old man has got eyes like an eagle."

Indeed, Finch was right. Pete had been peering keenly through the rifle slots all day and had accounted for more than his share of Indians. After looking long and intently for several moments, he leaned his rifle against the wall, sat with his back to the parapet, and lighted his pipe.

"Somebody's a-comin'."

"Where?"

"Who?"

"Southeast. A big bunch. But they ain't Indians."

\* \* \* \* \* \*

The Indians fired the barn that night. Finch felt a pang as the huge cottonwood structure was rapidly eaten by the flames, but he was thankful that the men and horses were no longer in it.

The men on the bunkhouse roof, who had been ensconced in the loft of the barn until Matt and Largo came to turn the horses out and instruct them to rejoin the others on the bunkhouse roof, stared in fascination at the holocaust.

"Whew!" one of them said fervently. "I shore am glad I ain't in that loft no more. That's as close to hell as I ever want to get."

"Probably won't be!" another responded laconically.

\* \* \* \* \* \*

It was a long and suspense filled night. The huge barn was only a pile of glowing embers, but eerie shadows danced in its glow. Several possibilities were discussed. They had no idea how many Indians surrounded the ranch headquarters. Finch was worried about Matt and was donning moccasins in preparation to go out into the darkness to look for him when Clem discerned his intention.

"Now, don't be a damn fool, Finch!" Clem said harshly. "That barn fire is a-givin' enough light for them Indians to see anybody a movin' out there. And we ain't lost a man yet, and there ain't no reason to now—not when that caravan will be here tomorrow."

"Matt may be bad hurt," Finch said tensely.

"And he may damn well be dead, too!" Clem said unsympathetically. "If he's dead, you shore can't help 'im none, and if he's hurt—then he's holed up where the Indians won't find 'im if he's smart as he ort to be."

"He's right, Finch." Shanker seconded Clem.

"Besides," Clem proffered the clinching argument. "Matt would be the first one to put the quietus to such a fool stunt—and you know he would!"

Finch sighed and discontinued his preparations to leave. "I reckon you're right," he admitted. "But it shore makes me feel like a coyote staying here where it's safe and not knowing."

"I doubt if Matt would give much of a damn how you feel," Clem said. "But he'd shore care a hell of a lot about how you acted if you went out there tonight."

\* \* \* \* \* \*

The men on the bunkhouse roof, with the exception of Pete, were taking turns at napping. One of them went below and brought coffee to the roof every hour or so. Pete did not drink the coffee, but moved from one rifle slot to another, puffing on his cold pipe. He dared not light it lest a keen-eyed Indian spot the glare.

As the moon rose higher, the eagle-eyed Pete could make out dim forms in the distance, and he increased his pace from one rifle slot to another. Once, he stopped and peered intently for several seconds.

"That there is one damn smart redskin that's a-leadin' this bunch," he said in a whisper loud enough for all to hear.

Every man was instantly alert, their coffee cups abandoned and their rifles ready.

"What are they doin'?" someone queried.

"They're a-sendin' out a scout." Pete did not leave his space. "I been a-watchin' 'im for quite a while. He was a-walkin' on his all fours like a damn coyote till he got so far away he thought we couldn't see 'im, and then he got up, and now he's a-runnin' like hell!"

"I can't see anything," one of the men who was peering into the dark complained.

"Well, I can," Pete answered firmly. "He's still a-runnin' like a rabbit, and he's circlin' to where they got their horses tied, down in the river brush."

"You must have cat eyes, Pete."

"I can see," Pete admitted.

"What will he do?" another asked.

"He'll ride out and circle the whole place, and he's sure to see that caravan, and then he'll ride like hell to get back here and tell the others."

"What do we do?"

"Nothin'!" Pete said. "Not yet, anyway. When he gets back and brings the news, then the Indians is a-goin' to start takin' their dead back toward their horses, and if it's long enough so's we can have a little light in the east, we ort to get some mighty fine shootin'—especially them that's a- carryin' their dead."

"I shore as hell hope you're right, Pete," a man said viciously. "I'd like to kill ever one of them red bastards. How many of 'em you reckon they is?"

"I been a-tryin' to figger that," Pete said. "I'm a-guessin' seven or eight hundred of 'em to start with, but they're shy about a hundred of 'em now. They is a lot of good rifle shots on this here ranch."

"A hundred!" a cowboy exclaimed in awe. "You think we've killed that many?"

"Yep."

"Will they try to carry off that many dead men?"

"They won't try," Pete said. "They'll do it."

"You sound as if you know Indians!"

"I've fit 'em afore!" Pete said dryly.

\* \* \* \* \* \*

True to Pete's prediction, the Indian scout returned just before daylight. His horse was lathered and panting for breath. He rode to a position well out of rifle range where a small knoll shielded him and his horse also. Pete surmised, correctly, that Yellow Wolf had been directing the attack—in a fashion that white men had not seen Indians use before.

Immediately, there was a wave of almost indistinguishable movement around the ranch compound. The movement was away from the headquarters. As soon as the Indians felt that they were out of rifle range, they stood erect and hurried toward the river, many of them dragging a fallen man.

But daylight was fast breaking, and the cowboys were able to see. They laid down a barrage of fire at the fleeing Indians, who had erred in their assumption that they were out of rifle range. Many were being killed as they sought the sanctuary of the shielding brush along the river. Yellow Wolf was paying a staggering price for his attempt to avenge his son!

When the sun was two hours high, Pete announced that the Indians had reached their horses and were retreating down the river, which ran obliquely to the approaching caravan.

Finch, too, had been searching the area with his glass and was reasonably sure that no hostiles were about.

"I'm going to see about Matt," he said.

"Dammit, Finch!" Clem addressed him. "One of them sneaky bastards may still be a-waitin' just to get a chanct at one of us when we step outside. Why don't we wait till—"

"Now that'll do" Finch said.

Clem had heard the phrase of finality from Finch before. He said nothing further, but started filling his pockets with shells and feeling his knife sheath, empty of the knife he had loaned Matt; he held out his hand toward Largo, who read the gesture immediately and correctly. He pulled his big knife from his belt and laid the hilt in Clem's hand.

"Now, what are you doing?" demanded Finch.

"I'm bein' a damn fool, as usual," Clem said gruffly. "I'm a-goin' with you."

"Now wait a—"

"I'll go too," Shanker said.

"Me too," Largo echoed.

"No, you won't—"

Finch was interrupted again, this time by Tonio, who was leaning against the parapet to ease his bandaged shoulder. "I think perhaps it would be best if some of us stayed here," he said. "It might be unwise to leave the women alone."

"You're right about that," Finch agreed. "Shanker, you and Largo and Tonio stay here. Clem and I will find him."

As Finch and Clem descended the inside stairwell, Mandy and Ellie met them.

"Where are you going, Finch?" Mandy's voice trembled with fear, and her large black eyes were luminous.

"We're going to see about Matt."

"Is it safe yet?"

"Nobody knows for sure," Finch said candidly. "But we've got to go out of here sometime."

"Please, Finch—Please just be careful!" Tears brimmed in Mandy's eyes. "I don't know what I'd do if—"

"We'll be careful," Finch answered as he patted her shoulder. "And we'll be back as soon as we find Matt."

They opened the door of the headquarters house and looked out cautiously. As they started to walk out, a young negroid voice stopped them.

"Mars Clem!" It was Ellie. Finch and Clem turned to her.

"Mars Clem," she said shyly, "yo be careful, too!"

Clem nodded, and Finch said nothing as they walked out into the sunlight.

\* \* \* \* \* \*

"Where do we look first?" Clem asked.

"Largo said Matt was going to put the jackass in your cabin. I bet the lazy bastard is still in there sound asleep on your bed. Anyway, I shore hope so."

They approached the cabin cautiously, looking about as they proceeded. When they reached the door, Clem opened it gingerly as Finch, just behind him, held guard. When Clem pushed the door wide open, he was greeted by a thunderous sound emitted by the jackass. He inadvertently retreated a step and backed into Finch. Both stumbled. The jackass completed his raucous braying. Finch and Clem grinned sheepishly at each other and entered the cabin. The jackass was tied to the stead of the one bed in the cabin, which gave mute testimony to the relationship of Clem and Ellie. Beside the bed was a crude crib. Matt lay on the bed.

Finch rushed to him, paying no attention to the pile of manure he stepped in. He knelt beside the bed and saw that Matt's face was very pale, and the cover under him was soaked in blood. Matt opened his eyes.

"That jackass scared you damn near as bad as that Mexican did a-poundin' on your door down in Santone, didn't he?" Matt grinned weakly.

"Dammit!" Finch said fiercely and with fear and dread in his voice. "Why didn't you come on back to the house and help out with the fighting?"

"This bed just felt too good," Matt replied.

"I told Clem we would find you lying in bed while we did all the work, you lazy bastard."

"I been layin' here a-thinkin' when was the best time for me to tell the boys in the bunkhouse how fast you could travel with your boots in one hand and your pistol in the other, and naked as a jaybird with your duds under your arm!"

Matt's voice was growing weaker and weaker. Finch had to lean close to hear. Matt coughed, and a pinkish foam boiled from his mouth.

"Well, you'll have plenty of time to think about it," Finch said. "Now get up from there, and let's go up to the house and doctor that scratch you got."

Matt opened his eyes again and grinned feebly. "You're wrong, Finch! I ain't got plenty of time. Fact is, I ain't got no time a-tall."

Matt closed his eyes. Finch held his hand and felt life leave him. It was a long moment before he could speak. Then, he took a deep, shuddering breath.

"He's dead."

Finch rose to his feet.

"What the hell was he a-talkin' about?" Clem asked curiously.

"Just something that only the two of us knew," Finch said. "And the son-of-a-bitch was just waiting to twist my tail telling about it," Finch said brokenly as tears ran down his cheeks.

"Well, he shore done one thing I told 'im to," Clem said as he picked up the huge knife he had loaned Matt. "My knife is as bloody as hell!"

\* \* \* \* \* \*

Two hours later they buried Matt in the ranch graveyard. Finch chose the spot that would give the best view of the river.

"He always said he wished he could see all the way to tomorrow. Maybe now he can."

The entire crew, including the Negroes turned out for the burial. Mandy looked pale and wan, but beautiful. She had done her hair up in a severe knot at the nape of her neck. Ellie looked frightened. The cowboys showed no emotion other than grim acceptance as the dirt was shoveled into the grave. Most of them peered cautiously about, lest an unfriendly approach while all of them were standing around the grave. Pete stood several yards away with his back to a tree; his eyes searched the area constantly.

When at last the dirt had been patted down on the mound, Finch said, "I reckon we ought to say something over 'im. I just wish Hump was here. He could say as good a funeral as anybody. But I don't know how. Not out loud, anyway."

"Then I will say it for your friend," Tonio said in perfectly modulated English.

The men all removed their hats and waited expectantly.

"Adios, amigo. Vaya con Dios!" Then he continued to intone phrases in various Indian tongues. And then, to the amazement of all, he repeated the 23rd Psalm and concluded with "Amen."

The men replaced their hats, and Tonio spoke directly to Finch. "I did not say any Cheyenne words over him."

Finch nodded, started to speak, but did not. The entire group walked back to their various quarters. Now it was time to look forward to the arrival of the caravan, which, if Finch had guessed correctly, would arrive before dark.

# CHAPTER 11

As the caravan crawled slowly toward the river, all hands watched eagerly from atop the fortress-like ranch buildings. When the caravan was within a mile or so of the ranch, which was still hidden from their view, Finch deemed it safe to cross the river to await their arrival.

Since there were no mounts available other than Hawk, who was still safely fastened in the half-dugout and the Beatenbow jackass in Clem's cabin, it would be necessary to walk across the river. Clem and Shanker both quickly volunteered to accompany Finch.

"You stay here, Shanker," Finch said. "Tonio and Largo both have wounds, and I wouldn't like to leave the women here without a good gun to protect them in case there are still some Indians hiding out in that brush. Clem can go with me, and we'll go by the bunkhouse and pick up a few more men."

"It'll be a damn few," Clem opined. "Most of them cowboys ain't walked that far since they was old enough to fork a horse."

Finch smiled wanly for the first time since he had found Matt in Clem's cabin. "Well, maybe so three or four of 'em won't be afraid to get their boots a little wet."

Finch and Clem walked out into the open and waved at the men on the bunkhouse roof. They made it known by gestures that they were coming over.

The bunkhouse door was opened for them, and they went inside. No one was downstairs except the man who had opened the door; he pointed silently toward the inside stairway. Finch and Clem mounted the stairs and ascended to the roof, to see most of the men leaning with their backs to the parapet. They were a scrawny looking lot, and those that did not habitually wear beards had a three day growth of stubble. Their clothes were wrinkled, and they looked very tired, which, indeed, they were. Only Pete was prowling like a huge cat from one slot to another. He did not even look around as Finch and Clem came up, but simply kept puffing on his pipe.

"Men," Finch said. "Clem and I are going to walk across the river and wait for the caravan, and we would like to have a few of you men go with us."

There were no immediate volunteers. Then one of the hands said incredulously, "You mean walk all the way across? Hell, Finch, that must be nearly a mile!"

"Well, we ain't got no horses; so I reckon it's walk or just stay here and set on your rump," Clem said sarcastically.

"Why couldn't we just let off a couple of shots when they're closer? They'd be sure to come over."

Three of the younger men reluctantly agreed to accompany Finch and Clem on their arduous trek across the river, but they were far from enthusiastic about it.

As they prepared to leave, Pete spoke up for the first time. "Might be you'd ort to keep your eyes about a bit when you're a-traipsin' through that salt cedar on both sides of the river. I been a- lookin' clost, and I ain't seen nothin' move—but that don't mean some of the red bastards ain't still out there."

"You can damn well bet we'll be a-watchin'!" Clem said grimly.

As the men left, they were in plain sight for a distance before they entered the brush on the river's edge."

"Now, you fellers," Pete addressed the remaining men. "All of ye but a couple to keep a lookout to our backs, come on over here to the south side and keep an eye on that brush. Likely our men will go straight to the river, and ye can see the cedars a-wigglin' as they walk through it. But if you see brush a-wigglin' off to the side, then we'd best put some lead in that wiggle."

"What if one of our men moves off to one side?" a cowboy asked anxiously.

"They won't," Pete said firmly. "Indians might, but they won't. Besides, them cowboys hate to walk so damn bad they're gonna step in Finch's tracks as best they can."

The men gathered behind the parapet on the south side of the bunkhouse, and true to Pete's prediction, the brush rippled like water in front of a floating chunk of wood as they walked. The men kept watching intently, but to Pete's disgust, they were watching the men and not scanning the area to each side of them, as they should have been.

As the men emerged from the brush and walked onto the sandy bed of the river, they stopped for a moment and waved back to the men on the bunkhouse roof, and then proceeded, Finch, in his long, smooth stride, and the rest of the men in their awkward and ungainly pace, to walk toward the south bank. As they came to the small stream that flowed down the river bed, they stopped, and, as Pete correctly surmised, were discussing whether to remove their boots. Finally, Finch stepped into the stream, and the others followed.

As they entered the brush on the south bank of the river, Pete's eagle eye caught a movement in the brush a hundred yards to the west of them. He knocked his pipe against the wall to draw the attention of the other men. They looked at him inquisitively, and he pointed to the movement he had seen. None of the others saw anything, but Pete never let his eyes wander from the movement that was progressing toward the hands. Suddenly, he chuckled and leaned his rifle against the parapet and lit his pipe. All the men looked at him curiously and questioningly.

"Our boys got a little surprise a-comin'," he said and chuckled again.

"How's that?" the men demanded almost in unison.

"I don't see a damn thing," one lamented.

"They is a rider a-comin' up on 'em from the west," Pete said, but there was satisfaction in his voice.

The men on the roof immediately laid their rifles on the parapet and were ready to begin firing.

"Ye can rest easy, boys," Pete said. "That feller that's a-comin' up on 'em is a white man and a good mountain, if I ever seen one. He don't let that hoss of his'n touch a bit of brush, and him and his hoss is about the same color as the land. I expect he's the scout and guide for that caravan."

"Hope one of the fellers don't shoot 'im when he shows up."

"They won't," Pete said confidently. "That feller has been around the mountain and up the river. Prob'ly seed 'em when they first started over. He knows they're white men, and they'll know he is too afore they ever see 'im."

\* \* \* \* \* \*

"Hold it right there, men," a deep voice to the rear of Finch and the men ordered. "And don't turn around. Leastwise, not fast, cause I got a buffler gun right on ye."

Finch and the men stopped so abruptly that they jostled each other. The voice continued, "I'm a white man and friendly—if you are. Now turn around, one at a time. Do it slow and don't make no foolish motions."

The men turned as ordered and gawked as they saw the buckskin clad figure sitting on a nondescript horse. His clothing looked as if it had never been clean, and the huge beard could not camouflage the big wad of tobacco in his jaws. Finch was startled at the resemblance of the man to Buff Larrigan, the old mountain men that had accompanied them from Fort Worth on their trek west.

"We're friendly," Finch grinned sheepishly. He was both humiliated and embarrassed that a man on a horse could approach them undetected. "Even if we wasn't, that big rifle of yours shore would make us friendly fast."

The rider looked at them keenly for several seconds, and then said, "You! The tall galoot with the hay-colored hair—pull off your hat!"

Finch looked puzzled, and the other men gaped. Finch knew that he could shoot the man out of the saddle before he could pull a trigger. Nevertheless, he complied with the order, lifting his right hand well away from his holster and raising it slowly to remove his hat. His yellow hair was fairly long about his neck, but was visibly receding from his temple.

"Ah, hah!" the rider said. "I figgered as much. Be ye Fauntleroy Finch?"

It was Finch's turn to gape. "That's right," he admitted. "Folks just call me Finch, though. How did you know?"

"I knowed Kit," the man said. "Heard tell a lot about ye." He holstered his rifle and stepped off his horse. "I reckon I'm glad to meet the only man that Kit ever admitted was faster with a pistol than him. They call me 'Pine'—short for Pine Tree."

He strode forward leading his horse and proffered a huge hand which Finch took eagerly. All of the men shook hands and said their names.

"I be a scout and guide for that there caravan you seed a-comin'."

"We saw them from the top of our ranch buildings," Finch said. "We came over to meet 'em. We've been in a squabble with some Indians and had to turn our horses out."

"So I seed," Pine affirmed. "Burnt your barn, too, didn't they!"

"How did you know that?" Finch asked.

"Waal now," Pine shifted his cud. "Like I say, I be scoutin' for that there caravan. I rid out early this mornin' a-lookin' for yore ranch. Kit, he told me about where it was. Whoever put up them adobes for you was right canny. A dozen men could hold off a passel of redskins from them roof tops."

"And we have been," Finch admitted. "A big bunch of Cheyennes hit us a few days ago. We been busy ever since."

"Looks like you done 'em some damage, too," Pine said with satisfaction. "I seed where they hauled off a lot of good injuns. Even found a couple that they missed. I reckon the buzzards will take care of 'em ."

"You've been around the buildings?" Clem's voice reflected his doubt.

"Aye, that I have. Seed 'em when their scout first told 'em we was a-comin', and they started high tailin' it."

"How big is the caravan?"

"Big. And we got a company of blue coats a-traipsin' along with us, too. Doubt if'n they'd do us a lot of good, though. Most of 'em is from way up north and don't hardly know that they're supposed to set astraddle of a hoss. And they got a young lieutenant in charge of 'em that ain't dry behind the ears yet and scairt as hell."

"A lieutenant?" Clem queried. "I figgered that they would be a least a captain in charge of a company."

"They was," Pine said laconically. "But we had a tussle with some Injuns a few days ago, and the captain was gonna show his troops how to fight Injuns, and got kilt for his showin' off."

"How many men in the company?"

"I dunno," Pine said with a notable lack of concern. "Usually, they is sixty to a hundred and twenty in a company, but we ain't got that many—around eighty, I'd reckon."

"That's enough to hold off a big bunch of Indians."

"Would be," Pine admitted as he squirted tobacco juice, "if they knowed a damn thing about redskins. But I doubt a dozen of 'em ever fit the red bastards afore they jumped us back on Red River.'

"Did you lose many men?" Finch asked.

"Naw. The captain, he got kilt and two or three of the soldiers. But we didn't lose none out of the caravan, except a few head of stock. Most of the men in the waggins know how to fight, and they can shoot—even some of the women. But we got a few Yankee drivers that don't know nothin'. But the waggin boss—he's a pure bastard, but he's smart—he put 'em in atwixt some old hands, and that helps."

As the men were talking, the caravan was inching its way toward them. The oxen and mule drawn wagons were strung out for almost a mile, and extra oxen and mules grazed alongside. When they were within a couple of hundred yards, the wagons stopped. Two men loped ahead and rode up to the small group. One was the lieutenant, the other a civilian.

They stopped a few yards away.

"Howdy," Finch greeted. He felt at a disadvantage standing and having to look up at the two riders.

"Howdy!" the civilian answered Finch's salutation. The young officer offered a half-hearted salute.

"What's the hold-up?" The civilian directed the question to Pine.

"That there is Gabe Elvers, the waggin boss." Pine motioned vaguely. "And the lieutenant, he's in charge of the soldiers. This here is Finch and some of his men," Pine said.

The wagon boss did not acknowledge the introduction, nor did he look at Finch. He was a big man with small eyes set close over a flattened nose and under bushy black eyebrows that met in the center of his forehead. He wore no beard, but the dark stubble on his face indicated that he had not shaved for a couple of days. Instead of a rope fastened to the pommel of his saddle with a leather thong, he carried a coiled and well-oiled blacksnake.

"I asked you what was the hold-up?" He spoke directly to Pine. His voice was unpleasant.

"Well!" Pine spat tobacco juice and continued. "These fellers here been havin' a bit of redskin trouble. They got a ranch a mile or so ahead. They lost their hosses, and I reckon they could stand a bit of help."

"We've had some Indian trouble of our own," Gabe said disagreeably. "And we took care of it. I reckon others can do the same. We got a long trip still ahead of us. We ain't got time to lose."

"Well, hell, Gabe!" Pine started to protest. "We cain't jus' leave these fellers here to—"

"You was hired to guide and scout, Pine," Gabe said harshly. "And I reckon you can just limit yourself to doin' that! I'll make the decisions!"

Finch and the cowboys had been observing quietly. It was the baby-faced young lieutenant who broke in. "Pine is right, Mr. Elvers." Even his voice sounded very young. "We can't leave these men without help."

Gabe stared incredulously at the young soldier. "Now that's a hell of a remark from somebody that damn near dirtied his pants when we was hit by them Indians."

"I was scared, all right," the embarrassed lieutenant admitted, and his face flushed. "But I did what I had to do."

"Which sure wasn't a hell of—"

Finch had had enough! His voice had a sharp ring to it when he interrupted. "Being scared isn't anything to be ashamed of," he said firmly, remembering just a flash of the terror that had engulfed him when his bedroom door was pounded in San Antonio. "And I reckon a feller that can do what he has to do—scared or not—is all right."

Gabe looked at Finch as if unable to believe that anyone would have the temerity to interrupt him! "Well, now, Slim." He looked at Finch contemptuously. "I wasn't a-talkin' to you—so's maybe you'd best just keep yore trap shut!"

"Gabe!" It was Pine who spoke. "I reckon maybe I didn't make it plain. These here folks is in trouble. Bad trouble, if'n they can't git their hosses rounded up."

"Well, their trouble ain't ours," Gabe rejoined harshly. "And we got our own job to do."

"Maybe their trouble is of interest to the army," the lieutenant said with all the grit he could muster. "We've been trying to rid this country of the Indian menace for a long time, and if these men are trying to ranch right here in the middle of the Indians, I think the army would expect us to help out."

"Why, you damn fool!" Gabe's harsh voice rasped like dead tree limbs rubbing together. "Don't you know that ever one of them men probably was in the southern army, and they was shore as hell trying to shoot everything that wore a blue coat just a few years ago."

Clem growled, and the men behind Finch started to spread out. The immature voice stopped them.

"I expect they were," the lieutenant said. "But that was before, and this is now. And if they need help, the army is going to give it."

The young officer's voice quavered a bit, but there was no mistaking his determination. He reminded Clem of young Brandy Wine defying the overbearing bully, Dutch Horst.

"Well, I will be damned!" Gabe said in astonishment. "The young rooster has got ruffle feathers, after all."

"Even if you and I are from the north," the lieutenant's voice was gaining more power, and the quiver was abating, "we are all Americans now, and the red man is our enemy. That's what they taught us at the point."

"You learned it pretty damn good, young feller," Pine Tree chimed in.

Gabe just gaped as the soldier continued. "Since Captain Moore was killed, I've been in charge of this company, and I intend to see that we all act like civilized human beings. So, if you want to go ahead, you will go without an army escort for a few days. We will try to catch up as soon as we have helped these men recapture their horses."

It was a long speech that had begun timorously, but had ended almost pompously. There was a ripple of sounds of approval from the few troopers who had ridden up during the discussion.

Gabe looked about and saw no sympathy or approval from any source. He capitulated. "All right, dammit! It's near time to stop for the night, and a day or so of rest won't hurt the mules or oxen, anyways. But don't expect no help from anybody in the caravan," he ended antagonistically as he turned his horse and rode back toward the wagons. As he did so, he uncoiled his blacksnake and flicked it viciously. It popped like a pistol shot. Horses and men flinched.

There was a long silence as the men watched Gabe ride away. Finally, Pine Tree said, "Lieutenant, I reckon I couldn't a-told that bull-headed bastard no better myself. Now git down off'n that hoss and meet some friends of a friend of mine—name of Kit Carson."

"You knew Kit Carson?" The young soldier was awed.

"That I did," Pine Tree said. "And Finch here," he pointed, "rid with 'im and fit injuns with 'im, too."

"We heard a lot about him at West Point. He was Brevet Brigadeer when he died."

"Well," Pine said. "I reckon he was more than that out this way, which is where he spent most of his time during the war. And now he's even got a town named after him—little place about a hundred miles from Pueblo."

The lieutenant had dismounted. Finch stepped forward and offered his hand.

"You actually knew Kit Carson?" the lieutenant asked as he took Finch's hand firmly.

"Sure did," Finch said, grinning. "Fact is, it was Kit that got the Indians to let me run cattle up here in the midst of all of 'em."

"I'll be darned! My name is Bob Seymour."

There was a general babble as the men introduced themselves. Clem Swenson paused perceptibly before he offered his hand to a Yankee soldier. He had thought that he would never do such a thing, but he did, and suddenly felt the weight of years of hatred vanish from him.

"Dammit, Lieutenant," he said as he shook hands. "I never thought I'd shake the hand of a blue coat, but I'm a-doin' it, and I reckon I'm glad."

"You must have been in the southern army," grinned the boyish lieutenant.

"I shore as hell was!"

"Then, I'm glad we didn't meet before this," Seymour said. "I guess you were in the Union Army, weren't you, Finch, if you knew General Carson."

"Nope," Finch denied. "I was in the Texas Rangers. Kit and I had a lot of tussles with the red men and Comancheros and other vermin out here on the frontier. We were more concerned about staying alive than what color coat anybody wore. All my men here were in the southern army."

"And right now everbody is all mixed up together and just a hoot and holler from hell if them Cheyennes come back with all of us out here in the open and some of us on foot," Pine Tree said sarcastically.

There was a general sobering; the laughter and talk quieted. The lieutenant ordered the troops to bring the army chuck wagon and twenty men, while the rest of them stood guard with the caravan.

In a short time, the order had been fulfilled, and the men all gathered around the wagon.

"Well, Finch!" the lieutenant said. "The U.S. Army is at your service! What do we do?"

"First," Finch said, "we've got to get some horses. We turned all ours out before the Indians burned our barn, but they'll stay in the valley, and it won't take a lot of riding to round some of 'em up."

"I doubt if my men will be very good at that, but we've got extra horses, and your men can ride them to round yours up."

"Hey, Lieutenant," one of the cowboys asked eagerly, "you haven't got some we can ride back to the ranch, have you? It must be forty miles from here the way my feet feel!"

Everyone laughed, and the lieutenant said, "We've got the horses, but we don't have extra saddles."

"Hell!" the cowboy said eagerly. "I'll shore be glad to ride bareback. I'd hate to be caught dead a-ridin' one of them flat saddles, anyway."

Enough extra horses were brought for the footsore cowboys. The army cook had a pot of coffee boiling. They stood and sipped coffee until Finch said, "It's the middle of the evening, Lieutenant. Why don't you come on over to the ranch and eat supper with us, and we'll talk about tomorrow. My partner's wife would like to meet you, I know."

"His wife? What about him?"

"He's dead," Finch said.

"Well, hell!" Clem Swenson sought to break the gloom that seemed imminent. "I have shook hands with a whole passel of damn-Yankees today, so I might as well go whole hawg. As many of you fellers as the lieutenant can spare, come over to the bunkhouse and try out some of that gut-shrinkin' grub that us pore cowboys eat all the time, while your boss and mine eat a good supper in the headquarters house."

\* \* \* \* \* \*

The day was waning as several cowboys, riding bareback, and a small group of blue-coated cavalrymen rode into the ranch yard. Finch and the lieutenant followed on foot and were talking amiably. Pine Tree followed, riding at a distance; he peered cautiously to both sides and to the rear.

"I'll be damned!" Pete, who had been watching from atop the bunkhouse exclaimed. "If that ain't old Pine Tree Phillips, then I'm blind as a one-eyed mule!"

"And if them ain't Yankees, then I'm blinder than you are, Pete."

There was a general growl of animosity among the men, who had fought so long, valiantly, and uselessly against them.

"Now, hold on, you men," Pete said urgently. "Them is friendly Yanks, and you can bet on it, else our boys wouldn't be amongst 'em. Lookee! One of 'em is a-walkin' and lettin' our man ride his hoss! And even Clem is a-talkin' to one of 'em!"

The men quieted and stared unbelievingly at the mixture of men below.

"Now you can settle down. Put your rifles up, and let's all go down stairs."

The men hesitated, but one of them finally laid his rifle down and started down the stairway. The others followed silently. When they were all on the floor of the bunkhouse, a voice yelled from without.

"Hey, you pore ignorant cow drivers—come on out and meet some new friends!" It was Clem.

One of the men opened the door and stepped aside. The others followed. They all wore their pistols.

"Fellers, we got company tonight; so tell cookie to put the big pot in the little 'un. We're gonna eat a-settin' down tonight—all of us!"

# Chapter 12

The Negroes had emerged from their cabins and stood staring, goggle-eyed, at the troops; they clapped their hands, laughed, and yelled. One youngster darted away and ran toward the headquarters house.

Finch and the lieutenant had been several yards behind the men when the Negroes came from their cabins. Lieutenant Seymour stopped abruptly.

"What are they doing here?" he asked suspiciously.

"Who?" Finch replied in surprise.

"Them." The lieutenant pointed. "The nig—the blacks?"

"Oh," Finch said in relief. "They're the blacks that my partner Hump Beatenbow brought with 'im from Louisiana."

"But they're free now!" the lieutenant said righteously.

"That they are," Finch agreed with a grin. "And they're all here because they want to be. They can leave any time they want, and they could have stayed in Louisiana. But they had been Beatenbow slaves, and when they were freed, they had their choice—to come west with Hump or stay back in Louisiana. As you can see, some of them chose to come with Hump. Some stayed."

"Well, I'll be darned!" The lieutenant expressed his surprise. "I would have thought that a free man would want to get as far away from his former owner as he could."

"Well, some did and some didn't," Finch repeated. "Fact is, all of 'em that came out here thought Hump was a great man—and he was. But, if you'd like to talk to some of 'em, you are welcome to do so."

"No. I mean, I wasn't doubting your word, Finch. It's just so incredible! I can't imagine a bunch of blacks out here in the west—especially with their former master."

"I reckon it is hard to figure out," Finch admitted. "But the fact is that one of the blacks was probably the best friend Hump ever had. Went all through the war with 'im, and then came west with 'im. Named Largo. He got an eye gouged out in a fight with an Indian."

"That's amazing! I didn't know Indians ever fought hand to hand."

"They don't ordinarily. But that one wanted Largo's wife for his squaw and challenged Largo to fight for her."

"What happened?" The lieutenant was fascinated.

"Largo killed the Indian. He was the son of Yellow Wolf, who is chief of the Cheyennes that attacked us."

"I guess I'm in for a lot more education than they gave me at West Point," Lieutenant Seymour said ruefully. "This has been one day I'll never forget!"

"Come on," Finch said. "I'll show you around the place. It's still an hour till sundown, and I see that your men and the cowboys have all gone into the bunkhouse. Besides, I need to put my horse in a corral."

"Your horse? I thought you lost all your horses!"

"Not that one," Finch grinned. "He's a stud and something special. We hid out a jackass, too. They're the two most important animals on this ranch. If it wasn't for a stud and a jackass, we'd be riding mustangs and working longhorns to our wagons."

"I never thought about that," the lieutenant said reflectively. "I guess they are pretty important at that."

"They are," Finch reaffirmed, then added grimly. "In fact a mighty good friend of mine got killed, getting that jackass before the Indians did."

"I'm sorry to hear that—when?"

"Come on," Finch said. "We've been standing here so long they'll think we're lost."

Finch and the lieutenant went first to the huge half-dugout where Hawk greeted Finch with a welcoming nicker when he opened the reinforced door.

"What a magnificent animal," the lieutenant said admiringly.

"Best I ever saw!" Finch was not modest about Hawk.

After they put Hawk into his stout corral, they went to Clem's cabin, got the jackass, and put him into his corral. Finch glanced at the blood-stained bed as he untied the jackass. A muscle twitched in his jaw.

"Now let's go up to the house. I want you to meet Mandy, Hump's wife. And I expect Largo and Shanker Stone and Tonio will still be up there, too."

"Who are Shanker Stone and Tonio?"

"Shanker is one of the best men on the place with a gun, and Tonio is our interpreter. He can speak a dozen different languages. But he was wounded. So I had Shanker and Largo stay with 'im to protect the women folks and kids, in case—"

"The women folks and kids!"

"Yes. Mandy has three little ones, two boys and a girl, all less than three years old. Then, there is Maisie—she's Largo's wench—wife, and they have a couple of kids. And there's Ellie—she's Clem's—she's Largo's little sister; and she has a little one, too. And I expect they're all waiting for us to show up."

"They don't even know we are here!"

"You shore don't know much about nig—blacks, Lieutenant. They've known since we came back across the river, and news flies on a bird's wing when blacks get hold of it."

They walked toward the big house. Finch stopped on the gallery to look about. He was gratified when he saw four men on roof guard. Thus satisfied, he turned and opened the door of the headquarters.

\* \* \* \* \* \*

There was no one in the living room that connected the Beatenbow wing with Finch's quarters. The lieutenant looked about curiously and was impressed by the spacious, cool room and the huge fireplace. Comfortable furniture, most of it made by Largo, was strewn about in strategic places. A man's hat hung on a peg of the rack by the fireplace.

"Whew!" breathed the lieutenant. "I never expected to see a room like this out here in Indian country. It looks so—so comfortable—lived in."

"It is," Finch agreed, "and it has been. This big room connects the Beatenbow living quarters and ours—mine, that is."

"You're not married?"

"I was once," Finch said quietly. "The Kiowas raided us about a year ago. That's when I got this white streak of hair. A rifle bullet burned me some, and O'oah, my wife, wasn't so lucky."

"I'm sorry," the lieutenant said quickly.

"Well, let's go up on top and see who is still up there."

He led the way up the inside stairway to the roof above. Only Shanker, Tonio, and Largo were there.

"Where are Mandy and the rest?" Finch inquired.

"They all went downstairs as soon as they heard the soldiers were coming," Tonio replied. "Maisie and Ellie are fixing supper, I imagine, and Mrs. Beatenbow said she was going to change."

"Men, this is Lieutenant Seymour. He's commanding the company with the caravan."

"We were mighty glad to see you all a-comin', yesterday," Shanker said as he shook the lieutenant's hand and said his name.

The lieutenant then shook hands with Tonio and extended his hand to Largo, who hesitated, but took the lieutenant's hand into his big, pink-palmed hand.

"How are you feelin', Tonio? That little nick you got hurt much?"

"No. It will ache a little for a few days, but it will heal nicely, I'm sure. Mrs. Beatenbow and the others did a fine job of bandaging it."

"How about you, Largo? That cut on your arm all right?"

"Yassuh, Mars Finch. It itch a little where Maisie sewed it up, but it don' hurt none too much."

The lieutenant was looking about the roof of the huge building with appreciative eyes. The waist high parapet with the rifle slots particularly impressed him.

"Man!" he exclaimed. "A few men could stand off a lot of Indians up here. Whoever built this house sure knew what he was doing."

"Largo and the rest of the blacks built it," Finch said. "And they did a good job, too. The walls are three feet thick, and adobe is cool in summer and warm in winter. Old Kate—she was Largo's dam—figured out most of the rooms. She even had hot water running in the bedrooms of each wing. The parapet and rifle slots were the only thing that I contributed. We have them on all the buildings except one—that's the one the jackass was in."

"Well, it sure looks like you came to stay!" the lieutenant exclaimed in satisfaction.

"We aim to," Finch said.

"I'll mosey over to the bunkhouse," Shanker said. "I expect the boys are about ready to eat, and I'm hungry enough to eat a saddle blanket."

"I'll go too," Tonio said.

"You men are welcome to stay and eat with us," Finch invited.

"Nope," Shanker said firmly. "Anyway, I've always wondered what a blue coat was like when you wasn't lookin' at it over a rifle barrel."

The lieutenant laughed politely, and Shanker and Tonio took their leave. Since Largo lived in the kitchen quarters where Maisie reigned supreme, he followed. When Shanker and Tonio went out the front door, he headed for the kitchen.

"I expect Maisie will have supper ready pretty soon," Finch said. "Let's go down and see."

They descended the stairs to find that a table was set for three people in the big room. Maisie appeared in the kitchen doorway.

"Miss Mandy, she be here right soon," Maisie said. "She gonna take a bath and change her clothes, an' she be right in. Ellie already fed de young uns, and dey is in der room. I brings yo some coffee while yo waits."

Finch and the lieutenant sat at the table and sipped strong coffee while they waited for Mandy. They talked for a few minutes. Finch's back was to the Beatenbow wing. Suddenly, the lieutenant's jaw dropped, and he gaped stupidly. He was staring past Finch; he gulped and rose so suddenly that he overturned his chair.

Finch turned to see Mandy entering the room, and he, too, stood. Her ash blonde hair was loose and fell to her waist; her wind-tanned skin and deep, dark eyes were an anachronistic picture of loveliness. She wore a gown that Finch had never seen before. Her step was firm as she walked to them and held out her hand to the lieutenant.

"Good evening, Lieutenant," she said. "Welcome to the HF ranch. You are our first visitor, and we have been here three years. I am Mandy Beatenbow."

The lieutenant struggled to compose his face and held out his hand. "I am Lieutenant Seymour," he gulped. "I mean I am Bob Seymour."

Mandy smiled at him brightly and turned to Finch. "Well, Finch," she said and turned her back to the lieutenant for a moment, which gave him time to set his chair upright and regain his stiff military stature. "I imagine that both of you are very hungry, and I'm sure that Maisie has our supper ready. Please be seated."

The lieutenant moved quickly to hold Mandy's chair, and she rewarded him with another smile. Unaccountably, Finch felt a slight pang of jealousy.

Maisie entered. "Is yo all ready fo de food, Miss Mandy?" she asked.

"Yes, Maisie. I'm sure that all of us are very hungry. Lieutenant, this is Maisie, our cook, and she is an excellent one. I think you will agree when you have tasted her food."

"Yes, ma'am," the lieutenant gasped. "I'll bet she is. I've met her husband, Largo. I think you are very lucky people." He held out his hand to Maisie, who looked startled and wiped her hand on her apron.

There was a tinge of mockery and sarcasm in Mandy's voice as she said, "I guess we are lucky—even to be alive. My husband was killed just recently, and a good friend of Finch's was killed yesterday, and his wife O'oah was killed less than two years ago."

"I'm—I'm sorry!" the lieutenant apologized. "I meant that you are lucky to have such a good cook and—"

"I know what you meant, Lieutenant," Mandy said contritely. "And we are lucky, too. I guess I was being just a bit bitter, and I'm not usually that way. Here's Maisie. Let's eat. I'm ravenous."

The meal proceeded, but the conversation was almost exclusively between Mandy and the lieutenant. Mandy was eager for news from the East, and upon learning that the lieutenant was from New York, she questioned him eagerly about the latest women's fashions and was enthralled by his description of the parties and social activities. Her eyes glistened, and she was more animated than she had been since Humphrey's death. Finch felt like an interloper. It was the first time Mandy had been inattentive to Finch's feelings.

Lieutenant Seymour could not keep his eyes off Mandy, and he had to ask Finch to repeat what he had said, when he occasionally tried, in vain, to enter the conversation. When the meal was over and they were having coffee, Mandy startled Finch by addressing the lieutenant directly.

"Lieutenant Seymour, do you think that you might have room in the caravan for another wagon? I'd like to take my children away from here."

Finch almost choked on his coffee. The lieutenant looked thoughtful.

"Mrs. Beatenbow," he finally replied. "I'm sure that we could add another wagon to the caravan, but we are headed west to Santa Fe. Most of the people in the caravan are from up north, and they intend to go on to the west coast."

"I want to go back east," Mandy said. "To New Orleans, if possible."

"Well, the lieutenant said eagerly. "Our company will be returning from Santa Fe in about six weeks, and I'm sure we would be glad to have you accompany us as far as Kansas City. I know we would if I am still in command. And I'm almost sure I will be, for there isn't a replacement for the captain in Santa Fe."

"Good," Mandy said with satisfaction. "We will have our wagons packed and ready. I expect quite a few of the blacks will want to go back, too."

Finch said nothing; his face was glum.

"Then you can count on the army to see you through to Kansas City, even if I'm not in command. My father is General Seymour, and I'll get word to him if necessary. But I don't think it will be."

"I can't wait," Mandy said eagerly. "I'll go tell the children right now."

Mandy arose from the table and walked quickly to the Beatenbow wing and disappeared through a door. The lieutenant kept staring at the place where she had disappeared.

"Looks like you got some passengers going back," Finch said grimly.

"What?" The lieutenant looked at Finch blankly. "Oh! Yes, I guess we do. And then he added lugubriously, "Finch, either I've been in the army too long, or that is the most beautiful woman I have ever seen."

"You haven't been in the army too long!" Finch said stoically.

\* \* \* \* \* \*

Finch and the lieutenant walked to the bunkhouse. They stopped just outside the door and listened to the loud talk and laughter coming from within.

"Sounds like the war is over," Finch grinned.

"It does, indeed," agreed the lieutenant. "And I'm glad. I was afraid there might be some trouble when your Rebels mixed with my Yankees."

"So was I," Finch said. "But it was Clem that broke the ice. He's our foreman and main Yankee hater. But he was so glad to see those blue coats I think he forgot he had a mad on, and I expect all the other boys did too."

Finch opened the door. He and the lieutenant stepped inside. The din quieted.

"Ten-shun!" a blue-coated sergeant yelled and jumped to his feet.

To a man, the entire group, with the exception of Pete and Pine Tree snapped to attention. The cowboys, who had all fought in the war, simply reacted automatically to their military training. It was Clem who first realized that they were standing at attention before a blue-coated lieutenant.

"You crazy bastards!" he yelled. "Set down. That feller ain't wearin' no gray coat."

The men looked at each other sheepishly, and one by one the cowboys sat on a bunk or slumped in a chair.

"At ease, men!" Lieutenant Seymour said, and the blue-coated soldiers relaxed. "Well, this has been quite a day! First, I find a regular stockade that's disguised as a ranch in the middle of Indian country. Then I find a whole passel of blacks that act like they are happy to be here. Then I eat a sumptuous meal cooked by one of them. And now, I've had a whole bunch of Rebels snap to attention in front of me!" He ended with a grin that made his face look even more youthful.

"You forgot a couple of things, Bob," Finch jibed.

"What's that?"

"You saw the best quarterhorse that's alive today. And you ate supper with a pretty good-looking woman."

"I did at that," agreed the lieutenant. "So, let's all forget the army for tonight and have a cup of that coffee."

The statement was greeted with cheers and yells. Laughter and a general babble of voices created a cacophony of sound.

Everyone was served coffee. Lieutenant Seymour sat beside one of the privates in his company. When the atmosphere was at its most congenial, the lieutenant stood up. The soldiers all started to rise.

"Forget it for tonight, men!" the lieutenant said, and the men relaxed again. "Just remember that we've got to be back over here by sunup tomorrow and go horse hunting. Finch may want to hire some of you when he sees how well you ride those flat saddles," he added facetiously. He was feeling good.

Raucous laughter greeted his statement, and a few minutes later the soldiers took their leave. The cowboys all walked outside to see them off.

As they rode out of view toward the river, Clem said with simulated disgust, "Damned if some of them bluebellies don't act part human. And I even shook hands with the sons-of-bitches."

"I expect they're like most folks," Pete said. "Some good, and some bad—but I think you just met a bunch of the good ones."

"I think so, too," Finch said almost sadly. Then he turned and made his way back to the headquarters house.

He paused on the gallery and turned to look about the headquarters compound, as he usually did before entering the house. The moon had risen and sent its gentle glow over the sprawling buildings. Faint wisps of smoke trailed upward from still hot embers of the burned barn.

Suddenly, Finch felt very alone and very lonely. He had always liked being alone for short periods of time, for it gave him time to think and plan and to marvel at the wondrous place the world was. But somehow, tonight was different. It seemed that this time loneliness was to be his constant companion. Though he enjoyed others and loved being around them, there had always been someone who was very special and close! First there was Chico Baca, his great Mexican friend who had been murdered on their way west; and Colette, whom he had been in love with and who died by a Kiowa arrow; O'oah, his beautiful Indian wife, who had her skull crushed by a Kiowa tomahawk; and Humphrey Beatenbow, killed by the very creatures he was trying to propagate; and then Matt, who had died by an Indian knife—and now Mandy!

They were all gone, or would be soon! Finch looked up at the moon, removed his hat, and took a deep breath. Then he said in a very low voice, "Much obliged, Lord—for letting me have them as long as I did!"

He turned and went into the house.

# Chapter 13

Several of the troopers, led by the lieutenant, arrived just at sunup the next morning. They were accompanied by a few civilians from the caravan. All were leading an extra horse. The soldiers rode the regulation saddle, while the civilians accompanying them rode stock saddles and had coiled ropes attached to the pommels. Finch surmised that they were good horsemen.

Finch and the HF cowboys were standing in front of the bunkhouse to meet them. Pleasantries were exchanged, and Clem invited them all in for coffee. They accepted with alacrity and handed the reins of their horses to several Negro youngsters who had come out to stare and giggle at them. Lieutenant Seymour looked at the headquarters house several times, and Finch knew that he was hoping to be invited to drink coffee with Finch and Mandy. But with a perverseness that was uncharacteristic of him, Finch refused to take the obvious hint.

After coffee, the cowboys chose a horse from the extras that had been led by the soldiers and civilians. There were not enough horses to mount all the cowboys, and some, including Pete and Pine Tree, had to remain behind as the group rode up the valley. One of the civilians who had accompanied the soldiers had a badly bruised face and limped perceptibly. When one of the HF cowboys offered to take his horse, the man accepted gratefully.

The cowboys who did not have a horse, knowing that it would be some time before the riders could return with any of the ranch horses, opened the corral gates and made sure that the jackass corral was firmly fastened. Since Finch was riding Hawk, they also opened his round corral, hoping that some of the horses might go into it. Wisps of smoke still trailed from the smoldering ashes of the burned barn; several men expressed concern that the odor of burned wood might "booger" the horses.

Having made all the preparations possible for the hoped for return of the mounts, the cowboys retired to the bunkhouse to drink freshly boiled coffee. One of them climbed to the roof to alert the others when he could see the riders returning.

"Waal," Pete said as he puffed at his pipe and drank the strong coffee. "Likely it'll be a couple of hours afore any of 'em starts a-comin' back, so I'd reckon we'd might as well set 'n whittle a while."

"I ain't never seen a better lookin' hoss than Finch was a-ridin'," Pine Tree, who had not removed his quid of tobacco from his jaw as he gulped the strong coffee, said to no one in particular.

"You ain't likely to, neither," one cowboy replied. "That there is an Old Billy stud out of that Paisano mare."

"Never heard of 'em," the man with the bruised face said. Speech was difficult with his swollen jaw. He had a Yankee twang.

"Then you ain't never been in south Texas!"

"I'm from Maine," the man said. "I've never been to Texas before, and wouldn't be now if that damn wagon master hadn't decided to cut south from Kansas City for some reason or other and hit the branch of the Santa Fe trail south of the Canadian that we are on."

"Looks like that would be a long ways out of the way."

"It is. But you don't argue with Gabe Elvers. He's the wagon boss, and he's the meanest son- of-a-bitch I ever saw. Anybody that bats a eye better hunt a hole. That's how I got this here swole up face and gimpy leg—he didn't want some of us to come help round up your horses."

The cowboys looked at the man in surprise. "Well—why don't you fire 'im?" one asked.

"We tried that onct, when we had been a few days on the trail. But he beat hell out of one man, and he shot another one."

"Well, I'm damned if I'd travel with a man like that."

"I dunno," the man said ruefully. "He's got a fist like a sledge hammer, and he's faster than anybody I ever saw with a pistol. So I reckon most is just gonna keep a-hopin' that we get to Santa Fe afore somebody else gits killed—which I damn near done this morning when I saddled up to come over here." He rubbed his swollen jaw.

"You ort not to of come over," Pete said.

"I reckon. But I ain't easy to talk out of doin' something. And I expect I'll have more a- comin' when we go back."

"You know," Pine Tree said, "that feller sounds like somebody that Finch ort to talk to."

\* \* \* \* \* \*

It was almost noon when the lookout on the roof reported a herd of horses about a mile up the valley. They were being driven by several riders.

The men all hurried outside and formed a wing on each side of the corrals to funnel the horses into the gate. Not all the ranch horses were in the herd, but it was a sizable bunch and included the gentle mares that Finch and Matt had brought from south Texas. As they neared the corral, several of them spooked at the burned barn, but the men pushed them hard. The soldiers were surprisingly competent in their flat saddles. Alf and Trey, the two Negro riders that Finch had chosen to go, did more than their share, even though the horses they rode had not been ridden with only a surcingle before. Finch and Hawk seemed to be everywhere. Hawk moved with cat-like quickness, his nose close to the ground, and turned back any horse that tried to break away. In a short time, all of them were in the big corral.

"Whew!" breathed one of the cowboys who had been left behind. "It's shore gonna be good to be a-straddle of a horse again. That walk all the way across the river damn near castrated me!"

The cowboys all laughed, but they too, were much relieved to have a corral full of mounts again.

Since it was noon, the corral gate was firmly fastened, and, leaving two men on guard, Clem invited the rest of the men to the bunkhouse to eat. The lieutenant looked at Finch almost pleadingly. Finch relented. "I expect that Maisie has dinner ready, and Mandy will be expecting us; so Bob and I will meet everybody in an hour."

The lieutenant smiled his pleasure, and he and Finch walked up the incline toward headquarters.

Maisie had the table set for three. After Finch and the lieutenant had washed their hands and faces, the lieutenant pulled a comb from his uniform pocket and carefully combed his dark, curly hair. Finch ran his fingers through his receding blond hair two or three times and led the way to the table. Mandy had not yet appeared; so they sat and were served coffee by Maisie.

The lieutenant kept looking anxiously at the door of the Beatenbow wing. When a broad smile broke across his youthful face and he rose from his chair, Finch knew that Mandy had entered the room, even though his back was to the door. For the first time since they had been eating together, he did not rise when the lieutenant held Mandy's chair and she sat down. Finch noted with no pleasure that she was wearing a different gown and that her long hair was tied with a blue ribbon at the nape of her neck. Her dark eyes were shining, and she looked very beautiful.

The meal was a replica of the night before. Mandy and the lieutenant kept up an animated conversation. Mandy avoided Finch's eyes. If the lieutenant noticed, he did nothing to include Finch in the conversation. Finch could not help but feel a bit of resentment. He knew that it was foolish, for Mandy had not seen anyone other than cowboys and blacks for a long time. Perhaps, too, he felt just a twinge of jealousy! It was an alien emotion for him. After all, Mandy was—. Finch did not complete the thought, for the lieutenant and Mandy were both rising from the table.

"I shall look forward to your return, Lieutenant Seymour," Mandy said as she shook his hand when he and Finch were leaving.

"So will I!" the lieutenant said eagerly. "And I do wish you would call me Bob. Lieutenant seems pretty formal to me."

"All right, Bob," Mandy smiled. "And please call me Mandy."

"Good! I'll see you in about six weeks, Mandy."

Finch said nothing as they took their leave.

The men were standing around the corral. Alf, the best roper on the ranch, had his lariat loose and was ready to catch a horse for each of the cowboys.

Catching the horses and saddling them took very little time, and soon all were mounted. It was decided that everyone who was not on guard would ride over to the caravan with their new Yankee friends. Pine Tree, who had been watching as they prepared to leave, mounted his nondescript horse.

"Reckon I'll just scout along the trail for a few miles ahead," he said as he squirted tobacco juice. As the men were riding away, he called to Finch, who turned Hawk and rode back to Pine Tree.

"Finch," Pine Tree began almost apologetically. "Mostly I figger on lettin' folks skin their own skunks, but I reckon maybe I ort to tell you about that yellow-bellied wagon boss. Not that I don't think you can take care of yourself," he added quickly. "Kit told me a-plenty. But that son-of-a- bitch is a back shooter. He carries that damn blacksnake all the time, and he kin pick a gnat off'n the ear of a ox with it—but he don't. Makes out like he's a-tryin' to, but he ain't. What he does is split the oxen's ears. He's just plain damn mean, and likes to hurt things. He's used that bull whip on a couple of men, and what he done to 'em wasn't pretty. And he's plenty fast with that pistol, too. Kilt one of the men back in Kansas—said he was a-reachin' for his pistol—but he wasn't. He just had a pretty wife, and Gabe figgered he might move in, it being such a long ways to Santy Fe. Anyways, you bein' a friend of Kit's, I figgered to have my say. I reckon I talk too damn much!"

"I'll watch close, Pine. And thanks!"

"Not none of my business, unnerstand!" Pine Tree said defensively. "Jist that I'd hate to see you ride up to a unfriendly a-thinkin' different. He didn't have no cause to beat up that feller this mornin' neither. Gabe jist didn't like the idea of him a-helpin' you."

Pine Tree lifted his hand in a half-salute and rode away. Finch looked after him thoughtfully.

\* \* \* \* \* \*

Finch lifted Hawk into a trot and caught the others as they reached the river bed. Clem cautioned all of them to be careful of quicksand. It was with some relief that all of them crossed safely. They were riding abreast when they neared the caravan. Finch and the lieutenant rode side by side. A rider that they recognized as Gabe Elvers rode out to meet them. They all halted a few feet apart.

"Well, it damn shore took you long enough!" he said harshly.

Then his eyes lit on Hawk, and a greedy and evil glint burned in them.

"They musta had a big bunch of 'em to take you so long, but I see you found one of our strays, too; so I reckon time wasn't plumb wasted."

"One of ours?" The lieutenant was nonplussed.

"That's right. The one that Slim there is a-ridin'. He strayed from the caravan a few days ago."

The ploy was obvious, and it was Clem who called it. "Mister, that stud ain't never been rode by anybody but who is on 'im. And he brung 'im all the way from south Texas. That there hoss is Hawk, the HF ranch stud."

"The hell he is!" Gabe rasped as he surreptitiously loosed the thong holding his blacksnake. "That horse belongs in our remuda. I've rode 'im before—"

"Yore a damn liar—" Clem got no further. The blacksnake lashed out wickedly and popped loudly as the tip of it bit a gash in Clem's cheek. Clem's horse reared and jumped to one side, unseating the unprepared Clem. Clem was reaching for his pistol when Finch's icy voice froze everyone.

"Now, that'll do!" he said evenly, but his voice was loud and carried to every man. His blue eyes shot sparks. "Mister!" He was speaking to Gabe Elver. "This horse isn't yours—and never will be. And if you think different, you'll have to use something besides that blacksnake!"

Gabe looked at Finch in astonishment. He could not believe that any man would challenge him! He had never heard of Fauntleroy Finch!

"Well, now, Slim," he said sarcastically. "You reckon to be man enough to keep 'im?"

"I aim to," Finch said.

Elver grinned evilly, dropped his blacksnake to the ground, and wrapped his big hand around his pistol butt. "Well, if it's gonna take more'n a blacksnake to convince you, then I reckon I jist have to use my pistol on a horse thief!"

With that, he started to jerk his gun. Pine Tree had said he was fast. And he was. He had the pistol almost clear of its holster when Finch shot him between the eyes.

Elver fell from the saddle, and his horse galloped back toward the caravan. Complete silence ensued for several seconds. Finch's face was pale and grim. As always, when he was forced to use his gun, he felt empty inside, but his hands were rock steady as he pushed the empty shell from his pistol and reloaded.

It was Pete who broke the silence. "What I seen just ain't plain damn possible!" he said in awe. "Elver had his hand on his pistol, and Finch had his on the saddle horn, but Elver didn't even clear leather."

"It's possible!" Shanker Stone said grimly. "And if the son-of-a-bitch had ever heard of Fauntleroy Finch, he would of knowed better!"

The lieutenant's face had lost its ruddy color, and he looked at Finch almost fearfully. "What will we do with him?"

"I'll take care of the sorry bastard!" Clem had risen from the ground and was mopping blood from his cheek with his bandanna. "If one of you boys will catch my horse, I know of a real good quicksand pool in the river."

"And I'll help 'im!" Shanker Stone volunteered. He had buried a man before in the quicksand.

"All right! You boys take care of 'im," Finch said. "We'll go find out who is to be in charge of the caravan now."

"Hey, Finch!" It was the man with the battered face and limp who spoke. "I reckon I'll be in charge now. I was supposed to be Gabe's segundo when we left Kansas City, but he ain't let me do nothin', and he beat hell out of me when I rode over to help you fellers out some."

"Good," Finch approved. "I expect the caravan will be in better hands now, anyway." Then, as an after-thought, he turned to the lieutenant. "Bob, do you boys have any say-so about a couple of fellers having an argument out here in the west? I mean, are you supposed to arrest me—or anything?"

"No, sir!" the lieutenant denied quickly. "I think all of us would agree that he was trying to kill you and steal your horse at the same time. Even the army can't condone that!"

There was a general murmur of agreement among all the men.

Clem's horse had been recaptured, and, as the rest of the men rode toward the caravan, Clem had his rope dallied around his saddle horn and the noose around Gabe's feet, He rode toward the river dragging the body behind him, and Shanker Stone rode alongside.

The caravan had been too far away for the people in it to see what had happened, but they had heard the crack of Gabe's blacksnake and a pistol shot. When Gabe's horse came running back with an empty saddle and the stirrups flapping, they gazed anxiously, almost fearfully, at the group of cowboys and soldiers who were riding toward the caravan. When they were within a few yards of it, the riders stopped their horses and sat in a group as a man from the caravan approached.

"What happened?" the man asked.

No one answered for a moment. It was one of the older sergeants among the troops who spoke. "Your wagon master got killed," he said.

The man stared in disbelief, and then a look of pure pleasure crossed his face. "He was overdue!" he said simply.

When the news was passed along the caravan, no one expressed regret at Gabe's demise, and several were openly pleased.

"Well, what do we do now, Art?" The question was directed to the man with the swollen face who was sitting his horse beside the lieutenant. It was the first time Finch had heard him called by name.

"You was supposed to be in charge if anything happened to Gabe," the man persisted.

Art was silent for a moment, and all eyes were upon him. Suddenly, he felt the crushing responsibility that he had inherited. He took a deep breath and looked at the sun.

"Well," he said. "We've got these cowboys enough horses rounded up so's they can make out, and there is still a lot of daylight left. So I reckon we'd best hitch up and make a few miles. I'd like to hit the main Santa Fe trail as soon as we can. Pine Tree says it ain't too far, and he's already scoutin' ahead."

"Good!" one of the men who had joined the group said. "Let's get started."

The men who had gathered around the cowboys and soldiers walked quickly to their wagons, and in a short time they were ready to pull out.

A corporal rode up to the lieutenant and saluted smartly. The lieutenant returned the salute. "How does the Lieutenant want the men deployed, sir?"

"Same as usual," Lieutenant Seymour replied. "Two men ahead, and the others strung out alongside. All of us here will wait and follow the last wagon."

The corporal saluted again and rode away. The caravan began to roll. Clem and Shanker, who had taken care of their grisly chore, had rejoined the cowboys and the troops who had helped gather the horses. The men were conversing in a friendly fashion as the wagons passed.

A variety of people made up the caravan, of almost every description. The men who sat on the driver's seats were usually accompanied by their wives, and many children peered from under the canvas, stood behind the wagon seat, or gazed out the puckered opening at the end of each wagon. Some of them waved at the cowboys and troops who still sat in a group.

Finch had been so engrossed in watching the passing parade that he was a bit startled when one of the wagons veered closer than the others. This wagon was pulled by mules instead of oxen, and a very pretty young woman sat on the wagon seat and held the lines. Beside her were two small children. The wagon stopped in front of Finch and the lieutenant.

"Are you the one who—did you—?" Her face showed traces of strain and weariness, but there was no doubt as to the question she was asking nor to whom it was directed.

"Yes, ma'am. I am," Finch said in a level voice that did not give any indication of emotion. "I'm sorry I had to—"

"Well, I'm not!" the young woman flared. "I'm glad! Glad, you hear! I know it's a sin to be glad somebody is dead—but I can't help it!" Her young and pretty face was flushed, and tears rolled down her cheeks. "That monster killed my husband, and he has been making life miserable for me ever since. He even took the caravan out of the way so we would be on the trail longer. I guess he actually thought—" She suddenly burst into sobs and covered her face with her hands.

The embarrassed men looked away. The lieutenant suddenly needed to check some of the trappings on his saddle. Finch sat in numbed silence. He removed his hat and pushed his fingers through his hair, as he tried in vain to think of something to say.

Suddenly, the young woman raised her head, brushed the tears away with her hand, and, slapping the lines on the mules backs, clucked to them. The wagon was only a few feet away when she turned on the seat and called back.

"Thank you, mister! Thank you, whoever you are!"

Finch watched as she drove away. He shook his head silently.

"Well," the lieutenant said. "I guess someone thinks you did a good deed, anyway."

"It doesn't make me feel good to kill a man," Finch answered grimly.

The last wagon finally pulled by. The soldiers and cowboys shook hands, and the troops rode alongside the last wagon. The lieutenant was the last soldier to leave the group of cowboys. He stuck out his hand to Finch.

"I'll look forward to seeing you in about six weeks," he said heartily as they gripped hands.

Finch just nodded his head, and the lieutenant rode after his men. Finch hoped he would never see the lieutenant again. But he knew he would.

\* \* \* \* \* \*

Finch ate supper in the bunkhouse that night. After all, Mandy had been too enthralled by the lieutenant and the prospect of going east to pay any attention. She probably wouldn't even miss him!

It was late when he went back to the headquarters house. He pulled off his boots lest his spurs jingle as he walked through the big room to his own quarters.

When he crawled into bed, he cupped his hands behind his head and stared into the dark. He knew that he was being childish, and he was a bit embarrassed by the feeling.

He tossed for a few minutes before turning on his side and closing his eyes. Then, for the first time since the caravan had left, he thought of the man that he had killed that day.

# Chapter 14

When Finch awakened the next morning, it was the first time in his life that he dreaded facing the day. He dressed slowly and carefully, then resolutely walked into the big room where Maisie had the table set for two. Maisie poured coffee, as he sat to wait for Mandy. Somehow, he hoped she would not come. But she did.

Finch rose, pulled her chair, and seated her.

"Thank you," she said formally.

Finch sat. Both he and Mandy were silent as Maisie served breakfast.

"Started packing yet?" Finch finally asked.

"I started last night," responded Mandy. She did not meet his eyes.

"I'll have Largo fit out a couple of good wagons for the trail. He knows how to do it. You and the kids can stay in one of them and haul all your gear in the other."

"I expect we will need more than two," Mandy said. "Maisie told me last night that she and Largo were going, too."

"What?" Finch almost yelped. "Largo and Maisie are leaving?" he asked incredulously.

"Yassuh. We is, Mars Finch." Maisie, who had come to pour fresh coffee had overheard them. "Largo, he say we be Beatenbow niggers, and wherever the Beatenbows go, we go too!

"But—but—Hump is—"

"Yassuh, we knows, Mars Finch," Maisie said sadly. "Mars Hump—he daid. But them little boys of his is Beatenbows, and allus will be, I reckon."

Finch and Mandy both looked at Maisie in surprise. It had not occurred to either of them that the Negroes would think of such a thing. Mandy had assumed that they were leaving because of the Indian menace.

"Well," Finch gulped in astonishment and disappointment. "Are any more of the blacks going?"

"Some is," Maisie answered. "Largo, he say dey talks some about it las' night, and some o 'em is ready to leave—especially de women who ain't got no man now."

Finch sat in stunned silence for a moment. Then he said, "I reckon we've got all the wagons and mules you'll need. I'll tell Largo to start working on the wagons. It will take some time."

"Lieutenant Seymour said he couldn't be back in less than six weeks," Mandy offered.

"That will give Largo plenty of time to rig wagons for everybody that wants to go," Finch said bitterly as he rose from the table. "I'll go out and get things started."

When Finch told Largo to start fixing wagons for travel, he was astounded when Largo said, "Yassuh, Mars Finch, I do dat. I done been a-figgerin' how many we gonna need."

"Who told you to do that?" Finch demanded a bit angrily, and then he was chagrined and a bit sheepish, for he knew he sounded like Humphrey Beatenbow.

"Ain't nobody tole me, Mars Finch," Largo said apologetically. "But I knows Miss Mandy and her young 'uns gonna need one or two, and then Maisie and me—we got some young 'uns, too."

Finch started to say something, but clamped his jaw. Largo could tell that he was irritated.

"Ain't like I was a-tryin' to be uppity, Mars Finch." Largo pleaded. "An' Maisie an' me sho does hate to leave yo out here by yoself—but we is Beatenbow niggers. Allus has been, and I reckon allus will be!" he ended with a trace of defiance.

"I know you are, Largo," Finch said as he mentally capitulated to the inevitable. "And I'm glad you are! I'll feel a lot better about Mandy—Mrs. Beatenbow—and her kids if you are with 'em."

"Yassuh, Mars Finch," Largo said with relief. "I takes care of 'em de bes' I can."

"I know you will, Largo. How many more of the blacks are going?"

"Ain't sho, Mars Finch," Largo said. "I reckon a few o 'em."

"Fix enough wagons for everybody," Finch said as he walked away.

\* \* \* \* \* \*

Finch kept as busy as possible after learning that Mandy was leaving, and he did his best to keep from thinking about it. He checked with Clem each morning and then scouted the prairie on each side of the valley. He rode many unnecessary miles each day and was grateful to be dog tired when he returned each night. He also stayed busy overseeing the blacks who were rebuilding the barn.

"I sees dat de barn be finished afore we leaves, Mars Finch," Largo said. He was directing the blacks who were working on the barn as well as those who were getting the wagons ready.

"I'll appreciate that, Largo," Finch said seriously. "I'm sure not much of a carpenter, and I doubt if any of the cowboys are. And if you do it, I know it will be done right."

"Thankee, Mars Finch." Largo grinned his pleasure at the compliment. "Dis time, we is a- buildin' it outta cedar logs and puttin' a sod roof on it, so's it won't burn so easy."

Finch nodded his approval and kneed Hawk to ride up the valley. He wanted to be as tired as possible when he came in each night. It made sleep come easier.

\* \* \* \* \* \*

Finch ate breakfast and supper with Mandy each day, but their relationship was no longer carefree and comfortable as it had once been. Mandy seemed preoccupied, and Finch did not try to reestablish their former camaraderie. He had admitted to himself that his feeling for her was no longer friendship. It was a great deal more than that, and her absence would leave a great vacant space in his life. Perhaps his depth of feeling for her had always been there, and he had stifled it because she was Humphrey's wife. His feeling of helplessness approached despair, and for the first time he wondered if the dream he pursued was worth the violence and heartache!

He and Mandy talked of trivial things at their meals. Each was polite, but distant, and they studiously avoided each other's eyes.

"I reckon the soldiers will be coming back by in a couple of weeks" Finch said as they ate breakfast early one morning.

"Lieutenant Seymour said they would be back in about six weeks," Mandy replied. "It's been four weeks and two days since they left."

"You have all your packing done?"

"Yes. I've been ready for a week. Largo has the wagons ready to go."

"Well, I hope he has plenty of them ready. I expect a lot of people are going to want to go."

"You will have enough people left to defend and run the ranch, won't you?" Mandy wasn't too interested.

"Yes. None of the white cowboys except one will leave. And Alf and Trey are both going to stay. They're the two best black cowboys we have."

"I'm sure that you will be able to manage. I'll write to you when I find out where I will be."

"I'll appreciate that," Finch said. "And I'll send your half of the money every time we make a drive."

"Which white cowboy is leaving?"

"Clem," Finch said tersely.

"Clem!" echoed Mandy in alarm, and for the first time, she looked directly at Finch. "Why— why—he can't do that! He's the foreman—and he's been with you since you started west from Fort Worth."

"He can," Finch said. "And he's going to. Says Ellie doesn't want to stay when Largo and Maisie leave."

"But what difference does that make to Clem? He's never cared anything about the blacks anyway."

"Ellie and Clem have been living together ever since Clem had that cabin built."

"I knew Ellie stayed there, but surely they aren't—" Mandy was aghast.

"Well, they are!" Finch said firmly. "And they have been for a long time. Clem is crazy about that kid of Ellie's—that was sired by Brandy Wine."

"But that child is half-black!" Mandy said incredulously.

"He's also half-white—and part Jewish and English, and maybe a lot more strains that we don't know about. But I guess he's a mixture just like the rest of us! Anyway, Shanker Stone will make a good foreman."

There was a long silence. Finch sipped coffee, and Mandy stared vacantly out a window. Finally, she looked at Finch again.

"Finch, you haven't visited White Horse since the Cheyennes attacked us." She reached over and put a hand on his. "Wouldn't you like to go see him again?"

"I reckon I'll not be visiting White Horse any more," Finch said firmly. Then he added a lame excuse. "Expect I'll be pretty busy around the ranch now?"

It was then that Mandy realized how devastated Finch had been by her preoccupation and coolness. What was more, she also realized that she cared. Deeply! Again, she reached over and squeezed his hand, and her eyes drew his like a magnet. She started to speak, and then tears suddenly appeared in her luminous dark eyes and rolled down her cheeks. She tried again to speak, but could not. She squeezed his hand again, quickly rose from the table, and ran to her room. Finch stared after her with puzzled eyes.

\* \* \* \* \* \*

An inexplicable aura of change pervaded the dining room when Finch and Mandy were eating together after that. Mandy had realized that both she and Finch had become uncomfortable in the presence of the other, and she was intent on making up for her indifferent and unresponsive mood. She again became animated and talked avidly as they ate. She asked questions about the ranch and what Finch did each day. Finch willingly capitulated, and soon they were friendly and congenial again, although the specter of Lieutenant Seymour's return and Mandy's departure hung heavily on the air.

The day the barn was finished, Mandy asked Finch to take her to see it. It was a puzzling request, but one that Finch gladly granted.

As they walked down the long building, Finch spied Largo, who was directing some of the blacks in building a long paddock that abutted the barn. Finch called to him.

"Yassuh, Mars Finch and Miss Mandy," he greeted them with a huge grin. "Mrs. Beatenbow wants to see the new barn," Finch said. "Maybe you could help out—you are the one that built it."

"Yassuh. I sho do dat." Largo's pleasure was obvious.

As they toured the huge structure, Largo pointed with pride to the various accommodations. "This here is Hawk's stall."

He stopped in front of the biggest one. "An' it open out into de paddock so he can git 'im plenty o exercise. An' he can come into his stall outen de weather, too. Well finish de paddock tomorrow fo sho; den we turn 'im in and see how he lak it."

Mandy expressed her delight in the ingenious arrangement.

"An' ever thin' is made outen cedar, too. We been a-sawin' ever cedar tree fo a mile up and down de river. An' it got a loft that yo can store a lot o hay in, too," Largo said proudly.

"I doubt if we will have much hay to store," Finch said ruefully. "The cowboys all seem to be afraid of a scythe—or anything else that they can't do from the back of a horse."

"I already got some niggers a-cuttin' hay up in dat little side valley where it's so tall," Largo said. "We'll have the loft mos' full if'n them army men don' come back too quick."

Finch and Mandy both expressed their satisfaction, and Largo grinned fondly at their backs as they walked back toward the house.

When they were inside, Mandy made another request that startled and delighted Finch.

"Finch," she said, taking his arm, "you said that you brought back a mare from south Texas just for me. Is she gentle to ride?"

"As a pup," Finch said. "I've been riding her a lot, and she's the easiest riding horse I've ever been on."

"Then, would you take me for a ride tomorrow up the valley? I'd like to see one more time the land that you love so much!"

"We'll leave right after breakfast," Finch said enthusiastically. "Have Maisie pack us a lunch in case we don't get in for dinner."

"I will," Mandy said gaily. "And I'll be ready to leave as soon as you are in the morning."

"Then, you'd better be ready early." Finch could not hide his pleasure.

\* \* \* \* \* \*

But they did not leave early the next morning, for some time during the night, Largo was killed.

Apparently, he had been to the Negro quarters, which he had often done after Maisie was asleep. He always took a circuitous route through the salt cedars so that he could not be seen on his nighttime escapades. He usually visited one or more of the single women in the quarters, for Largo was a virile man, and although Maisie was more than enough to satisfy him physically, he did like variety and availed himself of it often. He would have been astonished to know that his handsome wife knew of his nocturnal trysts and often feigned sleep so that he would leave and she could hang a dishrag out the window to let Alf know that the coast was clear. Maisie liked variety, too, and she, like Largo, had no repressive morals to bridle her animalistic instincts.

The moccasin tracks in the sand around Largo's body told their own story. He had been struck from behind, and his head was crushed by a stone axe and his body horribly mutilated.

Yellow Wolf had finally exacted his terrible revenge!

\* \* \* \* \* \*

The next few days were chaotic. The Negro population went into their ritualistic mourning for Largo's death. The entire day and night following, the eerie moaning and chanting could be heard from their quarters. No blacks appeared to work on the barn. Maisie was absent from the kitchen.

None of the cowboys, nor Finch, nor Mandy went to the Negro quarters. They knew that the ancient death ritual of the blacks, which had originated in Africa, prohibited a white man from their rites. They would not bury a person in the dark, nor would they work or eat until the body had been interred after sunrise the next day.

As soon as the mourning period was over, they buried Largo at the foot of Humphrey's grave, and the chanting and moaning ended, much to the relief of all the cowboys, Mandy, and Finch.

It was Alf who brought the blacks back to work. They did not fear him as they had the huge Largo and his hammering fists, but there was something about Alf that commanded their respect, and they worked, if not with their former vigor, at least acceptably.

When six weeks had passed since the departure of the caravan and soldiers, Finch kept looking at the west, dreading to see anyone coming. When another week had passed, Finch began to hope! Perhaps they had received different orders when they reached Santa Fe!

But they hadn't. Their delay was caused by Lieutenant Seymour's insistence that an army ambulance be fitted out with every imaginable convenience for a passenger he hoped to pick up on the way back to Kansas.

It was Pete who first spied the soldiers and wagons. When he reported it, Finch's heart sank.

The troops camped on the south side of the river. Lieutenant Seymour and four escorts crossed over. The four troopers with him dropped off at the bunkhouse and were greeted heartily by the cowboys who were not on patrol duty. The lieutenant handed the reins of his horse to an aide and brushed himself carefully before walking purposefully toward the headquarters house.

Finch had been looking out one of the deeply recessed windows in the big room. Mandy had been doing the same from her quarters. When the lieutenant reached the steps, Finch opened the door.

"Sorry I'm late, Finch," the lieutenant said. "But we had to make some additional preparations for the return trip. Is Mandy well?" The lieutenant proffered a gloved hand.

"Howdy, Bob." Finch shook his hand. "Yes, she is fine. Come on in."

The lieutenant accepted the invitation gratefully and looked quickly about for Mandy, who had not made her appearance.

"How was your trip, Bob?" Finch had to exert himself to be cordial.

"Fine! Fine!" the lieutenant responded enthusiastically. "In fact, much better after we left here. Art made a good wagon master."

"I would allow that he did," Finch said. Then he continued. "Mandy is all packed and ready—and has been for quite a spell. I expect you saw the wagons line up out front."

"I did," admitted the lieutenant. "But I don't see why she will require so many."

"A lot more folks are going than just Mandy and the kids," Finch explained tersely. "All of 'em black. Hope that's all right with you."

"Fine! Fine!" the lieutenant said. "My troops will see them safely through, no matter what their color," he added a bit pompously.

"Well, let's sit and have a cup," Finch invited. "I expect Mandy is fixing herself up some and will be out in a few minutes."

They sat and talked of mundane things for a few minutes. Then Mandy came into the room. The lieutenant rose quickly and stood almost at attention. Mandy looked more beautiful than Finch had ever seen her; she walked to the lieutenant and shook hands.

"We've been expecting you, Bob," she said brightly.

"We were a bit delayed," the lieutenant apologized. "I'm sorry!"

"Don't be," Mandy said graciously. "We've been busy, too. And we are all packed and ready."

"I saw your wagons outside," the lieutenant said. "Finch told me that some of the blacks are going too, and that's fine. But you won't need one of the wagons, for we fitted one out especially for you and your children. I think you will be comfortable."

"I'm sure we will," Mandy replied with a bright smile. Then she added, "It's a few minutes until meal time; so I think we should celebrate this occasion with a toast. That's what we did the first time I was ever in this room. Finch, will you tell Maisie, please?"

Finch raised his voice, and Maisie appeared in the kitchen door. "Maisie, bring us three glasses of whiskey," he ordered.

"Yassuh, Mars Finch," Maisie said quickly and disappeared into the kitchen, to emerge again with three glasses. All of them were more than half-full. She served Mandy first, then the lieutenant, and then Finch. She returned to the kitchen.

"That's one of the blacks you'll be having on your trip, Lieutenant," Finch said tonelessly.

Mandy looked at him quickly, but again turned her eyes to the lieutenant. "Would you like to give the toast, Bob?" she asked.

"I would, indeed," the lieutenant answered gaily. "Here's to a long and wonderful trip—and to a most gracious and beautiful lady," he toasted grandly.

The lieutenant and Mandy looked at each other as they raised their glasses to their lips. Neither noticed that Finch did not raise his.

When Maisie called them to supper a few minutes later, the lieutenant's glass was almost empty. Mandy had sipped gingerly at hers. Finch had not tasted his.

The meal was very much a repetition of the meals that they had eaten together before, except that the lieutenant became a bit garrulous from the effects of the strong liquor. Both he and Mandy ignored Finch almost completely.

"Well," the lieutenant said finally, "I will return to my troops for the night and return early in the morning, if that is satisfactory."

"We'll be ready," Mandy said. Finch blanched. Mandy saw the lieutenant to the door.

Mandy and Finch looked at each other silently after the door closed. Neither said good night as they left to go to their rooms.

\* \* \* \* \* \*

Finch stood and looked out the deep set window in the west adobe wall of his bedroom. The wind was blowing lustily and carried the redolent aroma of freshly sawn cedar logs. Finch wondered idly how long such tantalizing aromas had been held prisoner in the age-old trees before the Negroes had cut them to use in building Hawk's paddock.

It was well past midnight, and the moon rising in the east was not yet visible to him, but its glow lit the prairie that was visible out the west window, where the tall, lush grass bent to the wind's constant push.

Finch sighed deeply and felt the enormous burden that the death of Humphrey and the departure of the blacks would place upon him. Even with most of the blacks gone, the ranch was fairly well-manned by white cowboys, even for an Indian attack. But Finch had never felt so forlorn and lonely. It was a unique feeling, for he had been reckless and carefree all his short life.

But tomorrow! Tomorrow, he finally admitted, he would feel the greatest loss of his life— Mandy was leaving!

It was not unusual for Finch to stand at his window and look to the west at all hours of the night, for he had been like a caged puma since he had moved back into his wing of the headquarters.

As he gazed out at the moonlit prairie, he felt, rather than heard, someone enter the room. An aroma as tantalizing and as alluring as that coming from the freshly sawn cedar logs pervaded the room. And Finch knew, with primitive instinct, who it was. He did not move as Mandy walked quietly beside him. He stood very still for a long moment, and then placed his arm around her. Her flesh was warm and firm under the filmy night dress that she wore. Neither spoke, but Mandy sighed softly and laid her head on Finch's shoulder.

They stood for several minutes, looking out the window. Then Mandy took Finch's hand, raised it to her mouth, and kissed it softly. Then she slowly and gently moved it to her breast and held it there.

Finch was not startled, nor even surprised, for he intuitively knew that Mandy was as lonely as he—and she was frightened! Although fear was an alien thing to Finch, he could understand the emotion.

He squeezed Mandy's breast gently with his work-hardened hand. The breast immediately became firm. She turned to Finch and hugged him tightly. The bare nipples of her breasts pushed against his naked chest. They stood a moment longer without speaking. Then Mandy sighed, "Oh, Finch!" as she took his hand and led him to the bed.

There was no hurry to their love-making. Each seemed to be totally concerned with the needs of the other. When their mouths met in their first kiss, it was as though they had known each other from a timeless past.

There were moments when Finch felt a sense of wonder that few men are granted in a lifetime. Mandy's body was like a soft, warm cloud. She seemed to anticipate every need that Finch had ever felt, and Finch reciprocated in kind. The experience was both giving and taking and far surpassed lustful pleasure.

Two hours later, they were both sated and completely relaxed in each other's arms. The wind grew stronger and wailed mournfully around the window.

"Finch?" It was the first sound other than moans of ecstasy Mandy had uttered since they had gone to bed.

"What, Mandy?"

"I'm not going back to Louisiana tomorrow."

Finch tightened his arm around her.

"I'm glad," he said humbly. "I reckon I've been praying that you'd stay."

"I want to stay here with you, Finch! I want to spend the rest of my life up here where the wind lives."

The strong wind suddenly carried a sound that permeated the night. It began as a low moan, rose to a screeching pitch, and ended in a low rumble that echoed and re-echoed up and down the river, as the Beatenbow jackass roared his approval of the wild and wonderful world!